HERE AND NOW

complete series

HERE AND NOW

complete series

New York Times Bestselling Author

LEXI RYAN

Cover and Image © 2016 Sara Eirew
Interior Design and Formatting by:

www.emtippettsbookdesigns.com

LOST IN ME

Here and Now series, book one

LOST IN ME

Here and Now series, book one

LEXI RYAN

For Adrienne. Here's to writing dates, laughter, and dreams brought to life.

PROLOGUE

September—Eleven Months Before Accident

WHEN MAXIMILIAN Hallowell winks at me, my heart somersaults like an overzealous toddler at her first gymnastics class. Because, yes, when it comes to this guy, I am so over-the-top awkward that even the metaphorical tumbling of my internal organs is cringe-worthy.

I force myself to return his smile, but his attention has already shifted to my twin. My so-obviously-not-identical-it's-laughable twin.

"Go finish your drinks," Lizzy says, shooing the guys toward their table. "We need some time for girl talk."

I wish she wouldn't do that. Even if he hardly knows I exist, I want to be close to Max. When he's near, I forget how to breathe, yet I feel more alive than ever.

Lizzy slides into our booth and tugs me in beside her as Cally takes a seat across from us.

"What's that about?" Cally asks me, concern pulling on her features.

I shake my head. I should be glad Lizzy sent Max away. I'm so transparent. I probably would've made a fool of myself.

"She's got a crush on Max," Lizzy explains.

I jab my elbow into Lizzy's side—my crush on the unattainable Maximilian Hallowell is not for public consumption.

Lizzy ignores me. "Can't say as I blame her. You could bounce quarters off the boy's ass."

"He has no idea I exist," I whisper to Cally. "He's only had eyes for Lizzy since he came back to town and opened that gym."

Lizzy frowns, and I feel guilty for bringing it up. "I never would have gone on that date with him if I'd known Hanna liked him. I dropped him the minute I found out."

"Does he know how you feel?" Cally asks me.

"God, no!" Lizzy says before I can reply. "Are you kidding? Hanna doesn't tell guys when she's interested. She'd rather hide and believe she doesn't stand a chance. Which is stupid and a lie."

I shoot a conspicuous glance toward the guys' table just to make sure Max isn't listening in on this conversation. *Like he cares.* "What would he want to do with me anyway?" I mutter. "He's an athletic trainer who runs his own health club, and I'm a fat girl."

"Hanna!" Lizzy and Cally screech in unison.

I regret the F-word as soon as it leaves my lips. There are unspoken rules to being the chubby chick in a group of friends, and *numero uno* is that you never use the F-word. I can't do anything but shrug. The rule can't be unbroken. The ugly truth is out there. "Sorry."

"You're fucking gorgeous, and any guy would be lucky to have you." Lizzy gets so pissed off when I dare suggest her long, lithe limbs are more desirable than my size sixteen-to-eighteen "curves" ("curves" being the PC word for "extra layers of fat"). Reality doesn't even enter into her perception of the situation. Reality is that I've had a handful of dates that were terrible and two boyfriends who were even worse. Lizzy, on the other hand, has her pick of the lot. Including Max Hallowell.

There's honestly not enough beer in that pitcher for me to deal with this conversation tonight. "Time to change the subject, please."

Lizzy presses a kiss to my forehead and whispers so only I can hear, "My Hanna wants Max, my Hanna's gonna get Max."

Chapter
ONE

STORIES AREN'T supposed to start with the main character waking up. It's a rule I learned in my creative writing class in college. Something about boring the reader or being a cliché or... Actually, I don't remember the reason.

But dreams? A lot of my dreams start with me waking up, and this is too surreal to be anything but a dream. Opening my eyes, I find myself in the hospital, not knowing how or why, the nurse telling me that I've been here for over twenty-four hours.

"Mother's maiden name?" a nurse is asking me. She's been quizzing me for several minutes now. My name, my birthday, the freaking president of the United States.

I blink against the fluorescent overhead lights and supply, "Crossen." My head hurts like a thousand drunken clowns have been dancing on it. In cleats.

"Do you know the date?"

I grimace as I shift on the hospital mattress, and the movement sends pain ricocheting through muscles I didn't even know I had. I'm sure she has a good reason for these questions, but I'd like to ask some of my own, starting with, *Why am I in the hospital?* And, *Who beat the shit out of me?*

"September...twelfth, maybe? Thirteenth?" The words come out more like croaks than coherent syllables and they feel like a cheese grater against my throat.

"August," someone squeaks behind her. "She means August. Don't you, Hanna?"

Lizzy comes into my line of sight. Her blond curls bounce as she nods at me, as if it's *really* important that I agree with her. Of course, she's completely wrong. It's not August. It's September. We're a month into the fall semester of our senior year at Sinclair.

I try to frown but it hurts. My hand flies to my face, where the pain radiates like a mini explosion. I touch my cheek gingerly and wince.

Machines beep around my head, and even though I know I just woke up, all I really want is to take some good drugs for this headache and have a nap. "Why am I in the hospital? What happened?"

"Do you know who this is, Hanna?" The nurse motions to her right.

I roll my head to the side so I can more easily focus on my sister. Her curly blond hair frames her face at awkward angles, as if she's been sleeping on a park bench or something.

I'm trying not to panic, but again, I just woke up in a hospital, I don't know how I got here, they say I've been here for over a day, and they're asking if I know my name. My face feels like it's been introduced to a set of brass knuckles, and my skull is threatening to explode. These are not generally signs of a quiet night in.

Lizzy's eyes are red. She's been crying. I keep thinking of that second pitcher of beer we ordered at Brady's. Did we drink and drive? Lizzy looks well but really upset. Is someone hurt?

"Lizzy," I ask, "what happened?"

"She knows me, see?" Lizzy says. "She's fine."

"Can you tell me how Lizzy is related to you?" the nurse asks.

"She's my twin sister."

"Good," the nurse coos. "Good job. And can you tell me

the last thing you remember?"

I don't have long to consider her question before she's invading my personal bubble, her face too close to mine as she stares into my eyes. What? Did she lose something in there she's looking to get back?

"We were at Brady's. Girls' night. What happened?" God, I sound like a broken record.

"You've had an accident," the woman says, looking to my sister, who's shaking her head. A tear slips from the corner of Lizzy's eye. "A rough fall down some stairs. Can you tell me the last thing you remember before Brady's?"

"I was finishing up a paper for school. All the days blur together during the semester. I don't...I don't know."

"The semester?" Lizzy cries. "What are you talking about, Hanna?" She turns to the nurse. "I thought you said she'd be better once she was lucid?"

"It's okay," the woman assures her. "You're going to upset her."

"What happened at Brady's?" Lizzy asks me. "What do you remember?"

"We were hanging out with Cally, and the guys were there and they came over to join us."

"What were we talking about?" Lizzy presses.

She seems distressed, so I try to smile. That's my job, after all. I'm the one who makes things better. "We were trying to convince Cally that she should sleep with William."

"That happened *last September*," Lizzy whispers.

The nurse's brow creases. "Dr. Reid is on her rounds now. I'll update her, and she'll be in shortly."

Lizzy watches the woman leave then turns back to me. "Don't worry. Nix's going to fix you right up."

"Who's Nix?" I whisper.

Tears fill her eyes. "Our friend Nix. You know, Dr. Reid. She moved to town last winter?"

"I don't know any doctors named Nix, Liz."

Before she can explain herself, a pretty young woman enters in a dark dress and a white lab coat. She has long chestnut hair pulled off her neck in a twist and a warm smile. "I hear you're doing much better than last time I saw you."

I look to Liz, hoping she'll help me out.

"Do you remember her now?" my sister asks me.

I frown at the woman I'm supposed to know and shake my head. "I'm sorry."

"My name is Dr. Phoenix Reid. You call me Nix."

The nurse reenters the room and hands a clipboard to Nix, who scans it and nods.

"Why doesn't she remember you?" Liz asks the doctor.

Nix gives her a stern look. "Calm down. Hanna, do you remember anything else after your night at the bar?"

I shake my head, panic rising. "You guys are freaking me out. What happened? Did I drink too much?"

"You've had a head injury," Nix says, "and sometimes with head injuries you can experience a degree of amnesia."

"She doesn't have *amnesia*," Lizzy objects.

"There are different kinds of amnesia. There is no need to panic."

The room grows cold all of the sudden, and I'm overwhelmed with that anxious, claustrophobic feeling I've always gotten when I feel helpless and out of control. "Is this some kind of a joke?"

"She's awake? Talking?" The deep, familiar voice rips my attention away from Dr. Reid and to the other side of the room, where Max Hallowell is bursting through the door, worry creasing his gorgeous face as his eyes roam over me in my no-dignity hospital gown.

Not that my day was going great before this moment, what with the drunken, cleated clowns dancing inside my skull, and amnesia diagnosis and all, but Max Hallowell seeing me in this condition—and *especially* in this gown—sends my day from shitty to *you've-got-to-be-effing-kidding-me*.

"I'm sorry, sir," the nurse says. "Immediate family only. You need to leave."

Ignoring her, he rushes over to my bed and rests his big hand gently against my face. The feel of his rough palm against the skin of my cheek has my heart pounding fast and hard. *Max* is touching me.

This is definitely a dream.

"Sir!" the nurse scolds.

"I am her family," he bites out.

"It's okay," Nix tells the nurse.

Max's gaze drifts to my hand and he adds, "I'm her fiancé."

I draw in my breath so hard and fast that my bruised ribs wail against my expanded lungs. Then I see what he was looking at. The fat diamond winks up at me from my ring finger as if it knows all my secrets. My world is spinning. This all has to be some kind of elaborate joke, and I don't think it's funny at all.

"Baby," he whispers. "Do you remember yet? What happened?"

"She doesn't remember," Lizzy says, her voice cold.

I feel like everyone is twenty steps ahead of me. "Fiancé?"

"Hanna has a case of retrograde amnesia," Nix tells Max. "This can happen with head injuries."

"But it's not like *normal* amnesia," Lizzy objects. "She knows who she is. She knows who *I* am."

"Her most recent memory seems to be of a night in September," the doctor says patiently. "Retrograde amnesia isn't the same as global amnesia. Likely, her memory of everything before that point is just fine. That's why she remembers Lizzy and you, who she's always known, but doesn't remember me, since we just met in December."

"She lost only *part* of her memory?" Liz asks. "Will it come back?"

I'm too busy looking at the ring. A ring from *Max*. How could I forget that?

"There's a strong possibility most of her memory of the months in between will come back. Possibly in hours, but it could take up to a few weeks or months."

The blood drains from Max's face and his Adam's apple bobs as he swallows. "Last September?"

"*Most* of her memory?" Lizzy asks. "She won't remember

everything?"

I can't pretend to understand the emotions going over Max's face. Honestly, I don't know him that well. Or...do I? I shake my head, trying to focus as Nix explains my condition to Max and Liz. *Retrograde amnesia. Don't know when or if my memories will come back. Spontaneous recovery is likely. Little by little but not all at once. Timeline is different for every patient.*

"You remember Max, don't you, Hanna?" Lizzy is asking. She's moved closer to my bed now too. It's starting to feel crowded in here. Too many people and these things they're saying that don't make any sense.

"Of course I remember Max," I mutter. "We all grew up together."

"Do you remember this?" He picks up my hand and rubs his thumb over my finger. "Do you remember me giving it to you?"

"Yeah," Lizzy says. "When did that happen anyway? Was anyone going to bother to tell me my *twin sister* is getting married?"

I can barely process Lizzy's frustrated questions. I'm too focused on retrieving a memory of this ring. Max down on one knee, music, candlelight, anything. But the ring is as meaningful to me as the doctor who says I call her Nix. "I...I want to remember."

He closes his eyes, shielding them from me as his broad chest rises and falls on a deep breath.

"We'll need to run some tests," Nix says. "But the best thing you can do for Hanna is give her time. She needs rest and support right now. Not stress."

"We'll help you remember, Han-Han," Lizzy says.

"It doesn't work like that." Nix moves to the computer in the corner and types something in. "But tell her whatever she needs to return to living her life. Those memories might be back before you know it."

"Cally and Maggie are in the waiting room," Lizzy says. "I'm going to run out and give them an update. Can I get you anything?"

A healthy memory? Evidence that this isn't all just some bizarre dream? "No. I'm fine. Thanks."

Lizzy leaves, and exhaustion sweeps over me. My eyelids are heavy and my thoughts muddy with the implications of everything I've learned in the last fifteen minutes.

"When do I get to go home?" I ask in a whisper.

The doctor taps at the keyboard a few more times before turning to me. "Not today and probably not tomorrow. We need to run the tests and observe you for the next twenty-four to thirty-six hours. If everything goes as well as can be expected, you can go home after that."

Max takes my hand between his two warm ones.

Nix checks the display panel on the tower connected to my IV and presses a few buttons. "Let the nurses know if you need anything. Unfortunately, because of the head injury, we can't give you much for the pain other than Tylenol and ibuprofen, but try to sleep as much as you can. I'll see you on my rounds tomorrow." She flips off the lights at the door. "Rest. Take good care of her, Max. You know how to reach me."

I sleep fitfully, the pain in my head and ribs keeping me from settling into my dreams. When the early morning sun peeks in between the curtains, Max is still in the chair next to my bed. He's slumped over, sleeping, his dark hair falling into his face. I want to reach out and brush it back.

I try to roll to my side, but the movement puts pressure on my ribs and sends a jolt of pain through my center. I bite back my cry, but not before it wakes Max. He hops out of his chair and comes to stand by my side.

"Are you okay? What hurts?"

Eyes closed, I focus on my breathing. Inhaling. Exhaling.

"Do you want me to call the nurse? They can give you something else for the pain." His face is etched with worry as he scans mine.

"I'm okay," I assure him, because I know they can't give me anything else. "I'm just a little banged up."

"Okay." He lets out a breath and drags his hand through his hair. "This has been hell, you know. The last couple of days. You couldn't even carry on a conversation. They'd ask you one question, and by the time you answered it, you'd be confused all over again. I thought…" He shakes his head. "I didn't know if I'd ever get you back."

I have to swallow the thickness in my throat. "I'm here now."

After dragging the chair another foot closer to the bed, he sits and takes my hand. He toys with the ring on my finger, and a smile plays at his lips. "I like seeing this on you."

"You gave me this ring?" I whisper.

He lifts my hand and presses a gentle kiss to my knuckle right above the diamond. "I did."

"Why? I mean…how? I mean…" I bite my lip. My stomach is a mess of nerves.

He tucks a lock of hair behind my ear and gives a sad smile, his fingers working tiny circles on my palm. "How? I'm just a lucky bastard, I guess."

"Hmm." I rest my head back on my pillow and relax. "Sounds like it. Lucky guy is engaged to a girl who has a beat-up face and can't even remember dating him."

"Surely I can work this to my advantage." His eyes crinkle in the corners with his smile. He is so damn handsome. "Let me remind you all the ways I was the world's greatest boyfriend. The flowers, the foot massages, the…what else?"

"Coach bags," I supply. "The many Coach bags you bought me during our courtship."

"I'll admit, I never bought you a Coach bag."

I scoff. "And I accepted your proposal?"

"I love you, Hanna," he says softly, and more surprising than the words is this feeling in my chest. As if something there knows what he says is true, even if my mind can't remember how we got here.

"I…" What am I supposed to say? To echo the words back

to him would ring empty. We both know I don't remember being with him, let alone falling in love. *I'm sure I love you too?* That option seems like a kick in the pants.

"It's okay," he murmurs, kissing my hand again. "I know you don't remember. I'll win your heart all over again if I have to."

Chapter
TWO

OPEN MY eyes to see my sister Maggie's head bobbing to music I can faintly make out from her headphones, her gaze focused on the print-filled pages of a thick textbook.

"So what else do I not remember?" I ask groggily. "Are you having Asher's babies yet?"

She lifts her head and grins at me as she pulls off her headphones. "Hey, how'd you sleep?"

"Like a baby. In the literal awake-every-two-hours sense of the cliché." Hospitals have to be the worst places to get rest. Every time I would fall asleep, the nurse would come in to check something or change an IV bag. I tap Maggie's book. "What are you studying?"

"I'm doing an independent study in women in art history. Trying to catch up and make up for the year I took off."

"So that's a no on the babies?"

"Unless you count Zoe, no. No babies."

I nod thoughtfully. I remember Zoe. She's Asher's daughter who lives in New York. She spent most of the summer here— well, last summer at least. This gap in my memories is so bizarre. Not like forgetting what you did last weekend when you know time passed but just can't pin down any memories, but like the last year never happened.

I roll carefully to my side, mindful of my bruised ribs. No breaks, the doctor informed me. Just nasty bruises. Lucky me. Between tests and sleeping and being prodded by the nurses, I haven't gotten many answers to my questions.

"What happened to me, Maggie?"

"We don't really know." She closes the book and sets it to the side. "Lizzy found you at the bottom of the stairs behind the bakery. You were unconscious and looked, well"—she winces—"actually a sight better than you do now. Those bruises have gotten colorful."

"What bakery?"

"Your bakery." A slow grin lights her face. "You opened a bakery."

"I did? Mom didn't flip out?" I've always loved baking, much to the dismay of my fat-phobic mother.

She shrugs. "I don't know, but you wanted to do it and you did. It's downtown and does a nice little business. And your wedding cakes are gorgeous."

"My wedding cakes?" I've decorated cakes for friends' birthdays for years and always loved to play with frosting, gum paste, and fondant. I watched wedding cake shows on TV obsessively. But it was just a dream. Nothing I ever believed I'd be able to make a career out of.

She smiles. "We're all so proud of you."

"So then I have a bakery and I mysteriously ended up bruised and battered behind it."

"Our best guess is that you took a pretty good fall down the stairs."

I narrow my eyes at her. "So you're saying I didn't find gracefulness in those months I can't remember?"

She chuckles. "You're a hell of a lot more graceful than I am."

"What else did I miss?"

"You didn't miss anything," she says. "You were here for all of it, and that memory's going to be back in no time. I'm sure of it."

"Humor me."

"You and Liz graduated in May."

I lift my hand and study my ring. "And then there's me and Max."

"Yeah. Since, I don't know, maybe December or so? But the engagement is new. In fact, that's been a surprise to all of us. Mom came by while you were sleeping last night and she practically bawled when Max confirmed that the ring on your finger was from him and it was the real deal."

"Mom approves of Max, then?"

"That's an understatement."

I frown at my hand then stretch my arm out straight and study it. "I've lost weight." I sit on the edge of the bed and extend my legs out before me one at a time. They're long. Obviously I haven't grown in the last year, but they're so much thinner that they look longer to me. I've taken a couple of groggy trips to the bathroom with nurses at my side, but I didn't pay much attention to my body. I certainly didn't bother to look in the mirror. Thanks to my litany of aches and pains, I was too afraid to look.

I bring my hand to my stomach and draw in a breath. This isn't my body. I've never been this thin. Not as a teenager, not as a child.

I look to Maggie. "Did this happen before or after Max started dating me?"

"After," she says carefully.

I start to stand, and she takes my arm. "I'm fine," I assure her. "I just want to look."

She ignores my protest and escorts me to the bathroom, where I freeze at the sight of myself in the mirror. These bruises on my face aren't very pretty. In fact, they almost look worse than they feel—which is saying something. But what really has me staring is the shape of my face. My cheekbones are visible, the line of my jaw more defined.

"I'll give you a minute," Maggie says. "I'll be right on the other side of the door if you need me."

After the door clicks behind her, I lift my hospital gown

and study my body in the mirror. Frowning, I run my hands over my belly. It's flatter than I ever remember it being, and I can feel muscle definition beneath my stretchmark-wrinkled skin. The bruises at my ribs could get me a job starring in a domestic-violence video. Was this all really from a fall down the stairs?

I'll never have a model's body, yet I'm nearly giddy at the sight of myself. My waist is tiny for the first time in my life, my thighs toned, and the breasts I always cursed for making me look even bigger than I was are now nice curves. I'm actually excited to put on clothes and see my new body when I'm dressed like a normal person.

"It all seems too good to be true," I murmur as I study my reflection.

"Which part?" Maggie pokes her head into the bathroom just as I'm repositioning my gown. "The bruises or the traumatic brain injury?"

"You know what I mean."

She raises a brow. "You're the only person I know who could go through what you did and still think life is peachy. The rest of the world could learn a thing or two from you, Han."

I follow her out of the bathroom. "It's like a dream, you know. Suddenly, I wake up and, sure, I'm in the hospital and pretty banged up, but I have everything I've ever wanted. The business, the body—"

"You were gorgeous before," she tells me as I lower onto the edge of the bed. "You're the only one who couldn't see it."

"It's not just that."

"Max," she provides.

"Yeah." I sigh. "I feel like the universe wants me to see everything, to not take it for granted. The doctor said my memory will probably be back soon, so maybe this is the luckiest thing that's ever happened to me. How many of us get to step back from our lives and see how perfect they really are?"

"No one's life is perfect, Hanna."

"You know what I mean."

"I do know, and it worries me. You've got stars in your eyes about your life, and in a couple of days you're going to start living it again. I just don't want you to be disappointed if it isn't everything it seems."

I slouch into my pillows and take a deep breath in the silence of my hospital room.

Mom hosts brunch every Sunday at her house, and since I'm not expected to be released until tonight, she brought Sunday brunch to me this morning. My sisters were all here—Abby, Maggie, Lizzy, even Krystal, who came home from Florida when she heard about my condition. Asher stopped by. And of course, Max. Max, who hustled everyone out of the room just when I started feeling claustrophobic. Max, who managed to get my mom to change the subject when she didn't want to talk about anything but the wedding. Max, whom I caught watching me the way Asher watches Maggie, the way Will watches Cally.

A knock sounds on the door, and I expect to see Lizzy, but red curls, not blond, peek into the room.

"Are you okay?" Maggie asks. She steps in and closes the door behind her.

I swing my legs around to the floor and nod. "I'm good."

"It's all overwhelming, I bet."

"Does Mom still have him cornered?"

Maggie grins. "Yeah. I think she'd marry him herself if she could."

Toting the bag of clothes Max brought me into the bathroom, I crack the door so I can talk to Maggie. I do a double take when I see my reflection. I'll have to get used to this. I'd guess I'm at least fifty pounds lighter than I remember being. Maybe more. I knew I'd lost weight—I'd seen it for myself. Even so, when Max had first brought me clothes to wear, I couldn't believe the tiny jeans and tee in the bag would fit me. When I pull them over my hips, they slide on smooth and easy.

"She's trying to convince him to convert to Catholicism," Maggie is saying, "and Hanna, you need to tell him you don't want him to do it because I think, for you, he would."

I wash my face and brush my long hair into a high ponytail. When I return to the room, Maggie is sitting in a chair, flipping through a magazine.

Warm lips press against my neck, and I jump before realizing who's touching me. Max wraps his arms around me and pulls my back to his front. "Are you ready to get out of here?"

Leaning into his solid heat, I sigh. "More than ready."

"I have good timing, then," Nix says from the doorway.

I smile at her. After two days in the hospital and more tests than I've ever taken in my life, I've grown to like the woman. I guess this shouldn't come as a surprise, since I'm told we're friends.

"I just need to talk to Hanna about a few things and then she'll be free to go."

Maggie stands and grabs her purse. "I'll get out of the way. Call me if you need anything at all."

"I will. Thanks."

When she's gone, the doctor turns to Max. "Can I ask you to leave?"

Even though he releases me, I feel him stiffen. "She's my fiancée."

"And she'll still be your fiancée after you go down to the cafeteria for a cup of coffee." She gives him a reassuring grin. "Seriously, it's just those little HIPAA rules and my silly desire to keep my license to practice medicine."

He relaxes but seems reluctant. He brushes his thumb over my jaw and presses a soft kiss to my forehead. "I'll be back soon."

Nix follows him to the door and closes it behind him. When she comes back, she lowers herself into the chair by my bed and gives an awkward smile. "Your discharge planner met with you today and talked to you about resuming your regular activities?"

I nod. "None of that will be a problem. My whole family's on board with helping until I'm one hundred percent, and Max is just…amazing."

Nix nods. "How are you feeling about everything?"

"Other than feeling like someone decided to introduce my head to a baseball bat?" I attempt a smile.

"That's to be expected, unfortunately." She looks at her clipboard. "I wanted to talk to you about your blood work. There's nothing too alarming here, but there are some red flags with your electrolyte levels, possibly indicating malnutrition."

"Well, you're the first doctor who's ever accused me of being malnourished."

"You've lost a lot of weight the last few months, and rather quickly too. When you go home, I want you to make sure you're eating regular, balanced meals." Her brow wrinkles. "The imbalance isn't a cause for alarm at this point, but if it got worse, it could lead to kidney failure, so I want to run blood work again in a couple of weeks. I've already scheduled a follow-up appointment for you at my office." She hands me a piece of paper with a time and date.

"Thanks."

"I can only imagine what it's like to have everyone around you know more about your life than you do." She takes a deep breath. "Okay, here comes the awkward part. Are you ready?"

"Um, sure?"

She swallows and looks at her hands. "Normally, I'd call a social worker in to talk to you, but given the extenuating circumstances with your memory and our personal relationship, I wanted to do it myself. I need you to know that there are places you can call if you feel frightened or unsafe in any way. There are resources."

"Frightened of what? I don't understand."

"If there's someone in your life who's hurting you…" Nix trails off.

A chill sweeps over my skin until my bare arms are covered in goose bumps. "Who would want to hurt me?"

Nix cocks her head. "I know you don't remember your time dating Max, but I want you..." She takes another long breath and shifts awkwardly. "I'm sorry I have to ask, Hanna, but even without your memory, you know Max better than I do. Have you ever known him to be violent? Or quick to anger?"

I shake my head. "Not at all. He's just"—*the guy I always wanted*—"a really good guy."

She leans her elbows on her knees and nods. "Okay. I trust your instincts."

"What?" The implication clicks into place in my head. "You think he did this to me? You're wrong. Max is as nice as they come."

She nods again but doesn't look convinced. "Please don't be upset. I'm not making any accusations. I want you to know you have resources. If you don't feel comfortable calling the domestic abuse hotlines, you can always call me or—"

"Nix," I say. "I promise I'll contact you personally if I don't feel completely safe." She doesn't look convinced, so I add, "I just...fell down the stairs. I've always been clumsy."

"Hanna," she says carefully, "I am suspicious that there's more to these injuries than a fall."

"What? But you said—"

"Maybe you fell down the stairs and hit your face, your ribs, your hips in the worst conceivable places. It's possible. Or maybe"—she touches her own cheekbone, pointing to the location of one of my ugliest bruises—"maybe you were beaten and then pushed."

Chapter
THREE

I'm CONFUSED when we pull up outside a building near the town square. "Where are you taking me?" God, this is awkward. Max Hallowell is driving me home. Max Hallowell is my fiancé. Max Hallowell may or may not be abusive.

No. I don't believe that. I've known Max all my life, and he's sweet. Tender. He wouldn't have pushed me down the stairs. But who? And *why*?

It's all so unbelievable that, if it weren't for these bruises, I'd think this was all some sort of elaborate practical joke.

"You live here now," he says softly. There's a little crinkle between his eyes that tells me this is all as weird for him as it is for me. "You moved here in May."

"Oh." *I* moved here. Not *we*. Is it weird that I don't live with him? Probably not. Mom still thinks it's 1950 and disapproves of "premarital cohabitation" as much as she disapproves of premarital sex. Probably more, because at least you can hide premarital sex from the neighbors. "Does Lizzy live with me?"

He shakes his head and brushes a lock of hair behind my ear. "You live here alone."

That surprises me, but I can't think about it too long because the feel of Max's rough fingers on my cheek has my eyes fluttering shut. I wonder if I've come to take this for granted. Max touching me. Max looking at me with all that tenderness in his eyes. I can't wrap my mind around the idea of this being the new normal.

"Come on." He pinches my earlobe lightly between two fingers. "I'll walk you up." He climbs out of the car and rushes around to get my door, offering his hand as I step out.

He doesn't release me when I climb onto the sidewalk, just twines his fingers through mine. The storefront before us says *Coffee, Cakes, & Confections*, and the idea of it being mine takes my breath away. I've loved the simple chemistry of cakes and cookies and scones since I was a child. The smells comfort me in a way nothing else can. Feeding other people those delicious things? The best.

He nods to the glass double doors. "That's your bakery. You have an office there to meet with clients and a kitchen in the back where you do prep, but the front is all about coffee and baked goods."

"Any good?"

"The most amazing things I've ever tasted." He presses a hand to his stomach. "I think I've gained ten pounds since you opened it."

I quirk a brow. "Can't tell."

He squeezes my hand. "Your apartment is upstairs."

We walk to the paved walkway at the back of the building, and I have to stop and smile at the gurgling water of the New Hope River. I grew up here, playing along the banks, and nothing says *home* to me like the sound and smell of the river.

I slow as we approach the stairs. They're wooden and look sturdy enough. They aren't especially steep, and it's August, so it's not like they'd be slippery with ice. Was the doctor right? Did someone push me down the stairs?

Max touches my shoulder. "Are you okay?"

"This is where it happened?"

"Lizzy found you. Thank God she came by when you didn't answer your phone."

"Does that seem as weird to you as it does to me?"

He shifts awkwardly. "I don't know, Han. My best guess is that you forgot to eat again and maybe your blood sugar tanked." He strokes my cheek with his index finger. "You've been pretty bad about that since you opened the business."

Forgetting to eat? That doesn't sound like me at all. I've *pretended* that I "forgot" to eat before, but I've never truly forgotten. Eating is my coping mechanism. My go-to when all else fails. But then again, with all the amazing things happening in my life, maybe I didn't need to cope anymore.

We take the stairs to the second floor, and I find myself hoping to feel a faulty step or find something I could have tripped over. If I'd passed out from not eating and hadn't been conscious to catch myself, would that explain the force of my fall?

When we get to the door, I rummage through my purse for my keys, but Max just grins and opens the door with a key on his ring.

He has a key to my apartment. Of course he does. We're engaged.

He flicks on the lights, illuminating a spacious, open-concept loft. To the left is a little kitchen, the right a living room, and on the back wall, against windows overlooking the New Hope River, a tiny pub-height table and four chairs.

"Wow. This is… Wow."

He cocks his head, watching me as I take in our surroundings. "Doesn't ring any bells?"

I frown. "I'm sorry. I don't remember."

He nods. We went over this again and again at the hospital. What I remember (everything before a day approximately eleven months ago) and what I don't remember (everything since), but I imagine this is as difficult for him to comprehend as it is for me.

"Well, this apartment is yours, as is the bakery."

"I still can't get over knowing I started my own business." And not just any business. A bakery. The dream.

He steps closer. "A damn good one," he whispers.

I tilt my head up to look at him. He's half a foot taller than me. I wonder if that makes it difficult to kiss while standing. I'm sure I've kissed him before. How many hundred times do you kiss a man before wearing his ring?

My heart pounds as his gaze travels from my eyes to my mouth and back. For as sweet as he's been since I woke up in the hospital, for as many times as he's kissed my hand or cheek, for as many times as he's touched me, he has yet to properly *kiss* me.

And I want to properly kiss Max more than I want to breathe.

Without the memory of his kiss, this might as well be the first time.

He skims his thumbs along either side of my jaw. "When Lizzy called and said you were at the hospital and unconscious, I was so damn worried about you. I felt like I'd lost half of myself. Don't do that to me again, okay?"

I force a laugh. "Right. I'll try not to."

His gaze dips to my mouth again. "I want to hold you and never let go, and at the same time I'm too afraid that if I let myself touch you, I'll hurt you."

"You're not going to hurt me," I whisper. *Kiss me. Please kiss me.*

Then he does. He lowers his head and sweeps his lips over mine as if it's the most natural thing in the world. As if he's done it a million times. His kiss is soft but warm, and I slide my hand into his hair to encourage him. It doesn't take much before his mouth opens over mine and I can taste his gum, his heat, his carefully harnessed control.

He's good at this, and my heart quickly goes from a nervous hammering to a stuttering, aroused racing.

He pulls me close until my breasts are pressed against his chest and I can feel the long ridge of his erection against my stomach. When he breaks the kiss and nuzzles his face into the crook of my neck, he leaves one hand at my hip, his thumb skimming the skin just above the band of my jeans.

This is my life. It doesn't seem possible.

I know he's holding back, stopping himself. By the way his

fingers are curling possessively into my hip, I can tell he wants more—and I want to give him more. My heart stumbles at the idea. *More. With Max.*

Max lifts his head and runs his gaze over my face. His blue eyes have gone dark and smoky. Is that how he looks at me when I'm naked? God, I hope so. And yet, even with the changes in my body, the idea of his eyes on my nude form makes me painfully self-conscious. I've seen the women he's dated. I'll never compare to them.

"Do you need to rest or do you want me to stay for a little bit?" There's a painful edge to his voice.

"Stay." I flush and my teeth sink into my lip. "I'm a little nervous," I confess, but even as I say it, I tug his shirt from his pants and slide my hands underneath it. I've had a crush on Max since I was thirteen years old, and now I finally have permission to touch him the way I've only dreamed of before.

His stomach is washboard flat under my fingertips. As I trace the soft line of hair from his navel to the band of his jeans, his eyes float shut. His breath rushes past his parted lips. I remember admiring these abs when he was working on the deck at Arlen Fisher's cabin. I guess that would be almost a year ago now. He had sweat trickling down his chest, and he was laughing with William Bailey about something. I remember looking at him and wishing I was the kind of girl he liked. Wishing I stood a chance.

And now I'm wearing his ring.

That knowledge fills me with confidence I never imagined having, and I release the button on his jeans and slide my fingers into the band of his boxers. He hisses and staggers back half a step.

I flush with embarrassment. I shouldn't have been so bold. I shouldn't have assumed that—

"You just got out of the hospital."

One look at his face and my insecurities fall away. He's breathing hard, and there's something tortured about the way he's looking at me.

"You're not going to hurt me, Max. Please don't worry about that."

He takes my hand and leads me to the couch. He sits first, but instead of taking the seat beside him, I grasp on to this newfound confidence and straddle his hips.

He groans. "You're determined to tempt me, aren't you?"

I shift side to side, adjusting my knees until his erection puts delicious pressure between my legs.

"Hanna," he breathes.

There's something in his eyes. Something so much beyond the tenderness he showed me in the hospital. Heat. "I don't want you to hold back." I press my mouth to his, and his hands instantly find my hips, his curling fingers betraying his true desires. I want more of that, more of this evidence that this is really happening, that this is really my life.

"I can't wait to marry you," he whispers against my mouth. His fingertips roam over my jaw and across my collarbone as he shakes his head. "How did I get so lucky?"

"Tell me about our first date."

His face splits into a grin. "You want to hear about how nervous you were or where we went or—"

"How did it happen?" I settle my hand on his chest, loving the solid heat of it under my hand, the feel of his steady heartbeat. "I've had a crush on you for so long, but I thought you only had eyes for Lizzy. Did I finally work up the courage to ask you out?"

Some emotion I can't identify flashes over his face. "I asked you."

"Really?"

"You joined the gym, and I could tell you liked me." He shrugs awkwardly and slides his hands around from my hips to my ass. "Asking you to dinner was definitely the best decision I ever made in my life."

I'm engaged to Max Hallowell, and he says these amazingly sweet things to me. "Where did you take me?"

"Sebastian's."

My eyes go wide. "Fancy."

"I was determined to impress you."

"Ha! I liked you so much, you could have taken me to

McDonald's and I would have been impressed."

"Hanna—"

I cut him off with my kiss. I press my lips softly to his and feel him relax underneath me. When his lips part and his hands tangle in my hair, I'm not kissing him anymore. He's kissing me. His lips are gentle and persuasive, and I'm swept into that feeling that this is all some elaborate dream. And I don't want to wake up.

By the time our lips part, we're both breathing heavily, and I lean my forehead against his. "What are we going to do if my memory doesn't come back?" I whisper. The question has been nagging at me. "We're supposed to be getting married and I've lost the entirety of our relationship. This must be so terrible for you."

His eyes go wide. "You're worried about *me*?"

"It doesn't seem fair to ask you to start over."

"I'm not marrying your memories. I'm marrying you. And I would start over happily for you."

"This is all so surreal. I just keep waiting to wake up and find out it was all a dream."

He untangles his hands from my hair and slips them under my shirt. His touch is light and cautious of my bruises, but when his fingertips skim the underside of my breasts, he's confident and sure—a wanderer returning to familiar territory. His thumbs find my nipples and my breath draws in with a hiss. I collapse forward, resting my head on his shoulder.

"I'm here," he whispers in my ear as his fingers work delicious magic under my shirt. "And I'm real."

I roll my hips against his erection, and I can't deny it. He's real. And he's amazing.

I slide my hand between our bodies and find his hard-on.

"We shouldn't do this," he groans. His lips sample the side of my neck between his words. "Not until you're better. Not until we've really had a chance to talk."

I know this isn't the first time we've touched. It couldn't possibly be. If I wanted to release him from his jeans and take him into my mouth, it surely wouldn't be the first time for that either.

In the war between my desires and my self-conscious nerves, my nerves are winning, and I won't have that. If this is my new amazing life, I'm going to live it up.

"I guess it's stupid that I'm so nervous," I whisper.

"It isn't. Not at all."

Anything else he planned to say is cut off by his groan as I unzip his jeans and release him from his boxers with one bold move of my hand.

My breath catches at the sight of him, long and thick and hard. For me. I lick my lips, wrap my hand around his shaft, and stroke.

"Jesus." His eyes float closed and his hips buck instinctively, moving him hard against the grip of my hand.

My nerves flitter away as he gets lost in my touch. He fights to keep his eyes open, his control intact. I may be a little on the inexperienced side, but I know how to give a damn good hand job. I had one asshole boyfriend my freshman year in college who demanded them regularly. Once, I regretted that relationship, but suddenly it feels worth it because I love the pleasure on Max's face—the way he looks at me through his lashes, the way his nostrils flare as I use my thumb to test the moisture at the tip of his cock.

"Hanna," he chokes out, and I squeeze him a little harder. I can tell he's close by the way he's swelling. Harder. Thicker.

I push off him and to my knees on the floor, never releasing him.

He reaches for me, but I ignore his hands and lick the swollen head of his dick.

"Oh, fuck."

I grin because he's lost the battle with his self-control I never intended to let him win.

I release him just long enough to slide my tongue up the underside of his shaft, and his body shudders. When I stretch my lips over him and take him deep, he groans, and I feel beautiful and powerful. My body winds tight with arousal.

Max puts a gentle hand on my face. "You don't have to—"

I pull him deeper before he can say anything else. I don't

remember doing this before—blowjobs are definitely not in the limited realm of my remembered experience—but sixty seconds in, I can already tell what feels good to him and what makes him nearly lose control.

I work my tongue over the underside of him and add more suction to my movement. His gentle hand moves to my head and slides into my hair. He leads me to take him half an inch deeper. Before I can even adjust to the new depth, he's coming, filling my throat in a way I never would have imagined could be so sexy.

Yet a smile curves my lips as I release him, as happy as I am turned on. And *fuck* am I turned on.

He pulls me into his lap and gathers me against him.

"That was amazing," I murmur into his chest.

His body shakes with his nearly silent chuckle. "I'm pretty sure that's my line."

"I know you were trying not to go there tonight, but…" I sigh and grin up at him. "I couldn't help myself."

He kisses me firmly, tongue sweeping into my mouth, teeth nipping my lips. Then his hand is under my shirt again, doing delicious things to my nipples, and I hope he never stops.

"I like that so much," I breathe into his ear, and he moans and rolls a nipple between two fingers. He slides his other hand between my legs. I come up on my knees to get a better angle. As I rock into his hand, a desperate moan slips from my lips, and he gives me the extra pressure I need. My body might be beaten and tender, but I've had years of fantasies about this man. I don't have the patience to wait now that I have him at my fingertips.

More pressure between my legs. The hem of my jeans presses into my swollen clit, and I grind harder, but I need more. I need slick skin and rough fingers and—

"Ack!"

The sound of a woman's screech has me jumping off the couch. My feet tangle under me and I go down, falling to the floor and knocking my head on the glass coffee table.

Max's eyes go to the door, where my mom's standing, her

back already turned to us, her hand thrown over her eyes.

"Shit," he mutters.

"I didn't see anything," Mom sing-songs. "Just here to check on my daughter and drop off some groceries." She hoists a plastic bag into the air as evidence.

Max quickly pulls himself together, zipping his pants before sinking to the floor next to me. "Are you okay?"

I rub my head where it hit the table. "I'm fine." A little mortified that my mother just walked in on me grinding myself against Max's hand. But hey, I'm an optimist, and the optimist in me is just glad she didn't find her way in the front door, say, five minutes earlier—when I was on my knees.

"We didn't lock the door, did we?" he whispers.

"Apparently not."

"Yeah, next time—"

"Absolutely."

He helps me off the floor, and I give my girlie parts a silent little lecture about patience because they're down there whimpering, *"Not fair! Make her leave! Things were just getting good!"*

"Is everyone decent?" Mom asks, already turning around.

"Now we are," I say under my breath. "Mom, maybe you should knock next time?"

"You just got out of the hospital. I didn't think…" In her defense, her cheeks are beet red, and I'm fairly confident she will be knocking next time. And every time after. "I was young once too. I remember those weeks leading up to my wedding. Your father and I could hardly—"

"Mom. Please?" Somehow I don't think hearing about how horny she was before marrying Dad is actually going to make this situation less awkward.

"I'm just here to make sure you don't need anything, but obviously Max was taking care of you—"

"Mom!"

She throws her hand over her mouth, but I can see her smile peeking out the sides. "I didn't mean it like that." She drops her hand and sighs as she sets the single bag of groceries on the counter.

"Thanks for checking on her and"—Max rubs the back of his neck—"sorry about that."

She waves away his apology. "So we haven't had a chance to really celebrate your engagement, what with this accident nonsense. Max, would you allow me to host an engagement party at my house? I don't want to be the over-intruding mother-in-law, but I would really love to celebrate."

Max wraps his arms around me from behind and kisses my hair. I love that he seems to always be touching me. Like he can't help himself. "That would be wonderful, Mrs. Thompson. There's nothing I want to celebrate as much as Hanna agreeing to marry me."

She presses her hand to her chest and tears swell in her eyes. "It does my heart good to see you two together and so happy. The news of your engagement was what really got me through worrying about my daughter."

"I'm okay, Mom."

She nods and blinks away her tears. "I know, I know. But it was a shock. Oh, look at me! Keeping you up when you should be getting your rest."

Even after her touching display of emotion, I want her to leave so I can be alone with Max again. I blame those girlie parts down south. They apparently have a mind of their own, and an active imagination to go with it.

Mom adjusts her purse on her shoulder. "Try to sleep tonight. I know it's hard, but it's important if you're going to recover."

"I will," I promise.

Mom turns her smile on my fiancé. "Max, would you be a doll and walk me out? I know you need to get going too."

Max nods, and it takes everything in me to keep the smile on my face. *Effing seriously? He's leaving me?*

"Of course I will." He winks at me. "You know how to get me if you need me."

If I need him? I would have thought that was obvious.

Chapter
FOUR

ALMOST PERFECT.
I'm surveying my life as if from the outside, and that's how it looks to me. Almost perfect. Sure, I have these bruises and I'm banged up from my fall, but everything else? My apartment. My business. My body. *Max...*

He looks at me like I'm the most precious thing in the world. And I'm wearing his ring. I might not remember how my life got like this, but I'll do whatever it takes to keep it this way.

I wander around my apartment, feeling a bit like a rude visitor peeping in on someone else's life. The kitchen is clean, the refrigerator full of water bottles, apples, and carrot sticks. The freezer isn't much better, with little more than frozen berries and chicken breasts, and the pantry is sparse. Mom brought me a half-gallon of milk and some fresh fruit, but I still need to go grocery shopping. I find a notepad on the counter and start a list:

Grocery shopping: Bread, milk, cereal, pasta

I stop writing and stare at the list I've made. These were foods I ate before. What do I eat now? I'll have to be careful about what I buy. I'm sure I worked hard to lose this weight.

My mind goes to the stairs again. The fall. Max's words about low blood sugar and me forgetting to eat. Was that really all there was to it, or did I have to live on the meager basics in my kitchen to get this thin?

I shake away the thought. If I'd developed unhealthy habits, my sisters would have put a stop to it. Anyway, however I got here, I don't want to ruin my progress. Especially if we're planning a wedding.

A thrill runs through me at the thought. A wedding. I'm marrying Max.

But as I go to return the notepad to the basket, a small slip of paper falls out.

It's a prescription for an antidepressant. And it's dated one week ago. Why would I need that?

My phone buzzes on the counter, and I tuck the script into the bottom of the basket for safekeeping before grabbing my cell. I don't recognize the number on the display, and I'm not in the mood to chat anyway, so I send the call to voicemail.

As I wander the living room area, I spot a laptop on the desk in the corner. I immediately open it, ready to peek into the last year of my life the way a stranger might—social media. A dialogue box pops up on the screen and asks for my password. I tap in my birthday, but it doesn't take. I try my initials and my birthday. Still nothing. Those have always been my go-to passwords. I'll have to ask Max if he knows what it is. Maybe I used our first date or his pet name for me.

The bedroom is tidy, save for a basket of unfolded laundry in one corner. The closet isn't overly full, but I have a nice collection of jeans and shirts in my new smaller size and a slew of black workout capris and tank tops.

It's a small apartment so it doesn't take me long to see everything. I should take a shower and try to get some sleep. Tomorrow I want to learn all I can about my business and see what I need to do to catch up from my hospital stay. The idea of the water hitting my bruises with any pressure at all is more than I can bear, so I run a bath instead and sigh as I sink into the warm water. I release my hair from its clip and let it fall down my back.

When it's just me and the lulling beat of the water pouring into the tub, I let myself think about Max and what we might be doing if my mother hadn't come over tonight.

I skim my fingertips over my breasts and imagine him stripping off my shirt and releasing my heavy breasts from my bra. I squeeze my nipples with the thought of Max taking them into his mouth. Men have always liked my breasts, and I love having them played with, squeezed, sucked. Would he have kept me in his lap, his hand stroking me through my jeans as he sucked and played? Or would he have taken me to my bedroom so he could lay me down and explore my body?

My mind latches on to that image—a bare-chested Max hovering over me in bed, unzipping my jeans and dragging them down my hips as he sucked my nipple into his mouth, laved it with his tongue.

These aren't new fantasies, but knowing Max is mine now heightens their intensity. This "what if" could just as well be our "next time." Remembering how good it felt to have his hand between my legs and his breath in my hair, I'm already close when I slip my hand into the hot water and find my swollen flesh. I'm so wrapped in the fantasy that the hand isn't mine anymore. It's Max's. His hot mouth is open against my neck, and all he has to do is slip a finger inside me—*God, yes, like that*. I imagine his hand, his hot breath at my ear, his groan. I cling to the thought and I come.

After I wash my hair, dry off, and put on my pajamas, I lock the door and pad to bed with my phone in my hand. When I climb in, I pull up the text messages on my phone and enter Max's name.

> **Hanna:** *I hate that you had to leave when you did.*
> **Max:** *You and me both. Are you okay?*
> **Hanna:** *I am now. Took a bath and imagined how things could have gone if my mom hadn't shown up.*
> **Max:** *Want to tell me about it?*
> **Hanna:** *The bath? It was what you'd expect. Hot. Wet.*

Max: *You're killing me.*
Hanna: *That'll teach you to choose walking my mom to her car over finishing things with me.*
Max: *Lesson learned.*

I wake up to someone climbing into bed next to me, hot, hard muscle cozying up behind me.

I blink away sleep. Max is in my bed and I want to enjoy it, enjoy him, but sleep has such a tight hold on me I can hardly keep my eyes open. I snuggle as close to him as I can get, but sleep is already tugging me back down.

"Couldn't stay away?" I murmur in the darkness.

"You know I can't," he whispers against my ear. His voice is different somehow. Deeper? Maybe sleepy? I don't have time to think about it because I'm wrapped up in his heat, his bare chest against my back, one of his hands right between my breasts, and I can't fight it when my dreams suck me back in. But somehow, with his heat against me and his arms around me, my fitful dreams fade away and I don't just sleep. I rest.

When I wake again, the room is still dark, but Max's mouth is doing delicious things to the side of my neck. I arch against him and am greeted by the hard length of his erection against my ass. I have to bite my lip at the thrill that rushes through me. Not only can I do that to him, but he wanted me enough that he had to come back tonight.

Under my shirt, his fingertips skim the underside of my breasts, and a soft moan slips from my lips. He cups my breast in his hot hand and grazes his callused palm against my nipple, toys and teases until it's hard and tight under his hand and I am rocking back into him instinctively.

"Jesus, I missed you so much." His voice sounds funny, but I hardly have time for the thought to register before he's squeezing my nipples, sending electric jolts of pleasure from my breasts and right up through my center. His touch is harder than it was earlier. Rougher. But I like it. He's so good at this. He knows exactly how to touch me, exactly how much pressure I like. I wouldn't want him to ever stop touching my breasts if it weren't for this nearly painful ache that's been pulsing between my legs since we were interrupted in my living room—the ache my own touch couldn't quite ease.

I circle my hips and rub my backside against his erection. Thick and wild arousal buzzes through me, electric and sharp with its intensity. He wants me as much as I want him.

"Touch me," I whisper into the darkness. "I need you to touch me."

He groans against my neck and then his fingers are dipping into the waistband of my sleep pants.

I turn in his arms just as his hand meets the hot and needy place between my thighs. Our mouths touch in the darkness, and something niggles at the back of my mind. Something's changed between last night and now. Does he smell different or—

The thought disintegrates as he slides a finger inside me. I can't believe how slick and wet I am. Except that this is Max and I need his touch.

I rock against him, letting him touch me the way I touched myself in the bath. Only this is hotter. Sweeter. More intense. Not just because it's him. It's almost as if he knows what I like better than I do. His finger moves inside me and his teeth nip at my neck almost painfully. But I like it. I want more of this unbridled lust, more of his expert touch.

He withdraws his finger and replaces it with two, stretching me in a way that has my body pulsing around him in response.

"Yes," I whisper. I want this. Need it.

His thumb finds my clit and his fingers curl.

"Oh God…" Am I a screamer? I bite my lip, but holy shit, I can't—

"Let me hear you scream," he growls in my ear, his stubble scraping at the tender skin of my neck. "Let me feel you pulse around my fingers as you come."

I curl my nails into his forearm, not to stop him, but

because this pleasure inside me is so intense I have to do something, put this energy somewhere.

His other hand slides up my side and squeezes right at the bruise on my ribs. Pain vibrates through me, and I cry out.

"Hanna?" He pulls away and clicks on the light.

I'm still wincing at the pain from my manhandled bruise when I look at him through squinted eyes.

And then I scream.

I shove the man off me as hard as I can. My mind gropes for the lessons I learned in the personal defense class I took in college. I bring up my knee, aiming for his balls.

He lets out an airy *oomph,* and I flail, backing as far away from him as I can get. I fall off the bed, and the impact of my already-battered body slamming into the floor has me crying out.

"Jesus, Hanna!" the man—who is definitely not Max—says from the bed. "What the fuck was that for?"

Oh God. He knows my name.

I'm trembling.

My phone is on the bedside table, and I scramble to get to it before he can take it away.

"I'll call the police!" I warn, holding the phone up like it's a weapon.

The man on the bed is white-faced and stricken and looking at me like I've lost my mind.

"You can't just come into a woman's house and get into her bed." Shit. Now I'm trying to reason with a sex offender. Jesus. But he's just sitting there. Is that *normal*?

His expression goes from confused to desolate as he skims his eyes over my bruised face. "Damn. What happened to you, angel?"

I fumble with my phone, pressing the button on the side and trying to get it to light up. Nothing. It's dead. Why didn't I charge it before I fell asleep last night?

He pushes off the bed, and I back into a corner, arms wrapped around myself. "Leave. Please."

He holds up his hands and takes a step toward me. "Hanna,

baby. Tell me what happened. Tell me—"

I press my body as close to the wall as I can. I should have locked myself in the bathroom or something. I am one of those too-dumb-to-live heroines you see in horror movies. Especially since the thing keeping me here—keeping me from running to *safety*—is the hurt on his face. I've always been the kind of person who tries to make people happy, but this is ridiculous.

Think, Hanna. Okay, I'll need a description for the cops. Tall—taller than Max, maybe—messy dark hair, an Incredible Hulk tattoo on his right shoulder, some numbers tattooed above his left pec. God, is he an ex-con? Don't convicts get numbers tattooed on themselves?

He steps closer, and a shudder runs through me.

"Please don't hurt me." I sink to the floor and cross my arms in front of my face.

His gaze catches on my left hand, and his jaw goes hard. "I see." He backs off and grabs something off the floor. Then he's tugging a shirt over his head. It falls into place and covers that amazing body.

Amazing body? What the eff is wrong with me?

As stupid as it is, I don't believe this man is here to hurt me. There's nothing intimidating about his body language, and even though his face has gone hard and angry, there's no violence in his eyes.

He grabs his jeans. "You could have told me."

"I don't know what you're talking about." My voice cracks.

Jeans unbuttoned and half up his hips, he's heading toward the door. Stupidly, I follow him. My hands are shaking, my head spinning.

He grabs the doorknob and goes still, but he doesn't look at me. "When I was touching you just now"—he swallows—"you thought I was…"

"I thought you were my fiancé." The whisper seems to swell in the small space and vibrate off the walls.

He punches the wall beside the door. "You and Max have a nice life." Then he's leaving, slamming the door behind him and making the whole room rattle. And me right along with it.

Chapter
FIVE

"So did Max stay over last night?" Lizzy sets a steaming mug of black coffee in front of me and stirs cream into her own, all the while avoiding my gaze.

"Can I have some of that?"

"Cream? As in, empty calories? For healthier-than-thou Hanna?"

I've been drinking coffee since I was sixteen, and I've been taking cream in it for just as long. I try a sip without and shake my head. My memory loss apparently includes how to enjoy black coffee. "Yes, please." I snag the cream before she can make any more comments.

We're at a table in the front of my bakery, the OPEN sign glowing into the darkness of Main Street.

I convinced myself not to call her last night. I'd wanted to. I'd been confused and scared, and the most natural instinct had been to call Liz. After the man left my apartment, I ran to find my phone charger and plug in my phone. I stared at the screen as it came to life, but I kept thinking of the way the man's face had changed when his gaze landed on my ring. My mind kept repeating the deep rumble of his voice as he'd said, *"You and Max have a nice life."*

It wasn't confusion or fear that made me decide not to call her. As I sank to the edge of my bed and settled my head in my hands, adrenaline still hummed through my veins, but the frantic, clawing fear was gone. In its place boiled red-hot *shame*.

"So, Max?" Lizzy asks. She holds up her hands. "Not that it's my business."

There's something different in our relationship. We could always say anything to each other, though we often didn't have to. An exchanged glance was usually enough to let her know how I was feeling. But there's a rift between us now. I can sense it even if I can't explain it. I noticed first at the hospital—not so much by the way she acted when she was around, but more because of how often she *wasn't* around. I kept expecting her to be the one coming into my room to keep me company, but nine times out of ten, it was someone else.

All my life, people have asked me what it's like to be a twin. They want me to explain our connection. Trying to explain to someone what it's like to have a twin sister is like trying to explain what it's like to have a pulse. I don't know any other way. All I know is that her smile is attached to my heart. I float when she's happy, and when she's sad, my world is a puzzle with a missing piece.

But right now that connection is gone. I want to blame the amnesia, but I'm pretty sure that's just the optimism thinking.

"Max didn't stay," I say cautiously.

She rolls her eyes and mutters something I can't quite make out. "*Goody two-shoes*," maybe? She wouldn't call me that if she knew I woke up to another man in my bed. "Any progress with your memory?"

I shake my head. "Not yet. Patience, right?" Patience. I'm engaged to marry the man of my dreams, who I might or might not have been cheating on. Waiting for my memories to return should be a piece of cake.

"Well, patience isn't going to run this bakery," Liz mutters. "In the meantime, I'd better bring you up to speed."

She gives me a tour of my bakery. The front area is small

but serviceable. It has four tables and a bar along the wall with outlets. "So people who are working on their laptops don't hog the tables," Lizzy explains. The glass cases in the front feature everything from freshly baked Italian bread and croissants to cupcakes and fresh pastries.

"My mouth is watering just looking at all of it."

Lizzy snorts. "You don't touch it. Not a grain of sugar has passed those lips in at least three months."

"Nothing tastes as good as thin feels, I guess?"

"Clearly the amnesia has wiped away all memory of your cheese Danish. Maggie declared it foodgasmic, and she's not wrong. And your chocolate croissants?" She closes her eyes and bites her lower lip.

"You're making me hungry," I complain.

Her lips quirk into a lopsided smile. "Good. I didn't think you were capable of hunger anymore. Maybe the amnesia fixed you." She leads the way past the glass cases and through the doors to the gleaming stainless-steel kitchen at the back. Ovens line one wall, and another has a row of walk-in coolers.

"Holy crap," I breathe. "How did I afford this place?"

"You didn't. You had some silent partner backing you, so money wasn't an issue."

"Silent partner? Who?"

She shrugs. "I don't know. You were all mysterious about it. We thought it might have been Asher, but when Maggie asked him, he said he didn't have anything to do with it. Mom thinks maybe it was Max, but that doesn't explain why you'd be secretive about it. But *somebody* came in here and renovated the building and got you your little start-up."

"It's probably in my paperwork, huh?"

She shrugs. "I guess."

"I'm just surprised Mom didn't try to talk me out of it. You know how she's felt most of her life about my baking."

"She wasn't thrilled about your choice, but you could pretty much do no wrong in her eyes since you started dating Max." There's something snide about the way she says it, as if I dated Max and improved my relationship with my mom all to irritate her.

"I can't believe I took the plunge. That doesn't seem like me."

"You haven't seemed much like yourself for a while now," she says, but I don't think the words are for me. She shakes her head and waves away the subject. "You had a wedding last weekend while you were in the hospital. You'd already gotten the cake finished, so Maggie and I handled it for you, but you probably want to call the bride when she gets back from her honeymoon next week."

The bride. Because I make wedding cakes.

"I've been taking care of the bread orders for the restaurants and grocers who contract with you. Drew has been keeping up with the baking for the front, but school's going to start soon. She won't be able to put in the hours she has been."

"Drew?"

"Cally's sister."

I shake my head. "I know who she is. I guess I'm just surprised she works for me."

"She started the week you opened. She's a good little worker as long as you can keep her off her phone and away from the customers. Customer service isn't her forte."

I grin at the image of Cally's know-it-all teenage sister struggling to be kind to sorority girls ordering non-fat, sugar-free, extra-hot, double-shot mochas.

"You have a wedding this weekend, so we'll need to find time to get the cake made and decorated. I can try to help if you don't remember, but honestly, the decorating part has always been your baby and I pretty much suck at it."

"Wait. So you work with me?"

She lifts a brow. "I'm pretty sure you think of it as me working *for* you, but yes. I haven't gotten a teaching job, and I work for my sister like a loser."

"You work *with* me, and I think that's awesome."

She rolls her eyes. "Anyway, you have three meetings with upcoming brides this week."

"Wow." I turn a slow circle. "I can't believe how quickly it's taken off."

My stomach twists as I scan the gleaming stainless-steel countertops. I've been so hung up on my new body and my engagement to Max, I haven't had the chance to think much about this part of my life. How am I supposed to run my business if I don't even remember what recipes I use or what clients I've promised cakes to?

"I don't even know where I buy supplies," I mutter to myself.

Lizzy's cool fingers gently squeeze my forearm. "It's going to be okay." Her eyes connect with mine, and for a split second, it's back—that connection between us flickers like lights in a storm. "You should come to Maggie and Asher's with me tonight. Asher and Nate are having a jam session and they're making a get-together out of it."

"Nate who?"

"Crap. I guess you probably don't even remember him. Nate Crane? You know, sexy rocker?" She frowns. "I guess you wouldn't know. He was kind of an unknown before, but he's been touring with Asher, and his single is really shooting up the charts."

"Cool." I shift. Partying it up at Asher's doesn't appeal to me right now. After my middle-of-the-night visitor, I just want to spend my evening with Max and reassure myself that everything is okay. "I'll probably take a rain check, though."

"Oh." She sounds disappointed. Really disappointed. Like she was counting on me. "Okay, well, that's fine."

And just like that, the flickering light of our connection is snuffed out again.

"What happened to us?"

"What?"

"You and me. Why are you mad at me?"

"I don't know what you're talking about."

"Come on, Liz. This is us. Something's not right."

Lizzy shifts her gaze away. "Truth be told, you and I haven't exactly been close lately."

"Why?"

She shrugs. "I don't know. You started dating Max, and it was okay at first, but then you were running all the time and you were losing weight and—"

"You stopped being close to me because I lost weight?"

"Jesus! No. Of course not. You're the one who pulled away." She cuts her eyes to the floor and bites her lip. "At least that's how it felt to me, but I might have been uncomfortable with all the changes you were making. It just didn't seem healthy, ya know?"

"Getting healthy didn't seem healthy?"

She throws up her hands. "See? You're so defensive about it! We could never talk, and when we did, all you cared about was Max and running, and I didn't even recognize you anymore."

My eyes fill with tears. "I thought you of all people would be happy for me when I finally got some goodness in my life."

"Is it good, Hanna? Are you so sure?" She stares at me for a long time, that little wrinkle appearing between her blond brows.

The bell over the front door rings, ending our staring contest.

When we go out front, we find Mom and Granny behind the front counter, preparing themselves cups of coffee, Mom a flurry of anxious gestures in her pink business suit and Granny serene in her wrinkled cotton hippie skirt.

"Your first day out of the hospital and you're already back at work," Mom lectures.

"I'm fine," I assure her.

"You're not fine. You've had a bad fall and you need to recover."

"The doctor said I could get back to my normal routine. She said it might even be good for me."

Mom grins. "And you know what else will be good for you?"

"I can guess," Lizzy grumbles.

"I have appointments scheduled with three different possible wedding venues," Mom says. "I thought, what better way to recuperate than to focus on something that makes you happy? Something good."

"I don't know if I can—"

"I won't hear any objections. You're my daughter, and I'm going to make sure you take care of yourself these next few weeks." She tilts my chin up and moves my face side to side, inspecting my bruises. If she thinks those are bad, she should see what's going on under my shirt. "I bet you'll be healed enough for a wedding in as soon as a month."

Lizzy chokes on her coffee, and I gape at my mother. "A month?"

Granny tsks. "Don't rush the girl, Gretchen."

"Why you would drag your feet when a man like Max wants to marry you is beyond me."

"I'm not dragging my feet," I object, but I kind of am. Because don't I need answers before I can say my vows to Max? Don't I need my memories?

"So it's settled. We'll spend tomorrow looking at wedding venues."

"I can't just set a date without talking to Max," I object.

Mom waves away my concern. "It's the wedding. All men worry about is the bachelor party and the wedding night. Besides, we need to know what dates the venue you want is available. *Then* we'll talk about setting a date."

I try to take deep breaths, but I keep thinking about the man in my apartment, about all the things I *don't* know about the last year. My headache is back and nausea rolls over me. I brace myself on the counter.

"See, Gretchen?" Granny scolds. "You're stressing her out."

"I'm okay," I lie. "I'm just a little overwhelmed. I need Lizzy to bring me up to date on work stuff and I'll feel better."

Mom rolls her eyes then sighs. "Fine. I'll pick you up tomorrow at noon. Elizabeth, don't you dare let your sister do any work."

"Yes, ma'am," Lizzy says, irritation clear in her voice.

The women take their coffee and push through the door. A hot billow of August air fills the store as the door floats closed.

"Come on," Lizzy says. "Let's get some baking done before

you have to spend all your waking hours planning your happily-ever-after."

My phone buzzes from the pocket of my apron. I wipe my hands on a towel and pull it out.

Appointment with Doc Perkins.

I frown at the calendar reminder. Do I know a Dr. Perkins?

I move to the sink and turn the water on with the back of my hand. Once it's hot, I wash my hands with soap and water, dry them, and grab my phone again.

I have no idea how I managed to lose so much weight while doing this job. A single morning in my bakery and I'm jacked up on dozens of taste tests. A little bite of this treat, a sample of that frosting. I practically have a stomach ache. Thank God for my compulsive organization. It was relatively easy to find all my recipes. I was preparing gum-paste calla lilies for this weekend's wedding cake when my phone buzzed, but I can finish up later.

The reminder doesn't have a phone number or an address, so I pull up the browser on my phone and do a quick search. "Dr. Perkins New Hope" doesn't get me any hits, so I try "Dr. Perkins Indianapolis."

Dr. Perkins, MD, Psychiatry

A psychiatrist?

I scroll through my calendar, moving back through the past three months, but I only see one appointment with the doctor listed and it was a week ago. Was I going to start regular appointments? Why? For pointers on keeping brides calm? Or maybe the doctor is the silent partner Liz told me about?

Right. The relationship is a business one and you just happen to have a script for antidepressant in your apartment.

This doctor must have some answers to the endless questions that have taken up residence in my brain. I highlight the address in my browser and send it to my phone's navigation system.

I've already grabbed my keys when I pause. I'm not supposed to drive. But I'm not sure I want anyone to know I'm seeing a psychiatrist, and how can I have someone drive me without spilling the beans?

"Liz," I call to the front, pocketing my keys, "I need to leave for a few hours."

I wait for her to ask where I'm going, but she just shrugs. Her disinterest is another reminder of the distance between us. I'm not used to this, but I don't have time to think about it much. I'm too busy planning to break doctor's orders and drive to Indianapolis.

By the time I get to Dr. Perkins's office, I'm fifteen minutes late to my appointment. The receptionist's eyes go big when he sees my face. "What happened to you?"

"I got in a fight with a flight of stairs. I lost."

"Yikes." He stands and ushers me through a heavy walnut door.

On the other side, a woman is sitting behind a desk, tapping at her computer. Her face lights up then shrinks in rapid succession when she sees me. "Hanna! What happened?"

"I'll leave you," the receptionist says.

As the heavy door closes, the doctor motions to an overstuffed chair and steeples her fingers as I sit. "Tell me what's going on, Hanna."

"You're Dr. Perkins?"

Her tiny face draws into a tight frown. "Of course I am."

"And I'm…one of your patients?"

Her frown turns to skepticism.

"I took a fall." I motion to my face. I explain as briefly as I can about my amnesia, telling her I'm here because of the reminder on my phone.

"Oh, dear. I wish I would have known. I would have come to the hospital and consulted with your doctor."

I'm glad she didn't. I don't think I want my friends and family to know I've sought out therapy. "I don't understand." I don't want to offend this woman. She seems very nice. "It shows in my calendar that I've been here before, and I found a prescription for antidepressants in my apartment, but..." I'm not sure how to say it.

"Go on," she prods.

"My life seems perfect. I have my own business that seems to be going great, and I'm engaged to marry an amazing man. I feel okay about my body for the first time in my life. Why would I need to see a psychiatrist? Why would I need antidepressants?" *Why would I cheat on my loving fiancé?*

She folds her arms and studies me, her face a series of hard and soft lines I can neither read nor recognize. "Do you think only people who have something 'wrong' with their lives need to seek help for their mental health?"

"Of course not. I just—" I cut myself off at her raised eyebrows. Apparently she's a no-nonsense woman. "I wouldn't put it that way. I thought that if I was seeing you and you'd prescribed antidepressants, there had to be a reason."

She's silent for a long moment that catapults me back in time to just after my father's death. I was a teenager, and Daddy was my world. Back then, I never measured up with Mom. She was always trying to fix me—shrink me, tone me, dress me, make me an acceptable representation of her family. Something she wouldn't find so shameful. But Daddy was happy to let me be. Then he died, and after the funeral, the school therapist called us down one at a time. "Why do you think you're here?" he asked me, his voice sounding more bored than empathetic, and he let the silence grow bigger and stranger between us until I answered.

But I'm not that girl anymore. I'm not the fat teenager languishing in her gorgeous sisters' shadows. I'm not the ignored child striving for perfection in all things to make up for her appearance.

Sure, I'm overweight, but look at my grades!

Sure, I can't fit into the pants in your average store, but I'm always happy.

Sure, I can't get a date to save my life, but I'm the best friend a girl could ever have.

I'm exhausted just thinking about it.

But she isn't like the school counselor and she doesn't let the silence go on forever. "You came to me because you were battling depression and an eating disorder."

I feel myself wilt. I don't want to hear these things. I don't want her tainting my perfect world. I shouldn't have come. I should have ignored the reminder and carried on.

"Tell me what you're thinking," Dr. Perkins says.

I remember Nix's request for me to see her in her office about diet concerns brought on by my blood work. "An eating disorder? Depression?"

Something flicks across her features. Regret? Sadness? "There's no shame in getting help. Are you eating? Since your accident?"

I pause and turn back to her. "I am."

She smiles. "That's good."

"I wasn't before, was I? That's how I lost all this weight? I was starving myself?" Panic claws at me the moment the words leave my mouth because I know they're true. "This means I'm going to gain the weight back, doesn't it?"

"You came to me because you recognized something in your own habits that you knew wasn't healthy. You recognized there were parts of your life more important than numbers on the scale and you wanted me to help."

I swallow, but this information is a bitter pill that goes down rough and painfully. "Did I talk to you about…other things?"

"Like what?"

"This is confidential?" I whisper.

"Of course."

"Was I cheating on my fiancé?" I shake my head. "He's my fiancé now, but I guess he would have been my boyfriend last time I was here."

She crosses her arms over her chest. "You didn't share that with me if it was true, but you didn't mention a boyfriend either."

"Oh. Yeah. I guess this was just about the food."

"Eating disorders are *never* just about the food, Hanna. They're about more than your body and about more than losing weight. They're about control. And you've spent the last three months starving yourself so you would feel like you had control over your life again."

Chapter
SIX

WHEN I return from Indianapolis, the bakery is bustling with a crowd picking up lattes for their afternoon pick-me-ups and fresh pastries to go along with them.

Squeezing past the line, I slip behind the counter and tap Lizzy's shoulder. "I need to talk."

"Yeah, well, I'm a little busy running your bakery, so—"

I take the cup from her hand and slam it on the counter. "It's important."

"PMS much?" the ponytailed pretty girl at the front of the line says.

I narrow my eyes at her before sticking my head back in the kitchen. "Drew? I need you to work the front for a few minutes."

"That's a really bad idea," Lizzy warns.

I ignore her and drag her up to my apartment. It's tempting to meet her chilliness with my own, but right now I need my sister too much. I slam the door closed behind her.

"Listen." I wag my finger in her face. I've had enough. "I don't know who pissed in your Wheaties, but right now I need my sister, so whatever is broken between us, can we just put it aside for a while?"

Her eyes go wide. "I... You..." Her shoulders sag and she collapses onto my couch.

"You asked me if I was sure things are good. Well, I'm not sure." I pace in front of her. "Everything looks so perfect on the surface, but how am I supposed to know how I feel about anything when I don't remember?"

"I'm such a bitch, Hanna. I'm sorry. Don't listen to me. I'm jealous. You're engaged, Maggie's living with Asher... Any minute now, I'm going to be the last single girl standing. Maybe that's making me cranky, but it shouldn't ruin a happy time for you."

"I think maybe I'm cheating on Max," I blurt.

"Shit, Han-Han. What happened?"

I sink onto the couch next to her and lean my head on her shoulder. She combs my hair with her fingers, and even though the contact feels awkward and unsure, it relaxes me.

"It's going to be okay," she murmurs in my ear.

She doesn't rush me, and I let myself take my time because suddenly it's all too much—the last few days, the injuries, the amnesia, the engagement, the whole new life. As much as I'd like Max to be able to comfort me, he's still a stranger to me in a lot of ways. But Lizzy's part of me. We sit, letting the minutes pass and the silence slowly stitch us back together.

I don't know how much time has passed when I finally sit up and wipe my eyes.

"Coffee?" she asks.

I nod and follow her to the kitchen, where I sit on a stool as she prepares us a fresh pot. "While Max and I were dating, do you know if I was...seeing anyone else?"

She turns to cock a brow at me. "Seeing anyone else? Miss Goody Two-Shoes date two guys at once? *As if.*"

Right. It doesn't sound like me. But how does that explain what happened last night? *Better come out with it, girl.* "Max didn't stay over last night, but I didn't sleep alone either."

Her jaw goes slack and those gorgeous baby blues of hers widen. "What? Who? Why? Does Max know?"

"All very good questions."

She prepares my coffee and hands me my mug. I wrap my hands around it, letting it warm my hands instead of drinking it.

"Are you going to tell me who else you're sleeping with," Lizzy huffs, "or are you going to make me guess?"

"Someone slid into my bed last night. I was sleeping and assumed it was Max, but then we started fooling around in the middle of the night, and when he turned on the light, I realized it...wasn't."

"Someone slipped into bed with you while you were sleeping, and it *wasn't* Max?"

I watch her carefully. "No."

"Holy shit. Who was it?"

"I have no idea. He was a stranger to me."

She slams her mug down and coffee sloshes onto the counter. "Why aren't we calling the cops?"

"Because I don't think we need to."

"You're freaking kidding me, right?"

"I'm fine. Nothing bad happened. Just let me tell it before you freak out, okay?" I wait until the panic clears from her face before I continue. "He was a stranger to me, but I was no stranger to him."

"I'm not feeling better about this yet."

"I realized the guy who'd been touching me in...rather intimate ways...wasn't Max, and of course I panicked."

"I can imagine. I'm panicking now."

"I was thinking there was some rapist in my house, and I kneed him in the balls and got the hell out of the bed, but then my phone was dead and I couldn't call for help. And he was trying to get me to calm down and all the sudden he just...stopped." I make myself take a breath. "I wasn't thinking straight, but I think everything changed when he saw my ring."

"A rapist with morals?"

"He was no rapist, Liz. He looked at my hand and then he got dressed—pulled on his shirt and pants. What kind of sex offender strips down to his boxers and climbs into bed to cuddle with his victim half the night?"

"A really screwed-up one?"

"He held me," I murmur into my coffee, "and woke me up with sweet kisses on my neck. He knew my name, knew how I like to be touched. When he saw my ring, he said, 'You could have told me.' Then, before he left, he said he hoped *Max* and I had a nice life—mentioning Max by name."

Lizzy whistles long and low. "He knows about Max?"

I nod and add, "But does Max know about him?" I let that sink in for a minute. "Max is the love of my life. Why would I ruin that?

"Was he hot?"

I roll my eyes. "Yes, but that's hardly the point."

"So who was it? Anyone from town?"

"No one I recognized, but that doesn't mean anything when I can't remember the last year."

"Oh, good point." She sips her coffee. "What did he look like?"

"Young, probably my age. Dark hair, a little shaggy like Max's, I guess. He was tall, built."

"Again, like Max," Liz says.

"Maybe taller than Max and not quite that muscular, but impressive still."

"You're describing half of Max's workout buddies."

"Fuck," I groan. "Please tell me I'm not cheating on him with one of his friends."

"In what ways *didn't* he look like Max?"

"Tattoos!" I hold my hands together. Maybe this will be the piece of information that will help Lizzy identify my visitor. "He had several. Some numbers over his left pec and a Hulk tattoo on his right shoulder."

Lizzy raises a brow. "As in Hulk Hogan?"

"As in the Incredible Hulk. *You won't like me when I'm angry* Hulk."

"You're engaged to Max Hallowell and having an affair with a nerd?"

"Maybe?" I lift my palms helplessly. "Do you know who he is? I'm really freaking out here."

She shakes her head. "Not a clue."

"Stupid amnesia."

"No kidding." She paces. Stops. Paces. Looks out the window, toys with her hair, paces some more. Suddenly, her head pops up, making her curls bounce around her face. "Oh my God. So obvious!"

"What's obvious?" I'm so worried she's going to say, "Tell Max everything." That whole "honesty is the best policy" thing has always worked for me, but…

I'm not sure this is a the-truth-will-set-you-free kind of situation. And…

How can I tell Max the truth when I don't even know what the truth is?

"This is the twenty-first century, right? If you and some guy had a thing, there would be digital evidence."

"Digital evidence? You think I'd have let him take pictures? Oh God! Video?"

Lizzy winces. "Let's hope not, but that's not what I mean. You know, text messages and stuff."

I don't even bother replying because I'm scrambling toward my purse so I can look at my phone.

I scroll through my text messages. A conversation between me and Max, between me and my mom. Maggie, Cally, Lizzy, even Cally's little sister Drew.

"Any nude pics?" Lizzy asks. "Sexting? Anything?"

"There's absolutely nothing here to make me think I was having an affair."

She grabs my phone from my hand and does her own scroll-through. "Maybe the guy's just some nut job," she says, shuddering. "God. I hope he doesn't come back."

"Me too." But even if he is a nut job, that doesn't explain what he knew about me…or the way my chest ached when I watched him leave.

September—Eleven Months Before Accident

The minute I walk into Max Hallowell's health club, I feel like I'm wearing a giant neon sign that says I don't belong here. It's not that I don't work out. Hell, I work out more than most of the skinny girls I know. But I do it in private. At home or in my mom's basement. Never in a downtown health club where everyone can stare at me and wonder how soon I'll give it up and go on a Hostess run. Because that's what people think about fat chicks. They assume we're lazy and don't work out. They assume we eat Little Debbie Cakes three times a day and don't touch fruits or vegetables.

"Hanna!" Max calls from the back. He's squatting as he stacks weights by the chest press. "To what do I owe the honor?"

Returning his smile, I look around but don't see anyone I know. The club is slow right now, only a couple of senior citizens occupying the treadmills on the far side of the room. "I wanted to, um, maybe sign up for personal training."

He pushes off the ground and wipes his hands on his shorts as he crosses to me. His smile is wide and white and so damn sincere I want to melt under it. "Tell me what you have in mind. I'll see who I can hook you up with. I have a couple of female trainers but their specialties are different, so it just depends on what your goals are."

My heart stumbles in my chest from being this close to Max. I have to tilt my chin up just to see his face. "I was hoping you could do it?" It comes out as a question, a far cry from the flirty, suggestive tone Lizzy used when we planned this.

Surprise flashes over his face. "Me? Really?"

"If you can fit me in, that would be my preference." I can't believe this comes as a surprise to him. Women all over town pay to train with Max just so they can admire his body while he puts them through suicide drills. An hour of watching his muscles flex under his T-shirt is enough motivation to do most anything.

"I'd love to train with you. Let's sit down and talk about what you want to accomplish."

He pulls out a stool by the bar, and I climb onto it and cross my legs nervously. He takes the spot next to me.

"Okay." He grabs a notebook and pen from the other side of the bar. "Let's start with long-term goals and break them down to short-term. Where do you see yourself in twelve months?"

Sexy, skinny, and naked in your bed.

"Fitness-wise," he clarifies with a wink.

My cheeks burn as if he can read my thoughts. I tuck my hair behind my ear. I came ready to work out. Kind of. I'd normally wear my hair up to work out, but Lizzy insisted it was sexier to wear it down.

"I'd like to run a half marathon next summer."

Truth is, I have no desire to run a marathon—half or otherwise. I just want to lose weight and get Max to notice me. I exercise regularly, but I hate running with the fiery intensity of a thousand suns. But Max is a runner. He runs all the time, and since this is all about spending time with him, I've decided I'm going to be a runner too.

"That's totally doable." Max writes *Run half marathon* on his notepad. "Are you a runner now or are we starting from scratch?"

"Do I look like a runner?" I regret the question as soon as it's out of my mouth. Lizzy gave me strict instructions to leave my self-deprecating humor at home. She doesn't get that it's a Fat Girl Coping Mechanism. She wouldn't get that. How could she? "Sorry. I mean, I haven't done much running. My mom made me when I was in junior high—a mile every night after school. I hated it. I want to learn to love it—on my terms—but I haven't done much since I started college."

"A year is plenty of time," Max assures me. "I mean, you're obviously fit, so I bet we're still working with a pretty impressive baseline."

Obviously fit? No one has ever said that to me before.

He grins. "Why are you blushing?"

Because you're looking at me. "I guess this is all a little embarrassing."

"Don't be embarrassed," he says. "You know what you want, and I'll make sure you get it."

"I'm going to hold you to that."

Present Day

"I can't wait to get drunk," Lizzy calls from my bathroom, where she's putting on her makeup. "Are you going to get drunk with me or are you still obsessing about calories?"

"I might drink some." I force a smile.

I guess if I'm going to keep the body I spent the last year finding, I'll need to keep some of the new habits Lizzy finds so annoying. But right now I'm too worried about potentially being a cheating bitch to give my habits—new or old—much thought. Anyway, Dr. Perkins seemed to think I shouldn't be counting calories. Though I'm not sure a pitcher of daiquiris is what she had in mind either.

Truth be told, I'm terrified to go to this party. What if I run into Mr. Hulk Tattoo? What if he outs our relationship—or whatever it was—to everyone? But I can't spend the rest of my life hiding in my apartment, so I'm going.

"Is Max coming?"

I shake my head. "He has a late client and can't make it."

Lizzy flips her head upside down and adds some sort of magic curling goo to it. "You know what I'd like?" she asks as she scrunches handfuls of hair.

I plug in my flat iron and lean against the doorframe while I wait for it to warm. "What would you like?"

"One hot fucking night with Nate Crane."

I nearly choke on my tongue laughing. "Asher's rocker friend?"

"What? Maggie has Asher. Why can't I have Nate?" She

flips her head back up and wriggles her eyebrows at me. "Tell me you wouldn't sacrifice everything to have a night of dirty, no-holds-barred sex with Mr. Rock God."

I just shrug. "I have Max."

She rolls her eyes. "Right. Max and Mr. Hulk Tattoo, meaning you got more sexy male ass last night than I've had in the last six months. Yet another reason I deserve a night with Crane. I'm the only one around here who isn't getting any."

"Poor thing."

"You have no idea. Max can't keep his hands off you."

I frown at my reflection and run my finger along my newly defined jawline. Max can't keep his hands off me. I wonder if that started before or after I lost the weight.

She digs through my makeup bag. "So any revelations about last night's mystery visitor?"

"None." *Stupid amnesia.*

"Well, I vote that he was some nut job. You should really call the cops. The guy's probably stalking you or something."

"I don't think I want to do that. Not yet."

"But you're going to tell Max, aren't you?"

Anxiety lodges like a wet ball in my throat. "I just want to have more information before I tell him anything."

"Hanna, this is serious. I saw a *60 Minutes* episode once about a guy who imagined he had this whole relationship with the woman he was stalking. He watched her all the time, so in his mind they were together. Then she started dating someone and the dude flipped out and pulled a gun on him."

I turn and she's staring at me, worry in her bright blue eyes. I don't know how to explain to her that my heart told me I could trust this guy. "There's too much we don't know. I don't want to screw things up with Max for nothing. I need to get some facts straight. That's all."

"Okay." Her eyes brim with tears. She lunges forward and wraps her arms around me. "I've missed this."

"What?"

"My sister. I've missed talking about things. Confiding in each other. You have no idea how lonely it's been for me these last few months."

"I hope I never have to find out," I whisper, and she squeezes me even harder.

By the time the party rolls around, I'm already anxious for an excuse to leave. I just want to go home and make out with Max until I'm confident I haven't screwed up a good thing.

It's a hot night, and Lizzy vetoed my jeans and T-shirt for a short denim skirt and halter that look surprisingly impressive on my new body. The halter shows off my sculpted shoulders—apparently I've been lifting weights with Max—and the skirt shows my toned runner's legs. I top the outfit off with strappy black heels and throw my hair in a twist. Despite the bruise on my right arm and the side of my face, I feel so sexy I snap a picture of myself in the mirror and send it to Max with the caption, *Wish you were coming tonight.*

Two minutes later, I'm treated to his reply.

Max: *I don't want to wait any longer than I have to. The club closes at nine. Meet me here.*

His words send hot tingles of nerves and arousal rushing to my center.

Hanna: *It's a date.*

I'm still grinning at my phone when I hear Lizzy whistle. "Damn, girl."

"I know, right? Who knew I could look like this?"

She frowns. "You were sexy before you lost the weight. I was referring to the way you're glowing."

"Oh." I press my phone to my chest. "I hope I didn't screw things up. Max is... He's amazing."

She rolls her eyes. "I'm sure there's a perfectly logical

explanation for all of this. Come on. Let's get out of here."

When we walk into Asher's, Maggie greets us at the door in a white sundress and bare feet. "You made it! I'm so glad!"

"We're on a mission." I grin and nod toward Lizzy. "My twin would like to seduce your musician friend."

"You're going to seduce Nate?" Maggie asks, skepticism all over her face.

"Unless you're planning on sharing Asher."

Maggie snorts. "As if. But Nate? Really? The guy sitting in my basement in a Spider-Man shirt?"

Lizzy scoffs. "Have you heard that voice? God concentrated sexiness and gave it to the world through Nate Crane's voice. The boy could melt the panties off a nun."

Maggie rolls her eyes. "I think we all know you're no nun. Come on. Everyone's in the basement."

She leads the way into the house and to the stairs, where she stops and points at a small table. "House rules, no phones or other distracting electronics with the music." She digs her own out of her pocket and tosses it in the basket with the others. Lizzy and I follow suit then head down the stairs to where everyone is milling in the music room. Asher doesn't have big parties. In fact, his parties might better be described as "get-togethers" with most of the attendees being members of my immediate family. Tonight, there are more guests than normal—maybe a dozen total—probably due to his musician friend who's in town.

I look to the stage, where Asher is playing acoustic guitar and singing into a mic connected to a small amp. My gaze shifts to the man sitting next to him and I stop breathing.

"Asher's hot too," Lizzy's assuring Maggie, "but Nate could do *whatever* he wanted to me and I'd thank him in the morning."

Nate Crane. Dark, shaggy hair, deep voice, intense gaze. And no doubt a Hulk tattoo hidden beneath his right sleeve of his Spider-Man T-shirt. "Holy shit."

"He's got a nice voice, doesn't he?" Maggie says.

I nod dumbly. A nice voice that whispered sweet nothings

in my ear last night. Hot and dirty sweet nothings.

"You can't go being all star-struck when you're used to Asher hanging around." Maggie nudges me with her elbow. "You've met Nate. You two really hit it off."

"We hit it off? Why would you say that?" It comes out way too defensive, and I have to take a breath and force my shoulders away from my ears.

"He's a friend of Asher's. You kept me company when I went to see Asher and Nate perform in St. Louis a few months ago. God, that must be so weird, not remembering anything."

The guys transition into "Unbreak Me," a song Asher wrote for Maggie.

She bites her lip.

"Go on up there," Liz says. "You don't need to babysit us."

"Thanks." Maggie walks to the front of their makeshift stage and sinks to her haunches.

"Want something to drink?" Liz asks. "Because I'm at least three drinks short of the courage I need to approach that beautiful man up there."

"I'm okay for now."

"If you say so." She points toward the bar. "I'll be over there if you need me."

I nod but I can't take my eyes off the stage—off Nate. They finish the final chords of "Unbreak Me," and everyone applauds as Asher stands and kisses Maggie soundly.

When Asher leaves the stage, Nate stays behind, strumming chords to a song I don't recognize. He lifts his gaze. For five painful beats of my heart, our eyes lock. There's so much in his eyes. Pain, anger, frustration. I see it all there before he refocuses on his fingers and starts to croon the lonely lyrics of his song.

I'm nobody's hero, baby. Try not to fall too deep.
I'm nobody's angel, love, but you were crying in your sleep.
I'm useless, empty, nothing, sugar. Wait around and then you'll see.

You thought you'd find your answers, but now you're lost in me.

The words tap into me, loosening something in my chest until I feel like anyone looking at me can see my confusion and the inexplicable aching of my heart.

And when he lifts his head and watches me as he sings the last verse of his song, I don't move. I don't hide from those eyes that know too much. I don't run from that face that could destroy my whole world. I stand transfixed, the words rolling through my veins like they're part of my blood.

After he strums the final chords, he puts down his guitar and leaves the stage without explanation or promise to return.

My feet are following him before I've decided what to do. He heads up the stairs and out back, through the French doors and onto the patio, where he keeps going until he hits the path in front of the river.

He's trying to escape me. I should be happy, right? The past can stay in the past, and whatever mistake I made with this rocker can be left behind with it. But I can't let him walk away without answers.

"Stop!" I rush down to the river, my heels sinking into the rain-softened earth. "Who are you?"

He turns slowly, the confusion back on his face. "Is that supposed to be funny? Pretending there was nothing between us wasn't enough? You need to pretend you don't even know who I am?"

"I—" Oh my God. The hurt in his eyes. "I *don't* know who you are," I say carefully. "But maybe I should? I was injured and I have amnesia, so I honestly don't know you." And if that doesn't sound like a line from a Lifetime movie, I'm not sure what does.

"Amnesia? You're kidding me."

"I'm not." He starts toward me, and I hold out a hand to stop him. "I'd prefer you to stay over there. Please."

He pulls back, watching me. "Amnesia," he repeats.

"Yeah."

"You don't know who I am." It's not a question—more a realization.

"I don't know who you are or why you would crawl into my bed in the middle of the night. I don't understand why—" My breath catches and fat, hot tears spill onto my cheeks. Suddenly this is just all too much. "I don't understand," I repeat, and leave it at that.

"You don't remember anything? Do you know who you are?"

"Yeah. I remember everything up until about a year ago, but the last eleven months are just…gone."

He drags a hand through his hair, and I'm struck again by how gorgeous he is. Dark messy hair, dark intense eyes. His T-shirt clings to his sculpted arms. Tattoos peek out from the sleeves. No matter how hard I look, I can't remember being with him. So why do I have this feeling in my chest like my heart knows something I don't?

"Do I know you?" I ask.

He lets out a huff and stares at the starlit sky. "Yeah. You do." When he drops his gaze back to meet mine, his eyes are moist with unshed tears. "I'm the idiot who's in love with you."

In love with me? "But I'm engaged."

"I saw that," he whispers, his gaze flicking back to my hand. "Can I ask? Did that happen before or after the amnesia?"

"Before."

"Fuck." The word isn't screamed or thrown like a stone. He breathes it—exhaling the sound like so much disappointment.

To me, Nate's a stranger, but to him, I'm…*what?*

We just stare at each other, him looking heartbroken and angry, me trying to piece it all together in my head and make some sense of this. I'm engaged to Max Hallowell. I'm not the kind of girl who would get engaged to one guy when she's been sleeping with another.

Am I?

We stand here, the passing seconds measured by the chirp of a lonely tree frog. I scan my mind for anything. A memory, a piece of information, useless trivia—I search for anything at all I can take from my brain to make sense of this illogical ache in my heart.

Finally, he shoves his hands in his pockets and looks out over the water. "I've gotta get out of here, Han."

Han. He knows me. I can feel it. I know him. My heart does, if not my injured brain. "Please, tell me what happened. What did I do?" I whisper. "I don't understand."

He shrugs. "What's there to understand? You're wearing his ring."

Then he walks away, and I'm alone and confused. And I think I have a broken heart, but I don't know if it's breaking for me or for him. And I don't know who did the breaking.

Chapter
SEVEN

WHEN I return to the party, I immediately spot Nate sitting in a chair beside Asher, his guitar in his big hands, his dark hair falling over one eye as he jots notes on a piece of paper. Something twists in my chest at the sight of him. I want to tell myself it's regret or fear—anything but the longing I know it to be.

Maggie and Lizzy motion me over from the bar, but I shake my head and stay by the stairs. As if he senses me, Nate lifts his head and his eyes immediately lock with mine.

I might not understand the tangle of emotions in my chest, but there's no mistaking the anger that flashes over his face when he sees me, and because I'm a coward, I can't face it.

I run back upstairs.

"Where's she going?" I hear Maggie ask.

"She wasn't feeling great," Lizzy says. "I'll check on her."

I'm in the hallway when I feel her behind me, her hand on my shoulder.

"What's wrong?"

Everything. "Nothing. The doctor said the headaches and dizziness might give me a problem for a few days. A party probably wasn't the best idea."

Her expression is more worried than disappointed. "Let me take you home."

"No. It's a beautiful night, and I'd actually like the fresh air. And I think I'm going to swing by the club and see Max."

"Okay," she whispers. "Promise you'll call me if I can help?"

I take in a long, slow breath. "Go back down there and have a good time."

"Oh, right." Her eyes light up. "I have a rocker to seduce."

My stomach lurches, but I force a smile. "Right."

I watch her go back down before I turn back to the basket of cell phones by the stairs. After shuffling through it, I pull out the few phones I don't recognize as belonging to me or one of my sisters.

I hit the buttons to bring them to life and swipe all three screens to unlock them. One screen, no doubt Asher's, has a picture of Maggie and Zoe as the wallpaper, one has a young woman I don't recognize, and the other has Storm Troopers.

There's no question in my mind that the Storm Trooper phone belongs to the man with the Hulk tattoo and the Spider-Man shirt. The idea of this hard-ass rocker being a closet geek is so adorable. I soften toward him without wanting to.

Before I can think it through, I'm swiping my fingers across the screen and pulling up Nate's text messages. It doesn't take long for me to find a thread with my name.

The last one I sent was the day of my accident.

Hanna: *Left you a message. We need to talk when you get into town.*

What did I want to talk to him about? Was I going to tell him I was marrying Max? I scroll back through some harmless if flirty *Good morning* and *Good to hear your voice tonight* texts before I land on a conversation so damning it makes my hands shake.

The hallway is empty, but I can't risk anyone else seeing these. I take the phone out onto the back patio, sink into a chair, and scroll back to the beginning of the incriminating conversation. I don't take a single breath while I read it.

> **Nate:** *Did you remember to take your gift home with you?*
> **Hanna:** *I did. God knows what airport security thought of it when they searched my bag.*
> **Nate:** *I'm sure they've seen worse. Glad you have it with you.*
> **Hanna:** *It's a sorry substitute for you.*
> **Nate:** *I'll make it up to you when I get to Indiana. I'm coming straight to your place and keeping you in bed for days.*
> **Hanna:** *Hmm. That sounds kind of boring.*
> **Nate:** *Get naked, woman. I want to tell you how to use my gift.*
> **Hanna:** *Bossy.*
> **Nate:** *Only because it makes you wet.*
> **Hanna:** *Naked.*
> **Nate:** *In bed?*
> **Hanna:** *I've been in bed since you first texted. I have a 6 a.m. running date tomorrow.*
> **Nate:** *You should cancel it. I don't want you running off those curves.*
> **Hanna:** *You're the only one who likes my so-called "curves."*
> **Nate:** *Who else matters?*
> **Hanna:** *Good point. I miss your face.*
> **Nate:** *I miss yours too. You know what else I miss?*
> **Hanna:** *Tell me.*
> **Nate:** *The sound you make when I touch your breasts. The feel of your nipples against my tongue. I miss sliding my hand between your legs and finding you wet. I miss the taste of you. The feel of your heels against my back as I take your clit between my lips. But mostly, I miss holding you in my arms. So fucking perfect. So completely mine.*

I don't know what I expected. Maybe it was supposed to be like in the movies, where the amnesia patient sees something from her past and suddenly everything comes flooding back to her. But there's no memory here, and my half of this conversation might as well have been written by another woman.

When I lift my head, Nate is standing in front of me, hands tucked in his pockets, his eyes bored.

"See anything good?" he asks.

My heart is pounding and my breath is shallow and shaky. My cheeks burn and it has nothing to do with regret or guilt or embarrassment. The things he wrote. The things he said. There's a heavy tightness between my legs. My mind may still be confused, but my body? My body wants Nate as much as it ever wanted Max.

Oh God, Max. *I cheated on Max.* "Why would I risk everything?"

His jaw hardens and he shrugs. "You'd have to ask your fiancé."

"You *know* why I can't do that." I push my chair back, and the scraping of metal against concrete rends the air. I lift my chin. "I want to understand. I need you to talk to me."

He tenses at my demand. "No, I don't."

"You don't understand what this is like. Not remembering? I'm planning a wedding to this man I've wanted most of my life. Don't I owe it to him—don't I owe it to *myself*—to have the truth out there before we promise until death do us part?"

Even in the moonlight, I can see the pain in his eyes.

"I just need answers." I lift my chin and move toward the back wall of the house, toward him. Immediately, I regret the decision because his lips curve into a wicked smile and he closes what distance is left between us. "I need the truth," I whisper weakly.

"The truth? Is that what you really want, angel?" His deep voice dances over my skin like a caress. A little tender. A lot wicked.

I can't reply. I'm too busy holding my breath. Too deep of

an inhale might brush my breasts against his chest, and I'm afraid to touch him. Afraid of what it might make me feel.

As if he can read my mind, he takes another step closer, and when I step to the side to turn away, I'm against the wall and his body is against mine, his hot breath at my ear.

"Do you want to know what it was like between us?" he whispers.

"Yes."

I realize my mistake when a groan rumbles from his chest. "Should I start with how wet you were every time I touched you? Or maybe how you begged me that first night?"

"I didn't."

"Have you been telling yourself some wicked rocker seduced you? That I tricked you into my bed? Sorry. You asked for the truth. You begged. Right there outside the club, you begged me until I ripped your panties off and you were too busy biting my neck to talk anymore. Is that what you're hoping to remember? How you wanted me so badly you let me finger you out in the open, against that building where anyone could have seen?"

My breathing is uneven, my cheeks hot. When I press into his chest to put some distance between us, my traitorous hands curl into his shirt instead.

He makes a low growling sound at the back of his throat. His teeth nip at my earlobe. Lightning cracks in the sky behind him. "You might have forgotten me, but you still like dirty talk, don't you? And maybe if I made you come now, you'd still scream my name. Because you always screamed *my* name, Hanna. Never his."

I gasp. "You are horrible."

"What are you really upset about? That you wanted me? Or that even as you stand here wearing his ring, you're secretly hoping I'll tell you about it. Secretly wishing you could remember all the details."

"I don't," I bite out, the words edged with the sob I'm holding back. I shove him, and he steps away, but not because I'm strong enough to move him. I know better. But he steps back. He gives me that.

My legs are weak and I have to steady myself against the wall. I betrayed Max. Emotion riots in my chest, too much to contain. The worst is true. But the ache of arousal between my legs—that's the worst betrayal of all.

"Tell me why I did it," I say. "I need to understand."

He shoves his hands into his pockets and looks out toward the fenced area behind the patio, where Asher's hot tub gurgles as it spills into the pool. "I made you a promise," he says, his words measured. "I promised that when you made your decision, I would respect it. That if you took his ring, I wouldn't try to change your mind."

Seconds ago, I wanted his knowing eyes anywhere but mine, but now I wish he would look at me. I need to see the eyes of the man I feel this inexplicable connection to. The man I was considering leaving my fiancé for.

"I always knew you deserved better than me." His voice is a deep rumble that tries to hide behind the distant thunder. "I hope he's worthy of you. I sure as fuck wasn't."

Finally, he turns to me and takes my hands into his. His mouth is inches from mine, and his gaze rests on my lips. I wait for his kiss—wonder if I want it. Time snags on my indecision. Trips. Stutters. Slows to a crawl.

Lifting one finger at a time, he removes his cell phone from my grasp then steps away. He disappears into the darkness, his silence a promise I can't remember him making and the ache in my chest a regret I don't understand.

I walk around the side of the house, and drizzle fills the air and hits my hot cheeks. When it grows heavier, changing to rain, I don't run for shelter. Pausing, I look up into the dark, moonless night and let the rain shower my fears.

I'm soaking wet by the time I get to the gym, and when I push through the double doors, Max is squatting in front of a leggy blonde, his hand curled around her thigh. It's nearly nine p.m., and they're the only two here.

"Take it deeper," he says, his voice rough. "Yeah...just like that. Now really squeeze. Now go again."

The girl adjusts the weights on her shoulders and drops into a low lunge. "That *hurts*," she whines.

"Again," Max says. He turns his head toward the door—and me—and his face lights up. "Ten more on that side," he tells the girl. Then he's coming over to me.

"Sorry I'm early."

He doesn't look upset about it, and I can only hope he's not. After talking to Nate, I'm desperate to see Max again, to reassure myself that I haven't lost him. Whatever I've done, if he wants me, if he loves me, we can get through this. Can't we?

"No apology necessary." He runs his gaze over me and his nostrils flare. He laces a finger through one of the belt loops on my jean skirt and tugs me close. "Even hotter in person," he murmurs against my ear. "Did you walk through the rain just to make me crazy with wanting you?"

I bite my lip. I didn't give thought to anything other than getting away from the party.

"What now?" the girl whines.

He nips at my earlobe—the same earlobe Nate Crane just bit—and shame rushes through me in a tremor. Max misunderstands my tremble and whispers, "Soon," before pulling away and turning back to his client. "Other side."

The girl whimpers. Actually *whimpers*. "At this rate, I'm not going to be able to walk out of here."

"You said you wanted to be sore tomorrow." He cuts his eyes to me and winks before returning his attention to the girl. "I aim to please."

The girl flashes him a disappointed look, and I have to bite back my laughter. I'm sure she said that, and I'm sure she had a very different scenario in mind. I wonder if this is the first time a guy has ever turned her down.

"This is my fiancée," Max says, wrapping an arm around my waist. "She's just here to use the steam room."

"I am?"

"The cleaning crew just left, so it should be good as new."
He drops his head until his mouth hovers right over my ear
and whispers, "I'll meet you in there after I lock up."

Meet me? My heart kicks up a notch, as if I'm the one
doing the lunges. "Oh…"

"Come on," he tells the blonde. "You can go deeper than
that."

I slip past them and to the door that reads *Ladies' Locker
Room*. Max's gym is nice. Clean and shining, well maintained.
I don't remember working out here before, but Lizzy told me
I'd become quite the gym rat in the last eleven months.

The locker room is large. One wall is covered by a mirror
over three sinks. The other has a couple dozen wooden lockers.
I drop my purse on the bench by the lockers and follow the
hall back. There are three showers, all clean, with white towels
folded on racks between them. Beyond the showers is the
steam room. I hear the hiss of the steam before I see it.

I pull open the foggy glass door and am hit by a hot puff
of steam. Biting my lip, I scan the tile walls, the chairs, and the
two-tiered bench along the back wall. He wants me to wait in
here for him. Is this something we do a lot?

I have to let out a slow breath as my imagination runs
wild at the idea of waiting here naked for Max. Or better, Max
joining me naked.

He's going to expect me to have sex. I mean, of course—
that only makes sense. Engaged couples have sex. I'm nervous.
No, I'm terrified. No matter how many times I had sex in the
last months, I don't remember it, so I might as well still be the
virgin I was at the time of my last memory.

After talking to Nate tonight, I'm not worried he'll be
bothering me or running to Max. I should be happy. My secret
is safe, and I can focus on my upcoming marriage.

So why does the idea of having sex with my fiancé feel like
cheating?

Pushing aside the thought, I go back to the lockers to strip
out of my clothes. A towel secured under my arms, I return to

the steam room and step in this time.

Sinking into a chair, I lean back and close my eyes as the heat relaxes my muscles and quiets my mind.

I drift off to sleep, and just as my dreams tug me under, my mind skates along the edge of a memory—Max and me in the gym before we started dating. I asked him to be my trainer. It's there, a memory as clear as the ones I never lost, and I wrap myself in the comfort of it. Me. Max. No affairs. No angry rockers with broken hearts.

"Hey, sleeping beauty," someone whispers in my ear.

My muscles are so relaxed, I don't want to move. I stretch my arms and legs, and my towel falls to my waist as I open my eyes.

"Oh, damn, Hanna." Max stands before me, his chest bare, a towel tied around his hips. I can't quite make out his face in the steam, but I don't need to see his expression to know he wants me. Desire radiates off every water molecule in the room—a breath held and waiting for release.

I extend my stretch, arching my back in a move that thrusts my breasts toward him.

"Sorry it took me longer than I expected." His voice sounds strained as he offers his hand. "I had a new client come in just as I was trying to lock up."

I take his hand and stand, but when I reach to grab my fallen towel, he holds me fast.

"Please don't," he says.

Maybe I'd be self-conscious in another setting, but here in the steam, I turn sexy and wanton under his gaze. I feel nothing but determination under the weight of the unwanted ache in my heart while talking to Nate. Determination to prove to myself that *this* is the man I love—no one else.

With that first recovered memory in my grasp, I'm hopeful for the first time in days. I drop my gaze to his towel and arch a brow. "I sense a double standard."

He groans and drops his mouth to mine. His kiss is long and slow and thorough. He tastes like cinnamon gum and strokes his tongue against mine as he cups my breast in his hand.

"I believe it's my turn to touch you," he whispers against my lips. His thumb rolls over my nipple in the slow, sensuous motion of a man who plans to take his time. "And touching you in here ranks high on my list of fantasies."

I curl my nails into his back and nip at his bottom lip. Because I don't want him to take his time. I want him to touch me and kiss me until I've forgotten the sound of Nate's voice, until I'm so sure of our love and our future that my anxiety fades.

With his free hand, Max cups my other breast and treats it to the same slow torture.

"Max," I whimper, arching toward him, wanting more.

"How was the party?"

"What?"

His lips curl into a smile. "God, I love that I can make you lose your mind like that."

I slide my hands into his hair. "You can. You do."

Trailing kisses down my neck and over my collarbone, he makes his way to my breast and opens his mouth over my nipple. Slow, steady, achingly meticulous, he circles it with his tongue before pulling it into his mouth. My breasts grow heavier with every stroke of his tongue, the ache between my thighs more insistent. The steam has set my senses on fire, and the brush of his knuckles down my side is as thrilling as the first time a boy went up my shirt.

Just when I think I'm going to have to beg for more, he takes my nipple into his mouth and sucks—long and hard. My knees go weak and he has to hold me tight as I slip in his arms.

"Come over here," he murmurs. He leads me to the tiered benches and takes a seat on the bottom row. His erection is thick and tall under the towel, but when I reach to uncover it, he stops my hand. "Leave it. You tempt me too much."

"But I like touching you," I object.

"You like making me lose my mind."

A giggle slips from my lips. "It's a nice feeling."

"Come here." He tugs me forward until I'm straddling

him, the hard length of his cock needy and glorious between my legs. As he returns his mouth to my breasts, sucking and licking in turn, I rock against him. My thighs squeeze him as the sensation of his mouth on my breasts mixes with the pressure of his erection through the towel.

His hands slide around me and over my ass, kneading the flesh of my cheeks as his mouth works at my breasts.

Whimpering, I arch my back and shift my hips just so, and suddenly pleasure snaps through me like a whip. My hips want to rock, to circle, to grind against his length, but I force them to still.

"Move against me," he commands. "I want to feel you move."

The friction of the towel against my swollen clit is almost too much, almost uncomfortable, but it's a good kind of discomfort, and his cock swells bigger and more insistent between my thighs. I don't know if I could stop if I wanted to. Unless it was for something different. Something *more.* How easy would it be for him to move this towel and slide into me right now? My fear is gone, replaced by red-hot aching need. Doesn't he want it as much as I do? Maybe he doesn't have protection with him.

I can't think on the question for long before his hand is back at my breast, kneading and massaging. It takes my breath. Then he sucks me hard and mercilessly into his mouth and I buck against him. I circle my hips and rock, circle and rock. I'm so close to that edge, and as much as my body begs to slide over it, I don't want this to end.

Max grips my hip and rises off the bench to add another ounce of pressure between my legs. I cry out. In pleasure. In frustration. I need more.

"Please." My plea echoes against the walls.

He shifts us so quickly that he's moved me before I know what's happening. He lifts me onto the higher bench. I immediately miss the promise of him between my legs.

He sinks down as he spreads me open with a hand against each thigh. Then I'm open and exposed to him and his lips are close, the hot steam and his breath mingling and sweeping over my sensitive sex.

At first, his touch is tentative, his fingers tracing my folds before dipping into me. I bite my lip to hold back my cry, but then he lowers his mouth and wraps his lips around my clit at the same moment he slides two fingers inside me, demanding more with his touch. His fingers pump as his tongue strokes. Hungry, greedy.

Then, when I'm so full of tight-winding pleasure that I think I need to pull back, he takes my ankle and props my foot on the bench beside my hip. I'm stretched open and his fingers curl and coax and his lips wrap around my clit, and I can't stop myself from rocking into his face, fucking his fingers the way I want him to fuck me. I can't hold on anymore. I'm flying, falling, disintegrating until I'm nothing but the hot steam around us.

Chapter
EIGHT

I'M CURLED up against Max as he traces my spine with his fingertips and presses kisses along my hairline.

"Do we do this a lot?" I murmur against his chest.

He laughs, a silent chuckle I can feel more than hear. "Which part?"

"The steam room?"

"Never before, but I think we will now. In fact, I think I'll save my pennies so we can get one installed in our future home."

"Our home," I say, testing the words. "I like the sound of that."

"Me too." His voice is hoarse.

"Where will we live after we get married?"

"We hadn't really talked about it, but if it's between my tiny apartment above the club and your tiny apartment above the bakery, we should probably go with your place."

I frown. "I thought you had a house?" Not that I remember ever being there, but I remember seeing him work in the lawn of a tiny ranch off Main.

"I sold it. I was never there anyway." He tucks my hair behind my ear and cups my face in his hand. "I can't give you anything fancy yet, but I will. Whatever you want. I'll make it happen."

"I don't need fancy. Just you."

He wraps his arms around me and squeezes. "We should get out of here."

"Yeah, I think I'm out of sweat."

I grab my towel off the floor, but it's soaked and useless for drying me off. Max opens the door, and a shiver runs through me as the cool air hits my warm skin. He grabs a towel from the stand and wraps it around me.

His clothes are draped over a chair outside the steam room, and as he removes his towel, I can't help but let my eyes slide over his body, every inch of it toned and muscular. There's a three-inch tattoo of a dragon right inside the V of his hipbones. It must have been covered by his shirt when he was in my apartment last night. I want to lick it.

"You have a tattoo."

"I do."

"When did you get it?"

"Last December. I'd been thinking about it for a while, but you talked me into it."

I grin as I skim my fingers over it.

He releases a deep groan. "Hanna, you touch me like that and we won't make it out of here tonight."

I wrap my arms around his neck and rise onto my toes to kiss him. "Max Hallowell, I don't know how I landed a guy like you, but I promise I'm going to be the best wife you could ask for. I'm going to earn this."

Something flashes across his face—sadness, regret?—and he strokes his thumb down my cheek before gathering me against his chest and drawing in a deep breath against my hair.

"I'm the one who needs to earn this. Don't be fooled."

November—Nine Months Before Accident

The morning light reflecting off the river is quickly becoming one of my favorite sights. Even when the ground is covered with a thin sheet of snow and the air is cold enough that I can see my breath, I'm learning to like this time. I can't exactly say I love running, but I appreciate it, and I'm surprised how quickly I'm gaining stamina.

Max climbs out of his car, looking downright edible in his black, long-sleeved, moisture-wicking shirt and shorts. "Good morning!"

"It's a beautiful one," I call back. His smile warms me more than a cloudless spring day. I've become spoiled by this time with him, his attention on me.

We start jogging without preamble. At first I feel really good, but within less than fifteen minutes, my head gets fuzzy and my vision starts to blur.

My feet scuff the ground as I stumble mid-stride. Max grabs my arm and catches me before I can fall.

"Whoa, careful," he murmurs. "Easy there. Are you okay?"

The world spins off-kilter before righting itself, and I point to the ground. "I think I just need to sit down for a minute." I sink to the cold grass, the frozen earth solid and reassuring under me, and try to blink away a sudden wave of nausea.

"Hanna." Max squats before me and cups my face in his hand. Worry creases his brow. "Did you eat this morning?"

I blink. He's touching me, and I don't want to talk about my diet. I want to melt into his warmth. "I don't like to eat before I run," I admit.

"Okay, my lecture on that aside. What about last night?"

"Chicken breast," I answer, mentally amending *half* a chicken breast.

"What else?"

"What do you mean?"

"What did you eat with it?" His thumb strokes my cheek.

"Oh. I had it on about two cups of mixed greens."

"Any starch? Grains? Fruit?"

"No."

He takes a seat next to me and rests his forearms on his knees. "Lunch?"

"I don't know. I was busy. Maybe an apple."

He bows his head. "I'm the worst trainer ever. You didn't say anything about weight loss, and I just assumed you weren't looking to lose weight. But I should have known."

"Known what?"

He smiles at me. "You're just that kind of personality. You know? You decide you're going to do something and you go all in."

"You make it sound like a bad thing."

He grins. "It's not, but you can't starve yourself. If you really want to lose weight, that's okay, but you have to eat to lose."

I try not to roll my eyes at the advice I've heard again and again. I push myself off the ground. "I think I should just go home."

"Hanna, just promise me you'll start eating."

So I can stay this size forever? "Sure."

"Good. Then you can come with me to dinner on Friday."

Frowning, I turn back to him. "Why?"

He stands and brushes off his shorts. "I think it's called a date. I buy you dinner. We eat together. Maybe hold hands on the way home?"

I blink at him and the world spins in front of me again, but I soften my knees and draw in a long, slow breath. "That sounds nice."

"Pick you up at six."

Present Day

Liz: *Nate disappeared, so no sexy rocker for me tonight.*

Damn. I've known nuns who got more action than I've seen lately.

I grimace at Lizzy's text from last night. On the one hand, she makes me laugh, but on the other, I don't know what she's going to think when I tell her *Nate* is Mr. Hulk Tattoo.

I'm supposed to spend the day looking at wedding venues with my mom, and all I can think about is whether I cheated on my fiancé. Call me crazy, but I'm pretty sure I need to know if I'm fucking some rock star behind Max's back before I can choose the length of my veil.

I've been working in the bakery since four thirty this morning, and the clock reads twenty to six when Lizzy comes through the front door, her eyes half closed.

"Why couldn't your dream career have required me to sleep past ten every day, huh?" She pushes past me and to the coffee. "I swear, if I weren't an unemployed loser, I'd tell you to find someone else to wake up at the ass crack of dawn." She pours herself a cup of coffee and then dumps cream in it before taking a long drink. "Fuck me, that's good." When she finally opens her eyes and looks at me—really looks at me—she frowns. "What's wrong?"

"I know who Mr. Hulk Tattoo is," I whisper.

She straightens. "Really? Did he come back? Did you see him somewhere?"

"He was at Asher's last night."

She grins. "Oh, the plot thickens!"

"It's Nate Crane, Liz."

"What's Nate Crane?"

"Nate Crane is the guy who got into my bed like he belonged there. He's the guy I was cheating on Max with."

She squeezes her eyes shut and mutters, "God, you're such a bitch."

"What?"

"You're engaged. Sue me for hating you a little. You get the perfect life and the hottie on the side."

"The hottie on the side might ruin the perfect life!" As

much as I want to tell myself that my secret was safe, as much as I want to let go of what might or might not have happened with Nate, I can't stop obsessing over what I've done. What if my memories don't return? I need answers.

Liz frowns. "Yeah. I guess you're right. But come on. Who could blame you? Nate. Fucking. Crane. You were fucking Nate Crane."

"We don't know that for sure," I protest.

She cocks her head. "How familiar was he with your body when he was touching you in the dark?"

I wince. "This sucks."

She shakes her head as if still trying to clear away sleepiness. "Okay, so you saw him at the party and realized he was the guy. Then what? Did he approach you?"

"No. The opposite. He saw me and went in the other direction. But this is my life, you know? My future with this *really great guy.* And the more time I spend with Max, the more sure I am that he's the right guy for me, and I don't want to screw this up, but maybe I already have. So I followed Nate outside and told him I have amnesia and he asked when the engagement happened—before or after the amnesia, as if that made a difference—and I told him before and he was upset all over again and wouldn't talk to me about it. He walked away without answering any of my questions, but I got a hold of his cell phone and read through some of our texts to each other, and it looks really bad, and now I don't know who to talk to or where to get answers, but I'm scared I'll lose Max if I tell him and…" I take a long, gasping breath. "Help."

"Okay." She sets her coffee on the counter and comes over to put her hands on my shoulders. "This is going to be all right. We're going to figure this out. Together. But first you have to breathe."

"Right." I draw in another shaky breath. And another. I'm on my third before Lizzy's nodding and smiling.

"Okay. Now do you think you and Nate were just…"

"Just what?"

"Do you think he just came by for booty calls, or do you

think you had a relationship?"

"He said, 'I'm the idiot who's in love with you.' Those were his words, 'the idiot who's in love with you.' And then the text messages...?"

"Dirty?"

I nod. "Really dirty."

"Oh, damn, girl."

"I know. Right?"

She rubs her hands together. "Okay. I could talk to Nate, right? Feel him out?"

"He's hella pissed at me, Liz. I don't think he's any more likely to talk to you."

"What about Asher?" she asks, but my horror must be evident on my face because she says, "Okay, okay, bad idea. No one else needs to know until they need to know, right?"

"That's what I'm hoping."

"Your phone!" she exclaims. "We didn't know who we were looking for yesterday! Look in your contacts first. Maybe you have his name programmed as something else."

I scroll through my contacts until I see find his name staring back at me. "He's here. Programmed into my phone."

She makes a hurry-up gesture with her hand. "Well, click on the history."

I frown. I called him last Friday. That was the day of my accident. We had a three-minute conversation. About what? Judging from his reaction when he saw my ring, I obviously wasn't telling him about my engagement.

"Oh, hell, Liz. This doesn't make any sense."

She snatches the phone from my hand and starts scrolling through the history under Nate's contact info. "But you said there were texts from you on his phone?"

"Yeah. A lot of them. I didn't get very far back before he found me and took it back."

"But there's nothing on your phone, which seems to indicate you deleted the evidence."

I cross my arms. "It looks like it."

"Where's your laptop?"

"In the kitchen. I need to—"

I don't get a chance to finish before she darts to the back of the kitchen and opens my laptop. "What's your password?"

I shrug. "That's what I was trying to say. I haven't been able to get on because I don't know. Thank God my calendar is synched with my phone, but I brought it down today because I need to take it to the shop. I can't access my files."

"What have you tried?"

"All the usual passwords I've always used. Birthday, initials, HanHan, initials and birthday together."

"What about your anniversary with Max?"

I lift my palms. "No go."

"What about Nate? Or Nate Crane?"

"That's not it."

"You sure?"

I drop my gaze to the floor. "I tried this morning."

"Or…" She taps on the keyboard for a minute then presses ENTER. The computer beeps at her and gives her the "Wrong Password" warning message. "Hmm." She taps again.

"Let it go, Liz. I've tried."

She hits ENTER and the computer brightens as my desktop appears.

"What was it?"

"'Lost In Me.'" She forces a smile. "But that doesn't mean anything. It's a seriously popular song."

Maybe it's not incriminating evidence, but it doesn't look good either. "Go to my email first."

She opens the email client and loads the "Sent" folder. A quick scroll through shows messages from me to several potential clients, vendors, future brides. When she pulls up my contact list, Nate's name and email are listed, but a search for his email address gives us nothing from the history.

"Why would I have him in my contacts if I've never actually contacted him?"

"Let's check the trash," she says, moving the mouse to pull up the deleted messages. She looks at me. "Empty."

My stomach churns, bile crawling up my throat. "I've

never been good about clearing that stuff. Why would I do it here?"

"Because you were trying to hide something?"

"That's what I'm afraid of," I mutter.

A search of my Facebook profile yields similar results. Nate is in my friends list, but we can't find any evidence of correspondence between us. Of course, if we'd been having an affair, I can't believe I'd be stupid enough to flaunt it on Facebook. *Hanna is in a secret mostly-just-about-sex relationship with Nate Crane.* I'm pretty sure they don't have that option yet.

I want to scream. "I wish I were the kind of girl who kept a diary."

"What are you ladies doing?"

I jump at the question and turn to see Drew entering the kitchen from the back door. She's gorgeous, a younger, more petite version of Cally's dark hair and sultry curves. But she's certainly not dressed to impress anyone in her torn-up old jeans and raggedy T-shirt.

"Drew! Good morning!"

"Eh. If you say so. Coffee?"

"Up front," I say just as the bell at the front rings to let us know a customer came in. "And can you get that customer while you're at it?"

"Sure. I'm *great* with the public," she enthuses, with an eye roll thrown in for good measure.

I ignore her sarcasm. "Thanks, Drew," I say, and watch her push through the swinging door to the front of the shop.

"Let's think about this," Lizzy says. "Maggie says you met Nate three months ago at a show in St. Louis. That's also around the time you stopped *trying* to lose weight and started taking drastic measures to *be sure* you lost weight."

"Drastic measures?" Maybe the anorexia I was secretly seeing Dr. Perkins for wasn't much of a secret at all.

"You stopped eating, took your one-a-day workouts to two or three times a day. *Drastic.* That's also when you started pulling away from me."

The truth is that my anorexia is more believable to me than the idea of pulling away from Liz. "You think I did that because of Nate?"

"I didn't say that. I just think *something* happened three months ago and you changed." Her eyes light up and she's back at the computer, pulling up the web browser and typing madly.

"What?"

"Gossip sites." Lizzy's eyes scan the screen as she scrolls down with her mouse. "They're in love with Nate Crane for the obvious reasons, and I bet there's at least one pic of him while he was in St. Louis." She stops scrolling and her shoulders sag.

"What?" I step behind her to see what she found. She minimizes the window, but not before I see the headline.

The thing about being overweight, for me at least, is that I've spent most of my life strategically planning how I'm going to lose weight and change my body. Most fat girls don't like their pictures taken because they truly believe that soon enough they will be smaller, fitter, more toned—more aesthetically pleasing. No matter that I've been overweight my whole life. I wasted so much time and energy thinking about how to get rid of the weight that I never accepted my size.

Fitness people would probably say that's good. They would probably talk about the dangers of complacency and "giving up," blah blah blah. But they don't understand that always hating your size, always planning to change, translates way too easily to self-loathing and depression. And every time someone takes a picture of a fat girl, revealing her true fat-girl form, it feels like an insult, an intentional jab.

But one hundred times worse than the pictures is the commentary, as if we must be *reminded* of this completely unacceptable shortcoming. As if we don't spend the majority of our waking moments thinking about it.

My eyes sting as I blink at the screen where the picture was. Where the headline was.

"They don't know what they're talking about," Lizzy says. "They're fucking shallow idiots."

"Pull it back up, Liz."

She shakes her head. "No. It's stupid. Looking at it is only going to hurt you."

"Pull it back up." My determination must be clear in my voice, because she sighs and clicks on the icon. The browser pops back up on the screen.

The image shows Nate kissing a woman, his hand halfway up the black skirt that's creeping up and exposing her thick thigh. My face is obscured, but there's no doubt in my mind that I'm the woman in the picture under the soul-scarring headline: *Nate Crane's Secret Fatty Fetish.*

I reach over Lizzy and scroll down to the text of the article—a bunch of nothing trying to make legitimate journalism out of spotting Nate making out with an overweight woman outside a St. Louis nightclub. There's no mention of who the woman in the picture is—as if identity is irrelevant—and no mention of what Nate and the girl did before or after making out outside the nightclub. But Nate's words echo in my head.

"You begged. Right there outside the club, you begged me until I ripped your panties off and you were too busy biting my neck to talk anymore. Is that what you're hoping to remember? How you wanted me so badly you let me finger you out in the open, against that building where anyone could have seen?"

He wasn't lying about that. The evidence is right in front of me.

"Do you think I saw this?" I ask Liz.

She chews on her lower lip and shrugs. "It would explain your drastic diet changes."

"It doesn't answer any of my questions, though. Like why would I cheat on Max and how far did it go and...what the hell am I going to do?"

"We'll figure this out. Let me think. Three months ago seems to be when everything changed. That was our graduation, the night you met Nate, and—"

"She started taking those out-of-town baking gigs three months ago."

Lizzy and I turn toward Drew in unison as she pushes back into the kitchen, coffee in one hand, chocolate croissant in the other.

"That was even before this place was opened, but you were doing side gigs for people."

Lizzy's eyes are wide, her fingertips to her mouth. "I didn't even think of that. I found it weird at the time, but I was kind of pissed at you for dropping me. I didn't really give it much thought beyond that it was yet another reason you were better than me."

"I'm not better than you. I'm sorry if I made you feel that way."

She waves away my apology.

"Where was I going?" I ask Drew.

"Different cities," she says around a mouthful of croissant. "I bet you can find your flight information in your email."

Lizzy's already tapping at the keyboard, pulling up my travel folder in my email client. "Bingo."

I scan the destinations from the subject line. "LA, Seattle, New Orleans."

Lizzy opens a new tab and searches *Nate Crane tour schedule.* She clicks through a link and pulls up the calendar on his website. "The dates and cities of your gigs all line up with Nate Crane performances."

I step back and press my head against the wall before sinking to the floor. "Liz. What have I done?"

Chapter
NINE

"OH, CRAP, Liz! I need to get a shower and get dressed. I have a cake consult in fifteen minutes."

Lizzy arches a brow. "I think Cally will forgive you if you aren't looking your best."

"Not Cally," I say, grabbing my keys. "A wedding cake consultation."

Lizzy grins. "With Cally and William."

My jaw drops and my eyes water. Will and Cally visited me in the hospital. Cally even gushed over my engagement ring, but I didn't notice she was wearing a ring too. "That's... wonderful."

The bell rings, and Drew calls from the front, "Hanna, my sister is here!"

I rush through the swinging door without a word to Lizzy and practically tackle Cally into a hug. "Congratulations!" I screech.

Cally gives me a squeeze before stepping back and frowning.

"On your engagement," Lizzy explains behind me. "She didn't know."

"Oh!" Cally throws her hand over her mouth, and I see her

sparkling ring. "Of course she didn't!"

"How did I miss that when you visited me at the hospital?" I take her hand and study the ring. "God, it's gorgeous."

"I didn't have it on that day. The jeweler needed it so he could design my wedding band."

"Wedding band." I melt a little. William and Cally had to go through so much to get this far, and I can't think of any two people who deserve happiness more. "I'm so happy for you."

"Well, I'd hope so. You're in the wedding."

"Ooh!" My eyes fill with tears all over again.

Behind me, Drew grunts, and I can practically *hear* her rolling her eyes. "This would be so sweet if you hadn't already been through it all months ago. Seriously, it's the Twilight Zone around here."

"Come on." I wave Cally over to a table in the corner. "Let's talk about your wedding cake."

December—Eight Months Before Accident

Skinny chicks should be required to take a class in empathy. I'd call it Fat Girl 101 and I'd teach them all the secret rules fat girls live by:

1) Never use the word *fat*. It makes the skinny folk uncomfortable.

2) Pretend to be at peace with your body and size while simultaneously and continuously making your best efforts to reduce it to something more aesthetically pleasing.

3) Pretend to be attracted to the guys you stand a chance with and hide your attraction to The Unattainables.

I've spent most of my life following these simple rules, but tonight they're not coming easily.

I don't want to be *that girl*. The one who can't enjoy herself because she's too busy looking at how much thinner, prettier, or more fashionable the women around her are. The one who can't believe the man on her arm wants to be with her, so she spends all her energy feeding her jealousy toward the women he *should* want. But tonight, I'm all that and worse.

The gallery's winter opening is bustling, and William and Cally are glowing as people circulate through the new exhibit. Cally waves at me from across the room, her smile bright. Max and I are supposed to go out with them tonight after the opening, but Lizzy's here in a red dress that shows off her long legs and skinny arms, and all I can think about is how inadequate I am.

I'm about to smack myself.

I beeline for the bar and hand a ten to the bartender. "Your biggest glass of your sweetest red, please."

The bartender's eyes drop to my cleavage for a minute, and I actually smile. I forget how much men like tits. I forget that some men like tits enough to overlook everything else. And maybe I should be offended by this stranger's not-so-subtle appreciation of mine, but politically correct or not, knowing that he's looking seriously lifts my spirits.

I take a long pull off the wine and lean on the bar as I scan the room for Max.

"Waiting for your date?" the bartender asks. He's cute. Probably a student at Sinclair like me. He's got that disheveled surfer-boy look going on, even in his white button-up shirt and dress pants.

I take another healthy swallow. Wine goes a long way to make me forget my insecurities, and if I don't want to be *that girl,* I'm gonna need a vat of it tonight. "I am," I say with a sigh. "But last time I saw him, he was checking out my twin."

The surfer boy coughs and pulls at the neck of his dress shirt. He's so obviously uncomfortable in it, I almost feel bad for him. As if giving up, he unbuttons the top button. His eyes dip to my cleavage again, but he pulls them back up so fast it doesn't feel smarmy, just flattering and adorable.

"You have a twin?"

I roll my eyes. Boys and their twin fantasies. Seriously. "Yes, but we're not identical." *Not by a long shot.*

God, if Max had known I was behind him, he never

would have checked out Lizzy like that. He's not an asshole or anything. He's just a normal guy. And like any normal guy, he wants to fuck my twin more than he'll ever want to fuck me.

Three dates and he hasn't kissed me. Sure, he's held my hand, hugged me, kissed my cheek. But in three dates, his lips haven't touched mine. That wouldn't be the case if he'd had those three dates with Liz.

"Gah!" I growl. There may not be enough wine or cute-surfer-boy-tit-gawking to ever obliterate this mood.

The surfer boy's brows shoot up. "What?"

"I'm instituting my own drinking game." I prop both elbows on the counter and lean forward, grinning at my own clever idea. "Every time I feel sorry for myself because my date secretly has the hots for my sister, I'm taking a drink."

He shifts behind the counter and refills my wine without me asking. "Can I ask you a question?"

Max appears on the other side of the room and pulls William into one of those male-certified one-armed hugs. They're such a handsome duo—Will with his crazy blond curls, Max with his dark mop, both sporting bodies that belong in men's fitness magazines. Max looks amazing tonight in his pressed slacks and dark blue oxford. Flipping gorgeous and way out of my league. *Drink.* "Ask away," I say behind my wine glass.

"If he's into your sister, why are you with him? Why not be into a guy who's into *you*?"

Because guys aren't into me. Oh, shit. There I go again. *Drink.*

"I mean, if *I* were your boyfriend, for example, I wouldn't care what your sister looks like. Look at you."

I blink at him. Then it occurs to me that the wine is going to my brain. This guy is probably just trying to make me feel better. *Drink.* "I fell for Max when I was thirteen," I confess. "He smiled at me and I…" I take another drink. Really, if I'm going to tell him the story, he should save us both the trouble and hand me the bottle.

"Well, if you decide you want a date who's only interested

in you…" He walks around the bar and takes the phone from my fingers to tap on the screen.

I have to smile at him. It's been a long time since someone has gone this much out of his way to make me feel better. "You're really sweet, you know that?"

This time when his eyes drop to my breasts, they slide right down on past to my hips and then linger. "For those curves, I'll be whatever you want me to be."

"Who's this?"

I jump at the sound of Max's voice then back a step away from surfer boy, as if I've just been caught doing something wrong. "Oh, this is Max, my date," I tell the bartender. I widen my eyes and hope he can see the desperate *Please don't tell him what we were talking about* message in my eyes. "Max, this is the bartender, um…"

"Jimmy," the surfer boy replies. He's not bothered in the slightest by Max's presence. He winks at me like we have some sexy secret.

Max takes my hand and squeezes my fingers. "Will you come with me, please?"

I stop trying to figure out Jimmy's odd interest with me and look up at Max. "Sure."

He leads me through the gallery, nearly dragging me along behind his long strides. He takes the stairs two at a time to the loft, where there's a kitchenette and reception area.

When he finally stops and turns to me, I frown. "What's going on?"

"Let me take that." He takes the wine from my hand and sets it on the counter.

"Why?"

"Because I want your hands to be free when I do this."

And that's when it happens. He slides his hands into my hair and sweeps his lips over mine. But this is different than the chaste kisses we've shared before now. This is a hot *sweep, sweep, linger* that promises more. His thumb grazes the line of my jaw, and I open instinctively under him until he's kissing me full-on, his tongue against mine, his lips patient then coaxing, his fingers brushing up my neck and into my hair.

I've waited for this kiss since I was old enough to think kisses from boys were something worth wanting. I've waited for Max since I realized *boys* were worth wanting. And here he is. Kissing me as if he's craved me as long as I've craved him.

Slowly, he leaves my mouth and trails sweet kisses along my jaw and down my neck until his mouth opens against that tender skin at the crook of my neck. His hot tongue sweeps over it.

I close my eyes and try to catch my breath. But it's hard when he's this close and his mouth and teeth and tongue are doing things to my neck that feel so good my brain is imagining them everywhere else. Imagining them places I've never felt a man's tongue.

When he lifts his head, his blue eyes have gone smoky.

"What was that for?" I whisper.

"I think William's bartender was trying to steal away my date."

A puff of air slips between my lips. "He was just trying to cheer me up."

"Why did you need cheering up?"

I shrug. "I'm just in a mood." Or *was* in a mood. Clearly Max's kisses are a much more effective remedy than wine.

He skims his thumb over my bottom lip. "You look beautiful tonight."

"I do?"

Grinning, he tugs me toward the stairs. "Come on. I want to kiss you in front of that bartender."

Present Day

Mom, Granny, and I have been looking at wedding venues, and this is our last stop. I've been tense all morning, but the moment I stepped into the gallery, I remembered Max kissing me for the first time. The memory drained the tension from me like someone turned a release valve in my muscles.

I've always loved this place. William's gallery, the smile on Maggie's face when she works with art, the way the sun shines through the wall of windows at the back and reflects off the stained-glass art hanging from the ceiling. And best of all is the memory of that kiss.

"Hey, girlie. How are you doing?" Maggie asks as I step into the gallery. She's looking especially gorgeous today in a loose-fitting black tank, dark jeans, and strappy sandals.

"I'm good." I force myself to be positive.

Across the street, Max is standing outside the health club, chatting with a gorgeous, leggy blonde. The old Hanna would have felt twelve kinds of inferior to a girl like that. The old Hanna wouldn't have believed a guy like Max would want a girl like her. Too bad the old Hanna's mind is stuck in the new Hanna's body.

I shift uncomfortably as the girl leans in flirtatiously and presses her hand against Max's chest. I've never had the confidence to be a flirt, but that doesn't mean I don't recognize when someone is putting the moves on my man. Who is she? Some sorority girl he's training? Does he like her?

Max carefully removes her hand from his chest and takes a half-step back.

Next to me, Maggie follows my gaze and snorts. "Don't even worry about it, Han-Han. That boy only has eyes for you."

Mom paces a circle in front of us and frowns. "I'm just not convinced the gallery really gives you enough room for many guests. It would make for a gorgeous, intimate wedding, though, that's for sure."

"I didn't even know Will let people have weddings here," I whisper to Maggie. "I mean, I don't remember if I did know."

"We just started it maybe six months ago," Maggie says. "It works really well. The bride generally comes down the stairs instead of having a traditional aisle, and we have white chairs in storage we can set up here in the lobby for your guests."

"Sounds beautiful."

"It is." Maggie raises a brow. "Have you actually set a date?"

"No, but Mom's pushing me to."

"Nothing pleases that woman more than seeing her daughters marrying good men," Maggie grumbles. "I swear, if she keeps pushing Asher, I'm going to lose my shit."

"So no ring for you yet?" I ask.

Her shoulders tense. "Asher dropped some hints a couple of months back, and I freaked out. I think I scared him, and God knows if he'll ever ask now."

"I'm sure he just wants to make sure you're ready."

She shrugs and waves away the subject. After Maggie's history, I can imagine talk of weddings would panic her a little. I cut my eyes to Max. Only he's not outside anymore, and before I see where he's gone, the bell over the door chimes.

"Hey, Max!" Maggie calls.

From the door, Max grins and runs his eyes over me appreciatively. They're this gorgeous blue that made me weak in the knees back when he didn't notice me, but having them aimed at me like that nearly melts me to the floor.

"Max!" Mom calls, hurrying over to him. "You got my message. I'm so glad you could come over."

The way he just looked at me has my heart pounding triple-time in my chest. Or is that anxiety over what we found on my computer this morning, fear that I've screwed up a good thing?

Max escapes Mom's grasp and then he's spinning me around and grinning at me.

"Pardon me for a moment," he tells Maggie. "I need to kiss my fiancée." He presses his mouth to mine in a kiss that's sweet and tender and sizzles all the way down to my toes. Before I can kiss him back, he's pulling away.

"Hello there," I whisper.

His eyes have gone smoky. He brushes my hair off my shoulders. "I didn't know we were looking at wedding venues."

I settle my hands on his shoulders awkwardly, not sure what else to do with them. After last night, it's funny that I would feel unsure about touching him, but it's not natural to me yet. In my mind, Max is still more *crush* than *fiancé*.

"Mom insisted." I watch him carefully. "Does that make you uncomfortable?"

"We aren't in any rush." He smiles. "Well, *you* aren't. Personally, the sooner I have you sleeping in my bed, the better. Speaking of which, how'd you sleep?" His voice drops, low and husky. He may not have Nate's river-bottom bass, but sweet Jesus, Max does husky well.

"Okay." I force a smile. After he dropped me off at home last night, my conscience kept me up tossing and turning, and my four-thirty alarm came too soon. "What about you?"

He presses a kiss to the crook of my neck. "I would have slept better with you in my arms, but I managed okay." He inhales audibly. "God, you smell so good. What are you wearing?"

That makes me smile. "I think you're smelling sugar cookies and cinnamon muffins. Lizzy and I did a little baking this morning. Making you hungry?"

"Hmm. I'm hungry, all right." He snakes a hand under my shirt and brushes my navel with his thumb, and my mind flashes on the image from the gossip site—me pressed against the side of the building, Nate's hand creeping up my skirt.

I try not to tense. God. This is ridiculous. How can I feel so guilty when I don't even know if I've done anything wrong? *Right. Because there's an innocent explanation to all of this.*

"Mom's having girls' night at her house tonight. She wants to talk wedding plans."

"You should." He pulls his hand from my shirt and smooths the fabric back in place, but his expression is unreadable. "You've been working too hard lately. Not spending enough time with your sisters."

So I'm told. Why didn't he encourage me to spend more time with them back before the accident, when I was alienating Liz? Then again, I've probably been busy with the business and all the exercising. Not to mention a very serious boyfriend and a hottie on the side.

"Want to come with me? Mom wouldn't mind you crashing her dinner."

"I wish I could, but I have a late client again."

A late client. *The same woman as last night?* I bite back the question. I have no right to be suspicious of Max. Quite the opposite.

"The bride can enter from the stairs," Mom's saying. "Guests right there where you two are standing. It would be small but intimate."

"What are you thinking?" Max asks me quietly. "You seem distracted."

I force a smile. We're supposed to be deciding where we're going to exchange vows, and I'm too busy trying to figure out what I've done to pay any attention. "I'm just wondering when you can come by my place so we can pick up where we left off last night?"

"What do *you* think, Max?" Mom asks from the back. "Should we try to do this in October? Imagine the colorful leaves floating past on the river."

He never takes his eyes from mine. "The sooner the better."

"Great!" She claps her hands gleefully. "Maggie, pull out the calendar for October. Let's set a date!"

Chapter
TEN

"Listen." Max squeezes my hand and tugs me toward the side room and away from Mom and Granny, who are chattering with Maggie over the calendar.

It's done. We set a date. I have six weeks before I marry Max.

This is the room William uses for special collections. The first collection shown in here was of some shockingly intimate portraits of Maggie, but the artist kept it under wraps, so no one knew what he was showing until the opening. Asher bought them all that night, and rumor has it he burned them in a bonfire behind his house.

I don't know what happened between Maggie and the painter, but it sure looked like he'd put her secrets on display. As I scan the walls, now covered with a collection of Maggie's mosaics, I wonder what that would be like—your biggest secrets, your biggest shame on display to the world. Would it be painful, the shock of it? Or would there be an element of relief to know you didn't have to work so hard to hide anymore?

"We need to talk," Max says softly behind me.

I spin around and my stomach pitches at the worry written across his expression. Does he know about Nate?

About Sunday night? Does he suspect that another man's been touching me? Kissing me? Sliding his fingers inside me?

The memory sends a shudder through me that's equal parts arousal and fear. I've wanted Max my entire adult life, and I'm terrified I might have ruined my chance.

"What's going on?"

He draws me into his heat and nuzzles his smoothly shaved cheek against my neck. "You smell delicious. It feels so right to have you in my arms again."

"Who's the one with the faulty memory now?" I ask, trying for humor. "I believe you had me in your arms just last night."

He cups my face in his hand. "This is all happening so fast—the wedding date, the venue—"

"Oh my God. You want to call it off?" The words slip from my mouth on a squeak at the same moment my stomach releases from its panicked clench and takes a free fall to the floor.

"No. That's not it." His lips meet mine—firm and sure. It's not a kiss of seduction but one of demand. "I want to marry you. I wouldn't have given you that ring if I hadn't wanted that. But..." His hands fall from my face, and he drags one through his hair. "I know everyone thinks I just proposed last week, but they're wrong."

"What do you mean?"

"I proposed months ago."

Laughter carries from the hallway back to us, and I hear Granny say, "—young, lusty love. Let them have their moment!"

"I don't understand. Then why does everyone think we just got engaged?"

"I gave you the ring, and you..." He turns away, his broad chest lifting on a deep inhale.

Nate. I was going to throw away a life with Max for a fling with some rocker? Was he the reason I told Max I wasn't ready? How stupid could I be?

"I didn't accept," I whisper.

"I don't think you believed I was in love with you." He

runs his fingertips lightly over the swirls of yellow glass pieces making up a mosaic interpretation of *Starry Night*.

I'm such an idiot. Because that's something I would do—I'd deny a proposal from a man like Max, a man I've wanted my whole life, just because I didn't believe he really loved me.

"I'm so sorry," I whisper.

He turns back to me and tilts my chin up until he's looking in my eyes. "But I was in love with you, Hanna. And I am. Desperately, hopelessly, helplessly in love."

"Max." I put my hand on his arm. "I was an idiot. I—"

"I told you to keep the ring, that I would wait until you were ready. I was beginning to think you didn't want a future with me. You'd pulled away. We barely spent any time together. We were just in this hellish limbo while I waited for you to decide."

"I'm so sorry," I repeat.

"Don't be. Because then I got to the hospital and you were wearing the ring. You were confused and beat up and it was terrifying, but every time I saw that ring on your finger, I believed everything was going to be okay. It had to be."

"Sounds like I'd finally come to my senses." But what damage had I done in the weeks between?

"You needed to know. No one else does. We kept it quiet. I wanted the decision to be yours. All that matters is that you decided to put on the ring. And when I saw you in that hospital bed, my ring on your finger..." He shakes his head. Swallows. "God, it's such a cliché, but you've truly made me the happiest man in the world. You owe me no apologies."

"What I did hurt you." I glance over my shoulder to make sure our private conversation stays that way. "I owe you every apology for that." And maybe more than an apology. Maybe an explanation. Maybe the truth.

He draws me against him and crushes me to his chest, and I breathe him in and swallow back my tears. I could tell him. Maybe I should, but the idea of losing this...

I look up at him. "When *did* you propose?" I ask quietly.

"Three months ago."

"I brought the booze," Granny says when my mom leaves her dining room to retrieve dessert. She pulls a flask from her skirt, unscrews the cap, and takes a gulp before passing it to me.

I grin and take a swig myself before passing it on to Lizzy.

"Oh, Hanna, I've been dying to do something about this." She grabs at the air around my head, flicking away invisible pieces of God-knows-what.

"Granny, what are you *doing*?" Liz asks.

"Apparently Hanna neglected to keep her aura clean while in the hospital," Maggie grouses as she takes her turn with the flask.

"No, it's been like this for months." Granny shudders, flicking away more invisible aura ugliness. "Come to my office for a thorough cleansing. No bride should go into her wedding day with so much darkness in her aura."

"I'll think about it," I lie.

I have the world's coolest grandmother—as evidenced by the fact that she cashed in one of her investments to buy each of her granddaughters her own muscle car a couple of years back. But she's also the world's kookiest grandmother. I squirm under her assessing gaze, relaxing only when she shifts it to Maggie.

"Yours looks better than it has since you were fourteen," Granny tells Maggie. "I told your mother she shouldn't stop you from shacking up with that rocker. Best thing that ever happened to you."

Maggie blushes—a rare sight. "Thanks. I think so too." Then Mom's coming back into the room, and Maggie has to hide the flask under the table.

"Where is the Sexy Beast anyway, Maggie?" Granny asks, using Asher's music-world nickname.

"He has a concert in Chicago tonight," Maggie says. "It's sweet of you to ask."

Lizzy snorts. "Granny's only asking because she wants her eye candy back."

Granny winks. "Damn straight."

"Nanci!" Mom protests.

Granny shrugs. "What? I might be old but my eyes work just fine, thank you very much. And your daughters are doing a mighty fine job of giving me nice views as I go into old age."

"Well, it doesn't bother me at all if you want to check out my man," Maggie says. "But he and Nate are touring together for the next week and a half, so you'll have to wait."

"Will he be home a week from Saturday?" Mom asks. "I'm throwing a casual engagement party for your sister."

Casual. I'm sure. Mom doesn't know the meaning of the word. Case in point, the crystal goblet holding my water.

"When he comes back into town, he'll have Nate with him. They're trying to get a project finished up by the end of the month, so he'll be busy, but I'm sure he can get away for a couple of hours."

Lizzy and I exchange a look, and I force myself to relax as Lizzy leans across the table toward Maggie, an interrogator going in for the kill. "So Nate's coming back to town? Will he be staying at your house?"

Maggie rolls her eyes. "I think it's in Nate's best interest that I not tell you where he's sleeping, Liz. No offense."

"They'll probably have to work late into the night though, huh?" Liz asks.

Laughter bursts from Maggie's lips. "You're pathetic. If the guys emerge from their music-making cave long enough to have a beer, I promise to invite you over."

Lizzy squeaks, and I elbow her under the table. "Calm down," I say between my teeth.

"Thanks for dinner, Mom." She pushes her plate away and looks at me pointedly. "Hanna, were you going to come back to the bakery with me tonight? To work on the calla lilies for Saturday's wedding cake?"

"Sure." I'm halfway through the three dozen gum-paste lilies I need to decorate Saturday's monstrosity of a cake order.

"I'll see you later," Maggie calls.

As we head out the front door, I can hear Mom talking. "You could learn a thing or two from Hanna, Maggie. Instead of giving it up to Max the first chance she got, she's waiting until marriage. Maybe if you weren't living with Asher, you'd be wearing his ring by now. You know what they say about the cow and the milk."

I turn to Lizzy, wide-eyed, and she throws a hand over her mouth. I open the door just as Maggie says, "Mom, if you think sex is like milk, you're doing it wrong."

Lizzy and I are laughing by the time we climb into Lizzy's car, and I have to lean my head back against the seat and catch my breath.

"Here's the plan," Lizzy says when we're on the road and headed to the bakery. "We're going over there when Nate comes back into town. You'll corner him. Get some answers."

The smile falls from my face. "What if I don't want the answers?" I whisper. "I mean, I do. Of course I do. But I'm scared, Liz."

She pulls into a spot in front of the building and puts the car in park before reaching over to squeeze my hand. "You could just wait and see if your memories come back."

"They're starting to. I remember more every day, but it's all stuff from fall semester and the beginning of my relationship with Max. None of my memories are answering my questions yet."

We go inside the bakery and head to the back, working together to pull out supplies for Saturday's calla lily explosion.

"Today, Max told me something." I run my fingers along the prepared flowers, searching for imperfections. "He didn't propose right before my accident like everyone assumed."

Lizzy frowns. "Then where'd the ring come from?"

"He proposed before that. A *long time* before that. And I told him I wasn't ready."

She covers her lips with her fingers and studies me. "You've always wanted Max."

"I know."

"When did he propose?"

"Three months ago." I drop the flower I was inspecting and walk to the back door and push it open. I can't breathe. I need fresh air. "I didn't give him an answer and held on to the ring all this time."

"Three months ago?" She arches a brow. "As in, *after* you met a sexy rocker?"

"That's what I'm afraid of," I say.

"I think we're still missing something," she says.

"What do you mean?"

"That night you came home from the hospital and Nate climbed in bed with you in the middle of the night... Did you lock the door?"

"I did. I'm sure of it."

"So you gave him a key." She nods. "That says something about your relationship, I think."

"Why would I give him a key?" Panic starts that slow-clawing climb in my chest. "Didn't you say he'd never been to town?"

She shrugs. "Maybe you knew he'd be coming."

"And I gave him a key when *Max* already has one? Really? I mean, I was obviously being reckless, but that seems a little over the top."

"So you think he broke in?"

"I don't know," I whisper. "But I know I locked the door."

"What if he had a key for a different reason?" Liz asks.

"I'm not following."

"What if he has a key to your apartment because he owns the building? What if *Nate* is your silent partner?"

"Fuck," I whisper.

"Think about the timeline. You go to Asher's concert and meet Nate either shortly before or shortly after Max proposes, and within a couple of weeks, someone's buying this vacant building downtown and setting it up to be your bakery and apartment. Maybe you screwed around with Nate because you were feeling insecure and then he offered you your dream on a platter right before Max proposed."

"Why would Nate buy a bakery for a woman he just met? And if I was committed to Max, why would I let him?"

"Girl, your life has gotten better than my daytime soaps. *Days of Our Lives* cannot compete with this shit."

"Maybe I wasn't choosing Nate over Max. Maybe I was choosing my business over Max. I mean, what if Nate does own it and he was going to sell it or something if I married Max?"

"That would be pretty dickish."

"Yes, but he's a spoiled rock star. Of course he'd be a dick about getting his way, right?"

She frowns. "That's one big insult to his personality wrapped up in a clichéd assumption."

"Even if there were no strings attached to our agreement, that's gotta be awkward, right? What if Max marries me and finds out I'm in business with the guy I was once cheating on him with?" I gasp and throw my hand over my mouth. "Liz, Max and I are planning on living upstairs after we get married!"

"Shit," she breathes. "You need to find out if Nate's the silent partner."

I nod. "And I need to find out before the wedding."

Chapter
ELEVEN

"**I**T'S SO screwed up," Drew says. "The whole town hates her and thinks she's this total slut, but nobody really cares that it takes two, you know?" She scoops the cookies off the tray and slides them onto a cooling rack. "Can you imagine if we made all the cheating *men* walk around with a red A on their chests? No one would be ashamed. They'd just wear it all proud. Probably be embarrassed if they didn't have one. I swear. I hate the world sometimes."

I bite back my laughter. Drew's junior honors English class is American Literature, and she has to finish *The Scarlet Letter* before school starts on Monday. Just yesterday, she was groaning about having to read "this stupid old book," and now she's so into it she can hardly stop talking about it.

"I've made my last latte," Lizzy says, pushing into the kitchen. "I'm tapping out. Drew. You're up."

Drew groans but otherwise doesn't protest before going to man the front of the store.

"Thank God," Liz says when Drew's safely on the other side of the kitchen door. "I had to get her away from you before you started getting a complex and embroidering an A on all your clothes."

I wrinkle my nose. "I didn't even think of that, but thanks. Thanks a lot."

"So did you make an appointment with the lawyer to find out about the silent partner?"

I nod. "I'm going in next week."

"Good. Want me to go with you?"

I bite my lip and nod. "Is that pathetic?"

She rolls her eyes. "No. I'm, like, your assistant manager or some shit. What affects your business affects me."

"Thank you so much. The lawyer's in Indianapolis, and I'm not supposed to be driving."

"And you're a scaredy cat."

"True fact." I grab a hot pad and swat her with it before opening the oven.

The chocolate chip scones smell so delicious my mouth literally waters as I pull them out of the oven. I've been trying to be good about my eating. I haven't even been home from the hospital a week, and I've already gained weight. Dr. Perkins doesn't want me getting on the scale, but I don't need a scale when it's getting harder to button my jeans.

"Do it," Lizzy says behind me. She grabs one off the tray and breaks a corner off to pop it in her mouth. Her eyes float closed and she moans. "Jesus Christ, Hanna. I don't need a man. I just need your baked goods. *All* of your baked goods." She grabs my forearm and squeezes. "Promise me you'll never cut me off."

I giggle and break a piece off her scone. The butter and flour practically melt on my tongue. "God, I'm good."

"Are you sure you want to be eating that?" someone asks at the door.

Lizzy and I turn to find my mother walking into my kitchen with her old critical eyes on my baked goods. I'm not used to my mom looking at me with approval. She's terrified of fat, extra weight, and clothing sizes in the double digits. My inability to keep my weight down was always a point of anxiety for her. And I always felt like a failure. Until I woke up in the hospital with my new body. Then all that disappointment was gone from her eyes.

It's back now as she eyes the half-eaten scone in Lizzy's hand.

"She's sure," Lizzy says. "It's delicious, and she hasn't stopped working all day to eat lunch."

I think about it and realize she's right. I had some plain oatmeal for breakfast around five, but I haven't had anything since. No wonder I'm famished.

Mom lifts a brown paper bag and beams. "That's why I brought you a healthy lunch."

I have to bite back a groan. My old self hated the crap she used to feed me. Leafy greens without dressing, carrots, and way more chicken breast than any reasonable human would want to consume. Hell, the boob-loving men of the world should probably thank her. It was probably all those hormone-filled chicken breasts that gave me boobs by age thirteen.

"What did you bring?" Liz asks. "Some weeds and sticks for her to nibble on?"

"Elizabeth," Mom scolds. "We can't all have your metabolism. And that's going to catch up with you someday."

Lizzy glares defiantly and takes another big bite of her scone.

"Stop trying to make me out to be the bad guy here," Mom objects. "I'm just helping Hanna with something she decided was important to her *months* ago."

My size has always been important to me. Because she taught me to believe it was. But three months ago it must have become so important that I took measures I'd never stooped to before. Last night I found diet pills in the back of my cabinet. Add those to the starvation and unhealthy amounts of exercise. And so much of it cloaked in secrecy that it sickens me to think about it.

But Mom doesn't know about Dr. Perkins. She doesn't know I was making myself sick.

There's no reason to make her worry, though, so I paste on a smile and say, "What's for lunch?"

Mom smiles approvingly. "Chopped grilled chicken,

greens, and a tiny sliver of avocado in a low-carb, whole-grain wrap." She hands the bag over, and I dig out her homemade lunch. "Eat, and then we have an appointment at Cleanstein's."

I pause with the wrap halfway to my mouth. "At the wedding dress shop?"

"Of course. You're getting married in five weeks. We're going to have to buy off the rack as is. We need to start shopping last week."

I try to swallow around the tightness in my throat. Is no one going to ask if I *want* to be planning my wedding? If I *want* to rush my engagement?

Mom sniffs, and I realize there are tears in her eyes. "After Maggie's canceled wedding and Krystal's disaster of a ceremony, you can imagine how excited I am about yours." She squeezes my hand. "There's just something so special about Max."

"Speak of the devil," Liz mutters as Max pushes through the door into the kitchen.

My heart stumbles in my chest at the sight of him. He's got a light stubble going on today, and he's still disheveled from his run.

"Oh, hello, Max!" my mom croons. God, she loves him so much.

"How are New Hope's three most beautiful women?" he asks with a wink.

"We're peachy," Liz says. "How's New Hope's biggest suck-up?"

Max draws me into a hug and presses a kiss to my forehead. "Does your sister hate me?" he asks loud enough for her to hear.

"No. She's just cranky that Mom didn't bring her lunch."

Lizzy snorts at the same moment my mom says, "Oh, I'm so sorry, Liz! I won't forget you next time!"

"How are you?" I ask Max. We've barely seen each other the last few days. He almost always trains late at the club, and I get horrible headaches if I don't get enough rest, so I've been going to bed early. I haven't found the courage to ask him to sleep with me—in the literal or figurative sense of the phrase.

"I'm good," he says. "What are you up to this afternoon? Can I steal you away for a while? I miss my girl." He ducks his head and steals a bite of my wrap, and because there's something very twisted and wrong with me, I actually find the movement of his jaw as he chews sexy as all hell. Then again, it's Max, and everything he does is sexy.

"No horning in on our plans this afternoon," Mom says. "We are going wedding dress shopping."

Max's eyes light up and he looks at me like I've just given him some amazing gift. "Yeah?"

I'm gonna burn in hell for hurting this sweet, sweet man. "Yeah," I say, though I hadn't even decided until that moment that I was going to let my mom talk me into it.

Max grins. "Well, I guess I can sacrifice an afternoon with you if that's the reason behind it."

"There are plenty of plans you can join us for," Mom assures him. "I have appointments with three caterers lined up for next week."

"Wow, Mom," Liz says. "Whose wedding is this anyway?"

"This is really happening, isn't it?" Max asks, and there's so much joy in his eyes that I'm reminded of the day at the gallery when he told me about my initial lack of response to his proposal. *I was beginning to think you didn't want a future with me.*

He's had enough limbo, hasn't he? Can I really ask for him to endure more? And if Max is the man I want and he wants me, what's the harm in getting married quickly?

"Oh, Max, you sweet thing," Mom says, "of course this is happening."

"That is *the one*," Mom declares an hour into dress shopping.

I would have hated every minute of this at my old size.

Putting on these dresses and modeling them for my critical mother—it would have pretty much been my own personal hell.

But at this size, it's not so bad. The attendant brings in dress after dress, seemingly unconcerned about my own personal taste and style, and my mom dotes on me in every one. Even in the dresses she doesn't like, she squeaks when I walk out of the dressing room.

And the way she's looking at me in this one makes the little girl in me—the one desperate for her approval—so gleefully happy. I know this will be the dress we buy, regardless of how I feel about the style.

"Take your hair down," Mom says. She comes up behind me and releases my barrette to let my heavy, dark hair fall past my shoulders. "Get her a veil," she calls to the attendant.

The attendant rushes over with a veil in the same super-soft fabric featured on the dress and slides it into my hair.

"It's perfect, isn't it, sweetheart?"

When she turns me to face the big three-panel mirror, I can't reply. I look like…a bride.

"It's perfect," Mom says for me. "We're getting this one. No question."

It's not something I would have picked. It's fitted all the way down through the hips and is covered with twinkling rhinestones. It's one of those dresses I would love for someone else, but it's not really for me. I always pictured myself getting married in something softer. Simpler.

"We're in a tight timeline," Mom says. "What kind of discount can you give me if we buy off the rack?"

The attendant and Mom haggle over price as I stare at my reflection. It's just a dress. It doesn't really matter if it's my dream dress. All that matters is the guy. All that matters is Max.

February—Six Months Before Accident

"Would you get out from in front of that mirror?" Lizzy calls from the front room of our rental. "You look freaking gorgeous, and Max is going to think so too."

I blink at my reflection, as if moistening my eyes could make me see what Lizzy sees, but it's still me standing here. Me. Chubby. Plain. Trying too hard.

I chose black pants and a black scoop-neck sweater for tonight. No frills to distract from the two features of my outfit I do feel confident about: my cleavage and my sexy red heels.

I grab the curling iron and add a couple of fresh ringlets to hair. Max likes my hair. I said something about cutting it off last week, and he looked horrified. *"You have great hair. Why would you cut something so beautiful?"*

The ringing of the doorbell pulls me away from the mirror, and by the time I reach the front room, Max is already here, a bunch of red roses in his hands.

Lizzy shakes her head. "I fucking hate this holiday."

"I told you Sam wanted to take you out tonight," Max tells her.

Liz snorts. "Sam wanted to *fuck* me tonight. Pardon me for holding out for something more romantic than a low-budget porno on Valentine's Day."

Max laughs. "He would have given you all the romance you could handle."

"He asked if I was open to a threesome," Lizzy growls.

I bite back a smile. The relationship between Liz and Sam is a bit of a love-hate situation, and he likes to razz her by asking her for sexual favors.

"You know he really likes you," Max says. "He's just doesn't think you'd take him seriously."

Liz shakes her head and turns to me with a mischievous smile. "I'm out of here. You two have a nice night."

Then she leaves, and Max and I are left alone for the

Valentine's Day dinner I cooked for him. I liked the idea of being here and drinking too much wine. Maybe then I could get over myself enough to let him touch me. The high-school-caliber groping we have going on is nice, but I know Max is ready for more.

I take the flowers into the kitchen, where I've already set the small table for our dinner.

"It smells amazing in here," he says. "What are we having?"

"Filet mignon with green beans and a fresh French baguette and then chocolate lava cake for dessert." I fill a vase with water and arrange the roses in it before setting it on the table. When I turn around, Max is right there, his face inches from mine.

"Happy Valentine's Day," he whispers. He lowers his mouth to mine in a kiss so sweet my nerves fizzle away. And maybe it's how good he smells or the fact that I already had a big glass of wine before he got here. Or maybe it's because I'm standing and don't feel as self-conscious about my body like this. But when his hands find the hem of my sweater and slide under, I don't stop him.

He breaks the kiss and leans his forehead against mine, his eyes closed and lips parted a fraction of an inch as he cups my breast in his hand and grazes his thumb over my nipple. The contact makes my knees weak and I have to curl my hands into the thick muscle of his shoulders to keep myself upright.

"So we have the place to ourselves tonight?" he whispers.

Something thick lodges in my throat at his question and nerves flare back to life in my belly. "Yeah."

"Do you want to have dinner first or can I give you your present?"

"I thought the flowers were my present."

He grins and points to a gift bag sitting by the door. "I got you something else too."

"You really didn't have to."

He retrieves the bag and watches me carefully as I open it.

"Oh." It's pretty much the last thing I'd want him to buy me.

"Do you like it?"

"I…" I force a smile but it hurts when I want to die of mortification. "It's beautiful. Thank you." And it is. The silky gold material of the lingerie slip is rose-petal soft in my hands and beautiful against my skin.

"I know you're not ready yet. I don't want you to think I'm pushing you. But I saw it and I thought of you. You'd look gorgeous in it."

"Thank you," I repeat, dropping it back into the bag. I have to turn away from him. I can't let him know how horrified I am by the idea of him seeing me in that slip. I don't want him to see the parts of me that would be on display in it or to know how un-sexy a girl like me looks in lingerie.

I go back to the kitchen and busy myself with the steaks.

"Did I do something wrong?" he asks behind me. "Was that too much too soon or…?"

"No," I assure him. "You're wonderful. This is perfect." But the awkward silence as I get our meals on the table speaks volumes to how not-perfect this night is shaping up to be.

"Want me to pour some wine?" he asks as I take our plates to the table.

My shoulders drop in relief. Wine is just the Band-Aid we need here. "That would be wonderful."

He pours us each a full glass and we sit and stare awkwardly at our food. "I'm sorry about the lingerie. It's probably too soon for that."

Shit. I've ruined this. I keep reminding myself that I can't have it both ways. I can't be with Max in every way I want to *and* keep hiding my body from him. "I'm kind of…insecure," I blurt.

Looking up from his plate, he softens. "I noticed." He isn't cruel about it. It isn't an accusation—more of a sympathetic understanding.

"I saw the slip and instantly thought about how much I didn't want you to see me in it." God, that's terrible to admit.

"Hanna…" He exhales heavily. "I don't know what to say. I wouldn't have bought it for you if I didn't want to see you wear it."

"I'm not like the girls you usually date."

"Thank God." He grins. "You're you. And I happen to like that." His phone buzzes and he pulls it from his pocket. "Sorry," he says as he slides his finger over the screen and reads. "Crap."

"What is it?"

"Meredith thinks she's going into pre-term labor. She wants me to take her to the hospital."

"Meredith? The one who bought sperm to get pregnant and let everyone think it was William Bailey's baby?"

He taps something on his phone before sliding it back into his pocket. I wait for him to respond, but his mind is somewhere else already. "I'm sorry. She doesn't have anyone else to take her." He stands, and I'm so shocked I can only gape at him. "I'll make it up to you, okay?"

I shake my head as if the motion can send my confusion away. What is happening? Is my boyfriend seriously going to spend Valentine's Day with some pregnant bitch who tried to steal my best friend's boyfriend?

By the time I can gather my wits to follow him to the door, he's already in his coat and pulling open the door.

"It's Valentine's Day," I whisper.

He drags a hand through his hair, tousling it in the way that makes him go from handsome to devilishly irresistible. "She doesn't have anyone."

"What about her friends? I happen to remember her having a lot of those back when she was letting everyone think William was some jerk who got her knocked up."

His jaw hardens. "I know Cally's your friend, but Meredith is mine. You're going to have to deal with that."

He pushes out the door and pulls it shut behind him, and I'm left alone with a romantic dinner complete with wine, roses, and lingerie. Alone while he runs to rescue the gorgeous blonde.

Chapter
TWELVE

"IT'S NICE to see you again, Miss Thompson," the lawyer says as Lizzy and I settle into chairs in her comfortable Indianapolis office. "And it's nice to meet your sister. What can I do for you today?"

"We're kind of wondering who the silent partner is," Liz says. She points her thumb at me. "This one has amnesia and doesn't remember whether or not you told her."

Her eyes go wide. "Amnesia! That's horrible. I'm so sorry. What happened?"

"I'm a klutz and fell down the stairs."

"Goodness. Do they think your memory will come back?"

"The doctor said it will, but like Swiss cheese," I explain. "And so far that's been true. Lots of holes, including the details of my agreement with my silent partner."

"Well, to answer your sister's first question, the agreement was under the condition of my client's anonymity, so if you knew who was behind it, that information certainly didn't come from me." She stands and hands me a thick folder across the desk. "I'm sure you have this in your files somewhere, but those are copies with the details of our agreement. You may keep them if you like."

I open the file and flip through the first few pages, but my impatient twin cuts to the chase. "What's going to happen to the bakery when she gets married?"

She lifts a brow. "I'm not sure what you mean."

I shift awkwardly. "What my sister is trying to say is, not knowing who the silent partner is, I'm not sure if it would be okay for my husband and me to live in the apartment over the bakery. Or if my...partner would have an issue with that."

She frowns. "I'd be happy to check with my client, but I can't imagine he would object. Those living quarters didn't come with any stipulations that I recall."

Lizzy and I exchange a look, and Liz says, "You really can't tell us? Not even a hint?"

The lawyer looks unimpressed with my sister's adorable persistence. "Not even a hint, Miss Thompson. That's the definition of *anonymous*."

I dreamed about Nate Crane last night. We were swimming in Asher's pool and he stripped my swimsuit off my breasts and took my nipples into his mouth. I wrapped my legs around his waist and realized he was nude and his dick was cradled right between my legs.

"We can't have sex," I said in the dream. "I'm marrying Max."

"No you're not."

He slid the ring off my finger and threw it into the deep end of the water. Only we weren't in the pool anymore. We were in the river. The ring glinted against the moonlight before the dark water sucked it under, and I knew I'd never see it again. I just shrugged, and Nate slid his hand between my legs. Then we were in Max's steam room. I was sitting on the high bench just like I had the night I was there with Max, only it was Nate with me. Nate's face buried between my legs. Nate's fingers toying with my nipples.

And when Max walked into the room and called my name through the steam, I laughed. *"This is what you wanted,"* I said, grabbing a fistful of Nate's hair and holding him against me. *"You wanted me to find someone else, and I did. Now go fuck a blonde."*

I woke up confused, horny, guilty, and depressed. Did it mean something, or is my brain just screwed up from how crazy everything's been the last few weeks?

I've been home from the hospital for two weeks and I feel like I never see Max. He works late almost every night, and when he does come over, he doesn't stay long. And we've never had sex. I know he's turned on by me—it's evident—but it's almost like he's perfectly satisfied to stop things with a little groping.

In the meantime, wedding planning is going full speed ahead. I ended up having a meeting at the bakery during our caterer appointments last week, so Mom went with Max and they picked a caterer without me. I was relieved not to have to mess with it. Shouldn't I be more excited about my wedding?

From the edge of Mom's back deck, I scan the crowd gathered for my engagement party and try to push my anxiety to the side.

In just two weeks, Mom pulled together a party to rival the weddings of most girls in this town. I didn't give her any input on the event, but then again, she didn't ask for any. Not too different than my wedding, now that I think of it.

Nix Reid, my doctor and apparently friend, sidles up to me and puts her hand on my arm. "You look stressed. Are you okay?"

I force a smile. "I'm great. Turned out beautifully, didn't it?"

The evening is warm but not too warm to mingle out on the lawn. Servers circulate with hors d'oeuvres, and Mom hired a bartender to serve drinks from a makeshift bar on the deck.

On the lawn, a small band is playing in front of the temporary floor put down so our guests can dance under the stars. It's beautiful and perfect and terrifying.

"It's a lovely party." She smooths her hair and shifts awkwardly. She doesn't seem like a woman who's comfortable in dress clothes. "How are you feeling?"

"I'm doing great, really." I pause for a breath. "Do you have any guess as to when my other memories might come back?"

Nix looks around. "This is what you want to talk about right now?" She puts her hand on my shoulder and smiles. "Relax. Stressing about your memory isn't going to help anything."

"It's just weird," I say. "I'm getting these pieces back, but the last few months are still completely missing. Like they never happened." And the last few months are the memories I want the most.

"Memory recovery isn't an exact science. It's different for everyone, but it does usually happen chronologically—not always, but for the most part. Just because you don't have any memories from the last few months doesn't mean you won't."

"There's so much I still don't know. And the day of the accident? The day I fell down the stairs?" *The day I put on Max's ring.* "I want that back. I want it all back."

"Listen," she says. "The worse the head trauma, the less likely you are to remember the events leading up to it. You need to make peace with the possibility that you might never recover your memories of the accident or the days prior."

Including the day I chose Max. "This sucks."

She whispers, "I know, but let it go. For tonight at least, okay? Try to enjoy your party. I'll see you in my office next week."

"Where's the couple of honor?" the bandleader asks in the mic. "Because I understand this is their song." The guitar player starts into the first notes of Jason Mraz's "I Won't Give Up."

Suddenly, Max is next to me, taking my hand and leading me to the dance floor.

"This is our song?" I ask as I slip my arms around his neck.

"I gave you the ring three months ago, remember?"

Something squeezes in my chest as the man sings the line

about giving his love the space she needs to navigate. Is that what Max did for me? Gave me the space I needed to figure this out? I want to remember.

"You look drop-dead gorgeous tonight," he murmurs against my ear.

I'm wearing a red dress, a bold, daring color that draws attention to my legs and my curves. Not just any red dress. It's Lizzy's. The one she wore to the winter gallery opening. Now I remember the night I caught Max checking her out and felt twelve kinds of depressed about it...until he kissed me silly.

"You know what I think would be even more gorgeous than you in that dress?"

"What's that?" I ask.

"You out of that dress. In my bed."

A delicious chill runs over my skin, but he says stuff like that and then...nothing.

He pulls me even closer and I can feel that hard length of him through his dress pants. "That's all I've been able to think about since I had to leave you last night—undressing you and taking you to my bed, keeping you there all weekend."

"I think I'd like that." I've not pushed the issue of our lack of intimacy. My head's too busy spinning with what I have and haven't done, but I'm ready to put a stop to that hesitancy. I'm marrying this man, and none of my memories of making love to him have returned yet. I want to know what that's like. I want the *reassurance* of him making love to me.

He groans. "I'd make damn sure you liked it."

"Don't make promises you don't intend to keep."

His hands tighten on me, pulling me closer. "Don't tempt me. We've made it this far. We can hold out for a few more weeks, don't you think?"

I stop moving. Right there in the middle of the dance floor, my shoes might as well be filled with lead. "What?"

"Don't get me wrong," he says quietly. "I want you. You don't need to question that. I want you like I've never wanted anyone." He presses his nose to my hair and inhales deeply. "But there's something kind of special about waiting, about the anticipation of it. And I'm sorry if it's not politically correct, but I fucking love that I'm going to be your first and only."

I push back half a step so I can look into his eyes. "Are you saying we've never...?"

Confusion flashes in his eyes. Then he drags a hand over his face. "God, it never occurred to me that I needed to tell you, but how would you know if you can't remember?"

"Know what?" I need to hear him say it.

He smiles, as if he's about to tell me some delightful surprise. "You're a virgin," he whispers. "You wanted to wait for marriage." He pulls me back against him, and I press my hot cheek against his chest and squeeze my eyes shut.

"You're a virgin." But what he means is that I haven't slept with *him*. Did I sleep with Nate?

The song ends, and he tips my chin up to look in my eyes. "Are you okay?"

I don't trust myself to talk, so I nod toward the bar.

We walk hand in hand. Every brush of his thumb skimming over my knuckles digs a guilty dagger into my heart. Every day it becomes clearer to me that I have secrets I have to share with Max before we can get married, but it never occurred to me I might have to tell him I gave my virginity to someone else.

Lizzy's standing in front of the bar in a long, strapless black dress, tapping her foot to the beat. She takes in our joined hands and grins. "You two look nice out there."

Max presses a kiss to the back of my hand and winks at me. "This beauty can make anyone look good."

Lizzy's jaw goes slack and she flashes me a look as if to say, "How could you *doubt* a future with this guy?" Or maybe it's more, "You are such a bitch." As her twin, I'm excellent at reading her, but those are pretty similar looks.

"What can I get you?" the bartender asks.

Max stuffs a five in the tip jar. "A draft beer for me and a glass of Riesling for my girl." The bartender hands us our glasses, and Max presses a kiss to my bare shoulder. "I need to talk to William about our plans for his bachelor party. Sam made plans at this strip club in Indy and Will isn't having it.

Apparently, I'm supposed to be the mediator."

"Mediate away." I force a smile. "I'm not going anywhere."

"I love you," he whispers.

I wait until he's gone before I turn to Liz and drag her into Mom's house and all the way upstairs to our old bedroom.

"What's going on?" she asks as I shut the door.

"Max said I'm a virgin."

Her eyes go big and her jaw drops.

"He said I wanted to wait until we got married to have sex."

"Since…when?"

I let out a long breath and study the ceiling. This is all so weird. Some days it doesn't even feel like I missed a year of my life. It feels like I was dropped into someone else's.

"I just assumed you two had had sex."

"That makes two of us."

"You and Mom have gotten closer lately," she says. "Maybe she brought you over to the devout side?"

"I'm not buying that."

"Yeah. Me neither. But hey, at least that means you didn't have sex with Nate Crane either, right?"

"But what if I did?" I whisper.

"Oh." She plops down on the bed. "That would be really bad, wouldn't it? Max thinking you're a virgin and you actually already gave that up to someone else?"

"I have to tell Max what I know."

"Why?"

"Lizzy, I'm marrying him."

"Exactly."

"I need to be honest. I need him to know what I've done."

"If you had your memories, I might agree, but the truth is, until they come back, you don't know the whole story. The only thing you're going to accomplish by telling Max is hurting him."

"So you're saying I shouldn't tell the man I'm marrying that I was seeing someone else? Possibly *sleeping* with someone else? I shouldn't explain to him why I wouldn't wear his ring all those months?"

"That's exactly what I'm saying."

"My memories are starting to come back."

"More since last time?"

I nod. "It's weird, you know. I get these snippets, and a lot of them are insignificant. I remember jogging with Max in the mornings. I remember going into his gym and asking him to train me. I remember the first time he kissed me at the winter gallery opening."

"Anything about Nate?"

I shake my head. "And nothing to make me think I would have had a reason to cheat on Max." Except for my profound insecurity.

What if I never got over that feeling that I wasn't good enough for Max? What if those feelings made me do something really stupid? And what about Valentine's Day, when he left me alone to take care of Meredith? Is that just the price of dating a good guy? Or was something going on there?

She taps her knee thoughtfully. "None of this makes sense. Cheating? That's just not in character for you. Maybe you didn't realize things with Max were going anywhere. Maybe you didn't think he was serious about you."

"You forget that he proposed *three months* ago."

"Crap. That's right."

"Girls!" Mom calls from downstairs. "What are you doing up there? Come down to the party!"

"Coming!" I call back.

Lizzy's staring at me. "Are you sure you're okay with this? Not all the memory loss and bad crap, but marrying Max? Is this what you want?"

"Of course." But in that moment, with everyone waiting downstairs to congratulate me and ask questions about how many babies we plan to have, I'm not sure if this is really what I want or what I *should* want.

Chapter
THIRTEEN

MAX PROPS his bare feet on my coffee table and sips a beer. I had no idea a man's bare feet could be so damn sexy.

The engagement party couldn't have gone any better, but I'm glad it's over. As soon as we got back to my apartment, all my fears and insecurities faded away. Because Max makes me feel good.

"I hear you picked out a dress last week," Max says.

"I'm not sure if *I* picked it out or my mom did, but that's more or less true."

He frowns. "Do you like it?"

"It's beautiful, and hopefully *you* will like it."

I take the beer from his hands and set it on the end table before straddling him. I'm still in the red dress, in no hurry to put an end to the way his eyes roam over me while I'm wearing it.

I sink onto his lap, my knees on either side of his hips. His gaze floats down to the dress's low neckline and he swallows.

"I've missed you this last week." I rub my fingers over the stubble of his jaw. "Are you working a lot more than usual or is this normal?"

He shrugs. "Money's a little tight and I had to let a couple of part-timers go. Summer's always slow. It'll pick up when the semester starts and the Sinclair students decide they want to work out in something nicer than the dungeon that the college tries to pass off as a gym."

"Hmm. Well, we'll have to figure out how I can see you more."

"When your doctor says it's okay, we'll run together again. That was always *us* time."

I arch a brow. "No offense to your very healthy-sounding plans, but I had a different kind of exercise in mind."

His eyes darken, his pupils dilating, and I slip the dress's thin straps from my shoulders.

He slides his hands under the soft cotton and cups my ass. "Hanna?"

"Mmm?" My eyes float closed as his fingers massage into tight muscles.

"What happened to your underwear?"

I look up at him through my lashes. "I took them off when I got home. Seemed like they might just be in the way."

I kiss the corner of his mouth, the stubble at the edge of his jaw, and open my mouth against his neck. He yanks my hips forward and lifts his in one liquid movement, pressing my exposed sex to the hard denim of his jeans.

"You know the worst thing about our night in the steam room?"

I pull back. "I didn't know there was a worst thing."

"Oh, there was something." He traces my bottom lip with his thumb. "I couldn't see you. I want to see you."

He wraps his arms around me and stands. I squeak and wrap my legs around him, locking my ankles behind his back to hold on.

He carries me to the bedroom, lowers me to the bed, and clicks on the light on the bedside table.

Slowly, he trails his gaze over me, from my red-painted toenails to my thighs. I lift off the bed as he grips the hem of the dress and pulls it off over my head. His eyes are hot when they return to mine. Hot and needy. It takes my breath.

He pulls off his shirt and climbs next to me in his jeans. I wish he'd get naked, but his hands are on me before I can ask, his fingers following the path his eyes just took—from my toes, up my calves, to my thighs. He hesitates between my legs and skims a finger right over my center before resuming his northward journey over my navel and to my breasts.

I'm already wet and aching and breathing heavily, and he hasn't done anything but skim his fingers over me.

"Tell me what you like."

What I *like*? Who would know that better than him? "I just—"

His phone beeps and buzzes from his pocket. "Sorry." He digs it out and tosses it on the floor without looking at it. "You were saying?"

I shrug, suddenly self-conscious. "You. That's what I like. Just you."

He groans and lowers his mouth to mine, one leg nestled between my thighs.

His phone beeps and buzzes again, clattering against the floor.

"You should check that," I say against his lips.

He exhales heavily and climbs off me to retrieve it, but when he looks at the screen, something in his face changes. "I'm so sorry. I'm going to have to go." He taps the screen and shoves the phone back into his pocket. When he looks at me again, he rakes his gaze over me and shakes his head. "I don't want to, but I have to."

I push onto my elbows and frown. "What's wrong? Who was that?"

"It's a friend." He grabs his shirt off the floor and tugs it on over his head. "I'll fill you in on the details later, but I have to go help her out."

Her? My hands shake as I pull my dress back on and follow him to the door. He shoves his feet into his shoes, and my stomach twists. My voice is weak when I ask, "Who?"

I can tell by the way he stiffens that I'm not going to like the answer. "Meredith."

The name hits me like a punch in the gut. *Meredith.* My mind conjures the images of him leaving on Valentine's Day. His sweet attention completely diverted the moment she texted. The way he hurried out the door when she needed him. And now, on the night of our fucking engagement party, he's going to her.

"What does she need?" I ask, but my question is masked by the ringing of his phone.

"I love you." He presses a kiss to my forehead and pulls his phone from his pocket. "Hey... Yeah, I'm on my way."

Then he's out the door.

I watch him jog down the stairs, the phone to his ear the whole time. When he disappears around the corner, I return to my apartment. *Breathe. Just breathe.*

But the reminder doesn't help, and I have to rush to the bathroom to throw up.

I never thought I'd be engaged to a man I couldn't trust. I never thought I would doubt Max of all people. He hasn't done anything to deserve my suspicion, but I can't help it. The old insecurity is back, and it doesn't matter what I look like now or how many pounds I lost, because Meredith is everything I'll never be. Blond, slim, the kind of woman men's eyes go to when she enters a room.

And to top it off, she's a complete bitch. William Bailey dated her for a while before Cally came back in town, and when he broke it off for his first love, Meredith got artificially inseminated and let everyone in town think it was Will's baby.

After brushing my teeth and settling my angry stomach with Sprite, I found my underwear—so much for *that* seduction plan—and a pair of canvas flats and started walking.

Nothing calms me like the sound of the river, so I hit the path behind the bakery. Three times, I've pulled up Max's number on my phone, ready to call him and demand answers.

Three times, I've changed my mind. I don't want to be *that girl.* Insecure. Untrusting. He's marrying me, isn't he? And if he were doing something wrong, would he have told me where he was going?

I pull off my shoes and walk in the cool grass, the stars mocking me from above with their happy twinkling. I don't know how long I walk or how far, but by the time I've left the center of town and can see my mom's house in the distance, the bottoms of my feet are raw from walking barefoot.

In front of me lies the empty expanse of Mom's backyard. The party is over. The band's been packed up, the decorations taken down. All like it never existed.

I'm not ready to return to my apartment yet, so I stop at the dock just between Mom's and Asher's adjoining properties.

I sink onto the wooden planks, wrap my arms around my knees, lean my head against them, and tell myself everything is going to be okay.

I focus on breathing. *In. And out. In. And out.*

"You planning on sleeping there or just staying long enough to ruin that sexy dress?"

I lift my head to see a dark figure leaning against the rail at the end of the dock. I blink until Nate Crane comes into focus. He takes a drag off a cigarette—no, not a cigarette, a joint. I sneer in disgust. I hate drugs. I have no use for people who can't think of any better way to entertain themselves.

"You planning on getting stoned the rest of your life or actually doing something meaningful?"

He steps closer, and in the light of the moon, I can make out the half smirk, half smile on his lips. "Asher and Maggie invited me to your engagement party tonight, but I decided being stoned and useless would be more enjoyable. So would Chinese water torture, come to think of it. Looks like maybe you feel the same." He takes another step closer and offers the joint.

"Fuck no." I wave away the puff of smoke left behind and cough for good measure.

"Suit yourself," he murmurs. He shifts his gaze back to the

river, but instead of taking another drag, he pinches off the glowing tip into the water and tucks the rest into his pocket. "Do you want to talk about it?"

"I don't know what you're talking about." I sound like a sulking teenager.

He arches a brow but doesn't press.

Releasing my knees, I pull myself up and stand beside him at the rail. "That first weekend we met, did I tell you about how much I wanted to open a bakery?"

"You did."

I have to ask. "And you wanted me to do it?"

"I told you I thought you should." A frog sings in the distance, filling the silence. "You have talent."

"I love it, you know. Every time I walk in, I smile."

"Glad to hear it." There's a rough, pained edge to his words.

"And you made sure I had a chance," I say matter-of-factly.

"I'm not sure what you mean."

Clearly he's not interested in changing the "anonymous" part of our arrangement, and I'm too grateful to push the issue, but I can't help the sigh that slips from my lips. "I feel like everyone knows more about my life than I do."

He looks out over the water. "What do you want to know?"

"Everything," I whisper.

"Why?" If an open wound has a sound, it's the sound of his voice right now.

"You have no idea what it's like to be missing pieces of your memory, to feel like your own body is failing you."

He grunts. "Do you remember anything from our time together?"

"Nothing."

"Will it come back?"

The wind shifts, and a cloud blocks the moon and cloaks us in darkness. I'm standing in the dark with a man who's a stranger to me. I should be uncomfortable—cautious at the very least. Instead, my muscles relax incrementally. There's something comforting about darkness, about not being seen.

"The doctor says it's hard to say at this point," I say.

"Maybe, maybe not. The closer the memory is to the time of my accident, the less likely I am to remember it. Maybe I won't ever remember you. Maybe if you hadn't climbed into bed with me two weeks ago, I'd never have known about us."

"My life's biggest regret," he murmurs.

I wince. If he'd slapped me, it would have hurt less. "I'm your biggest regret?"

"No." He growls the word then takes a breath. "I'm not this great guy. I've made a lot of mistakes. Done a lot of shitty things, made a lot of selfish choices. But in the end, it's all worked out."

I wish I could see his face, read the nuance of his expression. Instead, he's only a silhouette in the night, and I'm left with nothing but his words and the low rumble of his voice.

"I don't regret much," he explains. "But I do regret crawling into bed with you when I came to town." He looks to the sky. "Your amnesia was a gift that I fucked up."

"You *wanted* me to forget you?"

His chest expands on his inhale, and I have to fight this irrational desire to lean my head against him. To comfort him with my presence, despite what he's saying. "It would be... easier."

"I'm not going to bother you, if that's what you're worried about. I won't be the girl who runs to the tabloids to tell about her hot night with Nate Crane."

"Hanna." He takes my shoulders and turns me to face him. He studies me for a beat. Two. Like he's trying to solve a puzzle and the answer is in my eyes. Then he drops his hands and turns away again. While he stares out into the stillness of the night, I'm left to guess what he might have been about to say.

"I might not remember what happened between us, but I feel something..." I make a fist and press it to my chest. "Something here. Every time you're close."

"And what about him? Do you feel it when he's close?"

Hot tears sting the backs of my eyes and I nod. "I do."

"There's your answer." His gaze settles on my hand, his eyes burning into the ring on my finger. "That's all you need to know."

"But I don't even remember putting it on. How can I trust a decision I don't remember making?" My question is punctuated by a distant owl call.

"You're the smartest girl I know. I trust your decision. Maybe you should too."

"I need to know something first."

He hangs his head. "You should talk to your fiancé."

"Did I sleep with you?"

The clouds shift again, and the moonlight casts shadows on the beautiful hard angles of his face. My heart pounds hard as he steps closer. He tilts my chin up until my eyes are on his.

"What do you think?"

"I think we all make mistakes."

Something flashes in his eyes, but it's gone as quickly as it appeared, his expression whitewashed by that stoner-may-care blankness.

I have to repeat the question. If I don't, I might lose my nerve and run away without hearing the answer. "Did we have sex?"

"No. We didn't."

There's no relief at his words. Not really. Only emptiness. Any way you paint it, I still betrayed my fiancé. I've been promising myself I'd tell Max the truth if I learned that I slept with Nate. Maybe I wanted the excuse to confess.

"Goodnight, angel."

"Don't go."

He closes his eyes, and I can't help myself anymore. I touch his face, carefully, tentatively. He stands stock-still as I skim my fingertips over the rough stubble of his cheek, study him while his eyes are closed. Then I just hold there, neither of us moving or breathing. Caught in the moment and the moonlight.

When he opens his eyes, they're filled with pain. With longing. Is that real, or am I seeing what I want to believe? He's as much a mystery to me as this connection between us.

He parts his lips and his eyes lock with mine. Just when I think we might stand here forever, a tragic tableau of secrets and heartache, he shifts a fraction of an inch and leans into my touch.

"Dammit, Hanna." The words are soft, tortured. "What do you want me to do?"

"Kiss me." And I can't believe what I'm asking, but the command is out there and I can't take it back. I don't want to.

"How am I supposed to say no to that?"

"You're not."

His gaze dips to my lips, and my heart races. A pace so painful and violent I fear it might burst from my chest right here and fall to his feet.

As his mouth moves toward mine, a sense of calm washes over me. My shoulders drop. My breathing slows. For a moment, my past doesn't matter. My future doesn't matter. Only here. Only now.

When his lips are so close I can almost taste him, he squeezes his eyes shut and leans his forehead against mine. "I love you too much to screw this up for you. I love you too much to let you beat yourself up over a stupid kiss." He staggers back.

"I'm sorry." My hand goes to my mouth. Shame washes over me, a hot rush followed by the icy-cold grip of loneliness. "I shouldn't have... I don't know why—"

"Go home, Hanna. Go be with your future husband."

Chapter
FOURTEEN

"HAS ANYONE ever told you that you work too much?" Max asks as the front door swings closed behind him.

I hand Mrs. Oaks her non-fat cappuccino and smile for her benefit as I say, "Takes one to know one."

She smiles back. "Could I also have the rest of your cheese Danishes, sweetheart?"

"Of course!" I grab a box off the shelf behind me and fill it.

"I'm going to surprise the ladies at Bible study with them," Mrs. Oaks says as I ring her up. "I brought them chocolate croissants last week, and you'd have thought I brought them each a piece of the moon."

"You're too sweet!"

"It's all true." She pays and tucks the box under her arm. "You two have a lovely day. Tell your mom I said hi, Hanna."

"I will. Thanks."

Max steps behind the counter as the woman leaves. We're alone in the front, only us and the sounds of Drew doing cleanup in the kitchen. He slips his hands under my shirt from behind me and draws me against him.

I tense.

Nuzzling the side of my neck, he takes a long, deep breath.

"You smell like clean sheets and flowers," he murmurs. "I just want to breathe you in for days."

The heat of his mouth against the side of my neck should be sweet and delicious, but instead it makes my stomach hurt. "You're distracting me," I protest lamely.

"Mission accomplished." His hand moves farther north and cups my breast, and even as part of my body reacts, warming and purring for more, another part of me is thinking about Nate. The way his whispers sent an electric buzz of pleasure through my veins last night. The regret in his eyes as he pulled away.

Max must sense something, because his hands still and he takes his mouth off my neck. "Are we okay?"

Three words. A simple question. My throat grows thick. "I didn't like the way you ran off to be with Meredith last night. It hurt me."

He withdraws, pulls his hands out from under my shirt, and steps back. "I didn't go off to *be with her*. It's not like that."

I set my jaw and cross my arms over my chest. I don't want to know his reasons or what kind of emergency she had. "It made me feel like I was less important to you than she is."

He exhales heavily and drags a hand through his hair. "I'm sorry you felt that way."

"That's not an apology." I spin and push into the kitchen. All my life I've struggled with telling people when their actions hurt me, and all too often it meant being used and trampled. The reason my twin sister is my closest friend is because she doesn't need to be told when I hurt. She can tell without me saying it.

I grab a tray and fill it with snickerdoodles from the cooling rack.

"I was just about to do that," Drew says, hands on her hips. She took the early baking shift this morning—thank God, since it was after two when I finally got to bed.

"I got it," I mutter.

"Don't let your shitty mood ruin my hard work," she grouses.

"Drew," I hear Max say, "can you cover the front so I can talk to Hanna?"

"Trouble in paradise?" she asks, but when I glare at her, she throws up her hands and scurries to the front.

"Did I miss something?" he asks. He crosses to me and turns me to face him.

Instead of meeting his eyes, I stare at his cheesy gym logo on his chest: *Hallowell Health Club, Fitness to the Max.*

"What's really going on here?"

I close my eyes. I feel so childish, like the teenager who throws a fit when she sees her boyfriend talking to another girl. "I remembered Valentine's Day," I admit.

"Valentine's Day?" He looks lost.

"You left to help Meredith." I shake my head. "I understand that I might seem irrationally jealous, but trust takes time to build. You have almost nine months of our relationship to lean on when you have a bad day. I have two weeks and a handful of memories. Last night made me feel unimportant, and I didn't like that."

His hard jaw softens. "I'm sorry."

"I'm not saying you can't help out a friend, but I need to know—I need to believe—I matter."

"Of course you do." He runs his finger over my cheek. "You're my life, Hanna. My future. You matter."

When he lowers his lips to mine, my anger has melted into a puddle at my feet. Maybe this shouldn't be the end of this fight. Maybe I should press the issue. But I'm so confused after last night that I just want the security of his touch. I let him kiss me and I kiss him back until the last of my hurt has evaporated into the sweet, sugar-scented air of the kitchen.

"You love birds can't keep your hands off each other, can you?"

The sound of my mother's voice has me breaking the kiss and backing away. She's already sipping a cup of coffee, her Bible tucked under her arm.

"Good morning, Mom. How was church?"

"Wonderful. Just wonderful. I wanted to invite you and

Max to Sunday brunch. Max, a few of the ladies from the New Hope Restoration Council will be there. Don't get me wrong, I think we're going to get you that grant for your gym—I've really been pulling for you—but it couldn't hurt to schmooze. A little insurance, you know."

This is the first I've heard of Max applying for a grant with the city restoration group, but I'm not surprised. Mom sits on the board, and it makes sense that they would give one of their grants to a business like Max's.

"I can't, Mom. I have too much to do here."

"You work too much," she says.

Max grins and winks at me. "That's what I keep telling her."

"Max, why don't you go without me? Mom's right. It certainly wouldn't be a bad idea to get some face time."

He nods and steals a cookie off the tray. "I can come by for a bit."

Mom brightens. "Wonderful! While you're there, I'll introduce you to Fred Wellings. He's the contractor who built my house. Built William Bailey's too. You can talk to him about building you and Hanna a house after your wedding."

Max lowers the cookie that was halfway to his mouth, cutting his eyes to me and then back to Mom. "Mrs. Thompson, Hanna and I both have new businesses. We're really not going to be in a position to build a house for quite a while."

"Balderdash," Mom says, waving her hand. "Hanna will get her trust fund once she's married. There's plenty there to build a home and have a little nest egg."

Poor Max looks so uncomfortable.

"We're going to live in my apartment for a while," I say.

"That will be great for while you're building, of course, but you can't raise my grandbabies in a tiny apartment above your bakery."

Max and I exchange and glance. "We'll talk about it," I promise.

She looks at her watch and squeaks. "I need to get going. Max, I'll see you at the house later."

When she's finally gone, I turn to him and wince. "I'm

sorry. She totally blindsided me with that, but that's pretty much Mom's MO."

He takes my hands and squeezes my fingers. "It's okay. Maybe we'll talk about it later."

I nod. "I never really think about my trust fund. That's money from Daddy's insurance. If he hadn't died so young, it wouldn't be nearly what it is, so it's not really something I like to think about. She's right, though. There's enough there for us to build a nice house if that's what we want to do."

"Well." He tilts his head, his eyes searching my face. "I guess it all depends on how soon you want to give her those grandbabies she's talking about."

"I—oh, um… I'm not sure I'm ready to be a mom yet. I mean, we're young still, right? And…" *And if I get pregnant, I'm going to get fat again, and what if you don't want me anymore?*

"Okay." He squeezes my hands again, but the gesture isn't reassuring when everything about his expression tells me I didn't give him the answer he was hoping for.

"So how are you feeling?" Nix asks when I'm sitting in her office on Wednesday morning.

"I've been nauseated a couple times, but I think it's just stress. You know, weddings," I say lamely.

"How are the headaches?"

"I haven't had a headache in probably a week."

"That's great news." She looks in my eyes and ears. "And you said you're getting some of your memories back?"

"Some," I say, "not all. It's frustrating, but I'm trying to be patient."

"What about the other thing we talked about in the hospital?"

I raise a brow.

"Do you feel safe?" She pauses a beat. "Is Max good to you?"

"Oh! Of course." I wave my hand. "Seriously, I'm sure I just fell down the stairs. Max is a prince."

She frowns. "Your sister says you've been spending time with her and Maggie again, not isolating yourself like you had been. That's a good sign."

"Of course. Other than Cally, my sisters are my best friends."

"Keep that up. It's important that you have a support system, not just Max."

"I will. I promise."

She nods, looking satisfied. "Did you fast this morning?"

I wince. "Crap. I totally forgot you wanted to do blood work."

"That's okay." She smiles and lowers herself into her chair. "You can swing by the lab any morning to get that done, but I can guess already that it's going to look better."

"Why do you say that?"

"Well, in the two and a half weeks since you've been out of the hospital, you've gained about six pounds. I know without seeing your lab work that you're eating again. That's good news."

"You're the first doctor who's ever called my weight gain good news." I can't handle the sympathy in her sad smile, so I study the blue specks on the industrial-grade flooring tiles. "Did you know? About the anorexia?"

Nix takes a breath, surprised at my confession, I guess. "I suspected, but you weren't very receptive when I tried to talk to you about it over the summer."

"Do you think I can start working out again? Running?"

"Let's start with a week of light, low-impact workouts. If that goes okay, you can try a short run. Just ease back in and listen to your body. But I don't want you working out more than once a day, got it?"

"I'm scared I'm going to gain it all back." I hate admitting this. I hate letting someone see how much my stupid body affects how I feel about myself. "But I think I'm just as scared of letting food control my life, letting my desire to be thin ruin everything else." When I lift my head to meet her gaze, there's more understanding in her eyes than I expected.

"You're probably going to put on some more weight, at least some of it. When you lose weight in such an unhealthy way, your body can't maintain it when you go back to eating and exercising normally. There will be an adjustment period where you figure out what weight you can maintain while eating regularly and having a healthy relationship with exercise."

I nod, but my eyes fill and I have to look away. I only have a few recovered memories of Nix, and I don't know how close we are. But if I voice my fears to Liz, she'll just be mad at me.

"What is it, Hanna?"

The floor's blue specks swim before my eyes. A tear plops onto the tile next to my sandaled foot. "What if the weight comes back and Max isn't attracted to me anymore?"

"Oh, sweetie." Then she surprises me by hugging me, wrapping me up against her.

"Are doctors supposed to hug their patients?" I ask, hugging her back awkwardly.

"I'm not hugging you as your doctor. I'm hugging you as your friend." She squeezes one more time before releasing me. "You need to talk to Max. You can't live the rest of your life fearing that he might not want you."

May—Three Months Before Accident

"I'm so pleased to meet you, Miss Thompson," the lawyer says. She gestures to the chair and takes her seat on the other side of her desk. "I'm sure you're wondering why I summoned you."

"I am." I lower myself into the wingback chair. Her office is slick and modern with just enough homey touches—throw pillows, framed snapshots—to make it comfortable. Well, to make most people comfortable. There's nothing comfortable about how I feel being called to Indianapolis to meet with a lawyer I've never heard of before. "I can only assume I have a distant rich relative who passed away and left me his fortune."

She laughs good-naturedly. "I keep waiting for that call myself, but unfortunately, that's not why you're here today."

"Bummer." I force a smile and shift in my chair. Waiting.

"I understand you just graduated from Sinclair and have a successful side business decorating cakes for friends."

"I did just graduate, though I'm not sure how successful I'd call my business. I do it more for fun than anything."

"You enjoy it, then?"

"Of course!" My cheeks warm. "It's fun to make something out of raw ingredients. And cakes just make people happy."

"And you have a dream of opening up your own bakery in New Hope. Is that correct?"

This will definitely be filed under Strangest Experiences Ever. "Yes, but it's really more of a pipe dream. Nothing serious."

"What if it didn't have to be a pipe dream?" She pushes a thin stack of papers across the desk. "My client who, let's be clear from the start, wishes to remain anonymous, thinks your 'pipe dream' bakery plans, as you call them, could really turn into a profitable venture."

I pick up the stack of papers and leaf through them, but I'm not really sure what I'm looking at.

"The one on the top is the New Hope revitalization project, explaining tax breaks and grant funds the town of New Hope will give to young entrepreneurs who want to help revitalize the historic square."

I scan the page, my eyes landing on the maximum dollar amounts the city will contribute. "I know about these grants," I say, nodding. "William Bailey got some grant money to open his art gallery. I'm familiar with the opportunities, but they aren't anything near what someone like me would need to open my own business." I'd be able to do it with the money in my trust fund, but I don't get that until I'm thirty or married.

Max's proposal flashes through my mind—the look on his face when I stared at the ring and didn't speak, the moment he rose off his knee and placed the ring in my hand, closing my fingers around it. *"Keep it. That's how much I want this, Hanna. Keep it. I'll wait."*

What was the "this" that he wanted? Me or my trust fund? I squeeze my eyes shut.

"That's why I'm here. My client would like to go into business with you, Hanna. He would provide the rest of the funds you need to open the bakery in the old Woolworth's building on Main. We've had a team of contractors give us estimates on turning around the space, and he'd even put an apartment for you upstairs to compensate for the minimal income you'd expect your first months in business."

"How can I go into business with someone who wants to remain anonymous?"

"He'd be a silent partner. He'd get a portion of your profits until you choose to buy him out or sell the business."

"But what if I don't make a profit? What's in it for him then?"

She shrugs. "Investments always come with risk, but my client believes you'll be successful."

"So if I want to make a decision, how am I supposed to talk to him?"

"Most things you'd be free to decide on your own, but there are major decisions he'd want to be consulted on, and those would go through me."

Who would want to go into business with me? Who do I know with the money to take on something like this? "Is Nate Crane behind this?"

Her face remains impassive. "Anonymous means anonymous."

It has to be Nate. And I should say no. I shouldn't accept his money. Only he's offering me something I want so badly. I can already picture my bakery on Main, Sinclair students hopping in between classes for a gourmet coffee, a glass case with freshly baked cookies and scones.

"Do you think you'd like to talk more, or is an anonymous partnership out of the question for you?"

"Tell me more."

Chapter
FIFTEEN

A<small>T FIRST</small>, I'm not sure if what I'm hearing is someone knocking on my door because the booming thunder of the storm masks it. Then it comes again. *Boom, boom, boom.*

I slide my laptop onto the couch beside me and rush to the door.

"Hanna?" Liz calls.

"What are you doing out in this storm?" I hurry to the door and yank it open.

Liz steps in, soaking wet but grinning. Maggie, Cally, and Nix pile in right behind her. "Impromptu girls' night!" Liz announces.

"Sorry, I couldn't hear the knocking over the thunder."

The girls shed their shoes and jackets by the door, and I grab towels for them.

"It's a mess out there," my sister says. She wipes the rain from her face and shakes her curls, not unlike a dog coming in from the rain.

Cally goes into the kitchen and plugs her iPod into the radio, and Maggie hoists a couple of canvas shopping bags on the counter and starts pulling out cream, Godiva liqueur, and vodka—ingredients for chocolate martinis, if I'm not mistaken. Nix removes a box of truffles, cheese, and crackers from another bag.

"You guys," I say. "I have a wedding dress to fit into in three and a half weeks."

Liz opens cabinet doors until she finds my martini glasses and sets them on the island. "You've never had us over here."

"We had to remedy that," Cally says, grinning.

"And Asher and Nate are working like fiends, so I was bored," Maggie explains.

"Where's Will?" I ask Cally.

"He's hanging with Max and Sam at Brady's."

I head to the island and pop a truffle in my mouth. "That is amazing!" I close my eyes and chew slowly.

"God, it's good to see you eat!" Cally says as she chooses a chocolate. "You were losing weight so fast. I was worried about you."

"She's doing really well," Nix says. She winks at me as she grabs a truffle for herself. "Oh, wow!"

"They're orgasmic, aren't they?" Maggie says. "Asher got them for me when he was in New York last month. There's this shop in the city that I swear does voodoo to make their chocolate."

"Let me try." Lizzy abandons her half-made chocolate martinis to try the orgasmic treat for herself. "Holy shit! I didn't know chocolate could be *better*."

The speakers click as Cally's iPod shuffles to a new song, and Nate Crane's "Lost In Me" begins.

I gasp.

Lizzy reaches over and squeezes my hand, and I close my eyes.

"That's it." Maggie slaps her palm on the counter. "What is going on with Nate Crane?"

Lizzy puts on her innocent face. "What do you mean?"

"Something's up with you two. You get all weird any time I mention Nate, and he gets all weird every time I say anything about my sisters."

"Weird?" Lizzy says. "We're just fans. That's all."

Maggie raises a disbelieving brow. "You are a shitty liar."

My twin sighs dramatically. "Fine. You know how I feel about his hotness. You caught me. I'm sleeping with Nate Crane."

"You wish," Maggie mutters before she zeroes in on me. "Hanna, spill."

"She doesn't—"

I hold up a hand. It was only a matter of time, right? "It's okay. I made this mess and now I have to live with the consequences. Maggie should know."

"It started in St. Louis, didn't it?" She looks heartbroken.

"She doesn't have her memory, remember?" Lizzy defends.

"I don't know much. But the night I got home from the hospital, I woke up with Nate in my bed, and he was really angry when he saw my ring."

"Jesus." Cally drags her hand over her face.

"You can't say anything to Will," I plead with her. "Not until I tell Max the truth."

"You haven't told Max?" Nix says.

"Amnesia, remember?" Liz says. "She can't even remember being with him."

"But he climbed into your bed," Maggie points out. "Did you ask him what's been going on between you?"

"He's not real keen on talking to her," Liz says. "You know, given that she chose the other guy."

"But you know for sure there was something going on between the two of you?" Maggie asks. "You and *Nate Crane*?"

"You're one to talk," Liz retorts. "You're fucking Asher Logan. Seriously, what's happened to this town? And when do I get a sultry affair with a sexy rocker?"

Nix shakes her head as if to clear it and grabs the martini shaker from Lizzy's hand. She pulls off the top and takes a drink straight from the shaker. "No wonder you're so anxious for those memories to come back," she mutters. "*I'm* anxious for you to get those memories back."

"I know, right?" Liz says. "I want details, and whether she remembers or not, I'm pretty sure I'm never going to get them."

"What about Max?" Worry is written all over Cally's face. "You *are* going to tell him, right?"

"I have to," I whisper.

"Hanna!" Lizzy says.

"I've made up my mind, Liz. I'm giving my brain one more week to share any details it has hidden in there and then I'm telling Max what I know. For better or worse."

Liz exhales heavily. "You're stressing me out. Thank God we have chocolate." She pops another truffle into her mouth and moans again as she chews. "Oh, hell, that's better than sex."

"No, it's not," Cally and Maggie say in unison. Then they giggle, and Maggie nudges me. "Come on. Don't make me feel like the dirty ho here. I know you guys agree with me. That chocolate is good, but it's *not* better than sex."

"I wouldn't remember," Lizzy says. She takes the martini shaker back from Nix and takes a gulp.

"Sisters in unwanted abstinence," Nix says.

Lizzy gives her a high five. "An exclusive club that no one wants to join."

"Tell me about it," I mutter.

The girls stare at me, and Liz bites back a laugh. "Hanna just found out she and Max don't have sex. She's not taking it very well."

Maggie's eyes go wide. "But you're, like, twenty-three. And you and Max have been together for *months*. How does that even happen?"

"She's saving herself for marriage," Lizzy says. "Who knew any of the Thompson girls would make it to marriage with her virginity? Mom would be so proud."

"So you weren't having sex with Nate Crane?" Cally asks.

"Apparently not," I say.

"How do you know?" Nix asks quietly.

"I saw him over the weekend and asked. He said we didn't." I frown. "You're my doctor. What do you know about this that I'm not remembering?"

Nix breaks a cracker in half and avoids my eyes. "We can have this conversation in private later."

"I want to have it now. These ladies already know my worst secret. Tell me what you know."

She holds up her hands in defense. "Nothing, really. I was not privy to the details of your sex life. And you certainly never told me you were involved with Nate Crane, sexually or otherwise."

"But..." I prod.

"But you came in at the beginning of August and talked to me about birth-control options. You'd had some problems with headaches when you were on hormonal contraceptives in high school, so you wanted to know about some other options and decided that condoms and a diaphragm was the right combination for you."

"So I got a diaphragm?"

"We fitted you for one."

"Did I tell you anything else?"

She breaks another cracker and sweeps a small pile of crumbs in front of her. "You were still a virgin when we talked, according to you. But you didn't think..."

"You're killing me with the suspense," Liz says. "She didn't think what?"

Nix shrugs. "She didn't think she'd make it more than a couple more weeks."

"That doesn't mean anything," Cally says. "She could have been planning to sleep with Max."

Thunder claps, and half a second later, the apartment goes black, blessedly ending the awkward conversation.

"Candles," I announce. "I'll find candles. And...matches or something."

I hear a click, and the next thing I know, a single flame is illuminating my friends' faces from the lighter in Nix's hand. "I've got us halfway there."

"You carry a lighter?"

"And a pocketknife," she says proudly. "I had four Eagle Scouts for big brothers. Always be prepared and all that jazz."

"Do you need help looking for the candles?" Liz asks.

"No. I know where to look."

I head toward the bedroom, my mind still churning on the implications of what Nix just told me. If I was getting birth control only a couple of weeks before the accident, that could mean I'd decided to accept Max's proposal. Or it could mean I'd decided to earn my scarlet letter after all.

"They're not in the kitchen?" Maggie calls, and I can already hear her opening drawers and rummaging through them.

"Maybe, but I know I store scented candles in my drawers. They work better than sachets for keeping clothes smelling fresh."

"She's so girly," Nix says. "I need you guys to teach me how to be girly. Could you? For my birthday?"

I feel my way to my dresser and pull open the top drawer. Fumbling through piles of cotton and satin and lace, I finally find what I'm looking for. "Found one! It's a taper candle, so we'll have to hold it until we can find a candleholder, but this should get us started."

As I leave the bedroom, lightning flashes and floods the apartment for two beats. Then we're left in darkness again.

I fumble with the candle as I scoot my way back toward the kitchen. It's kind of an odd shape. I wonder if it melted in the heat and re-formed or something. I hope no wax melted on my undies. "Nix, can you light your lighter again? I can't find the wick."

With a metallic click, the lighter blazes, and I lift the candle. "Do you see the wick anywhere?"

The room fills with Lizzy's peals of laughter. "What drawer was that in?"

My cheeks heat. "My underwear drawer."

"Lemme guess. It was tucked under your lingerie, maybe some sexy undies?" Even in the faint flickering of Nix's lighter, I can see glee written all over Liz's face.

"Oh. My. God." As the realization hits me, my hand opens and I release the *oh-my-God-that's-no-candle*. It falls to the floor with a thump.

Liz sinks to her haunches and picks it up off the floor with two fingers, the way one might hold a pair of someone else's dirty underwear.

"It looks like a taper candle in the dark," I say. "I don't even know where that came from."

Maggie snorts. "Amnesia is *such* a handy excuse now, isn't it?"

Kill me now.

"Is it…is it what I think it is?" Nix asks.

"I guess that depends what you think it is," Liz says. Twisting it at its center, she confirms my worst suspicions and sends it into a vibrating tizzy.

I back away. Horrified.

Lizzy giggles harder. "It doesn't bite."

"I didn't even know I had a… Why do I have that?"

My mind wraps around the words from the texts on Nate's phone. Nate asking if I'd taken my gift home. What had I replied? *"It's a sorry substitute for you"?*

Not just a vibrator. Worse. A vibrator that was a gift from Nate.

The girls are all giggling now.

"I know you two are close," Cally says, "but I absolutely cannot believe you're touching that."

"I don't get it," Nix says. "She gets buff, sexy-ass Max Hallowell and an affair with the sexy rocker. What's the need for the vibrating friend, Hanna?"

If the floor wanted to open up and swallow me right now, I'd be okay with that.

Another flash lights the room. I must look as horrified as I feel, because Lizzy's giggles go quiet. "Hanna, we're just giving you a hard time. Are you okay?"

"I'll go find your candles," Maggie says, taking the lighter from Nix.

I watch her silhouette move through the darkness and into my bedroom. I shouldn't let her rifle through my clothes— God knows what else she might find that I don't know about— but another flash of lightning fills the space and a memory comes with it. Not the memory of sending those texts to Nate.

A different memory. Clear and vivid and visceral.

Maggie is carrying a lit candle in each hand when she returns.

"We'll stop teasing you about the vibrator," Nix promises me. "We all have one."

"Those bitches probably don't," Liz says, pointing to Cally and Maggie. She tosses the vibrator onto the island. Right there between the truffles and cheese. "They have men to do that work for them."

Maggie snorts. "Where have you been, Liz? Men and vibrators go very well together."

"She's not lying," Cally says.

"I hate you all," Liz growls.

"Can we change the subject?" The question comes out of me with an awkward squeak.

"Sure," Nix says. "Let's talk about what we're going to do for Cally's bachelorette party."

The girls start chattering about their plans and ideas, but I can't seem to focus on the conversation. My mind is playing and replaying the memory of Nate Crane's wicked eyes watching me as he rubs the vibrator over my inner thighs.

"What do you think, Hanna?" Lizzy asks.

"Um, what?" *Stop thinking about the vibrator. Stop thinking about Nate holding the vibrator.*

Maggie laughs. "We're trying to decide whether or not we should crash Will's bachelor party. He's not going to be able to talk Sam out of the strip club, so we're thinking we should show up."

"Oh, that could be fun." *Stop thinking about Nate Crane.*

But it's useless. I finally have a memory of Nate Crane, and instead of helping me let him go, I'm so wrapped up in it I feel lost and confused all over again.

June—Two Months Before Accident

The ribbon-wrapped box sits on the crisp white linens of the hotel bed, and I creep toward it, unable to resist the lure of an unexpected gift.

Strong arms encase me from behind, and I feel Nate's breath hot in my ear. "I got you something." His mouth drops to my neck, where he nibbles his way down to my shoulder and sends little shivers whipping through me.

I close my eyes against the pleasure and moan. "I saw that. You shouldn't have."

"Hmm," he groans, his hands already sliding inside my shirt. "You shouldn't say that until you know what it is. It might be more for me than it is for you." His fingers skim over my belly then slide into the band of my jeans and sweep lower, sending my knees weak. "You want to open it?"

"You're kind of making me want something else right now."

He chuckles and nips my neck one last time before pulling away and grabbing the box off the bed.

"You should stop buying me things," I protest lamely.

"Don't steal my joy, woman." He nudges the gift toward me, and I take it in my hands and pull off the lid.

I'd like to pretend I'm one of those worldly girls who doesn't shock or embarrass easily, but I'm not. The gift inside this box both shocks and embarrasses me, but I make myself pick it up and hold it in my hand as I say, "Thank you?" Unfortunately, any attempt at sincerity is lost when the words come out like a question.

He chuckles. "You don't sound like you mean it."

"Um, no, I do mean it. Thanks." I put the box down on the bed and study the object. "I just... I'm not sure why..."

"It's a vibrator, Hanna. Not a medieval torture device." He steps closer and closes my hand over the toy, twisting its shaft under my fingers.

"Oh!" I squeak when it starts buzzing in my hands, but he holds tight, keeping my fingers wrapped around it. A giggle slips from my lips. "Um…should I be worried that you said this is more for you than me? I mean, I'm game to try new things, but I've never been with a guy who wanted—"

He grunts. "Not like that."

"No. I want to give you what you want. Um…" I motion toward the bed and bite my lip as laughter bubbles up in my chest. "Bend over?"

He grins and steps closer. "I have other plans, but thanks for the offer. Means a lot."

"I'm very open-minded," I say sagely.

"Your face when you opened it doesn't support that claim. Have you ever used one of these before?"

My lips part as his hands lead mine over the vibrating shaft in long, lewd movements that kind of turn me on. "I guess I would just prefer the real thing. You know. If someone would give it to me." I pout. "It's the least you could do when you're going to be leaving me for the Middle East in September."

"I promise, having sex now wouldn't make a month apart any easier."

My shoulders sag. "I hate that you're going. I'm going to be worried sick until you're home safe."

He groans and nips at my ear. His hot lips sweep over my neck and then his hands slip under my shirt, making circles around my navel. "You're cute when you're worried about me. Now get naked and lay your sweet ass on that bed so I can show you just what I want you to do with this."

"Oh." I grin and unbutton my jeans, watching him as I push them off my hips. I leave my panties and T-shirt on and climb onto the bed. "In that case…"

"You're not naked."

I lift a brow. "Neither are you." I love his hot eyes on me.

"Lie down."

I obey, and he runs his eyes over me again and again. Nate looking at me is as good as any foreplay I've ever known.

He hands me the vibrator then moves to the end of the

bed. "Put it between your legs."

"I'd rather you do it for me," I protest. Turning the device in my hands, I look up at him through my lashes. I know how badly he wants to touch me, how much self-restraint he's using to stay at the foot of the bed when he could be on the bed with me. Touching me.

"You're going to have to figure out how to use it yourself." He folds his arms and stares down at me like a warden supervising his charge.

I grin. "You think I don't know how to get myself off? Aren't you cute?"

A muscle in his jaw jumps, but he raises a brow and holds my gaze. "Prove it."

My heart leaps into my throat at the challenge, and I lick my lips. When I part my legs, his nostrils flare and his eyes go darker. "With this?" I ask, holding up the vibrator.

"Show me how you do it." He drops his arms and his fists clench at his sides.

I release the vibrator on the bed next to me. Keeping my eyes on him, I cup myself between my legs. I'm so turned on from all this talk of masturbation and the look in his eyes. I'm already slick and swollen, and if he joined me on the bed and put his hand between my legs, he could get me off in seconds flat.

But he isn't on the bed with me, and I'm not going to rush this. I rock my hand against myself, applying just enough pressure to my clit to make my eyes float closed.

"Here." His hard voice has my eyes flying open. He's leaning over the bed and tugging my panties from my hips in one smooth motion.

I squeak as my ass falls back to the bed, and he gives me that shit-eating grin.

"You have touched yourself without the panties before, haven't you?"

I take a breath and part my legs farther. He watches, and that's what does it for me—his gaze between my legs, like that private bit of me is the most beautiful thing he's ever seen, the rising and falling of his chest as I slide my hands up my inner thighs.

I've never done this before—never let a man watch me touch myself. I would have thought it would be awkward or that I'd worry I might look like I was enjoying my own touch more that I enjoyed his, but there's nothing awkward here, and we both know it's Nate's touch I want. All I feel is heat and lust and this need to give him anything he wants.

As I settle on hand over myself, taking my clit between two fingers, I bring my other hand up to my chest and squeeze my breast through my shirt. I'm not wearing a bra, and the sensation of my sensitive nipples scraping across the cotton makes my hips buck and my body ache for more. For his mouth on my breasts, his tongue toying with my nipples until he draws them into his mouth—hard and tight and merciless.

I enter myself with one finger as I imagine it, and he steps closer. I love that I can make him damn near lose his self-control. I imagine his mouth against the flat of my belly before dipping lower.

I squeeze my clit gently. Right where I want his lips. My hips rock faster and his eyes grow hotter.

I'm close. So damn close. But my own hand isn't enough when he's right there, when I can reach out and touch what I really want. "Nate," I whimper.

"Do it, angel." His nostrils flare as I pinch my nipple through my shirt again. "I want to hear you come. I want to watch."

"I want you to do it."

"Do this for me." His breathing is ragged. As if he's been holding me up and fucking me hard rather than standing here watching.

I can see what I'm doing to him. I can see it in his eyes, hear it in his voice.

"Fuck your hand for me, baby. Just like that." His words make me wild and my hips move faster, my hand at my breast pinches tighter, and then I'm gone—tightening, squeezing, and exploding into a hard and fast release that's better than any orgasm I've ever been able to give myself.

As I lie limp in bed after, he climbs in beside me and brushes my hair from my face. "I swear to Christ, you are a living fantasy."

I force my heavy eyes open. "That was amazing. I wouldn't have believed I could make myself..."

"Get off?"

I shake my head. "I knew I could do that, but it's never that good. But with you standing there..."

He presses a kiss to the side of my neck. "That's what I want you to think about when I'm gone. When you touch yourself, imagine me at the end of the bed watching you."

I hear the hum of the vibrator clicking on, and then he's pressing it against the inside of my thighs and sucking at my neck as he inches the vibrating wand closer to the apex of my thighs.

"What are you doing?" I whisper, reaching for the button on his jeans. "I think it's your turn."

"I might have had an ulterior motive for buying this for you."

"What's that?" My breath catches as he brushes it lightly over my clit before returning it to my thighs. I part my legs instinctively.

"I want to fuck you with this, Hanna. If I can't have my cock inside you, I still want to fuck you."

I slide my hands into his hair and lock my eyes on his. "If you want me, I'm yours. I've told you that."

His kiss is hard and sweet at the same time. I know he's trying to be noble, and I don't want him to be. I release him from his jeans, and he groans as I take his hard length into my hands.

"I'm ready," I promise.

He buries his face in my neck and presses the vibrator lightly against my entrance. The sensation is new and intense, and I cry out even as I rock my hips toward the intrusion.

"Just imagine it's my cock sliding into you."

I want to make a joke about his magically vibrating

appendage, but the words die on my lips. I'm too distracted by the round tip of the vibrator poised at my entrance. He slides it in, inch by inch, while kissing my neck. Slowly in. Slowly out. Long, languid movements that already have my body pulsing in response.

"Nate." I try to draw back, to escape the sensation before I'm lost in it. He lowers his mouth to my breast and sucks hard. Then instead of pulling away, I'm rocking forward. Instead of withdrawing from the pleasure, I'm running toward it.

"I can't stop thinking about how it would feel to be inside you," he whispers. "You are so fucking responsive, and I could get off right here just imagining that pussy squeezing around my cock."

I cry out, my hips rising off the bed. "Please."

He groans in my ear and rocks the toy inside me, moving it deeper this time. "I know, baby. I want it as much as you do. But you've done something to me." He removes the vibrator, and I cry out, hungry, empty, desperate.

"Fuck me, Nate." I wouldn't have had the courage to say those words to anyone before meeting him, but he brings out this bold side of me. This wicked side. "Don't make me wait anymore."

"It would be so damn good." He touches the vibrator to my clit and my body squeezes tight, climbing higher. "I'd never get enough of you. I'd fuck you from behind. I'd fuck you with your legs wrapped around my waist. I'd fuck you in the shower and until you thought you couldn't come again."

"Now. Please."

He slides two fingers inside me and holds the vibrator snug against my clit. "Not until you've made a decision. Not while his ring is waiting in your jewelry box." With those words, he rocks against my clit and curls his fingers, and I'm gone. Flying. Falling. Releasing.

Chapter
SIXTEEN

WHEN MY alarm beeps at four thirty on Friday morning, I roll over in bed and bury my face in the pillow, howling in frustration. I thought about Nate Crane all night—his eyes on me, his dirty words, his wicked touch. And when I managed to fall asleep, I dreamed about him.

My body is a live wire of hot need at the memory, an ache pulsing between my legs that I don't want to ignore. For thirty seconds, I lie there with my eyes closed and contemplate sliding my hand beneath the sheets to banish the ache, but guilt has me climbing out of bed.

I take a cool shower before dressing and heading for the bakery, where I lose myself in the comforting motions of baking.

Liz comes in at six and works the front while I experiment with a new cupcake recipe—stress management for bakers.

When Drew comes in after school, Liz hands over front-counter duties and drags me away from my flour and sugar. "Time to stop stewing and get cleaned up."

"What? Who said I'm stewing?" I let her lead me up to my apartment, and I unlock the door for us and push inside.

"You are, aren't you?"

My shoulders sag. "Totally."

"Want to share?"

"I had a Nate Crane memory."

She frowns. "Was it bad?"

I chew on my lower lip and shake my head. "No. It was good. Really good. And now I'm having memory guilt."

We sit in silence for a minute before Liz asks, "Does it bother you not knowing what made you choose Max?"

The question makes me uncomfortable in my own skin. I want to say no. To swear that I don't *need* to know. To say that every morning when I wake up, my heart chooses Max.

But that's not true. My heart? It doesn't know what it wants.

"You don't have to answer that," she whispers.

I sigh. "Bridesmaid dress fitting this afternoon?"

"Yeah. Yours is going to need to be taken in. We ordered them a couple months ago. I think we're going to choose bridesmaid dresses for your wedding while we're there."

"Oh. Yeah, I guess we need to do that."

She frowns. "Don't get too excited."

"What do you mean it doesn't fit?" my mom screeches from the other side of the dressing room door. "That dress fit you perfectly the day we bought it!"

The seamstress studies her shoes and shifts uncomfortably. "I could try the zipper again," she whispers.

I shake my head. "It's no use."

We met Cally, Maggie, and Nix at Cleanstein's to try on our bridesmaid dresses and see if they needed alterations. They pinned mine to be taken in. Then Mom showed up and decided that I should try on my wedding gown for the girls.

"Okay," Mom says, pushing into the dressing room. "We can put off final alterations for, what, another couple of weeks if we need to. You can get the weight back off, can't you, sweetie?"

I look to the seamstress. "Is it possible to take it out?"

"We have maybe half an inch to work with," the seamstress says. "It might just be enough, but in a dress this style, there's not much wiggle room."

"Let's wait," Mom says. "Hanna's going to fit into it, and if not, we'll take it out." She forces a smile and pats me on the shoulder awkwardly before leaving the dressing room.

The seamstress helps me out of the dress and leaves me alone to study myself in the mirror. Somehow it looks different to me now. The curve of my hips and my breasts. The returning softness of my belly. This is a body two amazing men lose their minds over. It's something beautiful. Something worth caring for.

"Are you okay?" Maggie calls on the other side of the door.

I shake my head to clear it and dress. "I'm fine."

She's waiting outside the door when I exit the dressing room. "I heard it doesn't fit," she whispers.

"I've gained weight." I lower my voice to make sure Mom can't hear. "There are probably only five pounds between me now and me getting that dress zipped, but just staying the size I am now until the wedding is going to be hard enough."

"Would you be offended if I offered my old dress from my canceled wedding?"

I draw in a breath, remembering how much I loved Maggie's dress. She ended up calling off the wedding, and I never thought about what happened to it. "Would it fit me?"

She nods. "It's a ten and it's an A-line, so it's only fitted right above your waist and at your chest. It's in the closet in the guestroom at Asher's if you want to try it on."

"You think Mom would flip out?"

She shrugs. "It's your wedding, Hanna. I think it's more important you wear what *you* want."

Maggie's wedding dress fits like it was made for me.

"Oh, Han-Han," Lizzy breathes. "It's perfect."

The A-line bodice accentuates my breasts while making my waist look small, and the basic bridal satin is covered with the most delicate organza I've ever touched. The satin bodice is heart-shaped, with only the organza continuing over my shoulders in wide, sheer straps.

"Do you want us to stay or do you want to be alone?" Maggie asks as I look at myself in the mirror. "Think about it for a little bit?"

I watch my reflection as I turn side to side. I've never felt so beautiful in my life as I do in this dress. So why does the idea of wearing it in three weeks make me want to weep?

"Can I have a few minutes?"

She nods and ushers Lizzy out of the room with her.

The bedroom has French doors that lead out onto a balcony overlooking the river. I unlock them and pull them open. Desperate for fresh air, I lift my skirt and step out onto the balcony.

I close my eyes as the breeze brushes through my hair. I concentrate on my breathing.

Everything is good. Everything is okay.

My mind scrambles through reassurances, but only one calms me—I don't have to go through with this. If, in a couple weeks, the idea of marriage still panics me, Max would understand. Wouldn't he? Or would I lose him for good? And what would my mom think? She'd be so embarrassed to have another daughter with another botched wedding. Maybe the Thompson girls are cursed.

"Hanna?"

I turn toward the voice to find myself face to face with Nate Crane.

His eyes take me in inch by inch, like he's drinking in what he sees. Me. The dress.

"What are you doing here?" After last night's memory, I'm simultaneously more drawn to him than ever and more wary of being near him. Stepping toward him is as instinctive as breathing, but I catch myself and stop. I clench my hands into fists at my sides. I want to smooth over the hurt between his eyes, to touch his cheek and feel the heat of his skin under my fingertips.

"You look..." His dark eyes scan over me again. "God, you're so beautiful it hurts."

Birds chirp happily and the sun warms my skin, and I hate myself for wishing I could be seeing him somewhere else. That I could be *someone else*.

"You probably shouldn't be saying things like that to me."

He must hear it, that brokenness in my voice, and he must care something for me, because he lets out this long, shaky breath, as if he's as fucked up over all this as I am. "You're really going to marry him." It's not a question. More like resignation.

I look down to my ring and remember Lizzy's question. *"Does it bother you not knowing what made you choose Max?"*

Nate turns to the river and squeezes the balcony rail until his knuckles go white. "When you told me you had amnesia, I wanted to believe he tricked you into taking that ring."

"Max wouldn't do that."

Nate cuts his gaze to me. There's something in his eyes—a secret locked away—but he doesn't disagree. "For the record, I knew this was how it would end. We both did. It's the amnesia that fucks it all up. Makes this harder than it needs to be."

"Max is perfect for me." I say the words because I don't know what else to say. I need to remind myself that I can't have this man take me into his arms, no matter how desperately I want him to. Not when I chose Max. "And I'm going to tell him the truth. I'm going to tell him that I cheated on him."

His face shifts, that sadness and resignation tightening, hardening into anger. "You didn't *cheat* on Max." He drags a hand through his hair, looking like he wants to throw something. "Jesus. Is that what he made you think?"

"He didn't have to. I remember."

He draws in breath in a sharp hiss. "Everything?"

"Bits. Pieces. Enough to know I was unfaithful."

His jaw ticks, and I can tell he's fighting some kind of internal struggle. Then, as if he can't handle looking at me anymore, he tears his gaze away. "You weren't unfaithful. Not at all. The night you met me—"

"Three months ago. In St. Louis," I supply.

"You remember?" The question is cautiously whispered, but I can't tell if he hopes I do or don't.

I shake my head. "Maggie told me."

"You'd just broken up with Max that night. Come on, Hanna. Use that amazing brain of yours. You aren't the kind of girl who would date one guy and mess around with another. You wouldn't have ever gone out with me that night if you and Max hadn't broken up."

"A breakup?" I almost laugh. "You don't understand small towns. If that were true, everyone would have known."

"But you two didn't want anyone to know. Your mom was helping him get that grant so his business could stay afloat, and you knew she'd stop if you two weren't dating anymore. Things had gotten bad for him—he sold his fucking house, for Christ's sake."

I don't like the logic of those words—the way they dig into my skin and crawl like a hundred parasites.

"You didn't cheat," Nate repeats. "Tell him whatever you want about us, but you weren't unfaithful."

"If we broke up, why wouldn't he have told me?"

"Maybe because he doesn't want you to remember that he broke your heart."

No. "He didn't break anything. He *loves* me. He's good to me. Better than I deserve."

He backs away. One step. Two. The invisible cords connecting us stretch and groan with every inch.

The feeling scares me so much, I lash out. "If you really love me, you'll do something for me."

He laughs, an empty, hollow sound. "You want a favor now?"

"I want you to leave town." It's not a fair request. He hasn't done anything to make me think he's going to disrupt my picture-perfect life. But I fear I'll do something disastrous if I keep running into him. "I want you out of my life." I pray that saying the words might make them true. They're the right words to say—I know that—but they hurt, like someone taking a dull blade to an exposed wound.

"As you wish, angel."

Angel. "Why do you keep calling me that?"

Silence pulses between us for a beat. A living thing. "Because you saved me."

Then I don't have to walk away. He leaves before I can process his words. And I'm grateful. I'm not sure I'm strong enough to walk away from Nate Crane while knowing I'll never see him again.

"Where are you tonight?" Liz asks, waving a hand in front of my face.

I take a deep breath and shake my head. "Sorry. I'm distracted."

We're at a club in Indianapolis—one of those honky-tonk places where they get female customers to dance on the bar. Maggie, Nix, and Cally are on the dance floor while Liz and I watch our drinks at the table.

Liz frowns at me. "Don't pull away from me again, okay? You can talk to me."

"Did Max and I break up before my accident?" I blurt.

She scoots closer. "I'm sorry," she calls over the music. "I thought you asked if you and Max broke up."

I nod. "Did we?"

She frowns. "Not that I know of. Why would you think that?"

"I've been feeling so guilty about Nate, but what if I don't need to feel guilty? What if I was only with Nate after Max and I broke up?"

She shakes her head. "Wouldn't people have known? And then there's the ring. Didn't Max say he proposed *months* ago?"

It's crazy to have this conversation here, in this bar that is so loud I practically have to scream my secrets to the world. But I've held on to Nate's words for over twenty-four hours now and suddenly I can't handle it anymore. I need answers.

"I saw Nate at Maggie's last night, and he said I never cheated on Max. He said Max and I were secretly broken up, and I didn't tell anyone because I didn't want Mom to find out. She was helping him get a grant—a grant that was going to keep his club open."

"The Healthy Tomorrow Grant," Liz says. She swallows hard. "They'll announce the recipient next week, but I'm pretty sure Max is going to get it."

I know this already, yet hearing Liz say it makes my stomach churn.

"Why did you break up?" Liz asks. "And why didn't Max tell you?"

I stare at my drink, Nate's words echoing in my ears. *"Maybe because he doesn't want you to remember that he broke your heart."*

Liz narrows her eyes. "What are you not telling me?"

I exhale a long breath full of worry and second guesses. "What if I'm not the only one in this relationship who hasn't been completely honest?"

"What did he do?"

I tell her about the random text message Max received the night of the engagement party and Max leaving because Meredith needed him. "It's not that I don't believe that's possible. We all know she thinks the world is her freaking oyster, but why is anything she needs more important than being with me? There was something about it that made me feel…"

"Like he was lying," Liz supplies.

Tears fill my eyes as I nod. "I know it's not fair. He's a good guy, and I'm sure I'm just projecting my own guilt onto him or whatever."

She opens her mouth then closes it again before reaching over and taking my hand. "We'll figure this out," she whispers.

"It might not matter anyway. Tomorrow I'm telling him

the truth about Nate. If Nate's wrong and Max and I weren't broken up, that might be the end of us anyway."

"He loves you," she assures me.

"Would you want me to marry him if things were the other way around?"

She doesn't answer. She doesn't have to.

I look down at my phone and see the notification light blinking at me. I have a voicemail. "I missed a call. I'm going to go outside and listen to this message."

I wedge my way through the crowd to make it out the front door of the club. My ears breathe a sigh of relief when the door floats closed behind me and takes the noise with it.

"Hanna Cakes!" the woman on my voicemail chirps. "It's Elle! I was hoping I'd catch you in person, but apparently I didn't. Tonight is Cally's bachelorette party, isn't it?"

I frown at the phone because I have no idea who Elle is or why she'd know about the bachelorette party.

She sighs heavily. "Well, I hope you're having a freaking fabulous time because you deserve it. Listen, I'm sorry to throw this at you tonight of all nights. I know you have your own shit you're dealing with right now, but Nate's a freaking mess since he got home last night. He's spiraling out bad. I tried to get him to snap out of it before I left, but he doesn't listen to me. You're the only person who can get through to him. Please go to the house and see what you can do. I don't like to imagine him leaving for his trip in this condition. I'm about to board my plane and then I'm en route to India, and I'll check in when I get there, but then I'll be MIA for a few weeks. Remember that spiritual cleansing I told you about? The one Madonna raves about? Well, they gave me a spot, though the timing is shitty because electronics are a total no-no through the program. Go take care of him, okay?"

I'm still frowning at my phone when Lizzy, Cally, Maggie, and Nix push out of the club, all smiles and excitement.

"Who was it?" Liz asks.

I shake my head. "Nothing important. What's up next?"

"We're going to crash the boys' party at the strip club,"

Maggie says with a grin.

Nix sidles up beside me. Her request for tonight was that we make her "look like a girl," and when we put her in fitted jeans and a fitted shirt, she said, "No, a slutty girl." So she's wearing a tight black skirt that shows her long, toned legs—apparently I'm not the only runner in this group—and a strapless pink top that shows off her shoulders. She wanted to wear sky-high heels, but we nixed that plan when we saw she wasn't able to walk in them without falling over.

"My nurse called me yesterday afternoon," she says as we move down the sidewalk toward the strip club where the guys are supposed to be. "Your blood work results are back. I'm sorry I haven't been in the office to look at them yet, but I'll be there tomorrow. I'll give you a call."

"I think they took enough blood to give someone a life-saving infusion," I inform her.

"Sorry about that. I wanted to do the whole workup again."

"Don't go into the office just for that. It's fine. I'm eating."

I take a deep breath of the cool night air and think about that voicemail. I scan my memory again and again, but I can't remember an Elle. Obviously it's someone I know from Nate's life.

"Have you told Max yet?" Nix asks quietly.

"Tomorrow. That's the plan." I wanted him to be able to enjoy Will's bachelor party without my nasty secret hanging over him.

"Huh. Maybe we should work out some sort of Bat Signal so I can interrupt with the blood work call if it's not going well."

"There it is!" Liz calls, pointing to the building in front of us.

There's a long line out front, but the bouncer waves us over.

"Does he know we're coming?" I ask Liz.

She snorts. "No, but we're a group of five hot-ass girls going into a gentleman's club. We probably won't have to pay for a drink all night."

I laugh, but my moment of good humor is cut off when a

familiar voice calls, "Oh, look who's there."

When my eyes land on Meredith coming out of the club, I want to puke. She might have just had a baby a few months ago, but she's as gorgeous as ever in a tiny black dress and heels, her long, silky blond hair hanging past her bare shoulders.

"What are you doing here?" I sneer.

She leans against the building and crosses her feet at her ankles. "Oh, nothing special. Just hanging with some…friends. I hear you lost your memory."

"What's it to you?" It's not just a smartass retort. I want to know.

She shrugs. "I was out of town when it happened so I just heard. Me and baby girl got back last weekend. But I guess you know that since Max came to help me out for a while. He's such a natural with kids."

She winks at me like we share a secret, and I want to slap her.

Meredith's eyes rake over Cally in her bride-to-be shirt. "What's up, Cally? Are you here to pick up your check?"

Cally's hands clench and her jaw ticks but she doesn't respond.

Meredith's glossed lips curl into an ugly smile. "Quite a step up from your…previous employment."

Cally seethes beside me, and Liz steps forward. "Don't you have a baby you should be home caring for?"

Meredith rolls her eyes. "That's what babysitters are for."

"You ladies coming in?" the bouncer asks.

"Have fun," Meredith calls. "I know I did."

I follow the girls into the club, but the energy of our whole group has changed. None of us are in the mood to party anymore. Instead, we all want to know what Meredith was doing here and if it had anything to do with our guys.

And that's just what she intended.

"I hate her," Lizzy spits.

Cally squeezes her shoulder. "Let it go. She's petty and shallow and not worth our energy."

Maggie forces a smile. "Come on. The guys reserved the

room in the back."

We follow her through the tables and past the stage to a private party room with its own bar. Will and Max are together at the back of the room filled with a dozen or so other guys I don't know.

"Damn, looking good, Hanna," Sam says when he spots me. He's almost vertical, though remaining upright appears to be a struggle, and he smells like a bottle of scotch.

"Thank you, Sam."

He winks at Liz. "You too, I guess."

"Gee, thanks," Liz drones. "I'm just wondering what Meredith was doing here."

Sam shrugs. "She just wanted to hang for a while. But watch out, Hanna," he says, raising his drink. "She's apparently given up on Will and set her sights on your man. She could hardly keep her hands off him tonight."

"Hanna," Liz whispers, but I'm already rushing away from them, hurrying toward Max before my fear of the truth trumps my need to know.

Max does a double take when he sees me. "What are you doing here?"

I hold out my hand. "Give me your phone." I'm not sure what's shaking more, my hand or my voice.

His smile falters. "What's wrong? Did something happen to Cally?"

A wave of nausea hits me hard, and I slide my hand into his pocket and retrieve the phone myself.

"Hanna, stop." His voice is hard, but before he can take it from me, Lizzy's there, pushing him back.

"What's going on?" Will asks. Then he sees Cally and grins. "My night just got a hell of a lot better."

I swipe my finger over the screen to unlock it, and Max whispers, "Can we talk about this?"

But it's too late. I've already pulled up the texts on his phone and found the messages that came after our engagement party.

Meredith: *I need a favor. Can you be here in ten?*

Meredith: Fuck you, Max. I'm losing my mind. She's your baby too. Come over here and give me a fucking break.

I lift my head, and Max looks so damn forlorn I'd feel sorry for him if it weren't for this terrible ache in my chest. "Is this a joke?" My whole world is this elaborately woven tapestry, and he's holding the single loose strand. If he tugs, it will unravel. If he pulls just right, it will all fall apart.

Liz takes the phone from my hands and reads. "Holy baby mama drama."

"But…she bought sperm, right?" I gulp in air and remind myself to breathe. "She was artificially inseminated."

Max looks to Will, who's holding Cally in his arms. Will looks confused. He can join the fucking club.

"I'm sorry, brother," Max says. "You weren't serious about her and you know I've always been hung up on Meredith. Like an idiot. But I swear I didn't sleep with her until after Cally came back."

Will's chest rises and falls and his jaw hardens. "Man, you're apologizing to the wrong person."

Max's gaze shifts back to me and he shakes his head. "I didn't know the baby was mine. I…suspected, maybe? But she said she'd been artificially inseminated. She didn't tell me the baby was mine until weeks after she was born."

"When was that?" I whisper.

"About three months ago."

My heart hurts.

Lizzy smacks Max in the chest. "And when were you going to tell Hanna, huh?"

"She already knew." He swallows but doesn't take his eyes off me. "I just hadn't told her *again* yet." He drops his voice. "I didn't know how. Say something, Hanna."

"I'm sorry," I whisper. "But I think I need to leave."

Chapter
SEVENTEEN

" **I** NEED A flight to LA, please."

The woman behind the counter at the Southwest Airlines desk takes my ID and credit card and clicks at her keyboard.

My phone buzzes in my hand.

Liz: What do you mean you're GOING TO LA?

Some mornings, I wake up with new memories. Usually, they're nothing important.

"I can get you on a one o'clock flight out," the woman says, quoting me a dollar figure that would send my rational self running in the other direction. But I'm not feeling terribly rational today.

"Sounds perfect. Put it on the card."

I went to sleep last night knowing I could forgive Max for his omission. I understood why it would have been hard to tell me about the baby. I could see that. And it hurt. But I closed my eyes, planning to talk to him today, to forgive him for his omission and make things right by telling him what I know about my relationship with Nate.

"Any bags to check?" she asks.

"Nope."

I went to bed feeling spent and hurt but hopeful. We were going to get through this.

She returns my cards and hands me a boarding pass. "Have a nice flight."

"Thank you."

I head for security and my phone buzzes again.

Liz: *Max just called me wanting to know if I know where you are. He was really upset. What the hell is going on?*

Some mornings, I wake up with new memories. Once, I woke up with the memory of Max flirting with me at Brady's, my cheeks burning as I realized maybe he was sincere in his attraction to me.

The Indianapolis airport is quiet this morning, and the blue-shirted guy at security checks my boarding pass and ID. "Los Angeles, huh? Business or pleasure?"

"A little of both, I guess." I force a smile. Because that's what I do. I smile to make people comfortable. I smile when my heart hurts, and I act like everything's okay when I've been betrayed.

"Think you'll see any stars while you're there?" the next guy asks while I take off my shoes.

"I'm almost sure of it." I plop my carry-on, purse, and cell onto the conveyor belt next to my shoes and inch through the metal detector.

Some mornings, I wake up with new memories. A couple of days ago, I went to bed without a single memory of my opening day at the bakery, and when my alarm went off the next morning, I could recall the terror of my first day with a new business like it was yesterday.

"Thanks, ma'am," calls the lady behind the metal detector screen. "Have a nice flight."

Nodding, I grab my shoes and bag. I'm reaching for my phone when it starts to ring. Lizzy's face flashes on the screen, though I didn't need to see her picture to know it was her.

I put it to my ear. "Hello."

"Talk to me."

"I'm going to LA."

"And you told your fiancé you couldn't marry him. What the hell did I miss?"

I scan the signs and turn right to head toward my terminal. "I need to see him."

"Did you have a new memory? Hanna, come on."

"I can't talk about it right now. I understand if you need to close the bakery while I'm gone. You've already done more than I should ever have asked."

"I'll run the bakery. That's not a problem." The line goes quiet, and I know she's picking up on how serious I am about being unable to talk. We're twins, after all. We have that connection. And now, more than ever, I'm glad it's back. Because I really can't do this. I can't talk right now. I'll lose it. "If you want me to come out there with you, you just say the word."

"Thank you." My voice glitches over the words like a scratch on a record. "I'll text you when I land."

"I love you."

"Love you too," I whisper. And I end the call, loneliness tearing at my chest.

Some mornings, I wake up with new memories. Usually, they're nothing. This morning when I woke up, I remembered the night three months ago when I ended my relationship with Max because he had broken my heart.

May—Three Months Before Accident

"God, I'm so jealous of you I could spit." Lizzy grabs Cally's hand and holds it in front of her to inspect her ring. It's girls' night at Brady's and the table is full of empty glasses and half-full margarita pitchers.

"I'm the luckiest," Cally says, grinning.

Lizzy snorts. "Pretty, lucky, and gracious. Almost makes you hate her. So did you have to train the muscles in that arm to keep that rock on there all the time?"

"Shut up! It's not that big!"

My phone buzzes in my purse, alerting me to a new text message. I grin, immediately thinking it's from Max. He wanted to see me tonight but didn't push when he found out the girls were getting together for margaritas.

I pull my phone out and open my text messages. I frown at the screen. I don't recognize the number.

Unknown Number: *When are you going to give it up? Max is way out of your league.*

My stomach pitches into my chest and drags my heart with it as it falls back down. The words are not only cruel, they're exactly what I fear. I've wanted Max since we were teenagers, and now that I have him, sometimes it feels too good to be true.

I'm still trying to decide whether to text back when another beeps through.

Unknown Number: *You can keep fooling yourself if you want, but while he's dating your fat ass, he's wishing he were with someone he's actually attracted to.*

"Hanna?" Lizzy says. "Is everything okay?"

I paste on a smile to cover the sick churning of my stomach. I could tell the girls about these messages, bask in the reassuring warmth of their righteous indignation. We could talk about lying, jealous bitches who will go to any length to drag happy people into their misery. The conversation would no doubt end in all of us laughing and me deciding to ignore this nastiness.

But what if the person on the other end of this text conversation is telling the truth?

"Yeah. I'm fine." I text back. I shouldn't engage. I should find out who these are coming from and show them to my friends, to Max.

Hanna: Who is this?
Unknown Number: This is the sexy bitch your boyfriend wishes he were fucking.

"I'll be right back," I say in a rush. It's not so much the text as the series of screenshots attached to it that has me shaking. I have to get away from this table before the tears come. I can't let the girls see.

I barely make it to the bathroom before I start crying, and Meredith is waiting on the other side of the door, a smirk on her face.

"Why so sad, Hanna?"

I stumble back. "You?"

She smiles prettily and touches up her perfect lipstick in the mirror. "I didn't think I wanted him," she says. "I mean, I'm more interested in a man who can really support me, you know. But then things didn't work out with William because apparently he has a thing for whores—"

"Don't!" I growl, my nails biting into my palms.

"You're all so cute. Sticking up for each other. Why don't you go get your friends? I can show them my old texts too. We'll see what they think about your perfect boyfriend then."

"Why do you even care about this? Didn't you just have a baby?"

"I did. Which is why I've decided it's time to be proactive."

"What do you want from me?"

"Max," she says simply. "I want what you have, and as you might have noticed from those messages, he wants me."

"Then why is he with me?" I force myself to ask. Because that's the only defense I have. Meredith is beautiful. She's thin and blond and perfect. Everything I'll never be. And the texts between her and Max are so damning that I want to wilt like an unwatered flower in the hot sun.

"Come on, Hanna. Everyone knows your family is loaded. Max's little health club isn't going to get him very far if he doesn't have a sugar mama to bail him out."

I open my mouth to defend him then close it. Because it's true. I've already called in a favor with my mom and her friends to try to get Max a grant to help him pay the mortgage on his club. And I can tell by the Cheshire Cat grin on Meredith's face that she knows that too.

"I'm done waiting, Hanna, and he needs your money too much to leave you. So…" She shrugs. "I figured it was time to let you in on our little secret so you could hurry things along my way."

It feels like there's a rabid animal frantically clawing its way out of my stomach. I can't look at her anymore. I can't stand here and listen to her.

I turn around and grab the door handle, but her words stop me.

"Oh, I copied Max on that last one. I couldn't risk you pretending you never saw it just so you could keep him. Now you can pretend if you want, but you'll both know and things will never be the same between you."

I don't look at her before pushing through the door and leaving the bathroom.

"I've gotta get going," I say when I reach the table.

Lizzy frowns at me. "Why? What happened? Who were those texts from?"

My twin knows me too well, but I paste on a smile and shake my head. "I'm just not feeling very well. I'll see you at home later."

I don't wait for their permission or even their goodbyes, and I head out the door and toward home. I've had too much alcohol tonight to drive, so I walk the half-mile through town to my rental house, my heels pinching my feet painfully with every step.

Max is waiting at the door when I get there, his face drawn with worry. "It's not what it looks like."

I nod and step into his foyer. "Good." My voice is clear and strong, and some distant part of my mind is just proud that I'm not collapsing in a pathetic heap at his feet, begging him to love me, pleading with him to explain this away. "Because it looks like you're a lying asshole."

He drags a hand through his hair. "Hanna, don't. Okay? You weren't supposed to see those texts."

"Oh my God. Seriously? That's the best you've got? I wasn't supposed to *see* that our relationship is a total sham? That it's *pretend*? That you—" A sob rips through my chest before I can finish. It hurts too much.

"But it's not," he growls. I try to step around him, but he grabs my hand and holds it tight. "This is real. Nothing about what I feel for you is pretend."

"But it was. At one point it *was*."

"I was an idiot," he whispers. "Such an idiot."

"You don't understand what it's like to feel like shit about the way you look. You don't understand what a leap of faith it was for me to believe you wanted to be with me when you could have had any woman you wanted in this town."

"Meredith and I have a long, screwed-up history, and until things were serious with Will and Cally—"

"Leave." I point to the door.

"Don't do this, Hanna. Those texts were from *December*. That was months ago. You and I hadn't even kissed yet. I had no idea I was going to fall in love with you."

"Stop. I can't do this." I shake my head. "I have spent too many years of my life hating myself. I can't be with you anymore. I can't..." I shrug and tears spill onto my cheeks. "Please leave."

"I'll give you time, but please—"

"It's over, Max. Leave." I sound wild. Crazed. Maybe I am.

When he walks out the door, I sink to the floor and wrap my arms around my knees as I sob. I don't need to look at my phone again to remember the texts. They're branded on my brain.

Meredith: *You're seriously going out with Hanna Fat Ass Thompson.*

Max: *You're seriously going to start this conversation by being a bitch?*

Meredith: *Just tell me how this happened.*

Max: *It's a temporary arrangement. She needs a self-esteem boost.*

Meredith: *I had no idea you were taking charity cases.*

Max: *No worries, I still prefer blondes.*

Meredith: *So what's it like to fuck a fatty?*

Max: *Don't be a bitch.*

Meredith: *He dodges the question.*

Max: *Trust me, I'm not going to let this charade go that far. She's a sweet girl, but she's not my type.*

Meredith: *Am I your type?*

Max: *You know you are. But last I checked you were still hung up on Will Bailey.*

Meredith: *That was so last month. Come over here and I'll prove it.*

Max: *What do you have in mind?*

Meredith: *You. My mouth. More specifically, your dick and my mouth.*

Max: *Shit. Don't say that when you know I can't.*

Meredith: *You said yourself that your thing with Hanna is just a charade.*

Max: *I don't want her hurt. Period. I'll have to take a rain check.*

Meredith: *I can keep a secret. I know when to use my mouth. And where.*

Max: *This is a bad idea.*

Meredith: *I'll see you in fifteen, then?*

Max: *Make that five.*

Chapter
EIGHTEEN

WHEN I climb into a cab at the airport and say, "Nate Crane's house, please," I almost expect the guy to laugh at me. Instead, he shakes his head, mutters something about tourists, and starts the drive to Hollywood Hills.

"Nate Crane lives right past those gates," he announces in a bored tone.

The house in question is lit up like Granny's last birthday cake, and the circle drive has so many high-end cars that it would make the nicest (er, *only*) dealer in New Hope weep.

"Where ya wanna go next? Eminem's home isn't far from here."

"No. This is where I'll get out, thanks."

"You know they don't just let you come party with 'em, right?"

I smile and hand him cash for my fare. He looks at me like I've lost my mind but shrugs as I climb out of the back.

When I walk up to the gate, there are two security guards in black suits. Big guys.

"Sorry, ma'am," a dark-skinned man calls from in front of the gate. "Private party."

"Keep walking," his white comrade instructs.

"Yeah, um." *Shit.* I didn't really prepare to face the Men in Black to get to Nate. "I—"

"Jesus, Hanna, girl? Is that you?" The first guy slides his sunglasses down his nose and peers at me over the tops. "What are you wearing?" He nods to one of the other guys then grabs me by the upper arm as the gates slide open.

So I guess I'm going to get in after all, because next thing I know, he's sitting me in a golf cart and driving me up to the house. Without a word, he leads me out, up the front stairs, and into the house.

"Nate lives here?" The massive marble staircase fills the entryway with all the pomp and circumstance of a grand museum. Crystal chandeliers hang overhead. Somehow, it doesn't seem fitting of the secretly dorky rocker I know so little about.

The man frowns at me. "What's wrong with you?" He shakes his head. "I can't have you going back there dressed like this. Not with all those hos hanging around."

It's my turn to frown. I wasn't exactly worried about my ensemble of a T-shirt and jeans when I left my house this morning. I was more worried about getting the hell out of Dodge. Anyway, I'm not here to compete with any "hos." I just want a chance to talk to Nate.

"Um, do we know each other?" I ask the man as we head up the stairs.

He leads me into an impressive, large bedroom with an even more impressive walk-in closet. "Oh, you think you're funny and you're going to act like you don't know me, huh? Well, play coy all you want, but those girls Crane has over tonight aren't playing games."

"What are—" I'm cut off by my own shriek as the man yanks my ponytail holder from my hair and my T-shirt off over my head.

I wrap my arms around myself, trying for what modesty I can.

He wriggles his eyebrows. "Well, at least you wore the good underwear." Then he's scanning the closet and I relax.

This man isn't interested in ogling me. In fact, if I had to guess… "Damn good thing you have a gay man around to dress you tonight, sweetheart. Because them bitches out back aren't messing around."

I gasp dramatically. "You're telling me there are both bitches *and* hos here tonight?"

"You think you're cute," he says, moving his head side to side, "but they're 'bout to steal your man."

"He's not my man."

The man rolls his eyes and waves away my objection. "This!" He pulls a bright red dress from the rack and offers it to me.

"Whose clothes are these?"

"Well, they're Janelle's, of course. Now get changed and walk by that boy before he does something he regrets. I don't know what you did to him, but he's been in a bad way since he got back here Friday night. Drinking, partying. Hiding from something." He raises an eyebrow and gives me an unimpressed once-over. "You know what you did."

"Actually, I—"

"Change. Then meet Jamaal in the bathroom to freshen that makeup."

He's halfway out of the closet when I ask, "Who's Jamaal?" It's only one question of the approximately 1700 that are floating around in my mind right now, but since I'm supposed to see "Jamaal" next, I guess it takes priority.

The man stops, turns, and glares at me. "I thought you were clean, girl? You know that's why Janelle liked you. None of the drugs and bullshit. Now get changed and meet me in the bathroom."

"Jamaal!" I hold my breath. Could this flamboyant man be such a walking cliché that he speaks of himself in the third person?

The man stops and turns. "Yes, princess?"

I grin. I can't help it. I like this guy. A lot. "I don't remember you."

He snorts. "Don't be a bitch. Nobody forgets Jamaal."

"No, I…" I shake my head and bite back my laughter. "I don't remember much of anything from the last year. I had a head injury, and I have amnesia."

His big brown eyes grow impossibly wider. "No shit?"

"No shit," I say solemnly. "And the more I find out about what I've forgotten…" I swallow, struggling to verbalize the strange but undeniable impulse that brought me here. "The more I learn, the more I realize I need to spend time with Nate before shutting him out of my life."

"Why would you shut him out? That's crazy talk," he says. I hold up my left hand, and Jamaal draws in a long breath, his nostrils flaring as he presses his hand to his chest. "Who gave you *that* pathetic excuse for a jewel?"

"Does the name Max Hallowell ring any bells?"

He shakes his head and makes a tsking sound. "You don't remember Nathaniel? Truly?"

Nathaniel. I like that. Fits with the comic book T-shirts and Hulk tattoo. *Nathaniel.* "When I woke up in the hospital, I didn't remember him at all. Now I only remember bits and pieces. I just want him to talk to me."

He hums, noncommittal. "Change and meet me in the bathroom." With a flourish, he shuts the doors behind him and leaves me alone in the brightly lit closet.

I like Jamaal enough that I decide to follow his directions rather than questioning him. I strip out of my clothes and pull the red dress overhead. It's too small for me, but he chose a dress that stretches nicely, and after a bit of yanking and tugging, it covers my hips almost respectably. I spot a pair of matching red heels on the shoe rack and grin when I see that they're my size. I might feel uncomfortable in this dress, but I love shoes. I've always loved shoes. Shoes always fit.

My phone buzzes in my purse and I pull it out to see a new text.

Nix: *You need to call me. STAT.*

I don't want to talk to anyone from home right now. I can't

handle the sympathy I know they want to deliver.

When I exit the closet, I don't have a chance to look for the bathroom before Jamaal is whistling at me—à la calling Fido, not à la catcall—and waving me into another room.

I gasp as I step into the glitzy bathroom. *Glitz* is the only word for it. Marble and glass, mirrors and crystal. It's a large, shining space that's too over the top to belong on anything but an episode of *Cribs*.

"If you're going to stand there with your mouth hanging open, at least turn to me so I can touch you up while you gawk."

I obey, and Jamaal's large hands begin applying mascara, blush, and lip gloss in a rather expert way. When he's done, I can only blink at myself in the mirror. In less than three minutes, he managed to transform me from Plain Jane to one of the LA-caliber women I saw milling at the airport.

"Wow."

"You're welcome. Now let's hurry down to the pool and find that fool man of yours before he does something really stupid."

"He's not my man, Jamaal."

He snorts in reply and leads me back out into the hallway, but instead of taking the stairs that brought us up here, he leads me to the back of the hall and opens a door to a small, narrow set of stairs.

"Be careful in those heels." When we hit the bottom, Jamaal points the way toward the back door. "There you go, kiddo. He's out there making an ass of himself."

I study the large French doors and the scantily clad women beyond. Some of them are dressed like I am now, in dresses and heels. Others are in bikinis and sarongs. Others still in bikinis and heels. Because bitches and hos, I guess.

They're *all* painted and more beautiful than I will ever be without surgical enhancement. Knowing I'm going to step out there like I'm one of them makes my stomach cramp painfully.

"You've got something none of those women have," Jamaal says from behind me, as if reading my thoughts.

"What's that?"

"A mind of your own, kid. Why do you think he likes you so much?" He tilts up my chin and studies my face in the light. "You really don't remember? That's not just a bunch of bullshit?"

"I really don't. Did I come here a lot?"

He shrugs. "A couple of times."

My gaze drifts back toward the door and the music trickling in from outside. Someone screeches, and I hear a splash.

"What am I going to do if he won't talk to me?"

Jamaal shrugs. "Janelle will call. We'll get her to help. He can't say no to her."

Right. Janelle. The woman whose clothes I'm wearing. "And who's Janelle?"

"Janelle Crane? How hard did you hit that head?"

He walks away as the name clicks into place in my mind. *Janelle Crane*. The actress. I struggle to keep my jaw hinged as I look down at my dress. I'm wearing Janelle Crane's dress. Janelle Crane's shoes. *Holy. Shit.*

"Martini?"

I jump at the voice. A woman is standing next to me with a tray of martini glasses filled with light pink liquid. "Um, no thanks."

She smiles politely and heads out the door.

Rolling my shoulders back and lifting my chin, I follow her.

The back of the house is as gorgeous as the front. A large pool sits off to the right, surrounded by several tables and countless loungers. The space is overwhelmed with people, mostly women, and pounding music fills my ears. Women dance against each other, drink, and splash in the pool. And at least three look at me like I have two heads and should leave immediately.

I lift my chin and scan the scene for Nate. The only man in a crowd of women shouldn't be that hard to find.

I spot him in the hot tub, using his mouth to take a shot glass from between a woman's breasts. I stamp down the jealousy I feel at the sight and want to kick the shit out of myself.

My ego was battered and beaten by my memory of what Max did. Naturally, I thought I'd make myself feel better by visiting a celebrity who buries his face in the tits of whatever woman is handy. This was a stellar plan. Yet I can't turn around. I keep moving, keep heading toward Nate and this I-don't-know-what I'm after.

The click of my heels against the stone patio is muffled by the music and chatter, but I narrow in on the sound, concentrate on it as I cross to him.

He's laughing about something, but when his gaze settles on me, his smile falls away. And after the way I treated him last time I saw him, who can blame him?

"Well, look who came to party," he says, his words only slightly slurred.

He's drunk. I can see it in his eyes. Hell, I can practically smell the booze rolling off everyone in that hot tub.

"Can we talk?" My words come out meek, and I wish I could take them back and replace them with a command. *We need to talk.* Something. Anything other than sounding and feeling weak and unwanted. I'm so sick of feeling unwanted.

"What do you think, ladies?" he asks the woman around him. "Is there room for one more?"

The women pout and crowd around Nate. "Aren't we enough for you, Crane?" one asks. Another says, "Things were just getting interesting." And another complains, "It's already crowded in here. There's hardly room for *her.*"

The jab at my size hurts worse than it would have fifty pounds ago. Because in my size tens, I'm bigger than the rest of them, the kind of women who scour racks for extra-small shorts. It hurts more than it would have before because this is as good as I get and I know it. In fact, *this* probably isn't going to last.

I'm so stupid. I have a man at home who loves me. Who is more than I deserve. Who looks at me like I'm his world. Max screwed up. He hurt me. Betrayed me. But I can imagine a life with him, raising our kids in New Hope alongside our friends. So why am I here?

Nate's gaze rakes over me, from my head to my toes, trailing electric fingers of need in its path. Why does my body react when he looks at me like this? "You want to talk?" he says, lifting heavy-lidded eyes back to mine. "Climb on in." He turns to the women around him. "Sorry, ladies. I'm gonna need you to leave for a bit. You're right. No room for her and all of you, and I like her more."

The women whine in unison and fawn at Nate. He locks his eyes on mine for two beats before pressing a hard, open-mouthed kiss to the woman next to him. It's wet, sloppy, and entirely for my benefit, and I won't give him the satisfaction of looking away.

My stomach clenches, but I keep my face impassive as he releases her and the three women climb out of the hot tub, seemingly unconcerned with their bare chests.

He doesn't even watch them go. He just leans his head back, closes his eyes, and says, "You wanna talk, you're gonna have to climb in."

"I'm—" I shake my head, which is stupid since he can't see me. "I'm not wearing a swimsuit."

He lifts his head, and this time his gaze lands on my left hand. "I guess it can wait, then."

"I came all the way here," I say in a hard whisper. I don't want to call too much attention to myself. "The least you can do is talk to me."

"A lot of people visit me here." He picks up a shot glass off the back of the tub and throws it back. "Too bad you didn't bring a suit. We could have that talk you're so set on."

Fuck it. Even in underwear and a bra, I'll be more modestly covered than most of the women here tonight. I kick off my shoes and peel the dress off over my head. I fold it neatly before setting it in a chair. The last thing I want to do is be responsible for ruining Janelle Crane's dress.

When I turn back to the hot tub, his eyes are on me again, hot and greedy and…something else. There's something more in those eyes this time. Sadness?

"Take the bra off too," he orders as I step in.

"Dream on." I sink into the water and have to swallow back a sigh as it bubbles around me and warms my skin. I've had such a long, shitty day, and I could really use a relaxing soak. Instead, I'll talk to this jackass. Did I actually believe he was the person I needed when my heart was hurting?

He's watching me carefully. "Last time we talked, you made it profoundly clear you didn't want to see me again."

"I changed my mind."

"Yet I don't remember inviting you here."

"You sure know how to make a girl feel welcome. And is this seriously your house? It doesn't seem like you at all."

"Oh, so you know me now? Is that memory back?"

My cheeks burn with my blush. "Some of it."

"Yeah?" He drops his gaze down to my breasts. "Anything good?"

"I remembered that I broke up with Max. I remembered that I never cheated on him. I remembered how much he hurt me."

He sighs and leans his head back on the edge of the tub. "I'm not interested in being some prop for revenge."

"This isn't about revenge."

He doesn't look at me. "Sure it isn't."

"I called off the wedding."

"I'll believe that when his ring's not on your finger. Why are you here, Hanna?"

"I'm here because nothing is as it seemed and..." And what? Why *am* I here? "You said you were in love with me."

"Yeah, well, what was it you said? *We all make mistakes*?"

"Was the mistake being in love with me or telling me that you were?" I don't know why it matters so much that I know, but right now it seems so important that I'd do almost anything to get an honest answer from him.

"What do you want from me?" He sounds almost bored.

I scan the party going on in full swing around us. The women, the booze, the superficial bullshit. "I just want to talk to you. Without all these people. Without all the secrets."

He lifts a brow and grabs a phone from the ledge of the tub. He taps the screen then puts it down, and within seconds, Jamaal is coming out the back door with several other men in black suits.

"Party's over," Jamaal calls. "Thank you for coming. We hope you had a good time. Now it's time to leave. You don't have to go home but you can't stay here."

I blink in amazement as everyone does as he says, and minutes later, Nate and I are alone, the music is off, and the only sound is the whir of the hot tub's jets and the hum of traffic in the distance.

"That better?" he asks softly. And maybe he's not as drunk as I thought. And maybe he's not bored with my presence. His eyes dip to my cleavage and back up, roaming over my face. Again, I get that feeling that he's drinking me in. Memorizing me.

I swallow. The truth is that I want to memorize him too. The hard angles of his cheekbones and jaw, the dark brown of his bedroom eyes, the softness of his beautiful mouth.

"Don't look at me like that," he whispers.

"Why not? Maybe I should have let myself look at you the night you showed up in my bed. Maybe I should have made you talk to me then. Maybe if I knew what *you* know, I'd understand why I chose him instead of you."

He lets out a breath and closes his eyes. I gather every bit of my courage and turn to him, straddling his lap and wrapping my arms behind his neck.

His eyes fly open. "What are you doing?"

"This isn't about revenge."

He brushes my jaw with the back of his knuckles.

I lean into his touch, the gentle reassurance of it. "It's not about Max. It's about us."

Pain slices over his face and he drops his hand. "There is no *us*, Hanna."

"I don't remember making that choice. Just—"

His expression hardens. "There was no *choice*. Not about

me. It was never a choice between me and Max. The only choice you had to make was whether to take Max back or not."

"I don't understand."

"I never offered you what he did. The life, the marriage, the commitment. The happily-ever-fucking-after. I can't. I won't. It wasn't a choice between him and me because I wasn't offering you those things."

I wilt and back away from him. If our relationship was purely physical, why do I feel this way? "You and me? This? It was just about sex?"

"Not even at first."

"Then how—" I squeeze my eyes shut as the memory crashes over me and the understanding right along with it.

It was never a choice between two men.

"I'm sorry," he breathes. "You have no idea how sorry." Water sloshes as he stands and climbs out.

I follow numbly, not sure what else I'm supposed to do with myself.

He hands me a towel but doesn't meet my eyes. "Come on. You can sleep in Janelle's room."

Into the house and back up the narrow stairs, he leads me to the room where Jamaal ushered me upon my arrival.

After clicking on a lamp, Nate disappears into the closet and returns with gray cotton pajamas. "These should fit," he says. "You can stay as long as you want. You're always welcome."

I'm still reeling from the memory. "I feel…really stupid."

"Don't." He tilts my chin until I'm looking at him. Then he drops his hand quickly, as if touching me costs him. "Please don't."

Chapter
NINETEEN

August—Five Days Before Accident

THE DELICIOUS smells of bacon, cinnamon, and pastry dough wake me.

I roll over and stretch, my body spent in that most delicious way, my muscles singing with happiness. If a weekend in bed doing everything *but* making love makes me feel this good, how good would I feel if Nate would sleep with me?

I don't want to go back to New Hope. I want to stay here in LA in Nate's big-ass house, where life seems less like this ominous dark cloud waiting to be confronted and more like when I played pretend as a kid.

I climb out of bed and head to the bathroom, where I wash my face, brush my teeth, and try to calm the worst of my bed-head. After throwing on a robe, I head down to the kitchen.

Nate stands bare-chested and beautiful behind the island, the muscles in his forearms flexing as his competent hands chop apples and peaches and throw them into a bowl. Behind him, bacon sizzles on the stove, the smell incredible.

My stomach rumbles.

"Looks like you're cooking for an army this morning."

He looks up, noticing me for the first time since I entered the kitchen. His eyes light with his smile. He wipes his hands on a towel and skirts around the island to pull me into his arms and kiss me soundly. When he breaks the kiss and steps back, I have to grab the edge of the counter to keep my balance.

If only this were real life.

"What are you doing with all this food?" I survey the pan of rolls cooling on the counter next to some sort of casserole that looks like it has more cheese than I've let myself eat in months.

"I'm feeding my girl."

My cheeks flush. I'm embarrassed that he thinks I require so much for breakfast. Downside of being a big girl. "I just need some coffee and maybe a little of that fruit salad."

He raises a brow. "What you need is a keeper. How much weight have you lost since we met three months ago?"

Thirty-eight and a half pounds. Add that to the ten I managed to drop the five months prior and I'm almost down fifty pounds. But I know Nate won't like my answer, so I avoid the question and cross to the coffee pot to pour myself a steaming mugful. The creamer sits next to the pot, and I look at it for a minute, tempted. *Empty calories.*

When I turn around, he's right in front of me.

"Hanna," he whispers, tilting my chin up so I'm looking him in the eye. "I'm worried about you."

"I needed to lose some weight. Trust me, I'm not going to waste away."

"You didn't need to lose an ounce." He *is* worried. I can see it in his eyes. "Did he do this to you? Did he make you feel this way?"

No need to say who *he* is. "It doesn't matter."

"Fuck, Hanna. What did this loser do to you?"

"He's not a loser!" I shut my mouth and study my coffee. Max is off-limits, and Nate usually respects that.

"So you haven't given him an answer yet."

I gasp, horrified that it's not obvious. "I wouldn't be here if I had."

Nate gives a sad sort of half-smile and backs up a step. "Yeah, but you see, that assumes you're going to take him back. If you'd answered and told him no, there'd be nothing wrong with being here with me."

He goes back to his breakfast preparations, the silence snapping between us with so many things unsaid.

When breakfast is done, Nate serves both of us. I know I won't eat much of the calorie-laden breakfast—doing so would make me sick at this point—but I don't argue when he fills my plate.

We sit at the glass table in the sunroom, the slow morning rain tapping on the glass. I wish for clear skies and sunshine to warm my skin through the glass. I close my eyes for a minute, imagining it, the hope it normally makes me feel.

"I'm sorry, Hanna," Nate says, and when I open my eyes, he's watching me. "I know you love Max. I just…" His jaw works as he shifts his gaze to something beyond the glass. The bird bathing itself in the garden? Maybe something that can't be seen.

"What do you want me to do?" My voice breaks on the question. I really want him to answer because I don't know what I'm supposed to do. I'm putting us all through this painful holding pattern until I can get my mind straight. I'm just waiting, assuming the answer will come to me. Or am I really waiting for Nate to offer me more than he has?

His fork clatters against his plate and he shakes his head. "Nothing. I'm not asking anything from you. I'm not him."

I close my eyes. It's not fair to want a declaration of love from this man. He was upfront with me from the beginning. He's not about the relationship, not about the forever.

Pushing back from the table, I stand up and head out to the patio. I stand under the awning and watch the rain dance on the water in the pool.

"It's not you." The sound of Nate's voice sends a tremor of sadness through me. Because he's never asked anything from me, but part of me wants him to. "You know that, right?" He stands next to me, head tilted back, eyes on the sky. "I can't offer you more than this. Even when you deserve more. It's not because I don't want it. It's because I made a promise to myself. To my son."

Turning, I run my fingers across the date tattooed above his left pec. He told me the significance of that date the first night we met. It's his son's birthday. The day he says his world changed. "I never asked you for more, Nate."

He grabs my fingers and squeezes them in his. "But you deserve it."

"I'm a big girl. Let me decide what I deserve."

"You deserve everything. Anything you could want." His grip is nearly painful on my fingers, but I don't pull away. I'm too worried he'll stop talking. "But I'm not the man to give that to you. I can't."

You won't, I think.

His eyes scan the dark and angry sky. "My dad left my mom when Janelle and I were eight. It always sucks for kids when their parents split, but he moved out of our house and into Jayda's. She was already pregnant with his baby, and I remember when my stepsister was born. You should have seen my dad's eyes when he looked at her. Like she was the most precious thing he'd ever been given. Then Jayda had a second child, and a third. He was so damn happy with them. For a while, he did his visitation with Janelle and me. We'd go over there on the weekends and every other holiday. But it was so painfully obvious that we were the *other* kids, the *other* family. We were an inconvenience. We were the mistake he had to deal with now that he'd finally found his real life."

I understand how it feels when your parent lets you down, and my heart aches for him. "I'm so sorry."

"By the time Collin was born, my relationship with his mother was already over. We were young, and we'd never been serious, but the first time I held him in my arms, his eyes locked on mine and I knew I couldn't do to him what my father had done to me and Elle. I promised myself *he* would be my family. Even if his mom and I weren't together. It didn't matter. I promised I would never make him feel like he was second best."

"You're a great dad, Nate. You'd never make him feel like that."

"It's hard enough to be a kid to celebrity parents. I won't pile that on too." His hair falls into his face as he drops his head. "Collin is the most important thing in my life. I can't give you more without taking something from him. I won't do that."

"I wish you'd quit making it seem like I'm asking for that." My voice breaks because we both know I want more than this. Need more. A home. A life. Babies.

"What happens if we don't end this, Hanna? You can't be my mistress for the rest of my life. You can't keep flying out here when I snap my fingers." His face twists in disgust, and he steps away from me and into the rain. "Every time I say goodbye, I tell myself that's it. That I'll end it. Because you deserve that. But I'm weak and selfish as shit and keep calling you back because I can't get enough of you."

"What are you trying to say?"

He tilts his head to the sky and closes his eyes, letting the rain shower down on his face. I study the ridges of his strong back expanding as he breathes in and out.

I step into the rain and press my lips to the damp skin of his bare shoulder.

When he speaks, his question is so quietly murmured I can barely make it out over the rain in my ears. "Are you still in love with him?"

It's my turn to tense. "I am." I latch on to the best of my bravery and whisper, "But I'm in love with you too."

"Don't say that."

I back away. Slowly at first and then fast. Then I'm turning and running. Back into the house, up the stairs.

I crawl under the covers still in my rain-dampened robe and curl into a ball on my side.

When I hear him pad into the room, I don't roll over to look at him. When I feel the bed shift under his weight, I don't open my eyes. And when his arms wrap around me from behind and he pulls me to his chest, I don't say a word.

"I was in such an ugly, dark place the night we met. I looked into your eyes, and you were right there with me—my angel in the darkness. You saved me." He buries his nose in my hair and inhales audibly. "You saved me and I love you."

I draw in a gulp of air, but it enters my lungs with a sharp, painful edge.

"I think I've been in love with you since the night we met. And I know that sounds crazy and implausible—like one of those things the guy says when he's trying to win the girl—but for me, it's just true. I love you and I'm terrified that you're going to ruin your life because of it." His arms tighten around me and he presses a kiss to my shoulder. "I'm not telling you to take his ring. I honestly believe that if he were worthy of you, you wouldn't be here with me. But don't let *me* be the reason you don't take the life you want."

"What if *you're* the life I want?"

His arms tighten around me and he presses his lips to my shoulder. "You're asking me for something I can't give."

Present Day

Nate's sitting on the edge of the big bed, elbows on his knees, studying the floor.

Rubbing sleep from my eyes, I push myself up and lean against the headboard. Next to me on the nightstand, my engagement ring stares back at me. I took it off last night. I should have left it at home. Ignoring it, I grab my phone to check the time. There's another message.

Nix: *Please call me soon!*

"I'm sorry. I'll get dressed and get out of here." I scramble to the edge of the bed.

He stops me with a hand on my wrist. "Are you going to

be okay?"

"Yeah." I nod, trying for chipper, but I don't feel it. "I'll be fine."

"You took off the ring." He massages the back of his neck. "It's over?"

"It needs to be. I don't know how I'm supposed to move forward when what we have behind us hurts so much."

He studies me, his eyes full of thoughts I can't read and know he won't share. "You can stay here as long as you want. Take some time. Think things through. Jamaal will be here. He'll get you anything you need."

I tuck my feet under me and sit next to him. He's already dressed in dark jeans and a white button-up dress shirt. "Are you going somewhere?"

"I leave for Afghanistan this morning."

A memory flickers. "You're performing for the troops?"

"Yeah."

"How long until you leave?"

He cuts his eyes to me and pushes off the bed. "My driver's waiting out front."

"Is this it? Is this…goodbye? For good?"

He closes his eyes. "It has to be. "

I slide off the bed and touch my hand to his face. "How am I supposed to let you go?" I run my fingers along his jaw. "It's the right thing to do, but—" My voice breaks.

He cups my jaw, his fingers sliding into my hair. "I know your memory isn't the greatest right now," he says. "So I'm going to tell you the things I need you to remember for me."

"Okay."

"You are the most beautiful woman I have ever met." He swallows and braves a tentative smile. "You're like the sun—completely blind to your own beauty because you are so busy making everyone around you shine. No matter how far we hide in the shadows, you share your light. That's how you stole my heart when no one else could find it."

It hurts to breathe. "Nate."

Steps sound outside the heavy bedroom doors. "The

plane's waiting, Crane." Jamaal's voice. "Time to head out."

Nate ignores him and keeps his dark eyes locked on mine. "You have to go."

He holds me tight. "One more thing."

"What?" I don't know if I can handle anything else.

"Thank you," he whispers. "Thank you for giving something I never thought I deserved. And for giving it without expectation or condition. You made me believe I was worth it."

I shake my head, unsure of this metaphor. "My light?"

"Your love." He drops his hands and steps back.

I gulp in air and watch him back toward the door. Turn the knob. Walk away.

When he shuts the door behind him, I race to the bathroom, turning on the shower full blast because I can't stand the idea of letting him hear me cry.

I bite my fist to block the sobs, but they come anyway—thick and angry, ugly sobs of grief and self-pity. Because I don't have to know anything else about Nate Crane to know I love him. And he just said goodbye.

When the mirror is obscured by steam, I peel off my sleep clothes and step under the spray, letting it pound against me. I close my eyes and imagine the water can wash away all my heartache, all my fears and confusion. I lean my head against the glass enclosure and let the tears come.

My body rocks with my sobs. They tear out of me like my body rejecting poison. I let them come, and I let the water wash them away until my breathing evens and my tears are gone.

I don't know I'm not alone until hot, rough hands are on my bare shoulders, and Nate is turning me around.

"Nate," I breathe.

He's fully clothed, the water streaming down his face as he looks at me. "Why'd you have to forget?" Then his mouth is on mine, lips and tongue and teeth, taking and demanding and punishing.

I want this kiss too much to do anything but return it in

kind. I suck at his lower lip and explore his mouth with my tongue. His taste is new and familiar all at once.

My hands go into his hair and I hold him close. I'm afraid he might disappear—that this might prove to be a hallucination—but he's solid under my hands. Water pours over us as we devour each other's mouths, and my hands find their way from his hair to his shoulders, his chest, and finally down to the hem of his shirt.

His mouth leaves mine just long enough for him to pull his shirt over his head and throw it to the shower floor. Then he's stepping into me again. One leg between my thighs, he presses me against the wall as his mouth returns to mine.

His kiss is softer this time. Slower, sweeter, and less desperate. If he was feasting on me before, now he's savoring me, and I let him. I savor him in return. The last sips of a precious bottle of wine, the last moments of a fleeting dream.

I don't know what I'm doing. I don't know what this means for tomorrow or next week. Right now, I don't care. I just need his hands on me, his taste on my tongue. I blindly grope for the button on his jeans. Releasing it, I shove them down his hips, and he kicks them away.

His hands grip my hips and he slides my body up the glass until my feet are off the ground and I'm resting on his thigh. The pressure is so perfect and so sweet. He rips his mouth from mine and moves to my neck as a hand cups my breast. I'm a mess of sensation and I don't want it to end—the press of his thigh between my legs, the tease of his thumb against my nipple, the scrape of his mouth against my neck.

"I've missed this," he murmurs.

Leaning my head back, I give up and let my eyes float shut. "What have you missed?"

"No, Hanna," he growls. "Look at me. I want you to remember who's touching you."

I force my eyes open and am treated to the sight of his head dipping to my breast. "Oh God." I should stop him. I shouldn't let it go this far. We both know what this is. A stolen moment. An extended goodbye. But his teeth scrape my nipple, and instead of protesting, I'm arching into his mouth, urging him on.

He squeezes my breast and groans as he lifts his head and returns his eyes to mine. He flicks my earlobe with his tongue. "I've missed your taste." He pinches my nipple between his fingers. "The way you cry out when I touch you." He repositions me between himself and the wall until my thighs cradle the bulge of his erection. "I missed the heat of your pussy when you're turned on."

Then his mouth is on mine again, his hands tangling in my wet hair as he devours me.

"The plane?"

"It's mine. It can wait."

Eventually, we make our way out of the shower and dry each other with fluffy white towels. Then he takes my hand and leads me to his bedroom. He slides under the covers with me. The frantic pace of the shower is gone and in its place is the steady beat of a grief-filled love song. He traces every line of my body with his fingers then his tongue. Love and need fill me so completely they hold together the pieces of my broken heart.

When Nate settles his head by mine on the pillow, his eyes are as tender as they are hot. "I have to let you go," he whispers. "This has to be goodbye."

My throat grows tight. "I know."

Chapter
TWENTY

I FELL ASLEEP in his arms.

When I wake up again, the room is quiet. Nate is gone, his absence nearly tangible.

The covers smell like him. I can still feel the scrape of his beard against my skin. And despite this grief that makes my limbs feel heavy and my eyes gritty, I feel a sense of peace I haven't in weeks.

I climb out of bed and pull on a robe before padding down the stairs and out to the patio. The sun is high in the sky, warming the air and reflecting off the surface of the pool. Crystal sun catchers hang from the awning and spin in the breeze, casting dapples of light into the shadows by the door.

I close my eyes and step into the sun, letting the light warm my cheeks.

Inhale. Exhale. Let go.

I'm going to be okay.

My head is clear, the fog of the last two days lifted. And with my clarity comes the understanding. I wish I could've had more time with Nate, yet I'm glad he had to go. He needed me to let him go. We needed to let go of each other. Holding on to him was hurting him as much as it was hurting me.

And Max...

I open my eyes and tilt my face to the sky. Fluffy white clouds roll across the endless sea of blue.

I can forgive Max. I love him too much to hold on to my anger. I can forgive him. But I can't marry him. Maybe that will change with time, but I'm not going to ask him to live in limbo for me again. I have to let Max go too.

Canceling the wedding will break my mom's heart, but I need to make this decision for myself, not her. And regardless of what I may have been thinking when I put on Max's ring before my accident, regardless of what emotions or revelations I can't remember, I'm not ready to get married. Not to Max. Not to anyone. I'm still figuring out who I am and where I fit into my world.

I'm giving myself the gift of time and no attachments. Maybe my memories will return or maybe they won't. But whatever secrets are lost in my damaged brain, I've let the person I am—the person I want to become—get lost there too. Or maybe she was lost before my memories were. Maybe I lost myself three months ago when my world spiraled out of control.

I need to call Liz and make arrangements for a flight home. I need to call Max and my mom. Suddenly, calls that terrified me twenty-four hours ago are simply steps on a new path.

I climb the stairs back to Janelle's room. My phone flashes wildly at me from the nightstand, and I pick it up and open the latest text message.

Nix: *Call me. Now.*

I straighten. What if something happened to Liz? I hit the button to call her, and as it rings, I imagine half a dozen different scenarios in which Liz or Cally or my mom could have gotten hurt.

Suddenly, my stomach clenches and the peace I was feeling moments ago flees. What if something happened to Max? What if he's in the hospital and thinks I don't care? I flinch as guilt punches me in the gut.

"Come on, Nix," I whisper against the ring.

I'm expecting her voicemail when she finally picks up. "Hanna!"

"Is everything okay?"

"Your blood work is back."

My shoulders sag in relief. No one is hurt. Nothing horrible has happened. Nix is just being doctor-ish. "Okay? Are my electrolytes still screwed up?"

"Your electrolytes are fine, but your hCG levels are elevated."

"What does that mean?"

"It means you're pregnant."

ACKNOWLEDGEMENTS

So many people help me bring a book together and this was no exception.

First, my husband, Brian, who never complains when date nights turn into brainstorming sessions and who is more than happy to tell me how he'd react to the drama I throw at my heroes. You, my love, are the real hero. Thanks for being awesome. I might keep you around after all.

To the medical professionals who helped me understand Hanna's condition and hospital protocol. To my sisters, Deb and Kim, and my mom—thank you for fielding my endless questions. Extra thanks to Eileen Dreyer, who didn't know me from Adam but happily answered my emails quizzing her about retrograde amnesia and dozens of what-ifs. These ladies provided me with more information than I could possibly include, steered me clear of plot holes, and inspired plot twists with their knowledge. Any errors are my own.

A huge thank you to my friends and family for being amazing cheerleaders. A special shout out to the "Indy Crew." I miss you guys and am so grateful to have your on-going support, virtual or otherwise. Justin, thanks for taking my plot question phone call while registering for your wedding gifts. That's above and beyond, sir.

To everyone who provided me feedback on this crazy twisty-turny plot—especially Violet Duke, Adrienne Hogan, and Annie Swanberg. Rock stars, all of you.

Thank you to the team that helped me package this book and promote it. Sarah Hansen at Okay Creations designed my beautiful cover, and if I have my way she will do many, many more for me. To my editing team, Rhonda Helms, Mickey Reed, and Arran Nicol, you make my books better. To Chris, my assistant, who keeps me organized against all odds. A massive shout-out to Julie with ATOMR for organizing my promotional events and to all of the bloggers and reviewers who help spread the word about my books. Amazing. Every one of you.

To my agent Dan Mandel and my foreign rights agent Stefanie Diaz for getting my books into the hands of readers all over the world—you're making my dreams come true.

To all my writer friends on Twitter, Facebook, and my various writer loops, thank you for your support and inspiration. Special thanks to the NWB—Sawyer Bennett, Lauren Blakely, Violet Duke, Jessie Evans, Melody Grace, Monica Murphy, and Kendall Ryan—you ladies make me smile on a daily basis!

And last but certainly not least, thank you to my fans all over the world. To those who read *Unbreak Me* and *Wish I May* and wrote begging for another New Hope story. To those who follow me on Facebook and tell me to write faster because you can't wait. You're the best fans an author could ask for. I couldn't do this without you and wouldn't want to. Thank you for buying my books and telling your friends about them. Thank you for asking me to write more. You're the best!

~Lexi

PLAYLIST

Anna Nalick—*Breathe (2am)*
Barenaked Ladies—*Odds Are*
Dave Matthews Band—*The Space Between*
Matchbox Twenty—*If You're Gone*
Shakira, Rihanna—*Can't Remember to Forget You*
Sarah Bareilles—*I Choose You*
Jason Mraz—*I Won't Give Up*
Nine Inch Nails—*Something I Can Never Have*
A Great Big World—*Say Something*
P.M. Dawn—*I'd Die Without You*
Jason Walker—*Down*
Macy Gray—*I Try*
James Blunt—*You're Beautiful*

FALL TO YOU

Here and Now series, book two

FALL TO YOU

Here and Now series, book two

LEXI RYAN

For Sue—the sweetest lady, the best mother-in-law, and the coolest nana to my kiddos. Thank you for all you do!

.

Part One:
BEFORE

MAX

Three Months Before Hanna's Accident

Mom's eyes water as she hands me the velvet box. "I wish your grandmother were alive for this," she whispers. "She always loved Hanna, and she would have been so happy to see you with her."

My hands are shockingly steady as I open the lid to reveal the modest ring my grandmother wore on her left hand until the day she died. Hanna deserves something with a little more flash, but I know she'll appreciate the sentimental value of this ring more than a giant rock I can't afford.

I close the box and clasp it in both of my hands, exhaling slowly. I never imagined I'd be anxious to get married. I thought I'd be the guy whose girlfriend would have to guilt him into it. But I've never been with anyone like Hanna.

"When are you going to do it?" Mom asks, tucking one leg under herself on the couch. I'm pretty sure I made her night tonight when I came by to ask for Grandma's ring.

"Next weekend."

"You don't need to be nervous. Hanna loves you."

My phone buzzes with a text alert. Once, twice, three

times—a sure sign someone is sending me a long text that has to be delivered in several pieces. I pull it from my pocket and unlock the screen.

At first, I don't understand what I'm looking at. Mom is saying something, but I can't make it out over the roaring in my ears. My eyes are glued to my phone. These texts were sent over five months ago, but it feels like eons, and looking at them now makes bile crawl up my throat. I'm not the same man I was then, but leave it to Meredith to never let me forget a screw-up.

> **Meredith:** *You're seriously going out with Hanna Fat Ass Thompson.*
>
> **Max:** *You're seriously going to start this conversation by being a bitch?*
>
> **Meredith:** *Just tell me how this happened.*
>
> **Max:** *It's a temporary arrangement. She needs a self-esteem boost.*
>
> **Meredith:** *I had no idea you were taking charity cases.*
>
> **Max:** *No worries, I still prefer blondes.*
>
> **Meredith:** *So what's it like to fuck a fatty?*
>
> **Max:** *Don't be a bitch.*
>
> **Meredith:** *He dodges the question.*
>
> **Max:** *Trust me, I'm not going to let this charade go that far. She's a sweet girl, but she's not my type.*
>
> **Meredith:** *Am I your type?*
>
> **Max:** *You know you are. But last I checked you were still hung up on Will Bailey.*
>
> **Meredith:** *That was so last month. Come over here and I'll prove it.*
>
> **Max:** *What do you have in mind?*
>
> **Meredith:** *You. My mouth. More specifically, your dick and my mouth.*
>
> **Max:** *Shit. Don't say that when you know I can't.*

*Meredith: You said yourself that your thing
with Hanna is just a charade.
Max: I don't want her hurt. Period. I'll have to
take a rain check.
Meredith: I can keep a secret. I know when to
use my mouth. And where.
Max: This is a bad idea.
Meredith: I'll see you in fifteen, then?
Max: Make that five.*

If I could go back to December, back to those early days
of my relationship with Hanna, back when I thought it was all
temporary, a favor for a friend. If I could go back there and
knock some sense into myself, I would.

At the very least, I'd tell myself to stay away from Meredith.
She's had her claws in me most of my life, and she can't stand
that she doesn't control me anymore.

It's not until my eyes skim over the screenshots of these
five-month-old texts a second time that I see it—the other
number in the recipient field.

Hanna's number.

And then, just like that, my world falls apart.

"Fuck," I growl.

Mom hops off the couch and props her hands on her hips.
"Maximilian!"

"Sorry, Mom." I push off the couch. "I have to go." My chest
feels tight. I have to get out of here. I have to get to Hanna.

"What's going on?" Worry etches lines between her brows.

I'm already halfway out the door and don't answer her
question. Hanna lives a few blocks from Mom, so I don't
bother with my car. I break into a run toward her house, the
velvet box holding Grandma's ring clenched in my fist.

I lost my grandmother my senior year of high school.
Before she died, she warned me that Meredith would ruin my
life. She was too kind to say it like that, but I remember it so
clearly. Grandma was standing in her little kitchen, thin gold
bracelets jangling at her wrists as she chopped apples for one

of those nasty salads that involved too much mayonnaise.

"Maximilian," she said, her voice creaking like the hinges on an old door, "you see someone drowning and you're gonna be the first to jump into the lake without a life preserver. I know this about you, but you can't save them all. Meredith is drowning, Max, and jumping in to save her is only going to destroy you both. Don't let her pull you under."

At the time, I wrote off her comments as those of an overprotective grandmother. She'd seen Meredith use me and drop me again and again, and she hated it. But she was right, and now Meredith is destroying the most important thing in my life—and me right along with it.

The house Hanna shares with her sister is dark, and when I pound on the door, no one answers. I use my key to let myself in. "Hanna?" I call. God, the fear is right there in my voice, making it tremble. How can I fix this? How can I stop her from seeing the screenshots of those old texts?

I sense Hanna before I hear her feet hit the steps behind me. When I turn, the truth is all over her face. She saw the texts. I'm too late.

"It's not what it looks like."

She steps into the house and nods carefully. "Good. Because it looks like you're a lying asshole."

Fuck. Fuck, fuck, fuck. I shove the ring box in my pocket. Panic tightens a hot fist around my heart. "Hanna, don't. Okay?" I just need a chance to explain, but my chest is so tight and it's hard to think. Hard to breathe. "You weren't supposed to see those texts."

"Oh my God. Seriously?" Her voice is hard. Distant. I want my soft, open girl back. "That's the best you've got? I wasn't supposed to see that our relationship is a total sham? That it's pretend? That you—" Then her brittleness shatters and she sobs. All I want to do is pull her into my arms. And I know I can't.

"But it's not," I plead. She tries to step around me, but I grab her hand and hold her fast. "This is real. Nothing about what I feel for you is pretend."

"But it was. At one point, it was." Tears leak out the corners of her dark eyes, and each one is a punch in the gut. Each one a nightmare come to life. I'm supposed to be the one to kiss away her tears, not the one who makes her cry.

"I was an idiot." It's a pathetic defense. The truth usually is. "Such an idiot."

She lifts her chin, and some part of me is proud of her for standing up to me. "You don't understand what it's like to feel like shit about the way you look. You don't understand what a leap of faith it was for me to believe you wanted to be with me when you could have had any woman you wanted in this town."

"Meredith and I have a long, screwed-up history, and until things were serious with Will and Cally—"

Her eyes flash, a wave of anger crashing over the hurt. "Leave." She points to the door.

"Don't do this, Hanna. Those texts were from December. That was months ago. You and I hadn't even kissed yet. I had no idea I was going to fall in love with you."

"Stop." She wraps her arms around herself and backs away as if I'm some asshole she needs to protect herself from. Maybe I am. "I can't do this. I have spent too many years of my life hating myself. I can't be with you anymore. I can't—" A new sob cuts off the rest of her sentence. "Please leave."

"I'll give you time, but please—"

"It's over, Max. Leave." She lifts her eyes to my face and winces as if looking at me causes her physical pain, and there's nothing I want more than to take that pain away.

So I do what she asks and leave.

I walk numbly through the darkness and back to my house, and I'm not even surprised when Meredith is waiting for me by the door.

Her lips curl into a smile when my feet hit the landing. "Why so glum, Max?"

"Get the fuck off my property," I growl. I swear to Christ I've never felt a single violent impulse toward a woman before. I'm not my father. But damn if I'm not feeling one hell of an impulse now.

"You don't really mean that." She steps forward and slips her hand under my shirt, scraping her fingernails across my abs.

The only thing keeping me from physically removing her hand from my body is the fear that, if I let myself touch her, I'll hurt her. When I back up a step, she follows.

"It's going to be okay," she whispers. She looks up at me through her lashes and goes for the button on my jeans.

I grab both of her wrists. "Don't fucking touch me."

Those calculating blue eyes turn sad and fill with tears. "You used to love me."

"So that gives you the right to fuck up my relationship with Hanna? To fuck up my life?"

"You don't even look at me anymore. You hardly reply when I text you." Her bottom lip trembles. "Why? You once told me I was the only one for you."

"I'm in love with Hanna. You can't change that by being a world-class bitch."

"Let me make this up to you." She steps closer, pressing her body to mine, and for the first time in my post-pubescent life, the feel of Meredith's body does nothing for me. "I know how you like it, Max. Let me make you feel good."

"Get the fuck away from me."

HANNA

Love is a manipulative bitch.

Love is what had me believing that a guy like Max could actually want a girl like me. Love had me walking on clouds for the last five months. And love is the reason I'm knocking on Max Hallowell's door at six a.m. the morning after he broke my heart.

"Hanna." He steps back and opens the door wider to let me in. His dark hair is tousled from sleep and his chest is bare. My gaze is instantly drawn to the soft trail of hair that disappears into the waistband of his sleep pants. His blue eyes are bloodshot. Like maybe he drank too much before climbing in bed last night. Or like he didn't sleep much at all.

Good.

I follow him inside, and my heart aches as I look at the stacks of boxes ready for the move. What did Meredith say to me after sending the screenshots of those texts? *"Everyone knows your family is loaded. Max's little health club isn't going to get him very far if he doesn't have a sugar mama to bail him out."*

Suddenly, it's so obvious. Max's financial situation sucks. He sold his house and is moving into the tiny apartment above the gym. He let go of a couple of his employees, picking up their hours himself to help with cash flow.

I'm the one who suggested he try to get the Healthy Tomorrow Grant, and I'm the one who talked my mom into pushing Max's application to the committee members over the other applicants.

Right now, it literally hurts to be near him, but the manipulative bitch that is love has me standing here anyway because I don't want him to lose his health club.

"Can we talk?" he asks softly. His voice still has that early morning rumble that makes me weak at the knees. He turns toward the little kitchen. "I'll make some coffee."

I follow him but try my best to keep my distance. Every second I'm here costs me. I need to keep this brief. "I can't be with you anymore," I say, repeating the words I rehearsed in my head on the way over. "But I don't want you to lose your grant, and you know how political those decisions are. I think we shouldn't tell anyone about our breakup until you're awarded the money."

He freezes, drops the coffee carafe in the sink, and turns to me, his hard jaw ticking. "You think I'm going to pretend you're my girlfriend just so I can get some stupid grant money?"

"It's not stupid and you know it." I close my eyes. He's so close, and all I really want to do is take a few steps forward and curl into him. I know how warm he'd be and how good it would feel to have his arms wrapped around me.

"Nothing happened with Meredith," he says softly. "I want you to know that."

"You went to her," I whisper.

He nods, and it hurts. Maybe I wanted him to deny it. To say that she fabricated the whole thing somehow. Instead, he says, "That's true."

"And you meant it when you said I wasn't your type."

"I…" He takes two long strides so he's standing in front of me. He tilts my chin up until my gaze meets his, and I can feel his warmth. So tempting.

I squeeze my eyes shut. It hurts too much to look at his beautiful face, to see those eyes that studied me as he touched me, played with my breasts, found me wet between my legs.

Suddenly, his arms are around me and he's pulling me against his chest, holding me against his heat like he has so many times. And because I'm weak, I let him. I let him hold me and I take in his scent, memorize it. Because I have to end this.

"I never meant to hurt you," he whispers. "I was trying to help, and—"

Even weakness has its limits. I shove him away and swipe at the tears on my cheeks. "Don't."

"I fell in love with you," he growls. "Don't you get that?"

"What? When? While you were making me into some kind of experiment? Seeing if you could cheer up the fat chick by taking her on a few dates?"

"You are fucking beautiful, and I hate when you talk about yourself like that." When I lift my chin, he shrugs helplessly. "I don't know when. After Liz talked me into—"

"Liz?" I feel like someone punched me in the stomach, and no matter how many times I try to draw in air, none makes it to my lungs.

Max winces. "I'd asked her out. She yelled at me. Told me I was an idiot if I thought she was going to go on a date with me when you were so hung up on me."

"She told you to pretend to want to be with me?" I'm surprised I can form the words with what little air I can draw into my lungs. Bad enough that Max always wanted my twin. Bad enough that I wasn't on his radar. But Liz—my sister and my best friend in the whole world—was behind the stupid idea to fake interest in me.

Max hangs his head and shoves his hands in his pockets. "She was sure that you'd worked me up to be better than I was. That if you went out with me a couple of times, you'd realize I wasn't this great catch."

"So you did it? To…what? Get rid of me?"

"It wasn't a hardship, Hanna. You're gorgeous and sweet and-"

"And you only went out with me because my sister told you that was the best way for me to get over you."

His jaw tightens and he locks his gaze on mine. "Does it matter? Sometime after that first date and before that first kiss, my reasons changed. And then I fell in love with you. Maybe I wasn't looking for it to happen, but it did, okay? I fucking fell in love with *you*. Whatever was once between me and Meredith is over. Once you and I were exclusive, there was no one else. I wouldn't do that to you."

"I know you wouldn't," I whisper.

"So why are you throwing this away? Why are you giving up on us?"

I cross my arms, shielding myself, my heart. "I didn't need you to save me from my insecurities, and by trying to, you've only made them worse."

"What do you want from me? Tell me and it's yours."

"All I ever wanted was you, Max."

"I'm yours. You are the only thing that matters in my world. Don't you see that?"

I shake my head. "I don't."

"Take some time. Think about it. Don't throw this away."

I wish I could believe he wanted me for the right reasons. "It's too late. Knowing the truth hurts too much."

"Only because you don't see yourself the way I see you."

"Please…" I take a step back.

I can't risk him changing my mind. And I love him too much to explain why I don't believe him. I love him too much to see the hurt on his face when I tell him what I understand now: that, whether he knows it consciously or not, he wants my money more than he wants me. Needs it more than he needs me. And I love him too much not to make sure he gets at least some of what he needs.

"Consider my request. Consider keeping this a secret until after you get the grant."

"No. Either you're mine or you're not." His voice is a low rumble. "None of this pretend bullshit."

A humorless puff of laughter escapes my lips. "The irony." Then I walk out the door before the last of my willpower dissolves completely.

NATE

Fans mourn the death of actor, producer, Dritts Crane.

The tequila warms my throat and belly as I glare at the screen and the picture of my father with his wife and three youngest children.

My phone buzzes with a text alert.

> *Janelle: Can you believe this bullshit? Like he was the world's best father or something.*

Looks like my sweet twin sister is watching the national coverage of my father's funeral too. She doesn't have a concert to perform in three hours, though. I, on the other hand, am going to be on Asher Logan's shit list if I don't stop drinking and start sobering up real fucking soon.

> *Nate: Turn off the TV. It's only going to piss you off. Go out with your friends or something.*
> *Janelle: I would bet money that you're no better. Probably drinking in your hotel bar and glued to the TV, just like me.*
> *Nate: Affirmative on the hotel bar. But why be*

glued to the screen when I can be glued to a
willing groupie?
Janelle: *I hate you.*
Nate: *Love you too. Turn off the TV and get*
out of the house.

Tucking my phone into my pocket, I scan the bar. Truth is, I have no interest in groupies. I'm here incognito in a hat and sunglasses, and I've done a rather fine job of avoiding them thus far. If I didn't have to perform tonight, my date with a bottle of tequila would start now.

I'm debating another drink when she walks in. Dark hair. Sunglasses. Strappy heels. Snug-fitting black dress and curves from here to California. *Damn.*

She heads straight for the bar and slides onto a stool two down from mine. "Vodka cranberry, please?"

I move toward her, taking a seat next to her as the bartender hands over the drink. "Meeting someone?"

She downs half the pink liquid in one long pull before settling it on the counter and studying the contents. "Just killing time while my sister screws her boyfriend in his suite." She doesn't sound spiteful or jealous, just matter-of-fact.

"And where's *your* boyfriend?" On the scale of lame to rock star, that line lands me closer to a pasty-faced gamer at his first Comic-Con.

She pulls off her sunglasses and studies me. Her eyes are a dark chocolate brown and her face sweeter than I expected—down to the faint freckles sprinkling the bridge of her nose. "If you're trying to pick me up, could we just skip to the hot-but-regrettable make-out session in the coatroom?"

My lips curve into a smile without my permission. It might be the first time I've smiled all week. And another first for the week? There's finally something that sounds better than another shot of tequila. I'm already imagining my hands on her curves as I taste those sweet lips. There's something about the fact that she said *make-out session* and not *fucking* that makes her even more appealing to me.

She's sweet, I realize. Sweet women are such a rare breed in LA. It's hardly something I have to worry about. But sweet means off-limits to men unwilling to part with promises and tomorrows. I can't remember the last time I kissed a sweet woman. Not worth it. And yet...

I stand and offer her my hand, but she just frowns at me like I've lost my mind. "Let's go find that coatroom," I say.

She grins—a big smile that stretches across her face and shows her white teeth. As far as smiles go, it's stunning. She's stunning without it. She doesn't need anything beyond all her long, dark hair around her shoulders and those killer curves. But that smile nearly knocks me off my feet.

"You are just that accommodating, huh?" she asks.

"I aim to please."

When she laughs—not a giggle, but a rich, deep belly laugh that carries across the room—I'm once again thinking, *Sweet*. And I'm feeling one hell of a sweet tooth coming on.

She shakes her head and offers me her hand. "I'm Hanna."

"Nathaniel," I reply. I'm not sure what makes me use my full name instead of Nate, but it's probably because I don't want this moment with this woman to have anything to do with my identity as a musician.

"Nathaniel," she repeats, as if testing the weight of it on her tongue. "You look like a Nathaniel. Honest to God, I don't know many guys who'd come on to a girl while wearing a *Star Wars* shirt."

"You should see my Incredible Hulk tattoo. It makes all the chicks swoon."

She grins again. "You're kidding me."

"I would never kid about the Incredible Hulk."

"Hmm... Prove it."

I raise a brow. "I'll show you mine if you show me yours." More laughter, and I feel like a small piece of me—one that once felt irrevocably hardened by this week from hell—warms and softens.

"What if I don't have a Hulk tattoo?" She takes another sip of her drink. She might be flirting, but she's still firmly planted at the bar, no real interest in finding that coatroom with me. *Damn.*

"That's disappointing."

"I bet. But good for you for showing your true colors. So many guys just try to be what they think women want."

"How do you know that's not what I'm doing? Haven't you seen *Big Bang Theory*? Nerds are all the rage right now."

She studies me for a beat. "Batman or Superman?"

"What's the metric? Basic coolness? Batman. Ability to kick the most ass and save humankind? Superman."

She snorts. "Best Doctor?"

Curves like that and she knows *Doctor Who*? I'm fucking toast. When she raises an eyebrow expectantly, I realize I haven't answered. "Well, I would say Peter Davison, but a more serious dork might say Sylvester McCoy."

"You're definitely not faking it." Her smile falls away and she swallows hard. "I needed this. Thanks."

"Needed what?"

She shrugs and her tongue darts out to moisten her bottom lip. "To smile. To feel…like some random guy—nerd or not— might be attracted to me."

"You find that coatroom you suggested and I promise to take the *might* right out of that thought."

She bows her head and studies her drink. Her cheeks blaze pink. So sweet. *Damn.*

My phone buzzes, and I know without looking that it's time to go meet Asher and warm up for our performance tonight. As much as I'd like to stay and flirt with this beauty, I owe too much to Asher to screw this up.

"I have to go," I say reluctantly. "Duty calls."

"Comic book convention?"

"Something like that. Have a nice night." Then I walk away because I don't have any tomorrows or promises to offer.

But damn if this sweet tooth isn't nagging at me.

MAX

We collapse onto the couch, breathing hard, sweating like fools.

"On second thought," Will grumbles, "this couch is a piece of shit and we definitely shouldn't bother moving it."

I push off the couch in question and every muscle screams. "I'll go grab the beer."

"I can't believe you sold your house," Will says.

I open up the little fridge, pull out two beers, and twist off the caps. "Grandma would understand."

He narrows his eyes at me. "You'll tell me if you need more, right? Because I can help."

"I'll make it work. I have some contingencies lined up."

Will downs half his beer in one gulp before leaning his head back into the cushions. "Next time, I'm just giving you the cash to hire movers," he mutters.

"And deprive me the view?" Cally calls from the door. "I watched you muscle that monster up those stairs. Sexiest thing I've seen all day."

"Haven't looked in a mirror, have you?" Will says. He pushes off the couch and groans. "Damn, Max. I thought I was in good shape, but now I just feel like a senior citizen."

"Come on, old man," Cally says. "I know someone who can give you a massage."

Will grins, gives his fiancée a once-over, then hesitates. "I'll meet you outside, okay?"

She nods and leaves us alone.

Will looks around the tiny studio apartment that sits above my health club. I'd been using it for storage since I bought the space a couple of years ago, but now it will be my home. For a while, at least.

"Is your mom upset about you selling the house?"

I shake my head. It was a hard choice to sell the house Grandma left me when she died, but it was the right one. Despite everything, I'm sure of that. "Mom understands."

"Are you going to tell me what's really going on with Hanna?"

I take a pull off my beer and attempt a smile, but a smile is a lie and I can't lie to my best friend. I've hardly slept, Hanna isn't returning my texts, and my life just isn't my favorite thing right now.

When I lift my head to look at Will, that big-brother concern is all over his face. "She broke up with me." I have to tell someone, and if anyone can relate to desperate, pathetic, heartbroken attempts to win back the woman you love, it's William Bailey. To think that once I didn't understand that about him.

"I didn't know. I'm sorry. I thought you were going to propose. What happened?"

I swallow around the tangled ball of emotion in my throat. "Meredith." I don't have to say any more before Will is wincing.

"What did she do?"

I shake my head. "She forwarded Hanna some texts from back in December. Pretty damning."

"You fucked around on Hanna?"

I study my beer. Really damn interesting, beer is. Much better than looking at your friend when you're telling him what a fuck-up you are. "When Hanna and I started dating, I was still hung up on Meredith. You know what a screwed-up past we have. And the first few times I went out with Hanna, I wasn't really interested. I didn't *see* her, you know? She was just that cute girl who'd always had a thing for me. I thought I'd give her a self-esteem boost."

William's breath draws in with a sharp hiss.

"I know. It's bad, but it didn't seem so terrible at the time. I figured we'd go on a few dates and she'd realize I wasn't what she built me up to be in her mind. Then we'd go our separate ways."

"But that's not what happened," Will says.

"No." I shake my head and lift my gaze to the ceiling. "I fell so hard for her. I mean, it's like she looked at me and saw this amazing man, and suddenly I wanted to *be* that guy. I wanted to be better. To earn it. Does that make sense?"

"Been there," Will whispers. "I get it."

I blow out a long breath. "So I'd gone on a couple of dates with Hanna when Meredith talked me into coming over to see her. At that point, I still thought nothing would come of me and Hanna. I got over there, and as soon as Meredith and I started messing around, all I could think about was Hanna. I kissed Meredith and wondered what it'd be like to kiss Hanna. I got out of there, but…now Hanna knows. She knows I asked her out for all the wrong reasons, and she knows I went to Meredith that night. I hurt her."

"Shit. So it's over?"

I nod. "Yeah. But she's so fucking sweet she swore me to secrecy about the breakup. She wants her mom to help me get that grant for the gym, and she's afraid I won't get it if her mom knows we broke up."

"You're going to stand for that? Some fake relationship just so you can get some grant money?"

"We both know this isn't about the money." I lock my eyes with his. "If you thought you'd lost Cally, wouldn't you carry on in a charade of a relationship if it meant you got more time with her? If you thought it might mean a chance to win her back?"

Will exhales heavily and nods. "Fuck. Yeah. I would." He

drags a hand through his hair. "If Meredith sent Hanna those texts, you can count on her being a problem. Watch out."

"I know."

"You'll let me know if I can help?"

I grimace. "Seriously? Your fiancée is outside that door, ready to take you home and get you naked, and you're still standing here trying to get me to take your money?"

Will grins. "Good point. See you later. I'm sorry about Hanna, but hang in there. She'll come around."

I pretend hearing her name doesn't make me want to double over. I follow him to the door, shutting it behind him. When I'm left alone in the silence, I sink to the floor and cradle my head in my hands.

Because this is my life now. Alone in this shit excuse for an apartment, up to my eyeballs in debt and secrets, and in love with a woman who wants nothing to do with me.

HANNA

A year ago, if someone had told me that my life would soon involve hanging out backstage with Asher "Sexy Beast" Logan right before one of his performances, I would have accused them of peeking into my fantasies. Of course, in those fantasies I would have been the one on the gorgeous rocker's arm, not my sister, Maggie. Also, in those fantasies, I was grinning and joyful, not sipping my vodka cranberry and quietly nursing a broken heart.

Asher's been touring to promote his new album, *Unbreak Me*, and though his fifty-show tour at small colleges across the US is small beans compared to the tours he used to do with Infinite Grey, he's still on the road more often than he's at home, and that's hard on Maggie.

So I agreed to drive the four hours to the tiny liberal arts school outside of St. Louis so we could see Asher perform. Because that's what I do. I make decisions that make people happy. Regardless of what I might need myself.

"Chin up, buttercup," Maggie says. "I want to introduce you to Nate Crane."

I lift my head and suddenly I'm sucking in air because my eyes are connected with the man who flirted with me earlier.

He'd had a hat and sunglasses on in the bar, and I hadn't recognized him, but this time his identity is clear.

"Hanna, this is Nate Crane. Nate, this is Hanna, my sister."

His eyes sweep over me the way a guy's eyes are supposed to sweep over a girl. The way Asher's eyes sweep over Maggie every time she enters a room. The way William's eyes sweep over Cally when he doesn't think she's looking. It sends a little buzz through me that's not quite a chill but not quite electric either. Just a nice, warm shimmy of sensation that starts at my core and radiates out through my limbs.

Then I check behind me because I'm sure I'm mistaken. He was just playing around at the bar, right? I mean, guys don't look at me like that. They look at my sisters like that; they look at my best friends like that.

"Maggie never told me her sister was so gorgeous," Nate says, putting an end to any debate over his attraction to me.

My cheeks warm with a flush I can feel all the way from my chest to my hairline.

"Maggie, I did tell you I have a thing for sweet girls who blush, didn't I? Is she my birthday present? I'd say you shouldn't have, but I'd be lying." He says all this without taking his eyes off me. His gaze drifts over me again, slower this time, lingering at my waist, my hips, my feet in strappy, heeled sandals. "I was a good boy this year. I deserve her."

Maggie thumps him in the chest with the back of her hand. "She's a woman, not some trinket or object that can be given."

"Oh," he says, his voice so low I can barely make it out, "I noticed she's a woman."

"We met earlier," I say quickly. "In the bar. He's just teasing."

Maggie huffs. "Deserve or not, you can't have her. Hanna has a boyfriend."

Oh, no. No, Hanna doesn't. But I didn't tell Maggie about Max. It hurt too much to share what I'd learned. I'm too proud to share it. And if I want to keep our split a secret, I couldn't really tell her if I wanted to. I can't risk telling anyone.

Nate takes my hand, clearly undeterred by the mention of competition. "Tell me she's lying. Please? It's my birthday tomorrow."

"And you wanted me to jump out of a cake for you?" I retort, but I let him play with my fingers and try to keep my breathing steady. His touch brings back something I didn't think anyone but Max could make me feel.

"I wouldn't complain."

I'm fresh out of spunk, and stare stupidly. Nate Crane is six feet some-odd inches of deliciously tatted, freshly showered rocker. In ripped-up jeans and a *Star Wars* tee, he exudes a geekiness that's only amplified by the tattoos peeking out from under the sleeves. The rest of him is essentially a catalogue of every woman's fantasy. Broad shoulders, narrow hips, shaggy, dark hair still wet from his shower and curling slightly at the ends. Those intense eyes that seem to be smiling at me as he follows the lines of my palm with his calloused fingertips. He hadn't really been on my radar until this year, when he started performing with Asher at a lot of his tour stops. They're old friends, apparently.

"You didn't tell me you were a rock star," I murmur.

"You didn't tell me you have a boyfriend," he counters.

"Come on, Crane," Asher calls. "It's time."

Maggie drags me back to the dressing room, shoves me toward the bar, and wraps herself around Asher. I'm not sure I'm up for watching them grope each other, but I don't want to rush them either.

The concert was great. No, it was effing amazing. Standing on the side of the stage while watching Nate and Asher perform was the experience of a lifetime.

I'm glad I didn't let my broken heart keep me at home.

I pour myself a vodka cranberry, deciding that, if she and Asher aren't unglued by the time I'm done with this, I'll get my own cab back to the hotel.

When I look up from my drink, Nate Crane is sauntering

toward me. He takes my fingertips, lifts them to his lips, and then actually kisses the back of my hand. Who does that? And who the hell knew the gesture could be so sexy?

He's in no hurry to release me, and I'm in no hurry to ask him to.

"Did you watch the show?" he asks.

"I did."

"So?"

"So what?" I smile.

He looks almost insecure, like he's seeking approval for something the world has applauded him for a thousand times over.

"What was your favorite song?"

"I really love 'Unbreak Me.'" I have to bite back my smile when I name one of Asher's songs and not one of Nate's. The truth is that the song that rocked my world, the one that had me sitting at the side of the stage, my jaw slack, and chills racing up my arms, was Nate's song "Lost in Me." Tonight wasn't the first time I've heard it. It's a hit, and they play it on the radio all the time—almost as often as "Unbreak Me"—but tonight was the first time I've heard it live. Tonight was the first time I watched Nate's face as he sang the words, the pain ripping across his features like the lyrics weren't words but blades digging into his skin.

"I also really liked 'Unforgiven,'" I say, naming another of Asher's songs.

Nate narrows his eyes. "If you don't want to talk to me, you can just say so."

I shrug. "If you want me to stroke your ego, you can just say so."

His lips curl in amusement, and he steps closer. "My ego could use a good stroking, now that you mention it. But not by just anyone."

"Who do you have in mind?"

He makes a sound that's somewhere between a groan and a moan and drops his gaze to the little hint of cleavage revealed above the neckline of my dress. I'm not the kind of girl who likes to show a lot of cleavage, but it's kind of hard to avoid in anything that doesn't accommodate an undershirt, and this black dress definitely doesn't accommodate anything.

Nate lifts his eyes back to mine and sends a thrill rushing through me. Hot eyes. Hungry. I'm experienced enough to know those are the eyes of a man who has sex on the brain. Sex with me.

"You really have a boyfriend?"

I shift awkwardly. "Hard to believe?"

"Hard to believe he'd not want to be as close to you as possible when you're dressed like that."

My eyes seek out Maggie, but she's in the corner straddling Asher's lap and definitely not paying me any mind.

Saying the words out loud—saying that Max and I broke up—makes it too real, and I'm not ready for that. When I bought the dress to wear tonight, I thought Max would be by my side. I wouldn't have had the courage to buy it at all if I hadn't seen the heat in his eyes as I stepped out of the dressing room. That had been real, hadn't it? And the way he responded when I touched him? Can guys fake that?

"Here..." Nate leads me over to the bar. He takes my drink from my hand and dumps it in the sink. After rinsing my glass tumbler, he fills it halfway with clear liquid.

"What's that?"

"Tequila *blanco*. The good stuff."

"You trying to get me drunk?" Not that I'd mind. A drunken night with Nate Crane? I could go for that. Especially after the week I had.

"It's for me," he grumbles. He shoots back the alcohol in two long swallows, watching me the whole time. When he puts the glass back on the counter, he says, "My consolation prize, since I don't get to spend my night seducing you."

"Why not?"

Our eyes lock, and I'm not sure who's more shocked, him or me. I wrap my fingers around the glass, resting my hand over his for a moment before I pull it away. Something pulses between us, electric and hungry.

After grabbing the tequila, I add a generous shot to the glass. Not as much as he had, but enough to take away my worries for a bit when the heat hits my veins.

"Lime?" he asks.

I nod, and he grabs a couple of wedges from the little glass at the back of the bar.

He's watching my every move like I'm the sexiest thing he's ever seen. Like I'm some sort of erotic film he can't look away from.

"We called these snakebites when I was in high school," I say. "We'd do them at parties. What do you call them?" I bring my wrist to my mouth and wet the inside of it with my tongue.

"Sexy." His voice is a low rumble. "But with your mouth, I might need to modify that name."

Raising a brow in question, I grab the salt and sprinkle it on my wrist. We used to do these as body shots. In fact, I remember Will taking one off Cally before they started dating. I remember standing there and thinking, *Someday, a guy is going to look at me the way Will is looking at Cally right now.* I'm not feeling quite brave enough for body shots, though, so I carry on, knowing he's watching me.

Slowly, I lick the salt off my wrist then shoot back the tequila. It's high-quality stuff and drinks smooth, a silky rush of heat down my throat then circling in my belly.

I lift a lime to my mouth and suck.

Nate's lips part. His pupils dilate. Max used to look at me like that.

When I pull the lime from my lips, I can see Nate's pulse thrumming beneath his Adam's apple.

I need this. I've been in such a dark place this week. Since I got that text message and my world imploded. I want to get lost in this man, to spend my evening reveling in superficial attraction—even if it's completely irrational coming from a music god who dates celebrities and can have any woman he wants. But it's there, thrumming between us as clear as the notes he played on his guitar. And that is exactly what I need.

"Hanna." Maggie's voice pulls my gaze away from Nate's

for the first time in too many heartbeats. "Asher and I are heading back to the hotel. You ready?"

I look at Nate and back to my sister.

"I'll take her," Nate offers. He shifts his attention to me. "If that's okay with you. I thought we could hang."

"That's…that's fine with me."

Maggie's studying us, a crease between her brows. "I thought you said you were tired?"

Asher slides an arm around Maggie's waist and squeezes. "Let them hang. Nate's harmless." He raises a brow in Nate's direction and nods toward the door.

Nate and Asher step into the hallway, leaving me alone with Maggie and her worried eyes. "You don't have to entertain Nate just because he's putting on the charm."

"I don't," I blurt. Taking a breath, I force myself to relax. "I don't feel like I have to. I just want to chat for a while."

She chews on her lip then nods. "Okay. But call if you need anything." She squeezes me into a hug and then heads for the door.

"Maggie?" I ask, stopping her. "He's like Asher, isn't he?"

"What?"

"Nate. I mean, he's a good guy like Asher is, isn't he?"

"What are you doing, Hanna?"

"I just need someone to talk to. Someone who isn't from New Hope. Nate seems…" I drop my gaze to the floor. I'm ridiculous. I just met the guy and I'm crushing so hard that I want to turn cartwheels. I'm pretty sure this is what they call the rebound.

"He's a good guy," she finally says. "But so is Max."

I don't know if that's true anymore. But I say, "I know," and watch her leave.

NATE

Asher's scowl isn't something I've been on the receiving end of many times. "Behave yourself," he warns. "That's my future sister-in-law you've been molesting with your eyes."

"Future sister-in-law, huh? Is that an official title?"

His scowl changes to worry and he shifts uncomfortably. "Not yet. Soon. I hope. If she says yes."

"Goddammit, why didn't you say something?" I pull him into a hug and thump him on the back. "You're one lucky bastard, you know that?"

He hugs me back briefly before withdrawing. Asher's pretty much the best friend I have in this world, and I've never seen him as happy as he is with Maggie. "I know," he grumbles. "Trust me, I know. I just don't want to scare her away."

"You won't." *Damn.* Who would've guessed that Asher Logan would ever be worried about a woman turning him down? "She's mad about you and your ugly mug."

He smirks. "I'm serious about Hanna, though. Be careful with her."

I nod, looking back into the room, where Hanna and Maggie are talking. "What do you know about the boyfriend?"

Asher shrugs. "He's a local. Good guy."

"Does he make her happy?"

Asher's face hardens. "No, man. Don't play that game. Taken is taken."

I hold up my hands, palms out. "Understood."

"Really? Because Maggie will have my ass if you seduce her sister."

I nod, but I don't make any promises. There's a sadness in Hanna's eyes that I recognize too well. She's not happy. She wouldn't be staying here with me if she were.

Maggie saunters out of the room, her eyes eating up Asher. He's worried she won't say yes? She's as crazy about him as he is about her. Lucky assholes.

She slides her arm through Asher's and tilts her face toward his, her eyes bright with adoration. "Ready to go?"

"Goodnight," I call as they walk away, but they're already so absorbed in each other that they don't notice me.

When I head back into the dressing room, Hanna has gotten herself a new drink. She's leaning against the wall with her eyes closed.

All that dark hair hanging down her back, her curves hugged tight by that killer dress, and damn—those shoes. Black strappy heels that show off her red-painted toes. Black heels I've imagined digging into my back since she first cracked that smile at me.

She's the most beautiful thing I've seen in months—hell, maybe ever—and I need beautiful after the ugly week I've had.

She opens her eyes and locks them on mine. Shrugging, she looks bashful for the first time all night. "Here we are." Her eyes skim over me, and her tongue darts out to wet her bottom lip.

Oh, damn.

I've never been the kind of guy who goes after another man's woman. I've known guys who get a thrill out of that— the conquest of it, the competition. Not me. But *damn.*

"My sister is going to be so pissed that she chose some club in Indy over coming with Maggie tonight."

I grab a beer out of the mini fridge. "Why's that?"

"If she finds out she could have spent the night hanging with Nate Crane? Are you kidding me?" Her purse buzzes and her smile falls away. "I bet that's her."

"You sure it's not your boyfriend?"

Shaking her head, she draws her phone from her purse. "'What am I missing?' she's asking. See? Twin think." But she doesn't smile when she says it. Instead, it's almost like the words are a painful reminder.

"You're a *twin*?"

She slides the phone back into her purse without typing a reply. "What is it with boys and their obsession with twins?"

I grin and shake my head. "I swear, my curiosity isn't rooted in a sexual fetish."

"Good. Because I'm not that kind of twin. Not by a long shot."

"Meaning she doesn't look like you?"

"If Lizzy had been here, you would only have eyes for her."

I grunt. "Don't count on it."

"Lizzy is… She's gorgeous. The classic blond-haired, blue-eyed beauty. She has a great sense of humor, and she's always smiling. Everyone is happier when Lizzy is around." She drops her gaze to the floor.

"Not all guys are hung up on blondes."

She snorts. "Trust me. Being a brunette is the least of my worries."

"I don't understand. You think she's more fun than you or what?"

She wanders over to the couch and sinks into the cushions, crossing one leg over the other and revealing another two inches of soft thigh while doing so. With some women, that would have been a calculated move meant to draw me in, but that's not the case with her, and knowing that makes it even sexier.

She settles her drink on her knee and studies it. "I think she's more attractive than me." She gives a smile that wouldn't fool a soul and shrugs. "No big deal. Is what it is."

"There's no one measure of attractiveness," I argue. "She might be more attractive than you to one guy, but you're going to be more attractive than her to another."

"Oh boy, do I know how to have a good time or what?"

I know she wants to drop it, but I can't. Not yet. "You're just so fucking stunning. I'm a little surprised at your insecurities."

She takes a long sip of her drink. "I could use a guy like you around, boosting my ego. It might be good for me."

"Your boyfriend doesn't?"

"I—" She squeezes her eyes shut. "We broke up. But don't say anything to Maggie. I haven't told her yet. Or anyone else, for that matter. It's complicated."

I'd like to say I'm not happy to hear those words, but I've never been a saint. "Damn. I'm sorry. Do you want to talk about it?"

"No." Ice clinks against the side of her glass as she tilts it against her lips. She sips and swallows, her tongue darting out to catch a stray drop. "I don't want to talk about it and I don't want to think about it. You know what I want to do? I want to…"

She trails off, and I wait to be disappointed. Wait for her to say that she wants me to fuck her silly, that she wants a rock star to prove that her idiot boyfriend should have appreciated her more.

Hell, I'd do it. If she wanted me to take her on this couch with her boyfriend watching on FaceTime, I couldn't bring myself to say no.

And that is insane, because I'm not some horny teenager desperate to get off.

I'd do it just to watch the way her eyes flare to life when I look at her. To see her blush and that pulse thrum a little faster at the side of her neck. I'd do it just to taste her.

"I want to have fun," she finally says, her eyes lifting to connect with mine. "I've been so busy with finals and graduation, and I haven't made time to let loose."

"And how do you let loose, Hanna?"

Her smile is so bright that it damn near punches me in the gut with desire. Goodness radiates off her, and I want to crawl inside.

"I dance."

HANNA

There are very few nights of my life that I'm confident I will remember forever. But tonight makes the list. It's a dream. A fantasy.

Every date and kiss and moment with Max always felt like it was leading to something more. Something bigger. I have no illusions here. This night has nothing to do with what comes after, and maybe that's why I'm so uninhibited. A single night. A fantasy. An escape from my heartbreak.

Sweaty, teeming bodies fill the dance floor that literally pulses with the bass from the music.

I move awkwardly at first. There's only room to dance against each other.

Taking a breath for courage, I step closer. My arms loop behind his neck and my hips rock to the beat.

From under his ball cap, he keeps his gaze locked on mine and slides his hands around my waist, resting them at the small of my back.

Our eyes stay locked as we adjust our movements to the music and the fit of our bodies. He smells so good. I want to bury my face in his neck and breathe him in until I'm intoxicated.

Time trips, stutters, stalls out, and then melts away entirely. At some point, one of his hands moves from my back to my hip, and our already-connected dancing becomes something more intimate.

I've been self-conscious all my life, but dance has always been the exception. There's something magical about music that masks everything else, and ever since I was a little girl all too aware of being the chubbiest in my ballet class, nothing but music and movement mattered once I started dancing.

Couples on either side of us are making out. The man to our right has his date's leg up around his waist as she grinds against him and he sucks on her neck.

Nate's hands drift to my ass and back up, down and back up.

His touch leaves me breathless and aroused, a hot ache settling firmly between my legs and inspiring me to match the pose of the couple next to us. I can feel the length of his erection against my belly, but I want to feel it nestled between my legs.

The realization makes me draw back a bit, put an inch between our bodies.

I never intended to make it to twenty-three as a virgin, but I have. Max and I could have gone there, but I was so terrified I'd disappoint him that I told him I wasn't ready. That I wouldn't be ready until after marriage. It was a lie. My body was completely ready. And my heart belonged to Max since the beginning. Maybe it still does.

"Where's that mind of yours gone, angel?" Nate's voice is in my ear again. Then his breath is sweeping over my neck, hot and needy, as if he's asking permission to taste me there.

Suddenly, my virginity is nothing more than a heavy coat in the heat. I want to shed it, to be done with it and put it behind me—a problem I won't have to deal with anymore.

I tilt my head up and rise onto my toes until my lips are a breath from his. He drops his gaze to my mouth for a moment, but instead of kissing me, he spins me around then grasps my hips with his hands, drawing my back against his front. The movement is so smooth and easy that it almost feels choreographed.

One of his hands slides around to lie flat against my belly. The other takes a tour of my body, dipping down over the tops of my thighs, sliding up over my hips and belly, his fingertips brushing the underside of my breasts. I can't breathe. Breathing feels inconsequential when every cell in my body is homed in on the sensations his touch sends through me.

Then his hand is on my neck and my chin, my jaw, turning my head so I'm looking at him again. His lips are so close. Rising onto my toes, I part my lips. An invitation.

But instead of bringing his mouth to mine, he drops his hands and steps away from me. "Can I get you a drink?"

"A drink?" I don't want a drink. I want him. His mouth against mine. His body. That sexy voice, low and gravelly, promising pleasure in my ear.

I shake my head and push past him, through the crowd, and out the side exit into the night.

My ears seem to sigh at the silence, and my heated skin practically steams in the cool air.

Several smokers mingle a few feet from me. I catch the scent of clove cigarettes and something else. Weed, probably. Long shadows wait for me around the corner, and I slip into them, leaning my head against the building and closing my eyes.

He flirted with me all night, didn't he? Made his attraction clear? Danced with me so close my body is buzzing, my skin hungry for more of his touch. He made me believe a guy like him could find me sexy.

But maybe it was all just pretend—a guy pretending to be attracted to me to cheer me up.

The thought makes my chest ache, throb like a thumb hit by a hammer. Why couldn't I have been made more like my sisters? Maggie doesn't have to worry about her weight and she eats whatever she wants. Krystal works hard to keep her body, but even if I eat the same things she does and follow her to the gym, I barely lose a pound. And Lizzy has been thin her whole life—my twin completely unaffected by my demons.

"Hanna."

My eyes fly open to find Nate standing in front of me, hands in his pockets. His eyes are unreadable, cloaked under the shadow of the ball cap. I'm so drawn to him that, despite the sting of fresh rejection, I want to step into his arms, rub up against him like a cat.

But I'm not the kind of girl who can rub up against guys and get them to respond. I just proved that, didn't I? How did I forget?

"Hanna, talk to me."

My heart pounds in my chest, and I want to scream. "I'm sorry. I thought…" I shake my head. "I misunderstood what was between us. Don't worry. It won't happen again."

"Shit." He steps forward, his body a breath from mine. "I've wanted to get my hands on you since I saw you walk into the bar at the hotel." Taking my hands, he hooks my arms behind his neck. The gesture works with his words to fill me with one last ounce of courage.

My stomach riots with nerves, but I lift onto my toes to get my mouth to his ear. "Then why won't you kiss me?" I hardly recognize myself in the boldness. It's him. He does this to me. His eyes and touch, his words, making me so sure of his attraction to me when it's ridiculous for me to be sure of any such thing.

Before he responds, his hands settle at my hips and tighten. He sweeps up my sides and back down. When he speaks, his words come out with something resembling a growl. "I've wanted to kiss you all night long. I've hardly thought about anything else since we started dancing. But I'm not just thinking about kissing you, Hanna. If I thought we would stop with kissing, I would have done it hours ago."

I'm so distracted by the heat of his hands through my dress. I don't understand. "Then why not?"

"Because I want to do more than kiss you. I want to touch you. Explore you." He dips his head, and his hot breath glides against my neck, his lips so close but not touching. "But I promised Asher I wouldn't."

"Asher? He thinks Max and I are still together. He—"

"He would have given me the same warning if he'd known the truth. You're heartbroken and on the rebound."

"I—" *Can't deny that.*

"I shouldn't do any of things I want to do to you." His voice drops lower, and he skims his thumb over my bottom lip. "I shouldn't taste these lips." He follows the words by brushing his mouth over mine.

A shiver of pleasure rushes through me as he repeats the motion. My lips part under his, and he draws my bottom lip between his teeth and sucks gently. Then his mouth is slanting over mine and our tongues meet in a hungry, desperate kiss. For a moment, my brain holds Nate's kiss up against Max's, the hungry to the gentle, the rough to the soft. But then that slips away and I'm not thinking at all, just kissing him back and clawing at his shirt, wanting him closer and closer. I wasn't wrong. This man wants me. And I want him so badly that the want is a live, pulsing thing, consuming me until I am nothing but desire.

When he breaks the kiss, his eyes skim over my face as if memorizing it. "I shouldn't put my hand under that skirt." And as he says the words, his hand connects with the sensitive flesh of my inner thigh.

I shift, instinctively parting my thighs for his touch. A moan slips from my lips, and I lean my forehead against his chest and close my eyes. "Why not?"

"Because you're sweet, Hanna." His hand moves slowly, torturously on my thigh. "Too sweet for me to touch right here." He finds my panties with his fingertips and, with whisper-soft pressure, sweeps over my center. His breath is hot and heavy against my ear. "Too sweet for me to finger fuck just because I want to feel how wet you are. Too sweet for me to make you cry in pleasure where anyone could hear. To make you come just because I want to feel you fall apart in my arms."

There's a tug on my panties. Then the lace is magically gone and his hand is against me, the heat of his palm then his fingers finding my clit. We both gasp at the touch. I am so swollen, slick, and I want nothing more than for him to do the very things he just described.

It's crazy. I shouldn't. Not here. Maybe not at all. But my body has all but shut off the function of my brain, and the only thing that seems to matter is getting his fingers inside me.

He toys with my clit, rubbing it between two fingers, and I curl my fingers into his arms. His triceps flex under my touch, and for a blip, my brain slingshots back to Max, his thick arms, his muscled body. Max touching me, Max kissing me.

Max breaking my heart.

"Please," I say, rocking my hips toward him. "I need this." I need to turn off my mind. To forget.

Nate draws back and studies me. I see the tension in his jaw and shoulders. He's holding back.

"Please, Nate."

NATE

At the sound of my name on her lips, what little control I have left snaps. I have to feel her. I step closer, one leg outside hers, my body angled to protect her from the curious eyes of anyone coming around the corner. I run my fingers over her wet sex one more time before I slide a single finger inside her.

"Jesus," I hiss against her ear. "You're so damn tight."

My cock aches against my fly at the feel of my finger sheathed in her. She's hot and wet, and she feels so good I'm nearly blind to anything but how soon I can be inside her. I want to hail the nearest cab and take her back to my hotel, let her crawl onto my lap and grind against me on the ride. Fuck, I want to unbutton my jeans and take her against this building, squeeze that amazing ass, and drive fast and hard inside her. Make her cry out as I make her come with my cock instead of my hand.

I take a deep breath, searching for sanity. Her scent nearly undoes any attempt to calm myself down. Her lips part and her lids go heavy. Pleasure washes over her face in waves. I move slowly, sliding my finger out as I circle her clit with my thumb, then back in, curling it just enough so she shudders in my arms.

"I love how wet you are," I growl against her ear. Words turn her on, and I'm not about to fail to take advantage of that. "I love how your pussy squeezes my finger, how you respond to my touch." I draw out again, and this time, I add a second finger.

At the added pressure, she opens her mouth against my neck and bites down softly. She works at my neck as I fuck her with my fingers, her mouth licking and nipping and sucking in ways that are giving my dick all kinds of ideas.

It's with the thought of that mouth on my cock that I use my thumb to apply pressure to her clit and move my fingers inside her. "Every second you danced in my arms, I was another second closer to losing this battle with myself."

"Please," she whimpers.

"You're too sweet for a mess like me, but every second I stand here smelling your perfume, touching your perfect body, my control slips another notch. Nothing will stop me from fucking you until you're coming and crying my name."

She buries her face in my neck and shudders again, rocks her hips into my hand as her body pulses around me. Then, just as she goes limp in my arms, the sky opens and rain pours down on us.

Hanna looks up into the downpour in wonder, and I slowly remove my hand from between her legs and smooth her skirt down to cover her.

She blinks at me through the rain, her wet cheeks flushed. Her tongue darts out over her swollen lips. "I don't know if I should be embarrassed or…grateful."

I chuckle and take her hand, kissing the soft skin over her knuckles. "Come with me?" My voice hitches at the end, and my suggestion becomes more of a question. There's something about Hanna that makes me feel vulnerable.

She grins. "Let's go."

By the time we get a cab, we're drenched, but she doesn't complain about her hair or makeup like most girls would. Instead, when we slide into the back, she keeps biting back a smile. *So damn sweet.*

Taking my hand, she intertwines our fingers. My plans for using the cab ride for another ten minutes of foreplay melt away. For now, I settle for breathing in her scent.

HANNA

We enter the hotel's glitzy lobby and make our way to the elevator hand in hand, leaving a path of damp footprints on the marble tiles.

When the elevator dings and the doors slide closed, Nate presses the P button and slides his room key in the slot. A shiver shudders through me. I was okay outside, but in the air conditioning, my skin is breaking out in goose bumps.

He rubs his knuckles over my bare shoulders. "We'll get you out of these wet clothes and warmed up." He cups my face in both his hands before kissing me.

My heart pounds and I can feel it in my ears. I'm really going to do this. I'm going to lose my virginity to a guy I just met.

He pulls back, concern twisting at his beautiful face. "Are you okay?"

I nod, but before I can figure out what to say, the doors slide open to a lush suite. I step inside, afraid I'll chicken out if I don't move quickly.

He's behind me, settling his hand possessively at my waist. "Do you like it?"

"It's really nice."

The elevator chimes, and I spin around and watch the doors slide closed again.

"Hanna." He tilts my chin so I'm looking at him. "Your room is an elevator ride away. We can say goodnight any time you want."

"I…" Why can't I feel like I did outside the club? Bold. Uninhibited. Ready to throw off the chains of my virginity. Instead, I'm a live wire of nerves and hyperaware of everything. The burbling of the saltwater fish tank set into the wall, the soft hum of the air conditioner, the way Nate's eyes are searching mine.

What will he think if I back out now? What will I think?

What if I'm wrong about me and Max and we end up together again? Will I tell him about tonight? Will he resent me for it? Or will I keep it to myself and let it be the secret that sits between us our whole lives, the something keeping us from truly connecting like we once did?

Pushing my thoughts aside, I rise onto my toes to press my mouth to Nate's. He doesn't take long to respond, and the feel of his mouth over mine, his tongue sweeping inside, helps to quiet the chaos of my mind.

"Shower?" he murmurs against my mouth.

"Mmm-hmm."

"With me?"

Another shiver rushes through me, as much from nervous anticipation as from cold. "If that's okay with you."

His eyes flash. "More than okay."

Taking my hand, he leads me farther into the suite, past the living room area and into a giant bedroom. The king-sized bed is made with fresh white linens and seems as enormous and frightening as what I'm about to do.

Any nerves I feel at the sight of the bed fall away when Nate continues on, flipping the lights in the bathroom and revealing an oversized en suite with a large glassed-in shower and Jacuzzi tub.

I watch in awkward silence as he turns on three different showerheads. What am I supposed to do with myself? Am I supposed to undress or wait or…?

Worry fizzles, because before I can decide what to do, he's back and kissing me again, pressing me against the long granite countertop. He pushes one dress strap off my shoulder and tugs on the fabric until one lace-covered breast is exposed.

He groans softly. "Your bra matches your panties."

"What happened to those?"

With a boyish grin, he produces them from the pocket of his jeans. I take them and hold them up. They're ruined. Torn at both hips. And I'm not the slightest bit upset about it.

I prop my hands on my hips in a pretend pout. "Now what am I going to put on after our shower?"

"If I have my way? Not a damn thing."

Dropping his head, he puts his mouth to my breast and sucks me through the lace. The sensation is too much—the wet heat of his tongue, the rough texture of the lace, the painful pleasure of his rough mouth. I cry out, and the sound echoes against the walls.

Before I realize what he's doing with his hands, my dress falls away, puddling at my ankles and leaving me standing there in nothing but my bra and my strappy heels. He slowly drags his mouth from my breast, and my nipple puckers harder in the cool air as Nate steps back to take me in.

This is the part I hate. Men's assessing eyes on all my imperfections—the stretch marks at my breasts, the extra fat around my stomach, the cellulite on my ass and at the tops of my thighs. There's nothing sexy about any of these parts of me. And there's nothing that turns me off more than the disappointment in men's eyes when they get me naked. It wasn't like that with Max. But then again, I've never let him see me naked—not entirely. And by the time he saw me semi-nude, he was already in love with me.

Or you thought he was.

I focus on Nate and will myself to stop thinking about Max. I won't let my broken heart ruin this night. This isn't about love or men who make you feel whole. This is about sex and pleasure and—

Nate lifts his eyes back to mine, and what I see there brings my overactive brain to a screeching halt. Not disappointment. No. The heat in his eyes is undeniable. And it's for me.

"You couldn't be more perfect, Hanna."

I look down, confused. Has someone else's body magically replaced mine, because…? It's true that I've toned up a bit in these last months while working out with Max, lost maybe ten pounds, but I still don't have anything near the bodies my sisters have. I'm still the size-sixteen embarrassment I've been since adolescence.

Nate tilts my chin up with his thumb. He cocks his head as he studies me. "You really don't know, do you? Our conversation earlier wasn't just an act. You have no idea how gorgeous you are."

I want to shrug it off, but he's looking at me so intently, I know he expects an answer. "I've never been with a guy who was…into big girls."

He grunts. "Is that what you think this is? Some sort of fetish?"

I shrug and drop my gaze to his throat.

"Hanna, I'm not 'into big girls,' as you put it. I like women. Beautiful women. Women who have curves." He steps forward and twists the front clasp on my bra until it releases. The straps slide off my shoulders, and the bra falls to the floor. "I like breasts," he murmurs, cupping mine in his hands and brushing his thumbs over my nipples.

I shudder at his touch, that knot of pleasure tightening between my legs.

He steps closer, and my breasts press against his chest. He slides his hands around my back and down until they're cupping my butt. "And I'm not ashamed to say, I'm a bit of an ass man." He squeezes. "Fabulous to look at and something to fill my hands when I'm fucking you from behind."

My breath catches at the image. *Fucking me from behind.* No doubt he wouldn't be talking to me like that if he had any idea how inexperienced I am.

"Nate—"

The sight of him dropping to his knees cuts me off. "And this." He presses his mouth against the curve of my belly. "I've been with women who have flat stomachs and women who are soft here. Beauty comes in different shapes, colors, and sizes. There's no cookie cutter for sexy."

At the gentle pressure on the inside of my thighs, I widen my stance instinctively, bracing myself on the counter as the most intimate part of me is exposed to him. I shudder as he takes two fingers and traces some invisible line from just below my pubic bone to my center.

"This," he murmurs. He lifts his gaze to mine and touches his fingers to his lips for a moment. "How turned on you get when I touch you? When I talk to you? It's is the sexiest fucking thing in world."

He kisses each hipbone. Then his mouth is on me, open and hungry, his tongue sweeping over my clit. He slides a finger inside me, and my legs tremble. I don't think I can stand here while his mouth is down there. My legs will give out.

But then he's standing and hoisting me onto the cold counter, and before I know what he means to do, he's dropping to his knees again.

"I've been fantasizing about getting you naked down to your shoes since I first spotted you tonight. Your legs in those heels..." He strokes the insides of my thighs, and my back arches instinctively, my hips rising off the counter and toward the hot breath of his mouth. His eyes flick up to meet mine for two heartbeats, and then he places my ankles over his shoulders.

"What are you—"

But then I get it because his face is buried between my legs and his hands are under my hips. He licks me—right up my center—and my whole body shudders.

My hips buck toward his face. I try to stop myself, embarrassed at my own lack of control, but he holds me tight, his fingers digging into my hips.

"Don't you dare hold back." His words are muffled, but I hear him. I feel him.

He nuzzles my clit with his nose while sliding his tongue inside me, and I'm lost. My hips jerk and rock, and all that heat and tongue and pressure down there feels so good that everything else slips away.

I lean back on my hands because it brings me closer to him, closer to the strokes of his tongue and the pleasure of his kiss. By the time he slips a finger inside me, I'm already halfway gone, and his lips wrap around my clit and send me over the edge.

When Nate stands, he's breathing heavily and his eyes are all over me. I scramble to right myself, but he steps between my legs before I can hop off the counter. He cups my face in his hands and kisses me—long and slow and steady. My disintegrated nerve endings fire to life again, one by one.

If I had any idea that letting a guy kiss me between my legs would feel like that, I might have gotten over my insecurities and let Max do it when he asked. *"You're always making me feel so good, Hanna. Let me return the favor. I'm dying to kiss you there."*

I kiss Nate harder and thread my fingers into his hair as if I need to hold on to him—to the here and the now—to keep the memories at bay.

Between kisses, I find the hem of his shirt and pull it over his head. The sight of him takes my breath away. He's not as built as Max, but he's still gorgeous—a date tattooed above his right pec, the glinting blade of a sword tattooed up his left side, the Hulk tattoo he mentioned in the bar on his shoulder. I promise myself I'll explore them all later.

My hands drop to the waistband of his jeans. I unbutton them and shove them down his thighs. I slide my hand inside his boxer briefs and wrap my fingers around him. He draws in his breath in a hiss that shoots something electric through my veins and emboldens me. I'm insecure about my body, but I know I'm good at this.

He sweeps his thumb over my shoulder. "You're cold."

"I'm fine," I promise, but he sheds his briefs and leads me into the shower.

The water rains down on us as he draws me against him, my back against his front. He lathers soap between his hands and slowly washes my body. His fingers knead small circles down my belly, slip between my legs, and trail back up. When his hands cup my breasts, I close my eyes and let him toy with my nipples.

"I could do this all day," he murmurs against my ear. "I love the way you respond when I touch you."

As I turn in his arms, his cock juts out between us, long and thick. I drop to my knees under the spray.

"Hanna." He reaches for me.

Before he can say anything else, I draw my tongue up the underside of him, from root to tip. I focus on the salty taste, the way he mutters "Jesus" and slides his hands into my hair, the memory of him touching me outside the bar, moving his fingers inside me, and making me come with people milling around the corner not ten feet away, the still-tender skin of my inner thighs marked by his stubble. It all compounds and gets my mind back where it belongs—on this man, this night, and the way he makes me feel.

I wrap my hands around him and squeeze, stroke, squeeze, stroke. Then I part my lips and taste the head of his cock, licking it, and then opening to take more of him in.

He leans back against the tile and tugs lightly at my hair. "Fuck, angel, I could come just looking at your lips stretched over my dick like that."

His words tie a knot of pleasure between my legs, and I suck him deeper. He's a big guy, and I use my hand to stroke the part of him I can't take. With my other hand, I gently cup his balls, and a long, pained groan rips from his chest.

All my life, I've had this need to please others, to do for them instead of myself. It's a characteristic I've cursed many times, but it made me damn good at this. Right now, being good at bringing Nate pleasure is the only thing that matters. I love the feel of his hands tightening in my hair when I pull him deep, love the taste of him on my tongue, the way his hips buck forward and pull back when I suck. He's struggling to hold on to his control, and that knowledge only makes me hungrier for him, for this, for what will come after.

"Hanna." His voice is rough, a painful scrape of control against pleasure. "Get up here, baby. I'm—"

I relax my throat and drop my hand, taking nearly all of him, farther than I thought I could. But I'm so turned on the discomfort barely registers. I add pressure to his balls, massaging them until he loses hold of that control and lets his hips rock toward my face. The movement pushes him deeper, and I swallow, knowing that the pressure will squeeze him. His hips jerk again, and I'm so turned on by what I'm doing that I moan, and the vibration of my lips and mouth pushes him over the edge. I swallow as he comes in my throat, his hand fisting almost painfully in my hair.

I withdraw slowly, and he draws me up until I'm standing, my needy and trembling body leaning into him.

He loosens his grip on my hair as he kisses me, long and thorough and a little rough. He bites my lip before pulling back. "I didn't think you could taste any better than you did." He presses another kiss to my mouth and growls. "But tasting myself on you... Jesus, Hanna, there's nothing as sexy as that."

"Hmm, I like the way you taste."

It's my turn to take the soap. To let my fingers explore his body while I clean every inch of him. He watches me through thick, dark lashes as I lather his shoulders, his pecs, the flat of his stomach.

I'm struck by the intimacy of this act—of how vulnerable we are when bathing. It's more intimate than what he did to me on the vanity. And here I am, sharing it with a man I just met. Showing him and giving him more than I ever gave Max. Because there's a security in knowing that this is just one night. If Nate doesn't like my body, or if he's disappointed that I can't do some yoga-inspired position in bed, I don't lose anything.

How many times did Max invite me to shower with him? I always declined because I passed on anything that involved getting nude with Max. I didn't want him to see my painfully imperfect body. I was afraid he'd realize I wasn't as beautiful as he thought.

I've circled around Nate and begun washing his back when he turns to me, takes away the soap, and rinses us both.

"I need more, angel," he murmurs.

I'm not sure what he means, but when he takes my hand and leads me out of the shower, I follow him. He dries me with a soft towel and pulls me into the bedroom.

My steps stutter just inside the door.

He turns to me, and my stomach clenches. He's hard again. Already. This knowledge has me equal parts elated and terrified. Am I really going to go through with this?

He's studying me, worry etching his features. God, he's gorgeous. I'd be foolish not to do this. Wouldn't I?

NATE

I don't know what happened between the bathroom and the bedroom, but Hanna looks terrified. Am I rushing this? Rushing her?

"What's going on in that head of yours?"

"Nothing. I mean…nothing bad. I mean…we can do this. It's okay."

Oh, hell. She's spooked. Her dark hair frames her face in long, wet waves that fall past her shoulders and nearly cover her breasts. She's so fucking gorgeous. Wet, nude. Like Aphrodite risen from the sea foam.

I cup her face with one hand and trace her lips with my thumb. She closes her eyes at the touch, and I can see some of the tension leak out of her. "Do you want me to take you back to your room?"

"You… I mean, I thought we were going to…" She motions toward the bed.

I could lead her there, touch her until whatever's got her tied in knots loosens. "Are you thinking about him? The ex?"

"No!" Her eyes widen and lock with mine. "I promise that's not what's wrong."

I nod. "So there is something wrong."

She frowns and worries her lip between her teeth for a solid thirty seconds before she speaks. "It's just…I've never done this before."

My shoulders sag in relief. The whole one-night stand thing is freaking her out. "I didn't think you had."

Her jaw drops. "You…knew?"

"That you aren't the kind of girl to have a one-night stand?"

"Oh. No. Not that."

"You have had one-night stands before?" I don't like the idea of that, though it's a little hypocritical of me to feel that way.

"No. I haven't. I've—" She rolls her eyes and takes a deep breath. "I guess I should just spit it out."

"Please?"

"I've never done this before." She waves to the bed again.

She looks such the perfect combination of sweet and sexy standing there, nude with her thick, dark hair falling around her shoulders, her hands twisting in front of her. But I'm so hungry to have my hands on her again that my brain is struggling to make sense of her words.

"Done what exactly?"

"Sex."

"Sex?"

"I'm a virgin."

HANNA

Nate drags a hand through his hair and lets out a long breath. "A virgin? Like…born again something?"

"Not born again. Just a virgin." This is a really mortifying conversation to have under any circumstances, but it's even more mortifying to have it while standing here buck naked. "Do you have a T-shirt I could throw on or something?"

He drops his hands to his sides and his eyes to his own naked body as if just remembering we don't have clothes on. "Um. Sure." He grabs something from his drawer and crosses to me. He's barely a breath away when he looks down at me and shakes his head. "I really hate to cover up all that gorgeous skin."

"Sorry." I snatch the shirt from his hand and yank it on over my head. It's soft blue cotton with a Superman insignia on the chest that stretches across my breasts. Though too snug at the chest, it falls to the tops of my thighs and makes me feel less exposed.

Nate stares at me for minute, running his gaze over me in his T-shirt, my bare legs down to my painted toenails. Finally, he grabs a pair of athletic shorts from his drawer and pulls them on, leaving his chest bare. Despite the awkwardness that hangs around us like a thick fog, and despite the fact that I'm pretty sure my confession put the brakes on tonight's sexy times, I want to lick him. Right between his toned pecs and over his hard abs. I want to lick those numbers above his left pec and the sword blade up his side.

A moan slips from my lips as I imagine what I'm likely going to be missing out on tonight. Hours in bed with Nate. Exploring his body while he explores mine. His face between my legs, his hands on my breasts…

"Can I just take back what I said just now?" I ask.

"About being a virgin?"

"Yeah. I'd like to rescind that statement."

He looks so hopeful, his dark eyes softening as they connect with mine. "Because it's not true?"

"Unfortunately, it's true. I want to take it back because it changed things between us."

He tucks my hair behind my ears. "I'm sorry, Hanna. I just…" He shakes his head. "Food. We need food."

"What?"

"Cooking relaxes me, so I only stay in suites equipped with full kitchens if I can help it." His bashful grin melts something inside of me. "Will you let me cook for you?"

Not where I expect this night to go, but… "Sure."

I follow him to the kitchen, a small but lush space with a single-burner gas stove, granite countertops, and a stainless-steel fridge. I wonder what "cooking" means to a celebrity like Nate Crane. More than throwing a pizza in the oven, sure, but can he really cook? To me, cooking is about sauces and tender cuts of meat paired with fresh, crisp vegetables. I love cooking in a way my mother could never understand. And even better than cooking—baking. The chemistry of flour and sugar and the perfect hints of flavors melting on the tongue. I was always trying to spend more time in the kitchen, and she was always trying to chase me out of it.

Nate washes his hands in the sink then pulls a sauté pan from the cupboard and sets it on the cold stove. He starts removing items from the refrigerator and placing them on the butcher block—fresh asparagus, bell peppers, thin-sliced chicken breast, strawberries, and heavy whipping cream.

As he starts washing, dicing, and chopping, the surprise must show on my face, because he winks at me. "Did you expect Pop-Tarts?"

I grin. "Maybe. Can I help?"

"You're the company. Sit and let me take care of you. Here…" He grabs a bottle of wine from the fridge and pours me a glass. Pinot gris. "Drink."

I pull a stool up next to his butcher block and settle in to watch him work. He has great hands. Nate chopping vegetables, flouring chicken, and drizzling oil in the pan to heat is far sexier than I would have imagined. Then again, it's a beautiful man cooking. What's not to love?

"Where'd you learn to cook?" I ask.

His lips quirk in a lopsided grin. "Here and there. Mom was always off on some movie set, and my dad, well…" He shakes his head. "I was close to our housekeeper. She let me help her in the kitchen, taught me to cook."

"Your mom's an actress?"

He nods. "Film and TV. Family curse, and I count my blessings to have escaped it."

"Where was your dad?"

He shrugs. "Busy." He exhales, and his shoulders drop as if he released his frustrations with the breath. "So I learned to cook young, and I liked it. I started watching cooking shows and shit. Just getting ideas."

He places the flour-dredged chicken into the sizzling oil and gets to work washing strawberries and removing their stems.

"I love cooking," I confess. "Well, baking, really. I always dreamed of opening my own bakery. I love making my friends cakes for special occasions, and I can just picture a little bakery on the main strip at home."

He lifts his head and grins at me. "Why can I imagine you as a child, baking cookies with your mom?"

"Hardly." I sigh and roll back my shoulders. "No, Mom

doesn't bake. In fact, she pretty much hates any food that tastes good. And it always seemed like the more my mom tried to teach me that food was the enemy, the more I loved it."

"Food is life." He grabs a freshly rinsed strawberry from the bowl and offers it to me.

I open my mouth, and he places it between my lips for a bite. Sweetness explodes on my tongue, and I close my eyes.

"Food and sex," he murmurs. "I never understood why people have to demonize something meant to be enjoyed."

NATE

I want her. *Fuck*, do I want her. I watch pleasure flash across her face as she chews, and my mind instantly conjures an image of her enjoying a different kind of pleasure. It was too dark outside the club, and I wanted to see more. I want to know how she looks when she comes. I could hardly give my attention to her face while mine was buried between her legs. And then her confession pretty much spoiled the rest of my plans.

I can't take her virginity, and if I would have known earlier…

No, I can't lie to myself and say that I'd have resisted. Asher warned me off and I still didn't stay away. I needed her tonight. Needed to escape in her, and she proved to be so much better an escape than tequila.

Her eyes stay on me as I work. I'm so hard and so uninterested in this food. All that interests me is being inside her. I can only imagine how good she'd feel. As fucking tight as she was around my fingers, as much as she responded to my touch, she's a fucking fantasy. And I'd watch that sweetness in her eyes turn to heat as I slowly stretched her out.

I have to get my head together. If I study her lips for

another minute, I'm either going to lose my mind or kiss her, and we both know it wouldn't end with a kiss. I add wine and cream over the chicken and whisk it into a sauce before adding the asparagus to the pan. When it's all ready, I place it on small plates that I take to the suite's dining table.

Hanna hops off the stool and walks over to join me, the shirt shifting with every step to reveal another inch of her thighs before hiding it again.

She heads to the chair opposite me, and I say, "Nuh-uh. Come here, gorgeous." I drag the chair between us a little closer to mine.

She grins as she sits. "Okay. If you don't bite."

"I never made any such promise."

"Oh. Well, in that case." She scoots the chair another inch closer and traces the numbers tattooed on my chest. "What are these?"

"My son's birthday."

Her lips part in surprise, and she studies the numbers again. "You have a son?"

I nod and swallow the thick knot in my throat. I don't tell many women about my son. Not because he's a secret, but because he's none of their business. Telling Hanna about him feels like cutting myself open and exposing my soul for her inspection.

"He's an amazing little kid. Wicked smart, clever, great sense of humor if you aren't too mature to laugh about bodily functions."

She grins. "What's his name?"

"Collin."

"And have you introduced him to *Star Wars* yet?" she asks, her face a mask of seriousness.

"Not yet," I murmur. "I will when he's ready."

Her smile lights up her face and her laughter fills the room.

I'm so done for. "Wanna talk about the boyfriend who's not really a boyfriend anymore?" It's not my style to ask about old boyfriends, but I need to get my mind off the bed waiting for us in the next room and the sounds she made when I used my tongue between her legs.

Frowning, she pokes at her food, so I scoop up a bite on my fork and offer it to her. She parts her lips and closes them over the tines so slowly that my brain slingshots right back to the shower, to Hanna on her knees, her lips stretched around my cock.

"You are such a good cook," she says on a moan. She chews slowly, and when she swallows, she sighs and shrugs. "I don't want to talk about Max. He screwed up, but he's not a bad guy. In fact..." She pokes at her food again.

"I promise it was dead before I put it in the pan." That earns me a smile. I love washing the sadness from her face. More than I should.

"Maggie took Asher home with her the first night they met." She keeps her eyes on the table and smiles softly. "She stripped and told him she wanted him."

"Seems like that worked out for them."

She nods. "But I'm not like that. Maggie knows men want her. *Knows* it. I've never had that kind of confidence, and for months, I've been holding back with Max and..."

"He broke up with you because you wouldn't have sex with him?"

Her head snaps up and her eyes meet mine. "No. I broke up with him."

I raise a brow. "And here I thought he broke your heart."

"That's why I had to break up with him," she whispers. Then her cheeks flush and she shakes her head. "I am officially the worst date. How many rules have I broken? The V-word—that was a bad call. Then talking about my boyfriend? Crying into my dinner?"

"I'm sorry I freaked about the virgin thing." I clear my throat. This isn't exactly a conversation I've had to have before. "Your first time is kind of a big deal. Add that to the fact that you just broke up with your boyfriend and I'd be a total asshole to sleep with you now."

"I had to follow the *sweet* rocker back to his hotel room, huh?"

HANNA

"I'm not sweet," Nate says, but even as he says it, he offers me another bite from his fork.

I take it, watching his eyes flare hot as I chew. It's almost like everything I do is sexual to him, and I love that feeling.

"I'm a fucking no-good bastard. That's why we have to put on the brakes. Don't let the dorky shit fool you. I'm that guy who isn't going to call you tomorrow. I'm that guy who isn't going to return your texts. I'm that guy who's going to fuck you silly and then act like it never happened. That's who I am. That's how I live."

"I have trouble believing that."

"Believe it, sweetheart. Damn it." He drops his fork, takes a handful of my hair, and twirls his fingers in it. "I knew you were too sweet for me."

I run my fingertips over the stubble on his jaw. How would I feel if I slept with him tonight and he acted like it never happened? My body is so full of hormones and longing right now that it doesn't seem like it matters.

"I didn't come here looking for forever. I came here looking for tonight."

"And tomorrow I'm just going to be this mistake you made

once. Normally that wouldn't bother me, but you're special."

"I'm not worried about tomorrow. Worrying about tomorrow never got me anywhere. The only thing that matters is here and now."

I scoot forward on my chair and kiss him tentatively. I don't know if he wants to touch me anymore. I don't know if I should stay back, but I want to kiss him. I want him to kiss me, rub his scruffy cheeks against my neck before he bites it.

His hand loosens in my hair and he kisses me back gently, softer than he's kissed me all night. I miss the frantic pace of our earlier kisses. I miss the rough way he tugged at my hair. But I'll take this.

As if reading my mind, he pulls back and studies me. "I was too rough with you earlier. Jesus. I—"

I cut him off with a finger to his lips. "I liked it. Especially the part where you kind of pulled my hair while you were coming in my throat."

He groans. "You're killing me, Hanna. You're this angel who could tempt a saint, and I'm no saint."

"Maybe you're right," I say, tracing the blade tattoo on his side. "Maybe it's not a good idea for us to have sex tonight."

"I know I'm right. And I'm showing an uncharacteristic amount of restraint, so I should probably take you back to your room before that fades."

His biceps flex under my fingers as I move to trace the Hulk tattoo on his left arm. God, he's like this impossible combination of sexy-cool rocker and nerd.

"You weren't lying about the tattoo."

He raises a brow. "You won't like me when I'm angry."

I snort. "You're a pussy cat."

He stiffens. "Don't try to pretend I'm something I'm not."

With a deep breath, I remind myself of the look in his eyes after he surveyed my nude body. To this man, I'm as good as any of my gorgeous sisters. Better, maybe, though I'll never understand why. It's only with that in mind that I can muster the courage to slide off my chair and onto his lap. I straddle him. I'm so close that the stiff ridge of his dick presses between my thighs, only the soft cotton of his sleep shorts between us.

"So maybe we shouldn't have sex, but I was having an awfully good time doing all the not-exactly-sex stuff, and I think you were too."

"You *think*?"

"I *know*," I whisper. "Because I can still taste the evidence."

"Hanna." There's a warning in his voice that neither of us wants to listen to.

"I could get turned on by the sound of your voice alone." I lick my lips and slip my hand into his shorts, finding the slick head of his cock with my fingertips.

"Fuck." His hips jerk, and then my fingers are sliding around him.

I look to the clock on the wall. Three in the morning, and I'm not the slightest bit tired. He's already hard, but I feel the blood pumping into his dick, making him even harder, thicker, as I stroke.

"Is it really your birthday?"

He's watching me with heavy-lidded eyes as I work him over with my hand. "Yes."

"And what if I told you I wanted to stay? What if I told you I wanted a second round of what we did in the bathroom?" My old insecurities sneak into my voice on the last question. I would elaborate, would tell him how turned on I am by the idea of his mouth between my legs, but I've already stretched my bravery to its limits.

"I won't take your virginity," he warns.

"I'm not asking you to." My heart pounds in my throat as his eyes roam over my face, and I kiss him before he talks himself out of it.

I sweep my lips over his and nip at his bottom lip. Slowly, his mouth opens over mine, and then he's kissing me and his fingers curl into my hips, and I know the night's just begun.

NATE

I haven't slept all night with a woman next to me since before my son was born, yet here I am, holding her like I'm some closet romantic who doesn't plan to send her on her way in a couple of hours. I loved every fucking minute of sleeping with her in my arms. I love how she reached for me in her sleep, how she rubbed her ass against my cock as if trying to wiggle a puzzle piece into place. And maybe a puzzle is the right analogy, because her body fits so damn perfectly against mine that I feel like something's missing when she rolls away.

She's on her back now, a hand reaching out, fingers resting on my bicep as if she's afraid I might escape. The women I take to my bed tend to react that way, but I know it has little to do with my mad bedroom skills. For them, it's about status, a notch in their bedpost of celebrities. What's it about for Hanna?

The air conditioner cycles on, parting the curtains and bathing her in morning light that reminds me I should be urging her out of my bed. Only I don't want her to go anywhere. I'm too enthralled by the dark smudge of her lashes against her cheeks and the soft parting of her full lips. She has these faint freckles across the bridge of her nose, another detail in this study in contrasts—the sweet, insecure virgin who doesn't understand her own appeal and the wanton goddess who sucked me so hard and pulled my dick so deep she's no doubt ruined me for all other blowjobs. And the way she responds when I touch her...

Hanna's a virgin, but she was made for sex. Damn, how I envy the man who will get to introduce her to that pleasure. Will it be the ex? Max?

Something flames in my gut at the thought, but I ignore the flare of jealousy. She still loves him. I'm nothing more than the rebound guy, and I should be glad for that because I can't offer her more than this.

"Mmm," she moans, her eyes fluttering open and closed again as if she can't quite convince them to greet the day. "What are you looking at?"

"You."

She pats her hair before tugging the sheet up to cover her bare breasts. "Not much to look at before coffee. I'm probably a mess."

"A beautiful mess," I growl, tugging the sheet back down. "Don't interrupt me. I was trying to play connect-the-dots with your freckles."

She raises a brow but doesn't try to re-cover herself. "How's that work?"

"Well, they obviously start here," I murmur, touching the bridge of her nose. "Then they pick up again here..." I drag my finger down her nose, over her soft lips, and to her collarbone, where a few more freckles are sprinkled.

"Not much of a treasure hunt."

"Oh, you see, the amateur might think that's the end of the trail, but I am an expert at connect-the-dots, and I don't give up so easily."

"Oh. Good. I was worried."

I shake my head and press a quick kiss to her lips. "I won't let you down. But are you ready for the next part?"

"I don't know? Is it hangman? I'm not sure I want you playing hangman with my freckles." Her smile damn near bowls me over.

"Still connecting the dots, but you see, it's about intuition when the going gets tough like this, and for my intuition to work at its best, I need to stop searching with my fingers and take over with my tongue."

She giggles. "Oh really?"

I climb on top of her, resting on my elbows, and she instinctively draws up her knees so my torso rests between her thighs. My cock aches, demanding that I slide up her body and get closer. Fuck. It wants more than to be close. It wants inside her. Tight and hot and deep. But I ignore it and lower my mouth to the freckles on her collarbone.

The taste of her skin on my tongue makes me hungry for more. I want to lick her clit again, to slide my tongue inside her until she loses control and rocks her hips in that sweet rhythm of fucking.

Instead, I trail my tongue down between her breasts and to the lone freckle beneath her sternum. "Found it," I murmur before gently nipping her skin.

She arches toward my mouth. "Your tongue has a rather impressive intuition."

"Oh, and it's not even done yet."

I sweep my mouth lower, nipping at each hipbone before pressing my face right between her thighs and finally finding what I'm craving. Licking her clit, I slide my hands under her ass and lift her toward my face.

She moans and her hips buck. I want more than that. I want crazy, needy, desperate. So I draw back and blow softly. She gasps, and I follow my breath with my mouth and taste her with my smile.

"Nate," she says, arching off the bed. "Aren't you bored with... *Oh, God...*"

I wrap my lips around her swollen clit and suck, and she grabs a fistful of my hair and starts that desperate movement I've been after, but I can't stand not seeing her face. I want to know how she looks when she comes, so I reposition myself next to her and slide two fingers inside.

"Nate." Her eyes glossy as she turns to me. "I—"

"Sorry, sweetheart." Her slick heat squeezes around my fingers. "I'll get back to tasting you later, but right now, I want to see what you look like when you come."

Her lips part and her eyes flutter shut. Then a phone rings.

She stills. "That's probably Maggie." She sinks her teeth into her lip.

"Let it go."

She shakes her head and slides away from my touch. "I'm sure she's worried about me if she's gone to my room and I wasn't there." She finds her purse and pulls out her phone. "Hello?" Her face falls and her body language changes. "It was good... Yeah... I'm sorry. I'm not up for that..." Her gaze flicks to mine then back to the floor. "I don't want to talk about it right now... I love you too," she whispers, and then she ends the call. Covering her mouth with her hand, she squeezes her eyes shut and draws into herself.

"The boyfriend?"

"*Ex*-boyfriend," she corrects, still not looking at me.

"You regularly tell your exes you love them?" I'm not the jealous type. You wouldn't fucking know it by the tone of my voice.

She meets my gaze. "Love doesn't go away just because you realize you can't be with someone."

Don't I know it.

She finds my T-shirt on the floor and pulls it on over her head. "Listen, could we keep what happened here between us? I really don't need my sister freaking out about it."

"And you don't want it getting back to Max," I say flatly.

She shrugs. "It would only hurt him. I don't want to hurt him."

I nod, ignoring the knot in my stomach. "It's our secret," I promise.

"I should get dressed."

I'm not ready for her to shut me out. I'm not ready for this time together to end. I'm trying to come up with an excuse— any excuse—to get her to stay.

And for that reason, more than any, I say, "I'll walk you to your room."

HANNA

Candles. Music. Rose petals.

Am I in the wrong house? But my key hanging from the door confirms I'm at the right place. Maybe I'm interrupting some romantic evening of Lizzy's—she's overdue for one of those. But then Max is walking toward me, his face serious, his eyes soft.

From the living room speakers, Jason Mraz croons about not giving up.

"What is this?" I ask stupidly. Maggie just dropped me off. I'm still buzzed on another man's kisses, can still feel the beard burn between my thighs when I walk, and here's Max setting this romantic scene.

He drops to one knee and—

"Holy shit." The ring in his fingers sparkles in the candlelight as he lifts it toward me.

"Hanna Thompson," he says, his eyes locked on mine. "I love you. I love you more than I've ever loved anyone. I didn't have any idea that love could be like this. That it could make me a better man in every way. You showed me that. And I'm so sorry that I hurt you. You're the only one I want. From now until forever."

I can't breathe. Can't think or process his words. This is a dream, right? Because I'd effing swear to you that Max Hallowell is in my living room proposing. And that can't be. Can it?

He draws in a ragged breath. "When I picture my life, when I imagine waking up next to someone, when I imagine my children in their mother's arms, I picture you. I've known for months now that you're all I want. All I need. And maybe I don't deserve you, but I'm selfish enough to ask for you anyway. Marry me, Hanna. I want to make a life with you. I want to be by your side while your dreams come true."

I manage a breath, but it enters my lungs in a thick and ragged gulp. My limbs are so heavy that it's hard to move.

"Say something," he whispers, still looking up at me, his gorgeous blue eyes wet with unshed tears.

"I..." What do I say? Last night, I was begging another man to take my virginity, and now Max—gorgeous, amazing, all-I-ever-wanted Max—is on one knee, promising me forever. "I can't," I whisper.

His shoulders sag and he drops his head. I stand there and watch his chest rise and fall with his breath. Pain rolls off him in such intense waves that it threatens to bowl me over.

"I'm sorry," I say, but what I really mean is that I wish he had done this before Meredith and those texts. Before he broke my heart and became desperate to win me back. Before I stopped believing in him.

He shakes his head and stands. "You don't owe me any apologies. I'm the one who fucked up." He lifts his hand to my face, and just before his fingers touch my cheek, he drops it.

"I don't want to say no," I admit. "I want to believe you really mean it, but, Max... Part of me will always believe you proposed out of guilt. Part of me will always believe this is all a charade to you. Some sacrifice you're making to help the fat girl feel good about herself." Part of me would always believe he was marrying me for my money.

"Hanna. You're beautiful." He squeezes his eyes shut, and

when he opens them again, they're soft and sad. "I don't know how to make you believe how beautiful you are. You hardly let me touch you, and I was okay with that because not touching you is one thousand times better than losing you. But don't think for a second that means I didn't *want* to touch you."

I keep my hands at my sides, clenching my fists because I really just want to reach for him, to curl into him. But I can't.

He rests his forehead on my shoulder. "I was an idiot, and I am so sorry."

"Me too," I whisper, and suddenly, hot tears are rolling down my cheeks. Because I love this man, and I want everything he's offering. "But your timing is terrible."

He takes my hand and presses the ring into my palm, curling my fingers around it. "Keep it. That's how much I want this, Hanna. Keep it. I'll wait."

MAX

When Hanna's door closes behind me, I feel like I've been gutted, and I'm leaving here without my heart. I have to stop on the steps. I close my eyes and try to remember how to breathe, how to take a step and live without the only thing that matters.

I'll give her the space she needs. God willing, she'll find her way back to me.

The sound of someone crying pulls me from my thoughts, and when I turn to the street, I see a figure leaning against an old maple a few houses down. Her face is hidden in the shadows of the night, but her shoulders are shaking and there's no mistaking the sound of sobs.

I approach slowly. "Are you okay?"

"*Fuck. Off.*" Meredith's voice catches me by surprise, and I stumble back a step. Two.

"What are you doing here?" I can't help the angry edge of my voice. I accept responsibility for the decisions I made in December, but I can't forgive Meredith for how Hanna found out.

Sniffing, she wipes her face with the back of her hand and

turns to face me. "I was…on a walk. The door was open. I saw…" She draws in a shaky breath. "That ring should have been for me."

I drag a hand through my hair, trying my damndest to ignore the way my chest pinches at her tears. Too many years of giving a shit what Meredith thought and how she felt. Old habits die hard, I guess.

"Why now, Meredith? I've chased you for years, and you'd never let it be anything more than sex. You say that ring should have been for you, but you weren't interested in that kind of relationship with me. You only wanted it once I found it with someone else. It doesn't work like that. I'm in love with Hanna, and I'm not going to let you destroy what I have with her." *Too late*, something whispers at the back of my mind, but I ignore it.

"What about what you have with me?" she whispers. "You're going to destroy that?"

"A long line of drunken hook-ups and rejection? Years of you calling me only when the guy you really wanted wasn't available? Last I checked, that's all I have with you."

"No, it's not." She takes a step forward, and the light from the streetlamp slashes across her features. Mascara stains her cheeks, and her eyes are filled with hurt she never lets the world see.

This is the real Meredith. The one I knew in high school. The one who would come to me when the screaming got too loud, who would hide in my room when her father was on a drunken terror. The one who knew about the kind of bruises fathers can leave that no one else can see. These are the eyes of the girl who understood me when no one else did. The first girl I fell in love with.

"What am I missing, then?" I ask, softening. "And I'm not talking about the past. I'm talking about today. What do we have together now?"

"A baby," she whispers. "We have a baby."

"No. *You* have a baby. And I'm sorry if the idea of single parenthood is suddenly freaking you out, but you made the choice. You bought the sperm and dove right in."

"I never bought any sperm," she whispers.

"Bullshit. I know you want to pretend the baby is Will's, but—"

"It's not Will's, and I didn't buy sperm. I just told people that because I didn't want them to know the pregnancy was accidental. The baby's yours, Max. You're the father."

A car rushes past, splashing yesterday's rain puddles onto the grass. Laughter rings out in the distance.

"I don't believe you."

She shrugs and swipes at her cheeks. "Well, some things are true whether you believe them or not."

Then she walks away.

HANNA

Nate Crane's Secret Fatty Fetish

I don't know what made me look him up online. Maybe having Max's ring in my jewelry box is messing with my head. Maybe I just wanted to pull up pictures of a sexy man who actually seemed to want me for me—not for what I can do for his future.

Regardless, when I sat down with my computer this morning, something made me go to Google and enter Nate's name. There it was, one of the top hits—a website known for celebrity gossip featuring a picture of Nate holding me up against the side of that building, my thick thigh practically wrapped around his waist.

Fatty fetish.

Shit. Who am I fooling? I'm no one special, and whatever Nate seemed to see in me, the rest of the world doesn't see. I sure don't see it.

I close my laptop and fold my legs under me, my brain already piecing together a weight-loss plan. Maybe Nate thought I was gorgeous, but I'm never going to see him again. It was one night, and now I'm facing the rest of my life in a world where I'm the chubby chick at best, the "fatty" at worst. I won't do it. I won't live like that.

"I brought us donuts!" Liz calls from the kitchen.

The sound of rustling bags tells me that she's unloading groceries. "Thanks." But a donut is the last thing I need. What I *need* is a few hours on the treadmill. And why not? I have free access to Max's health club, don't I?

My phone rings, and I pull it from my pocket and see an Indianapolis area code. Who's calling me from Indy?

"Hello?"

"Is this Hanna Thompson?" the man on the other end asks.

"It is. Who is this?"

"I'm calling from the offices of Smith, Peterson, and Frank in Indianapolis. We'd like to arrange a meeting with you to discuss a business matter on behalf of one of our clients."

Liz walks into the room, a half-eaten chocolate Long John hanging from her fingers. "Who's that?" she whispers.

"Who's the client?" I ask, ignoring Liz.

"We'll explain everything when you arrive," the assistant says. "Can you make it in this afternoon? Say, around two?"

I frown. "Sure. I guess."

The assistant gives me the address, and I jot it down while Liz stares on with growing impatience.

"What was that about?" she asks when I hang up the phone. She takes another bite of donut, and my stomach growls. I haven't eaten anything since the banana I had for dinner last night.

"A lawyer in Indianapolis wants to meet with me."

"Did some rich relative we don't know about die and leave you his fortune?"

I smile. "I'm hoping."

"Let's assume that's what it is. Then you can open your bakery and give me a job, since no one in this town wants to hire me to teach."

"You know that none of the teachers make a final decision about retiring until the start of the new school year," I say.

"Something will come around."

"We'll see." She shrugs. "Donut?" she asks, holding it out for me.

I'm nearly nauseated by the sight of it and how much it reminds me of my chunky thigh on display for the world in that picture. "I'll pass. Want to go running with me this morning?"

She wrinkles her nose and casts a glance over her shoulder. "Do you see someone chasing me?"

MAX

She found out. My stomach churns at the idea as I step into the old Woolworth building on Main. *Hanna found out, and it's going to ruin everything.*

She turns to me when I enter, and for a minute, it's like the last two weeks never happened. She grins and steps toward me, hand outstretched. Then, as if remembering herself, she stops and drops her hand.

"Hi," she whispers. "Thanks for coming."

I swallow. Hard. One more step and she would have been in my arms, an old habit that would have given me a hit of her scent, the both calming and arousing contact of her body against mine. But she stopped because, no matter how sorry I am, no matter how much I try to explain how I feel, she can't forget. She can't forgive.

"What are we doing here?" I ask.

"What would you say if I told you I was going to open a bakery?"

I smile. I can't help it. Joy rolls off her when she says the word *bakery*. "I would ask how I could help."

She hops up and down and clasps her hands together. "I want to do it. I really want to do it. And someone's offering to back me. To get this building remodeled and ready to open up as a bakery. But it feels too good to be true, and I called you because…" She trails off, the smile falling from her face.

"It's okay." I know what she's thinking. We talked about her opening a bakery, but always in the context of our future—together.

"Do you think it's crazy? I don't even know who the silent partner is. It's anonymous. Though I have a pretty good idea."

"You do?"

"I think so." She shrugs as if it's not important. "Is this crazy? Going into business with some anonymous partner? What if I totally screw it up? What if I fail?"

"I think anyone who's going to make this kind of investment would know what he was investing in." And *whom* he was investing in.

"Right. Market research and stuff, right?" She nods. "It's hard to wrap my head around the chance to open this bakery, to run my own business in New Hope, to feed people the kind of food that brings comfort. I can't even describe what it's like to want something as much as I want this."

"I think I have an idea," I say, but the words catch on something in my throat and come out rough. Her eyes lock with mine and soften. "Hanna…"

"I miss you." She squeezes her eyes shut and shakes her head. "Sorry. I shouldn't—"

"I miss you too."

"You haven't told anyone about the breakup, have you?"

"Only William." As much as I believed it when I told her I wouldn't pretend, the truth is that telling people we broke up makes it too real. It feels like giving up.

"Good." She bites her lower lip, worries it between her teeth. "Will you promise me you won't tell anyone else?"

I step forward and take her hand, graze my thumb over her knuckles. "If we're going to let the world think we're together until September, you need to understand something."

"What's that?"

"Every time we go to dinner at your mom's, every time

we hang out with our friends, I'll be by your side. You'll have to let me close if you're determined to do this. They'll know something's wrong otherwise."

She nods. "I know. It's okay. It will be worth it."

I take another step closer, trace her jaw with my fingertips, slide my hand into her hair. She tilts her head back. Parts her lips. "I'll be using every moment of that time to win you back," I warn. "And I'll insist that you hold on to that ring until September. It might be pretend for you, but for me…" I dip my head until my lips are a breath away from hers. "For me, it will be a second chance."

It doesn't take much to close the distance between us, and when my lips touch hers, she sighs against my mouth. I want to kiss her hard and deep and long. What if I press her against the wall and remind her just how much passion there is between us? I could wrap her legs around my waist until she's cradling my hard-on and forced to understand that there's nothing *pretend* about my attraction to her.

But I keep it soft. Light. I let her take the lead and set the pace. She opens under me and slides her hand into my hair. When she arches her back and her breasts press against my chest, I have to pull back and end the kiss before I ask for more than she's willing to give.

She brings her fingertips to her mouth as she opens her eyes to look at me. "That was a mistake."

"No," I whisper against her mouth. "*That* was everything that's good in the world. Meredith was the mistake."

"Don't confuse me, Max. This is hard enough."

I brush my knuckles across her cheek, and all I can think is, *Three months.* I have three months to win her back.

Part Two:
AFTER

HANNA

S he isn't dead. She isn't dead.
    These are the words I've repeated to myself over and over again on the drive from the airport to the hospital. Lizzy was waiting for me at baggage claim when I got off the plane, her face sheet white. I could hardly register her words. *Mom. Chest pain. Hospital.*

We drove back to New Hope in silence, terror choking the words before they could slip past our lips.

What was there to say, anyway? *Is this a nightmare? Will we lose Mom like we lost Dad?*

"She's down here," Nix says when we step off the elevators and onto the second floor.

"Is she conscious? Is she in pain?" Lizzy asks. She was pulling into the parking garage at the airport when she got the call from Nix.

"She's conscious and she's in no immediate danger," Nix says. "We did an EKG and are running some blood tests. We'll keep her overnight for observation." Her gaze drops to my naked left hand.

"Ohmigod!" Liz squeaks. "Your ring, Han."

My breath catches. "It's in my suitcase."

"It's okay," Nix says. "I think she has more important things to worry about than your jewelry. Come on." She leads us into Mom's room.

I'm not sure what I expected to see, but Mom doesn't look like a woman who just suffered a heart attack. A little pale maybe, but otherwise she looks almost serene propped up in her hospital bed, flipping through a house and garden magazine.

She sees Nix first and greets her with a smile. Then Liz gets the same. But when she spots me, her smile falls away. "Where have you been, Hanna?" The disapproval on her face is the windshield and I am the bug. Story of my life.

"I… Well…" She just had a heart attack and she wants to talk about my spur-of-the-moment trip to LA?

"She had some business to take care of out of town," Liz says. "How do you feel?"

Mom adjusts her hospital gown and straightens her necklace. She's so vain; this is probably hell for her. "I'm embarrassed, mostly." Again, she looks at me. As if I'm somehow the cause of her embarrassment. "I had no idea I was at risk for a heart attack. I'm a healthy weight. I eat right, exercise, never smoked a day in my life."

"Some of heart health has less to do with your choices and more to do with your genetics," Nix explains. "But let's wait and see what the cardiac cath shows us in the morning."

Mom waves away her explanation. "I'm fine now, just a little tired," she assures us, fidgeting with her bracelets. Does the woman ever lose the accessories?

I nod and stare awkwardly at Mom, unsure what to do or say.

We were sixteen when Daddy died of a heart attack in our backyard. I found him—hand clutched to his chest, an ugly scowl on his face. I called 911. Attempted CPR. At the funeral several days later, Mom made a comment about my outfit not flattering my "unique shape," and for a moment, I wished it had been her in the casket and not my father. It had been a fleeting thought, the ugly, angry sister of grief rearing her head when I was weak. I dismissed it a split second after I'd thought it. Of course I didn't want that. All I wanted was for both of my parents to be healthy.

But I've never forgotten that moment. Those moments of weakness have a way of defining our relationships, and I've always felt guilty for wishing—even for a moment—that I could trade my mother's life for my father's.

Mom's studying me, eyes narrow, calculating. "The timing couldn't be worse. What with the wedding so close." She drops her gaze to my hand—to my naked ring finger. "There is still going to be a wedding, isn't there, Hanna?"

Liz looks at me, and I blurt, "Of course!" because despite that horrible moment seven years ago, despite the weight of my grief for my father on the day we put him in the ground, I don't want my mother to die. As much as I'd like to get the whole *my engagement is over* conversation out of the way, now is not the time. I don't know what would happen if I told her the truth right now.

"You left your ring on the counter at the bakery again," Liz says, fumbling for an explanation. She nudges me. "I told you to buy a chain to wear it around your neck while you work."

My thumb rubs my bare ring finger. "Good idea," I mumble.

"Well, the doctor said they won't be letting me go today or tomorrow, so I'll have to make you a list of the things that need to get done before the wedding. It's coming up fast, and it's time you take a more active interest in the plans anyway."

Nix gives Mom a smile. "Right now, you should rest." She turns to me and Liz. "I need to get back to the office. Your mom is working with a fantastic cardiologist, and she's in good hands, but you know where to find me if you have any questions you don't want to ask him. Hanna?" She tilts her head toward the hallway.

"I'll be right back," I tell my mom. Then I follow Nix into the hallway.

"How are you doing?" she whispers after the door closes behind her.

I cross my arms. "What do you mean?"

"How are you handling the news of your pregnancy?"

"I'm not pregnant," I tell her flatly. "Virgins don't get pregnant."

There is so much pity on Nix's face that I nearly squirm under the weight of it.

"That would have shown up before if it was true, right?" I point out. Because I've been thinking about this a lot since she called with the news yesterday. "If I were pregnant, we would have known when I was in the hospital. You guys test for that kind of thing, don't you?"

"We do." Her words are cautious. Measured. "Your hCG levels were normal when you were in the hospital."

That's what I thought, and if it weren't for my worry over my mom, I might actually smile. "So I'm not pregnant. There was a mistake. The blood work must have gotten mixed up or something, because I remember every day since the hospital, and trust me, there's been no sex."

"Or," Nix says, looking over her shoulder to make sure this conversation is still private, "you were so newly pregnant when you were hospitalized that your hCG levels hadn't yet elevated. Pregnancy isn't just a snap occurrence. It's a process. Egg meets sperm, moves down into the uterus, implants in the uterine wall—"

"I took bio in high school."

"Then you know there's a window between conception and when the body starts producing the pregnancy hormone."

I shake my head. I can't deal with this right now. It can't be true. "Someone's screwing with me. They switched my blood work or something."

"That only happens in the movies."

"Well, virgins only get pregnant in the Bible, so..."

She studies me for a beat. "Are you sure you're a virgin?"

"I haven't slept with Max and I haven't slept with Nate, so unless I'm an even bigger ho-bag than I thought and there's a third guy I'm not remembering"—I meet her eyes and speak slowly so she understands—"I. Am. *Not. Pregnant.*"

We stare at each other, engaged in a battle of wills.

"Call my office and make an appointment," Nix says. "If you're so convinced we ran the wrong person's blood, we'll need to do it all again anyway."

"Fine."

"Hanna." The voice calling my name makes me close my eyes. It hurts too much to hear his voice.

When I open my eyes, Nix must see the question on my face. How much did Max hear? She mouths, "It's okay," then says out loud, "We'll talk to you tomorrow."

Slowly, I force myself to turn around and face Max. He's carrying a vase of colorful roses, and even though he attempts a smile when I look at him, he can't mask the hurt in his eyes or the questions there.

"Is she okay?" he asks quietly.

I nod. "I think so?"

"Do you mind if I go in there with you?"

"That would be good."

He opens the door, and I step in before him.

"Max," Mom says, delighted when she spots him behind me.

"How are you feeling?" he asks Mom.

"Better now that I see the bride and groom standing together again."

I feel Max stiffen next to me, but he doesn't say anything. Instead of correcting her, he steps forward and sets the flowers on the nightstand next to her bed.

"You didn't have to do that," Mom says.

"I wanted to," he assures her.

Mom sighs and leans back against her pillows. "Thank you all so much for stopping by, but I'd like to rest, if you don't mind."

"Of course, Mom," I whisper.

"I can't help but worry about my girls," Mom says as we're heading to the door.

"You don't need to," I promise, but I'm wondering what she means by that.

After we exit, Liz closes the door behind us and exhales heavily.

"I'm sorry she still thinks we're getting married," I whisper to Max. "I can't bring myself to tell her the truth right now."

He winces. "Of course. I wouldn't expect you to..." He drags a hand through his hair and exhales slowly. "I wouldn't expect you to break it to her while she's in the hospital."

"It's just for now," I promise. "I'll tell her when the doctor says she's in the clear."

Lizzy's eyes grow big. "The wedding is in three weeks. You can't put it off for long."

Liz is right, but I can't wrap my brain around a solution. My mind is swimming with everything that's happened in the last few days. "I know."

Liz smacks Max's shoulder. "I'm pissed at you."

"Liz!" I hiss. I wave my hand, leading the two of them away from Mom's door. This is probably the worst possible place to do this.

"A baby?" Liz growls at him when we reach the elevators. "With Meredith?"

Max doesn't say anything, but his jaw hardens.

"Liz, let it go," I warn.

She pokes Max in the chest. "Maybe Hanna's not upset anymore, but I—"

"Stop!" I say. She must hear the desperation in my voice, because she does. She steps back and drops her hands.

The elevator dings, and I force myself to follow Liz and Max inside.

"Can we talk?" Max asks. "Tomorrow?"

I nod dumbly. As confident as I was just yesterday in my decision to end this, anxious even, now I want to drag my feet to the finish line. Not only because of my mom, but because I love Max.

We climb out of the elevator and head toward the parking lot. When we arrive at Lizzy's car, Max studies me for three beats. Four. Like he wants to say more but doesn't know how. "I'll see you later, then."

I watch him walk away and feel half of my heart leave with him.

MAX

The sight of Hanna in a wedding gown steals my breath and makes my chest ache. She's so fucking perfect—dark hair flowing down her back, lips parted as if the photographer caught her mid-sentence.

Meredith hoists her purse on her shoulder and flips her blond hair. She's carefully put together, as usual, and smugger than ever. She was heading in to see Hanna's mom and caught me in the parking lot.

"Gretchen was looking at that headline right there when she started having chest pain. The ambulance had to come to my salon and get her."

I'm trying to tear my eyes off the pictures on the cover of the gossip rag, but I can't. Not when right next to the picture of Hanna in a wedding gown, there's a picture of her straddling Nate Crane's lap in a hot tub. The picture is only a couple of days old if this piece-of-shit publication is to be believed.

"This is the woman you're promising your tomorrows to?" Meredith asks.

I exhale slowly and force my shoulders to release. I can't believe I ever thought Meredith's nastiness was an admirable quality. "I'm sure it's not what it looks like."

She crosses her arms and shakes her head. "You said I treated you badly, but what about this?" She throws up her hands and turns to the hospital entrance, leaving me alone with this fucking magazine.

When I look down at the publication again, my heart plummets. For the first time, I understand why I once preferred women like Meredith to women like Hanna. It wasn't their hearts I was trying to protect. It was mine.

HANNA

"Can we go get coffee somewhere?" I ask as Liz puts the car in gear.

"Coffee?" She blinks at me. "Screw that. I vote for drinking martinis until we can't feel our faces. Considering the day we've had—hell, the *month* we've had—I'd say we deserve it."

I shake my head. "No martinis."

She arches a blond brow. "Tequila?"

"Coffee?"

"Buzzkill," she mutters, turning the key in the ignition and bringing the car to life.

When we finally get settled into a booth at the greasy spoon by campus, she's practically vibrating with all the questions she's not letting herself ask.

I make her wait and order decaf coffee and a milkshake. She orders coffee and a mountain of fries with liquid cheese, and we stare at each other while we wait for our food to come.

"Meredith's baby isn't the reason I called off the wedding," I tell her. "Meredith was pregnant in October. Max and I didn't start dating until November."

She frowns. "Then why?"

I take a breath and wrap my hands around my coffee mug,

needing its heat. "Because it hurt to find out that he only ever started dating me because he felt sorry for me. That he didn't intend for anything to come of it."

She draws in a quick breath but doesn't lift her eyes to mine.

"But you already knew that, didn't you?"

"I didn't realize you knew," she finally says. She dumps three sugar packets in her coffee and follows them with as many tubs of creamer. "About me telling Max to date you."

I sigh. "It wasn't that you told him to date me, Liz. It's that you told him to fake interest in me."

Her eyes fill. "It worked out, didn't it?"

"I had to find out from Meredith of all people. And it hurt."

"I'm sorry," she says. She exhales heavily. "How long have you known?"

"I found out last May the first time. Then I remembered Sunday morning." I show her the text messages between Meredith and Max.

"That son of a bitch," she breathes.

Watching Lizzy read the texts is like seeing them for the first time all over again. "I didn't tell anyone back then because I was afraid Max would lose the grant for his club."

"So you remembered this and went to see Nate?"

I nod. "It seemed like the logical choice at the time." A moth has taken up residence outside the window, and I watch its fluttering wings.

I've felt strangely calm since Liz told me about Mom's heart attack. The same calm I felt when I saw my father unconscious in our backyard. It was like my brain put all of my emotions to the side until I did what needed to be done—call 911, check his pulse, start CPR. *Triage.* Nothing is real during triage. Nothing can hurt you because you're operating like a machine, going on to the next necessary task and the next.

With Dad, it wasn't until later that it all hit me. After the ambulance pulled away, my father already pronounced dead. After my mother collapsed and we had to call the doctor to get her a sedative. After my sisters clung to each other and cried. Only after did the emotions hit—the fear, the anger, the terror. And finally, the soul-ripping grief. I'm still waiting for the news of Mom's heart attack to hit me, but right now, I'm still numb.

"So are you two an item now?" Liz asks. "You and Nate?"

The sound of his name makes my heart ache. "We were never together. Not really. It wasn't supposed to be more than a fling. The night we met, he was very upfront about what he could and couldn't offer me." I exhale slowly. "Whatever it was between us is over now anyway. We said goodbye."

She stirs her coffee. "So…you're staying with Max?"

I shake my head. "How can I?"

Of course, now there's the question of my pregnancy, but I'm not ready to tell Liz about that until I know for sure. Could Nix be right? I can't help but hold out hope for the lab mix-up.

When our food comes, we eat in silence. Lizzy takes mercy on me and doesn't ask any questions.

We're both exhausted, worried about Mom, and emotionally spent. But when we leave the restaurant, Liz drives to the drugstore instead of my bakery.

"Come in with me?" she asks.

I nod and follow her into the store, where she heads straight to the back and stops in front of the pregnancy tests. "A one- or two-pack?"

My breath catches. "I'm not pregnant," I object, but the words sound weak even to my ears.

"I'm your twin," she says quietly. "I can sense these things. Have you taken a test yet?"

"Nix said that the blood work…" I shake my head. "It can't be true. She's wrong."

She takes my hand and squeezes. "It's going to be okay."

My eyes fill. How is it that four weeks ago I woke up to my dream life and every day it becomes more of a nightmare? "What am I going to do if I am, Liz?"

"Don't borrow trouble. We'll cross that bridge when we get to it."

We pay for the tests and head back to the restrooms. Lizzy

tears open the box, hands me a stick, and slips the other one in my purse.

"For emergencies," she says with a half-smile.

I almost laugh, but it doesn't quite make it from my lips. "Are there directions?" I ask, frowning at the test.

"It's a pregnancy test, not rocket science. Pee on it and wait"—she looks at the box—"two minutes. One line is negative. Two lines is…"

"A problem."

"We're going to figure this out, Han. Okay?"

I swallow, but I can't agree. I don't see how this is going to be all right.

Lizzy squeezes my hand then nudges me toward the stall.

My hands are shaking as I hold the stick between my legs. I don't look at it as I set it on the back of the toilet, just sink to a ball on the floor and wait for it to process.

I've been going to church all my life. I've never been good about saying my prayers, but in this moment, there's nothing else I can do but pray. I draw my knees to my chest and lean my head against them. William and Cally would make great parents. They have an amazing relationship, and I know how much a baby would mean to them. Cally told me that William can't have kids because of some football accident when he was in high school, but I know they want babies badly. Why doesn't God give *them* an unexpected pregnancy? Why me?

I lift my head and stare at the stick. I should stand and look. One line or two. That simple.

But it's not simple at all. Two lines means not knowing whose baby I'm carrying in my belly. Two lines means having to figure out whose baby this is, and one possibility is more complicated than the next.

What if it's Nate's? Nate, the amazing man who doesn't want to have a family of his own because he doesn't want his son to feel second best. If it's his, I can't tell him. Because he'll believe he has to break the promise he made to himself and his son. And he'd resent me forever.

And what if it's Max's? Max, who wants me for all the

wrong reasons but still holds my heart. Should I cancel a wedding to a man I love if I'm carrying his baby?

Two lines means telling my mother that I'm going to have a baby out of wedlock. It means disappointing her. Two lines means the end of this charade and the beginning of something terrifying and unknown.

My knees are wet with my tears when Liz knocks on the stall door. I reach up to unlock it for her, and she frowns when she sees me curled up on the floor.

"What did it say?"

"I'm supposed to be a virgin," I whisper as if that answers her question.

I don't have to say anything else before she's picking up the stick.

Emotions flash over her face in quick succession. Disappointment, sadness, frustration, and finally happiness.

"So?"

A tear trickles down her cheek. "I can't bring myself to be disappointed about having a niece or nephew."

A sob tears from my chest, and then my whole body is shaking as she sinks to the floor and wraps me in her arms.

"Shh," she whispers. "We're going to figure this out. Shh."

When Liz drops me off at my apartment, I find Max sitting in the dark, elbows on his knees, head cradled in his hands. "How long have you been seeing him?" he whispers. "Did it start after you broke up with me or before?"

"What?" I flip on a light and drop my keys and purse on the island. I wish he'd told me he was coming over. I wasn't prepared for this tonight. It hurts to look at him, to have him so close when everything about the last twenty-four hours has turned my world upside down.

He lifts his head and tosses a magazine onto the coffee table. "Nate Crane? The fucking rocker?" He releases a humorless chuckle. "And here I am, this fool who thought he had a chance to win you back. I thought all I had to do was prove my love, but there was someone else all this time."

My heart doubles its pace and every beat aches like someone pounding on a bruise. "I didn't meet Nate until after you and I broke up." I realize I sound defensive, and shake my head. "I don't owe you an apology. For the last month, I've been walking around sick with guilt because I thought I'd betrayed you. But I didn't cheat on you. We were broken up. And worse than that? We were broken up because you never wanted me to begin with."

"Never wanted you? You're fucking kidding me, right? I want you, Hanna. I want you so badly I'm consumed with it. I want you and no one but you."

"I know *you* believe that."

His jaw hardens and he drags a hand through his hair, making a mess of it. "Let me fill you in on some of the pieces you might have forgotten. Three months, I waited for you. I wanted to marry you or, at the very least, have you give us another chance. Three months, Hanna. And I would have waited even longer if that's what it took. But to know that while I was waiting—while my ring was in your jewelry box—you were playing house with some asshole rocker, a guy I could never compete with."

"Compete?" I laugh, but it sounds ugly. Sick. "You never would have had to compete with him if you'd just wanted me from the start. You were the only thing I ever wanted, Max, but you ruined it when you hurt me."

I stomp across the room and snatch the magazine from the coffee table, but the indignation drains out of me when I see the two pictures on the cover. In the first, I'm in a wedding dress on Asher's balcony, right next to Nate. It's not terribly incriminating as far as pictures go—and the headline about Nate's secret marriage is just ridiculous. But combined with the picture next to it—me straddling Nate in his hot tub, my arms wrapped around his neck…

"That's what your mom was looking at when she got her

chest pains. She was getting her hair done at Meredith's salon and picked up that magazine to see her daughter on the front." He moves to the picture window and looks out into the black night. I wait for him to turn, wait for him to look at me. He doesn't. "Apparently she was a little shocked to discover you'd been hooking up with Nate Crane." His voice drops. "She's not the only one."

I only speak when I can't stand the silence anymore. "Didn't you know?" I whisper.

"I suspected there was someone. You said there wasn't."

I wince. I lied to Max?

"Are you in love with him?"

"Yes." I know how much that admission is going to hurt, and my voice breaks on the word. And maybe my heart.

His head bobs as he nods. "Okay. And me?" The pain's right there in his voice, but it's not the hot and fresh wound I expected. It's hard and calloused. Old hurt brought to the surface.

"I love you too." It's the first time I've said it since I lost my memory, and he bows his head at the words. I whisper, "But love isn't enough. The way you really feel about my body, about the real me. That will stand between us." I swallow hard. "I know you believe that I'm what you want. And maybe I am. But you don't want me the way a man should want his wife. Maybe it's stupid that I care. But I want someone who's going to be as crazy for my body—in all its flaws—as he is for my mind."

He turns and drags his eyes over me. Slowly. Deliberately. "You don't believe I'm crazy for your body?"

"She said, 'What's it like to fuck a fatty?' and you said, 'I'm not going to let it get that far.'" Hurt slices through me at the memory. "How the hell else was I supposed to take that, Max?"

His jaw hardens. "Don't pretend that *her* words were my thoughts."

"They might as well have been." Anger bubbles into my voice, making my words pop and snap. "You have no idea what it's like to always fall short. To be the reason your mom won't serve full-fat anything at family functions. To be the one who never had a date to prom. You have no idea what it's like to be so in love with the same guy since you were thirteen years old and have him look at your twin sister like she's the sprinkles on a sundae. You have no clue what it's like to have someone you want find you unattractive."

"I never said I found you unattractive," he growls.

"You said I wasn't your type."

"You *aren't* my type, Hanna."

The words hit me like a bucket of cold water against my anger-heated cheeks. "Exactly." I turn to leave the room, the conversation—because *fuck him*—but suddenly he's there, his body in front of mine so I'm looking at his chest.

"Ask me what my type is," he says, but his voice isn't gentle anymore. It's low and foreboding, the rumble of thunder before the wild storm.

"I don't have to ask. I know."

"Do you?" He steps toward me, and I find myself backpedaling until I'm against the wall. He stalks closer until he's leaning over me, a hand against the wall on either side of my head, pinning me in. "You aren't my type."

"I heard you the first time." I'm trying to sound fiery, but the words come out weak. *Damn it.* "Why are you doing this?"

"You have never been my type."

"Because you like blondes. Like Meredith. Like Liz."

"Because I don't like women who are as soft as you are."

That's it. I smack his chest with both hands, but he doesn't budge. "Fuck you. There are men who like my body."

"You think I don't know that? You think I'm blind to the way guys look at your ass when you walk across the room? You think I don't hear the guys at the club making comments about your tits?" He scoffs at my grimace. "No, don't play politically correct on me now. You started this conversation, and now we're going to finish it." His gaze is on my mouth. Hot. Hungry. Wanting. I don't understand, but I know what I see. "I'm well aware that men want you. Because I'm one of them."

"You just *said* I'm not your type." God. I don't want to

have this conversation. He's not making any sense, and every reminder about my imperfections is another splinter digging into my battered heart. "You just *said* I'm too soft for you."

"I wasn't talking about your body. I was talking about your heart."

"That's ridiculous."

"My mom has a soft heart too, and she let my father beat her down every day because of it. He may not have used his fists, but he didn't have to. Words are so much crueler. She took the blame for every insult he threw, swallowed every manipulation. And when he left, she believed it was because she wasn't good enough. He nearly destroyed her. You aren't my type because you give and give and give, and that scares the fuck out of me. Someone like Meredith could never hurt me. She's too hardened to get close enough to hurt me. But you? You open your heart so much and get so close that I'm more vulnerable than ever."

"I don't make anyone vulnerable." I'm confused. I want to believe what he's saying, but it doesn't fit with what I've spent my whole life believing about myself and how men see me.

"You do," he says softly. "You make me vulnerable and you hurt me more than Meredith ever could. And fuck it if you're not worth every bit of pain I feel right now."

"You don't understand what it's like to feel so completely inferior to everyone around you just because of the size of your body. And to know that it was all some ruse, that you weren't even attracted to me when you asked me on that date—"

"Does it matter when I'm attracted to you now?"

I shake my head. "I'm not the same woman I was then." I drop my gaze down to my body, the weight creeping back on little by little every day. "And I had to starve myself to get here."

"I loved you before you lost the weight. I asked you to marry you before you lost the weight." His lips hover over mine, and I so badly want him to come a breath closer. My knees are weak with need, and I *crave* his lips on mine. Instead, he asks, "Do you remember the first time we kissed in the gallery?"

The memory flashes through my mind, sizzles. "Yes."

"Do you know why I kissed you that night?" The blue of his irises thins as his eyes heat.

"You were trying to make me feel better about myself."

"Not that night," he whispers softly. "That night, I saw you laughing with the bartender and suddenly I saw you for the first time. Before that night, I hadn't seen you as anything other than a little sister, a friend. But suddenly, something clicked and I really looked. When I dragged you upstairs that night, I wasn't thinking about babies or the future. I sure as hell wasn't thinking about your self-esteem. In that moment, all I wanted was to get my hands on this body, make you scream, and fuck you till you were exhausted in my arms."

A shiver runs through me, leaving heat in its wake, and my breathing goes shallow. "But I didn't let you do any of that."

He flicks his tongue over my earlobe, and one hand comes to my side, his thumb skimming the underside of my breast. "I'm well aware of that."

I arch toward his touch. "So why'd you stay with me?"

"Because it's more than sex with us, Hanna. You're amazing, and I fell in love with you, and I couldn't imagine being with anyone else. I didn't want anyone else."

Suddenly my heart is a twisted mess and my tongue is heavy with words I can't find. "I'm so confused."

"I can see that." He drops his gaze to the magazine still in my hand and sighs heavily. "I hope he's good to you." Then he backs away and walks out the door, leaving me scared and confused and lonelier than I've ever been in my life.

MAX

I don't want to talk to anyone, but when I get to my apartment, William is waiting on the balcony in one of my cheap plastic deck chairs with a six-pack of beer.

"What are you doing here?" I sound as exasperated as I feel. I'm pissed and hurt and just fucking exhausted. I don't want to have a beer with Will. I just want to open a bottle of Jack and drink until I've forgotten my own name. Until I've forgotten how good she smells and how right she feels in my arms.

"Meredith is telling everyone in town about that magazine." He pulls a beer from the pack and hands it to me. "I figured maybe you could use a beer."

What I could use is a fucking scouring pad to scrub my brain. Every time I close my eyes, I see Hanna half nude and draped over Nate Crane. *Fuck.*

"It's over." I take the beer and sink into the chair next to him. "I thought I could win her back, but I was wrong."

"The wedding is off?" Will asks.

I open my beer and nod. Something clicks in my mind and I release a dark laugh. "Huh. I guess you know all about some rocker asshole stealing away the girl you want."

Will shrugs. "Maggie meeting Asher was one of the best things that's ever happened to me. If she hadn't, everything would have been different when Cally came to town. Cally is all that matters."

I take a sip of my beer because it's too dangerous to speak with this tightness in my chest.

"But Hanna's your Cally," Will says.

"She is," I whisper. "And after three months of waiting for her to make a decision, watching her waste away… I thought I'd lost her. And then I get the call about her being in the hospital and I walk in and she's wearing my ring and all doe-eyed when she looks at me and—" Again, that fucking tightness in my chest, burning behind my eyes. I'm not going to lose it here in front of Will.

"And she didn't remember what you did to hurt her," he supplies.

"I'd been given this second chance. She was wearing my ring." For four weeks, those words were my mantra, and I wanted them etched into stone so I could wrap my fingers around them like a talisman, a reminder. *She was wearing my ring.*

"So give her some time to digest everything and have faith that she'll choose you again." Will clacks his beer bottle against mine. "She's your Cally. It'll work out."

I wish I could be as confident as he is. But I'm in a nightmare stuck on repeat. Tonight's argument with Hanna felt like one we've already had, only this time I know what she was doing with her weekends out of town over the summer.

"How can I compete with Nate Crane? He could give her the world."

"Sure," Will says, "but you can give her the life she wants in New Hope. I think we both know which Hanna would rather have."

HANNA

"It's called broken heart syndrome," the cardiologist says.

Mom's hospital room is packed this morning. Lizzy, Maggie, and Krystal are gathered around Mom's bed, and Max and I are standing in the corner. I was surprised when he showed up at my apartment this morning, but he simply said, "Your mom needs to see us together right now," and since I couldn't argue with that, I followed him to his car and let him drive me to the hospital.

Now we're all standing around, waiting to hear the results of the cardiac cath they performed on Mom this morning. Abby's staying with Maggie while Mom's in the hospital. She wanted to be here too, but Maggie played her big-sister card and insisted Abby go to school. In addition to four of her five daughters, Mom's old friend, Carol Standers, is here, anxious as the rest of us to hear the news.

"Essentially, we see the same elevated enzymes that we would in a regular heart attack, but it's brought on by stress rather than any blockages that you'd see in a traditional heart attack."

"Broken heart syndrome," Maggie says. "So what can we do to make sure it doesn't happen again?"

I gave my mom a heart attack. The doctor's talking and I can hardly process his words with the blood rushing in my ears.

"We're going to have her wear a monitor for a couple of months," the doctor continues. "This way, we can monitor her heart activity and it will give her a jolt if her heart isn't functioning properly, but of course, I need you to limit your stress as much as possible."

Carol lifts a brow. "With her daughter's wedding coming up?"

"I'll be fine," Mom insists.

"No offense," Carol says, patting Mom's hand, "but your daughters have a track record of bringing on the drama when their weddings are approaching."

"Jesus!" Maggie hisses. "Seriously?"

"Don't swear, Margaret," Mom scolds.

"I'm just saying that with *two* daughters who called off their weddings at the last minute, it's no wonder she was feeling so stressed before Hanna's big day."

"Don't put this on Hanna," Lizzy growls.

"Come on, you guys," Krystal says. "Just let it go. Carol is just a concerned friend, but in this case, she doesn't need to be worried. Max and Hanna are in love."

All eyes turn to Max and me—every pair seems to be asking a different question, but the only one that matters is Mom's.

A couple of days ago, I was confident in my ability to tell my mom that I was canceling my wedding, but now I have to tell her that I'm canceling my wedding *and* I'm pregnant. *Oh, and guess what? I don't know who the father is!*

Max wraps his arm around my waist and squeezes. I'm not sure if the gesture is for my benefit or my mom's.

Thankfully, the doctor quickly gets us off the subject of my upcoming wedding and the attention returns to him as he explains that Mom will need to stay in bed today and will be released to go home with her new vest tomorrow. Max keeps his arm around me, and I let myself take comfort in his warmth.

When we leave the room, he steps away as if touching me cost him.

"Let me know if you need anything," he says softly. "I'll be at the club." Then he tucks his hands into his pockets and leaves.

"Mom's asking to see you," Krystal calls to me from the doorway to Mom's room.

Oh, shit. I knew this was coming. But luckily I called Liz last night and we came up with a plan.

I step into the room and pull the door closed behind me. "I hear you saw that ridiculous article," I say. Because I'm more of a "rip off the Band-Aid" kind of girl.

"I did." She's not looking at me, just out the window. But I've been trained well, and after twenty-three years of her disappointment, I don't have to see her face to sense her disapproval.

"It was stupid, wanting to be an extra in that music video, but I guess it's just something I've always wanted to do." I hold my breath, waiting.

"You were in that man's hot tub for a music video?"

"Oh, yeah." I'm pretty sure I'm going to burn in hell for lying to my bed-ridden mother, but that's better than having to live with myself if my mistakes kill her. "We'll see if they even put me in it. You know how those things go."

She turns back to me and nods, but I can't tell if she's buying my story or not.

My sisters decided that the "It's five o'clock somewhere" rule totally applies on vacations, wedding days, breakups, and weeks your mother is in the hospital for a heart attack. So they called Cally and Nix, who cleared their schedules for the rest of the day and met us at Brady's.

Krystal already headed back to the airport, so it's just Liz,

Maggie, Cally, Nix, and me, all squeezed into a booth with three pitchers of beer. At noon, but whatever.

Cally fills the glasses, and I put a hand over mine. "Water for me."

Maggie gawks at me as if I suddenly started speaking in tongues.

Best to just spit it out, I guess, but I lower my voice and lean over the table so curious ears don't hear. "I'm pregnant."

Maggie chokes on her beer and the mug clatters to the table, its contents sloshing. "Pregnant…like metaphorically, right?"

I look to Nix, who's nodding in confirmation. "Nix called me in LA. My blood work came back and everything looks good…except that."

Maggie blinks at me. "But you're a virgin."

"So they say," Liz mutters.

"One of them must be lying, right?" Maggie says.

"Which one?" Cally asks.

Liz raises a brow. "Kind of an awkward question to ask."

I fill them all in on the memory that had me leaving for LA and the truth about how Max and I were pretending to be together before my accident so he'd still have a good chance at getting the grant money.

Cally's studying her beer.

"You knew, didn't you?" I ask Cally. "You knew we'd broken up."

She worries her lower lip between her teeth and shrugs. "Will and Max are best friends. Max needed someone to confide in when it was all going down."

Liz gapes at her. "And you didn't think you should've mentioned it to her after the accident?"

Cally shows her palms in defense. "I didn't know until the night of the bachelorette party. Will told me then."

"So why didn't Will say something when Hanna woke up without her memory?" Maggie asks. "Didn't he think she should know her relationship was pretend?"

Cally shrugs. "But it wasn't. Not anymore. Hanna was

wearing the ring. Will thought she'd finally taken Max back."

We're all silent for a bit. I sip my water while the girls nurse their beers.

Then Cally asks, "Have you told Max about the pregnancy?"

I shake my head. "He's going to meet me here later, and I'm planning to tell him then. He came over last night, but we were a little busy arguing about Nate, and I never got around to telling him."

Maggie's eyes go wide. "Max knows about Nate?"

I pull the magazine from my purse and plop it on the middle of the table. "Apparently that's what Mom was looking at when she started having chest pains."

"Oh, shit," Cally says.

"I told her I was there as an extra for a music video."

"Good cover," Maggie says. "I didn't know you had it in you."

"I don't know if she believed me or not," I admit.

"I'm sure she believed you," Liz says. "She wants to see you marry Max too badly to believe anything that doesn't align with that goal."

"Speaking of marrying Max," Maggie says. "I presume that's over now that the thing with Nate's out of the bag?"

"It's over," I admit. "He wants me for the wrong reasons." Or I think he does. Our conversation last night left my mind spinning with confusion and my body hungry with wanting. "He has so many financial problems."

"He doesn't want you for your money," Cally says. "If that's what you're thinking, you've got this all wrong."

I smile at her and shrug. Max is her fiancé's best friend. Of course she's going to think the best of him.

"But what if Max is the baby's father?" Liz asks.

Cally frowns. "You need to ask him again if you ever had sex. Maybe he had a reason for lying."

"Or maybe Nate had a reason for lying," Maggie says.

Liz turns to me with wide eyes. "What are you going to do if it's Nate's?"

I shrug. "Maybe I'll pull a Meredith and tell everyone I

bought sperm." My joke falls flat and the girls just stare at me. "I'm not telling Nate. And you all have to promise me you won't either."

Maggie studies me, her face sad. "I don't think that secrets are the right answer here."

"If this baby is Nate's," I say, "secrets are the *only* answer. When we were seeing each other, it was so important to him that I understood he didn't want commitment or a family. You have no idea how much it would screw up his world if this baby's his and I told him."

"Promise me you'll tell him." Maggie's face is so damn serious that I can't refuse, even if I know I can't do that to Nate.

"I'll think about it."

"Damn." Liz clunks her nearly empty beer on the table. "I just want to know who had sex with you and lied about it."

"She could still be a virgin," Nix interjects. "I mean, technically, you can get pregnant without penetration."

Liz looks horrified. "You're fucking kidding me."

"Like all the consequences of sex with none of the fun," Maggie says.

Nix nods. "If there was ejaculate that made its way to her vaginal opening, there's a chance it could happen. Not a *good* chance, mind you, but a chance."

Liz cocks her head. "*Ejaculate* and *vaginal opening*. That's some sexy talk there, Phoenix. You pull those ten-dollar words out in bed too?"

I laugh. I can't help myself. Nix's cheeks flush pink, and it's just a relief to think about something other than my broken heart and baby-daddy drama.

"What words should I use?" Nix asks.

"*Come*?" Cally offers.

"*Pussy*," Maggie adds.

Liz bites back a laugh. "*Spooge*?"

At that, we *all* burst out in laugher, and Nix's cheeks flare to a darker red. "Oh my God, you guys," she whispers. "Someone's going to hear."

We're all giggling like schoolgirls when Max walks up to the table.

MAX

Her smile is so beautiful, but the moment she sees me, it falls away.

"Hey," she says softly.

"Hi." I nod to the other girls, but the fucking magazine with Hanna's picture is right there in the middle of the table, and my stomach twists painfully with the reminder of how the woman I love spent her weekend.

They all wave awkwardly, and Hanna steps out of the booth and follows me to another, more private booth at the back of the bar, right by the space we use as a dance floor when we've had too much to drink.

"Thanks for coming this morning," she says softly. "I just can't disrupt my mom's world with the truth right now."

"And the truth is," I say carefully, "you aren't going to marry me."

"Right." She traces a gouge in the wooden table again and again and avoids meeting my eyes.

I take a deep breath. "Is this because of him? Is he offering you a future? Does he love you like I do?"

"He's not offering me anything. It's over between Nate and

me. This isn't about him."

We're both quiet for a long time before I speak. "The Friday night of your accident, I was training someone at the club, and you left me a voicemail. You said you'd made some decisions and wanted to talk. I was about to call you back when Lizzy called and told me you were unconscious at the hospital. When I got there, you were wearing my ring and your memory was gone."

"Convenient," she whispers. The word cuts me.

"*Convenient?* You're kidding me, right? You think I was happy you had brain damage?"

"You got a second chance," she whispers. "I didn't remember how you hurt me."

I wish she could understand why I handled everything like I did, but I'm in my own fucking head and even *I* think I screwed up. "You also didn't remember deciding to put on my ring."

"I didn't. I still don't, and Nix says I probably never will remember the day of the accident. You should have told me the truth."

Of course I should have. And I meant to. I planned to. But how do you find a good time to break the heart of a woman you'd do anything to protect?

"You know what you said to me that night I brought you home from the hospital? You said, 'You're not going to hurt me.' Those words killed me. You didn't remember anything from the last year—not a single kiss or date or touch—but you had so much faith in me. I should have told you the truth, but how would you have felt if I had? How would you have felt if I'd sat there and explained how we started dating and why? If I'd shown you those texts? You'd been through that once. *We* had been through that once. Telling you when you couldn't remember would have meant sending you through that pain all over again. I couldn't do that. Not intentionally."

"Were you just going to let me marry you? Without telling me?"

"No." *Fuck.* When did everything get so screwed up? "I

guess I hoped that when you remembered the bad parts, you'd remember the good parts too. You were wearing my ring. Don't you see that? You'd spent months putting off making a decision. Whatever happened that day you fell down the stairs, you'd put on my ring first—*before* you lost your memory."

"I wasn't seeing clearly," she whispers, and I feel like I'm slowly bleeding out. "Meredith helped me understand something."

I don't know where she's going with this, but if it involves Meredith, it can't be good.

"What's that?" I ask, despite myself.

She's quiet for too long, studying that gouge in the wood again, and I know before she speaks that I'm not going to like it. "She made me see how marrying me would solve every single one of your financial problems."

My stomach heaves and thrusts my breath from my lungs. "You believe I want to marry you for your trust fund?"

She looks sad but firm. "I believe my trust fund may be making you misinterpret your feelings for me. Consciously or not."

I push out of the booth. I love this woman. I would give her everything I have, and she thinks I want her for her money.

"Think about it," she whispers to my back. "Wouldn't you have spent more time with me these last few weeks if you really wanted me? I was *yours*, but you were barely around."

I turn slowly because I need to look her in the eye when I say this. "I never wanted your money, Hanna. I just wanted you. That's always going to be true, whether you believe it or not."

HANNA

Tension radiates off him in hard waves that would knock me over if I weren't sitting. I ball my hands into fists to keep myself from touching his cheek and his two-day growth of beard. I have to remind myself to breathe. *In and out. In and out.* Because giving voice to my suspicions hurt a thousand times worse than letting them simmer in some dark corner of my brain. But I had to do it. I had to explain why I can't marry him.

He turns on his heel and walks away.

Breathe in. Breathe out. It takes all of my courage to stand behind my words when I just want to chase after him and take back anything that might have hurt him.

William arrived sometime while we were talking, and he stops Max at the bar. Max is nodding, listening, occasionally eyeing the door, but not sparing me a single glance.

Shit. I need to tell him about the pregnancy. I push out of the booth to make sure I stop him before he goes.

Lizzy spots me heading toward the bar and hops out of the booth to join me. "How'd it go?" she whispers.

Brady grins at me and pours a shot of tequila *blanco.* "I

heard about your mom," he says, nudging it toward me. "That one's on the house."

I catch the scent of the tequila, and it jiggles a memory loose. I pick it up, intending to take another whiff and see if I can break the memory free, and Lizzy says, "Hanna, the baby!"

She realizes her mistake at the same moment that her words register in my mind. Both of us turn our eyes to Max, who's gone statue still next to William.

The air seems to dance in the tension between us. I wait for him to take a breath, for some evidence that he didn't understand what she said or that he thinks it's a joke. But he's frozen for so long that my heart is stuck on a never-ending free fall into the infinite depths of my stomach.

Finally, Max slowly lowers his glass to the counter, turns, and walks out of the bar without a word to any of us.

"I'm so sorry," Lizzy whispers. "It just came out. I didn't realize you hadn't told him yet. I suck and I'm the worst."

The door swings closed behind him as he leaves in no apparent rush and with no apparent destination. I can't even imagine what he's feeling.

"I hadn't gotten to that part yet."

"Well, I know it must be a shock, but I'm a little pissed. Could be he's going to be a dad, and unexpected or not, he doesn't have to be a dick. Men. I swear."

"It's not his baby," I whisper. Because I remember now.

Five days before my accident. At Nate's house. It was a memory I thought I'd recovered, but I was missing so much of it. The second half. The part that changes everything.

"What do you mean? How do you know?"

"I never slept with Max, but I'm not a virgin." Something clenches, tight and painful, in my chest.

"The baby is Nate's?" All the horror I've felt in the last few seconds flashes across Lizzy's face, but I can't stand here and talk about this with her. I need to go after Max.

I rush out of the bar and spot him on the sidewalk less than a block away. I jog until I catch up.

Sensing me, he stops and turns to me when I'm still a

few steps away. "Is it true?" he asks, his eyes dipping to my stomach.

"I'm sorry," I whisper. "I'm so sorry."

When he lifts his icy-blue eyes to mine, they're hard. "When did you find out?"

"While I was in LA."

His jaw ticks. "Were you planning to tell me?"

"Yes. Of course. I just—" I have no excuse, so I go with the truth. "I didn't know how."

He steps off the sidewalk into the grass and sinks to his haunches. "It's his?" He pauses a beat and shakes his head. "Of course it is. Who am I kidding?"

I close my eyes against the onslaught of emotions I'm feeling. Pain—for him, for me. Guilt. Regret over how I've handled this from the beginning. And frustration that there's still too much I don't know and don't remember.

His jaw goes hard and he pushes to standing. "You deserve better than to get knocked up and abandoned."

"It's not like that."

"Then how is it? You just told me it was over between you two."

"It's complicated." Even more so now with my latest memories clicking into place.

"No shit." His body deflates a bit, the fight draining out of him. "What is it about me? Why could you give him…"

I know what he's asking. Why could I have sex with Nate when I couldn't even let Max see me naked? I understand the question, but I don't say anything because I don't know the answer.

He shakes his head and drags a hand through his hair. "Never mind. I have to get out of here, Han. I can't… I just can't."

HANNA

When I return to the bar, the whole place is quiet but for the sound of an anchorman on the TV hanging above the bar. At first, I think they all know about my pregnancy and the drama between Max and me, but then I realize all my friends are standing too, their eyes glued to the television.

I follow their gaze and watch the "Breaking News" banner run across the bottom of the screen.

Someone turns up the volume, but I can't hear a thing over the rushing of blood through my ears and the shattering of my heart.

Tragedy in the Middle East: Helicopter carrying musician Nate Crane and others shot down in Afghanistan.

I catch snippets. Crane and three other musicians were in military transport to a performance. Authorities haven't released any further information at this point. Waiting for military to report if there are any survivors. Then they have some military weapons expert explaining the precision of surface-to-air missiles.

I don't know when I collapsed. I don't remember sitting or falling. But suddenly Lizzy is behind me, putting a glass of ice water to my lips. "Drink, Hanna."

I part my lips instinctively, taking the smallest sip past my lips, but I shake my head when she offers it up again.

"We need to get her out of here." Nix's voice.

Then hands lifting me, leading me. My feet are working. Moving. But I feel disconnected from my body. Above it and beside it all at once.

Time passes in still frames. Lizzy helping me off the floor. Maggie's tear-soaked face as she helps me into her car. Lizzy brushing my hair behind my ears, tears in her eyes as I look up at her from her lap.

There's a bed and blankets, and I don't understand why they're bundling me up, but then I realize I'm shivering. Violent, body-racking shivers that are so exaggerated it almost seems like I must be faking it—no one shivers like this—but I can't stop.

Then Lizzy climbs in bed behind me, pulling me into her arms, whispering reassurances in my ear.

Time passes and freezes. Minutes slide by without notice and hang suspended in the air, punishing me with their brutal stillness. Someone offers me a pill, and I shake me head.

"Nix said it was okay. The baby needs you to sleep." Lizzy's voice. And Maggie is next to her, holding a glass of water.

I swallow it down, and later—minutes, hours, seconds, it doesn't matter—sleep comes and releases me from the torment of consciousness.

Part Three:
BEFORE

HANNA

Ten Weeks Before Hanna's Accident

The box is wrapped in ribbon and was delivered by courier. A freaking courier delivery in New Hope. I didn't even know that was a thing.

Inside, I find a black slip and panties in the finest black lace nestled under a thin envelope.

"Courier deliveries of expensive panties?" Liz says, startling me. She comes and stands next to me in the dining room, and I shove the envelope into my pocket before she can see it. "Did you finally let Max get to third base and just not tell me? Damn. I want a man who will send me expensive lingerie." She picks up the slip and fingers the whisper-soft lace. "Lucky bitch."

I force a smile and shrug.

She frowns at me. "What's up with you lately? You're acting weird."

"Nothing. I'm just busy." I've been keeping my distance from Liz since I found out that it was her idea for Max to ask me out. I can't let her know about the breakup anyway. I can't risk that information getting back to my mom.

"Well, next time I see Max, I'll tell him he needs to hook me up with a friend who has as good of taste in lingerie as he does. Because *damn*."

I open my mouth to ask her not to, then close it again. First of all, asking her not to say anything to Max is practically admitting that the gift is from another man. Second, some small, shallow part of me likes the idea of Max knowing I got a gift like this from someone else. And yes, I know this makes me small and terrible, and all-around unworthy of both of these guys, but maybe after all these years living in the same town as Meredith, some of her bitchiness is rubbing off on me.

I take the slip back from Liz and return it to the box. "I think I'll take these to my room."

"Okay," she mumbles behind me. *Crap.* I've hurt her, and she has no idea that she hurt me first.

After padding to my room, I close the door behind me and pull the envelope from my pocket, my nerves buzzing. I don't need a tag to know this box isn't from Max. And maybe it's crazy for a girl like me to believe that a rocker I spent a wickedly sexy night with would send me a gift...but I *know*. I just know this is from Nate even before I open the envelope.

But even as sure as I am, when I pull out the paper inside and see a handwritten note, I gasp a little. His writing is tall and narrow, the words scratched with a black felt-tip pen.

> *Angel,*
> *A pair to replace the one I ruined—I regret nothing—and the slip that goes with it because I spent five minutes in the store staring at it and imagining how it would look on you. After that, I either had to buy it dinner or send it to you.*
> *Maybe you're back with the ex by now, but I have a concert in Chicago this weekend, and when I imagined you waiting in my room after... Well, let's just say I liked the idea a hell of a lot.*
> *I'm staying at the Waldorf Astoria. They'll have*

a key and concert tickets waiting for you at the
front desk.
-Nate

MAX

Hanna's on the treadmill. Again. That's twice today. At least a dozen times so far this week. She's practically taken up residence on the damn thing in the weeks since we split.

I put my hand on the rail and look at her, but she's got her earbuds in and doesn't even notice me. The club closed fifteen minutes ago.

What's she running from?

My stomach knots as I think of those old texts between me and Meredith. Is that what has had her working out two to three times a day?

Her ponytail bobs as she runs, and her eyes seem vacant without her ever-present smile. That smile's been a rare sight these last weeks.

Suddenly she realizes I'm standing next to her, and she slows the treadmill to a crawl and takes in the empty club. "You're closed," she says, pulling the earbuds from her ears. "I'm sorry. I'll get out of the way."

The treadmill beeps as she shuts it down and hops off.

She grabs her purse off the floor and starts toward the door, but I touch her arm to stop her.

"I need to show you something."

Her gaze drops to my hand on her arm then back to my face. Tiny splinters of regret drag through my heart at her expression. Every time she looks at me, I feel like I've smacked her. I can't undo the past. I want to. I would. But I can't, so I'm left here, helpless.

"Come with me," I whisper. I lead her into the women's locker room and past the showers to the floor-to-ceiling mirrors at the back. The silence pulses around us like an unwelcome visitor. I turn her toward the mirror and stand behind her.

She frowns at my reflection. "Max, what are you doing?"

My heart slams in my chest as I study her. There's nothing I want as badly as I want to kiss her again. I want to taste the tender spot at the crook of her neck. I want to hear her soft moan as I pull her bottom lip between my teeth. I want to get her naked and touch her until she's breathless and turned on, make her beg until she understands how fucking beautiful she is.

"Look." The word comes out harder than I intended, a brusque command.

"At what?" Her gaze skips over her reflection quickly, dismissing it.

"Look at yourself, Hanna." When she tries to turn, I hold her shoulders and make her face her reflection. "Look at the woman you are, not the woman you think you are."

Her breath catches and she tries to turn away, but I hold her still, make her look. "I know what I look like."

"Do you?" I skim my knuckles over her jaw. I can't help myself. It's been too long since I've touched her, and I miss the feel of her skin under my fingers. I miss her kiss. The way she'd curl into my chest and sigh like she'd found heaven and I was some sort of a god. I miss her laugh and her smile. I miss my girlfriend. "I don't think you have any idea how beautiful you are, Hanna."

Her eyes brim with tears. "Why are you doing this?"

"I see you out there, running like a woman possessed. Pushing yourself until your legs shake and you can hardly stand. Lizzy tells me you're hardly eating. If you would just look at yourself. If you would see what I see and—"

"Stop." She steps out of my grasp and turns her back to the mirror. "You don't get to give me this speech, Max. Not you."

"Why not?"

She crosses her arms under her breasts and lifts her chin. "Because it's bullshit. We both know this isn't about my so-called beauty. It's about your guilt, but you don't get to pretend anymore. I know the truth."

My jaw hardens. "*Pretend?*"

"You know the truth. You know I'll never be your type." She pauses for a beat. Two. As if she needs a few seconds to remind herself to breathe. "And that's okay. I've made my peace with that. But please don't try to rewrite history and tell me that I was always the one you wanted."

"I never said that. My biggest crime was being so hung up on Meredith that I didn't see what was right in front of me. But I opened my eyes and realized what an idiot I was. I'd been on two, maybe three dates with you. I didn't intend for anything to come of it. Then Meredith called me over—"

"I saw the texts," she bites out. "I don't need the play-by-play."

"I went over to her house," I growl, barreling forward. "And she kissed me. That's all that happened. She kissed me, and I kept thinking about you. So I left."

"So fucking noble of you." She tries to push past me, but I grab her and wrap my arms around her, holding her tight against my chest.

"I'm done letting you blow me off. You're going to listen to me this time. I left because I realized I wanted *you.*" She goes perfectly still in my arms, and I drop my mouth to her ear. "I know that doesn't seem like much to you, but I've been in love with Meredith for years. And now she wants me for more than the occasional good time. She wants the life I wasted years dreaming she'd let me give her."

"Then go to her," she whispers.

"I can't. I've felt real love with you. Good, healthy love.

Love that makes me think about making babies and growing old. Settling in with someone whose hand in mine is the most comforting thing in the world. That's what I want now, and I want it with you. All of it."

"I don't want a husband who sees me as the best companion. The best mother for his children. I want more than that. I want someone who wants me—physically—as much as you used to want Meredith."

"I want you more than I ever wanted her."

She scoffs. "Right."

"I can't believe how wrong I was."

She shakes her head. "I don't know what you're talking about."

"I thought I was being the good guy by not pushing you about sex. I thought you needed me to be patient. To be okay with your rules, to be okay with you barely letting me touch you. But I was wrong. You needed to know. You needed me to show you how much I want you." I drop my mouth to just above her ear. She smells so damn good. "I think about it all the time. My hands on your body. My mouth. The way you'd taste if you'd just let me kiss you everywhere." I pull back, breathing heavily, fighting to keep myself from touching her, from kissing her until she listens to me.

She squeezes her eyes shut. "You're confusing me."

"Good. Maybe that means you're finally listening to me."

"Max…"

I step close, skim the shell of her ear with my lips "How can I prove it to you?" I whisper. "I'd think knowing how hard you made me when we touched might be enough evidence, but apparently not. Maybe you need more than that. Maybe you need to know how much self-control it took me not to seduce you. Or maybe you need to know that when you sucked my dick, the sight of your lips stretched over me turned me on so much that I had to close my eyes so I wouldn't embarrass myself. Or maybe that's not enough for you. Maybe I also need to tell you about what I think about when no one's around. Maybe if you could see what I'm picturing when I jack off—if you had any idea how much I fantasize about driving inside of you, sucking those tits, making you come—maybe *then* you'd believe me."

NATE

Hanna's naked, sitting on the edge of my bed and staring at her phone.

I rub my eyes and look at the clock. It's six in the morning. I came back to my room last night and found her waiting for me. I stripped her bare and kissed her until I couldn't think anymore. Every day since my father's death, I've felt myself sink a little further into the darkness.

Vivian doesn't want Collin to be raised in LA, and I can understand that. Hell, I agree with her. But the week my father died, Vivian and her new husband started looking at houses in Tennessee. When Collin told me about it, he slipped and called Vivian's husband "Dad."

It was an accident, and Collin caught himself and giggled away his mistake. I tickled him and acted like it didn't matter, but the slip ate at me. The fact that he said it by mistake and not deliberately proved something, didn't it? And the more I thought about their move, their happy little new family, the more I realized I've lost my place in my own family again. Right now, I'm Collin's second family, but soon, I won't even be that. I'll be tertiary. An afterthought.

Unwelcome at my own father's funeral and soon to be an afterthought to my only son, I slipped deeper and deeper. The night I met Hanna was a bright spot in the darkness, and when I made myself say goodbye to her, it came back—suffocating me until not even the sound of Collin's voice was enough to let me draw a full breath.

So I summoned my angel, knew I could climb out of the depths on the sound of her moans alone. I had her coming for the first time before we ever left the foyer, and by the time I had her in my bed, I felt like I could breathe again.

But I'm so fucking selfish that I didn't think until now how much, by saving me, she's tormenting herself.

Rolling over, I brush my knuckles across her shoulder blades. "What is it?"

She doesn't look up from her phone. "It's Max," she says softly. "He wanted to check in and make sure I'm having a safe trip."

I tense. If I've ever been used before, I've never cared. But the idea of my time with Hanna all working to manipulate the ex? The idea grates on me.

"What does he think of you being here with me?"

With a click, she places the phone back on the bedside table. "He doesn't know. Everyone thinks I got an out-of-town wedding cake gig."

I want to reach for her. Last night, I was so wrapped up in my own grief and my own need, I was so busy running from my own demons, that I didn't think to ask about hers. But now I want to touch the tight lines around her eyes and make it better. To trace my thumb down her cheeks until I find the tracks of the tears he made her cry.

"I almost didn't expect you to come," I confess. "I thought you'd be back with him by now."

When she turns to me, there's an apology in her eyes. "I kissed him."

"Okay." Her words have jealousy eating at my gut. And *fuck that.*

"It just happened."

"You can kiss anyone you want, you know," I say carefully. "You don't owe me anything."

"I know but...this is different for me. I've never..." She shakes her head.

I had no right to invite her here. I need to back off. Leave her alone. I'm not interested in being involved with a girl who thinks she can't kiss her ex-boyfriend. So I have no idea why I ask, "What's his hold on you?"

Standing, she shakes her head and turns away, blocking her face from my view. "It doesn't matter. It's over."

"You're a terrible liar," I say flatly.

She releases a humorless chuckle. "Better than an accomplished one, I guess." She's silent for a beat, and I wait, knowing she's building to something, collecting her thoughts. Finally, she lets her gaze meet mine. "He proposed. After I got home from St. Louis."

I blink. I'm not even sure what to do with that information. I'm not one of those guys who claims all women confound him. I like to think Janelle taught me the basics of understanding the female psyche. It's one thing for Hanna to keep me secret from an ex. It's quite another for us to have a secret fling when she has a fiancé.

"I told him I couldn't," she says.

I don't like the relief I feel. "But you wanted to say yes."

"I don't know." She worries her bottom lip between her teeth. "He told me to keep the ring. To give it time. He said he'd wait for me."

Something knots in my stomach at that. "And do you want him to wait for you?"

"I shouldn't, but I do."

"Then I guess I only have one more question. Why are you here with me?"

She flicks her gaze to mine. "Because I wanted to say yes, and you remind me why I need to say no."

Oh, damn. Fuck, fuck, damn.

I'm not even sure what she means by that, but I do know it should have me running in the opposite direction. Instead, I find myself gathering her against me and whispering, "Come to LA with me."

This sweet virgin from Nowhere, Indiana, gave me one night, and now she owns me.

HANNA

Opulent. That's the word for Nate's house. Marble floors, crystal chandeliers, soaring ceilings, walls decorated with paintings that would probably send Maggie into fits of envy.

I love looking at it, gawking at all the glitz, yet I can't imagine living here. It would be like living in a museum. I'd rather have my tiny little rental house in New Hope with Lizzy.

"What do you think?" he asks me as we end our tour.

"It's gorgeous. I've never seen anything like it." By New Hope standards, my family is "rich." But there's *New Hope* rich, and there's *Hollywood Hills* rich.

Nate sighs. "Yeah. I guess it is."

"You don't like it?" A strange question to ask a man about his own house.

He shrugs. "It's a house." Then he pulls me against his chest and crushes his mouth to mine in a kiss that has me forgetting my name. His hands find their way to my hips and ass.

"Well, isn't this a cute picture?"

When I try to back away at the sound of a woman's voice, Nate takes my shoulders and turns me around while still keeping me close. "Janelle," he says. "I'd like you to meet my guest. Hanna, this is my sister, Janelle Crane."

The second he says her name, I see her face, and my jaw comes unhinged at the petite raven-haired beauty in front of me. Maybe I should have known that Nate's sister was actress Janelle Crane. He mentioned his mom was an actress the night we met, so it's not much of a leap to think he might have an actress sister as well. If I kept up on those weekly gossip magazines like my mom, I'm sure I would have connected the dots.

"Uh...wow...um..." I blink at her and search my brain for those things, the, um...words. Yes. I need words. Maybe a few of them. In a row.

Janelle raises a brow and shifts her gaze to her brother. "She looks smarter than your usual conquests, yet she doesn't seem to know how to speak in complete sentences."

"Don't be a bitch," Nate warns, but his tone is light.

My cheeks burn. "I'm just...a fan." I swallow so hard you can hear it in the quiet room.

She sighs heavily. "*Roommates*, right?" she asks, referring to the popular sitcom my friends and I watched through college.

I nod stupidly. I mean, I'm here with Nate Freaking Crane, a celebrity in his own right, but I'm going all speechless over his sister.

"Hanna is a twin too," Nate tells Janelle.

I snap my head in his direction. "You two are *twins*?" The night we met, he said that his curiosity about my twin didn't come from a sexual fetish. Now I understand what he meant.

"I'm not trying to interrupt your romantic weekend or anything," Janelle says. "I just couldn't take another minute in *his* house."

I bite my lip to make sure I don't nose in where I shouldn't. But seriously, it's all I can do not to tell her that I was totally Team Janelle through her nasty, way-too-public divorce from actor Tom Comer. (Okay, so maybe I do sometimes check out the headlines on Mom's gossip rags.) Whatever. He was blatantly cheating on her, and if three out of four nationally distributed publications sold at my grocery store are to be believed, the ass thought she should be okay with his infidelity.

"Why don't you just move in here for a while?" Nate says. "You can lie low. You know I have more than enough room."

Most of the sneer falls off her face and her eyes fill. "You mean it? I don't want to get in the way of…" Her scrutinizing eyes try to figure me out. "Whatever this is."

"Oh, no." I shake my head. "This isn't anything. I'm just a friend. I'll be out of here in a couple of days."

Nate tugs me closer, holding me against his chest. "Of course I mean it. Make yourself at home."

"Nathaniel Crane, you did not invite company into this house without even giving me a word of warning!"

The three of us turn to see a large, muscular man step into the foyer, his ebony face a mask of disapproval, his hands on his hips.

"Hanna," Nate says, "this is Jamaal. He's my groundskeeper and head of security."

Jamaal rolls his eyes. "Fancy title, but it really means I pick up Nathaniel's dirty underwear and keep the screaming fangirls from breaking in to steal it."

Nate grunts. "Will you please show Miss Thompson to my room, Jamaal? I need to talk to my sister for a minute."

Jamaal takes my bags, and I follow him up the stairs and through the long hallway to the west wing of the house. The room is as magnificent as the rest of the house, and I can't help but take in all the little details—the crown molding, the polished wooden floors, the marble-faced fireplace across from the giant bed.

Too late, I realize Jamaal is watching me. "Sorry," I mutter. "I've just never seen a house like this."

He only grunts in response. It doesn't take a genius to see that he doesn't trust me. "How long do you plan on staying?" he asks, clasping his hands in front of his body.

"Only a couple of nights." I told my family I was going out of town to make a wedding cake for a college friend whose baker had to cancel at the last minute. They bought it, but the excuse only buys me two or three days if I don't want anyone finding out about Nate. And I don't. He has to be my secret if Max is going to get that grant.

My stomach twists at the thought of Max, but it's a different kind of tummy twist since he pulled me in front of that mirror and said those things to me. Did he mean what he said or is it all part of his plan to win me back? Is he still trying to give me that confidence boost he set out to give me in the beginning? He seemed so…sincere. And hot. Since when is the idea of a guy thinking about me when he jacks off so freaking sexy?

"She can stay as long as she wants," Nate says from the doorway. Guilt has me spinning around and turning off my thoughts of Max. Nate grins at me as he enters.

"Right," Jamaal says. "Please let me know if you need anything." He turns to Nate. "Could we speak in the hall?"

Nate nods, and the two file out into the hallway. I'm not trying to listen, but I'm not trying to not to either.

From Jamaal, I hear "bad idea" and "dealing with grief," and Nate spits, "This isn't about him." Then there are murmurs and the door is opening again as Nate returns.

"How are you doing?" he asks, closing the door behind him.

"What was that about?"

Nate shrugs. "Jamaal doesn't trust people. He's worried that you're taking advantage of me at an emotionally vulnerable time."

"How does he know I'm emotionally vulnerable?"

"Not you. Me." He sighs and crosses to me.

"What happened?"

He shrugs. "My father died a couple of weeks ago."

"Oh my God." I feel like an inconsiderate bitch. Not to mention self-centered. I mean, he's a celebrity, so it's probably all over the news, but I had no idea. "I'm so sorry."

"Nothing to be sorry about. I'm fine."

Before I can say more, he's gathering me against his chest and burying his nose in my hair.

I wrap my arms around him and squeeze. Because I've lost a father too, and I understand that grief isn't always simple. Then something clicks in my head and I pull back.

"But you've been in the Midwest the last two weeks."

"I have. Did you get enough sleep on the plane, or do you want to take a nap?" He grins as if he didn't just change the subject from the death of his father. "I'll join you if you'd like some company in bed."

I don't push it. It's not my business, and he clearly doesn't want to talk about it.

Yawning, I stretch my arms above my head. "Now that you mention it, I could use a nap."

His hands find their way under my shirt. "Fantastic. I did mention my no-clothes-in-bed rule, didn't I?"

His hands have found the hook on my bra when we hear a knock at the door and we both freeze.

"Yes?" Nate calls.

"He asked her to marry him," Janelle says, her voice small. "He just called me to let me know she said yes. Does he really think this is what I need right now?"

Nate squeezes his eyes shut and curses under his breath.

"It's okay," I promise. "Go be with your sister. She needs you. I could use a shower anyway."

By the look on his face, I might as well have told him I was going to torture his puppy. "Fine, but tonight I'm getting you naked and making you come so hard you can't remember your own name."

NATE

"Tell me about this house," she whispers as she settles against me in bed.

It took me way too long to get her here tonight. It was like Janelle was on a mission to be the world's biggest cock blocker. "What do you want to know?"

"It's not you, and you don't like most of it. You could live anywhere, buy any house you want, but you live here. Why?"

I thread my fingers through her hair, grateful for the darkness. "My father bought it for me. We weren't very close, and the fact that he thought I'd like this place proves that you know me better after a couple of days than my father ever did." I sigh. "But I can't bring myself to sell it or remodel."

"You miss him, don't you?"

My jaw hardens. "My father was an asshole. It's hard to miss an asshole."

She brings her hand to my face. "Just because we have a difficult relationship with someone doesn't mean we grieve them any less when they go."

My chest tightens. Because that's exactly what my stepmother didn't understand. She told Elle and me that we weren't welcome at the funeral. She didn't understand that we needed closure as much as the children he'd given his time and attention to. Maybe more.

"Are you in a hurry to get home?" Maybe it's a change of subject or maybe it's very much on subject. Because I've had a shitty fucking month with Vivian's wedding—her happy little family—and my father's death. And Hanna's smile, the way she needs to be desired like no woman I've ever known. She makes me feel needed and necessary for the first time in too damn long.

"I have absolutely no plans until I have to meet the inspector at the end of the week." She tilts her head and studies me like we share a secret. "I'm really excited about my bakery."

"You're shitting me. You're doing it? That's amazing."

She lifts her head and meets my eyes with a small smile. "Right. Because you don't know anything about it."

"Should I?"

"Hmm. Well, I have an anonymous investor, and it's happening. They're preparing the building now."

I press a kiss to the top of her head and hold her against me, breathing her in. "You deserve it, angel."

She pulls back and gives me a sad smile. "*I'm nobody's hero, baby. Try not to fall too deep*," she says, reciting my lyrics back to me. "*I'm nobody's angel, love, but you were crying in your sleep.*"

"Oh, but you are." I nuzzle her neck. "You came along right when I needed an escape. You smile and I forget the bullshit of the world. And the sounds you make when I touch you? I could drown in that alone. Lose myself in the sound of your screams when you come." I slip a hand between her legs and roll her clit between two fingers. "Just the taste of you and I forget all the shit this life has waiting for me."

"Did you ever think that maybe you're an angel for me in the same way?" she asks. Her lips curve into a smile. *So. Damn. Sweet.*

"How do you figure?"

"Because angels don't stay forever. They're there when we

need them, and then they let us go." She studies me. "I need you to be temporary in my life as much as you need me to be temporary in yours."

HANNA

The library smells like books and cinnamon cookies. I sink into a chair and tuck my legs under me.

I dreamed about Max last night. His breath hot against my ear, his dick in my hand as I stroked him between our bodies. *"Fuck me, Max,"* I whispered in his ear. *"Show me you want me."* And he did. He pulled up my skirt and fucked me right against the wall, whispering dirty things in my ear. When he pulled out of me, Meredith tapped him on the shoulder and asked, *"Me next?"*

I woke up with an angry scream in my throat and Nate sleeping next to me.

My conscience isn't comfortable with dreaming about one man while sleeping next to another, so I slipped out of bed.

I've been dreaming about Max a lot since the night at the gym. Some of the dreams are good, some bad, but they're always sexy as hell, and I wake up wanting him and…missing him.

So why am I at Nate's Hollywood Hills home? With the bakery opening soon, I need to be in New Hope preparing my business, but I can't resist Nate's invitations. Can't resist his hands or his mouth. Can't resist those precious moments I'm in Nate's arms and I forget about my damaged heart.

Sooner or later, I'm going to stop taking these trips and accept the truth. No matter how many nights I spend with Nate, no matter how much more I feel for him, my love for Max doesn't diminish.

I thought Nate could push Max out of my heart, but I fear that Nate's taking up residence there without budging Max from his position. Yet every time I touch my lips to Nate's or let his touch me, I feel like I'm putting another nail in the coffin of my relationship with Max.

The library is my favorite place in this big house. Well, my second favorite place. Nothing beats Nate's bedroom. When I woke up this morning, I padded down here and grabbed a book off the shelf in a section that seemed to be filled with nothing but romance novels. Whoever filled this library had good taste in books.

Now I'm curled up in front of the fireplace, a steaming cup of coffee beside me, my book in my lap.

"You're still here?"

I look up to see Janelle settling into the chair across from mine. She's in black yoga pants and a thin, wide-necked tee, her dark hair thrown into a sloppy bun on top of her head, yet she's still stunning. I'm more than a little jealous.

"Do you have a problem with that?" I ask.

She lifts a shoulder. "It's Nate's house. It doesn't matter if I have a problem with it."

"Do you have a problem with me?" But I don't even care if she does. My time with Nate isn't reality. This is just temporary. Just pretend. What some actress thinks of me will have no bearing on my life.

"No." Her shoulders sag. "I don't have a problem with you, Hanna. But I'm really damn curious about what hold some random chick from Podunk, Indiana, has on my brother."

"I don't have any hold on Nate. We're just…" I search for a word, but there isn't one. Fuck buddies who aren't fucking? "We're friends."

"The way he looks at you is pretty damn friendly, all right."

Jamaal appears with a silver tray holding a ceramic teapot and a mug. He sets it onto the coffee table between us and turns to me. "May I get you anything, Miss Thompson?"

I shake my head. "I'm fine."

"Nathaniel is cooking breakfast. He's asked me to tell you two to join him in the sunroom in thirty minutes."

I can't help the smile that comes over my face at the mention of Nate.

Janelle looks skeptical. "Nate's out of bed? Before nine in the morning?"

"It appears so," Jamaal says. He looks at me pointedly. "Someone appears to be a good influence on your brother."

"It has nothing to do with me," I protest. "He's probably still on Eastern time."

"Mmm-hmm," Jamaal says. Then he turns and leaves the library.

When I look back to Janelle, she's staring at me.

"What?"

"You know what I think is hilarious?" she asks. "All these women who throw themselves at my brother—the groupies and shit? They all think Nate's this bad-boy rocker, when the truth is, half the time he'd rather hang with his comic books and his Blu-ray edition of *Firefly* than party with them. They have no idea who he really is or what he really likes. And he lets them believe what they do because he has no interest in letting a single one of them close to him. But then there's you..."

"What about me?"

"You don't think he's some bad boy."

I raise a brow. "He doesn't exactly hide his inner nerd."

She nods slowly and purses her lips.

"People see what they want to see," I say. "If those other women think he's a badass rocker, maybe that's the fantasy for them."

"Or maybe he's just letting you close the way he's never let anyone else."

I shake my head. I don't want to talk about this. Nate and

I know where we stand with each other, and that's all that matters. I don't want to try explaining it to Janelle.

"Nate doesn't bring women here," she says carefully. "You know that, right?"

I frown. "The tabloids are always talking about crazy parties at his house."

"Out back—on the patio and sometimes in the pool house. But you're the first woman I've ever known him to allow inside."

"Oh." I'm not sure what to make of that. Nate, with his aversion to commitment and his refusal to take my virginity. "Well, maybe I'm the first woman who didn't want anything from him."

"Nothing but sex, I hope," Nate says from the entrance to the library. He narrows his eyes at his sister as he crosses to us then turns his attention to me. "Don't believe anything she says about me. It's all lies. Except the good stuff. The good stuff is totally true." He takes my hand and pulls me to my feet before kissing me soundly right in front of Janelle. "Come to the kitchen. I want to feed you."

MAX

I'm not the kind of guy who dreamed about becoming a father. I guess I figured I would someday, but it wasn't something I thought much about. I definitely wasn't in a hurry, and I certainly never thought it would happen like this.

Even after I fell for Hanna, when I knew I wanted to marry her and could see what an amazing mom she was going to make, I wasn't in any hurry.

If I had to put money on whether or not this baby is mine, I'd feel safe wagering a good chunk on Meredith being a fucking liar. I mean, the timing makes sense—we screwed around at precisely the time she was telling Will she bought sperm—but she's just that level of evil that I can't take her word for it.

Fuck. It's not her fault. She's evil because she had to be. She had to be tough to survive. And once upon a time, that's why I was drawn to her. We understood each other.

I tense when I hear the bell ring. It's Meredith. I told her we could talk, and now I'm regretting doing it here and not somewhere public.

I open the door and find myself faced with a bundle of

pink sitting in a floral stroller.

"Meet Claire," Meredith whispers.

In that moment, I know without a doubt she's mine. Hell, I've seen my baby pictures enough times to know what I looked like as an infant, and here's this newborn with the same big blue eyes, the same impossibly thick mop of dark hair.

Meredith leans down, lifts the baby out of the stroller, and hands her to me. I take her, awkwardly at first until I figure out how she fits in the crook of my arm and against my chest.

She smells like baby powder, and her eyes lock on mine. Her little fingers wrap around my thumb.

Then in the space of two heartbeats and one long, ragged breath, I fall in love.

I've heard people describe moments like this as a moment when something shifted inside of them. But it's not like that for me and Claire. Quite the opposite. For the first time in my life, I'm still. Everything changes. The world shifts around us and we click into place. Daughter. Father. Just like that.

"You should have told me," I whisper. "I deserved to know."

"I won't let everyone in this town think I got knocked up."

I tear my gaze away from Claire to look at her mother. "You were willing to let them believe that when they thought Will was the father."

She frowns. "That's different." She holds out her hands, ready to take Claire back.

I shake my head and find my way to the couch. Claire is a month old. I've already missed too much. "Different because he has money," I say softly because I don't want to upset Claire.

"We could be together," she says. "I'd tell everyone she's yours if you were with us. If we could be a family."

"I will be her family," I tell Meredith without taking my eyes off Claire. "I don't have to leave Hanna for that to be true."

"Why does that fat cunt have such a hold on you?"

The fact that Claire is in my arms is the only thing that keeps me calm. I look at Meredith. I once thought she was the standard of beauty. Blond hair, blue eyes, lithe figure. But now all I see is an ugly, angry person whose former strength turned her hard and brittle.

"Get out of my house," I say calmly. "You're not welcome here if you talk about Hanna that way."

"Then give me my daughter."

I shake my head. "Go get yourself a cup of coffee or something, Mer. Claire and I have some catching up to do."

HANNA

Meredith: Just left Max's place. Thought you might want to know.

My stomach sinks as I read the words of Meredith's text. Maybe she's lying or maybe she's telling the truth, but the fact of the matter is that, even though I'm the one who insisted things be over between me and Max, my stomach turns sour at the idea of him touching anyone else. Especially Meredith.

I am *such* a hypocrite.

Nate comes up onto the sun porch and wraps his arms around me, pulling me close until my back is against his chest. "Thank God she went to bed," he whispers in my ear. "I thought she'd never leave."

I lean my head against him, and he presses his mouth to the side of my neck. "Be nice to your sister," I whisper. "She's going through a hard time."

"So am I," he protests. "I've barely gotten to touch you all day. These are the sacrifices I make for her, and she doesn't even appreciate it." His hands slide under my shirt and flatten against my belly. "Come swim with me."

"I don't have a suit," I object.

"Even better," he murmurs. Then he's pulling my shirt off over my head.

I squeak in protest, but he's already tossed my shirt to the floor and moved to the button on my jeans. "Fine," I say, wriggling out of my jeans, because this is just what I need to forget about that text from Meredith. Kicking my jeans to the side, I rub my backside against him and find him already hard. "But you should know I've never been skinny dipping before. If there's some sort of etiquette, you need to tell me now."

He groans and squeezes my hips to still them. "You keep rubbing that excellent ass of yours against me and I'm going to embarrass myself."

I turn in his arms, biting back my grin. "Really?"

His gaze dips to my breasts. Then he steps back. I'm in nothing but my black satin bra and matching panties, and his eyes flare with heat as he runs them over me. "Take off the bra, Hanna," he whispers.

I swallow hard and obey, unhooking the clasp at the front and freeing my heavy breasts. The bra falls from my shoulders and I wait. I've never liked men to look at me nude or nearly nude. I became a pro at avoiding it with Max. Why is it so different with Nate? Because he's just a fantasy and this is just temporary?

"What about your shirt?"

He pulls the shirt off over his head and throws it across the room. "Panties," he says, nodding.

I hook my thumbs into the satin at each hip and slowly slide them down. Nate's gaze follows as they drop to my ankles and I step out of them.

He steps forward and crushes his mouth against mine. His fingers trail down between my breasts and over my belly. "I need to taste you," he murmurs.

His hand dips lower, and I back away, sidestepping his touch. "I thought we were going to swim." I rush toward the doors, grinning at him over my shoulder.

"Imp," he calls after me.

I run outside and across the patio to the pool. When I step into the heated water, it swirls around my ankles and my nipples harden in the cool night air. Before I make it down the steps, Nate's behind me. When I turn, he's nude—glorious—his cock jutting out between us. I want to touch him. To sink deeper into the pool and take him into my mouth while the warm water kisses my skin.

Resisting temptation, I take a shallow dive and swim to the far end before surfacing. I grab the edge of the pool then squeak when a hand wraps around my ankle.

Nate turns me around from under the water. He slowly kisses his way up my body—my thighs, my stomach, my breasts. By the time he's broken the surface, I'm trembling and clinging to the edge.

He grins and settles his hand either side of me, blocking me in until I lace my arms behind his neck. "You've really never been skinny dipping?"

I shrug. "Now I have."

"So I'm your first."

"You're my first a lot of things," I whisper, my eyes dropping to his neck.

He tilts my chin up with a finger so my eyes meet his. "Like what?"

"My first rocker. My first trip to LA. My first..." I'm embarrassed to admit the truth.

"What?" he prods.

"Oral sex." My cheeks burn.

His eyes go wide. "I've heard of beginner's luck, but there's no way—"

"No. I'd given a blowjob before. Many times. But I'd never..." This conversation is growing increasingly awkward for me, and I try to back away, but he holds me fast.

"Your boyfriend didn't go down on you? Is he one of those idiots who thinks it's gross?"

"No. He wanted to. I..." So embarrassing. Why did I bring this up? "I wouldn't let him."

"Shit," he breathes, but he doesn't look upset, just

astonished. "Then why'd you let me?"

"I didn't have anything to lose with you," I admit. Letting Max do it would have meant letting him get me naked. Letting him look at parts of me I didn't think he'd like.

He shakes his head. "I wish you would have told me."

"I'm glad I didn't." Because I know he wouldn't have done it if he'd known, and that experience—being up on the vanity of that fancy hotel bathroom, spread wide as he licked and kissed me to orgasm—I wouldn't want to give that up.

I wrap my legs around him instinctively and a shudder of pleasure shimmies through my body at the pressure of his hard cock between my thighs.

He closes his eyes. "I'm not sure what I've done to deserve it, but it's clear that I'm being tested."

"Yeah?" I bite my lip and cautiously roll my hips, grinding our bodies together. "Who said this was a test you needed to pass?"

"Hanna…" He brings his mouth down to mine and kisses me hard. His hands squeeze my hips, and I love the way he holds me tight. "Thank you," he murmurs against my lips. "For trusting me." Then he's kissing me again, and one hand moves up to my breast, cupping, squeezing.

I gasp as he pinches. He drops his head to my breast and draws my nipple into his mouth.

Before I realize what he's doing, he's holding me and swimming to the shallow end of the pool. I squeak when he lifts me and settles me onto the top stair, my feet dangling into the water.

"You're kicking me out of your pool?"

He sinks down and gives me a wicked grin. Floating closer, he parts my thighs and the smile leaves his eyes and is replaced by heat as he draws a finger down my center. My hips tuck forward instinctively and my legs part, giving him better access.

"I love knowing mine is the only mouth that's ever touched you here." He leans forward and presses his tongue to my clit—not licking, not sucking. Just tasting.

I wriggle my hips, attempting to return to the pool, but he holds me fast with a hand at each hip. My nipples pucker in the cool night air.

"Relax, angel. I want to make you come while you look at the stars."

MAX

Sunday means family dinner at Hanna's mom's. It also means pretending we're still together. And that—being so close to her that I can smell her, so close that her hand brushes my arm when she talks—is heaven and hell all wrapped into one.

"Let me get you some potato casserole," I say to Hanna. "Isn't it your favorite?"

She shakes her head. "I don't need it. I ate breakfast at home."

I don't believe her, but now is neither the time nor the place.

"Krystal!" Lizzy shrieks. She drops her silverware and hops up from the table to meet her sister at the door. Hanna follows, and her smile is bigger than I've seen it in weeks.

"Oh my God, Hanna," Krystal shrieks. "You're really dropping weight."

"Too fast," Liz grumbles, and I'd have to agree but I know better than to say anything.

"I still have a long way to go," Hanna says.

"I'm so glad to see you finally paying attention to your health," Hanna's mother says, nodding with approval toward her daughter's plate of raw vegetables and a small pile of fruit salad.

I struggle to bite my tongue. I've seen Hanna on the treadmill in my club, and I've watched her avoid food like it's the enemy. I'm an idiot if I thought my little speech in front of the mirror was going to do any good.

Hanna blushes. "I've just been so busy getting the bakery up and running."

"How's that going?" Krystal asks as the girls settle at the table.

"It's amazing," Hanna says. She practically glows when she talks about it. "I really love it."

"I heard you've been taking a bunch of out-of-town clients too," Krystal says, which makes Hanna's blush turn from pink to red.

"I have no complaints," she says.

Later, when I pull up to the bakery, silence pulls between us, stretched thin under the weight of a thousand things unsaid. She stares out the window, lost in her own mind.

I pull the key from the ignition and lean back in my seat. "Is this it for us? Is it over?"

She practically jumps at my words. "What?"

"I don't want to pretend anymore. Not if you're only doing it for me. Screw the grant, Hanna. If you don't want me, if you can't forgive me, I'll let you go. But I can't stand seeing you on edge like you have been. I can't stand seeing you starve yourself."

Her face goes angry, defensive. "I'm not starving myself."

"Are you in love with him?" The question is out of my mouth before I decide I'm going to ask. I don't know that there is a *him*, but I suspect.

"What?" Her eyes go hard. "I don't know what you're talking about."

I close my eyes and take a breath. "All I know is that the only thing that makes you happy is that bakery and…whatever it is you're doing with your weekends."

"You want the ring back?" she asks weakly.

"I want you to live your life. You deserve more than to put it on hold for me."

Her lips part and she studies me.

"I'll be okay," I promise. And it's true. One way or another, I'll make it work. I can let the maid go and start cleaning the club myself or…something. There's always a way.

"What if you're still the only man I'm in love with?"

My heart stumbles, full and clumsy. "I love you too."

"I'm trying to let you go," she whispers. "Then I see you with my family or remember the way we used to laugh together. The way you touched me…"

I swallow, afraid to hope. If there's any chance she'll take me back, I'll take it. "Then don't let go."

"I love you too much to give up, but I don't trust you enough to take you back." She climbs out of my car and I watch her walk away as I try to breathe around the bruises on my battered heart.

NATE

She's still in love with him.

The words have repeated like an ominous drumbeat in my mind since I saw Hanna walk into Asher's house on Max's arm. She and I have been playing at this thing between us for over two months now. Every time I say goodbye to her, I swear to myself that it's the last time, but inevitably, one or two weeks later, I'm summoning her again.

It's selfish and unforgivable. She drops everything and rearranges her life to come meet me for a night, two if we're lucky. But I can't stop. She's my breath.

And she's still in love with him—should be marrying him.

"Hey, you doing okay, bud?"

I yank my gaze up from where I was studying my beer to see Asher frowning at me. "Fine. Just…" Just what? Heartbroken that the woman to whom I'll promise nothing looks really damn happy with a guy who'd be one hundred times better for her than I am? Surprised that the woman who made me keep our relationship secret is still in love with the other guy? Fuck. Did this really come as a shock?

"Hey, Nate." Maggie is all smiles and happiness as she heads toward the bar. People are chatting, music is playing, but it's clear as day that the source of her happiness is being this close to Asher.

Asher wraps his arm around her waist and draws her in for a quick kiss. They're absolutely, nauseatingly, deliriously happy together. Normally I'm glad for that. Asher deserves happiness. But tonight, I hate them both a little for having something I could only pretend at having.

When their quick kiss turns into something longer and steamier, I clear my throat.

Maggie pulls back, her cheeks burning red. "Sorry," she murmurs.

"I'm not." Asher grunts and pulls her back to him so her back is to his front. "You're always welcome here, but I'm not going to stop touching my girl just because you need to hide from whatever Hollywood diva is giving you trouble this week."

Hollywood diva. If only.

Maggie narrows her eyes at me. "Who is it this time? I heard rumors about Cyrus, but…"

Not my type. My type is curvier with dark hair and darker eyes, like black coffee but sweeter. Like dark chocolate but warmer. "Who says I'm running from a woman?"

Maggie and Asher exchange a look, and I'm pretty sure they're laughing at me in their own secret couple code. Assholes.

"It's so good to see Hanna here tonight," Maggie says. "I've been worried about her."

Asher nods. "She's under a lot of stress. All you can do is make sure she knows you're here if she needs you."

I want to ask what kind of stress. Do they know about her breakup? Do they know Max proposed and his ring waits for Hanna in her jewelry box? It feels so important that I know, but there's no way I can ask that without tipping off Asher and Maggie to my relationship with Hanna.

Relationship? She'd probably call it an affair. Fuck, *I* should be calling it an affair.

Across the room, Lizzy, Hanna's twin, says something that makes Max laugh, but he can't keep his eyes off Hanna. Like he's afraid she might disappear if he looks away too long. I don't know what happened between them, but I convinced myself that he wasn't attracted to her—or at least that he made her think he wasn't. That was the only explanation I could come up with for her insecurities and relative lack of experience. Now that I see them together, I know it's not true.

"See if she and Max want to stay after and use the pool," Asher says, completely oblivious to the knife he's digging into my back. "We'll be on our way out of town, and Nate won't mind."

Maggie nods, worry creasing her brow as she studies her sister. "That's a good idea. She's been so busy with the bakery. They could probably use the extra alone time."

Well, fuck this. "I think I'm going to crash." I dump my beer in the sink. When I told Hanna I'd be in New Hope this week, she warned me that I might see her with Max and that they were trying to look like a happy couple around her family. I promised that I wouldn't say a word. That promise is starting to feel like a deal with the devil.

What am I even doing? Vivian called me yesterday and told me that they're not moving to Tennessee. She's getting a divorce.

"*Why?*" I asked. "*What happened?*"

"*He can't handle the fact that I'm still in love with you.*"

Before I could even process her words, her whispered apologies, I was accepting flying to Indiana, pushing Vivian's words from my mind to make room for thoughts of Hanna.

"*We were good together. Why didn't we try harder?*"

Vivian is offering me something I've wanted for years. The chance to make a real family with my son. And the only thing I could think was that I didn't want to let Hanna go.

I have to end this. I've told myself that a thousand times, but it's never been so obvious as it is tonight. I pull my phone from my pocket.

> **Nate:** *Can't meet up tonight. Something came up.*

Across the room, Hanna looks at her phone and blinks at the screen. Her eyes meet mine, her expression full of hurt and resignation. That's the look of a woman who expects men to hurt her, who expects to be left alone. And I feel like fucking shit for being the one who put it there.

HANNA

"Are you sure you should be drinking another?"

Maggie, of all effing people, is looking at me like some concerned mother hen. Maggie, of all people, is hinting that maybe I'm drinking too much.

I glare at her and throw back the tequila. The white kind. Like Nate introduced me to.

Fucking asshole.

As soon as I think the words, I'm swamped with guilt. He made the score clear from the beginning, didn't he? He showed his cards, and I still insisted on playing the game. But damn did it hurt when I saw that magazine cover. I was at the drugstore buying some of those diet pills that help keep my appetite in check and there it was, right by the checkout.

I did a double take.

No. Not Nate. Someone who looks like Nate...

That's an old picture...

It's been digitally altered. It didn't really happen...

Eventually, I was out of excuses. While I stood there staring at the newsstand, the diet pills and the contents of my purse scattered across the floor.

That was definitely Nate. I know that jaw. That hair. Those biceps.

It was definitely not an old picture. Vivian's latest haircut made headlines, so I'm well aware that the picture couldn't be more than two weeks old.

And if it was digitally altered? Well, if it was, it was a damn fine job.

But why wouldn't he kiss the mother of his child in front of that swanky LA restaurant? Why wouldn't he let her slide her hands into his hair and press her breasts against his chest? Why wouldn't he do anything he pleased with anyone he pleased?

He hadn't promised me anything, and in the last two weeks, he hasn't called or texted, hasn't invited me to meet up with him. It's over, and that shouldn't take me by surprise.

"I'll take another shot," I call out to no one in particular.

Brady, the owner of this little drinking hole, wanders toward me on his side of the counter. "No. I don't think you will."

"Are you kidding me? You're cutting me off?"

"Someone needs to," he grumbles, all fatherly and disappointed.

I wince because I'm not used to disappointing anyone but my mom. And I don't care for the feeling. Then I shake my head and hop off the stool. *Fuck it.*

I'm not going to be that girl anymore. I'm not going to be the one who bends over backward to make everyone happy. I'm not going to be the one who lives in the shadows because she's too afraid that, if she steps into the light, people might see her for who she really is and disapprove.

I'm worth a little disapproval, aren't I? And I might not be better than some actress, but I'm *something*. I'm *worth* something.

"Hanna," Brady says carefully.

"No. No worries, Brady. I'll be down the street at The Wire. They'll let me drink, and they have better service anyway."

I right myself and find the door. Only instead of going to The Wire, I find myself headed toward Max's health club and climbing the stairs to his little apartment above it.

Max opens the door as I reach the landing, and I stall, my feet glued to the decking as his eyes travel over me, taking me in inch by inch as if he thinks he's seeing a ghost. He almost smiles, but then his lips go flat and he just stares at me, hurt in those gorgeous ice-blue eyes.

Why is *he* the one so hurt? He's the one who started this relationship under false pretenses. He's the one who wanted another woman while he was supposed to want me.

He's the one who broke my heart.

I want to hate him *and* Nate, to lump them both in the category of *asshole men who aren't worth my time.* But I love them.

I stumble back a step as the thought registers. I love them both.

When did I fall in love with Nate? That wasn't supposed to happen. He was just the rebound guy—there to make me feel good about myself while my heart mended.

Max steps closer and steadies me before I can hit the railing.

I swallow—hard—his words from last month echoing in my head. *"Maybe if you could see what I'm picturing when I jack off—if you had any idea how much I fantasize about driving inside of you, sucking those tits, making you come—maybe then you'd believe me."*

"Do you want to come inside?" he asks carefully.

Licking my lips, I nod as he holds the door open for me.

His living room speakers click, and a new song starts. Jason Mraz's "I Won't Give Up." Wasn't this the song that was playing the night he proposed?

My stomach tangles into a mess of knots as he closes the door. He looks so sexy tonight in jeans and a gray button-up shirt, his sleeves rolled to his elbows. My eyes follow the path across his broad shoulders and down to his thick forearms and big hands. I miss those hands. I miss Max.

I miss lying in his arms and talking about our dreams for the future. His plans for his club, my dreams of a bakery, our speculation of what our children might look like if we had them together.

Something catches in my throat, and the could-have-beens are so heavy in my heart that I can't breathe.

"Did you mean what you said? Was all that…true?"

"What I said when?"

I swallow. "A few weeks ago in the club. When you made me look in the mirror and you said…you thought about me."

His chest expands with his deep inhalation. "Every word."

"I don't believe you," I whisper. Because that's really the problem, isn't it? The reason I can't be with him isn't because he kissed Meredith in December. We weren't really a couple at that point. We weren't exclusive. What I don't believe is that, somewhere in those months between, I became the type of woman he wants. I don't believe he could really desire a body like mine. "I want to. But I can't."

"I know." He shoves his hands in his pockets, his face resigned. "Aside from ripping off your clothes, I'm not sure how I can prove it to you."

A giggle slips from my lips. Maybe it's the tequila or my decision to say "fuck it" to what everyone else thinks. But I grin because I like the idea of Max ripping off my clothes. Or I like it in theory. In reality, it would mean he'd see me and all my imperfections, and that wouldn't end well.

"You don't even know what I look like naked," I protest. "I'm pretty sure if I'd ever let you get me naked, you wouldn't be saying that now."

"Tell yourself what you must, Han." He drags a hand through his dark hair. God. He's so flipping gorgeous. Why do I have to be attracted to men who are so completely out of my league?

"Lemme prove it to you."

Stepping toward him, I tug my shirt off over my head and toss it to the floor. His lips part and his breath escapes in a rush. Before my brain can catch up with my hands, I kick off my shoes and unbutton my jeans, shoving them down my hips.

The months we were together—really together, not this pretend we've been playing since the texts—I hid myself from him. I was so terrified that if he saw all my dimples and soft spots, cellulite and imperfections, he would lose all interest.

But now what do I have to lose? He needs to see me as I really am.

"Hanna," he whispers, his eyes running over me. "What are you doing?"

"I'm proving that you aren't attracted to me. Not the real me, at least." I unhook my black bra, and I hear the hiss of his inhale as I let it slide from my shoulders. Next, I remove my underwear and kick it to the side.

My heart slams as I finally force myself to lift my head and meet his gaze, and I'm shocked by the heat I see there, the desire.

"Is that real?" I whisper. "I want to believe you're not pretending. I want to believe…"

He closes his eyes for two thuds of my heart, and when he opens them, he steps closer. "I couldn't fake this if I wanted to."

"Make love to me, Max. Have sex with me. I want to believe. Make me believe."

"Hanna," he breathes. He steps closer, pulls my body against his—my bare flesh against his denim-and-cotton-clad heat—and buries his nose in my hair. He leans in, brushes kisses along my jaw, and lets his mouth hover just above my ear.

"You standing here naked and begging me to fuck you," he whispers, his hands skimming up my bare sides and sending shivers of pleasure through me. "You have no idea what that does to me. I want it as much as you do. *More*. But I won't. Not while you're drunk and not while you're pretending my ring doesn't belong on your finger."

I stumble back. "Really? Because that just sounds like a convenient excuse."

"Try me. Come back here sober and test me, Hanna."

"Well, isn't this…cozy."

I spin around to see Meredith standing at the door, baby in her arms, and for a minute, I'm so caught off guard by her appearance, so blown over by my hatred for her, that I forget that I'm standing here completely nude.

Max steps in front of me to block me from her view. "Meredith, give us a minute."

"Nobody wants to see that anyway," Meredith sneers as she backs onto the deck.

Max pushes the door closed behind her and turns to me. "I'm sorry. This is terrible timing. I just…"

I scramble to gather my clothes. Tears burn the backs of my eyes. "I was so stupid. So, so stupid." With shaking hands, I fumble with the clasp on my bra then reach for my shirt.

"The truth is," Max says, "we need to talk."

"No, we don't." I shake my head as I shove my feet into my jeans. *Fuck, fuck, fuck.* What was I thinking? He's not mine anymore. I broke it off. So of course he's with Meredith now. "You want her. You can have her."

He grabs my hand. "Stop. Please?"

There's something in his voice that makes me lift my eyes to his. "Don't lie to me. I can't handle another lie."

He drags a hand through his hair. "This isn't how I wanted to tell you."

My stomach folds in on itself and I double over. "Tell me what?"

"Meredith and I aren't together. You're the only one I want." He stares at me, as if willing me to believe his words. "She's here to drop off the baby."

"So you're her babysitter now?"

"No. I'm the father." Maybe the apology that's all over his face should soften the blow of that news, but it doesn't.

Max and Meredith had a baby together.

I back toward the door.

"Hanna," he whispers. "Can we talk about this?"

I shake my head and grasp for the knob. Rushing out onto the deck, I come face to face with Meredith, her pink-painted lips pursed in a self-satisfied smirk.

"Desperate much?" she asks.

"Fuck you," I breathe.

She cuts her eyes to the door then back to me before she smiles. When she speaks, it's for my ears only. "Thanks, but I'll leave that to Max."

I don't believe her. Not really. But her words still make me feel small and ugly, and when I make it back to my apartment, I do the only thing I know to soothe the hurt. I text Nate.

NATE

Five Days Before Hanna's Accident

Here I am again. Another night with her in my bed. Another weekend with her at my house. Another morning waking with Hanna in my arms when I know damn well she belongs somewhere else.

I don't want her to leave. The realization hit me hard when she walked in my door last night, and I haven't been able to shake it. She's amazing. I've watched her win over Janelle, and now they talk like old friends. Then there's the way I feel when she's around—like I've been breathing with collapsed lungs and suddenly they're expanding again.

Here we are, suspended in time. Both of us escaping from the real world waiting on the other side of the door. Right now, I just want to watch her sleep and indulge in the fantasy of this being my life. What would that be like? Every morning waking up to her smell, my hand between her full breasts, her ass nestled against my cock. What would it be like to walk in the door and hear her laughter carrying through my house?

She saw the pictures of Vivian kissing me. They were all over the freaking magazines, but when I asked her about it, she shrugged it off. Didn't say a word. Part of me wanted her to be pissed. To see her throw things and tell me I'm an unworthy asshole. I wanted to be worth that kind of reaction, which is completely unfair when I'm the one who keeps insisting that we can't be more.

Vivian wants more, but I told her that she needs to take some time and finalize her divorce. She's a good woman—one of the best—and an amazing mom, and part of me will always love her, but we can't rush into a relationship that could confuse Collin. We both need to be *sure* that's what we want.

"Something's holding you back," she said after I ended the kiss that was splashed all over the internet.

I shrugged. "This isn't a decision we can make on an impulse."

"You're in love with her," she said.

"Who?"

She gave me a sad smile. "I don't know. I just know you love her. I can see it in your eyes."

"It's not serious. She's hung up on somebody else, and…"

"Tell her how you feel," Vivian said, squeezing my arm. "She needs to know."

"How do you know I haven't already?"

"Because I know you."

I nodded. "I won't do that to Collin. He's my family. I don't need anyone else."

Vivian's sweet face was sad as she studied me. "Don't use Collin as an excuse to put walls around your heart. Whoever she is, she's already found her way in. Think about what you're doing before you push her away." She stepped back and released my arm. "She's a lucky girl."

Hanna smiles in her sleep and settles her hand flat against her belly, her fingertips meeting the hair between her legs. What does a woman like Hanna dream about? The ex-boyfriend she won't tell her family is an ex? Or have I found my way into her dreams? She moans as her hips lift off the bed and toward some invisible lover. Jealousy flashes through me. I don't want her dreaming about anyone but me. Not while she's in my bed.

I sweep my lips across hers and down her neck, licking and nipping at the sensitive skin until she arches under me, and her hands roam over my bare chest.

"Good morning," I murmur.

"Morning." She's got the sexiest flush to her cheeks when she wakes up.

Our eyes lock for a few moments and my heart feels full and torn all at once. "What are you going to do when I let you go?"

She grins at me. "What do you mean?"

"When this is over and we stop meeting each other all over the country, are you going to put on his ring?"

She doesn't answer, and for the first time, I realize I want her to say no. I want her to ask me for the things I've told her I can't give. It's foolish and reckless and everything I swore to myself I wouldn't do, but I'll be damned if I don't feel like one of those lovesick idiots who says, "We'll make it work," and finds himself months later dealing with the consequences.

Giggling, she rolls to her back and stretches her arms above her head. "I slept so well. Did you?"

Very little. I spent an embarrassing amount of time watching her sleep. "Better than usual."

"Dream about anything good?"

"The dreams couldn't compete with the real thing lying next to me."

She snorts and rolls toward me, sliding an arm around my waist. "I bet that's what you tell all the girls."

Not at all. In fact, aside from kissing Vivian, I haven't touched another woman since my first night with Hanna. No other woman has appealed to me since I touched her.

"Tell me about your dreams, angel. What does your future look like in that amazing brain of yours?" I ask because I want to know and to remind myself why I need to keep my distance from her.

She snuggles closer and traces my tattoos with her fingertips. "Hmm, I don't know. I feel silly saying it out loud."

I tilt her chin up so she's looking at me. "Try. For me?"

"Okay… My bakery is successful. Days that start at four a.m. The smell of bread and pastries. Happy brides and wedding cakes that are so beautiful no one wants to cut into them." She smiles, lost in the image. "A little house for me in historic New Hope so I'm close to my bakery but still have space for kids, a backyard for a big dog. Evenings walking along the river and Sunday brunch, where I see my sisters and our kids grow up together—cousins who play and fight like brothers and sisters." She shakes her head, as if to shake away the thought, and releases a breath. "Probably sounds pretty lame to a big-shot celebrity."

"Not at all. It sounds…amazing." There's reverence in my voice. I don't know what that's like—the small-town life, the tight-knit family—and I envy the simplicity of it.

But she chuckles softly. "You don't think less of me because I don't want to escape the little town where I grew up?"

"I couldn't think less of you." I press a kiss to her mouth then move my way down her body, stopping to lick each nipple and suck at the sensitive skin above each hipbone. When I sink between her legs, she parts them easily, and her cries fill my ears as I explore her with my fingers and tongue.

And after she comes, I softly bite the inside of her thigh, suck until she gasps and then moans with pleasure. I'm marking her. Do I want her so-called ex to see I was here? Or do I just want her to remember me when she sees it? I don't need to understand *why* I'm doing it to know that I am. Marking her. Because knowing I can't have her doesn't change that I want her to be mine.

"Looks like you're cooking for an army this morning."

I look up from the fruit covering my cutting board and see Hanna walking into the kitchen. She fell back asleep and I came down here to make breakfast. She's not eating enough, so

I made bacon, hash brown casserole, cinnamon rolls, and fruit salad. She's wearing a robe—with nothing else if I'm lucky. I wipe my hands on a towel and skirt around the island to pull her into my arms. She has that effect on me. I see her and need to touch her. She melts into me as I kiss her, sweeping my tongue inside to taste her, to drink her in. When I break the kiss, it's only because I want it to be so much more.

"What are you doing with all this food?" she asks.

"I'm feeding my girl."

She blushes. "I just need some coffee and maybe a little of that fruit salad."

"What you need is a keeper. How much weight have you lost since we met three months ago?"

Ignoring my question, she goes to the coffee pot to pours herself a cup.

"Hanna," I whisper as she turns around. I tilt her chin up so she's looking at me. "I'm worried about you."

"I needed to lose some weight. Trust me, I'm not going to waste away."

"You didn't need to lose an ounce." My gut burns with rage at whoever made her feel this way. That rage used to be directed at the ex, but I'm not sure anymore. "Did he do this to you? Did he make you feel this way?"

"It doesn't matter."

"Fuck, Hanna. What did this loser do to you?"

"He's not a loser!" She snaps her mouth shut and drops her gaze to her coffee.

My gaze floats to her naked ring finger. "So you haven't given him an answer yet."

She gasps. "I wouldn't be here if I had."

I am such a hypocrite, because *fuck* that hurts. "Yeah, but you see, that assumes you're going to take him back. If you'd answered and told him no, there'd be nothing wrong with being here with me."

I return to the fruit salad, and the room is tense with our silence.

I make us each a plate and take them to the sunroom. No

sun this morning. Rain has been falling since last night, and I'm not sure when it's supposed to stop. She settles into the chair across from me and closes her eyes.

"I'm sorry, Hanna," I say. "I know you love Max. I just…"

"What do you want me to do?" she asks.

I drop my fork and shake my head. Because that's just it. "Nothing. I'm not asking anything from you. I'm not him."

Pushing out of her chair, she goes outside. That came out wrong. *Shit.* I just mean that he's better than me. He's the better choice, the choice that makes sense. I follow her to the patio, where she's watching the rain.

"It's not you," I say softly. "You know that, right?" The sky is gray, the rain coming down in a constant melancholy drizzle. Miserable day for a miserable conversation. "I can't offer you more than this. Even when you deserve more. It's not because I don't want it. It's because I made a promise to myself. To my son."

When she turns to me, confusion is all over her face as she traces the tattoo with Collin's birthday. "I never asked you for more, Nate."

Her touch is killing me. Making me want what I can't have. I grab her hand and squeeze. "But you deserve it."

"I'm a big girl. Let me decide what I deserve."

"You deserve everything. Anything you could want. But I'm not the man to give that to you. I can't." I take a breath and study the sky because I can't look her in the eye when I tell the story—when I explain how easy I am to leave behind. I tell her about my dad leaving, about being the second family, explain that I can't do that to Collin, and with every word, I hear Vivian talking over me in my head. *"Don't use Collin as an excuse to put walls around your heart. Whoever she is, she's already found her way in. Think about what you're doing before you push her away."*

"You're a great dad, Nate," she says when I'm finished. And even though she really doesn't have any evidence for her claim, it still means the world coming from her. "You'd never make him feel like that."

"It's hard enough to be a kid to celebrity parents. I won't pile that on too. Collin is the most important thing in my life. I can't give you more without taking something from him. I won't do that."

"I wish you'd quit making it seem like I'm asking for that."

I stare at her, long and hard. I know she's not asking for more from me. Isn't that why I'm so scared to offer it? "What happens if we don't end this, Hanna? You can't be my mistress for the rest of my life. You can't keep flying out here when I snap my fingers. Every time I say goodbye, I tell myself that's it. That I'll end it. Because you deserve that. But I'm weak and selfish as shit and keep calling you back because I can't get enough of you."

"What are you trying to say?"

I close my eyes and tilt my face to the sky, letting the rain wash over it. Then I feel her behind me. She kisses my bare shoulder and my heart snags between fear and hope.

"Are you still in love with him?"

I feel her tense behind me as she removes her mouth from my skin. "I am. But I'm in love with you too."

I squeeze my eyes shut. "Don't say that."

Before I know it, she's gone—running into the house and away from me. How did I let this get so fucking complicated? I knew I would only hurt her, and I was right.

"Shit," I breathe, chasing after her.

I find her in bed, curled onto her side, eyes closed. I climb in and wrap my arms around her. "I was in such an ugly, dark place the night we met. I looked into your eyes, and you were right there with me—my angel in the darkness. You saved me." I breathe her in, a man taking his last breaths of pure oxygen before going underground. "You saved me, and I love you."

She doesn't reply, so I keep going. Because she needs to know. "I think I've been in love with you since the night we met. And I know that sounds crazy and implausible—like one of those things the guy says when he's trying to win the girl—but for me, it's just true. I love you and I'm terrified that you're going to ruin your life because of it. I'm not telling you to take his ring. I honestly believe that if he were worthy of you, you wouldn't be here with me. But don't let *me* be the reason you don't take the life you want."

"What if *you're* the life I want?"

There it is again. That snag on my heart, a tiny tear at the top as it's caught in the middle of this internal war. "You're asking me for something I can't give."

HANNA

I wait until he loosens his hold and then I turn in his arms. "Okay. But there is something you can give me."

His brow furrows and his eyes drop to my lips. "What's that?"

"Make love to me, Nate. I want you to be my first."

Holding my breath, I wait for him to respond. His breathing changes, and he threads his fingers through my hair and tucks it behind my ear. "Hanna," he murmurs, and I know from the way his voice breaks that he's lost the battle with himself.

I close the inches between our mouths and sweep my lips over his. Before I can pull away, he fists his hand in my hair and holds me tight. The kiss turns hungry and desperate, and I understand. For three months, we've been building up to this moment, and as much as I'm sure of my decision, my belly is a bundle of wild nerves.

He rolls us until I'm on my back and he's hovering over me. He parts my robe with one hand and lowers his mouth to my neck, my breasts, my belly. I shove his pants down, and he kicks them to the side. I'm trembling by the time he tugs my panties from my hips and pushes my thighs apart.

"Once won't be enough," he murmurs as his mouth skims

my hipbones. He rocks his hand against me, and I raise my hips off the bed.

"Please," I whisper. "Don't make me wait."

After grabbing a condom from the drawer, he sits back to slide it over his thick erection. Then he lifts his eyes to mine. "There's so much I want to show you, and you're going to be sore tomorrow."

I grin. "Pretty confident, aren't you?"

He moves back up my body until he's framing my face in his hands. I'll never forget the look in his eyes the first time he saw me naked, the intensity, the heat. But it's different now. There's something else in those dark, expressive eyes. Tenderness. Love.

Maybe I thought it would be rough and crazed if Nate and I ever made love, but he's not in any hurry. His mouth on mine is slow and thorough and full of promise, and when he breaks the kiss, I feel him poised at my entrance. He watches me as he slowly slides in, and I'm so desperate for more that I want to arch my back and push him deeper.

"Please," I murmur.

He shuts his eyes for a breath, and his lids are heavy when he opens them again. "You feel so fucking amazing. But I'm afraid I'll hurt you."

"It's okay," I whisper. "It feels good. I want more."

He hesitates a moment. Then he sinks all the way in. There's a stretching and pulling sensation, but it's not pain, not exactly. It feels too good to be described at pain. It's just adjustment as my body stretches to accommodate him.

He's completely still inside me as he sprinkles kisses across the bridge of my nose and down the crook of my neck. When I lift my hips, he groans. "Do you feel okay?"

"It's good," I whisper. I draw up my knees, and we both lose our breath for a second as our positions adjust and he's fully sheathed by me. I lock my ankles behind his back. "So good."

He lowers his mouth to my ear as he finds his rhythm. Each time he presses into me, fills me up, he touches some deep spot that begs for more. It's a new sensation. Deep and unexpected. I wouldn't know how to describe it if I had to.

"I've dreamed about this," he murmurs against my ear. "I'd dream that we got carried away, and it felt so damn good." He nips at my ear. "Then I'd wake up and you'd be next to me. So fucking sweet and beautiful. I've wanted to do this since that first night. And knowing that you were a virgin…" He groans in my ear and slips a hand between our bodies, finding my clit with his thumb.

I cry out and squeeze around him.

"I wanted to be the one to show you how good this feels." He adds more pressure to my clit and drives deeper with those words. I feel myself coil tight, so close to release. "I've spent months imagining what it'd be like to have you squeezing my dick when you come."

My body quivers with orgasm, and I can't help but rock my hips as I ride it out. I expect him to come with me or right after, but when my body has turned to mush and the orgasm has passed, he pushes up on his elbows and smiles at me. It's not his normal cocky grin. It's this sweet, vulnerable smile that seems to say I've just made him happy.

"You are so sexy," he whispers. "So fucking sexy you make me lose my mind."

I lick my lips. "I like it when you lose your mind."

He pulls out almost all the way, and I gasp with the loss. He grips my hips and rises onto his knees, lifting my hips up off the bed and keeping us connected. For a second, I think he's going to stop, that he's done with me, but then he's filling me again, driving into me at this new, deeper angle. His eyes are hot and his gaze is locked on that spot where our bodies meet, and I suddenly understand the appeal of the position. They say that women aren't visual, but seeing all of Nate, watching him lose his control as he thrusts his hips, is so hot it has me climbing again.

"That's right, angel," he growls, lifting his eyes to mine.

He strokes my clit, and his movements grow rougher. This time as I come, he slams into me, the muscles in his neck straining as his fingers curl deeper into my hips, and he comes.

After he cleans up in the bathroom, he slides back into bed next to me. He wraps his arms around me and nuzzles my neck. "I don't want to let you go."

My body is sore and sated, my heart full, my eyes closed as I'm curled against him. I breathe him in and remind myself to stay in this moment—here and now. No regrets or longing for a future that can't be.

"If only you weren't still in love with him," Nate whispers.

I picture Max—the big grin, the intense eyes. No matter how much I want this moment to be about me and Nate and no one else, it can't be that way when my heart is divided.

"I can't help that."

I can tell by the way his body stiffens that he thought I was sleeping and didn't expect me to hear his words. "He's waiting for you." It isn't a question, more like a reminder.

"Why are we talking about this?"

He finds my left hand and takes it in his, rubbing my bare ring finger. "Because I'm in love with you."

My heart swells at his words, threatening to burst at the fractured seams. "I love you too."

"What if I told you I needed you to choose?"

I turn in his arms so I can see his face. "I don't understand."

He slides a hand into my hair and brings my head to rest against his chest. "This is hard for me. I've never wanted..."

I want to look at his face, to try to understand what he's saying, but he clutches me tighter against his chest, and all I can do is wrap my arms around him and hold on.

"My decision not to start another family wasn't a difficult one for me," he says softly. "Collin is my world, and I never thought anyone would matter as much as him. But then I met you." He loosens his hold, and I draw back so I can see his face. There's torment in his eyes.

"What are you trying to say?"

"I'm saying I've fallen in love with a girl who makes me want to figure it all out and find a way to make it work."

My chest tightens with hope, confusion, terror. Because...

me and Nate for real? How would that even work? "Nate, you don't have to—"

"I want to. Fuck, angel, I *need* to."

"Then why do you look so sad?"

"Because you're still in love with him, and I'm not sure I'm the guy you'll choose." He brushes his knuckles across my cheek and lowers his voice so I can barely make out his words. "I'm not sure I'm the one you *should* choose."

"I love you." I feel the tears on my cheeks. The panic in my chest.

"You need to talk to Max. Before I come to New Hope to work with Asher next week. You need to put it out there. Tell him what you're scared of. As much as I want to believe he's just some asshole after you for the wrong reasons, I don't think that's true. I've seen the way he looks at you, Hanna. You have to hear him out because you deserve better than to let your insecurities keep you from the life you deserve."

"And what if I choose him?"

He studies me in the silence, his eyes roaming over my features. Memorizing. "I'll let you go. I know this is hard for you, and you have my word that I'll respect your decision once you've made it. I'll still feel like the luckiest bastard in the world because you trusted me with something precious."

"My virginity?"

"Your heart, angel." He swallows. "But here's the deal. If you choose *me*, I want all of you. Mind, body, and soul. I won't settle for less and I won't share."

MAX

The notification light on my phone is flashing at me when I get back to my office. Shit. I missed a call from Hanna.

I dial the voicemail and listen.

"Hi, Max. Can you swing by my place tonight? I need to talk to you about some things. You're right. I needed to make a decision, and I did."

My stomach knots and I have to sink to my chair. She made a decision. I've wanted this, but I've dreaded it just as much.

I'm halfway through texting a reply when my phone rings and Lizzy's number pops onto the screen.

"Hello?"

"Max? Hanna…" I can't make out her words. All I know is that she's crying, sobbing, and repeating Hanna's name and *hospital.*

"I'll be there in two minutes." I don't bother putting away my files, shutting down my computer, or even telling anyone where I'm going. My mind is in such a fog that the drive to the hospital is a blur. I'm in constant motion until I make it to the hospital and I find her in a temporary room beyond the ER.

For the first time since I got Lizzy's call, I stop moving. Hanna's in a hospital gown, unconscious, her lip bloody, her face battered. "Where am I?" she murmurs, turning her head toward Liz.

"You're in the hospital," Liz replies. "You've been in an accident."

"My head hurts," Hanna whispers. Then she closes her eyes again.

Finally my feet obey my brain and I step into the room. "Is she okay?"

"Does she look okay?" Liz sniffs and doesn't bother looking at me.

Then I see it. Right there on Hanna's left hand—my grandmother's engagement ring. She made a decision.

Part Four:
AFTER

MAX

The axe splits the wood again and again, the boom and crack comforting me, the burning in my arms and shoulders distracting me from the fucking aching in my chest.

How long can you fight for someone before it kills you inside? How long can you hold out before it isn't devotion but pathetic desperation?

"I thought I'd find you here."

I look up to see Will pushing through the gate to my mom's backyard. He eyes my growing wood pile and raises a brow.

"Planning a fire?"

"No. Just…" My throat thickens, and I rest the axe on the trunk of a maple and grab my water bottle. I guzzle half of it before trying to talk again. "What are you doing here? Don't you have a wedding to prepare for?"

Will shrugs. "I'll pick up my tux on Friday, but we have a wedding planner who's pretty much taking care of the rest."

I grunt and start stacking wood under the awning by Mom's back porch.

Will doesn't ask any questions, just starts grabbing wood

with me and adding it to the pile. We work together seamlessly, the only sounds the chirping of the birds and the rumble of the occasional diesel truck passing on the street out front.

I only speak when the wood is all stacked and my hands burn from handling the rough logs. "She thinks I want her for her money."

Will coughs on his water. "What?"

"Yeah. Apparently Meredith planted this idea in her head, and she can't let it go."

"Tell her everything. Make her understand."

I let out a long breath. Leave it to Will to figure that the truth will set me free and all that shit. "It's more complicated than that," I mumble.

"If by complicated, you mean she bruised the shit out of your ego, I'd believe that."

"By complicated, I mean she's pregnant."

Will's brows shoot up, hiding under his messy blond mop. "Say what?"

I've had less than twenty-four hours to process the fact that my fiancée spent her summer with another guy, and the news of her pregnancy isn't going down real smooth. "Nate Crane got her pregnant."

"Are you serious? I thought she was waiting for marriage to have sex."

I nod, swallowing around that lump in my throat. "Apparently that only applied for me. *Fuck*." I punch the wood stack then regret it when my knuckles feel like they're going to explode. "She says it's over between them. Doesn't she deserve better than that? I swear, if I get my hands on him—"

"Nate is dead," Will says softly.

"What?"

"He was supposed to be performing in Afghanistan this week with a couple of other musicians. Their helicopter was taken down by a surface-to-air missile. No survivors." He studies me closely as he shares this news, and I feel my heart slow down to a dangerous crawl.

"Fuck," I mutter. "Is Hanna okay?"

Will shakes his head. "She saw the news report at Brady's. She's in shock, but they got her home and into bed."

"Shit." I squeeze my eyes shut. Worse than my own pain is the knowledge that Hanna is hurting.

Will shoves his hands in his pockets. "She's going to need you."

HANNA

When I wake, sunlight is slicing across my blankets and I can hear voices outside my bedroom. My sisters, Nix, Cally.

"The military has issued an official press release that there were no survivors." Maggie's voice, soft, full of grief. "They have to do…" A ragged intake of breath. "…to do DNA testing to confirm who was on the plane. Because—" She breaks off on a sob, and I squeeze my eyes shut.

I push out of the bed and pull on a robe before rushing into the bathroom and vomiting. My stomach heaves and cramps and shudders, and when there's nothing else left inside, I wash my hands and face, brush my teeth, and study my reflection in the mirror. The perpetual flush has left my cheeks, and I'm pale and ghostly, my eyes vacant.

Yesterday, when the girls tucked me into bed, my heart hurt so much that I couldn't feel anything else. That ache is gone now. I can't feel anything this morning, not numb but empty.

In the living room, Lizzy, Maggie, Cally, and Nix greet me with worried eyes, and I hold up a finger. "Don't," I warn.

My twin rushes forward and folds me into a hug, but I keep my body stiff. If I bend to this, even a little, the darkness will come back. I have to keep moving forward. I have to erect my walls and fortify them with ambivalence.

"Max called," Maggie says softly. "He's worried about you."

Max. Max, who knows my heart is breaking over another man. Who knows I'm pregnant with that man's baby. And he's still calling to check on me.

"I'm okay," I manage. "I need to get showered. Who's running the bakery?"

"Drew's down there right now," Liz says. "She said she couldn't sleep anyway and offered to run the front this morning. I was just about to head down so she could get to school."

"Thanks for taking care of that."

"Of course," she says helplessly. "Anything for you, Han."

I walk to the kitchen and fill a glass of water to take my prenatal vitamin. When I close my eyes to swallow, I see Nate's face. Tender and sweet as he enters me for the first time. This baby is never going to know his dad. Never going to hear him sing outside of recordings. Never going to know the feel of his hand ruffling his hair.

Having the choice ripped from my control made me realize just how terrible it would have been to keep this baby a secret from Nate. Maybe I would have come to that realization on my own, but it's painfully clear now. Especially in light of my newest memory.

Nate lied to me. The reminder sparks something like anger inside me. It's not enough to fill the emptiness, but it's *something*, and I'd rather be angry than be nothing but a void. When I was in LA, he lied.

"I never offered you what he did. The life, the marriage, the commitment. The happily-ever-fucking-after. I can't. I won't. It wasn't a choice between him and me because I wasn't offering you those things."

But that wasn't true at all. He told me that I needed to make a choice just days before I lost my memory, but he knew

I couldn't remember. Why? I took off my ring when I was in LA. I told him that I realized I couldn't be with Max anymore. Was he stepping back because he thought I'd change my mind and go back to Max? Or did he change *his* mind and decide he didn't want me after all?

What did he say that night at Asher's? *"I promised that when you made your decision, I would respect it. That if you took his ring, I wouldn't try to change your mind."*

Why couldn't he just have been honest with me? Yes. Anger. Anger is good. Without it, I'm afraid I'll just disappear.

"Will you still be coming into the office today?" Nix asks.

Closing my eyes and clinging to that sliver of anger toward Nate, I nod.

"Do you want me to go with you?" Liz asks.

I shake my head. "No. I think I need to do this by myself."

She frowns but doesn't argue.

"I'll be there. You won't be alone," Nix says, but I think the assurance is more for Liz than for me.

I'm vomiting in the trash can when Nix enters the exam room.

When I finish and look up, she's tucking my chart under her arm and shaking her head. "I guess I don't need to ask how you're feeling."

"I'm dying." I run water in the sink and scoop handfuls into my mouth until the bitter chalk taste of bile leaves my mouth. I've vomited four times since I woke up this morning. Zero morning sickness yesterday, and today, I feel like the toilet is my new best friend. "This baby obviously wants me dead."

"Well, there is a baby. Your dipstick read positive, confirming your blood test results. But I don't think the baby wants you to die."

"Easy for you to say," I mutter, but my hand settles over

my stomach. *Pregnant.* How many times do I have to hear that news before it starts sounding real to me?

"We'll do an ultrasound today and figure out exactly how far along you are."

"I know when I conceived," I whisper.

Her lips part. "Oh."

"I remembered."

She nods. "Okay, well, we'll confirm, then. And if we're lucky, we might hear the baby's heartbeat."

"We don't need to do that. I'd rather not, actually." I've imagined this moment—the first time I'd get to hear the steady heartbeat of my child—but I never imagined I'd be facing it alone. It's just too much for me today. "I shouldn't have come. This was a bad idea."

When I look up, Nix is studying me. "You're not thinking what I think you are, are you, Hanna? Because I know your mother won't approve of the timing, but I'm not the right doctor if you're looking to terminate this pregnancy."

"What? No! Of course not. I—" Her words have me clutching my stomach as if they were a threat.

Her shoulders relax. "Good to know. Now lie back so we can measure this little bean in your belly and see when he or she started growing."

I lower myself onto the table, taking the ever-awkward, time-honored position of my feet in the stirrups as she prepares the wand for a transvaginal ultrasound. I turn off my mind to anything other than Nix's commands. *Don't think.*

"Relax," she orders, pressing my thighs apart.

I squeeze my eyes shut. Lying on a table and getting my first ultrasound has to be the loneliest place in the world. I know Liz could have been here, would love to be here, but having her by my side would have been even more painful, the Band-Aid that chafes the open wound.

"Are you ready?" Nix asks.

I open my eyes and mouth, "No," but she's not looking at me. She hits a few keys on the keyboard, and a fuzzy black-and-white image pops onto the screen to my left.

At first, all I see is a black void with occasional white patches. But then she coos, and I see something that looks very much like a little lima bean.

"See that?" She points to a flashing green light on the screen. "That's your baby's heartbeat. Let's see if we can get a listen." She taps the keyboard again, and then suddenly the thumping of a fast-beating heart comes over the room's speakers.

The sound spins my emotions on their head and the moment transforms from surreal to wonderfully and painfully real. It's not just a sound. It's a part of me.

Nix gives me a sad smile before turning her attention back to her computer screen. "Let's take some measurements to see how far along you are." The image on the screen swishes from right to left as she maneuvers the wand and uses the mouse at the computer to measure this little bean inside me. "Oh... oooh."

I tense at the surprise in her voice. "What? Is the baby okay?" My mind immediately shoots to the diet pills and starvation. Could the damage I did to my body then be hurting my baby now?

"See that?" She taps the flashing light on the screen again. "That's your baby's heartbeat." She taps another blinking light on the screen. "And that's your baby's heartbeat."

"What's wrong with it? Why does my baby have two hearts?"

"Your *babies*," she says. "You're pregnant with twins."

MAX

"You don't have to do this." She pokes at her crawfish étouffée and scans the crowd of Cajun Jack's, where she asked me to meet her for dinner. She's been quiet since we took our seats in the little booth, but it's not a distant kind of silence, just an unreadable one.

"I don't have to do what?" I ask.

"You don't have to pretend we're together." She abandons her fork and sips at her Sprite. "Especially now that you know about…" She drops her eyes toward her stomach. "I understand why you'd want to be done with the charade. As soon as they announce that you got the grant, I'll figure out a way to break it to my mom gently."

"I didn't get it," I say softly.

She sits back. "What?"

"They announced the grant recipients yesterday. The Healthy Tomorrow Grant went to someone else."

"But my mom… I thought…"

I knew there was a good chance I wasn't going to get it, but Hanna seemed convinced from the beginning that her mom could make it happen. "Your mom is only one vote. Everyone else on the committee got a vote too." And who wanted to vote for a sweaty gym when there were community gardens and nature trails applying for the same money?

"I'm so sorry," she whispers. "What are you going to do?"

I shrug. "What I've always done. Work my ass off until things pick up again. I never expected this to be easy, and I don't mind the work."

She stares at me, her lips parted. "I wish I could give you some money."

"I don't want your money. I'm okay. Things aren't as bad as they seem."

"If they already announced the grant recipient, why are you willing to keep pretending to be with me?"

I wince. I wish she'd just punch me in the balls. It would feel better than this. "It was never about the grant money. I wanted a chance to win you back."

"I'm hurting you, aren't I?" She shakes her head. "I was too insecure to believe you could really want me for me, and I screwed up everything. I broke *your* heart too."

"You were worth it."

"Was I?" she whispers, looking down at her plate again. Fat tears rolls down her cheeks, and I feel like someone is taking a cheese grater to my heart. "I don't feel like I'm worth much right now, and for the first time in my life, those feelings have nothing to do with my body." She laughs, but it's not the normal bright laughter I'm used to. "I was such an idiot. You and I could be happy, but I let my fear destroy something good."

"Nothing's destroyed, Hanna." I take a breath and study her. "I'm not saying everything is going to be easy, but nothing is destroyed."

"It's twins, Max. Nix did an ultrasound today, and I'm having twins."

Twins. Jesus. *My* head is spinning, and I can't think of a single response to that news. I can't imagine how she must feel.

"I'm sorry you had to find out like you did—about Nate and the pregnancy. You didn't deserve that." She draws in a shaky breath. "God, how did everything get to be so screwed up?" She smiles for a second before she remembers herself and it falls away. "He defended you. Told me I was too good inside to be able to love an asshole. He and I never planned to have a relationship. Just a fling, I guess. He was supposed to be my rebound guy. Someone to make me feel better about myself after you and I split."

"I'm sorry." I say the words without meaning to, and flinch. This conversation isn't about me. It's not about us.

"For…what?"

"For screwing up our beginning. For making you feel unworthy in any way." My throat is thick, and I have to stop talking, force myself to breathe. "Take as long as you need before you announce anything. Not just as long as your mom needs, but you too. I'll be here for you. However I can help you."

"Thank you."

We give up the pretense of eating and I take her home. Just the sight of those narrow steps up to her apartment makes my stomach flip. It's bad enough that she fell down them before, but now that we know she's pregnant, the idea of her falling is enough to keep me up at night. Maybe we could rent out that apartment to someone else and use the money to get her a place without stairs.

"Let me walk you up," I say, taking her arm.

She gives me a half-smile. "Thanks."

When we reach her door, our gazes lock and I have to swallow something thick in my throat that feels a whole lot like regret.

HANNA

His eyes search mine, and they're full of so many emotions I don't dare analyze.

I can't ask him to stay. I wouldn't. But I'm terrified to go into that apartment and spend the night alone. The future stretches out before me—an endless landscape of terrifying unknowns that I have to brave alone.

"I'm scared."

The moment his fingers touch mine, my heart slams in my chest and some frozen part of me begins to thaw. He brings my hand to his mouth. It's just a kiss, a brush of lips against my knuckles, but there's so much in that one gesture.

"I'm here, okay?" He grazes his thumb over my cheek, and I feel the moisture of tears I didn't realize I was shedding. "However you want me to be."

I wake in the middle of the night and bolt upright in bed to horrible, ugly sobs. It sounds like someone is having her heart ripped out and it's terrifying. Only when Lizzy wraps me in her arms and murmurs in my ear do I realize they're coming from me.

"Shh." Liz holds me, rocks me back and forth. "Shh. You're not alone. I've got you."

When the sobbing subsides, I lie back down, and she lies next to me and laces her fingers through mine. "My heart hurts," I whisper into the darkness.

I can't see her face, but I know from the way she's sniffling that she's been crying too. "I know."

"He lied to me." I close my eyes and squeeze my sister's hand. "He said he wasn't offering me commitment, but that's not true. A few days before my accident, he told me he was in love with me and wanted to find a way to make it work."

"Oh, Hanna," Liz says. "I'm so sorry."

I shake my head in the darkness. "I was supposed to be making my decision. I was supposed to choose, and the next time he saw me, I was wearing Max's ring. I can't imagine how much that must have hurt him, but I don't understand why he lied about it when I told him I needed to remember why I chose Max. Why would he lie?"

"Maybe he thought you'd be better off with Max."

"I think I was wrong about Max's reasons for wanting me." I draw in a ragged breath. "I never realized how much my own self-hatred could damage everyone around me."

"You don't need to worry about that," she murmurs, smoothing my hair.

"I love them both. Nate is dead, and I still feel like my heart is torn between two men."

"Shh." She squeezes my hand. "It going to be okay."

I shake my head. Nothing's okay. I love two men and can't be with either. If accusing Max of only wanting me for my money didn't destroy everything between us, the fact that I would be choosing him after Nate's death does. And now I'm grieving another man, pregnant with his babies. Twins. I shouldn't be surprised. Nate and I are both twins. But that doesn't make it any less of a shock. I'm not sure I'm ready to be a mom at all, and suddenly I'm going to be a mom of two?

"I'm so fucked up."

"You're tired. Close your eyes."

"It's twins," I whisper into the darkness.

I know she heard me because I hear her soft gasp, but I can't see her face. Then she throws her arms around me and we're lying in bed, hugging so tight that right in that moment it feels like maybe—despite the grief tearing me apart inside, despite the heartache that makes me want to cling to Max, despite the fear of what will happen when I tell my mom the truth—for just a minute, I believe everything is going to be okay.

HANNA

William and Cally's rehearsal dinner is full of food and wine and laughter, and I'm sitting here fighting the urge to lean my head against Max and close my eyes. I didn't know it was possible to be this tired. Last night, after I woke from nightmares three different times, Liz stayed in bed with me like we used to when we were kids and scared of the dark.

I've been next to Max all night and it's starting to get to me—the smell of his cologne, his drop-dead-gorgeous grin, his thick forearms exposed by the rolled cuffs of his dress shirt. I see his arms and want to crawl into them and hide from the world.

This afternoon, Liz made me go upstairs and take a nap, but instead of sleeping, I lay in bed wondering about those five days before my accident. Since I was living a life veiled in secrecy, I don't have much to go on, but I know two things to be true: Nate told me that it was time to make a decision, and sometime shortly before I fell down the stairs, I put on Max's ring. I gave my virginity to Nate and, less than five days later, chose Max. And the day I put on Max's ring is a day Nix tells me I'll probably never remember.

The servers are clearing our plates when Will stands from his seat next to Cally at the head table. People clink their forks against their glasses, and he smiles as the room grows silent.

"I just wanted to say a few words before we send you all on your way tonight," he begins. "As you all know, I've been in love with Cally since high school."

"Poor girl moved across the country and still couldn't escape you," Sam calls out.

Will chuckles, but his face goes serious again as he turns to his bride. "Love isn't easy. Not the good kind. At least it hasn't been for us. There have been a lot of obstacles, but we made it here. Cally and I?" He grins at her. "We're meant to be together. I knew that from the beginning. When I was a teenager, I thought that was all it took, but I learned that destiny—or whatever you want to call it—that's not enough. We had to fight for each other." Cally looks up at him, adoration clear in her eyes, and when he meets her gaze, it's so clear the feeling is mutual that my chest aches with envy. "I'm not perfect, Cally, but you do make me better. If I have to, I'll fight for you over and over again, and I'll point to every battle scar and tell our kids, 'Totally worth it.'"

I feel Max's eyes on me, and when I turn to him, the intensity in his gaze takes my breath away. I can't imagine what this weekend must be like for him when our own wedding is supposed to follow in only two weeks.

Will turns to the rest of the room. "We owe so much thanks to you all too. The Thompson girls—Hanna, Liz, and Maggie—you gave Cally the friends she needed when she returned to New Hope, and I thank you for that. To the jerks I call my friends—Sam, Max, Asher—I know this wedding stuff isn't your favorite, but you're here anyway. In the time we've been friends, you've proven you'd drop just about anything for me if I asked you to. I appreciate you. Everyone, thank you for being here. It was tempting to skip the whole to-do, especially after my...*ahem*...prior difficulties with weddings." His cheeks actually turn a little pink as the crowd laughs. "But we decided not to get married on the beach in Maui. We wanted you with us. You've helped make our lives so awesome. Now let's drink some wine and hurry toward the part of this weekend where this woman becomes mine forever."

Applause fills the room as Cally hops out of her seat, wraps her arms around Will's neck, and kisses him silly.

Again, there's that ache in my chest. I don't begrudge them their connection or their happiness. I wouldn't want any less for my friends. But I do envy them. Just last week, I thought my life was headed in the same direction as theirs—not just the wedding and honeymoon, but the shared life. The laughter and connection. The inside jokes and…togetherness. Having a partner when life throws shit at you. I thought I'd have that with Max.

He's watching me, but his face is unreadable. Is he thinking the same thing? Or does he resent me for betraying him with Nate?

"Why don't you two go dance?" Mom asks.

Max stands and offers me his hand. "May I?"

I nod, place my hand in his, and follow him to the dance floor, where I wrap my arms around his neck and pretend we're the engaged couple Mom thinks we are.

"Relax," he murmurs in my ear. "It's just a dance."

I didn't realize how stiff I was holding myself. I rest my head on his shoulder. My whole body is exhausted after a day that started before five a.m. and has been go-go-go ever since, and my body turns to mush as I melt against his heat and the comfort of his breath against my ear.

MAX

Hanna smells so damn good. I don't want to let her go. Which is a really fucking bad idea. I *need* to let her go. I need to put some space between us, go home, and try to sleep—something I haven't done much of this week. But instead, I'll stay here as long as I can, holding her in my arms and pretending this is real.

Pretend. After months of pretend, I thought we were past that, but here we are again, and maybe it serves me right. It's my punishment for not seeing what was in front of my nose for so many years.

"They're perfect for each other, aren't they?" Hanna rests her cheek on my chest and watches Cally and William on the other side of the dance floor. "He loves her so much. She didn't believe he'd ever be able to forgive her for her mistakes, but look at them now."

I don't know the whole story of what happened between Will and Cally, but I know enough to understand that their love is truly unconditional. "When you love someone, you can forgive them anything."

She lifts her head, her dark brown eyes locking on mine.

"We both screwed up, didn't we?"

I nod, my throat thick as she reaches up to brush my hair from my face. Earlier today, I was thinking how much I needed a damn haircut, but now I'm glad it's falling in my eyes.

"Do you ever wonder if things could have gone differently between us?"

"Every day."

She nods. "Me too."

"Things have a way of working out," I promise, brushing her stomach with my thumb. "No matter what happens, you'll never regret them."

"What's it like?" she asks, fingertips still resting on my jaw. "Being a parent?"

"It's…awesome." I clear my throat and swallow back emotion. "But in the literal sense of the word, not the clichéd sense. You're going to make an amazing mother."

My eyes burn at the thought and my chest feels too full. How many times have I pictured Hanna's stomach rounding out with a child? How many times have I rocked Claire to sleep and wanted to share the feeling with the woman I love?

"Can I ask you a question?"

I nod. She can ask me anything she wants if it means I get to keep her in my arms.

"When everything settles down and we don't have to pretend anymore…will you be with Meredith?"

"No." I hate that she even has to ask. I've tried to make it clear that I'm not interested in Meredith anymore, but I obviously haven't done a very good job.

"But she wants you. And you said yourself you've been in love with her most of your life."

Three soft little tendrils have slipped from her twist at the nape of her neck, and I take one between my fingers as I respond. "I thought it was love once. But that was before I knew what it was like to be in love with you."

Her lips part and her gaze dips to my lips. "You say these things—"

"Go ahead and kiss her, Max!" Sam calls from the other

side of the dance floor. "You guys are next!"

Several people around him call out in agreement, and all eyes land on us.

Hanna nods almost imperceptibly, giving me the permission I need before I lower my mouth to hers. I mean for it to just be a touch of lips, enough to appease the curious people staring at us, but the second my lips touch hers, she melts into me, and I can't resist tasting her for another second, memorizing the sweetness of her mouth under mine. I'll be there for her. I'll be the friend she needs when she raises her babies, but she's made it clear that's all we can be. I can't rush this last kiss before I have to let go of this part of our relationship forever.

HANNA

"I have a buttload of flowers to pick up from the florist to put on Cally's cake tomorrow. Would you mind the extra stop?" The sky is filled with stars tonight, and I take a minute to breathe it in as Max opens my door.

"Flower shop and then the bakery?" he asks as I climb in.

With a grateful smile, I nod. Then, for some reason I'm not entirely sure of, I lift onto my toes and press my lips to his. He freezes for a moment. Probably because no one's watching and there wasn't any reason for me to kiss him.

Slowly, he cups my jaw with his big hand, and when I part my lips under his, he sweeps his tongue inside my mouth. The kiss is slow and tender, and it reminds me of the early days of our relationship, when I was so nervous about my body that kissing and over-the-clothes groping was as wild at it got.

When we break the kiss, I can't deny the sadness in his eyes, and guilt sweeps over me. What's wrong with me that I couldn't see his love for me for what it was? Why did I let Meredith control my perception of Max?

I want to apologize, but the words turn to dust on my tongue. Are there any apologies more difficult than the ones we owe the most?

He kisses my forehead before heading around to his side of the car.

"Thank you for tonight," I whisper as he starts the car. "It meant a lot to me."

He takes my hand and presses my knuckles to his lips. Then he puts the car in gear and starts driving to the florist.

"We're here," he whispers, lightly brushing my hair from my face. "I'll take the flowers into the cooler. You can go up to bed."

I blink at him. I was so tired that I must have fallen asleep. I shouldn't let him do this without my help, but every cell in my body seems to be demanding more sleep now.

"Okay," I murmur.

He helps me out of the car and watches me walk up the stairs before he turns back to get the flowers.

At my door, I dig in my purse for my keys, and when I wrap my fingers around them, I realize my mistake. He's going to need the key to the bakery. I peek over the balcony and frown when I see the back door open and light flooding into the alley as Max hauls the giant flower box inside.

I look down at my keys then back at the door. "How...?" Slowly, I make my way back down the stairs and into the bakery. Max is locking up the walk-in cooler when I step inside.

He gives me a soft smile. "I thought you were going to bed."

"You know," I start carefully. I look around my commercial kitchen with new eyes. "I really thought Nate Crane was the silent partner. I thought he just wasn't admitting it. But I was wrong."

"Hmm." He shoves his hands in his pockets and shrugs. "Maybe it's just a private investor and nothing personal."

I take a breath, my heart heavy and full. "This was personal. The apartment upstairs, the care that was put into the remodel."

He turns his head and studies the gleaming stainless-steel countertops. "Whoever it was should have spent the extra money on putting those stairs inside the building. Then you wouldn't have to go outside every time you needed to get between the apartment and the bakery. And maybe you wouldn't have fallen."

"I think he did more than enough," I whisper.

He shrugs. "I'm just glad you get your bakery."

"Were you ever going to tell me that you're the one behind all this? That you're the one who set it all up for me to live my dream?"

He drags a hand through his hair and studies the ground.

"Max. Look at me."

He shifts his eyes to meet mine. "It was your dream. I knew you didn't believe in yourself enough to do it on your own. But I believed in you. I've always believed in you. You're the most amazing person I've ever met."

Oh, God. How could I have been so wrong about him? "Why didn't you tell me?"

"I didn't really intend for it to be a secret. I was in the middle of investigating the opportunity to buy this building when you broke up with me, and when it looked like it could work, I didn't want you to think there were strings attached. I had to find a way to give this to you without you believing the gift was contingent on marrying me." He shrugs awkwardly.

"Max," I whisper. And then I can't help it anymore. I cross to him, wrap my arms around his neck, and kiss him hard. Because Max gave me something more than a dream. He gave me the dream and put it in New Hope the way only someone who was raised here would understand to do. Any other investor would have wanted me to go to the city or take a bigger location off the historic New Hope square. Max didn't just give me the dream. He gave me the dream wrapped up in home.

I make myself pull away and leave it at a chaste kiss, but as I lower back down to my heels, his hands come up to cup my face, and then he's lowering his mouth to mine and kissing me back—sweetly, softly, and with a tender love I'm not sure I deserve.

His fingers slide into my hair and he releases the clip and lets it fall down around my shoulders. Then his hands are sliding down my body and under my ass and he's hoisting me up on the counter and parting my thighs to step between them. When he returns his mouth to mine, his kiss is harder than before. Deeper. Stronger. It's the kiss of a man who has found something he thought he lost. The kiss of a man who will do whatever it takes to hold on.

And I kiss him back in the same way, the love and the pain in my chest wrapping around and through each other until they are one and the same. They are the disease and the remedy. They are the poison and the antidote. They fill me and whisper to me until I know the only thing that can make the hurt go away is this man's kiss.

"Come upstairs with me," I whisper against his lips.

He releases his breath in a rush. "Hanna. That's not why—"

"I know." I want to kiss away the sadness in his eyes. I want to take away the pain I put there. "I know," I repeat, taking his hand.

Carefully, he helps me off the counter. "Okay."

He follows me up the stairs, and the minute the door closes behind him, my fingers start at the buttons on his shirt. I need Max. Naked. Against me. Now.

He stops my hands with one of his. "Can we just…" He closes his eyes like he's not sure where to start. "I love you. I don't want to rush this." He brushes his knuckles over my cheek. "I don't want to scare you away."

"I'm right here," I whisper. "And I'm not going anywhere."

He tugs on my dress, and I lift my arms as he pulls it off and tosses it to the side. His smoky eyes drop to my breasts, skim over my belly. His fingers tighten on my hips. "I can't tell you how many times I've fantasized about this. You. This body. The sounds you make when you're about to come. The way you taste here." He brushes the pad of his thumb over my nipple. "And here." Grazes my navel. His voice drops deeper, and he slides his hand between my legs and cups me. "Imagined how you'd taste here."

"Max," I whimper, my hips rocking into the pressure of his hand.

"Don't ever doubt my attraction to you. You are *it* for me, Hanna. I don't need anyone else, and I don't want anyone else." He drops his head to my breast and sucks me through the lace of my bra. Pulling my nipple into his mouth, he sends a painful pulsing and vibrating between my legs, where his hand rubs me over my panties.

I fumble with the remaining buttons on his shirt, yanking it down his arms until he tosses it onto the floor. His skin is smooth and hot over thick muscle, and suddenly I need to memorize it. My mouth and hands are all over him, my fingers skimming across the flat plains of his abs as I take his shoulder into my mouth and bite softly. He groans as I nip, bite, and suck my way up to his neck and my fingertips slides under the waistband of his pants.

I unbutton his pants and draw his dick from his briefs, and he steps back.

His gaze roams over me, hungry and greedy, but he doesn't step closer. He nods approvingly and eyes my bra and panties. "Let me see all of you."

I release the clasp on my bra first and let it fall to the floor. Then I hook my fingers at each side of my panties and wiggle them off my hips. I don't turn off the lights and hurry into bed and under the covers. I stand exposed in the light, wanting him to see the softness in my belly and the stretch marks at the tops of my thighs. This is my body, for better or worse.

When I meet his gaze again, his eyes have gone darker, his pupils dilated, his nostrils flaring. He grunts and steps closer. "My attraction to you has never been pretend. You're fucking beautiful, and you always have been. And when I imagine your belly round with these babies…" He brushes his fingers across my stomach, and my eyes fill.

"I want you," I whisper, wrapping my fingers around that thick length of him again. "Here. Now."

His eyes darken and his nostrils flare. "Don't test me."

"I'm not testing you. I'm asking you." I stroke him, squeeze and releasing, squeezing and releasing. "I never wanted to wait until marriage to have sex."

Hurt slashes across his face at my words.

"Max, I was scared that you'd see me naked and realize I wasn't as beautiful as you'd convinced yourself I was, scared that I wouldn't be able to make up for it with my seduction skills. I was terrified I'd disappoint you."

"Jesus. You're the sexiest woman I've ever touched. You would never disappoint me."

"I finally believe that." And I finally see how much damage I did by not believing it sooner. I press a hand to his chest, and his skin is hot against my fingers. I trace the line of hair between his pecs and over his stomach, down to the dragon tattoo on the V of his pelvis, and he draws in a sharp breath. "Do you mean what you said about that night at the gallery?"

"The gallery?"

I take him in my fist. His eyes shut and he clenches his fists at his sides, hanging on to control.

"What I said?" he manages.

"About the first time you kissed me? About what you wanted from me that night?" I move over him in long strokes. "Do you still feel that way?"

"It's different now," he says. "I want you just as much—more—than I did then, but I love you too. I love you so much that I want to give you everything. I want to make you happy and safe. And when you told me that you wanted to wait for marriage, those two desires came into direct conflict with each other." He kisses the inside of my wrist, then my palm. "I guess I'm a little slow, though. I thought what you wanted was to wait. But what you really meant"—he forces his gaze back to mine—"and help me out here, because I'm not fluent in female—"

I giggle, and the seriousness of his expression breaks for a minute.

"—you meant that you needed to believe you were beautiful, needed to see what I see, before we made love."

I can't do anything but give him a sad smile, because that's exactly what I needed. He dips his head and brushes a kiss across my lips and in the corners of my eyes.

"I think you speak female okay," I whisper.

He cuffs both of my hands behind my back with one of his. "I can't think when you're touching me like that." He runs his free hand up the side of my body and works his tongue at my neck, and I arch toward him in response, my breasts pressing against his chest.

"Please," I murmur as his thumb circles my navel.

I can feel his sigh in the crook of my neck when he says, "I love you, Hanna."

"I love you too." A single, hot tear rolls down my cheek. "I'm so sorry. I'm so, so sorry."

"Me too, baby. Me too."

MAX

'm kissing her. My hands are in her hair and my mouth is on hers, and I'm so desperate to drink her in that I don't stop her when I feel her reaching for my cock again. I'm already lost.

She tears her mouth from mine and presses kisses to my neck and across my pecs and abs. When she skims her tongue over my tattoo, I have to pull her back to me. All those months we were together, she insisted any time we touch be about me. I can't let this first time back together be that way. I need to show her.

I lead her to the bedroom and turn on the lights.

When I step back to look at her, she lets me. None of the insecure covering or turning off the lights she used to do. She lets me look my fill.

I rake my eyes over her again and again, drinking her in. "You woke up without your memory, and you just assumed you'd gotten over all of your hang-ups over the last year." I step closer so I can feel her breasts against my chest. I slide my hand between her legs as I whisper in her ear. "It was a miracle to me because you were suddenly willing to let me see you. To let me touch you. And when we were in the steam room and

I got to kiss you for the first time here..." I brush my knuckles over her. She's already wet, and I'm dying to slide my fingers inside her, to feel her wrapped around them as I make her come. She digs her nails into my shoulders and shudders in pleasure at the faint contact. I want more. Need more. "I felt so damn guilty for keeping the whole truth from you, but I'm an asshole, Hanna. I'm a fucking selfish ass who had to bury his face between your legs before you remembered—to show you pleasure, to prove to you how fucking much I want you." My knuckles brush again, and she gasps, her fingers curling into my triceps now. "I crave you. I fucking *need* you. You accused me of keeping my distance from you after the accident, said I would have spent more time with you if I'd really wanted to be with you. The truth is that, after the night in the steam room, I didn't trust myself. I knew you'd let me take you. You would have let me that night. I didn't trust myself to keep touching you without fucking you."

She whimpers. "You could have."

"Exactly. I *dream* about fucking you. Your legs wrapped around me while I slide into you or biting this sensitive spot on your neck while I fuck you from behind." I nip to show her where, and she rocks her hips into my touch. "You're looking for someone who loves your body as much as your mind? I'm your man, Hanna. Just give me a chance to show you."

When I pull back, her eyes are half closed, her lips parted. "Show me," she whispers.

I shouldn't. Not when things are so confused and complicated between us. Not when she's so emotional and vulnerable.

"It's okay." She brings her hand to my cheek. "I need this. I need you. More than ever."

I kiss her then, trailing kisses along her jaw and down her breasts. When I stop and draw a nipple into my mouth, she cries out and buries her hands in my hair, holding me there. My cock is so damn hard it aches, but I lower to my knees and press my mouth between her legs. She gasps as my tongue hits her clit. Widening her stance instinctively, she keeps those hands in my hair as I lick her, taste her, find her with my hand, and pump my fingers inside her. She tightens her hand in my hair, and I wrap my lips around her clit and suck.

There is nothing as sexy as fingering Hanna while she rocks her hips against my face. She tugs at my hair, and I know she's close. I slide a second finger inside her while I add suction to her clit. She screams and bucks, and it's the fucking sexiest thing I've ever experienced in my life.

When I stand, she wraps her arms around my neck and kisses me hard. I move us to the bed and pause when I'm hovering over her. "I didn't bring a condom." I didn't expect tonight to end like this. "I'm clean, but if you want…"

She shakes her head. "I've never had sex without a condom. I want you to be that first."

My chest is tight, and I swallow hard as I slowly slide into her. She's so tight and slick, and I don't know how I'm going to last, but she arches against me and moans, and I know I'll find a way to make this last—to make sure she comes again while I'm inside her.

I watch her as I move, and she holds my face in her hands. When tears trickle out of the corner of her eyes, I kiss them away, and she smiles at me.

"They're happy tears," she promises. "I love you."

"I love you too," I murmur.

Her eyes float shut, and I can feel her tightening around me. I kiss her as she comes. Kiss her as I sink deep and pray to God that this is real and not some amazing dream.

HANNA

Lizzy adjusts the diamond pendant on my necklace and sniffs back tears. "You look beautiful."

"Thank you." This is really it. My wedding day. The first day of the rest of my life with Maximilian Hallowell.

Liz sniffs again and wipes away tears. "He'd better know how lucky he is."

"He knows," calls a deep voice.

We both gasp and turn toward the back exit to the area above the gallery, toward the sound of Max's voice, deep and sure as he walks in the door.

"You're not supposed to be here," I object, but the words don't hold much conviction because, truth be told, I need to see him. I need to see the confidence in his eyes when he talks about our future. My stomach is a mess of butterflies and rattlesnakes and I'm not sure which will win.

He draws in a long breath as he looks me over. "You're so gorgeous."

"I'll give you two some privacy," Lizzy says. She presses a kiss to my cheek and whispers so only I can hear, "You deserve this."

I have to look at the ceiling and breathe long and slow. I just did my makeup. I don't want to have mascara streaming down my face when I walk down the aisle.

Lizzy closes the door behind her as she leaves, and Max and I just stare at each other for long seconds before he steps closer and takes my hand.

"Are you ready?"

I nod, and when he presses his lips to mine, I return the kiss. Something in the back of my mind tells me that I'm a liar, but I ignore it because Max's lips are on mine, taking little sips from my mouth until the tension starts draining from me.

The door opens again, and Liz slides in. "It's time."

"I'll see you downstairs," Max says.

I watch him leave, even though I want him to stay. I want him to hold my hand and walk me down the aisle. I want him to get me to the spot I know I need to go. Because Max is going to take care of me, love me. But can I really marry a man, even a man I love more than myself, when I'm only in possession of half of my heart?

The music starts playing downstairs, and Liz grins at me. "That's my cue."

She leaves me to begin her descent down the stairs into the gallery, and I back against the wall and remind myself to breathe.

The music changes to the bridal march, and I right myself and take a step forward, but someone grabs my wrist and tugs me back. Turning, I gasp at the sight of Nate's dark brown eyes connecting with mine.

I try to breathe, but I can't. I try again, but something's weighing down on my ribcage.

Nate flicks his gaze over me, and I realize I'm naked in my bed with Max's arm wrapped around me. Nate climbs into bed on the other side of me. He lies on his side, not touching me with anything but his eyes. I slide Max's arm off me and reach for Nate, and he disappears.

My eyes open to darkness, loneliness, and guilt. Max is sleeping next to me, naked and beautiful, his hand reaching for me in his sleep. My heart is hammering and I feel like I've just run up three flights of stairs. *Breathe*, I remind myself. *Just breathe.*

I want to fold myself into his arms and let him soothe the anxiety away, but the dream has left me feeling too guilty to take the comfort of his arms.

I climb out of bed and lock myself in the bathroom before I start crying.

MAX

I don't open my eyes until I hear the bathroom door close. Rolling to my back, I thread my fingers through my hair and press my palms against my eyes.

She whispered his name in her sleep. One word. One syllable. *Nate.*

My chest is torn by conflicting emotions. Jealousy—because we made love last night and then she dreamed about another man. Heartache—because she's hurt and grieving, and I'd do anything in my power to make it better. If I could, I'd deliver Nate to her door alive and well just to erase the pain from her eyes.

But I can't do that, so I'm left here, helpless in the darkness, jealous of a dead man.

HANNA

Maybe it's the hormones, but looking at William and Cally's wedding cake has my eyes watering and my chest feeling painfully full. Simple tiers of white cake covered with silky fondant, it's beautiful—just like they are together.

"It's done," Liz says behind me. "And it's gorgeous. Quit fussing and go get a shower."

The gallery is decorated for the ceremony, and since this is where the reception will be as well, I set up the cake in the back corner by the big windows that overlook the New Hope River.

"Need any help?" a deep voice asks behind me.

I turn and see Max holding a baby girl with a mop of dark hair.

I open my mouth. I should say something. Anything. But I can't. My mouth is dry and my heart feels like it's trying to claw its way out of a shallow grave because Max is holding a baby—cradling her in his arms—his lips curling into a smile every time his gaze dips to her face, and she keeps reaching her pudgy little fist up to touch the scruff along his jaw. The sight has so many conflicting emotions racing through me that I can hardly stand up straight, let alone sort them out.

"Is that Meredith's baby?" Liz asks, maybe a little too much hostility in her voice.

Max raises a brow. "This is my daughter, Claire," he says patiently.

I reach for her. It's instinct. I *need* to hold that baby. I'm rewarded with Max's slow, easy smile as he settles Claire into my arms, and as soon as I feel her warmth and smell her skin, I remember that I've held her before. And I loved her then too.

That doesn't even make sense, but she's a baby, a part of Max. Loving this child is as natural as breathing.

"How can something that came from Meredith be so cute and loveable?" Liz asks under her breath.

"She gets it from me," Max says, winking at my sister. "Do you two need any help this morning? I was about to take Claire to my mom's for the day, so I'll be available."

Reluctantly, I hand Claire back to Max. "I think everything's set here. I'm going to go grab a shower and then start getting pretty."

"Too late," he says. "You're already beautiful."

I look down at my yoga pants and my stretched-out old T-shirt covered in smudges of white flour and frosting. "You need to raise your standards."

Max drops a quick kiss on my forehead before leaving. It's not until he's gone that I realize Liz is staring at me like I have two heads.

"You want to tell me what that was about?" she asks.

Feeling my cheeks warm, I shrug and turn to pack up my supplies to haul back to the bakery.

She gasps. "You had *sex* last night."

My cheeks go from warm summer day to inferno. "He *is* my fiancé," I whisper defensively. I grab a towel from my supplies and wipe at my shirt, more for something to do than anything.

Liz clears her throat. "So how was he?"

Is there something hotter than an inferno?

"Man!" Her blond curls bounce as she scoops a box of supplies into her arms. I load up too and we head toward her car. "I am so freaking *jelly*. Do you know how long it's been since I had sex?"

"I've offered to help with that."

Somehow, I'm not surprised that Sam appeared on the sidewalk at just that moment. He has a tendency to appear any time Lizzy is complaining about her sex life.

Liz shoves the box she is carrying into Sam's arms. "Thanks."

He doesn't even complain, just loads it into the trunk when she opens it then helps me load mine. "Need anything else, ladies?"

"I think that's everything," I say.

"Anything else at all?" he asks, running his eyes over Liz.

"You're gross." She smacks him in the chest with the flat of her hand. "Come on, Han."

We climb into the car, and I grab my bottle of water from the console. I drink and wish I loved water as much as coffee.

She's starting to pull away from the curb when she says, "I am totally fucking Sam tonight."

And that's why her dashboard is now soaking wet.

When I get out of the shower, I find Meredith sitting on my couch, tears swelling in her big eyes as she looks at a piece of paper.

I left Liz down in the bakery putting things away so I could grab a shower, but now I wish we had some sort of secret code because *Meredith is in my fricking apartment.* I must have left my door unlocked. *Eff it!*

Tears spill onto her cheeks and she drops her gaze back to the paper in her hands. "You're lucky, you know. I had to go through all this alone." Her head bobbles a little as she looks up at me, and I'm pretty sure she's drunk. Before noon.

I have bigger things to worry about today than some bitch who's dead set on ruining my life. She doesn't deserve any of my energy. She's not worthy of the anger that boils up inside me until I want to punch her. I've never gotten into a fight, never been a violent person, but right now, it would feel so good that I have to grab my jeans to keep my hands at my sides.

"What are you doing here?" I want her out of here. Away from me. Looking at Meredith brings back all sorts of pain I don't want to deal with right now.

"I just wanted him to choose me." Her tears spill onto the paper—no, not paper. My ultrasound images. I snatch them from her hands before she can ruin them, and she releases an empty laugh. "I wanted him to choose me, and now he's going to marry her." She shakes her head. "I mean, you."

"Leave." I bite out the word, my stomach convulsing on itself, nausea pushing up into my throat. Because it's so clear now that this was never about Max. Max is just the substitute for William—the man she really wants, the one who's getting married today, the one who had *just* proposed to his girlfriend when Meredith decided to blow up my world. "Get out of here."

"William doesn't talk to me anymore, and Max only ever calls because he wants to see Claire. Will and I were good together, you know."

"Do you even hear yourself? He's in love with someone else. He never wanted you."

She stands and has to catch herself on the couch when she loses her balance. "You know what's amazing about *you*?" she slurs. "Everyone thinks you're this amazingly sweet and giving person when you're so self-centered."

"You don't know me."

She smiles sickly. "But I do. And you know who else I know? I know your sister."

"Leave her out of this. She doesn't have anything to do with what's between us."

She arches a brow. "Doesn't she? She's the reason Max asked you out, isn't she? Even though she had it *bad* for him, she backed off and had him go out with you, and you didn't even see that because all you could think about was yourself. *Poor Hanna* can't date the guy she likes. *Poor Hanna* doesn't get noticed. Never mind *poor Liz*."

"Shut up, Meredith."

I spin around at the sound of Lizzy's voice and see her walking into my apartment. Her face twists into a snarl as she props her hands on her hips.

"Get out of here," Liz barks. "He didn't pick you. Now stop trying to fuck up everyone else's life just because you're such a bitch you've already screwed up your own."

Meredith shrugs. "Whatever."

I watch her leave before turning to Liz. "Is it true?"

Liz chews on her lower lip and shrugs. "It's ancient history."

"You liked Max?" The bottom has fallen out of my stomach, and I hate it because this is exactly how Meredith wanted me to feel. She still knows right where to hurt me.

"I would never have gone out with him if I didn't like him, but it's not like I was in love with him."

"But you like him, and when you found out I did too, you never saw him again."

She shrugs again. "You're more important to me than any guy, Han."

I cross to her and wrap my arms around her. "Best. Sister. Ever," I whisper. "I'm so sorry."

The wedding dress doesn't quite want to zip.

"Exhale hard and suck it in!" Cally's sister Drew commands, her voice a little nasally with the head cold she's been fighting all week. "Liz, hold here at the top. We're going to make this work!"

Cally sucks in her nonexistent stomach, and Drew and Lizzy work together to battle the zipper up.

"I'm bloated because I'm going to start my period soon," Cally says when she's allowed to breathe again. She presses her hand to her white-satin-covered stomach. "I can breathe later, right?" But she grins.

She's so happy to marry William that nothing is fazing her today. Not the chaos that broke loose when the florist mixed up two orders and brought someone else's flowers. Not the awkward breakfast where Will's grandmother apologized for the way she once treated Cally—but not before detailing why it was so hard for her to trust a girl whose mom used to run a shady massage business.

I envy Cally's impenetrable joy. I love Max, and I know we're going to have an amazing life together, but Cally doesn't just love Will. She believes they're destined to be together. And maybe I'd believe in destiny too if I'd had to go through what they did to get to my wedding day.

"I am so tired it's ridiculous," Cally says, stretching her arms over her head and yawning. "It's my wedding day, and I'd pay any one of you fifty bucks for twenty minutes to take a nap."

Drew straightens her dress and frowns in the mirror. "You haven't been feeling well for weeks. Are you sure you shouldn't go to the doctor?"

I take a step closer to Cally. "Not feeling good how?"

Cally shrugs. "Nauseated in the evenings sometimes. It's no big deal. Drew keeps me on my toes, and I think I've just been worrying about her."

"Huh." Lizzy looks up from the bag of makeup she was digging through. "Sounds like you're pregnant."

The whole room goes still, and Cally freezes, her mouth open as she stares at Liz.

"Could that be it?" Drew asks. A smile tugs at her lips and she can't hold it back. "When was your last period?"

"Weeks ago." Cally frowns. "But that couldn't be it." She lowers her voice. "I mean, Will can't…"

Lizzy drops her mascara and spins around. "Holy shit, I was *joking*."

Cally's hand drops to her stomach. "Do you think we could be so lucky?"

"This is nuts," Lizzy says. "We don't have to sit here in suspense when there's a CVS a mile down the road that sells perfectly good pregnancy tests."

"I can do you one better," I say, grabbing my purse. "I have one with me." I pull out the unused pregnancy test from my two-pack, and Cally takes it with shaking hands.

We all wait anxiously outside the bathroom as she takes the test, and when she comes out two minutes later, she's grinning so big she doesn't have to tell us what it says.

There are lots of hugs and squeals and carrying on, and no doubt the guests waiting downstairs in the gallery think we've decided to start the party early, but we don't care. This is Will and Cally, and they deserve this.

"I can't believe we're *both* pregnant," she squeals when it's my turn for a hug.

I nod and blink back tears. "Stop. You're going to make me ruin my makeup."

"Drew, are you crying?" Liz asks.

"No." Drew rolls her eyes, but she can't hide the truth. She's as happy for William and Cally as the rest of us are. "It's just that Asher promised me a dance at the reception, and I'm starting to worry he'll forget."

Sniffing, Cally grabs a tissue, and I grab one for myself.

"Okay, ladies!" the wedding planner says. "Let's get lined up. It's time."

It's only as I turn to take my place in line that I see my mother standing in the doorway, her eyes wide, her mouth agape as she stares at my stomach. How long has she been standing there?

She flicks her gaze to my face and back to my stomach. "Are you? But you're not married…"

Behind me, Maggie draws in a sharp breath, apparently realizing what our conversation is about. "Shit," she mutters.

The music starts to play, and the wedding planner nudges me forward. I give one last apologetic glance toward my mother and head down the stairs.

There are few sights in this world as gorgeous as Maximilian Hallowell in a tux, and there he stands, his dark hair falling into his eyes, his broad shoulders filling out the black tuxedo. He stands on the dance floor, holding the microphone and speaking to the small gathering of guests filling the gallery.

"I've been friends with William my whole life," he says. "And he's been his happiest when he's with Cally. I would tell you that I think they're lucky for the happiness they've found, but the truth is this: I'm the lucky one. Watching Will and Cally love each other taught me what love can be." His eyes find mine across the room and my breath catches at the intensity I see there. "Every guy should be lucky enough to have a friend teach him that love is worth risking everything for." He raises his glass and smiles at the bride and groom. "Here's to Will and Cally. We love you guys."

When Max returns the mic to the DJ, he catches me staring and grins. My heart does a painful little flip-flop as he comes over to me.

"Dance with me?"

I nod, not trusting myself to speak, and he leads me to the dance floor.

Leaning my head against his shoulder, I let the heat of his body seep into mine. His breath dances in my hair as we move.

He holds me close as we dance, his mouth against my ear, his fingers grazing down my spine. "You look beautiful tonight."

I smile into his neck and sigh. Despite everything else, it was a good day. William looked like the happiest man in the world as Cally came down the stairs. Seeing them exchange vows after all they've been through... Heck, I even think Drew had tears in her eyes. And if I just hold on to that feeling, I can almost believe that everything's going to be fine. That everything's going to work out.

"So do you." I tuck my hand inside his jacket to feel the

hard heat of him. I want to curl up in Max tonight. I want to forget the rest of the world and the rest of the heartbreak and grief and breathe him in until nothing else exists.

"I've missed this," he says. "I've missed feeling you in my arms. The way you smell. The way my whole world feels like it's righted itself when you're near me. How are you feeling?"

"I'm okay. Tired." His question reminds me of my mother, whom I've skillfully avoided since her unfortunately timed appearance before the ceremony. "Cally's pregnant," I say, pulling back to look at him.

His grin is slow and wide as he lifts his head to find the couple in question on the other side of the dance floor. "Will must be over the moon."

"She is too," I say. "But when we found out, Mom heard Cally say something to me and now Mom knows I'm pregnant."

He frowns. "She's okay, though, right?"

I shrug. "I've pretty much been avoiding her, but I can't put it off much longer. I'm going to invite her to the bakery tomorrow before church. I need to tell her the truth. I need to tell her there isn't going to be a wedding."

"I'll be next to you when you tell her."

"Really?" I ask.

"I should have never let her rush this. It was too soon after the accident, too soon after...everything." He studies me for a long time, and when he speaks, his voice cracks a little, like maybe he's nervous. "What if the truth was that you and I aren't ready to get married just yet, but we're still planning on making a family together...in our own time. On our own schedule."

My stomach clenches and my heart does a few more acrobatic moves.

"I didn't ask you to marry me on a whim. Forever doesn't have a deadline." Slowly, he lifts my hand to his mouth and kisses my engagement ring. "You and me, Hanna? We're right together."

I shake my head. "You don't have to do this. No one would blame you if you walked away. Not even me."

He gives me a sad smile. "You hear what song is playing, don't you?"

I wasn't paying attention, but I listen and realize we're dancing to Alicia Keys and Adam Levine's cover of "Wild Horses." The lyrics tug at my heart.

"Just think about it, Max." I stop dancing, but he holds on to me. "I don't want you to spend the rest of your life regretting your decision to marry me."

He kisses my neck then whispers in my ear, "The only decision I would regret is letting you go. I'm not swimming in money, but I can give you a good life. If you want more babies, I'll give them to you. If you want a career, I'll support you. I'll eat peanut butter sandwiches every night for a year if it means you can afford to do something you love. I would do anything to see you happy, but I'd sure as hell like to be the one who wakes up to your smiles." When I don't speak, he pulls back to show me an awkward grin. "Think about it. You don't have to decide tonight. If we do this, it's on *our* timeline. No one else's."

"Max, I chose you."

"I don't begrudge you your grief, Hanna. He's part of your past. I—"

"No, I want you to understand. I *chose* you. Before the accident."

"Are you sure about that?"

I nod. "Five days before, Nate decided that he wanted more from me. He told me I needed to choose. To make a decision. I might not remember the days after, but I chose you. I put on your ring."

He toys with my ring and kisses the top of my head. We hold each other tight as we dance.

MAX

Next to me in bed, she moans softly in her sleep, her dark hair fanned out around her head. I want to touch her—trace her soft lips, the line of her jaw, the roundness of her breasts, all the way down her soft thighs to the arch of her foot. I want to taste her again, to wake her with the soft flick of my tongue against her pussy.

I barely slept last night. I kept waking up and staring at her, pulling her tight against my chest to make sure she was still there. Still real.

I start at her breasts. The sweep of my tongue across her already-taut nipple as I cup her between her legs.

Then I move lower, positioning myself at the end of the bed and parting her thighs before lowering my face to taste her.

"Well, good morning to you too," she whispers, drawing up on her elbows.

I lift my eyes to meet hers, and lick her clit. "Relax," I murmur against her. "I have some things I need to do."

I test her wet core with my fingertip and my cock throbs. She's already so turned on, and if I wanted to take her, she'd be ready for me. I squeeze my eyes shut against the image of Hanna underneath me as I enter her, and instead, I slide two fingers inside her.

She gasps at the sudden intrusion, and her muscles grip my fingers so tightly my cock aches. When I lower my head and wrap my lips around her clit, she grabs a fistful of my hair. I know it's reflex—a base instinct demanding more from me— but I fucking love that I can do that to her. I suck on her clit gently as I pump my fingers in and out of her in a rhythm so much like fucking that my own damn hips are rocking against the end of the bed.

Her grip on my hair tightens and her hips rock until she's fucking my fingers and my face in the sexiest way possible.

I drew her a bath last night and climbed in behind her. I washed her and explored her then used the showerhead to rinse her off before sliding it between her legs. She was shocked at first, the sensation of the pulsing water too much against her sensitive flesh, but I held her still, sucked at the tender skin at the side of her neck until she relaxed into the pleasure, until she was rocking her hips for more. Her moans grew louder and her ass rubbed against me, harder and more frantic as her orgasm built. I rolled her nipples in my fingers and whispered dirty words in her ear, and when she came— violently, beautifully—I imagined her pussy squeezing my cock. It was so fucking good—touching her, feeling her—I could have come too, right there in the water like some teenage virgin, from nothing but the sound of her moans and the pressure of her ass rubbing against me. I was rewarded for my self-control when she turned in the water, wrapped her arms and legs around me, and guided me into her.

After, she lowered her head to my chest and I watched her hair fan out in the water behind her, measured her breaths until she feel asleep.

She's not sleeping now. Her hand is in my hair, her soft little cries echoing in the silence of the bedroom.

HANNA

"Can I get you a latte?" I ask Mom. She met me at the bakery like I asked her to, though she looks like she'd rather be anywhere else and she hasn't made eye contact with me once since she arrived. "Or I could get you a muffin, maybe?"

"You know I don't eat sugar," she snips.

I take a breath. Yeah. I do know that. If I thought news of giving her grandbabies was going to change that, I guess I don't know her very well.

"It's true? You're pregnant?" she asks. She's still not looking at me. She's staring out the window like she's waiting for someone to pull up and rescue her from this conversation.

I lower myself into a chair at the little table where I imagined we'd hash out the challenges ahead of us. Clearly I've been delusional if I thought my mom would see my canceled wedding as a "challenge" we could problem solve together.

"I'm pregnant," I confirm.

Max stands behind me and squeezes my shoulders, and I'm so grateful for him being here right now. Part of me thought I should do it alone—it's not like they're his babies—but it's a relief to have him close.

Mom spins on us suddenly. "Well, no one else needs to know. Your wedding is in two weeks. Everyone will think you got pregnant on the honeymoon."

Right, about that...

"We're canceling the wedding," Max says, sparing me from finding the words. "It's too soon and too fast, and Hanna needs to focus on the pregnancy right now."

Mom's jaw drops. It's such a dramatic expression that I almost want to laugh, but I've probably pissed her off enough for one day. "This is a mistake."

"No, it's not," Max says. "The mistake would be rushing into this like we have been. I want to spend the rest of my life with Hanna, but she's been through a lot in the last month and we both have some things to figure out before we say our vows."

She worries her lip between her teeth. "Okay. We could push it back a month, maybe use my heart attack as an excuse. Then we'll just pretend the baby came early."

I shake my head. "No, Mom. I'm not getting married until after the babies are born, and that would be the soonest."

"Babies?"

"Twins," I whisper.

I didn't think it was possible, but her face goes even harder. "Then you're a bigger fool than I thought. You have *no idea* how hard it is to have a baby, let alone two at a time." She turns her scowl on Max. "How are you going to let her have your babies without being married?"

"They aren't his," I blurt before Max can respond. "I slept with someone else and got pregnant. This isn't Max's fault."

She presses her hand to her chest and sinks into the chair across from me, and I think, *I am going to kill my mother. This might really kill her.* So much for finding an easy way to break my news.

"Could I speak with my daughter alone, please?" She's looking out the window again. Apparently, she can't tolerate the sight of me.

Max squeezes my shoulders, and there's so much in that

tiny gesture. He's saying that he'll be here if I need him, that he loves me, that he's proud of me. Then he presses a kiss to the top of my head and goes to the kitchen to give us some privacy.

"What will people think?" Mom says as soon as we're alone.

I shrug. "I spent my whole life worrying what people would think. You taught me that. Since I was ten years old, I wondered if I was too fat for people to like me, believed I had to make up for it by being kind, by pretending I didn't have any feelings of my own. I can't tell you the number of decisions I made just to please *you*. I am so *over* what 'people' think, because 'people' really means *you*, and you should love me unconditionally. Screw-ups and all."

"I do." Her eyes well with tears, but she pushes out of her seat and turns her back to me. "I just want to protect you from bad decisions."

I'm not surprised when she leaves, but just because you expect something doesn't mean it doesn't hurt. Max must have heard the bell over the door because he's beside me, pulling me against his chest and stroking my hair before I even realize I'm crying.

By the time Liz comes in the back door, I've settled down but I'm sitting in Max's lap, snuggled against his chest.

"Go," she says, pointing to the ceiling. "Go back upstairs and get to sleep or screw like rabbits or whatever you have to do, because it's way too early for people to have to look at that."

I grin. "You look like you just rolled out of some guy's bed." And she does. In jeans and a man's white button-up shirt, she looks, in fact, like she crawled out of bed and scrambled for something to wear. I arch a brow. "How'd it go last night?"

She crosses her arms. "You can't prove anything."

Max and I laugh, but then I sober when I tell Liz, "We're calling off the wedding. We told Mom this morning."

She flinches. "But you guys look so happy."

"We don't have to get married to stay happy," Max says.

"Take off your dress," Max whispers behind me.

A thrill rushes through me at the command. It's been a week since Cally's wedding, and every night, Max has come to my apartment when he gets off work. Some nights he has Claire and we hold her and feed her and generally spoil her rotten. And some nights it's just him and he takes off my clothes and does these amazing things to my body.

I obey. I pull the black sundress off over my head and let the fabric spill to the floor.

He takes me by the shoulders, and I feel his eyes on every inch of me as he slowly turns me to face him.

He tilts my chin up with his fingertips and lowers his mouth to mine. Our kiss isn't easy or sweet. It's not the coaxing kiss of seduction or the lazy kiss of long-time lovers. No, this kiss is a cocktail of need and regret and desperation. It's the hard kiss of two people grasping on to something they thought they'd lost. It's the demanding kiss of lonely hearts offered a second chance. It's lips and tongues and teeth, and before it's over, my arms are wrapped around his neck, my legs wrapped around his waist, while he hoists me up and carries me to the bed.

He settles me on the edge, and I lie back and let him look his fill. In the last two weeks, my breasts have grown firmer than normal with pregnancy, and they're extra sensitive when he grazes my nipples with his fingers.

"So fucking beautiful," he whispers.

He trails a hand between my breasts, over my belly, and circles my navel with his thumb. I can't believe I ever doubted his attraction to me. It's everywhere—in his touch, in his eyes, in the way he talks to me to turn me on.

I reach for him. "Come here."

He pulls off his shirt and unbuttons his jeans, pushing them and his briefs from his hips in one fluid movement. But when he's nude, he doesn't settle over me. He lowers to his knees and places his face between my parted thighs. I love his face between my legs, but I had an especially lonely day, and I need him close to me tonight.

I urge him up, and he kisses me one last time before climbing up my body and settling on top of me. I draw up my knees, and he slides into me with one long, hungry movement. His lips find mine as he pumps. His hands tangle in my hair.

"I've thought about this all day," he whispers in my ear. "Getting inside you, feeling you wrapped around me, making you come."

I whimper under him, and he hooks his arm under my knee and drives into me farther, deeper, harder. "Please," I murmur.

"Please what, baby?" His mouth is on my neck, his teeth nipping at my earlobe. "This?" He finds my breast between our bodies and toys with my taut nipple. I gasp, and he groans against my ear. "You are so sexy. So amazing."

He shifts slightly and suddenly he's deeper, pressing into me harder, and I lose control as my hips dance to their own rhythm against his, desperate, hungry, demanding. I curl my fingers into the thick, corded muscles of his arms and meet him stroke for stroke.

When he slows and circles his hips, I can't hold on anymore, and I let the orgasm tear through me and bring with it all the joy and love and regret I feel for this man.

He cleans us up after and we lie next to each other in bed—nude, fingers exploring each other.

"Did you know I used to think you didn't like me?" he asks.

That makes me smile. "What? No. Why would you think that?"

He toys with my fingers. "Back in high school. You'd be laughing with your sister and Cally. You've always had the most beautiful smile, and it makes people want to be around you. Want to have that smile aimed at them. And you'd be laughing and smiling, and I'd walk up and you'd stop. Like you were just waiting for me to leave so you could have fun again."

I laugh and bite my lip. "I didn't want you to leave. I wanted you to notice me, and I was so nervous."

He nods. "I noticed. I just didn't think I could love someone like you. I didn't think I could handle it."

"I am pretty demanding."

He gives me a sad smile and brushes my hair from my face. His eyes fill with tears, and he kisses me right over my heart then trails down until his lips are against my stomach. "I know I don't deserve this. I don't deserve you. But I swear to you I'm going to earn it. Our life together. Waking up next to you. I'm going to earn it, Hanna."

"Max, I—" Someone is knocking on the front door. It's after ten p.m. Who would be visiting me this late?

As Max climbs out of bed and pulls on his jeans, my phone buzzes on the nightstand. "I'll go with you," I tell Max. I shove my arms into my robe, grab my phone off the nightstand, and read the text as I follow him toward the door. "Liz says we need to turn on the news."

Max frowns and the deadbolt clicks as he unlocks it. "Why's that?"

"I don't know. She didn't say, but—" Whatever words I was going to speak are lost with my breath as Max opens the door.

There he is. My most desperate prayer and my life's greatest complication.

Nate Crane.

ACKNOWLEDGEMENTS

I wish I could say I do all this by myself, but the truth is, none of my books would have made it into the world without the assistance of countless people.

First and always, my husband, Brian, and our kids, Jack and Mary. I have the best little family and I'm so lucky to share my days with you. Thank you for cheering me on, lifting me up, and reminding me what really matters in this life.

To my brother-in-law, Gary, for answering questions about travel across the Middle East. Thanks for sharing your experience and knowledge. Any errors are my own.

A huge thank-you to my friends and family for being amazing cheerleaders. I couldn't ask for better book pimps.

To everyone who provided me feedback on this crazy twisty-turny plot—especially Rhonda Helms, Adrienne Hogan, and Samantha Leighton. Rock stars, all of you.

Thank you to the team that helped me package this book and promote it. Sarah Hansen at Okay Creations designed my beautiful cover, and if I have my way she will do many, many more for me. To my editing team, Rhonda Helms, Mickey Reed, and Arran McNicol, you make my books better. To Chris, my assistant, who keeps me organized against all odds. Thank you to Christine at iHeartBigBooks for designing my gorgeous promo materials, and a massive shout-out to Julie with AToMR for organizing my promotional events. To all of the bloggers and reviewers who help spread the word about my books—you're amazing. Every one of you.

To my agent Dan Mandel and my foreign rights agent Stefanie Diaz for getting my books into the hands of readers all over the world—you're making my dreams come true.

To all my writer friends on Twitter, Facebook, and my various writer loops, thank you for your support and inspiration. Thanks to Emma Hart for raving about book one and beginning the #TeamNateinmyPanties hashtag—my mom is proud. Special thanks to the NWB—Sawyer Bennett, Lauren Blakely, Violet Duke, Jessie Evans, Melody Grace, Monica Murphy, and Kendall Ryan—you ladies make me smile on a daily basis!

And last but certainly not least, thank you to my fans all over the world. To those who read *Unbreak Me* and *Wish I May* and wrote begging for another New Hope story. To those who read *Lost in Me* and said you couldn't wait to get your hands on *Fall to You*. You're the best fans an author could ask for. I couldn't do this without you and wouldn't want to. Thank you for buying my books and telling your friends about them. Thank you for being gracious and kind in your letters. You're the best!

~Lexi

PLAYLIST

New Politics—*Tonight You're Perfect*
Snow Patrol—*Chasing Cars*
Sarah McLachlan—*Angel*
Christina Perri—*Human*
Brooke Fraser—*You Can Close Your Eyes*
Ed Sheeran—*Kiss Me*
Coldplay—*Magic*
Ed Sheeran—*Lego House*
John Legend—*All of Me*
Alicia Keys, Adam Levine—*Wild Horses*

ALL FOR THIS

Here and Now series, book three

ALL FOR THIS

Here and Now series, book three

LEXI RYAN

For Annie. You're a great cheerleader, and when it comes to brainstorming, you're the bee's knees. But mostly, I'm just glad that, after all this time, I can still call you my friend. Love and miss you.

ONE

NATE

S he's wearing his ring.

Hanna's hand shakes as she presses it to her lips and her engagement ring flashes at me. She's in a thin pink robe, her hair falling in wild waves around her shoulders. Max stiffens next to her, bare-chested and protective. It doesn't take a genius to know what they were doing before they answered the door.

The sucker punch to the gut is too much, and I take a step back despite myself.

I shouldn't have come here. LA is too insane right now and I need to lie low until this madness settles. But I never should have come to Hanna's apartment.

It was instinct. As soon as I talked to Vivian and made arrangements for Collin, I came here.

"You're supposed to be dead," Hanna whispers.

"I'm not." But I can't decide if she wishes I were.

Our eyes are locked. I need to break free and leave—go back to Asher's and hide from the world while I wait for Collin to arrive.

Max turns to the living room, where he clicks on the TV, and while I'm trapped in the torment in her eyes, the news anchor tells the world that I'm alive and well.

Hanna finally releases me from her gaze and whips around to take in the TV, as if it might provide her with better evidence than my standing in her doorway.

"I just wanted to make sure you're okay." The lie scrapes across my heart as it passes my lips. I wanted so much more than to make sure she was okay. There's something about discovering that you should be dead that changes the way you look at the world. Changes what you're willing to risk.

"I'm okay," she says, her gaze still on the TV screen.

Suddenly, she throws her hand over her mouth and runs to the bathroom, and the sounds of her retching carry down the hallway.

Max throws me a look I don't understand. Maybe he too needs confirmation that I'm really at their door. Then he follows her.

When they return, his arm is wrapped around her shoulders, and she's leaning against his chest. I want to rip him off her and take her into my arms, where she belongs, but she sinks into his embrace as if she needs him to stand. Another reminder that I don't belong here.

Hanna might be the best thing that ever happened to me, but maybe for her, that's Max. Hell, Asher told me Max was no money-grubbing asshole after Hanna for the wrong reasons. And I already suspected that, didn't I? It was just further evidence.

And here he is—fucking Good Guy of the Year—holding her up when her lover stands at the door.

My hardened heart threatens to crumble.

Fuck. "I'll be at Asher's if you need me." I nod and back away as Max stares at me, his face a mask, his eyes unreadable.

I rush down the stairs before my heart can keep me where my brain knows I don't belong.

HANNA

He's gone. He came long enough to turn my world upside down and then disappeared.

Max kisses the top of my head, and I'm so conflicted by the intimacy of that single gesture. I want to curl into his sweetness, let him protect me the way I know he wants to. And at the same time, I want to push him away and tell him that he can't touch me like that anymore. Because Nate is alive.

"What can I do?" Max asks.

I shake my head and make my way to the bedroom to get dressed. "I need to go after him." I pull on a pair of jeans and a T-shirt and slide into my tennis shoes. When I reach the front door, I sense Max behind me and stop. "Will you be here when I get back?"

He's silent for a beat, and for the space of a breath, I wish we could go back to the simplicity of the moments before Nate knocked on my door. The wish disintegrates the moment I think it. Even the part of me that loves Max and craves a life with him wants Nate alive.

"Do you want me to be?" Max asks.

"Is it that simple?"

"For me it is. If you want me to be here, I will be."

I meet his eyes for the first time since our world imploded. "It's not that simple for me."

"I love you," he whispers. He hands me my car keys then reaches around me and opens the door. "Be careful."

I pocket my keys to appease him, but I have no intention of taking my car. I walk through the darkness, taking the path along the river and hoping the cadence of my steps might calm the riot in my heart.

I find Nate standing on the dock near Asher's house, his hands wrapped around the railing as he looks across the water. I knew he'd be here. Did he know I'd come after him?

The wind runs its fingers through his tousled hair, and I'm so overwhelmed with the need to touch him—to make sure he's real and alive and healthy. I shove my hands into my pockets so they can't betray me.

"You lied to me."

He nods without turning to me. "Seemed like the right thing to do at the time." His deep murmur floats on the breeze and wraps me in its embrace. Right now, Nate's voice is the most beautiful sound in the world, the only thing I want to hear.

"I understand why you would lie to me about taking my virginity if you thought I was going to marry Max," I say, standing next to him at the rail. "I don't agree with the decision, but I understand. But you lied to me about what was between us—about what you'd been willing to have with me. Why?"

"You'd made your choice," he whispers, his knuckles tightening around the wood.

I shake my head. "Not when I came to LA. I'd called it off with Max, and you made me believe that you'd never changed your mind about us."

"Did you really call it off, Hanna? Did you tell people you weren't going to marry him? Or was it a secret again?"

"I…" I force my lungs to take air. "That's not fair. You knew I couldn't remember, and you lied."

He studies me for a minute. "And how much do you remember?"

"I remember the day we made love. I remember you telling me that it was time for me to make a choice."

"After that?"

I shake my head. "Nothing."

He looks back to the water. "Let's just say that by the time you left my place, it was pretty clear I couldn't give you what you wanted. And after five days of you not answering my calls or texts…"

"Yet a week later, you were at my house, climbing into my bed?"

"Foolish optimism."

"What happened? Why did you have to lie?"

"I was right, wasn't I? It didn't take you long to take him back." His gaze flicks to my hand, and I realize his jaw is hard—angry. "You didn't wait long to put his ring back on your finger. I'm not the only one who lied."

The wind whips my hair around my face and stings my eyes. "What's that supposed to mean?"

"You're fucking kidding me, right? You took off his ring and told me you weren't going to marry him. But what you really meant was that you wanted your rebound boy again. That's all I am to you, the guy you like to screw around with when Max hurts your feelings."

"That's unfair," I breathe.

"Is it? How long after my supposed death did you wait to fuck him, Hanna?"

Hanna. Not *angel.* I've lost that label. "You walked away from me."

"I didn't walk away. I let you go."

"What's the difference?"

He shakes his head. "Go home. I'm sorry I interrupted you. Go back to fucking your fiancé."

His words hurt. They make me feel dirty and ashamed when I've done nothing wrong.

"Why did you even come here tonight? To hurt me? To make me feel guilty? Mission. Accomplished."

He turns and closes the distance between us, sliding his fingers into my hair and cupping my jaw in his hands. "I came because I thought you would be grieving me and I couldn't stand the idea of you hurting." His eyes dip to my mouth. "But I guess I didn't need to worry about that."

I swallow hard and wait for my feet to obey my mind—to back away before he can kiss me. But they don't. I've never had any willpower to resist this man, and I wonder if that weakness will be my undoing.

"You have no idea what the last ten days have been like for me."

"No. I guess Max is the only one who knows that." When

he lifts his eyes back to mine, the pain there rips me in two.

"I won't apologize for loving him. He's a good man."

"I'm glad," he says. "I hope you two have a good life."

Another punch in the gut, but my gut's practically numb by now, so I hardly wince. "So this is it, then? You're just going to show up on my doorstep—alive when you're supposed to be dead—make me feel like shit, and then walk away?"

He leans his forehead against mine and our breath mingles. His hands tighten in my hair almost painfully. "Are you asking me to do something else?"

"No," I whisper, and that's it. That's all I have left. All my will and all my strength go into that single word.

He releases me and steps back. I wait for relief, but it doesn't come. His eyes are resting on my left hand, and I want to cut it off for the pain it puts on his face.

"Goodbye, Hanna."

TWO

MAX

The clock's second hand mocks me as I sit in Hanna's otherwise silent apartment and wait for her to return.

I wanted to tell her not to go, but I knew she needed to. I wanted to go with her, but I would have just been in the way.

What the hell am I going to do now?

I'm not a fool. I know she still loves him, and I know she wouldn't still be wearing my ring if he hadn't been presumed dead. What I don't know is how this changes things. Am I supposed to step aside so she can be with the father of her children? Am I supposed to hold on tight and pretend it doesn't kill me to see the way she looks at him—as if he's some gift, a miracle from the heavens? As if no one and nothing exists for her when he's near?

In the cupboard, I find the wrapped jewelry box I positioned by the coffee and tuck it into my pocket. I have epically bad timing. I'd just gotten the ring and made plans to propose when Meredith decided to throw a wrench in my world, and tonight, I'd hidden the house key when Nate showed up at her door.

I shouldn't have signed the lease, but it seemed like the

perfect surprise. We spend more nights together than apart, and I hate the idea of her using those stairs several times a day. And with the babies coming…

The door groans softly as it opens. Hanna's face is pale, her cheeks wet with tears.

I stand without thinking.

What a fucking asshole. It's all I can do not to track him down and punch him in the face. Because she's standing here pale and limp, and he did that to her. He showed up on her doorstep without warning and then walked away like he didn't just turn her world upside down. And whatever he said when she went to find him made her cry. *Asshole.*

I wrap my arms around her and she clings to me—her nose against my chest, her hands curling around my arms. I stroke her hair and wait for her to break down, for these quiet tears to turn to sobs. But they don't. She just holds on, her slow and steady breaths warming my chest.

"How did my life get so screwed up?"

"Are you okay?"

When she lifts her eyes to mine, there's so much sadness in them that it makes my chest ache. "Can you forgive me for loving him too?" she asks. "Can we really survive this?"

Relief hits me center mass and splinters out through my limbs. Because there's still a *we.* I bring her hand to my mouth and press my lips to her knuckles. If I could package the intensity of my love in a single gesture, if I could prove to her how hard I'm willing to hold on, she wouldn't doubt us for a second.

When she settles her head against my chest again, I squeeze my eyes shut and say a prayer that I'll be enough for her.

"I'm not going anywhere," I whisper into her hair.

NATE

"Fuck, it's good to see you." Asher pulls me in for a hug

and slaps me on the back.

"You too."

Maggie waits behind him, half sniffling, half smiling, and when Asher doesn't release me soon enough for her liking, she pulls him off me and curls into me. "You scared the shit out of us," she growls into my chest.

I grin and stroke her hair. "I think your girl likes me, Asher."

He grunts, and Maggie says, "Shut up, Crane. You couldn't handle me."

"No doubt," I mutter.

She pulls out of my arms, grabs me by the wrist, and leads me into the kitchen while Asher takes my bags up the stairs.

After pouring herself a shot of tequila, she hands one to me. I throw it back without question. I haven't had anything alcoholic to drink since the night Hanna showed up at my house in LA, only half of her memory intact. I relish the warmth of the alcohol as it sinks to my stomach.

"What the fuck happened?" she asks. "How was it that you weren't on that helicopter?"

Asher joins us and stands so Maggie's back is against his chest. They're so damn good for each other, it eats at me.

"I was supposed to be," I begin. I pour myself another shot because, fuck, if anything calls for alcohol abuse, it's finding out that you're supposed to be dead and the woman you love—the woman who's the only reason you aren't dead right along with the rest of your tour—has moved on with another man. "I decided I couldn't do the tour and chartered a private plane to get me to Janelle in India. She was at this spiritual retreat and I was staying there, but they don't allow technology, so I…I had no idea the helicopter went down until someone arrived to deliver the news of my death to Janelle."

"Where is Janelle?" Maggie asks.

"She's still there. I told her to stay, and she was shaken enough that she didn't feel like she wanted to be anywhere else."

"Why couldn't you do the tour?" Asher asks.

Maggie says, "Because of Hanna, I bet."

I look to Asher, who shakes his head. He didn't tell her.

"Why would you say that?" I ask Maggie.

"I know about you and Hanna. Everyone knows." She digs through a stack of magazines and hands me one.

My gut burns when I see it. "Fucking privacy-invading assholes," I growl. My gaze snaps back to Maggie. "Max knows too?"

"Yeah," Maggie says.

Then she smacks me on the right shoulder. "That's for scaring me." Then again on the left. "And that's for screwing around with my sister and not even telling me about it."

Asher grabs Maggie's wrists and pulls her back against his chest. "Quit beating on the company." Then to me, he says, "You can stay as long as you want. When will Collin get here?"

"Vivian's bringing him in the morning."

Maggie's eyes fill. "That poor kid. I can't imagine what a rollercoaster this has been for him."

My throat is too thick, and I can't risk speaking, so I only nod. Vivian said Collin never cried. He insisted Daddy wasn't dead because Daddy would never leave him without saying goodbye.

One impulsive decision is the only reason my son still has his father, and that fact makes me feel so insanely helpless I want to scream.

"I'm ready for him to be here," I finally say. "And thanks for letting us stay awhile. LA is a madhouse. Vivian's been hounded by paparazzi since the helicopter went down."

Asher nods. "Of course. You're welcome as long as you want."

We all say our goodnights, and the happy couple makes their way to their bedroom, leaving me with the bottle of tequila and memories of Hanna's mouth under mine.

NATE

Five Days Before Hanna's Accident

"Stay one more night?"

She rolls to face me and runs her fingers over my stubble. I need a shave, but I can't bring myself to have a smooth face when Hanna's around. She can't keep her hands off my face when it's a little rough.

"You're sure you want to be with me before I've made my choice?"

My gut burns. Of course, I want her to make her choice *now*. I want to be the easy choice and for her to say she doesn't need to think about it. But it's not that simple. Hanna's heart is too loyal for that, and that's what I love about her, isn't it? Her big heart. Her loyalty. And a goodness that runs so deep and so steady that, when she's close, it becomes part of who *I* am.

"Stay with me. One more night," I repeat, and the unsaid words *in case this is goodbye* electrify the air between us.

I trace my hand down her body, and the tension seeps out of her with a soft moan that gets me hard every time. Maybe I shouldn't have taken her virginity. Maybe she'll regret that after she leaves, but I know I never will. Being inside her, watching the pleasure wash over her face as her body adjusted to mine and I finally sank deep… It was the most beautiful gift I've ever been given, second only to a woman like her loving me.

She grabs the tequila we left on the bedside table last night and says, "Cheers," before taking a swig.

Taking the bottle, I grin and splash some between her breasts. "Cheers," I murmur before I lick away the liquid, following it as it trails down her belly and sides. By the time I'm done, she's squirming under me.

Gently, I cup her between her legs, where she's wet from our lovemaking. "Are you sore?"

She shrugs. "A little, but it's not a bad feeling. More like muscles after a long workout. The good kind of hurt."

The good kind of hurt. Yeah, I'm feeling that too, even if my pain is more of the existential variety.

"Hmm." I roll on top of her and pin her hands to the bed as I murmur against her skin and kiss my way down her body. "Let me kiss it and make it better." Releasing her hands only so I can part her thighs, I sink to my stomach on the bed and position my head between her legs. "Right here?" I trace her opening, and she gasps and parts her legs farther.

When I replace my fingers with my mouth, she fists her hands in my hair, and *fuck,* do I love that. I stroke her with my fingers and tongue until she's moaning and so close to coming that she's fucking my face with jerking, desperate movements. Only then do I pull away and slide back up the bed next to her body.

"Better?"

She pries her eyes open and frowns at me. "You're...you're done?"

I have to laugh. "You're so fucking cute when you're trying to pretend you don't care about getting off."

"I don't want to be...greedy. I mean, I know we just had sex, so maybe you're not interested."

I grunt and lead her hand to my aching erection. "I'm interested, angel. With you, I'm always *interested.*"

She licks her lips as she wraps her fingers around me and strokes. "Then why did you stop again?"

My hips thrust, moving in her hand. "Because I want to be inside you when you come but I don't want to make you too sore. I'm trying to be a gentleman."

"A gentleman? Oh." She releases me, and I nearly grunt in disappointment. "In that case, I'm going to be a lady. And this lady needs a shower."

I stay in bed as she saunters into the bathroom. Not because I'm going to lose the opportunity to shower with Hanna—fuck no—but because I like watching her ass jiggle as she walks. There are very few perfect sights in this world of imperfections, and as such, I will never take Hanna's ass for granted.

By the time I pull myself out of bed and meet her in the bathroom, she's already in the shower, water sluicing over her curves. I'm jealous of the damn water because it's touching her everywhere I want to. I'm going to have to lap it all up with my tongue.

I step in behind her and press my mouth to her neck, sucking at the sensitive spot before knotting my hand in her wet hair and turning her to face me. "I love you," I say against her mouth.

"I love you too."

The tenderness that swamps me is terrifying. I don't want to let her go, and the fear that I might have to consumes me. I slant my mouth over hers, pouring everything I have into the kiss—all my love and fear, my vulnerability and desperation. I can't handle the power of what I'm feeling, so I put it into my kiss.

Soon, her back is against the glass, her leg is hitched around my waist, and my dick is nestled right against her hot, slick pussy.

"Mine," I growl against her lips.

Then I slide into her and it feels so fucking good I almost come right then and there. I lift her other leg—greedy for more, desperate to bury myself as deep in her as possible—and I fuck her against the glass. Her mouth is on my neck, her hands in my hair, her ankles locked behind my back.

"Mine," I repeat.

Her moan echoes in the shower, but I need more. I wrap my hand under her thigh and stroke her where our bodies are joined. Her pussy squeezes around me violently, and she bites the side of my neck as she rides out her orgasm. And I'm so wild with lust and jealousy and this soul-shredding love I feel for her that I've come inside her before I realize I'm not wearing a condom.

I pull out of her and slowly help her feet to the ground. "I'm sorry," I whisper.

She cocks her head. "Why? That was…amazing." She winces a little. "Okay, so I'm sore, but it's really okay."

I drag a hand through my hair. The shower is still running, and I turn it off before I answer. "I'm sorry because I wasn't wearing a condom."

Her lips part as she registers my words.

"There's probably nothing to worry about," I say, but I'm thinking of the one other time in my life when I forgot to wear a condom. I was nineteen, and nine months later, Collin was born. Best mistake I've ever made, but still. "We'll be more careful. Are you… You're on something, right?"

She opens her mouth and closes it. Goose bumps prickle on her arms as she shivers. I lead her out of the shower and wrap her in a towel.

"I'm sorry," she says. "I didn't even think…"

Oh, damn. "*You're* sorry? Angel, you didn't do anything wrong. I should have…" Then it hits me. "You're *not* on birth control."

She shakes her head, and I pull her against my chest and squeeze my eyes shut, cursing myself over and over in my mind. I want Hanna. I want to find a way to make it work with her. But another kid? That's leaps and bounds beyond what I'm ready for. *Fuck it.* I can't even let my thoughts go there.

"It's going to be okay," I promise. "The chances of this resulting in an accidental pregnancy are so small."

She wraps her arms around her middle, holding the towel against her breasts. She studies the floor. "What would happen if I were? What if we had shitty luck and the small chance turns into a baby?" When she looks up at me through water-dampened lashes, I can see the confusion in her eyes.

"It'll be okay."

"But what if it's not?"

Fuck, fuck, fuck. "Do we really have to have this conversation right now? Isn't that just borrowing trouble?"

She squeezes her eyes shut and turns away from me. "I'm not trying to be melodramatic, but it matters."

"I won't ruin today. I'm not going to have a fight over

nothing."

"Why does it have to be a fight? I'm just asking what you'd do. What *we'd* do."

"We'd figure it out. I have more than enough room here. You could move in with me or—"

"You think I'd move to LA?" The horror in her voice is a backhand to the face, a reminder of all the reasons I've kept this part of my life inaccessible to women. She points to the bedroom. "Is that what you meant when you said I had to choose? You want me to give up my life for you?"

"I didn't say that."

"But you're saying it now, aren't you?"

I set my jaw. I wish she'd turn around and look at me. "I said I want to find a way to make it work. I don't know what that looks like because I've never allowed myself to consider it."

"Consider it now," she whispers. "In your mind, do I have to give up my bakery and move to LA if we're going to be together?"

"My son is here," I say slowly. "So in my mind, that's the easiest solution. Can we please end this conversation? We're arguing over a hypothetical—"

"No. This isn't just a hypothetical. This is something I need to know." She squeezes herself tightly and lowers her head. "If I'm going to choose, I need to know."

I spin her around and squeeze her shoulders as I growl, "*I. Love. You.*" Anger tears through me with my frustration. I want my love to be enough for her. *I* want to be enough for her. But here we are, minutes after making love, and she's holding me up to this other guy. "Why can't that be enough for you? Not forever but for now. *Please.*"

She lifts her eyes to mine, and pain slices through my gut at the doubt I see there. Doubt in *us*. Doubt in *me*. "I think it's time for me to look beyond here and now. Here and now is all I let myself think about this summer, and look where that got me."

I flinch. "It got you here. With me. Is that so terrible?"

"And what happens next year? The year after that? What happens when I'm ready to have the house with the picket fence and you're still in LA? What happens when I'm ready for babies?"

"Don't do this. Don't destroy what's between us by asking it to carry more than it can hold. This is new, and it's not fair to push it like this."

"You're the one who told me you wanted me to choose," she whispers. "These are things I need to think about."

I crush my mouth to hers and yank the towel from her body. I expect her to push me away, but I'm wrong. Jesus, am I wrong. She's just as greedy for me as I am for her. Her hands go to my hair. Her breasts press against my chest. Her tongue slides against mine, desperate. This is where we've always been good. There's never been a question of the heat between us. Here's where we can always find our way—this kiss, the heat of our bare skin pressed together. How can this be so powerful and mean nothing? I know it's the question we're both asking ourselves as terror holds us in its steely grip.

"Was it like this with him?" I ask against her ear, my hand skimming her side. "Did you need him the way you need me?"

"Don't."

"You didn't, Hanna. There's a reason *I'm* the one you let kiss you here." I settle my hand between her legs, and her eyes float closed. "There's a reason you never fucked him and were ready to let me inside you the first night we met."

"It's different."

"Damn straight it is." I want to slide my fingers inside her, feel the slick walls of her heat, feel evidence of the need I won't let her dismiss. But I know she's gotta be sore and I settle for cupping her and the satisfaction of the needy rocking of her hips. "It's different because you're *mine* more than you were ever his. You might love him, but you *need* me. And if you choose him, you'll always wonder if you and I could have made it work."

She wraps her hand around my wrist and slowly removes it from between her legs before stepping back. "And what if I choose you? Will I spend the rest of my life wondering if I could have a family and kids if I'd chosen him?"

I fist my hands at my sides because I'm afraid that, if I let myself touch her, I'll pull her into my arms and refuse to let her go. I'm afraid one hit of her scent will make me promise things I know I can't give.

"I don't want any more kids, Hanna. I have Collin and I can't do that to him."

"Can't or won't?"

"Don't," I plead.

"There's a difference," she whispers. "An important one."

"Maybe I'll change my mind, but right now…"

She swallows and her eyes well with tears. "Thank you for your honesty." Then she leaves the bathroom.

I feel like an idiot and an asshole, but I won't lie to win her. She deserves better.

After I wash my face and dry off, I return to the bedroom. She's dressed and her bag is thrown over her shoulder.

"Hanna, I'm sorry."

She shakes her head. "Don't apologize for being honest."

"If I changed my mind for anyone, it would be for you. Don't go. Not yet."

"I'm going to fly home tonight. I need to think."

Stepping forward, I cup her jaw in my hands and tilt her face up to mine. "I wish I'd met you before you started dating him."

"And I wish we could just be a normal couple in love. But we're not." She touches her hand to my cheek. "There's never been anything normal about us."

"Only because this is better than normal. You know it is."

"Give me time. I need to think."

She's ending this. She's fucking leaving me and ending this. "Don't do this. Hanna…"

"We'll talk when you get back from London." She turns toward the door.

"Angel," I call. She stops but doesn't turn to me. "You can leave, but you're taking my heart with you. You can choose him, but part of you will always be mine."

THREE

HANNA

The first time Max and I made love, I told him I'd never had sex without a condom.

I was wrong.

I lie in bed with the memory searing my brain like a hot iron. When I close my eyes, I can feel the goose bumps on my arms, the cool tile under my feet, my skin still wet, my body sore from making love to Nate, my legs sore from being wrapped around his waist as he took me in the shower.

"I don't want any more kids, Hanna. I have Collin and I can't do that to him."

Then when I returned to LA after the amnesia, when we were saying goodbye, he met me in the shower again. *"Why'd you have to forget?"* At the time I thought he meant *forget us,* but he meant more than that. He meant…everything. His offering more, his taking my virginity, his making love to me in the shower and the conversation that rendered him silent when he discovered I'd made my choice.

I settle my hand on my stomach and imagine the little lives growing inside. My pregnancy was hard for me to accept, and the idea of having a baby at all—let alone twins—still terrifies me. But, despite all of that, these babies feel like a miracle and a gift to me. And to Nate, they'll be nothing more than a slight to his firstborn.

When my alarm goes off, I'm relieved. I may have spent more of the night pretending to sleep than actually sleeping.

Max reaches for me as I slide out of bed, and I squeeze his hand before padding through the dark to get ready in the bathroom. If I worried that he'd want to have sex last night, I needn't have. He held me in his arms and fell asleep, and I lay there wondering how I ever made a choice between two halves of my heart.

In the bakery, I find comfort in my morning routine—warming the ovens, pulling the ingredients for today's recipes, listing the outside orders for the following week, and penning them into my schedule.

As I bake, my mind turns, and to keep myself from spinning my emotional wheels, I make a mental list of what I know to be true.

I chose Max once and I have no reason to doubt that decision given what I know now about the bakery and how he feels about me. Especially considering Nate doesn't want any more children and I always hoped to have a big family.

Max is exactly what I need now. My future with him will be stable and secure, and most importantly, it's a future here, at home.

Despite all of that, I find myself trying to make the choice all over again. Maybe because I'm pregnant with Nate's babies and that complicates things. Or maybe for another reason altogether.

I need to tell Nate about the pregnancy, regardless of how he feels about having more children. When I talked to him last night, I was still trying to digest the fact that he was alive. And trying to defend myself against his accusations. He thinks I just jumped into bed with Max the second I learned his helicopter went down. It's not that simple—nothing is. He walked away from me. He said goodbye.

I would have ended up with Max again, even if the whole

world hadn't thought Nate was dead.

Wouldn't I?

And it's in the space of that tiny question, in the hesitation between the beats of my heart, that my kernel of guilt sprouts poisonous blossoms in my heart and leaves my relationship with Max in its shadow.

Telling Nate about the babies while keeping Max's ring on my finger is about the cruelest position I could put him in. I'll be making him the second family—again and forever—when he deserves so much more.

At six, I go to the front to unlock the door and turn on the sign, and I find my mother standing at the entrance in her church clothes. The moment I open the door for her, she wraps me in her arms.

I will never be too old or too broken to be soothed by the comfort of my mother's arms. She strokes my hair, and I let quiet tears leak from my eyes.

"I might not approve of your relationship with that rock star," she whispers, "but I thank God my grandbabies won't be deprived of knowing their father."

That makes me cry harder.

She smooths my hair and gently pats my back. "How's Max holding up?"

I withdraw from her embrace. "He's fine." And he is. Poor guy doesn't even get the opportunity to be pissed off. If Nate had never been presumed dead, no one would have questioned Max's right to be angry as hell about my summer with Nate. Maybe it wasn't cheating, but it wasn't honest either. And that was stolen from him. Since Max isn't enough of an asshole to wish someone dead, he's left having to be okay with Nate's reappearance in our lives.

"I just don't understand," Mom says as she walks over to the coffeepot.

I get to work on filling the bakery cases. "Don't understand what?"

"How all of this happened. The pregnancy, the postponed wedding, your whole relationship with Nate Crane. A few days before your accident, you couldn't *wait* to marry Max."

I freeze with a tray of scones in my hands. "I couldn't?"

"The sooner the better, you told me. You weren't even wearing a ring yet, but you just wanted to start your life with him."

"I said that?" I whisper.

"Yes. And it didn't surprise me that you felt that way. Of course you would. You and Max were always so good together." She looks down at her coffee and draws in a breath. "Then you had that horrible accident. You seemed so reluctant to make wedding plans, but I thought it was because you couldn't remember. Then, suddenly, you were pregnant with another man's baby. It didn't make sense to me."

"When did I tell you I wanted to marry Max?" I ask, pressing. Would I have told her that to help with his chances to get the grant? No. That doesn't make sense. She would have been just as likely to support Max as my boyfriend as she would have if he were my fiancé.

Mom frowns at me. "Shortly before your accident."

"But *when*?" I squeak. Mentally, I'm calculating what I know, what I remember, and trying to fit it in.

Mom props her hands on her hips. "Why does it matter?"

"I still don't remember everything," I explain. "And those last four days are still completely gone. I want to know."

Her eyes tilt to the ceiling. "Well, I guess it was after Abby's party. The day after, maybe? Because you'd forgotten to bring her gift to the party and you were swinging by the house to drop one off. Gosh, you know, maybe it was the day before your accident. That evening."

"And I wasn't wearing the ring?"

She shakes her head. "The first time I saw your ring, you were in the hospital. Why don't you ask Max when he proposed? He can fill in some details."

Because he proposed months before.

Mom cocks her head. "You look pale, Hanna. Are you sleeping enough? You need to make sleep a priority for those babies. Pregnancy is hard on the body."

"I will," I promise. I hand her a cup of coffee and lead her out the door.

It's so tempting to hold on to the secret as long as I can. I force myself to pick up my phone and text Nate.

NATE

"Daddy!"

My heart swells as Collin runs to me across Asher's backyard. I squat and open my arms, and he throws himself in them, hugging me as I lift him off the ground. I can breathe easier when he's close to me. He's the reminder of all the reasons I needed to let Hanna go. All the reasons I should wish her well in her life with Max. He's the only thing that matters.

"I knew you weren't dead," Collin says, his face buried in my neck. "I just knew it."

I stroke his dark hair, close my eyes, and say a prayer. "I love you, buddy."

He gives me one more squeeze before pulling back and grinning at me. "Mommy said I can stay here for a while. Is that true? Do I get to sleep over at Uncle Asher's house?"

Five minutes ago, I didn't feel like smiling, but Collin's happiness is contagious, and nothing matters now that he's here—safe and with me, where he belongs.

"It's true," I answer. "How was the flight?"

"Awesome! Mommy let me drink champagne and then she played DS with me! Did you know she can beat all the levels on *Luigi's Mansion*?"

I lift my gaze to Vivian, who followed Collin into the yard. "Ginger ale," she explains. "Extra yummy in a champagne flute."

"Drake," I say, nodding to her personal security guard.

The tall man straightens his sleek leather jacket and nods as a greeting. He's been Vivian's bodyguard since we were teenagers, and I've seen him bloody faces of men who dared get their hands or their cameras too close to Vivian. His flowing, platinum-blond hair and ghostly blue eyes make him a more likely candidate for a retro romance novel cover than a security guard, but he's good at his job.

"Is that Collin I see out there?" Asher calls from the patio.

"It is!" Collin squirms, and I set him on his feet so he can run after "Uncle" Asher.

"Thanks for bringing him," I tell Vivian. After over a week in silence, speaking still feels odd. When I went to India to join Janelle at her little spiritual retreat, I had no idea I'd be handing over my electronics and my right to speak for the foreseeable future. Not that I cared. I didn't want to talk to anyone anyway.

"The last thing you needed was a paparazzo catching your reunion or, worse, following you here. It was better this way."

I nod, watching as Collin follows Asher into the house. "Jamaal will be here soon, and Asher and I are hiring extra security. They'll find me here, but I don't have to let them get close."

Her shoulders drop a little, and I know she's relieved. She's never been fond of what she sees as my "lax" security measures. "I'm glad to hear it."

"How's he handling the divorce?" I ask, looking at Collin.

She shrugs and puts on the brave smile I recognize so well. "Better than expected, I guess. Except he seems to think this means you and I are getting back together, and I try to explain that sometimes mommies and daddies love each other but can't be together."

"Viv," I whisper.

She shakes her head. "Don't apologize. That makes me feel worse."

"I need to apologize, especially about what happened in London. It was—"

She puts her fingers to my lips. "Stop while you're ahead. Please. I'm just glad you're not dead. The rest is irrelevant."

I pull her into a hug and press a kiss to the top of her head. "I'll always love you. You gave me my son."

"Be careful."

"I'm not getting in a helicopter anytime soon, so you don't need to—"

"With *her*, Nathaniel. Be careful with that girl. I don't trust her."

"Hanna?"

She nods. "I don't want to see you hurt."

Too late. "You're the one who insisted I tell her how I feel."

"That was before I knew she was seeing someone else. I saw them together."

"I know about her fiancé, Viv. Just...back off, okay?"

"She's engaged to him?" She smacks me in the chest. "Why are you messing around with a woman who's engaged to someone else?"

"She wasn't engaged then."

My phone buzzes. Hanna's name scrolls across the screen, making my gut flip and clench all in one riotous movement. All summer long, texts from Hanna were the highlight of my days. How long has it been since I received a text message from her?

> **Hanna:** *Can we talk tonight?*
> **Nate:** *What's there to say?*
> **Hanna:** *Please.*

I swallow as I stare at the single word in her last message. *Please.* I can't say no to her, even if seeing her with his ring on her finger will kill something inside me.

"Is that her?" Vivian asks. She reaches for my phone, and I sidestep her.

"Back off, Viv. Don't try to mother-bear me. This doesn't concern you."

"You said you told her how you felt."

"I did," I growl. "Drop it."

"You see? It's better. Now you know and—"

I don't hear the rest because I'm walking away. The last thing I need right now is to hear Vivian's opinion of my relationship with Hanna. When I'm alone in the house again, I reply to Hanna's last text.

Nate: *The dock. Nine thirty.*

FOUR

MAX

"How are you holding up?"

I'm quiet for a minute, looking around Brady's. There have been plenty of curious glances thrown my way since William and I sat down with our beer. The news of Hanna's and my canceled wedding spread across town like the best kind of gossip.

By now, half the town knows Hanna is pregnant with another man's baby, though I'm not sure who leaked that information. Not that it was a secret, but the summer breakup was. The story of her pregnancy is irresistible to the gossip hounds.

"I'm good," I finally say. William is studying me as if he doesn't trust my words. "Relieved, honestly."

He raises a brow. "Yeah?"

I'm not sure how to explain it. I want Hanna, but I want her to be with me because I'm her choice, not because a tragedy made me the default choice. Every night I slept with her in my arms felt like a miracle made possible by the death of someone she loved. His death tainted what we had.

I only say, "It's better this way."

"You two are okay?"

I wish I knew. "She's still in love with him."

"She's still in love with you, too," Will says, and I nod because that's what I've been holding on to. "Where is she tonight?"

"She's meeting Nate." I swallow. "She needs to tell him about the babies." I offered to go with her. I wanted him to see that I'm standing by her side through all of this, but she declined. *"Having you there will just hurt him more."*

"He's going to fight for her," Will warns.

"I'll fight harder."

Will grins his approval.

I have to change the subject. If I think too much about Hanna meeting Nate tonight, I'll lose my mind. "How's Cally feeling?"

Will beams at the mention of his pregnant wife. "Tired, nauseated, anxious to grow a belly so the whole world knows she's pregnant. How's Hanna?"

"Same. Tired. The nausea comes and goes, but cold washcloths help a lot."

"Shit," Will grumbles, looking to the door. "We have company."

"Hi, boys." Meredith is all smiles as she slides into the booth next to me. She smells of rum and her eyes are drunken and glazed. "I heard the good news about Nate Crane. Didn't you?"

William stiffens. He and Meredith used to be friends— more, even—but after the way she treated Cally, he can't stand her anymore. "I don't remember inviting you to join us."

"Where's Claire?" I ask. I refuse to take her bait, and she scowls.

"I dropped her off at your mom's."

My jaw ticks in annoyance. "I thought you were going to spend some time with her before your business trip."

"Don't tell me how to be a mother and I won't tell you how to be a fiancé. You are still engaged, aren't you? Or has she come to her senses and left town with that sexy rock star?"

"Go away, Meredith," Will mutters.

She ignores him and looks at me. "Is it true you rented the old Blackman house?"

"It is."

"Well...I'm pretty sure once Nate Crane finds out your *fiancée* is pregnant with his babies, you're not going to have the need for three bedrooms anymore."

"Go. Away," Will repeats, and I add, "What he said."

She shrugs and slides out of the booth.

Will watches her go, only turning back to me when he's convinced she's far enough away. "She's poison. I know she's the mother of your child, but you need to find a way to keep her from contaminating your relationship with Hanna."

Across the bar, Meredith is flirting with a young professor who's new to town. Poor bastard doesn't even know what he's getting himself into.

"Congrats on the new house. I had no idea."

"It was supposed to be a surprise for Hanna. I thought we could rent out our apartments and live together. I was going to take her there today, but then Nate showed up last night and I decided to wait."

"Understandable."

"I need a big favor," I admit.

"Anything."

"Hanna wasn't the only reason I decided to get the house." And I hate this. William has been my best friend for most of my life, and I've prided myself on never taking advantage of his generosity. "I'm talking to a lawyer about pursuing physical custody of Claire. I'm sick of her using my daughter to manipulate me, and I can't stand the thought that she could take her away from me."

"Of course. That's wise. And you need money for the lawyer?"

"I have an offer for the club. Someone who's willing to buy it."

Will leans back in the booth and shakes his head. "Don't be stupid, man. This is your future. Let me lend you money."

I take a breath. Borrowing money from Will would make me feel even worse than this. I don't want it to come to that. "Remember when I was looking into opening the club and you offered to buy in?"

"Sure." His brows shoot up, disappearing under his messy mop of blond curls. "Are you saying I can buy in now?"

"If you're interested. It would take a lot of pressure off, but I don't want you to feel pressured."

"Don't even think about it. This is important, and I'd love to do it. What does Hanna think about the custody situation?"

I release a slow a breath. "I didn't want to bring it up until I knew I could do it. We'll have three babies under the age of one. Am I crazy?"

"Fucking nuts," Will says. "But would you have it any other way?"

I grin. "Not a chance."

NATE

I didn't want to leave Asher's until I was sure Collin was asleep, and by the time I make it to the dock, Hanna's already there. She's sitting against the railing, looking out over the water. Her dark hair is off her neck in a twist, and my fingers itch to toy with the little tendrils that have escaped. I miss the way her hair feels, miss the way her eyes float closed as I comb it with my fingers.

The night is clear and the moon reflects off her pale skin, and looking at her hurts so much that I wonder for a few breathless seconds if I can breathe near her, knowing she's not mine.

"It's a beautiful night." I consider sinking onto the planks next to her but dismiss the idea. I don't trust myself to be that close. I take my station on the other side of the dock instead.

"It is." She stands and crosses to stand next to me. Her smell slingshots me back to weekends waking up in hotels with Hanna's hair fanned across the pillow, her soft curves under my hands.

"Why are we here?" If the question comes out harsher than I intended, it's because I'm desperate to get away.

She reaches in her purse and hands me a folded piece of paper. "Because I need to tell you about this."

I unfold the paper and my hammering heart is blindsided by the black-and-white image. I can barely make it out in the moonlight, but I know what it is.

"Mine?" My voice breaks on the word.

"They don't have to be," she whispers.

I rip my gaze away from the ultrasound image to see her face. "What's that supposed to mean?"

"I'm telling you because it's the right thing to do. But I'm not asking anything of you. I wouldn't do that."

"You think I'd just walk away from my child?"

"Children." She points to two spots on the image. One gray lima bean and the other.

My breath is trapped in my lungs, and I have to close my eyes to remember how to breathe. "Children?" When I open my eyes again, she's staring at me, trying to read my expression.

Finally, she nods. "Twins."

My stomach feels like it's stuck in an endless free fall as I study the little, colorless splotches in the moonlight. Twins. *My* twins.

"Does Max know?"

"Yes."

"He knows they're mine?"

A breeze picks up off the river, and a wispy lock of hair blows across her face. "Yes."

"When are you getting married? Wasn't that supposed to be soon?"

She shakes her head. "We called off the wedding. Postponed it indefinitely. I can't move forward with anything like that until after the babies are born. Right now, they're my only priority."

"And then?"

She shrugs. "We're engaged. I plan to marry him eventually. Just not yet."

"Do you expect me to just walk away? Let you two create your happy little family with my children?" Hanna is one of three people in the world who could understand how much that hurts me. Yet here we are. Here I am—on the outside again.

"I don't know what to expect from you. I just know the choice needs to be yours, and that's why I'm telling you."

My whole body tenses and an ugly laugh slips from my lips. "My choice? What if my choice is to be in their lives every day? What if my choice is to have them in my house? What if I want to be a real father and not just someone they visit from time to time? Are you giving me that choice?"

"You are their father, and I won't keep them from you. But I am their mother. If you fight me for custody"—she lifts her eyes to mine and I see her determination—"I will fight back just as hard. You will lose."

"What if I don't just fight for my kids?" I ask. Vivian says I keep walls around my heart, but I would take a sledgehammer to those walls for Hanna. I would tear them down and stand completely exposed, all to get closer to her. "What if I fight for their mother too?"

HANNA

Will I ever be able to look at Nate and not feel this painful tugging in my heart?

"Didn't you already have your chance?" My fingernails bite into my palms as I force my hands to stay at my sides.

"I couldn't fight for you before."

I draw in a breath, and he opens his eyes to meet mine. The question I can't ask pulses in the air between us. *Why not?*

"What if I won, Hanna? What if I fought for you and I won? I'm not the prize here. *You* are." He turns then, reaches out, and his fingers stroke the side of my cheek. My eyes float closed because it's too much—having him here when he's supposed to be dead, having him touch me when I'm supposed to let him go. "It would be different if you hadn't chosen him, if you weren't in love with him." His fingers take my chin and tilt it up until I open my eyes and look into his. "It would be different if I didn't know that you're too damn good for me. I came here, and you had made your choice and forgotten me. I knew I didn't deserve your heart, and I didn't want to risk breaking it."

I step back until his hand falls away from my face. "Too late."

"That's why you chose him? Because I didn't fight for you? Come to LA with me. Be with me. I will fight for you every day."

"Would you even say that if you didn't know about the pregnancy?" My voice is cold even to my own ears. Instinctively, my hand splays over my stomach, where my babies grow. According to all the pregnancy websites, today my little ones are no bigger than the size of a kidney bean. Not much. Yet...*everything*.

"I'm supposed to be dead." He squeezes my hand when I try to pull away. "As soon as we arrived in Afghanistan, I realized I couldn't do the tour. I was a mess. I needed some time alone, so I went to India to join Janelle and left my agent behind with the other musicians..." He closes his eyes. "I should have been on that helicopter and I should be dead right now, and the only reason I'm alive is because I'm so fucking in love with you that I couldn't face my tour. Don't you see? You save me. Over and over again."

I lick my lips and taste the salt of my tears. Maybe I'll always love Nate, and maybe that love for Nate will destroy what I have with Max. But this isn't about Max. This isn't as simple as choosing between two men. I'm not willing to move to LA, and I won't ask him to leave Collin to be here. I love him enough to let him go.

I understand the difference now. I'm not walking away

from him. I'm letting him go.

"I want to go to your next appointment," he says. "I'm their father. I want to be part of this."

"Okay."

"But do me a favor. Don't bring him with you."

I take a breath. "If I marry him, he'll be helping me raise them, regardless of how you feel about that."

His gaze settles on my left hand. "*If?*"

"*When*," I whisper, but the word feels like a lie.

FIVE

MAX

When I hear the click of the shower door opening and closing, I get hard instantly. Because the thought of Hanna joining me in my shower does that to me.

I haven't touched her since Nate appeared on her doorstep Friday night. I called her last night after she met with Nate, but her mind was somewhere else. I wanted to go to her apartment, to hold her and reassure us both, but I didn't want to push her when I knew she was emotional and confused.

"Want company?" she whispers.

As I turn to her, I'm already filled with thoughts of pressing her against the tile as I kiss her. I want to remind her how it feels when we're together. I want to sink to my knees so I can put my mouth between her legs as the hot water spills over her.

When I wipe the water from my face, I freeze. "What the fuck?"

Meredith skims her eyes over me, all the way down to my cock, and grins. "Good morning." She reaches for me, and I shove her aside and leave the shower.

Hanna's supposed to meet me here so we can head over to brunch at her mom's together. It's become our Sunday routine—as Meredith well knows, since she's met us here on the last two Sundays to hand off Claire. No doubt she hoped Hanna would find us together, wet from the shower.

I wrap a towel around my hips and storm from the bathroom, determined to put distance between Meredith and me before I do something I regret.

I have my jeans on by the time she joins me in the bedroom.

"That didn't turn out how I was hoping," she grumbles, plopping her nude, wet body onto my bed.

I throw my towel over her. "Was that supposed to be sexy? Did you think you could climb into the shower with me and I wouldn't be able to resist you?"

Her lower lip sticks out in a pout, and she removes the towel and uses it to dry her hair. "I thought maybe you could use some cheering up."

"Would you just stop for a minute and imagine if our roles were reversed? If I were trying to reconcile with you and got naked and joined you in the shower?"

"I'd be down for that."

Feeling her eyes on me literally makes me sick to my stomach. "If *you* do it, it's supposed to be sexy, but you know what it would be called if a guy did it to you?"

Her eyes go hard and her nostrils flare. "What?"

"Assault, Meredith. I'm going to say one more time that I'm not interested. I want you to stay away from me. This shit isn't sexy and it doesn't turn me on. It's sad and pathetic." I tug on a shirt.

"Her baby daddy is alive, Max. You're living in a fantasy world if you think she's going to marry you when she could have him."

I force myself to take a breath before I talk. "Are you listening? I need you to hear this. Whatever Hanna decides— whether she marries me or Nate Crane or the fucking man in the moon—I will never, ever be with you again. I would rather be alone than be with you. I would rather be abstinent for the rest of my life than have you in my bed. I tolerate you because you're my daughter's mother. That's it and that's all, and the next time you enter my house without my express permission, I'll call the police and have them drag your delusional ass to jail. Do I make myself clear?" I leave the bedroom before she can answer.

Hanna's waiting for me in the living room, her eyes wide. Of course. *Fuck.*

"Hanna, I can exp—"

"I heard. All of it. She's lost her mind."

My shoulders sag with relief and I gather her into my arms. "She's never known how to be alone. But this is a new low. I think..." I take a breath and slowly let it out.

Meredith has always been one to go after what she wants, and she never paid much mind to anyone who stood in her way, but it's been different since Claire was born. More desperate.

"Would you quit talking about me?" Meredith emerges from the bedroom, fully dressed, her hair hanging in wet clumps around her shoulders. She narrows her eyes at Hanna. "How's Nate?"

"Alive," Hanna says dryly.

"So I hear. Have you even told Max about your fun little trips this summer? All over the fucking country. Or should I say, all over the country, *fucking*?"

"Did you need something?" Hanna asks her, and I'm proud of her. Six months ago, Meredith would have had Hanna turning away to hide in a corner. She's changed. She's stronger now, more confident. Did I do that, or was it Nate?

"Fine," Meredith says. "I'm out. Where's Claire?"

"She's napping." I nod to the Pack 'N Play on the other side of the room. "I'll bring her by your place later."

"Fine."

"I need to tell you something," I say when we're alone.

Her teeth sink into her bottom lip. "Okay?"

"I'm getting a lawyer and pursing custody of Claire. I know it seems crazy with the twins coming, and I hope you understand—"

"I think it's wonderful." Her face lights up with her grin. "You're an amazing father, and I hope you win."

I release a breath and tension I hadn't realized I felt dissolves from my shoulder. "Thank you," I whisper, "for understanding."

She splays her fingers over her belly. "I understand more than you know," she says with a sad smile.

"How are you holding up? Did it go okay with Nate last night?"

She stiffens at his name. "He asked me to move to LA."

Of course he did. "And what did you say?"

She blinks at me. "I'm not leaving New Hope. This is my home."

"He wanted more than for you to move to LA." I take a step closer. I need to touch her. I wonder if she knows she's pulling away from me, if she can feel it like I can. It's as if we're connected by a thousand little threads like those in a woven rug and they've been breaking one at a time since the moment Nate came back into town. With every breath, I feel another thread snap. "He wanted *you*."

She shrugs. "I'm already taken."

I draw in a deep breath. She lifts her hand to my face and skims her fingers along my jaw.

I groan softly and slide my hand into her hair as I lower my mouth to hers. She's soft and sweet, and I need more of her.

Taking a fistful of her skirt, I yank her dress up around her waist and find the cotton of her panties. She gasps, and I rub her through the fabric as her fingers curl into my back. My lips find her neck and the skin in the sensitive juncture of neck and shoulder.

"Max," she says. But it's not the normal breathy, needy whispering of my name. The word is a warning. A yield sign. "Max."

My hand stills and I pull back to look into her eyes. I'm blindsided by the apology I see there. "Let's move in together."

"What?" She blinks at me. If she's thinking I have the world's worst timing with important proposals, she's not wrong.

"We could rent out our apartments and use the money

to rent a little place together. Someplace without those stairs that scare the living shit out of me every time I think of you climbing them. Someplace we can make our own." I take her hand and squeeze. "You didn't want to move in together last spring because you knew your mom would flip if you lived with a guy before marriage, but we're not trying to maintain appearances anymore, are we?" She looks at the floor, and I tilt her chin back up so her eyes meet mine. "I could give two shits about appearances. I want to wake up with you in my arms, Hanna. I want to know I'm going to be right there when you need me, every time you need me. You and Claire are all that matter in my world. I want everything that matters to be what I come home to every night."

"I'm sorry." She steps back. "I just can't. I'm too confused right now."

My lungs burn as I fill them—it hurts to breathe in a world where Hanna isn't mine.

"I know it's not fair. And I want a future with you, but…"

"But you can't stop thinking about him."

"I can't move in with you right now," she says softly. "That wouldn't be fair to either of us. It's not that simple."

"You keep saying that."

I swallow back the rest of what I want to say right along with my anger, frustration, and the betrayal I've never allowed myself to feel. While I was waiting for her to take my ring, she was with another man, and I was never allowed to be angry because that man died and she needed to grieve.

I drag a hand through my hair and look at the ceiling. "Was it that simple when you made love to him?"

"Can we not do this?"

Torment is etched across her face, and I can't stand to know I'm the one who put it there. I pull her against my chest.

"I won't rush you, but remember something for me," I whisper into her hair. "You put on my ring."

NATE

Collin tosses the stones into the river and claps when each splashes into the water.

But fuck if my stomach doesn't pitch every time I think of Hanna and Max having a life together, laughing together, in bed together. Raising my children together.

"Hey, sexy," a tall blonde murmurs from behind her stroller. And I'll give her credit—it takes one hell of a lot of self-confidence to try to play the slut while walking your infant through the park.

I turn away, silently dismissing her.

"We have mutual friends." She parks the stroller and sinks onto the bench beside me, but not before giving me an obvious once-over. "Congratulations on the whole avoiding-a-fiery-death thing."

"Thanks," I reply dryly. I keep my eye on Collin.

"So you're in New Hope for a while, probably hoping to win Hanna back, huh?"

My jaw tightens. "I don't know what you're talking about." Then I stand because I'm not in the mood.

"Oh," she calls to my back. "Because the rest of the town seems to think those are your babies she's carrying."

I stop and slowly turn to her, and I can tell by her face that she expected this to be news to me. "I don't know who you think you are or why you think I care about your opinions about my private business, but you're mistaken. You can leave now."

She attempts to look innocent and adjusts her baby's blanket. "Twins—can you believe it? Surely you're going to want to be in those babies' lives, though, right? I mean, it won't be easy now that they're moving in together, but I bet you and Hanna have worked something out."

My stomach clenches, and surprise must show on my

face because she smiles—slow and wide. It reminds me of the hyenas in the Disney movie Collin loves to watch. She finally hit her mark.

"Who are you?" I ask.

"I'm a friend who wants to see everyone get what they deserve. Nothing less. Nothing more."

MAX

Hanna's mother beams as she opens the door for me. "So glad you could make it for brunch."

"Thanks for inviting me, Gretchen."

"We missed you at church." She turns to the living room. "Hanna, Max is here."

Hanna pushes off the couch to greet me with a kiss on my cheek.

"Hi," she says. "How was your morning? Post-crazy-baby-mama drama?"

"Good." I spent it in my office at the club, trying to work magic with numbers and not succeeding. "How was church?"

She shrugs. "Mom is worried for the souls of her sinner daughters. We like to throw her a bone once in a while."

"Food is ready!" her mom calls. "Everyone in the dining room, please!"

We file into the dining room behind Gretchen—Granny, Liz, Abby, Hanna, Maggie, Asher, me, and a couple of Gretchen's friends—and line up at the buffet to fill our plates.

Gretchen takes Hanna's plate from her before she can fill it. "I want you to try this new recipe."

Liz and Hanna gape as their mother heaps hash brown casserole onto Hanna's plate. The potatoes are bubbling with cheese and butter.

"The baby needs the calcium," Gretchen says.

"I think hell just froze over," Liz mumbles, and her mom shoots her a stern glare.

When our plates are full, we find our seats around the table.

"Liz," Gretchen says, "I thought you might bring that nice gentleman you danced with at Will and Cally's wedding. That friend of yours... Max, what's his name? Sam something or other."

"You don't want me bringing Sam Bradshaw to a family brunch," Liz says next to me, scowling at her food.

"Why not?" her mother objects.

Hanna bites back a smile.

"He really likes you, Liz," I tell her, not for the first time.

"You're blushing!" their little sister Abby says. "You never blush!"

"It's hot in here," Liz grumbles.

Across from me, Maggie moans softly. "These potatoes. Oh my God! Mom, I had no idea you had it in you."

"She let me cook today," Granny says. "That's how food is supposed to taste."

My phone vibrates in my pocket and I pull it out to see a message from Meredith. *Can you come get Claire? A client has an emergency.*

"A haircut emergency?" Liz says, shamelessly reading from my phone. "Whatever."

Who knows if it's true or if Meredith just knows that this is my time with Hanna's family.

"My apologies, Gretchen." I stand and slide my phone back into my pocket. "I need to get my daughter. Her mother has to work."

Hanna stands. "I'll give you a call later."

I'll give you a call. Not, *I'll see you.*

She kisses me on the cheek, and I stop her before she can pull away. I press my mouth to hers. It's not a long kiss or a passionate one—her family is right here—but it's firm and sure and right. It's everything my love for her is.

SIX

NATE

I scratch out the last four lines on the page, pushing the pen so deep it cuts through the paper. I'm working on this collaboration with Asher and I'm stuck on the ballad.

All week, all I've been able to think about is Hanna moving in with Max, Hanna waking up next to Max, Hanna raising my babies *with Max*.

It's a good thing Collin is here. Otherwise, I probably would have already left Asher's in favor of getting trashed in a hotel room somewhere.

I stare at the marked-out lyrics and then throw the notebook across the room.

"What did that notebook ever do to you?"

I'm probably scowling when I look up at Maggie, but scowling is pretty tame considering how I'm feeling right now. How I've felt all week.

"She's having my babies and she's marrying him." I can tell by her face that this isn't news to her. Fuck. Of course not. "What am I supposed to do with that?"

She plops into a chair across from me and folds her legs under herself. "Asher told me that he warned you to stay away from her."

"I don't need a lecture tonight, Maggie."

"Asher also told me that ignoring a friend's wishes for a girl wasn't like you. But something about Hanna made you do it anyway."

I lean my head back and look at the ceiling, remembering that night, remembering her body moving against mine as we danced, the pitch in her voice when she asked me to kiss her. "She's my kryptonite."

"You're such a dork."

"Are they really moving in together?"

Maggie frowns. "Isn't that what people do when they get married?"

But Hanna said she wasn't moving forward until after the babies were born, and I hoped that meant... "Does she really love him?"

She picks at the seam of her jeans, and just when I think she's going to avoid answering the question altogether, she says, "I don't know Hanna as well as Liz does, so maybe I'm not the one to ask, but she's going through a really hard time right now. She spent her whole life believing she was undesirable because no one noticed her, and no one noticed her because she hid in the shadows, and she hid in the shadows because she didn't think anyone would want her." She lifts her eyes to mine. She's trying to read me. To decide if I'm worth her interpretation of the truth. To decide if I'm worthy of Hanna.

"What does all of that have to do with Max? With me?"

Maggie shakes her head and gives a sardonic smile. "Men," she mutters. "Of course you don't get it."

"Enlighten me."

"She doesn't even know who she is anymore. Her whole perception of herself has been blown to pieces because now two great guys want her. And to answer your question? Yes. She loves him."

I tear my eyes away from her and grab my guitar because I need something to do with my hands.

"She loves you too. You know that. You can't tell me you

can spend two seconds around her without feeling it."

"But?"

Maggie shrugs. "The choice isn't mine."

I strum a chord on the guitar—the opening chord to the song with the elusive lyrics. In my mind, it's always been "Hanna's song," but I never called it that. The first chord, then the second.

"I never believed she'd choose him," I say softly. "Maybe I didn't realize it at the time, but in retrospect, I know I thought I was the easy choice."

"Why?"

"Because she fits me. Because life was this crazy, chaotic disappointment and then Hanna came along and everything got quiet. Everything slowed down. It's like I spent my whole life only half filling my lungs because I was too busy running to the next thing. She makes me take a deep breath. She silences the bullshit and washes away my ambivalence." I drag a hand through my hair. "And I assumed that I did all of that for her too."

Maggie studies me for a quiet minute. "You're not so bad, Nate Crane."

"I'm a fuck-up," I mutter. "A fuck-up who can't keep his promise."

"What promise is that?"

"I promised that, if she chose him, I'd let her go. I promised that I wouldn't make her second-guess her decision."

"You think you broke that promise?"

I shake my head, grinning now. "No. But I plan to."

HANNA

"Somebody had a late night," I call when Liz pushes into the bakery.

She looks like hell warmed over this morning. Her blond curls are pulled back in a ponytail and her eyes are barely open.

And thank God she's here. Mom showed up twenty minutes ago and has been quizzing me about my plans for the twins. It's not even seven a.m. and my brain is spinning with information on breastfeeding and the dangers of co-sleeping as well as her opinions about the attachment parenting movement.

"It's not the late night that's the problem," Liz mutters. "It's the early morning."

Mom frowns at her and clears her throat. "Claudia Bauer saw you leaving Sam Bradshaw's apartment the other day. Sam's a nice boy, but if you give him what he wants now, he's never going to marry you."

Liz narrows her puffy eyes at Mom. "I don't want to marry Sam," she growls, heading for the coffee. "I just want to fuck him."

Mom gasps, and I have to bite my lip to keep from laughing. Seriously, the woman should know better than to pick a fight with Liz this early in the morning. Liz and mornings are mortal enemies, and she takes her loathing out on everyone stupid enough to get too close.

Mom huffs. "I'll say an extra prayer for you at church, Elizabeth. Your sister Maggie went through this phase too. And now Hanna's having babies out of wedlock. Heaven help me, you'd think I didn't bring my girls up in the Church."

Liz mutters something unintelligible under her breath. Probably for the best that Mom couldn't hear.

I pack up an assortment of pastries and see Mom to the door. "Take these for your Bible study group," I say. When she's gone, I turn to Liz. "I cannot believe you just told our mother you were using Sam Bradshaw for sex."

She chugs half her cup of creamer-and-sugar-filled coffee before replying. "I didn't say I was using him for sex. I said I don't want to marry him. I want to fuck him. And the look on her face was totally worth it."

"You're going to burn in hell." I giggle.

"Well, I'll have the best company." She laughs, but then her face goes serious again. "I have to tell you something."

"I don't know if I like the sound of that."

Sighing, she avoids my gaze. "You know how much I appreciate my job, don't you? I mean, you took me in and gave me work when you were pissed at me for the whole Max thing. Even though I totally wish you would have *told* me that's why you were pissed, I still think it's pretty awesome that you did that for me."

"Are you quitting?"

"Yeah," she says. "Kind of. Do you hate me?"

"Of course not! Did you get a new job? That's great!" I hug her, and when I draw back, she's grinning.

"I'm so excited. One of the girls who graduated from the El Ed program with me is starting a preschool, and she wants me to be her partner. Isn't that awesome?"

"Oh, Liz! That's great! I'm so happy for you!"

She frowns. "But you already work too much, and now that you're pregnant, I really hate leaving."

"Don't worry about it," I insist. "I never intended to have you here forever. You were helping me with my dream, and now it's time for you to go after yours."

"Best. Sister. Ever," she whispers.

"Just tell me what I can do to help."

"How about you start by planning to enroll those babies of yours in my preschool when the time comes. I'll hold their spot."

I feel the blood drain from my face. "I never realized how many decisions and plans are required when you're a new mother. It's just overwhelming. I know I won't be doing it alone, and I know Max would help me with anything I wanted, but I feel guilty because it's all I ever talk about and they're not even his babies." I take a breath and then another. Then I go to the kitchen to get a cold washcloth for my face because that's the best thing I've found for these nausea spells.

Liz follows me and beats me to the sink, wetting a towel and handing it to me.

The bell in the front rings, letting us know someone just arrived.

"I'll get it," she says.

"Thanks." I drape the washcloth across my forehead and close my eyes, listening to Liz talk to the customer.

"Oh," she says. "Hmm. Um. How are you?"

"Where's Hanna?" I know the voice, and an unwelcome thrill dances up my spine as Nate pushes into my kitchen and stalks toward me.

"Customers aren't allowed back here," Liz says behind him.

"Don't do it," he says, and those dark, broody eyes are all over me like he's trying to take me in, memorize me.

I take a deep breath and look to my sister. "You should probably go." Then I turn to Nate. "Don't do what?"

"Um..." Liz looks Nate up and down. "Are you sure? Because I can stay to protect you. Or...try." God bless her, she's standing behind Nate with her hands on her hips, ready to swing on my behalf.

"Why don't you give us a minute?"

She narrows her eyes at Nate. "Hurt her and I'll cut off your balls in your sleep." Then she pushes out of the kitchen, the door swinging wildly behind her.

"Don't move in with him," Nate says.

"What are you talking about?" I ask.

"I thought you said you weren't moving forward with Max until after the babies were born. Don't you think moving in is moving forward?"

"I don't know where you get your information, but I'm not moving in with him."

"You're not?"

I shake my head. "He asked me to, and I said no."

He must have been expecting a fight, because his shoulders relax and he drags a hand through his hair. "Thank you."

I toss my washcloth into the sink. "Is that all?"

"No." He lifts his eyes to mine. "I need to apologize."

"For what?"

"For this."

In two long strides, he closes the space between us and presses his mouth to mine. His lips are hot and hungry as his tongue sweeps inside—coaxing and demanding all at once.

And it's so good. So sweet and easy and safe that, for a breath, I forget how wrong it is. I'm back in the hotel in St. Louis, finding myself in the fire between us. For a breath, I forget that I'm wearing Max's ring.

I shove at his shoulder and push him away. "Don't do that again." My stomach squeezes, and my heart is so battered and beaten that it's unrecognizable.

NATE

Her eyes flash with anger, disappointment, and heat. "Do you think you can win me with a kiss? Did you think I'm so fickle that your mouth on mine is enough to convince me to break Max's heart?"

I step forward, blocking her between me and the counter as I lower my mouth to her ear. "I thought maybe you needed a reminder."

"What do you want from me? You want me to admit that I want you? You know I do. You want me to tell you I'm still in love with you? It's true."

My heart swells and hammers at her words. I don't know if I'll ever feel worthy of Hanna's love, but that doesn't change that I want it, *need* it like I need air.

"Isn't that enough? Is it like this with him? When he's whispering in your ear, does your body hum with need? We both know I could kiss you again and make you forget him. I could kiss you until you wanted me so badly you climbed onto that counter and let me touch you everywhere, let me do anything I wanted with your body."

"You won't," she says, her voice shaking slightly.

"Are you so sure?"

"You won't," she repeats, "because I'm asking you not to. You won't because you're too good not to respect that."

"I don't want to be *good*," I growl. I step back so I can see her face—her parted lips, her smoky eyes. "I want *you*."

"I'm taken."

"What happened?" I ask, scanning her face, trying to read her shielding expression. "Between when I left LA and when I came back to New Hope, what happened to make you take him back?"

She's silent for a minute, and I wonder if she's going to tell me the truth. "I found out he bought me the bakery—that all my worries and insecurities about our relationship were totally unfounded."

"I'll buy you a hundred bakeries."

"But I don't want a hundred bakeries. I only want this one."

Here. In New Hope. I close my eyes because I can't deny that geography still stands between us.

"Please don't kiss me again."

"What if you ask me to?"

She swallows. "I won't ask."

SEVEN

HANNA

The wind is cool as it rolls off the river and through the changing leaves. Autumn in New Hope has to be one of the most beautiful things I've ever seen. The leaves turn orange, red, brown, even purple, fall from the trees, and float by on the river. I'll always associate the sound of leaves crunching underfoot with my childhood, with home.

But today, it doesn't bring me the comfort I need. My conversation with Nate demands too much of my attention for anything to comfort me.

"Between when I left LA and when I came back to New Hope, what happened to make you take him back?"

You died. They were the words I didn't say, but they've been there, in my mind and on my tongue, since he asked the question. Are they true? Did I only go back to Max because I thought Nate was dead?

"How are you holding up?"

I look up to see Maggie pulling a chair up to the patio set behind William's art gallery. She asked me to meet her here, and something about my carefree sister scheduling a conversation has left butterflies in my stomach.

"I'm okay," I answer. "Emotional, but I blame the hormones."

"Yeah," she says, "not the fact that you're in love with two men, wearing one's ring, and carrying the other's babies?"

"Well, that sums it up rather nicely." I've been trying to convince myself that nothing between Max and me has changed, but I don't invite him to stay over anymore, and every time he kisses me, I feel ashamed and confused.

"Sorry." She shrugs. "I know something about loving two men at once. Listen," she says after studying me for a minute. "Before you dig your heels in about staying with Max, I want you to think about it."

I stiffen. I know Maggie loves me and has my best interests at heart, but after today, when I can still feel Nate's lips press against mine, when his scent lingers on my skin, this is the last thing I need.

"I have thought about it, and I made my decision—weeks ago, before the accident. I put on his ring."

"I'm saying don't blindly trust a decision you can't remember making. Ask yourself if you would choose Max again today—at this very moment—if you had to make your decision again."

"I don't know." If I'd known that my night with Nate left me pregnant, who knows what my choice would have been? "No matter what I do, someone gets hurt."

"Stop trying to figure out why you made the choice then and start trying to figure out what choice is right for you now. You're trying to protect Max, and as much as he wants to marry you, I don't think that's where he would want your decision to come from."

"I don't want to hurt him," I whisper. "He's too good. He doesn't deserve to be hurt."

"I know, sweetie."

I watch a young couple jog by along the river. "How did you know? When you decided to be with Asher, to move in with him, how did you know it was the right decision?"

"Hanna." She waits until I look at her. "I knew because I

didn't have to ask myself if I was making the right decision. When I was engaged to Will, I kept asking myself over and over again if I was doing the right thing. I would mentally tally all the reasons I should marry him and feel guilty for questioning it, and then the next day, the next hour, sometimes even the next minute, I'd do it all over again. But that should have been my first hint." She smiles then takes my hands in hers. "I know you're a grown woman and you have your head on your shoulders better than I probably ever will, so it seems ridiculous for me to give you advice, but I'm going to anyway. Give Max his ring back."

"Maggie—"

"Hear me out. Please?"

"Okay." But my stomach twists into a painful knot because I'm scared that I won't want to hear what she has to say.

"Maybe you're meant to be with Max. Maybe you two will work this out and you'll have these babies and find that all you want is to spend your life with Max at your side. Maybe there will come a day that he'll tell you all he needs is you and you'll be as sure as I am with Asher." She cocks her head and gives me a sad smile. "But, sweetie, it's all over your face that you're not there now. I'm not saying this because I'm Nate's friend and trying to give him a foot-up. I'm saying this because you're my sister and I love you, and I refuse to see you make the mistake that Krystal and I almost made. You owe it to yourself and to Max to give back that ring until you know for sure what you want."

A tear splashes onto the glass tabletop, and I stand up and walk down the stairs to the lawn. Maggie's not telling me anything I don't already know. But I've been putting off the inevitable.

Maggie wraps an arm around me. I lean my head against her shoulder as she smooths my hair and we watch the wind play in the leaves and the blue evening sky turn to the pink and orange of the setting sun.

It's been ten hours since the kiss, but when I open the door to meet Max at his new rental house, I can still feel the pressure of Nate's lips against mine. I can still smell his clean scent as if it's been branded to my clothing.

The house is nice. Nothing fancy, but it's clean and functional. The table is set, the candles are lit, and the wine is chilling in a bucket of ice on the island.

Max is at the stove, cooking dinner, with Claire strapped to his chest in a baby carrier. He's humming softly as he stirs chicken and vegetables in a sauté pan, and Claire's eyes open and float closed again and again.

I'm slammed with a vision of our future together, raising Claire and the twins side by side. Max is the kind of guy who would treat them all as his own, and he'll be the kind of husband who cooks dinner when I have to work late or just because. I'll have my bakery and he'll have his health club. Once we're married, I'll have access to my trust fund, so money won't be so tight, and even if it were, we'd make it work. He'd hold my hand when I worried about something, kiss my forehead and reassure me. He'll be an amazing husband and father. Everything I could have ever wanted or dreamed.

But he'll never be Nate Crane, and every day we're together, I will hate myself for being so completely and painfully aware of that.

Max shouldn't have to be Nate. Because he's an amazing and wonderful guy just as he is.

I press my hand to my lips and stumble back a few steps because things could have been different. If I'd figured out how to accept myself, my body, before he asked me out, they *would* have been different. I'd be looking at a future with an amazing man holding my hand rather than bracing myself for one where I raise my children alone.

Max wouldn't want me to marry him if he knew the decision was motivated by my desire to protect him.

He takes the pan off the stove and turns to pour its contents into a bowl on the island. When he spots me, his face lights up, and that makes me feel even worse.

Maggie's right. Whatever I decided before the accident and why I made that decision is irrelevant.

MAX

"Let me put her down." Hanna reaches her arms out for Claire, and I gently remove her from the carrier.

She is going to make an amazing mother. She snuggles Claire against her chest and hums softly as she paces around the living room. The two people in this world I would do anything for. My woman. Holding my daughter.

"Goodnight, Claire," she whispers, carefully lowering her into the crib in the corner. "You sleep well knowing you have the best daddy ever."

"Come over here," I murmur.

She's in a red, strapless sundress tonight, and the sight of her legs and the bare, soft skin of her shoulders is slowly making me lose my mind.

She scans the table and then meets my eyes as the music kicks on. "Max…"

"I wanted to do something nice for you." I take her hands and squeeze her fingers. "Someday, I'll be able to take you to fancy restaurants in Indianapolis and Chicago instead of cooking for you. Someday, I'll be able to buy you the kind of gifts you deserve and surprise you with weekends away at luxurious spas. You deserve it, and I'll make it happen."

She closes her eyes, and I count the beats of my anxious heart as I wait. "I don't care about all that."

"I love you, Hanna. I just want you to wake up every day and know—without a doubt in your mind—that you're engaged to a man who loves you and wants to make up for being blind for so many years."

"I've loved you since I was thirteen." She removes her hands from mine, and the first prickling of dread starts its ominous crawl toward my heart. "And I still think you're one of the best men I have ever met."

"Hanna." We both know where this is going. "What happened?"

Her eyes fill with new tears, and I see what's coming all over her face. I've seen it coming all week.

"Don't do this."

"I have to." She puts her hand to the side of my face then drops it quickly, as if touching me costs her. "You loved me and sacrificed for me—you knew the bakery was my dream and you went to extraordinary measures to make sure I got it. I'll pay you back and I'll never forget."

My lungs are tight and I can't make them take air. "You changed the way I see the world. You made me see what love could be. The bakery is nothing compared to that. I would do anything for you."

"I know," she says, and fat tears roll down her cheeks. "And don't you think it's time that goes both ways?"

"Don't."

"You deserve better than me."

I want to object. To tell her she's so wrong—that a future with her in any form is better than I deserve—but my throat is thick with emotion and there's no room for words.

She tilts her head to the side, and more tears stream from her eyes as she pulls my grandmother's ring from her finger. She may as well be ripping out my heart.

She takes my hand and presses the ring into my palm. "I can't be with you when my heart's not mine to give, and I won't ask you to wait for me anymore."

"Are you leaving me for him? Is he going to give you a future? Commitment? Raise the babies by your side?"

She shakes her head. "This isn't about him. New Hope is my home, and LA is his. I'm not going anywhere."

I can't help myself anymore, and I gather her into my

arms, pulling her against my chest. "Don't do this. I know you don't remember, but you chose me. There was a reason you chose me."

She lets me hold her for a few breaths, and I can feel her tears soaking through the cotton of my shirt. I breathe in her scent, and when I pull away, regret is all over her face.

"I never wanted to hurt you," she says, her eyes moist.

I want to kiss her. Hold her. Beg her to reconsider.

"I need to leave," she whispers. "I'm so sorry."

My grandmother's ring bites into my palm as I watch her head out the door.

EIGHT

HANNA

Four Days Before Hanna's Accident

When I knock on Max's door, it occurs to me that this is probably a terrible place to do this. I could have waited until tomorrow morning and caught him at the club. I could have called and asked him to meet me at the bakery. Instead, I came to his apartment.

The last time I was here, I took off my clothes and begged him to have sex with me. The last time I was here, he turned me down.

"Try me. Come back here sober and test me, Hanna."

Ever since I got back from LA, I've been thinking about that night at Max's house. Did I really want him to make love to me, or did I only say that because I knew he wouldn't do it when I'd been drinking? I think part of me meant it at the time. I love Max, and if Meredith hadn't screwed everything up, we'd be on our way to a wedding by now.

And now I'm here to give him back his ring.

When Max pulls the door open, he looks exhausted, but he grins as soon as he sees me. "Hey," he says softly.

"Hey."

He pulls the door wider, his gaze skimming over me. I'm in a jean skirt and red wrap shirt, nothing special, but his eyes on me make me feel beautiful. Sexy. Wanted.

"I don't suppose you're here for the same reason you were last time?"

My heart thuds, stumbles, and trips in my chest, and I can feel my cheeks burn. "I'm afraid not."

He makes some sort of unintelligible sound at the back of his throat then says, "You want to come in?"

"Yeah. I mean, assuming Meredith's not hiding in there somewhere." I regret my joke when his face falls.

"There's nothing between us but Claire."

I follow him into the apartment and notice he has a Pack 'N Play set up in the corner and a diaper bag on the counter. Was all of that there when I was here last week and I was just too drunk to notice?

"I'm pretty sure Meredith wants me to think there's more," I say.

"What did she say to you?"

"She likes to send me texts when she's over here. Implying… things."

Max's fingers are on my chin, tilting my face up until my eyes meet his. "I haven't touched her since before I kissed you for the first time in November."

My gut twists with guilt. Because maybe he hasn't touched anyone else, but I can't say the same. How would he feel if he knew I gave my virginity to another man? That I've been dating someone else all summer?

I shrug and drop my eyes to the ground. It's not that I can't face him. But there's such a fierce intensity in his blue eyes I'm afraid I'll kiss him if I don't look away. I want to remember what his lips feel like on mine before I say goodbye. I want to have his arms curl around me and hold me tight so I can remember all the good days and stamp them into a safe place in my memory.

"I haven't touched any woman but you, and that will remain true as long as my ring waits in your jewelry box."

I press my palm against my thigh and finger the ring in the pocket of my jeans. I'm not here because I'm choosing Nate. After yesterday, I know Nate and I can't be together. He says he loves me, but he's not willing to sacrifice anything to be with me.

I'm here because I can't choose either one of them, and I need to break it off with both.

Max's gaze drops to my mouth and his eyes turn from warm and tender to hot and hungry. "I miss you, Hanna."

"I miss you too."

He traces my bottom lip with his thumb. My eyes float closed and my muscles soften even as my conscience bristles. I can't keep this up much longer.

"I wanted to talk to you about Abby," I say, and my conscience sings, *Coward!*

"Is she okay?"

"Yeah, but she's taken some pretty radical measures trying to stay thin, and I'm worried about her."

He raises a brow. "I know how you feel."

I frown. "You knew about Abby?"

"I'm talking about being worried about you."

"Oh. No, don't worry about me. I'm fine." Or I will be. Catching Abby with those diet pills was a wakeup call for me, and I made an appointment with a psychiatrist in Indianapolis. "I was hoping you'd talk to her. Maybe go through a healthy, balanced diet and exercise plan. That kind of thing?"

"And would you be there to hear my lecture?"

I draw in a shaky breath. "Sure." Our eyes lock for a minute before I say, "I am working on it. I know I haven't been the healthiest role model for her."

A phone starts ringing in the bedroom and Max sighs. "I need to grab that. Don't go anywhere, okay?"

I nod, and he heads to the bedroom to take the call.

His shoulders are so broad, so strong. I know Max would give me everything Nate wouldn't, and it's so tempting to take what he's offering me.

I wander over to his kitchen table and my gaze catches

on a piece of mail at the top of the stack. *Smith, Peterson, and Frank Law Offices of Indianapolis.*

I know that law firm. That's the place that's managing the arrangement with my anonymous investor for the bakery.

What business could Max have with them?

I can hear Max's low murmurs coming from the bedroom. When I slip the papers from the envelope, I don't even feel guilty for snooping—not much, at least—because I already know what I'm going to see. Max's name and the name of my bakery all on the same letter with the lawyer's letterhead.

I don't get to do more than skim the letter before I hear him end the call. I have to shove the papers back into the envelope and drop them to the table.

"Sorry," he says as he emerges from the bedroom. "That was my mom. Her air conditioner is on the fritz again, and I was troubleshooting with her."

"No, not at all. It's fine. No problem. I hope you can fix it." I'm rambling.

He cocks his head to the side. "Are you okay? You look like you've seen a ghost."

"I'm fine." I nod once, twice…six times like I'm a freaking bobblehead. I was so wrong about Max, and everywhere this summer took me, every decision I made, branched from my disbelief that he ever wanted me for anything more than my money.

But there it is, right on his kitchen table: evidence that he wasn't ever after my money. He was sacrificing his own to make my dreams come true. Evidence that I let my insecurities ruin my future with an amazing man.

"Hanna?"

My eyes fill, and I step forward, wrap my arms around his neck, and hug him as I'd hug any friend who I learned had given me such an amazing gift.

Max wraps his arms around me and presses a kiss to my hair. "What's this for?"

"I'm sorry I took you for granted."

He slides his hand along my jaw and tilts my face up to his.

"Ditto," he whispers.

Then he skims his lips over mine in a movement that's so gentle and so tender I nearly disintegrate under it. I kiss him back, unsure whether I'm saying goodbye or welcoming something new into my life.

When he pulls back, his eyes are full of questions, but he only asks one. "Stay with me tonight? We don't have to do anything. I just need you in my arms again."

I don't know what I want, but he takes my silence as my answer and his expression changes and becomes guarded. "I'm sorry," I say, and turn to leave.

"I love you," he calls to my back, and I can only nod. I walk out the door, his grandmother's ring still in my pocket.

HANNA

Present Day

"So freaking *good*," I moan. I let the pure, unadulterated pleasure of fine chocolate ripple through my body.

After I left Max's house, I called Liz, who promised she was on her way, but she brought the whole crew, and now Liz, Maggie, Cally, and Nix are all gathered around my kitchen island with drinks—martinis for the three who aren't knocked up and herbal tea for the rest of us—and pounds of those gourmet chocolates Asher buys Maggie when he's in New York.

Liz raided the bakery and brought up an assortment of cookies and pastries, and Nix brought a silly card game that we haven't bothered playing.

Without my having to explain, they all understand how hard it was for me to give Max his ring back.

"So what happens between you and Nate now?" Nix asks.

Liz is shaking up a new batch of chocolate martinis, and Nix raises her glass to signal she wants another.

"Nothing," I say. I cut a piece of the cheese Danish and hand it to Nix. "This is my new recipe. Tell me if it's too sweet."

"What do you mean, *nothing*?" Nix asks before taking a bite. Then, with her mouth half full, she says, "Oh my God. This isn't food. It's an orgasm in your mouth."

When Liz reaches for the rest of the Danish, Cally smacks her hand away and takes it from the plate. "Pregnant ladies get first dibs."

"Nothing?" Maggie asks. "Are you sure?"

"I didn't break it off with Max so I could be with Nate." Though I'm sure Max believes I did. I'm sure everyone in town will think I did, once word gets out.

"What did he say when you told him you were pregnant?" Nix asks.

"He wants me to move to LA."

"What?" Liz squeaks. "Like you're going to totally throw away your business—your *life*—for him?"

"You can't blame him for trying," Maggie says.

"He's only interested because of the babies. When I went to LA and told him I wasn't going to marry Max, Nate still said goodbye. He doesn't want to be with me—not enough to fight for me when it counts." And not enough to figure out a way to make it work that doesn't involve my moving across the country.

"I'm not sure you're being fair, Hanna," Nix says. "When you went to LA, he thought you'd chosen Max before the accident."

Maggie nods. "I think he was trying to let you go since you wanted to be with Max."

"I didn't walk away. I let you go."

Is that what Nate meant? He let me go so I could be with Max?

"I still don't understand why I chose Max," I say quietly, and the admission fills me with guilt. "Don't get me wrong. I don't know how I could have chosen Nate either. It's an impossible choice. My missing memories are leaving me with a lot of unanswered questions. I still have four days of my life that are missing. I wish I knew what happened in those days."

"Have you thought any more about how the accident may have happened?" Nix asks.

Liz tenses. "What do you mean by that?"

Nix just studies me, so finally I say, "Nix thinks my injuries were too severe to be from just a fall. She suspects that some of them were…inflicted intentionally."

"What? By whom?" Liz asks. "How?"

I nod at Nix, silently giving her permission to talk about it, and she takes a breath. "I think maybe there was foul play—a fight with punches thrown, that kind of thing. I'm not excluding the possibility that Hanna took an accidental fall down the stairs, but given the state of her injuries, I suspected there might be more to it than that. Not knowing Max very well, I immediately asked about him."

"We can rule out that possibility," I say softly. "Max would lay down his life for me."

"What about Meredith?" Maggie says. "You were stealing her man."

Cally snorts. "I'm no defender of Meredith, but a fistfight? That doesn't seem her style."

"True," Liz says. "She might break a nail."

"I'm not convinced there was anything more than a fall," I say. "I wasn't eating and I could have passed out and fallen."

"Even if that's true, that doesn't answer the question about how you came to choose Max," Liz says. "I think it's reasonable to want to know, even if you aren't marrying him."

Maggie's frowning into her wine. "Am I the only one who thinks it seems unlikely that Hanna would give her virginity to Nate and, less than a week later, decide to marry someone else?"

"Maybe," I say softly. Nix, who was about to chime in, shuts her mouth. "Maybe I wanted to make love to Nate for the same reasons any woman wants to have sex with a man she loves. I know that might be hard to understand, but I do love them both." I look at my friends' and sisters' faces. "Letting go of either one of them seemed impossible the day Nate told me

I needed to make a choice." *It still seems impossible*, but I don't say that aloud.

Liz refills her wine. "Maybe it came down to which guy could give you the future that you want."

"Probably." I thought of that too.

I don't want to leave New Hope for LA or anywhere. How would a real relationship with Nate even work? Would he want me to move to LA or would our life be a series of two- or three-day visits here and there? Him coming to New Hope when he didn't have performances or need to put time in at the studio, me flying out to see him perform when I could get away from the bakery?

"Max looks better on paper," Cally says. "Except for Meredith, of course."

"Maybe Hanna found out about the bakery," Liz suggests. "I mean, the guy sacrificed his house just so she could have her dream."

"I did," I admit, thinking of my most recent memory. "I was at Max's apartment and I saw a letter from the law firm that handles the arrangement with the bakery. But would that be enough to make me choose to marry him?"

Maggie cocks her head. "So you believe you chose Max over Nate before the accident, and you want to know what finally brought you to your final decision."

I nod. "Wouldn't you?"

Liz opens a drawer and removes a pad of paper and a pen. "Okay, let's figure out what we do know." She writes *HANNA'S MISSING DAYS* at the top and draws a line under it. Down the side, she writes the days of the week through Thursday, and next to Thursday, she writes *Accident on stairs*.

"Can we assume that's when I put on the ring too?" I ask. "Did anyone see it on me before that?"

Liz shakes her head. "That was the day. I would have noticed if you'd had it on sooner." She adds *Puts on ring* to Thursday.

"When did you sleep with Nate?" Maggie asks.

"Saturday," I say, pointing. "And that's when he told me I

had to make a choice. Then, later, we…" I swallow. "We got caught up in the moment and had unprotected sex in the shower."

"And hello, twins," Nix says.

"Hello, horribly timed baby conversation," I reply. The girls all stare at me expectantly, so I explain, "It's a new memory. And not a good one."

"How can shower sex with Nate Crane be a *bad* memory?" Nix asks.

My cheeks burn. "Well, *that* part isn't bad."

"I hate you a little right now," Nix says.

"It was the after," I say, "when we realized what we'd done and I…" I swallow hard. "I pushed him about what would happen if I got pregnant, and we had this terrible fight because he didn't want to talk about it and I insisted. I needed to know."

"Of course you did," Liz says. "And you were right to ask."

"I guess," I say. "But think about it from Nate's point of view. He's been commitment-averse since his son was born. He didn't want a long-term relationship, marriage, kids, none of that. Collin comes first. Then, just hours after he said that he'd change his rules *for me*, that he'd find a way to make it work for me, there I am, talking about babies and the future."

"Not for nothing," Maggie says, eyes dropping meaningfully to my stomach. "Turns out it was a conversation you needed to have."

Liz writes *Baby fight* on the chart. "What else?"

I shrug. "I remember going to Max's and finding out about the bakery and then waking up in the hospital."

Cally leans forward. "What if we could help? I mean, we all see you almost every day, right? What do *we* remember about those days before the accident?"

Liz huffs. "She was hardly talking to me. I'm sure I don't know anything of any use."

Maggie chews on her bottom lip, thoughtful. "What was going on that week? I need a frame of reference for my memory."

Cally taps on her phone and studies the screen.

Liz looks over her shoulder. "That would have been the week of Abby's birthday," she says, referring to our youngest sister. She straightens a little. "We had a party at Mom's."

Maggie nods and her face brightens. "You were there, Hanna. And something happened, because you were upset."

"I remember that," Liz says. "She took Abby aside after we sang 'Happy Birthday,' and when you two returned to the party, you both looked happier. Like you'd settled something."

Next to Monday, Liz writes *Abby's party*.

"What else do we remember?" Maggie says.

The girls look to each other, and after several beats of silence, I sigh. "It's okay. I'll figure it out."

Cally yawns. "I'm so flipping tired. You guys mind if we call it a night?"

Liz raises a brow. "It's seven thirty."

Cally shrugs. "I'm pregnant."

"So," Maggie says, crossing her arms, "am I the only one who wants to know how *that* happened?"

"Yeah," Liz says. "I thought Will couldn't have kids. Weren't you guys looking into adopting?"

Nix frowns. "Does someone want to fill me in?"

Cally's cheeks turn pink. "William had a football injury in high school that made it highly unlikely he'd ever be able to father children."

Nix inclines her chin. "Yes, but medically speaking, *highly unlikely* is not the same as *impossible*."

Liz smirks. "Especially if you're fucking like monkeys."

Cally puts her hand on her stomach and smiles. "As it turns out."

When the girls leave, I stare at the notes Liz left behind. My eyes skim over *Abby's party* and land on all the blank spots. Something filled my time and my head during those days, and something led me to put on Max's ring when I knew that would mean saying goodbye to Nate. *Something*. But what?

I'm climbing into bed when my phone vibrates on my bedside table.

Nate: *Meet me at the park for lunch tomorrow.
I promise I won't kiss you unless you ask me to.*

NINE

NATE

The leaves crunch under my feet as I pace in front of the swings, waiting for Hanna to meet me.

I texted her the invitation last night, but she didn't reply until this morning, and when she did, all it said was *1:30.*

My watch says it's twenty-five after, and my empty stomach is yelling at me about the breakfast I was too nervous to eat. Whether Hanna can understand it or not, today is a big day for me.

"Beautiful day, isn't it?"

I spin around at the sound of her voice, and for a moment, I can only stare at her. She's in jeans and a pink T-shirt that says *Coffee, Cakes, & Confections*, and she looks so damn beautiful with the autumn sun shining on her skin that I want to break my second promise this week. I want to kiss her.

My gaze drops to her left hand and her bare ring finger.

"Who told you?" she asks.

"Asher."

He found me out back late last night, after I'd put Collin to bed. He told me that they broke up and warned me to be careful. When I promised I wouldn't hurt her, Asher grunted and said, "Maybe it's not her I'm worried about."

Hanna sighs. "This doesn't change things between us. The babies are my priority right now. I don't need any additional confusion in my life."

And that's pretty much what Maggie told me this morning. I don't know much about fighting for women—it's never been something I've wanted to do. But with Hanna, I know that fighting for her is going to mean equal parts patience and persistence. I'll give her the space she needs.

"I know," I say. "That's not why I asked you here."

"It isn't?"

"Collin," I call to my son. "Come meet my friend."

Collin hops off his swing and runs over to us, his dark mop of hair falling in his face.

"Hi." Hanna looks stunned. "You look so much like your daddy."

"Hi!" Collin replies. "I'm Collin, and you're very pretty."

"I'm Hanna," she says, dropping to her knees. "You're charming like him too."

Collin grins. He loves it when people tell him he's like me in any way, so Hanna's just outdone herself without knowing it.

"When I get big, I'm going to get a Hulk tattoo just like his, but he said I have to wait because it hurts a lot."

Hanna nods. "That's a good plan. Do you like the Hulk like your dad?"

"Of course," he says. "Don't you?"

Hanna smiles and stands. "I guess I don't really know enough about the Hulk to feel one way or another about him."

"We'll teach you." Collin looks up at me. "Won't we, Daddy?"

Swallowing the lump in my throat, I nod. "If she wants us to."

"She wants us to," Collin says. "Don't you?"

"Sure."

"Hanna's the friend I was telling you about, Collin. She's very special to me. Do you know why?"

Collin studies Hanna for a minute then looks up at me. "Because she knows Spider-Man?"

Hanna bites back a grin. "I'm sorry. I don't know Spider-Man or any of the superheroes, actually."

"Hmm," Collin says thoughtfully. "Then it must just be because you're so pretty."

I have to bite back a grin of my own. She's going to think I told him what to say. The truth is, my kid just has really good taste.

"Hanna's pregnant," I finally say. This is going to affect Collin's life, and I have no intention of keeping it from him. "She and Daddy made babies, and those babies will be your little siblings."

"Really?" Collin asks, staring at Hanna's belly.

Hanna looks up at me, caution all over her face. "It's true. They'll be twins, like your dad and your aunt Janelle."

Collin's eyes go big. "I'll have a brother and a sister?"

"I don't know," she says. "Maybe. Or maybe two brothers or two sisters."

"Will you live with us in our house?" Collin asks.

Another look from Hanna, this one less cautious and more apprehensive.

I jump in. "No, buddy. Hanna lives here in New Hope, and we live in Los Angeles."

"Then we'll have to visit a *lot*!" Collin looks at me. "Can I go play some more?"

"Sure," I reply. "Just stay where you can see me."

Collin loves New Hope. He's spent more than his share in the concrete jungle of cities, and he loves walking down to the river or even just going to the park, where the playground is surrounded by trees and filled with kids whose parents have never hired a nanny in their lives.

When he's across the playground, Hanna expels a long breath. "He's precious."

"He's my world." I need her to understand. "Or he has been until now."

She studies me for a minute. "You didn't have to do that."

"Do what?"

"Introduce me to your son. Tell him about my pregnancy."

"He was my everything, Hanna. But the day I met you, my world expanded."

"Nate—"

"Whether you're going to be with me or not, you're going to be part of my life." I close the space between us and press my hand to her stomach. "*They* will be part of my life."

"At least they'll have a big brother who loves them."

I swallow.

"Having three children in two different parts of the country is going to be a lot more complicated than what you're used to."

"My invitation stands. I would love to have you live with us in LA. I would give you anything you need, anything you want."

"Except my life in New Hope," she says softly. "You can't give me that in LA."

"Daddy!" Collin calls from the top of a twisty slide. "Look at me!"

I watch Collin slide down. "When is your next doctor's appointment?"

She drops her gaze to her hands. "Three weeks."

"I'll be there." And maybe by then she'll have had enough space and time from her breakup to reconsider my offer. "In the meantime, promise me you'll let me know what you need. Say the word, Hanna."

HANNA

I've always felt a special bond with my youngest sister. She's twelve years younger than I am, so we're not super close the way I am with Liz, but we understand each other in ways our other sisters can't.

Abby is petite, where I've never been, but we've both had

to contend with the efforts of our fat-phobic mother our whole life. In my case, it was because I was actually overweight, but Abby's love of dance gives Mom the excuse to harp about calories. We're both a little screwed up as a result.

I find Abby in the basement doing a Zumba video, which, I must say, is a marked improvement from the running Mom used to make me do. At least Zumba is fun for kids.

"Hi, Hanna!" she says when she sees me. She grabs the remote and clicks off the TV then dries herself off with a towel. "No worries," she says, still out of breath. "That's my only workout for today and I ate breakfast."

"Gotta have fuel," I say softly.

After collapsing onto the couch, she grabs her water bottle from the end table and unscrews the top. "I hope you're here to tell me your *news.*"

Well, I wasn't planning on having this talk today, but I suppose she'll want to hear it from me. "Sounds like you already know."

She rolls her eyes. "I heard Mom crying to Carol about it on the phone. Is it true? Nate Crane is the father of your babies, and that's why you and Max aren't going to get married?"

"Nate Crane is the father," I say carefully.

"How did that happen?"

How do you explain to your eleven-year-old sister that you're a dirty ho-bag who was sleeping with one man while pretending to be with another?

"It's complicated," I answer. "Definitely not the way I intended to start a family."

She sighs dreamily and leans her head into the couch cushions. "As if Max wasn't amazing enough, now you have Nate Crane. I mean, come on! How lucky are you?"

"I don't exactly *have* Nate." Guilt twists my gut, but I smile and say, "But I'm not here to talk to you about that."

"Okay, then what?"

"I'm trying to piece together what happened those last few days before my accident, and I'm wondering if you could help."

She frowns. "How?"

"Your birthday party was that week, right? The girls told me I talked to you alone that day, and it seemed like it might have been something important."

The smile falls off her face and she drops her gaze to study her hands in her lap. "Yeah, I guess so."

"Abby, would you tell me what we talked about?"

She shrugged. "I don't want you getting mad at me again."

My stomach squeezes in dread. "Why was I mad at you?"

"Because I was exercising too much and wasn't eating, and you caught me stealing your diet pills," she says in a rush. "But you don't need to worry anymore. I'm being real healthy."

Oh, God. I pull her into my arms and stroke her hair. "Because you saw me doing all that stuff, right?" I whisper.

She nods against my chest and sniffs before pulling away. "But you said being thin wasn't making you any happier and your habits weren't healthy."

I bite my lip, emotion threatening to spill over. "They weren't. Not at all. But I bet you're the reason I went to the psychiatrist to get some help. I bet you're the reason I decided to be better to myself."

She gives a half-smile. "You promised you would. We both promised." She leans into me, and I wrap my arm around her, hugging her again. I'll have to keep an eye on her now that I know, but I believe what she's telling me.

"It's hard living with Mom, isn't it?" I ask. "She isn't the most reasonable mother around."

Abby snorts. "I caught her researching Paleo diets and children. I know she means well but…"

"Yeah, I know what you mean. When I was a teenager, I wanted to change the spelling of my name to H-A-N-N-A-*H* because the missing last *h* felt like she was trying to make me smaller from the moment I was born. Everyone knows Hannah's a palindrome." I chuckle softly at the memory.

"Why didn't you change it?"

"Because it makes me different." I smile. "And I didn't want to disappoint Mom. I make a lot of decisions because I don't want to disappoint someone. I see you doing that too."

Abby shrugs. "We talked about that already."

"We did?"

She nods. "Yeah, and you promised me you'd always be here for me, whether I disappointed you or not," Abby says. "You said you were going to stop traveling so much."

My breath catches. "I did?"

"Yeah. You said you wanted me to be able to come to you when I was feeling depressed about my weight and stuff. Of course, then you had your accident, and I didn't want to remind you that you were ever mad at me."

"Well, I'm not *mad*," I tell her. "Only concerned because I've been through exactly what you're going through now."

She sighs. "Yeah, and look at you now."

I swallow. "Yeah. Look at me now."

TEN

NATE

"Turn around and close your eyes," Hanna instructs.

I lift a brow. "And miss the show?"

She props her hands on her hips and points to the opposite wall of the doctor's office. "Around."

"Killjoy," I mutter, and to make it clear just how much I resent having to look the other way while she strips, I rake my eyes over her before I turn.

Being in the doctor's office with Hanna is bringing back memories of Vivian's pregnancy. Only everything is different this time. When Vivian found out she was pregnant, we weren't really even dating anymore. I was young and terrified, and I had no idea how much a baby was going to change my life—no idea that a child could change the very construction of my heart.

It's different with Hanna, and not just because I'm experienced. It's different because I'm so painfully in love with her that the idea of her and two of my babies all being in that one body nearly paralyzes me with fear. Keeping my distance these last few weeks was harder than I'd anticipated, but I knew she needed the time.

"Okay," she says, and when I turn back to her, she's sitting on the edge of the exam table, covered by an ugly, white-and-beige-checkered gown. Her cheeks are flushed and she's avoiding my gaze. "Thank you for coming today."

"I wouldn't have missed it." The words surprise me by catching in my throat, and she finally lifts her eyes to mine.

Anything Hanna was about to say is lost when the doctor walks into the room. She does a double take when she sees me. "Oh. Hi. Mr. Crane. Wow. Hanna's told me a lot about you. I'm Dr. Reid, but you can call me Nix. I'm a friend and a fan."

I grin as I take her hand. By her blush, you'd think I was looking up her skirt. "It's always nice to meet a fan."

She chews on her bottom lip for a minute, and when I'm convinced she's completely forgotten the reason we're here, she turns to Hanna. "Congratulations on making it to your second trimester. How are you feeling?"

"Pretty good," Hanna says. "The morning sickness has let up and I'm not quite as tired anymore."

"That's great news!" Nix looks at me. "And how's Dad handling the pregnancy? Are you ready for this?"

Hanna's eyes dart to me then Nix. "He's not… I mean, we're not living together or anything, Nix. He's just the dad."

Just the dad sounds way too much like *just the sperm donor,* and I don't like that. "Yet," I mutter. "Not living together *yet.*"

Nix's eyes go wide for a moment. Then she begins her exam—poking at Hanna's hipbones and feeling her belly as she asks questions. Hanna hides it well beneath her clothing, but when her belly's exposed, I can see where it's begun to round with pregnancy, and I'm irrationally jealous that Nix gets to touch her.

"Shall we take a listen?" Nix asks. She pulls a giant bottle of jelly from the wall and uses the Doppler to smear it over Hanna's stomach. While she searches for a heartbeat, we listen to the *whoosh-whoosh* of the womb, and I take Hanna's hand.

Our eyes connect as the *whoosh-whoosh* becomes the sound of our baby's heart. *Dear God.* I forgot how amazing that sound is. How inconsequential the rest of the petty bullshit feels when you're listening to the tiny, miraculous heart of an unborn child.

"There's baby one," Nix says. "Sounds great."

Hanna squeezes my hand as Nix rubs the Doppler over a different location on her belly, and again, all the whooshing is replaced by the beautiful drumbeat of a baby's heart.

"And there's baby two."

HANNA

I wish I knew what he was thinking. His face looks almost pained as Nix turns off the Doppler and wipes off my belly, but I can't read him.

"I did some research," Nix says. "I didn't want to refer you out to just anybody, but I called some colleagues who work in Indianapolis and found an awesome obstetrician for you."

Frowning, I reposition my gown and sit up on the table. "What do you mean, refer me? I want you to be my doctor."

She tugs her bottom lip between her teeth. "I can't do that. Not in good conscience. Even if there weren't other concerns about your pregnancy, the fact that you're pregnant with twins is enough of a reason for you to see a high-risk doctor. Add to that the less-than-ideal health you were in when you got pregnant and I think it would be best for you to be in the hands of a specialist."

I feel the blood drain from my face. "You think there could be something wrong with my babies."

"That's not what I'm saying." She places her hand on top of mine. "I'm just saying I want you to have the best care possible. You have enough to worry about. The quality of your prenatal care shouldn't be on that list. Shall we set up your appointment for you?"

I nod. "Okay."

Nix grins. "Don't look so glum! You're in your second trimester—this is as good as it gets. The morning sickness will go away, and the worst of your breast tenderness along with it. You'll get your energy back. Enjoy it. Do you have any questions for me?" She looks back and forth between Nate and me.

"Not right now," I say.

"You can get dressed, then. I'll see you out front."

I wait until she leaves the room before turning to Nate, and I find him staring at me.

"May I walk you home?" he asks.

"Sure."

Without being asked, he turns around while I get dressed. We make our way up front, bundle into our coats, and step outside.

"I have to leave in a couple of days," Nate says after we've walked a couple of blocks. "Collin misses his mom, and I need to take care of some things in LA."

"Oh." I shake my head, trying to make the disappointment scatter. He sends texts to check on me, but it's not like we've been spending time together over the last few weeks. I guess I just found his nearness a comfort. "How long will you be gone?"

He shoves his hands in his pockets, and his breath puffs out like smoke in the cool air as he exhales. "A couple of weeks at least. I've been away too long, and I need to take care of some things if I'm going to spend time here after the babies are born."

I draw in a breath. "You're going to spend time here?"

We're outside my bakery, but he stops and turns to me, tilts my chin up with his fingers. "When I say I'm going to be in their lives, I don't just mean I want my name on their birth certificates. I mean the dirty diapers and the sleepless nights."

"It's just...not convenient."

"Worthwhile things rarely are." His eyes go hooded, and his hand doesn't leave my face.

"What are you thinking about?"

His gaze drops to my lips. "You."

I swallow. "What about me?"

"How much I want to kiss you."

My heart stumbles. Because I want him to kiss me. And I shouldn't.

"Do you remember my kisses, angel?" He skims his thumb over my lower lip, and something churns in my belly—hot and low and hungry.

"I remember." My mind instantly conjures a catalogue of kisses. Outside the club, the cool air on my face, the brick against my back. In his pool, my naked body pressed against his. On his bed, his dark eyes intense as he slid into me for the first time.

He lowers his mouth until it's just above mine, his breath warm and sweet against my lips.

"Don't."

He groans so low I can hardly hear it. "You want me to."

"You promised you wouldn't until I asked," I remind him.

His mouth moves to my ear, and his lips graze the sensitive shell as he speaks. "You're going to ask, Hanna. We both know you're going to ask."

"We can't be lovers."

"What *can* we be?"

"Friends."

HANNA

"Now you can open your eyes."

I do as my mother says and find myself face to face with... an open field. "Okay..."

"This land is for sale. I thought you could build your house here." She picked me up from the bakery, and we drove for thirty minutes. Out of New Hope and into stretches of cornfields that are conveniently located near more cornfields.

"Where are we?"

"Just a little drive outside of New Hope, but isn't it beautiful?"

"I don't have any money to build a house," I say cautiously.

"Well, sure you will—after you and Max get back together and you get married. You'll have your trust fund. I can just see you building out here, raising the babies in it, having a big yard for them to run in, and you can host dinners and we'll all drive over to see you."

I burst into tears, but it feels more like I'm smacked upside the face with them. "I don't want anyone to have to drive to see me," I snivel. "I don't want to live in LA and I don't want to live in the middle of a bunch of cornfields half an hour from my family. I want to live in New Hope. I want to be there when Abby starts dating and when Maggie has babies. I want to be here to watch Lizzy's preschool turn into the best preschool for miles and when you get old and senile." I draw in a ragged breath. "I don't want to leave. Is there something so wrong with that?"

Mom's face softens. "No. There's nothing wrong with that at all." She draws me into her arms and strokes my hair. "Nothing at all."

"I'm not going to get back together with Max," I say. "I can't marry him. It's over."

"What? Why? Is this about that rocker? Are you going to be with *him*?"

"No. Yes." I shake my head.

It's been weeks since I gave Max his ring back, and he's been as wonderful as he ever was before. He's been helping at the bakery while I've been doing interviews to replace Liz, he's brought me groceries when he thought I might be too tired to shop, and two nights ago, I caught him applying non-skid surface to the stairs to my apartment. He's sweet and wonderful. The terrifying months waiting before me would be so much easier if he were by my side.

"You still love him," she says into my hair. "I don't understand why you're doing this to yourself."

I pull out of her arms and take a deep breath. "I need to ask you a favor, and I want you to consider it before you say no."

"Okay."

"Max is the silent partner for my bakery, and I want to buy him out. He's trying to get custodial rights to his daughter. He needs the money." If he had the money, he might be able to hire more help at the club again, and he needs time more than he needs anything else. Sam and Will have been helping when they can, but that only goes so far. "Could you give me access to my trust so I can buy him out? I'm not asking for any more than that. Just enough to buy out his portion and pay off the mortgage on the building."

She studies me for a minute then shakes her head. "I would if I could, but those trusts were established by your father. We'd have quite a court battle on our hands if we wanted to go outside his terms, and we'd probably lose." She sighs. "I know this is important to you, and I'm sorry I can't change that."

My eyes burn with tears. Stupid hormones. "It's okay. I'll figure out another way."

ELEVEN

HANNA

The night is gorgeous. The stars twinkle on the river and the moon bathes Asher's backyard in a soft glow. Maggie and Asher have been in New York together the last week, and they've invited us all here for an early Thanksgiving gathering.

Nate's been gone for nearly four weeks, and I keep finding myself wandering around the party, looking for his face. I know he's coming back to town soon because he said he'd be back in time for my ultrasound next week, but every time I scan the faces in the crowd, I come up empty.

"We want to thank you all for coming," Asher announces to his guests. "We're thrilled that you could come on such short notice. You see, this isn't just any party. We wanted you to celebrate with us."

"Go ahead," Mom calls. She's practically bouncing in her seat. "Tell them your news."

Asher and Maggie exchange looks, and Liz says, "Holy shit. You're pregnant too?"

Maggie laughs. "No. That's not it. But"—she sticks out her left hand toward the small crowd—"we're married."

"No way," Liz breathes, and then, suddenly, everyone

is clapping and cheering, and Liz and I are rushing toward Maggie to hug her.

When I get my turn, I squeeze her tight. "Congratulations. You deserve this."

Maggie returns my hug. "I'm so happy. I never thought I'd get to be this happy."

"We want details," Liz demands.

Maggie beams. "We were in New York visiting Zoe, and Asher took me to this gorgeous little vineyard upstate. He had everything arranged—the flowers, the location, the photographer. He said he knew I was afraid of weddings because of…well, you know…but he didn't need a big crowd. He just needed me. If I would have him."

Tears spill from my eyes because I can picture everything she described, and as much as I would have loved to be there, I also know that Asher gave Maggie exactly what she needed.

"What did you say?" Liz asks.

Maggie looks at Asher. "I said, 'I do.'"

Before long, music is playing, drinks are flowing, mounds of food cover the buffet tables at the back of the house, and Liz and I have found our spots near the dance floor in the basement where she has access to the bar and I can more easily do my pathetic crowd-scanning thing without being obvious.

"Hey, Liz," Sam says, running his eyes over her in her black dress. "That dress looks terrible on you. Want me to help you out of it?"

"You wish," she grumbles.

He grins and dips his head to her ear to whisper something I can't hear. Whatever it was makes her smile despite herself, but she shoves him softly and says, "Go hang out with your boys. I'm talking to my sister."

When he's gone, I raise an eyebrow at Liz. "So, are you going to tell me what's going on there?"

She crosses her arms and frowns. "Nothing. It's *Sam*."

I sigh. "Well, if you aren't going to use what he's offering, can I borrow it?"

"No," she snaps. Her eyes track Sam across the room.

Holy crap. I think Liz has a thing for *Sam.* And not just an "I'd fuck him" thing. An *emotional* thing. Where have I been?

Some emotion I don't recognize flicks over her face before she pastes on a smile that would probably fool anyone but me. "I mean, I think you could do better, but go for it."

Not a chance. Not when my twin is giving him the hot-and-needy eyes. I don't need Sam anyway. Just sex.

I sigh. "I'll find someone else. Why did no one ever tell me how horny being pregnant makes you? Because this is ridiculous."

"Seriously?" Liz snorts. "You've got two sexy guys who'd kill to climb into bed with you and you're going to complain to *me* about being horny?"

I wave away her objection. "Too complicated. I just want sex. A lot of it. As often as possible."

"You called?" a deep voice says behind us.

I turn and find myself staring into Nate Crane's intense, brown eyes. Holy cow, he's sexy, and the way he drags his eyes over my body makes me want to strip off his clothes, crawl on top of him, and take exactly what he's offering. What was I saying about complicated?

Nate nods toward the dance floor and offers me his hand. "You owe me a dance, angel."

Mute with longing, I follow him and let him pull me into his arms. He's warm and his chest is solid against my cheek. He smells so good it makes the muscles between my legs clench.

"God, I missed you," he murmurs in my ear.

My stomach flip-flops. "You shouldn't say that."

"What? I can't miss my *friend*? Are you going to tell me you didn't miss me at all?"

Only every other second and the ones in between. "A little, I guess."

"How are you feeling?" he asks against my ear. Then I can feel his lips curve into a smile as he adds, "Other than painfully horny, that is."

My cheeks burn. "You weren't supposed to hear that."

"Maybe I'm glad I did. Maybe I wanted an excuse to talk

my way into your bed."

I bite my lower lip. Hard. Because I would gladly take him up on that—even if I know I shouldn't. And it's not just because pregnancy has left me as horny as a teenage boy at prom. It's because it's Nate, and I know a little bit about what would happen if I let him talk his way into my bed. But I'd like to know more.

"We can't," I protest lamely, because apparently my brain has conquered my girly bits in the battle for control of my speech. "You know that."

NATE

When I walked into the party tonight, she was the first thing I saw. In a black dress and bright red heels, she'd catch any man's eye. With her belly rounding with my babies, I could hardly see anything else.

I brush a lock of hair behind her ear. "All I know is that we're two consenting adults who want and love each other. All I know is that you're having my babies, and I'm going to be part of your life from here on out, whether you want me or not." It's one thing if she doesn't want to be with me, but I'll be fucking damned before I let her fantasize about screwing some other man just to get off. "Come with me," I say, taking her hand in mine. "I need to show you something."

She narrows her eyes. "What?"

I don't answer, but she doesn't argue as I lead her away from the party and up two flights of stairs from the basement to Asher's second floor.

"Nate," she says, the warning apparent in her voice as I lead her into my bedroom.

"The balcony," I say, pushing the doors open.

The night is balmy and the cool air nips at my cheeks, but I needed to get her away from everyone else. I needed to get her alone.

Her shoulders relax a bit as she walks to the rail and settles against it. "It's beautiful tonight," she murmurs.

There she stands. Gorgeous and framed by moonlight that shimmers on the water and stars that spread out across the black sky.

"Stunning," I whisper. Coming up behind her, I place my hands on the railing on either side of her. "And so are you." She stiffens slightly, and I graze the side of her neck with my lips—not kissing exactly, but definitely pushing the limits of her "friendship" rules. Damn, she smells good. Like vanilla and lavender. But I want her to smell like sex and me.

She's so fucking beautiful in that dress—a black thing that shows off her curves and ties above her rounding belly. It's grown in the weeks that I've been gone, and since I walked into the party half an hour ago, all I could think about was getting her alone and tugging on that bow, getting my hands on what waits beneath.

"What are you doing, Nate?" she asks, but even as she says it, she's tilting her head to the side and giving me better access to her neck. *Hell yes.*

"I'm trying to help a friend," I whisper against her ear, my hand finding the tie in the front of her dress. "You said we're friends, right?"

She stiffens slightly.

"Don't overthink this, Hanna. Just relax." I tug on the tie, and she gasps. The dress loosens and opens.

"We shouldn't," she says as my hand closes over her breast.

"Are you asking me to stop?" I pinch her nipple, and she moans, arches into me. I release her breast and trail my hand down her body, circling her navel.

"Didn't you say you weren't going to do this unless I asked?"

"I said I wouldn't *kiss* you unless you asked. I didn't say anything about putting my hands on your body."

"You don't play fair."

"Fuck fair. For you, angel, I'll play downright dirty."

She places her hand over mine and guides it farther south

until my fingertips are brushing the satin band at the top of her panties. It's all the permission I need.

Sliding my hand into her panties, I find her wet and swollen. "Is this what you need?"

I roll her clit between two fingers, and she gasps. "Please."

"I'm the only man for this job. Do you understand?" I release her clit and cup her softly.

"Nate, please."

"Please *what*, angel? Tell me."

"Touch me," she whimpers.

"I don't want anyone else touching this body," I growl, sounding and feeling more possessive than I ever have in my life. The idea of her fucking Max, the idea of him inside her, his hands on her body—it's enough to make me crazy. "No one but me."

"I don't want anyone at all," she objects, but her body betrays her and she rocks into my hand, begging for more.

"But I think you do." I run a finger along her clit, my touch light, more a tease than a gift. "I think you want me very much." Then I slide my fingers inside her, and she's so wet and so tight that my cock aches.

She lets her head fall to the side. I kiss her neck and play with her breasts as I fuck her with my fingers, making her mine in this simple way.

"Tell me you don't think about me when you're alone in your bed," I whisper. "Tell me you don't imagine my cock inside you when you're getting yourself off."

With a soft moan, she rocks her ass back, grinding against my hard-on.

"I'll tell you what I think about. I think about my face between your legs. Your clit under my tongue." Taking her earlobe between my teeth, I suck hard, showing her exactly what I'd like to be doing to her clit, and she comes, her pussy pulsing tight and hard against my fingers.

She turns in my arms, and the movement pulls my hand from her panties. Her teeth are sinking into her bottom lip and her eyes are still dark with lust. "Thanks, I think."

I raise a brow. "You *think*?"

She bites back a smile. "I don't want to encourage you."

"I don't need any encouragement to get you off, angel." I slide my hands down her back to cup her ass. "Just permission. Let me take you home. Let me..." I stop the words before they can leave my tongue. *Let me make love to you.* "Let me fuck you, Hanna."

She draws in a ragged breath. "I need to get back downstairs before..."

I wait for her to finish. *Before someone realizes we're both gone.* The words hang between us unsaid.

MAX

Will can't take his eyes off Cally. Asher can't take his eyes off Maggie. And, in a new and unexpected development, Sam can't take his eyes off Liz.

I need to get away from all the sexual tension in this party, so I wander the house. I haven't seen Hanna since I arrived late. I was hoping for a dance or, hell, just a smile. I'd take it.

She's been so tired lately with the pregnancy and putting in too many hours at the bakery. I wouldn't be surprised if she went home early. But when I pass the guest room on Asher's second floor, I hear her voice out on the balcony.

I smile as I follow it and then freeze when I spot her. She's standing at the railing, but Nate is behind her, his body pressed against hers, his mouth at her neck...and his hand between her legs.

Jealousy blazes through me at the sight. It doesn't matter that she's not wearing my ring anymore. The moan that slips from her lips feels like a betrayal, and I have to turn and leave the room before I yank him off her and throw him off the fucking balcony.

HANNA

"You don't need to go anywhere but my bed." Nate's breathing is hard and his eyes are hot. He leans down and brushes his lips against my ear. "Tell me you don't need me inside you."

I shiver, and when he offers his hand, I take it.

He leads me into his room. After swinging the door shut and locking it, he slips my untied dress off my shoulders. "Lie down," he commands, his voice rough.

I glance at my red heels.

"Don't touch them," he commands. "Last time I had you keep your heels on, I didn't get to fuck you. This time, I'm going to."

I know I should object. This isn't smart when we both know this will only complicate our future relationship, but I can't muster the will. When he removes his clothes and settles onto the mattress next to me, I can't bring myself to feel anything but gratitude.

"Have I ever told you how beautiful you are?" he murmurs. His hand sweeps over my collarbone, between my breasts, and over my belly, and when it dips lower, I part my legs instinctively, needing his touch there.

"You're beautiful too." And it's beyond true, but maybe the more amazing thing is the "too" on the end of my statement. Because I've never doubted Nate's attraction to me. It's been there from the beginning—from that first moment our eyes met in the bar. When he's looking at me, I am beautiful, and maybe that shouldn't matter, but after a lifetime of feeling unattractive, he was exactly what I needed. Maybe what I still need.

His fingertips are following invisible paths up and down my thighs, his eyes locked with mine. I arch my hips off the bed, telling him with my body where I need his touch. He just smiles.

"Don't rush me, angel."

I trail my fingers down his solid chest and follow that soft trail of dark hair south of his navel until I find what I'm looking for. "You sure?" I ask, wrapping my fingers around his thick shaft. A thrill flutters through me at the raw need that comes over his face as I stroke him. "Now," I whisper. "Please. I need you."

He groans and finally—thank you, God— settles his hand between my legs. He moves his fingers over my clit, teasing me before sliding a finger inside me.

My breath leaves me in a rush because, *damn*, I needed this. I needed what he did on the balcony, and I need this, and I need more. His hand rocks over me, his palm applying just enough friction against my clit as his finger pumps in and out. I keep my hand wrapped around his dick. I stroke and squeeze, desperate to bring him the same pleasure he's bringing me.

His teeth nip my ear. "I wanted to do this all night," he whispers, his fingers still working their magic between my legs. "I heard what you said to Liz, and I wanted to kill Sam and then take you to a dark corner and fuck you so hard your legs wouldn't hold you up."

I gasp as he shifts the angle of his hand, and I can hardly *think*, let alone explain that what I said about borrowing Sam was a joke.

He moves so quickly—drawing up my knees and positioning himself—that he's inside me before I realize what's coming. The quick and unexpected stretch and pressure of him filling me throws me over the edge. I cry out, squeezing and pulsing around him as I fly over that amazing edge of pleasure, and my body spasms.

When I recover and open my eyes again, he's resting on one elbow and stroking my cheek. His eyes are dark and hungry, and he slowly resumes his movements and thrusts into me, pressing deeper with each thrust.

"Again, angel." He hooks one arm under my knee and draws my leg up higher, and when he fills me, it feels so good

I scream.

I rock against him as he murmurs dirty encouragements into my ear, his words urging me along.

"Your body was made for mine," he whispers against my ear. "Just enjoy this." Then he thrusts hard and deep and we come together, my orgasm squeezing him as he comes inside me.

Only after does he break his promise. He takes my face in his hands, gentle and sweet, and he kisses me like I'm the only thing in the world that matters.

"I didn't ask you to," I object when he pulls back.

His lips curl in a self-satisfied smirk. "I'm not even a little bit sorry."

TWELVE

HANNA

"I want to know exactly what happened between you and Nate at Asher and Maggie's party," Cally says to me, wriggling her brows.

"I think he fucked you silly," Liz adds, "and you don't even have the courtesy to let us live vicariously."

The Wire is crowded tonight, and despite the ruckus around us, I still feel like everyone can hear our conversation.

"Can we please talk about something other than my love life for a minute?" I plead.

Liz sticks out her lip like a pouting child. "Your love life is the most interesting thing happening around here at the moment."

Cally raises a brow. "I'm not sure that's true. I heard you're sleeping with Sam Bradshaw."

"What?" Nix crosses her arms and glares at Liz. "I thought we were sisters in sex deprivation?"

"No offense, Nix," Liz says, "but that's not a club I'm that interested in being a part of."

Maggie snorts. "Preach."

"I want details," Cally says.

I bite back my grin and toy with my straw. "Details would be good. Come on, Liz. Have the courtesy of letting us live vicariously."

"I was horny. I slept with Sam. The. End."

"Lame," Nix mutters. "Vicarious sex is all I've got right now, and you're totally failing me."

Liz drains her chocolate martini and stays silent. *Stubborn.*

"I could use some vicarious sex too," I admit. Because my stolen moments with Nate were gone too quickly and only left me wanting more. "Is it normal to be this horny while pregnant?" I ask Nix.

"Biologically speaking?" she asks.

"Totally," I say.

"It's normal to be that horny when a guy like Nate Crane is looking at you like that."

I follow Nix's eyes to the other side of the bar, where Nate and Asher are sitting in a booth, and Nate's eyes are glued to me. The girls look too, and Cally and Maggie fan their hands in front of their faces.

"Tell me again why you aren't fucking him silly," Liz says. "Because there are desperate, undersexed women at this table who are offended by that sexual tension going to waste."

My cheeks burn as I study my virgin daiquiri, but Nix saves me by moving the conversation away from me and Nate again. "You," she says, pointing an accusing finger at Liz, "don't get to call yourself undersexed if you've recently fucked Sam Bradshaw."

"I'm sure he'd fuck you too if you asked," she mutters. She waves to the waitress and holds up her empty glass, signaling for another drink.

Cally snorts. "I'm not so sure he's interested in anyone but you, Liz."

"We're not surprised that you did it," I say, nudging my twin under the table. "More that you waited so long."

"It wasn't the first time," Liz grumbles, avoiding our eyes as the waitress hurries with her fresh martini.

"You had sex with Sam before and you didn't tell me?" I

squeak. "What else are you keeping from me?"

"Is he as good as the rumors suggest?" Maggie asks.

Liz scowls. "Why do you think I went back despite my better judgment?"

"Details," Nix demands.

Liz takes a sip of her martini and licks her lips slowly. I can't tell if she's remembering or trying to figure out how to change the subject. Then Maggie gets struck with the same revelation I had at her party.

"You *like* him," she whispers. "This isn't just sex. You really like him."

Liz shakes her head. "I'm a grown woman, and I'm done playing games. I want something *real*. Wicked-hot sex and handcuffs and the best orgasms ever aren't really a foundation for a successful relationship."

Across from me, Nix actually whimpers. "I really hate you."

"Doesn't sound so bad to me," I say.

Liz shrugs. "I shared. On to someone else, please." She looks to Maggie. "How about you? Can you share some dirty newly married sex stories for Nix to live vicariously through?"

"Do you really think I'm the kind of girl who would kiss and tell?" Maggie asks.

"Yes," we all say in unison.

She snickers and turns in the booth to eye her husband across the room. When she turns back to us, she has that wicked smile on her face. "He's still got it." She turns to Cally. "And married sex is the best, wouldn't you agree?"

"Yes." Cally grins. "But married, pregnant sex is even better."

I sigh. "Lucky bitches."

"Where are we?" I rub my eyes, trying to wake up.

After he promised he wouldn't try to get in my pants again,

I let Nate drive to my doctor's appointment in Indianapolis. We had lunch afterward, and I must have fallen asleep on the way home. Now, we're parked on the street in front of a house I don't recognize, and the sun is sinking lower in the sky. We're in the newer part of New Hope, in the recently developed area by the river where my mom and Asher live.

"Are we visiting someone?"

Nate doesn't answer me. Instead, he climbs out of the car and walks around to open my door. When I step onto the sidewalk, I see a "For Sale" sign in the front yard and a "SOLD" magnet across the center of it.

I turn to him and narrow my eyes. "What is this?"

He shifts awkwardly and gives me a tentative smile. He actually looks *nervous*.

"What are we doing here?" I ask again.

The house is beautiful. Not as big as my mom's and definitely not the size of Asher's, but it's a Cape Cod-style home with a covered wraparound porch and blue shutters.

I follow Nate to the door, and he produces a key from his pocket to unlock it. "Why do you have a key?"

"I know the owner," he says, pushing through the front door.

Whoever sold the house must not have moved their furniture out yet, because right inside the door is a fully furnished living room—fluffy, overstuffed couches, oversized chairs, all situated around a soft beige rug.

I'm still not sure what we're doing here, but I follow Nate into the kitchen. He turns on lights as I take in the dark cabinets, gleaming countertops, and shining appliances. The sink sits under a big picture window that looks out into a large, fenced backyard.

"Could you live somewhere like this?" Nate asks quietly. "It's not right on the river like your mom's and Asher's places, but I thought this might be safer for the twins. You can let them run out back and play without having to worry about them going too close to the water."

"Sure," I say. "Someday, this would be great." But this is a house for a family—a couple of kids and their parents. Not a screw-up single mom who loves two men and doesn't deserve either of them. Someone with a steady job who can pay the mortgage, not a floundering new business. "For now, I'm fine in the apartment above the bakery."

Nate shoves his hands into his pockets and his shoulders draw up around his ears. "No, you're not."

"That's hardly your choice to make."

He raises a brow. "You think I shouldn't have a choice in where my children live?"

"That's not what I meant."

"No? I think it was. I think you're still convinced that, by the time you have those babies, I'm going to be back in LA and out of your life for good." He stalks up to me slowly, determination in his eyes. "Sorry to disappoint you, angel, but that's not going to happen. You can't push me out of your life."

"I'm not trying to!" I squeeze my eyes shut and take a breath. We had such a nice, pleasant day, and I don't want to ruin it. "I never want to make you feel like you aren't welcome in the twins' lives. You're their father. They'll need you." I lift my gaze to his, and he drops his shoulders.

"So let me do this," he says softly. "If not for you, then for them."

"Do what?"

"Give them a home. This home. I know you think you can make it work in that little apartment, but even if it weren't way too small for two children, it also has those damn stairs. Have you really thought about what it's going to be like, lugging two babies up those stairs along with strollers and groceries? And what about when it gets icy in the winter? What if you fell again? What if you were holding the babies when you fell?"

I let out a long, slow breath. He's right. That apartment isn't going to work once the twins are here. "Okay," I agree. "I need a different place to live, but I'm not in a position to have a place like this yet."

"I am."

I wrap my arms around myself and shake my head. "No.

It's too much. I can't let you do that for me."

"I already have," he says softly.

He takes my hand and leads me through the house—the breakfast nook beside the kitchen with a great view of the backyard, the dining room.

"The master is on the main floor," he says, "but there's an attached office you can use as a nursery until the twins are old enough to move upstairs." He takes me into the large bedroom.

The attached bathroom is gorgeous—stone countertops, a jetted tub, and a large tile shower that has room for a small family. Off to the left of the bedroom is a sunny room with dark mahogany nursery furniture—two cribs, mechanical swings, a rocking chair, and a changing table.

"Do the current owners have twins too?" I ask.

"I'm the current owner," Nate says. He watches me carefully. "I bought the house and furniture for you. I hope you like it. I didn't get any of the bedding or decorations because I thought you'd want to choose that."

My breath feels stuck in my throat and my eyes burn with unshed tears. "It's too much."

He gathers me against his chest and wraps his arms around me. I'm so overwhelmed that I let him, breathing in his good, clean scent and wishing life were simpler.

Suddenly I'm hit with a memory of Vivian crying in my office, asking me to give her a future with Nate. He deserves that future. And if it weren't for me, he'd want it.

"It's not nearly enough," he whispers against my hair. "You're carrying my children. There is no gift that amounts to that."

"Thank you."

"I tried to remember everything you told me you wanted in your life. It's close to your family, so someday, when Maggie has kids, the cousins can play. It's a five-minute drive from the bakery. The fenced backyard will be perfect for a dog when you decide you're ready for that."

I pull out of his arms and wipe my eyes. "You thought of everything."

"I tried." He studies me. "There are four bedrooms upstairs, so the twins can each have their own room when they're older, but there's still room for more kids if that's what you want."

I chuckle softly. "And who exactly would I have these children with?" I regret the question as soon as it's out of my mouth.

Some emotion I don't recognize flashes over Nate's face, and then he's stepping toward me, cupping my jaw in his big hand, skimming his thumb over my lips. "May I, angel?"

I'm too caught up and trying to process his nearness—the amazing and forbidden unfurling of need low in my belly—and before I realize what he's asking, his mouth is on mine. Warm and tender, coaxing and wicked, the kiss is everything that turns me on about this man. It's the sweet against the sensual, the protective against the need to consume. His lips sweep over mine and his tongue slides into my mouth, and I feel wanton and sexy and cherished all at once. I want to stay here, locked under the power of his kiss as his hand slides under my shirt. I could. I know he'd take me as far I as I wanted to go, and it would feel so damn good.

Between my shirt and bra, his thumb grazes over my sensitive nipple, and I gasp at the faint contact. My knees go weak and the hot, needy ache between my legs turns molten.

Somewhere deep within me, I find the will to step away from his kiss, and we stare at each other, chests heaving, eyes hot, bodies on fire.

"You bought me a house," I say. "You didn't buy me." But my mind is already conjuring up all the things we could do in that bathroom, and some really horny, slutty part of me is whispering that it wouldn't be right to let him buy me that big four-poster bed without trying it out.

Some of the heat has dissipated from his eyes and his jaw is hard. "I'm not some asshole who's trying to buy you off. I didn't kiss you because I think you owe me."

"Then why did you do it?" I ask.

"Because you were looking at me like you wished I would."

I swallow the guilt gathering in my throat. "It's too

complicated. We're going to be in each other's lives. We need to set boundaries."

"You still want Max."

For a minute, I can only blink at him and wonder how he thinks Max has anything to do with this. I'll accept this gift because it's done and I know he can afford it, that he'd insist if I argued. In reality, I'd rather have him—here, in New Hope, making *me* his first family. I'll accept the house because I can't ask for more.

"I don't want anyone."

He flinches, and for a moment, I wonder how I learned to lie so quickly.

HANNA

Three Days Before Hanna's Accident

The bell at the front of the bakery dings, and I head up front to find a leggy, raven-haired beauty, her lips parted slightly as she studies my shop. A tall, blond Viking of a man follows behind her, his broad shoulders filling up the doorway. There are more dead-sexy men in this city every day.

"May I help you?" I ask, tearing my eyes off her young-Fabio companion.

"This town is unreal," she says. "Like something out of a movie. So flipping cute."

I can't help but grin because most people dismiss New Hope as a dumb, little hick town. I appreciate anyone who can see it the way I do. "Thank you. I think so too. Would you like some coffee? Breakfast? The scones are especially delicious, I'm told."

"Oh, I'd love a cup of green tea if you have it." She flushes sweetly. As she looks at me straight on for the first time, it hits me—this isn't just any out-of-towner. This is Vivian Payne.

The actress. The mother of Nate's child. "Does asking for green tea make me sound like Los Angel-bitch? Little bit, right?"

"Not at all." I fill a cup with hot water with remarkably steady hands and grab a tea bag before handing them to her across the pastry case. "On the house. What brings you to New Hope?"

"I'm hoping to track down Hanna Thompson?"

That's what I was afraid of. I force a smile. "You're looking at her."

"Oh! Wow. Crap. Well, no wonder."

I arch a brow. There is no way I can dislike this woman. Sweetness and goodness roll off her in waves. Why couldn't she just be a bitch?

"No wonder what?"

"No wonder Nathaniel's in love with you," she says softly.

Nope. Definitely not a bitch. "Thank you...I think." I can't risk having anyone overhear this conversation. I've worked too hard in the last few months to make sure everyone in this town thinks that Max and I are still together, and now that I know what Max has done for me... "Do you think we could talk somewhere private?"

Her eyes light up. "I would so appreciate that!"

I call to the back for Drew, and she scowls at me as she takes her place in the front. Her aversion to working with the public isn't as bad as she likes to let on, but she still likes to make a big deal about it every time I ask her to work the front.

Her scowl falls away when she spots Fabio. "Can I get you anything?" she asks, teenage lust dripping off her words.

"Drake," Vivian says, and I'm honestly disappointed his name isn't Fabio. "Get yourself something. I'll be back up shortly."

While leading Vivian to the back of the kitchen, I do my best to act casual, as if having her here isn't completely intimidating to me. "Have a seat," I say when we get into my office.

"This place is just adorable," Vivian says. Maybe from any other Hollywood starlet, that would sound condescending, but it doesn't come across that way from Vivian. She sips her tea and looks around my office with what appears to be sincere interest. "Why would you want to leave this behind?"

I frown. "What?"

She blushes. "I don't mean to presume, but I thought you'd be moving into Nate's house?"

My stomach pitches. "Did he tell you that?"

She bows her head. "Listen, he'd be really upset if he knew I was here. I had to harass Jamaal just to find out anything about you. But I'm sure you understand that I have good reason to be worried."

"Worried about what, exactly?"

"Nate doesn't fall in love easily. I just want to make sure that you're after him for the right reasons."

I shift in my chair and attempt to lower my hackles, but it doesn't matter how sweet this woman is. The assumptions behind this conversation are insulting.

She raises a hand. "I know how that sounds, and I apologize."

"What makes you think I'm *after* Nate at all? Maybe he's the one *after* me." Yeah, my attempts to calm myself? Big, fat fail. But *damn*.

Vivian's eyes fill with tears. "Must be nice."

Well, crap. "Do you want to tell me what this is really about?" I ask, calmer now.

"My husband and I divorced."

"I'm sorry to hear that."

She shakes her head. "No, don't be. It's what everyone expects of an actress anyway, isn't it?" She sighs. "I want my son to be raised seeing what love can be. How intense and beautiful, and how deep it can run. I didn't have that with my ex-husband. Maybe I could have, but you can't love someone the way they deserve when half your heart still belongs to someone else."

"And you love Nate."

"I never stopped," she whispers. When she lifts her gaze to meet mine, her lashes are damp. I swear I've never seen anyone look so pretty from crying. "But loving someone means wanting what's best for him, and if that's you, I won't confuse the issue. But if that's not you…" She studies me for a moment. "If that's not you, I'd really like you to step aside so my little family can have a chance." Her voice pitches at the end, and a tear escapes and rolls down her cheek. "We *are* a family, you know. Despite everything. I just want to be sure you know that."

I think of Nate's face when he talks about Collin. How desperately he wants to be the best father possible to his son, how he'll do anything to be part of Collin's life. "It was nice to meet you, Vivian." I stand and open the door to the office, motioning her out.

We walk up to the front together, and Max and my mom are at the front, chatting with Drew. Max's face lights up when he sees me. He skims his eyes over me in a way that reminds me too well of what used to be between us.

"Hey, beautiful," he says softly, pressing a kiss to the corner of my mouth.

Vivian's eyes shift between us, confusion on her face. "You'll think about what I said?" she asks. She doesn't wait for an answer before pushing out the door and leaving.

"You can't love someone the way they deserve when half your heart still belongs to someone else."

I'm already thinking about it.

I thought this would be an impossible choice, but there's only one choice that will give both of the men I love the lives they want.

I grab Max's hand and drag him to the back and into my office.

"Are you okay?" he asks, grinning.

I push the door shut behind him and shove him against it as I press my mouth to his, searching for answers in the kiss of a man who used to be my whole world.

He doesn't hesitate but slants his mouth over mine. His hands seek out my curves immediately, one settling on my ass, the other under my shirt just beneath my breast.

He rubs his tongue over mine, and I want to crawl into all his heat and goodness and warmth. I want this to work. I need it to.

He kisses the corner of my mouth and down the side of my neck, and a little moan escapes my lips. His grip on me loosens as he looks at me. "Marry me," he says softly. If I thought he was releasing me, I was wrong, because the hand under my shirt skims the underside of my breast before finding the front clasp of my bra and unhooking it. "And not just because you want me as much as I want you." Hand against my bare breast, he cups me and rolls my nipple in his fingers.

I whimper, but I make no move to escape his touch.

"Not just because I'm dying to get inside you and make you come."

"Max," I warn. My knees are unsteady, but when I wobble, he pulls me closer to him, still torturing my breast and making the whirl of desperate, achy, needy pleasure spiral tighter between my legs.

"The sex is going to be amazing," he whispers, his mouth brushing my ear. "Waking up with you in my arms is going to be a dream."

Effortlessly, he spins me and lifts me onto my desk, sending paperwork scattering across the floor as he steps between my legs. My skirt bunches at my hips, and he slides his hand up my inner thigh.

I grab his wrist and our eyes lock in that moment before my decision. I can stop him or I can let him touch me.

I lead his hand farther north. He groans as his hand connects with the damp lace of my panties. My sweet, tender Max vanishes. He tugs them to the side and sinks his fingers inside me.

I cry out, and the sound echoes in the small office. He sucks my earlobe between his teeth as his fingers pump in and out of me. If he stopped now, I'd die. I need this—and him. My heart hurts, and I need to know that this man can fill the hole Nate Crane will leave behind.

"God, I missed the way you feel wrapped around my

fingers," he groans in my ear. "So. Fucking. Sexy."

His thumb finds my clit, and I slide my hips forward, giving him a better angle while pushing my body closer to his.

With his free hand, he yanks my shirt over my head and tosses it to the side. Then he dips his head and sucks my nipple between his teeth—as hard and relentless as the hand fucking me between my legs.

Back arched, hips bucking, hands in his hair, I come. My world shatters into a brilliant blast of light, but as it slowly pieces back together again, nothing feels like it fits.

Max runs slow, soft kisses up my neck and back to my ear. "We're good together, Hanna. And our life together, here in New Hope? I'll do everything in my power to make it all you ever wanted."

I draw in a breath—thick and shaky and ragged.

Suddenly he's holding me in his arms, murmuring, "Don't cry," and kissing away my tears.

I am a collection of mismatched puzzle pieces, and all I want is to feel whole.

THIRTEEN

MAX

"Max! I have great news."

I frown at my phone. Other than when she called to tell me that Hanna had decided to go ahead with the bakery with me as her anonymous investor, I don't think my lawyer has ever left me a voicemail message with good news.

"A lawyer from California has contacted me, and her client is offering to buy you out of the bakery. The numbers she's throwing out are almost too good to be true. They'll more than cover the mortgage and your initial investment and leave you with a nice nest egg for your investment. As we prepare to move forward with your custody case, this would put you in a great position. I think you should take the offer. Give me a call."

I squeeze my eyes shut. An offer on the bakery. Probably from Nate Crane—this would cut me out of Hanna's life, and I'm sure that's what he wants.

My lawyer's right. I need the money. But the bakery is my last connection to Hanna's life, and selling it makes the end of our relationship feel too final. And who is the client? I'm not turning over half ownership of Hanna's *life* to just anyone. If it's Nate, would he use his ownership as leverage to get Hanna to move to LA?

I dial my lawyer, but she doesn't answer. She left the message on my office phone last night—a habit we formed when my involvement in the bakery was still a secret—and I doubt she's in her office this weekend.

After locking up my office, I find Sam at the front of the club. He's covering the front for me this morning—something he's done most Saturdays since I bought the bakery and didn't have the money for staff.

"I need to run over to the bakery," I tell him. "Are you okay to open if I don't get back in time?"

Smirking, Sam nods. Saturday mornings aren't a hopping time for fitness. "Whatever happened to your plans to offer classes on Saturday mornings to get traffic in here?"

I shrug. "I've just had other priorities."

"Like paying the bills for the bakery instead of hiring someone who could bring you new business here."

"Shut up."

"I'm just making an observation. Grab me a cup of the good stuff while you're over there."

"Should I assume Liz knows how you like it?"

"Fuck off," he mutters, but there's a hint of a smile behind the command.

The bakery smells amazing this morning—always, really, but there's an extra hit of vanilla in the air this morning, and it reminds me so much of Hanna's smell that it makes my chest ache.

"Oh, hey!" Hanna pushes through the swinging door from the kitchen and gives me a tentative smile. For a moment, I forget all the bullshit and almost expect her to come around the counter and rise onto her toes to kiss me.

I wish she'd forget too—just for a moment—that those days are behind us. I'd hold her fast and keep her close. I'd deepen the kiss until she softened and moaned against my mouth. I'd remind her what's worth fighting for.

"Thanks for helping me out while I did interviews last

week," she says.

"It's not a problem."

"Yes, it is. You have your own business to run, and I know it's hard for you to get away. But I appreciate it. Can I get you some coffee and breakfast as a thank-you?"

"I'll take a coffee. Thanks." She pours me a cup, and we both do our best to pretend this isn't as awkward as hell when she passes it across the counter. "How's the hunt for new employees going?"

"It's frustrating. I've found a couple of part-timers, which is great, but I really need a manager who can take care of the front of the house while I do the baking, and I need a second baker to take over for a few weeks when the babies are born. Drew is good, but she can't put in the hours I'll need."

Nate Crane pushes out of the kitchen, and the sight of him hits me like a punch in the gut. She said she wasn't leaving me for him, and he hasn't been around, so I was starting to believe it was true. Until I found them on the balcony at Asher's last weekend.

"Hey," he says, locking his gaze with mine.

I lift my chin as we appraise each other. He looks at Hanna, and I want to pull her into my arms and hold her tight, to keep her close until he leaves. But I don't have that right, and Nate's not going anywhere. I can tell by the way he looks at her—all that unveiled love and longing. I know the face of a man who would slay dragons for Hanna Thompson, because I see it every time I look in the mirror.

"Do you have any more boxes stashed in the back?" Nate asks.

Hanna shifts awkwardly and shoots me a look. "No, but Liz is bringing some any minute now." She points behind her and edges toward the door. "I have cookies that need my attention."

Then she's gone, leaving Nate and me staring at each other. He opens his mouth like he's about to tell me something, but then he shakes his head and goes back to the kitchen.

I need to follow Hanna and find out what she knows about

the offer. Hell, I should have saved myself the trouble and asked Nate. Buying me out would be nothing for him.

But I'm a fucking coward and I'm afraid to go through that door. Will he be kissing her? Touching her? Hanna's probably baking cookies—nothing more—but what I saw at Maggie and Asher's has tormented me for days. A repeat performance might destroy me.

"Hello?"

I turn to the door and find a customer. The petite brunette looks familiar, but I can't place her. Did we go to high school together? Or maybe college? High school's a better bet. Over half of my graduating class left New Hope for college and never came back.

She frowns at me and rises onto her tiptoes to peek over my shoulder. "I'm looking for Hanna. Will she be back soon? I could just wait."

I lift a brow. "I'm sorry, do I know you?" Forgetting people always makes me feel like an ass.

"Oops! I'm Elle." She smiles, and again I feel that sense of recognition, but I just can't place her. "Janelle Crane. Nate Crane's sister."

"Oh." Nate's sister. And a famous actress—thus the recognition. "Nice to meet you."

The bell over the door rings as Sam and Liz come in, their arms full of collapsed boxes.

"I stole Sam so he could help me with these," Liz says from behind him. "I promise I'll get him back in time to open the club."

Sam stops in his tracks two steps in the door, and Liz runs right into his back. "Ho. Lee. Shit," Sam manages.

"Walk much?" Liz says, skirting around him. "Geez." She turns to Janelle. "Have you been helped?"

"Yeah. This guy here is helping me. I'm so rude." She shakes her head and gives me an apologetic smile. "What was your name?"

I fold my arms and watch her as I say, "Max Hallowell."

Her brows shoot up and her jaw unhinges. Suddenly

she looks just like her character from *Roommates*. "Oooh," she whispers. "Holy crap. And you're here. Are you…? Did Hanna…? Oh, shit. Wow. Well, who can blame her for ditching my dorky-ass brother? You are a fucking *fox*. Look at those shoulders. Damn. How much can you bench-press?"

I don't answer or correct her. I'm not sure what she knows or when she last talked to Hanna. Sam's still gawking, and Lizzy is scowling.

"Who are *you*?" Liz asks Janelle.

"Elle," she says, offering Liz her hand. "Nate's sister, Hanna's friend. You're Lizzy, aren't you? I've heard so much about you."

Lizzy's eyes go wide and she stares at the woman's hand. "*Janelle Crane*," she says, putting it together. "Janelle Crane knows who I am."

"Janelle fucking Crane," Sam mutters. "Holy hell. You're even more gorgeous in person, which, for the record, I wouldn't have thought was possible. Damn."

Lizzy elbows Sam in the side—hard, judging from the way he doubles over—then drops the boxes and takes Elle's hand. "Have you talked to Hanna since the accident?"

Elle shakes her head. "No, but Nate told me briefly about it when he came to see me in India. Does she remember me?"

"I don't know. Probably. She has most of her memory back."

Sam gathers Lizzy's boxes with hers and stacks them in the corner. "What are all these for, anyway?"

"Hanna's moving," Liz says. Then she shoots me a look and winces—no doubt my surprise is all over my face. "And she probably wanted to be the one to tell you."

"Where's she moving?" I ask. "Someplace without stairs, I hope."

"No kidding," Liz mutters. "There are stairs, but she won't need to use them. I'll let her fill you in on the details."

"Is she in the back?" Janelle asks. "I have to talk to her." Without waiting for an answer or, you know, permission, she pushes through the swinging kitchen door.

Liz and I exchange a worried look before I follow Janelle.

The sounds of squealing women greet my ears as I come through the door. Nate's nowhere to be seen, and the women are hugging like old friends. I'm reminded of those months of Hanna's life that I missed. While we were only pretending to be a couple, she was forming new friendships, falling in love with another man…and getting pregnant.

"I am so glad to see you," Janelle says. "And you remember me, so obviously the *important* parts of your memory are back."

Hanna shrugs. "Most of it, but there are still missing pieces."

"Do you know what caused the accident?"

Hanna shakes her head. "Nix said I probably never will remember that day, unfortunately. What are you doing here? How long are you staying?"

"I had to come see the bakery I've heard so much about—and see my idiot brother—but I came here first. Did the lawyers contact you with the news yet?"

"What news?"

"I'm going to buy out your silent partner. Well, assuming he takes my offer, but it was way generous, so I'm sure he will."

Hanna's eyes connect with mine over Janelle's shoulder. The offer didn't come from Nate. It came from Nate's sister, a sister who thinks Hanna dumped Nate for me.

"Actually," Hanna says, "Max is the silent partner." She nods toward me, and Janelle spins around, her eyes wide.

"Oh. My. God. How romantic is that? Did you know that when you decided to marry him? And I owe you an apology! You know when I called and asked you to go check on Nate, I had no idea about the accident and that you had freaking *amnesia*. Nate was more interested in tequila than filling me in on the pertinent details, but he told me when he came to the retreat in India." She shakes her head. "And I'm sorry I had to ask you to do that. Considering the decisions you'd just made, you were probably a terrible person to ask, but I couldn't think of anyone else he'd listen to."

Hanna smiles, but it's forced. "Do you know about my

decisions, then?"

"Nothing was official, but you were pretty determined about your choice."

Hanna's eyes flick to mine and then back to Janelle. "My choice to marry Max?"

"Of course. Where's your ring, anyway? Did you set a date yet?" She flashes me a grin over her shoulder then lowers her voice. "He's so gorgeous, I can't even. And is that why you're moving? Are you going to live together?"

"She's going to live with me."

The girls turn toward Nate's voice at the back door, but I don't turn. Any kernel of hope Janelle's rambling gave me is crushed. Hanna's moving in with Nate.

HANNA

Max looks to me, Janelle, and finally to Nate. Then he turns on his heel and heads out the door to the front of the bakery. I hear the front bell ring as he exits to the street.

Crap. That's not how I wanted that to go.

I don't know how long Nate's been there, but judging from the look on his face, I'd say it's fair to say he heard his twin going on about my choice to marry Max.

I hate the idea of hurting either of them, and I'm killing them both.

"I'm not moving in with you." I stalk toward Nate and prop my hands on my hips. "That was never part of the deal."

Nate raises a brow. "You really think I'm going to buy a house in this town and then bunk with the newlyweds when I visit?"

"What's going on?" Janelle asks behind me. "Hanna, I thought you were marrying Max."

Nate snaps his mouth shut at those words and his jaw ticks.

"I called it off," I whisper. "Excuse me. I need to go tell Liz to stop packing my stuff."

I leave, but I don't go to the front, where I can hear Liz talking to Sam. I climb the stairs to my apartment, shut the door behind me, and sink to the floor.

"She's moving in with me."

If only he meant that as it sounded. If only he meant we could be together, a family who lives in the same house in the same town. But he's committed to another family, and I'm plagued by these questions about a decision I can't remember making.

FOURTEEN

NATE

"See everything you miss when you hole up for months without access to the outside world?" I attempt a smile but it falls flat.

Janelle, on the other hand, is having no trouble smiling. In fact, she's grinning like a madwoman. "It worked!"

"What are you talking about?"

"When I sent her to pull you from your drunken pity party, I was hoping she'd…you know, come to her senses and decide not to marry Max. Of course, I had no idea about the amnesia at the time, and that must have complicated things. But God, you were being such a whiny loser."

"She chose him," I growl. "I made a promise to respect that decision and I was trying not to break that promise."

"What did you promise, exactly? To be a loser who wouldn't fight for the woman he loves? The only woman in the world who makes him happy?" She attempts a scowl, but it's washed away by a smile she can't seem to resist. "But you two are moving in together now, so it's all good, right?" She frowns. "Or are you? She didn't seem so sure."

I drag a hand through my hair. "I bought her a house. I

assumed she knew I planned on staying there while I was in town."

"You bought her a house? And she accepted?" She frowns. "That doesn't sound anything like Hanna."

"She's pregnant." The words pummel my heart because I know that, if it weren't for those babies, Hanna would have never agreed to move into a house I bought.

"Get the fuck out. Seriously? And the baby is yours?"

"Babies," I correct. "Twins. I bought her a house so she'd have someplace safe to raise them since she won't leave New Hope."

"Of course she's not leaving. Who the hell wants to live in LA? You're going to have to move out here. It'll be good for you."

"I'm not leaving Collin. I'll just have to visit here as much as I can."

"You can't make a life with someone by 'visiting' them."

"Then I guess it's lucky that she doesn't want a life with me," I mutter.

"You're so sure about that?"

"Where have you been?" I glare at her. "You were just standing there, telling her all about how she chose Max."

"You're kidding me, right?" She points to the door where Hanna left. "She's pregnant with *your babies*. Stop letting your fear of rejection rule you. You love that girl, and she loves you."

"And she loves Max." *She chose Max.* Part of me never believed it. Part of me wanted another explanation for that ring being on her finger when she woke up.

Janelle grabs my shoulders. "When she chose Max, it had as much to do with trying to give *you* the life you wanted as it did with loving him."

"How do you know that?"

"We're friends," she says. "We talk. Man up and fight for her." Silence pulses between us, and when I meet her eyes, she looks as sad as I feel. As if she just realized she lost a battle she thought she won.

"I can't leave Collin."

"I get that you want to be Dad of the Year. We had the same asshole father, remember? But what's better for your son than seeing his dad with someone who makes him happy? You're going to stand there and tell me you think Collin's better off with the miserable lump you become when Hanna's not in your life? Better off with a dad who gets drunk every time his kid's not around because nothing else about his life is worth staying sober for? Make him see that Dad's worthy of love and happiness, and when he's an adult, he'll believe the same of himself."

I shrug her hands off my shoulders and turn away. Fuck. I need a drink. But seeing as how it's not even nine a.m., I opt for a deep breath instead. "What if I'm *not* worthy?" My voice breaks on the question. I might as well be a pubescent boy— Hanna makes me feel about that vulnerable.

"You really think he might be better for her?" Janelle asks, and I don't answer because if I didn't believe that, I would have fought for her from the first.

NATE

Four Days After *Hanna's Accident*

I'm half lost in Asher's song when I see Hanna coming down the stairs with her sisters. The sight of her catches me off guard and makes me miss a whole verse. She's grinning and beautiful, her legs on display in that sexy-as-fuck jean skirt. Happiness radiates off her as if she doesn't have a care in the world. As if she didn't just break my heart.

Asher narrows his eyes at me, and I tear my gaze away from Hanna and find my place in the music, hide behind lyrics and harmony like I have most of my life.

Asher transitions into "Unbreak Me," and I follow, harmonizing as he sings to his woman. When the song's over, he leaves the stage to kiss the shit out of Maggie, and jealousy rips through me. I've always appreciated what they have, but I've never been jealous of it. I never thought I could have it for myself, so I didn't bother with wanting it. But then there was Hanna.

I start playing her favorite song before I realize what I'm doing, and when I lift my gaze to hers, she's looking at me, and I'll be damned if I don't understand a single emotion on her face. I should have seen this coming. She hasn't answered my calls or texts since our fight in LA. Then, when I got her message saying she hoped we could talk when I got to town, I assumed the best.

But she chose him and didn't even have the courtesy to warn me, and now she's looking at me like my mere existence confuses her.

It hurts too much to look at her. She's everything I want and can't have. She's everything I would turn my world around for, and I fucked it up.

So I refocus on my song and the lyrics she loves so much.

> *I'm nobody's hero, baby. Try not to fall too deep.*
> *I'm nobody's angel, love, but you were crying*
> *in your sleep.*
> *I'm useless, empty, nothing, sugar. Wait around*
> *and then you'll see.*
> *You thought you'd find your answers, but now*
> *you're lost in me.*

I wrote this song for Vivian before Collin was born. She wasn't in love with me. She was in love with the idea of me. And then she got pregnant and was tied to me—a man who was nothing like the man she deserved. Not so unlike Hanna.

My throat grows thick, but I swallow back the emotion and lift my head to watch her as I sing the last verse. I'm almost surprised when she keeps her gaze locked on mine—that same pain and confusion in her eyes that I saw earlier.

I end the song and leave the makeshift stage. I can't do this. I can't pretend I'm not in love with her. I can't pretend she didn't steal my heart and throw it away.

Up the stairs and out the back door, I find myself heading down to the river that runs behind Asher's house. I have to leave, because if I stay, I'll drink, and if I drink, I'll drag her into my bedroom and beg her to reconsider. If I drink, I'll break the only promise I ever had the courage to make to her.

To think I climbed into her bed last night, ready to promise so much more.

"Stop!" The sound of Hanna's voice stalls my feet, and for a moment, I dare to hope she's following me to tell me she's changed her mind. "Who are you?"

I wince and then turn to her. "Is that supposed to be funny? Pretending there was nothing between us wasn't enough? You need to pretend you don't even know who I am?" And *fuck fuck fuck,* this hurts. Did I really let myself believe it could work out differently? That she might choose me? That, for once, I'd be first choice and not the castoff?

"I—I don't know who you are," she says slowly. "But maybe I should? I was injured and I have amnesia, so I honestly don't know you."

What the hell? "Amnesia? You're kidding me." I take a step forward, remembering the bruises I saw at her apartment last night.

"I'm not." She holds up a hand to stop me. "I'd prefer you to stay over there. Please."

"Amnesia." Please God, let this mean she didn't choose him.

"Yeah."

"You don't know who I am."

"I don't know who you are or why you would crawl into my bed in the middle of the night. I don't understand why—" Her eyes fill and tears stream down her cheeks. Tears I'm desperate to kiss away. I just want to hold her, to whisper in her ear until her body relaxes in my arms. "I don't understand," she repeats.

"You don't remember anything?" God, what are the odds? "Do you know who you are?"

"Yeah. I remember everything up until about a year ago,

but the last eleven months are just…gone."

Which means every single moment with me is gone. I drag a hand through my hair and exhale slowly as I try to wrap my head around this new information.

"Do I know you?" she asks.

Better than anyone else in the whole world. "Yeah. You do." My chest is tight and my throat thick, but I take a chance and say, "I'm the idiot who's in love with you."

"But I'm engaged."

"I saw that." I look to her hand again, and again, that damn ring is staring back at me. But maybe… "Can I ask? Did that happen before or after the amnesia?"

Her tongue darts out to wet her lips. "Before."

Any hope her amnesia story gave me deflates just like that. "Fuck."

I hold her gaze for a minute, wishing her memories back. I need Hanna, my Hanna, whole, complete, and with her memories—if not for forever, then for the goodbye her injury stole from me.

I'm the one who looks away. "I've gotta get out of here, Han."

"Please, tell me what happened. What did I do?" she whispers. "I don't understand."

I shrug, but I don't look at her again. I can't. It's already too hard to breathe. "What's there to understand? You're wearing his ring."

When I rejoin the party in the basement, Asher narrows his eyes at me then looks at the stairs and back to me. He must have seen Hanna follow me out. I just shrug and head to the bar.

I've been seeing Hanna for three months, and the only people who know about it are Hanna, my sister Janelle, and Jamaal. I was just the rebound guy, and she didn't want anyone to know. I had no idea how much I could regret such a secret. Would she be engaged to Max now if he knew she spent her summer naked in hotel rooms with me?

I turn to the bar and reach for the tequila. I stop because

it reminds me of Hanna. Of the first night we met and the day we made love. I snag a beer instead and lean against the wall to drink.

A clean-cut guy in a navy dress shirt sidles up to me. "I'm Sam, a friend of Asher's," he says.

"Nice to meet you, Sam." He offers his hand. I shake it reluctantly. I'm really not in the mood. "Nate Crane."

"See that blonde over there?" Sam says, nodding his head to the side.

Liz, Hanna's twin, stands beside Maggie, sneaking glances at me and giggling. From the way she's looking at me, it's fair to say Hanna never told her about what is—*was*—between us. Never told her twin and best friend in the world. This should tell me something about just how much I meant to her.

"She's got her eye on you," Sam says. "But she's mine. I just want that to be clear."

I raise a brow. "Isn't that hers to decide?"

Sam just grins. "Oh yeah, and she will. Don't worry."

I shrug. "No problem, man." Not that I'd go near her anyway. Maybe some guys like that kind of revenge, and God knows that, if Hanna had her memories, nothing would hurt her more than my sleeping with her twin. But no matter how battered my heart, I'd sooner shoot off a testicle than hurt her like that.

Asher waves me back over to the stage, and I go reluctantly. Better if I don't let on about my broken heart.

"How about this," he says as I sit down.

I take the paper from his hands and study the lyrics. Then I grab the pencil and make some modifications. "I love it. Wanna try—" The words get lost because Hanna's on the stairs again, her eyes locked with mine.

She turns around and jogs back up the stairs as if she can't bear to be this close to me. When I look back to Asher, he's watching me. He saw the way we were looking at each other. He knows me.

Pretending the silent exchange between Hanna and me didn't just happen, I jot down the last line of the chorus and hand the paper to Asher.

He sighs. "Your lyrics suck today."

"Thanks."

His eyes go back to the stairs as if asking if Hanna's the reason, but I play dumb.

I have to get away from this fucking party, from Asher's knowing eyes asking questions I don't have the right to answer. I head upstairs to call Janelle, but my phone isn't in the basket where I left it. Before I can think where it might have gone, I spot Hanna on the patio, my phone in her hands, and I'm instantly moving in her direction. She's staring at the screen, scrolling through something, and I hope to God it's our text messages. I want her to see. I want her to remember.

Her cheeks are flushed and her lips are parted, and when she lifts her head, she pulls in this little gasp. It sounds so much like the noise she makes when I put my mouth between her legs that my fucking cock goes hard.

"See anything good?" I ask.

Her pink cheeks turn crimson. "Why would I risk everything?"

Right. Losing Max is the risk. Fuck. Nothing changes. "You'd have to ask your fiancé."

"You know why I can't do that." Standing, she pushes her chair back and lifts her chin. "I want to understand. I need you to talk to me."

"No, I don't." Because she's made her choice. What would come of rehashing our mistakes?

"You don't understand what this is like. Not remembering? I'm planning a wedding to this man I've wanted most of my life. Don't I owe it to him—don't I owe it to myself—to have the truth out there before we promise until death do us part?"

Planning a wedding. The words are like red-hot ice picks in my chest.

"I just need answers," she says. She steps closer, tempting me without knowing it. "I need the truth," she whispers.

"The truth? Is that what you really want, angel?" Suddenly, I want to give it to her. I want to put my mouth against her ear and describe in outrageous detail all the things I did to her body. I want to slide my hand between her legs and prove she still wants me—even if she can't remember.

I take another step closer, and when she turns away, I close the distance between us, trapping her between the house and my body as I lower my mouth to her ear.

"Do you want to know what it was like between us?" I ask.

"Yes."

I groan. "Should I start with how wet you were every time I touched you? Or maybe how you begged me that first night?"

"I didn't."

"Have you been telling yourself some wicked rocker seduced you? That I tricked you into my bed? Sorry. You asked for the truth. You begged. Right there outside the club, you begged me until I ripped your panties off and you were too busy biting my neck to talk anymore. Is that what you're hoping to remember? How you wanted me so badly you let me finger you out in the open, against that building where anyone could have seen?" I just want her to remember. I need her to remember it all and then look me in the eye and tell me she's choosing him.

She lifts her hands to my chest, but right when I think she's going to push me away, she curls her hands into my shirt, and I groan again because my control is hanging by a thread and threatening to snap.

I can't help myself and I put my mouth to her earlobe, nip at it with my teeth in the way I know makes her crazy. The crack of thunder overhead reminds me of our first night together, the way the sky opened up outside the club and we got soaked. Then, later, when I peeled those wet clothes off her and warmed her with my hands and mouth.

"You might have forgotten me," I whisper now, "but you still like dirty talk, don't you? And maybe if I made you come now, you'd still scream my name. Because you always screamed my name, Hanna. Never his."

She gasps. "You are horrible."

"What are you really upset about? That you wanted

me? Or that even as you stand here wearing his ring, you're secretly hoping I'll tell you about it. Secretly wishing you could remember all the details."

"I don't." She shoves me back then, and I'm grateful because I was seconds away from taking her mouth like I'm so desperate to. "Tell me why I did it," she says. "I need to understand."

Looking away, I fight to steady my breathing. What the fuck did I think I was doing? "I made you a promise," I say carefully. I'm reminding myself more than telling her. "I promised that when you made your decision, I would respect it. That if you took his ring, I wouldn't try to change your mind."

A promise I all but broke just now. And as much as I want her—need her—more than she'll ever know, I could never forgive myself if I stole the future she chose.

"I always knew you deserved better than me," I say, still not looking at her. "I hope he's worthy of you. I sure as fuck wasn't."

Only when my breathing is steady and I think I have the strength to touch her without losing my mind do I turn. I take her hands, meaning to retrieve my cell phone, and for three painful beats of my heart, my gaze snags on her lips and I indulge in the fantasy of one last kiss. She'd let me. I can see it in her eyes. She feels something for me, even without her memories. I want to tell myself that means something. If we have a connection without her remembering anything about me, doesn't that have to?

But nothing changes the fact that she chose him.

I take my phone and walk away into the night. When the skies open and rain pours down, I welcome the deluge and wallow in the memories it brings.

I'm sitting in the dark on Asher's front porch soaking fucking wet when Asher finds me.

"I'm sorry I bailed on the rest of the party." I offer him the joint burning in my hand, and he sneers at me.

"You're fucking kidding me, right?" he asks.

"Sorry." I snuff it out and slide the rest of the joint into my pocket. It wasn't doing shit for me anyway. Nothing can erase Hanna from my mind. "Didn't mean to piss off the straight-edger."

"This isn't about the pot and you know it."

I lift my gaze to his. "What's it about, then?"

"What's between you and Hanna?"

"Nothing," I mutter.

"I saw the way you looked at her tonight, and you're a terrible fucking liar."

"Better than an accomplished one, I guess," I say, parroting Hanna's words from the night we met.

"What are you doing?" Asher presses.

"I'm not doing shit. She chose him." I release a humorless chuckle. "And now, conveniently, she can't even remember me."

"Please tell me you haven't been fucking around with Hanna. I told you she has a boyfriend."

Yeah, he told me that the night we met, but it wasn't true. But that's Hanna's secret to share, not mine. "I believe he's now her fiancé."

"He's a good guy, you know," Asher says.

"That's what everyone seems to think."

Asher turns his back to me and looks up at the starless sky. The rain has stopped, but the clouds loom overhead, dark and ominous. "Did you know an anonymous investor set Hanna up with the bakery?"

"Yeah."

"It was Max. That's the kind of guy we're talking about here. The kind of guy who would sell his house and live in a shit apartment to give the woman he loves her dream. The kind of guy who would do it without getting any of the credit or the glory."

"Then how do you know?" I ask.

"I know people." Asher shrugs then turns back to me. "I'm not trying to be an ass, but I care about Hanna, and I want what's best for her."

"And you know that's not me?" That hurts. Especially from

Asher.

"Think it through for a minute. You dodge commitment, and Hanna deserves better than that. And even if you were willing to give her more, how's that going to work? Are you going to move to New Hope to be with her and leave Collin in LA?"

Resting my elbows on my knees, I lean forward and study my shoes. Asher's pulling out the logic I've been trying to make myself accept ever since I saw that fucking ring on her finger. Hanna belongs here, in this little picture-book town with its friendly people and quiet streets. And I belong in LA. Near Collin.

"Do you have any idea how much I hate being away from my daughter?" Asher says. "Three months in the summer, two weeks over Christmas and a couple of long weekends here and there—that's all I get until I can convince her mom to give me custody. You know I have reasons beyond Maggie for staying away from the city, but I don't see you making that kind of sacrifice for a woman. Am I wrong?"

"She chose him," I repeat, because—*fuck*—I don't need to hear this. There's nothing to figure out. She doesn't want me. She's wearing his ring.

And I have to find a way to be okay with that, because a big damn part of me knows she chose right.

FIFTEEN

HANNA

My apartment is a clutter of half-packed boxes, and my mind is a jumble of questions and missing memories.

When I walk into my living room, Nate is bare-chested and sitting on the couch with his bare feet propped on the ottoman. For a minute, I forget how to walk. My feet seriously don't recall the order of operations necessary to get me from this spot at the edge of the kitchen island to the family room coffee table, where I left my cell phone.

Because Nate. Because bare-chested. Because hormones eating away at all the functioning parts of my brain and leaving only the parts that want sex.

I don't know if his presence—his *body*—is evidence of a divine power that loves me or one that wants to torture me. My mouth is dry and my hands itch to touch, to trace the lines of his tattoos and the faint trail of dark hair from the center of his chest all the way down past his navel and into his jeans.

I've followed that trail with my mouth before, and sweet, sweet memory, I know what waits on the other side.

When I drag my eyes back up to his face, he's smirking at me. "See anything good?"

"I was going to ask you the same thing. And then I was going to ask you to please refrain from watching porn in my family room."

"Wanna watch with me?" He wriggles his eyebrows and spins his iPad so I can see the screen. Comics. Of course.

"How'd you get in here?" The question comes out with a squeak.

"With the key you gave me last summer. God forbid anyone see us together if I was in town, so you gave me a key so I could come in the middle of the night."

I draw in a ragged breath at the bitterness in his tone. *"God forbid anyone see us together."* I wonder if it occurred to me how selfish I was being. "Did you ever use it?"

"Once," he says softly. He sweeps his eyes over me in my robe and lets them settle on the knot tied across my growing belly. "I got off the plane from London and hired a driver to bring me straight to you." He sighs. "My phone was dead, so I used the driver's, but you didn't answer. When I got here, I let myself in with the key you gave me and climbed into your bed. Unfortunately, you didn't know who I was, and we both know how that ended. Frankly, if you would have given me that knee to the balls before, you probably wouldn't be pregnant now."

I bite back a guilty laugh. "Sorry."

He shakes his head. "No. I'm sorry. I shouldn't have assumed you wanted me there."

My legs seem to be functioning again, so I walk over to the living area and sit on the chair. He's filling in blanks for me, and I'm desperate to see them filled.

"Tell me what else you remember from those days."

Apprehension flashes across his face. "You'd called me in London. You'd left a message saying you wanted to talk. It was the first time I'd heard your voice since you'd left LA after our fight. You'd been ignoring my calls and my messages. The only reason I knew you were okay was because you were still talking to Janelle, and she assured me you weren't dead in a ditch somewhere. She said you were thinking. You were trying to make some hard decisions, and I needed to give you space.

At one point, she even suggested that she could fly out here herself and check on you if it would make me feel better. But then you left that message, and I thought maybe..." He shakes his head. "Obviously, I thought wrong."

"I would have had to leave you that message before my accident."

"Yeah. It was Thursday."

I lift my eyes to his. The day of the accident. Was I calling to tell him I was going to marry Max? "Why didn't you call me back?"

He stares at me a long time then blows out a long breath. "I thought it would be best if we had the conversation in person. And then it turned out you were engaged to him and it became a moot point."

He's silent for a minute, and then his serious face transforms to a smile.

When I realize his eyes have settled on the cleavage peeking out the top of my robe, I pinch it closed. "Sorry. I'll go get dressed."

"I wasn't complaining."

"Yeah, well..." I shake my head. "I'm not going to tramp around in my robes if you're going to be spending a lot of time at the house."

"So you'll move? You'll take the house?"

I've spent most of my day thinking about it, and I nod. "I can't deprive my children of that home when their father wants to provide it. It's not reasonable. And when I stepped back and thought about it, it makes sense that you'd want to stay there when you visit. There's plenty of room and there's no reason you can't claim one of the bedrooms as your own. I just wish you'd considered how you phrased it when Max was listening. I'm sure the idea of us *living together* was a slap in the face to him. We're friends and we're parents together, but we're not a couple. I want that to be clear."

"Crystal clear," he murmurs gently, so much the lion to the sheep.

I sigh and continue. "And when I can, I want to pay you

back for the house."

"Hanna—"

"Please." I'm quiet for a moment, trying to figure out how to explain it to him. "You are the father of my children, and I will let you provide for them, but I never want to feel like you're my sugar daddy, providing for his woman on the side." I drop my gaze to the floor because I sure as heck can't say the rest while looking at his bare chest. "And that's why we can't sleep together again. You can't move here. I get that. You'll visit as much as you can, and I'm sure you'll be an amazing father near and far. But if we make a habit of sleeping together when you visit, I'll just feel…convenient."

He pushes off the couch and comes to stand in front of me. My eyes are glued to his bare chest, so he tilts my chin up. "Are you sure you want to make that rule?"

I nod and meet his dark, smoky gaze. "I'm sure."

"If that's what it takes to get you to move into the house, I promise I won't sleep with you until you ask me to."

I snort. "I think I remember you making—and breaking— the same promise about kissing me."

A slow smile spreads across his face as he traces the line of my jaw with his thumb. "It's true. I'm pretty terrible about keeping promises that involve staying away from you." He lowers his mouth to my ear, and I shiver. "How about I just say that, when I touch you, I promise to make it inconvenient as hell." His mouth hovers over mine for a moment, and I can't think or breathe. Just when I've prepared myself for his lips, he steps back and grins. "I guess that means sleeping in your bed tonight is out of the question?"

I blink at him. "I— What?"

"Tonight? I'm not staying with Maggie and Asher. Newlyweds don't need me around. Do you want me in your bed or on your couch?" He drops his gaze to my lips. "I'll do *whatever* you want, angel."

"I—" I swallow. Then again. Because I *want* a lot of things. And he knows it. "The couch."

He rakes his gaze over me one last time before turning

back to the living room. "Sweet dreams."

MAX

I'm beating the shit out of the punching bag when Will finds me. He doesn't say anything, just holds the bag and lets me go at it until my knuckles ache from hitting and my shoulders burn from swinging.

"Wanna talk about it?" he asks when I finally admit defeat and sink onto the bench.

"He bought her a house. She's moving in with him."

Will exhales slowly and sinks onto the bench beside me. "Well, fuck."

And that about sums it up. It's not so much that Nate bought her a house. God knows that, with his money, he could buy her any damn thing he wanted. It's that she accepted. Her willingness to move in there proves more than she realizes.

"You bought her a bakery," Will says hopefully.

I grunt. "Not for long."

My lawyer emailed with details of Janelle Crane's offer, and not long after, the actress called me herself about it. I already know that, if Hanna wants me to take it, I will. I need to.

HANNA

The shower rains down on me, hot and delicious on my sensitive skin. Having Nate in the apartment with me last night was enough to make me lose my mind. I lay in bed waiting for him to come into my room, climb into bed with me, and whisper something sexy in my ear.

But he didn't. He stayed on the couch all night long, giving me the space I asked for, even as I wished he wouldn't.

Then we had a long day of packing and unpacking, moving

and organizing my belongings in the new house. Liz, Sam, Maggie, and Asher helped, and Cally and Drew took care of the bakery. Janelle helped a little, but she had to leave to meet with Max about her offer.

"You've got a really cool thing going here," she said. "I want to be part of it and never want you to feel beholden to some man."

"I don't feel *beholden* to anyone," I said, but in the end, I agreed that she'd be a less complicated choice as a silent partner and promised I'd talk to Max.

Though Nate and I were too busy to talk much during the move, I'd catch him watching me, and then he'd wink and rake his eyes over me in that way of his. My cheeks would burn and every cell in my body would click into overdrive.

My new shower is amazing. I relish the hot spray coming from three directions. I wash my hair and body, shave my legs—a task that's getting more difficult by the day—and then turn off the water. After drying my body, I apply lotion, giving special attention to my growing stomach. I spent most of my life hating my stomach and wishing it were flat, but now my round belly makes me smile. I'm more than okay with it. I feel beautiful with it. Is that because of how much I already love these babies or because of the way Nate looks at me?

After we got everything moved, Nate went across the street to Maggie and Asher's house. He and Asher are still working on songs for their collaboration, but he made me promise I'd call if I needed anything.

I dry off and dress in maternity jeans and a sweater before walking across the street. It's dusk, and my breath freezes as it hits the air. I knock and no one answers, so I let myself in. The house is quiet, and I assume everyone's downstairs. I head in that direction and find a tall, blond man standing in front of the stairs. It takes a minute before I remember how I know him. Fabio…er…Drake. Vivian's bodyguard.

Before I can ask where they are, I hear Vivian's voice floating up the stairs. "Please reconsider. I'll do anything to make this work."

Murmurs. Nate's voice. But I can't make out his words.

Drake crosses his arms over his broad chest and gives me a look that tells me what he thinks of my presence. "I thought you were marrying the other boy." His voice has the low, gravelly rasp of a pack-a-day smoker, and I think it's the first time I've heard him talk.

I frown. "When did I say that?"

He shrugs. "Last time I visited, you were wearing his ring."

"You ever think she got pregnant on purpose?" Vivian asks in the basement.

I gasp, and Drake says, "That's a private conversation."

"Right," I whisper. Then I turn to the door and hurry across the street to my new house.

Less than half an hour later, Nate finds me in the kitchen. I'm sipping a cup of herbal tea and trying to figure out what to do about what I overheard.

He grabs a beer from the freshly stocked fridge, pops the top off with a bottle opener, and joins me at the table. He looks stressed and frazzled.

"Rough night?" I ask softly.

"You could say that." He takes a long pull of his beer. "Collin told his mom that you're pregnant. She isn't handling the news very well."

"Oh." I didn't really expect him to tell me about his conversation with Vivian, but I like that he is. "What did you say?"

"That it wouldn't change my relationship with Collin. That I owe as much to these babies as I do to him." He picks at the label on his beer. "She didn't care, though. It's my fault she's reacting like this. I shouldn't have let her find out like that. I just wasn't sure how to tell her."

We sit in silence for a minute. I'm unsure of what to say. Nate's picking at his beer label, aggravation rolling off him in waves.

I clear my throat and nod to his beer. "You know they say that people who pick at their labels are sexually frustrated."

My attempt to clear the tension falls flat when he lifts his eyes to mine. There is so much longing and heat and desire in them that it nearly bowls me over.

"*They* have no fucking idea." His chair scrapes across the floor as he stands. "Goodnight, Hanna."

NATE

"It's a nice house," Janelle says, scanning the living room. "You seem at home here."

Hanna's out with the girls, and Collin's asleep with his head on my lap, his chest rising and falling with the steady breath of sleep. I brush his hair out of his eyes and study his face. He stayed with his mom in a hotel last night, but he'll spend the next week at Hanna's new house with me. With Hanna. Then I'll take him back to LA, where he'll stay for a few weeks before Janelle brings him out to visit again. And so begins our new life.

"How's Hanna?"

"She's okay. Exhausted from the move." I shift Collin in my arms and stand. "Let's get him to bed." I take him to his bedroom, Janelle walking ahead of me to draw back the covers.

We head back out to the kitchen, and I pull a beer out of the fridge for myself and pour a glass of wine for Elle.

"Max is letting me buy him out," she announces.

I raise a brow. "You didn't have to do that."

She snorts. "Are you kidding? That woman works magic in the kitchen. This is the best investment I've made in years."

"I have to agree. She's amazing. So, are you planning to move here to be her business partner?"

"Me? In Middle of Nowhere, Indiana?" She shrugs. "God, sounds nice, doesn't it? But no. I'm a silent partner. I don't imagine I'll be around much more than I would have been otherwise."

"Vivian found out about the pregnancy," I say.

She sucks in air through her teeth. "And how'd that go? I'm

half surprised she left Collin here with you. I'd expect her to get all Münchausen-by-proxy kind of psycho after that."

"What's that supposed to mean?"

She rolls her eyes. "Seriously? The woman would do anything to keep you to herself."

"I think you're wrong."

She gulps her wine and shakes her head. "And I think *you* are blind."

SIXTEEN

HANNA

Every cell in my body is exhausted. I never would have thought it was possible to be exhausted on the cellular level, but after making Christmas cakes and pastries for every freaking family in New Hope, I have zero energy left and every intention of peeling off my clothes and climbing into bed. When I step into the bathroom to brush my teeth, that gorgeous soaker tub stares back at me, calling my name.

A soak in Asher's hot tub would feel amazing right about now, but since that's off-limits with the pregnancy, a warm bath is as good as it's gonna get for me.

I turn on the water and wash my face and brush my teeth while the tub fills. I strip off my clothes and wrap my hair into a loose knot on the top of my head. I have to grin at the sight of my stomach in the mirror. It's hard to miss. I'm only halfway through my pregnancy, but I already get comments from strangers about how I must be getting close.

As I step into the tub, I actually moan in pleasure at the feel of the warm water on my skin. I turn on the jets and sink into the soft eddies of water.

Without my permission, my mind immediately fixes on

Nate shirtless and beautiful sitting on my couch, Nate winking at me as he helps at the bakery, Nate sleeping in the bedroom over mine. Suddenly I'm not so tired and my skin tingles in the whirling water, so ready for human touch.

NATE

I have developed this nightly habit of tucking Hanna into bed. She goes to bed early, and half the time, I find her under the blankets with a book before eight. Being with her like this—close enough to touch at all times but off-limits—is making me lose my mind, but if my mind's gonna go, I couldn't think of a better way.

I head straight to the master. It's later than usual, so I expect to find her asleep, her book on the pillow beside her. Her bed is empty, but I can hear the jets running in the tub on the other side of the bathroom door.

I knock softly. "Hanna?"

No answer.

I knock again, a little louder this time. "Hanna, are you in there?"

When there's still no answer, my heart kicks into panic mode and I'm picturing her asleep in the tub, sinking into the water and drowning. "Hanna?"

I open the door, expecting to see the worst.

Instead, I find Hanna soaking in the tub, the jets stirring the water around her. But it's her hands that steal my breath—one between her legs and one at her breast, pinching her nipple.

God, she's so fucking beautiful it hurts. Every day that I'm in this town and not touching her causes me literal pain, but seeing her like this—the pleasure on her face as her hips lift and she moves her finger inside herself—is the most delicious kind of torture I could imagine.

Her eyes are closed, and I can't make myself move any

direction but forward. I want it to be my hand between her legs, my fingers bringing her that pleasure, and my mouth at her swollen breasts.

Hanna's always been beautiful to me, but round with pregnancy—ripe with *my babies*—she's over-the-top gorgeous.

She shifts her hand between her legs, changing her angle. Her moan is so soft I can barely make it out over the jets.

I'm so fucking hard. My cock strains painfully against my fly. I need to leave. She doesn't want me here. God knows I've made it clear where she can find me if she's interested. But my feet don't obey, and I can't take my eyes from her. What is she thinking about? Who is she imagining touching her?

Max? Me?

She murmurs something. Was that my name on her lips?

I don't dare to hope, yet I hear myself say her name. I speak it softer than I did outside the door, but she hears me this time, and her eyes fly open.

Her lips part and she says my name on an exhale. If I thought she was beautiful before...*damn*. Her eyes are dark with desire, and little tendrils have escaped from her hair tie, curling against the smooth skin of her neck. Her breasts rise and fall with her breath, her nipples teasing the water's surface as she takes me in.

"You're so beautiful."

She surprises me by crooking her finger at me. I step toward the tub as she rolls onto her knees. When I'm near enough that she can reach, she tugs on my belt and pulls me another step forward until she's looking up at me through her lashes and her face is level with the belt she's pulling from my jeans. She unbuttons my pants and tugs them down my hips.

"Jesus," I hiss. But her hand is already sliding between my legs and cupping my balls in her palm as she wraps her other hand around the length of my shaft. "Hanna..."

Her eyes flash to my face briefly before she's positioning her mouth over me—taking me in and stroking me with her lips and tongue—and my hand knots in her hair and tightens because *Christ, that feels good.*

I spread my legs to keep my balance and watch her lips move over me, feel her tongue wrap around the underside of my cock. God, I've wanted this—needed it. Not the blowjob, but Hanna. Touching me, letting me touch her. When she adds suction, a growl tears from my throat and my hand tightens in her hair. Then she moans too, and the vibration sends a current of pleasure right through me, knotting tight and low in my balls.

The hand that was stroking the base of me falls away. She dips it into the tub and slides it between her legs and—holy fuck—she's stroking herself while she's sucking my dick.

My eyes want to close because it's good. So damn good. And knowing that doing this turns her on that much makes it all the hotter. But I force them open and keep my eyes glued to her—so fucking beautiful. And, for the moment at least, mine.

She pulls me deeper, moaning as she strokes herself, and my control snaps and I thrust my hips—once, twice—as she swallows around my swollen cock and I come.

HANNA

When I pull back and lick my lips, Nate's looking at me like I'm a goddess. Like I'm the most amazing woman he's ever been with or near.

"I wanted to make sure you were okay," he says.

"I'm not," I whisper. "I'm not okay at all."

He cups my face in his hand. "How can I help?"

"Sleep with me tonight," I whisper. I'm sick of being alone. Sick of knowing he's so close and feeling like he's so far out of my reach. "No expectations, no confusion. Just…stay in my bed."

Then his hands are under my arms and he's kissing me and drawing me from the tub. He takes his time drying me off before leading me into the bedroom. I climb into bed, but he doesn't follow. He stands beside it and trails his eyes over me again and again, finally letting them rest on my stomach.

I settle both of my hands on my slightly rounded belly. "Imagine how big I'll be by the end."

He laces his fingers through mine and moves my hands before he lowers his mouth to my navel. "So. Beautiful."

Goose bumps run across my skin under the ceiling fan. He explores me with his mouth—his hot, open, miraculously talented mouth—and trails kisses from my collarbone down my arms. By the time his mouth finds my breasts, my skin is warm and I'm impatient for more.

He cups my breasts in his hands, his lips parted, his nostrils flaring. When he places his open mouth over my nipple, it's with the same tenderness he used on the rest of my body, and it's good—so good—and still I want more. My hands go to his hair and I arch into the sensation. While he draws one nipple into his mouth, he caresses the other, brushing the rough pad of his thumb against the taut peak, and that swirl of warmth in my belly becomes larger, hotter, and more intense as it finds its way between my legs.

"Am I too big?" I ask.

He lifts his head. "Too big for what, angel?"

"I want you to make love to me," I whisper. Then, with a hand to my belly, I laugh. "I'm wondering if I waited too long."

He sighs dramatically and rolls over onto his back. "I guess I'll just have to be on the bottom, but you should know this is terribly *inconvenient.*"

Giggling, I follow him and straddle his hips. "I'm not sure if it's inconvenient or impossible."

He lifts his hips off the bed at the same moment he grabs mine, and in the next moment, he's sliding into me, and I gasp. "Nothing's impossible."

Pleasure knifes through me as I sink onto him, but I force my eyes to stay open. He's grinning, and that smile makes me feel like the most precious thing in the world.

"Inconvenient," he whispers, lifting his hands from my breasts, "but damn if the view isn't spectacular."

NATE

She's curled into me, eyes closed, her hair fanned across my arm, and I want to hold on to her forever. I'm afraid that, if I leave her bed, she'll forget how good we are together, and God knows how long it'll be before I get to touch her again.

"I don't forget to use condoms."

She lifts her head and frowns at me. "I think it will be okay. Unless you're afraid you're going to get me pregnant?"

I chuckle and smooth her hair out of her face. "I'm saying I've never forgotten to use a condom before. Vivian and I didn't, but she was on the pill and I was young and stupid and didn't realize how unreliable the pill is if the person taking it is flighty and forgetful."

"I don't blame you," she whispers. "I forgot too. And now that I have them"—she takes my hand and places it on her belly—"I wouldn't want it any other way." She giggles. "They always get so still when you touch my stomach."

I swallow. I haven't felt them kick yet, though Liz and Maggie have. "I don't forget," I repeat. "And I think some subconscious part of me was very aware of what I was doing the day I took you in the shower. Part of me knew I was risking you being tied to me forever. And that part of me would do anything to make that tie."

Her breath catches and she lifts her eyes to meet mine.

"I'm sorry how I handled everything that day. The truth is, I still don't know what our future together looks like, and that scares me. I'm afraid that, if I don't know exactly what's coming and how we'll handle it, I'll lose everything that matters the most. I panicked, and I almost lost you because of it. And, angel, you're one of those things that matters most to me."

"I panicked too," she admits, "because I was scared I wasn't good enough for you to give everything I wanted."

"I should never have gone to London." I wrap my arms

around her and pull her against my chest. "I should have tracked you down here and insisted you talk to me. Insisted we work it out. But I thought I'd already lost you."

"You haven't lost me," she says, yawning against my chest. "I'm right here."

I focus on her breath against my skin, the heat of her body curled into mine. I try to live in this moment, to let the here and now be enough. But as the minutes tick by, contentment remains just beyond my grasp, hiding behind a question I only have the courage to speak into the darkness. "Why did you choose him?"

Her only answer is the steady rise and fall of her chest in sleep.

SEVENTEEN

HANNA

I pad down the hall and up the stairs to his bedroom and find the door cracked. I knock softly before stepping inside. I pick up a shirt from the folded stacks in his closet and press it to my nose, inhaling deeply, taking a hit of his scent. There's a picture of Collin on the dresser, his big grin eating up his face as he points to his Captain America T-shirt.

I'm not sure what I expected to find in here. Pictures of Vivian? A journal confessing that he wishes I'd never gotten pregnant? Some evidence that I've made him feel trapped? I am so terrified of trapping him. But there are no answers here. Only his scent and reminders of what a good father he is that make my heart tug.

What would it be like to let this be real?

I sit on the edge of Nate's bed and bury my nose in his T-shirt. His scent relaxes me so much that I find myself lying down. Just for a minute. Just a little rest before I go to my own bed.

"Angel?"

The whisper pulls me from a dream. Then there's a hand on my face, someone stroking my cheek. My eyes are heavy, but I force them open. I see Nate before I close them again.

"What are you doing in my room?" I mumble.

"You're exhausted," he whispers. "Close your eyes."

I obey because it's too hard to wake up and sleep feels so good. As I drift off to sleep, I feel arms wrap around me, warm breath against my neck.

NATE

I wake to the feel of Hanna's soft curves in my arms, her firm, round belly under my hand.

She slides her hand into my boxers and traces the length of my cock, strokes the tip with her thumb. "I want to touch you," she murmurs. Then she cups my balls, causing me to draw in a breath with a hiss. "I want to put my mouth on you."

My sweet girl and her dirty mouth. I'm a goner.

She takes my hands and positions them above my head, wrapping my fingers around the slats of the headboard. I don't object. I would do anything to keep her in this bed with me, and if that means keeping my hands off her a little longer while she straddles my hips—well, I might die from wanting to touch her, but it wouldn't be the worst way to go. The tie on her robe has come loose, and from this angle, I can see the creamy skin of her breasts. She doesn't stay there long. Stealing my view, she scoots down my body and shucks off my boxers.

"Hanna," I growl. I miss the view and the heat of her against my cock. I release the headboard with one hand and reach for her.

She looks up at me from between my legs, her cheeks flushed, her hair wild around her face. "Behave," she clucks, nodding to the headboard.

"You're wicked." Then I decide I've never been any good at following her rules. Grabbing her, I pull her up my body and roll until I'm on top of her.

She grins. "I might be wicked, but you're naughty."

"Damn straight." I kiss her as my hands work to untie the knot on her robe. I kiss my way south until I've found her breasts. When I suck one pebbled nipple into my mouth, she moans.

"Maybe this isn't so bad," she murmurs. "Sometimes."

Lifting my head, I take her face in my hands and shake my head. "No," I growl, and her smile falls away. "I want more than sometimes and I want more than to be friends and parents together. I want you. Completely and always."

"What if we can't figure it out?" she whispers.

"We will," I promise, sliding my hand between her legs. She opens her thighs and lifts her hips off the bed. "We will."

HANNA

Three Days Before Hanna's Accident

I wait until Max leaves for work before I let myself into his apartment and lock the door behind me.

I head straight to his bedroom and the desk in the corner. Max is neat, and there are only a couple of stacks of papers on the desk—a meal and exercise plan for a client and some information about a new piece of equipment he has in the club.

I turn to the filing cabinet and start thumbing through files, not sure what I'm looking for. He wouldn't exactly label it "Secret File About Hanna's Bakery." But I find a file labeled *Smith, Peterson, and Frank* and pull it.

There's a copy of the agreement I signed when I agreed to start the bakery with the anonymous investor and some other paperwork from the lawyer, but instead of a deed to the bakery, I find papers from New Hope Bank and Trust.

My stomach twists painfully. It's bad enough to know that he sold his grandmother's house to get me the bakery, but knowing that he had to take out additional loans makes me sick to my stomach. No wonder he's been letting employees go in favor of putting in long hours at the gym himself. He's busy paying on the loan he took out for me.

For some reason, my gaze catches on a letter stacked neatly on the corner of the desk. It's addressed to Max, but the name of a local investor jumps out at me. I unfold it carefully, and my stomach sinks.

> *This letter contains the details of the offer we discussed over lunch. I think this deal could be beneficial for us both, and I look forward to speaking with you further.*

"No," I whisper. He can't sell his club. He can't sacrifice his dream for mine.

My phone buzzes, and I pull it from my pocket to see a text from Nate.

> **Nate:** *Heading to London. I miss you already. Been thinking a lot about our conversation. Call me?*

I bring my hand to my mouth to stop the sob that threatens to escape. When I was a little girl, I imagined that one day I'd fall in love with an amazing man and he'd love me in return. I believed love was enough to overcome anything. But love isn't like that. The heart has the capacity to love beyond anything my little-girl self could have dreamed up. And where I once thought love was a journey and the destination was being together, I now know that love is more like a state of awareness, and sometimes its best expression is in releasing the person from your life.

I read the text a second and third time and then delete it before I can torture myself with another read. The text disappears, but the history of our texts stays on the screen.

In one hand, my texts from Nate. In my other, the evidence of what Max has sacrificed for me to have my dream.

I hold my breath as I hit the commands on my phone to

delete the entire thread. Then I delete my entire call history, and just like that, my phone's memory of my relationship with Nate is gone.

HANNA

Present Day

"Hey, Hanna." Sam stands to greet me at the bank and shifts uncomfortably as I stare him down. "Is this about Liz?" He's really adorable in that clean-cut playboy-banker kind of way. His light brown hair is clipped short, and his strong jaw is shaved clean. Broad shoulders fill out his suit and tie.

"Not about Liz," I say, and he relaxes visibly.

New Hope Bank and Trust is where Max does all his banking—unsurprisingly, since one of his best friends will inherit the whole thing someday.

Sam motions to his desk, and I shake my head. He works out in the open, and I'd rather keep our conversation between us.

"Somewhere private?"

He nods and leads me into a little office where they talk to clients about loans and such.

"Why didn't you tell me?" I ask the moment he closes the door.

He cocks his head. "Tell you what?"

"When Max got the loan for the bakery, why didn't you tell me he was doing that?"

His smile is so fake that it wouldn't fool a blind person. "I don't know what you're talking about."

"Cut the shit, Sam. Why'd you let him do it? He sold his grandmother's house for a down payment, didn't he? Do you realize what kind of a position that's put him in financially?"

His jaw tightens. "Max is a grown fucking man, Hanna. He

makes his own decisions. He didn't exactly consult me before throwing the whole damn world at your feet."

"And you don't approve?" The question comes out too snippy. The fact is, if I'd been in Sam's position, I wouldn't have approved of Max's decisions to fund my bakery.

He shakes his head. "I didn't say that."

"He's in debt up to his eyeballs, and I came to you, didn't I? I see it in my planner. Before the accident, I came here and talked to you about what I'd found in his apartment. He was thinking of letting someone buy the club."

Avoiding my eyes, he nods. "You wanted to know how much he owed on your bakery."

"How much?"

"I wasn't at liberty to tell you then, and I'm not at liberty to tell you now. But I promised you I wouldn't let him sell the club. Will and I had offered to be partners before. I made sure he knew our offers stood."

"Is that all I wanted to know?"

He studies me for a minute before finally admitting, "You wanted to know if you had enough in your trust fund to buy out your silent partner."

Bile rises in my throat. "And what was the answer?"

"More than enough."

"That's why I decided to marry him," I whisper, though I've suspected it for a while now. Ever since I remembered finding that letter in his kitchen. "I was counting on a decision I made for all the wrong reasons and you didn't even warn me."

"I didn't know for sure, and you *were* in love with him." He rubs the back of his neck. When I don't reply, he says, "Max misses you, you know. He's just waiting around like some lovesick puppy, and if you decided you still wanted him, he'd be yours."

"I can't," I whisper.

"He would take good care of you. He loves you so much."

"I know that." My throat grows thick and I swallow back tears. "Is there anything else from before my accident that you think I might want to know?"

"Meredith," he says. "The day you fell, I was jogging on the trail behind the bakery and I saw you two arguing."

All eyes are on me when I walk through Meredith's salon and back to her office, but I don't care. For the first time, I'm taking Nix's concerns about my "fall" seriously.

Meredith's sitting at her desk, but her head snaps up at the sound of the door closing. "What are you doing here?" she asks.

If I expected her to act like the snotty Meredith who's tormented me most of her life, I was wrong. Instead of sharp, her voice is distant, resigned. Maybe months of rejection are starting to get to her after all.

"I want you to give Max custody of Claire."

She raises a brow. "The choices I make for my daughter's life aren't your business."

"If you don't, I'll tell everyone that you were at my apartment the day of my accident."

Meredith's face goes white. "I thought you couldn't remember that day."

"I don't have to remember to know what happened."

She drops her pen. "How's that even possible? No one else was there."

"Sam saw you there. He saw you push me against the wall and yell at me. Why would you do it? I know you hate me, but I never would have thought you'd try to physically hurt me."

She sits back in her chair. "Clearly you underestimate how serious I am about Max."

I gasp. Because even though I'm here, I didn't really believe Meredith was guilty. "So you pushed me down the stairs?"

She pushes out of her chair. "I didn't do any such thing. I came to your apartment and fucking *begged* you to get out of the way so I could have Max back. And, sure, I punched you in that chubby face of yours, but you had on his ring and..." She clenches her hands. She's sneering now, her hatred and disgust toward me evident on her face. "Whatever. You gave as good as you got. You gave me a fucking black eye, and then you ended up in the hospital and I had to leave town so no one would think I tried to kill you. And after all that, you didn't even want him." Her face crumples and she points to the door. "Get out of here. I'm sorry your fat ass couldn't navigate a simple set of stairs, but I won't listen to you blaming me for that."

"I can't believe I used to be jealous of you." I shake my head slowly. "Now I just feel sorry for you."

"Why? Because I'm a single mom? At least I'm not some whore who got knocked up with a rocker's babies."

"I feel sorry for you because you're ugly, Meredith."

She snorts. "Look who's talking."

"Oh, no. You're plenty beautiful on the outside. Anyone can see that." I put my hand on the knob and pull the door open. "But inside, you're as ugly as they come. That's why Max doesn't want you."

Her face blossoms red. "Get out."

EIGHTEEN

MAX

Brady's is crowded tonight. Everyone who's here visiting family for the holidays fills the bars to escape them.

I scan the crowd, but before I spot Will, Liz grabs my forearm and drags me to the dance floor.

I raise a brow as she wraps her arms behind my neck. "No offense, but my years of crushing on you came to an end when I fell in love with your sister."

She snorts. "This isn't about you, Max. Get over yourself."

I follow her eyes to the other side of the bar, where Sam is watching us with an uncharacteristic amount of jealousy on his face. "I see." Not that I'm terribly surprised. Sam's had a thing for Liz for quite a while. "So what's happening between you two?"

"Nothing." She closes another inch between us and leans her head on my shoulder. "He's not what I'm looking for."

I lock eyes with Sam and raise a brow in silent question. The fact that he shrugs and walks away is more telling than he knows. Sam's never been shy about staking his claim, but the way he feels about Liz has evolved over the last few months.

"Can you imagine what would have happened if it weren't

for Hanna?" she asks. "Would those casual dates have turned into something more?" She removes her arms from around my neck and shudders softly as we leave the dance floor. "No offense. It's just that, these days, you feel more like a brother than a potential screw."

That makes me grin. "Damn. If you'd told me two years ago that you saw me as a 'potential screw,' it's fair to say things would have been *much* different between us."

She groans, and Cally hands her a drink. "And then I'd be the one dealing with Meredith's bullshit."

"Yeah," Cally says, "and maybe *you'd* be the one with amnesia."

I frown. "What do you mean, she'd be the one with amnesia?"

"Oh, who knows," Cally says, "but there will always be part of me that suspects Meredith was the one who pushed Hanna down the stairs."

Liz shifts uncomfortably. "I don't think Max needs to hear your crazy conspiracy theories."

"The one who pushed her down the stairs? Are you saying the accident wasn't an accident? Are you saying someone pushed her?"

Cally's face goes blank. Then she mutters a curse under her breath. "I thought he knew."

"Knew what?" The women just stare at me, so my voice holds warning when I say, "One of you, tell me."

"We don't know anything for sure," Cally says. "None of us was there except Hanna, and Nix says Hanna will probably never remember that day, but the nature and extent of her injuries indicated foul play."

"Like someone pushing her down the stairs." *Jesus.* Why did Hanna never tell me this?

"And maybe like someone knocking her around a little before they pushed her."

Liz winces. I feel like the wind's been knocked out of me. Because I know who was at Hanna's house the night of the accident.

When Meredith climbs my front steps, I'm waiting at the front door, my arms folded across my chest. The days are short and the streetlights are already on even though it's barely seven. They throw just enough light on her face for me to see the confusion on her face.

"Where's Claire?" she asks.

"She's sleeping." I don't budge from my spot.

"Well, move over. I want to get her."

"I don't think I want her going home with you."

Her eyes flash with anger. "You can't keep my daughter from me."

"I'm pretty sure the police would have my back on this if they knew what you did to Hanna."

"I seriously doubt the police care about some stupid drama. I don't even think I care about it anymore."

"Assault doesn't fall into the same category as 'stupid drama.'"

"What the fuck are you talking about?"

"Hanna's accident. Her fall down the stairs? You went to her house that night. I know because you came to the gym afterward and mentioned you'd been there. Then you left town for two weeks. I'm guessing with a guilty conscience."

"The only thing I feel guilty about was not acting on my suspicions that she was cheating on you. I could see it in her eyes, in the way she was always mentally somewhere else when she was next to you. I only felt guilty that I'd screwed up too much for you to take me seriously when I told you about my suspicions."

"She never cheated on me."

"Just because she was keeping you in limbo about the engagement doesn't mean it wasn't cheating."

"We were broken up," I growl. She stumbles back and grabs the porch rail, so I soften my voice when I say, "No one knew, but we were broken up."

She blinks at me. "You deserve better than that."

I wave away her objection, trying to get us back to the point at hand. "You're telling me you went to confront Hanna and the same night she happened to fall down the stairs and get bruised up like someone was beating on her?"

"I'm telling you I'd never do anything like that, and you're a fucking asshole for thinking I would." She rolls her shoulders back and lifts her chin. "Now move aside. I want my daughter."

She pushes past me and into the house, and I let her. What else can I do? Claire is her daughter, and I have no evidence that my accusation is true. I can't quite wrap my mind around the idea of Meredith using her fists when she prefers words, dirty looks, and carefully crafted manipulations.

When I enter the house, she's buckling Claire into the car seat.

"You all deserve each other. You deserve Hanna and she deserves her cheater asshole baby daddy."

"What's that supposed to mean?"

"It means everyone knows he's still screwing Vivian Payne. Everyone but Hanna. Hell, if she just looked at the magazines from the week she was in the hospital, she'd know what he was doing in London. But, hey, maybe none of you care about something as silly as *fidelity*."

"Meredith," I begin, but she avoids my eyes and pushes past me as she takes our daughter to her car. "Please stop," I call.

She ignores me, climbing into the driver's seat and pulling away without a word.

NATE

The Day of Hanna's Accident

Hanna's curves slide under my soapy hands. Every sweet moan that passes her lips feels like my reward for the shitty parts of my life.

I step back to get a better look at her and the shower water changes to rain and we're outside the club in St. Louis again, but she's nude and there are cameras everywhere.

She mouths my name but no sound passes her lips. Those deep, dark eyes stare into my soul.

"I'm scared," I say, my voice hoarse.

She nods sympathetically and shifts her gaze to someone standing behind me. Two women appear, and she's in a wedding dress, crying tears I never meant to make her shed.

My phone rings and drags me from the convoluted dream. I force my eyes open and reach for it, but my hand connects with flesh instead of phone.

My head is pounding like a son of a bitch, but I force my eyes open.

The woman moans and curls into me.

Fuck, fuck, fuck.

I haven't slept with a woman since I met Hanna. She walks away from me, avoids my calls for five days, and I'm waking up with some strange woman?

I spring out of bed and drag a hand over my face. My head doesn't appreciate the sudden movement, and I have to catch my balance against the wall as I search my mind for answers.

The phone goes silent, thank Christ. I scan my mind for any remnants of memories from last night. I remember the concert. Then after, I found a pub and some tequila.

I was so fucking lonely.

I called Hanna and got her voicemail.

Stumbling across the room, I find my phone peeking out from under the nightstand on the opposite side of the bed. Seeing the notification light flash at me, I hit the button for my voicemail.

"Nate, this is Hanna." She sounds exhausted. The clock tells me it's noon here, which means it's seven a.m. in Indiana. "I'm sorry I missed your call last night. You must have been out late." Out and lonely as hell, thinking I'd lost her, wondering if I was being irrational. "Are you still coming to New Hope when you get back to the States? We need to talk, but I don't want to do it on the phone. Okay. Just…call me when you can."

I feel like I'm sixteen again, because all I want to do is listen to her message on repeat. Revel in the sound of her voice and dissect every word placement, every breath.

But I don't let myself indulge in the comfort of Hanna's voice.

I was lonely last night.

Then I wasn't alone anymore, because—

"Good morning, sexy." The woman in my bed sighs softly as she sweeps her eyes over me.

I close my eyes, unable to look at the evidence of what I've done after hearing Hanna's voice. I was wrong. I didn't go to bed with a strange woman.

"Good morning, Vivian."

MAX

Present Day

It's eleven o'clock when my phone buzzes with a text. I'm half asleep and consider ignoring it, but I grab it on the off chance that Hanna is texting or something happened to Claire.

> **Meredith:** *You need to come get Claire. I'm so sorry. I'm terrible at this. At everything.*

I frown at my phone and reread the message three times, willing my brain to clear from the fog of sleep. Suddenly, the *not-right* feel of the text clicks in my sleep-riddled mind, and I hit the icon to dial her.

Listening to the ring, I tug on jeans and pull a T-shirt over my head.

"Come on," I growl. I run out to the front of the house to snatch my keys out of the basket and slide into my tennis shoes. Her phone clicks over to voicemail, and I hang up and dial again as I run for the car.

The phone rings ominously in my ear. I start the car and head for Meredith's apartment to the sound of her voice telling me to leave a message. Ugly chills of foreboding wriggle up my spine.

"Pick up the fucking phone, Meredith."

Dialing again gets me the same results. The voicemail is clicking on again when I reach her door. Dropping my phone and keys on the table, I head straight to Claire's room.

My daughter is sleeping in her crib, her little belly rising and falling with the soft breaths of a restful sleep.

I tear out of the room and search for Meredith. Her bedroom is empty, but I find her in the bathroom. She's nude, passed out in a tub full of water, her chin and lips immersed and slowly sinking deeper.

"No!" I lunge for her. Grabbing her under the arms, I yank her from the tub and against my body.

Her eyes flutter open before I can check her pulse. "You'll take good care of her."

"What have you done, Meredith?" The words break, each a crystal dish shattering as it falls from my lips. "What are you *doing*?"

I carry her to the bed, and then I see it. A note placed under an empty bottle of pills.

> *Dear Claire:*
>
> *I wish you the best life…*

I grab the bedside phone and dial 911.

> *You are the best thing I've ever made, and I'm sorry I couldn't be—*

I throw it across the room, as if reading it makes what she's done real.

"911. What's your emergency, please?"

"I think she's trying to kill herself. I think she overdosed." I grab the bottle and read the name of the prescription painkiller to the operator, and then I give Meredith's address.

"Max," she whispers, her hand settling against my jaw.

Her eyes float closed again, and I hold her against my chest, my fingers on her pulse.

NINETEEN

HANNA

The shrill ring of my phone jars me from a sound sleep. I grope for it in the dark and answer without looking at the display.

"Hello?"

"Hey. It's Max."

I reach across the bed and click on the bedside light. His voice sounds funny. "What happened?"

"I need you to come watch Claire. I wouldn't ask, but it's an emergency and you can get here faster than my mom."

I'm already out of bed, looking for my clothes. "Sure. Of course. Your house?"

"Meredith's apartment. The complex on College, unit 302. They're taking Meredith to the hospital, and I want to follow."

"What happened?"

His breathing is choppy, like maybe he's been running or maybe he's trying not to cry. I can't tell.

"I can't talk about it right now, Hanna."

"I'm on my way."

I dress in the bathroom and am halfway to the door before I consider that Nate might worry if he checks on me in the middle of the night and I'm not here. When I return to the bedroom, a sliver of moonlight is slicing across his bare chest. My heart stops for a minute at the sight of him—strong and solid, yet almost vulnerable in his sleeping state.

I bite my lip, not wanting to wake him up but not wanting to worry him either. Finally, I decide to leave him a note, and I'm heading toward the kitchen for a notepad when I hear him shift in bed.

"I wanted to let you know I'm leaving. I didn't want you to worry."

He sits up and drags a hand over his face before grabbing his phone. "What's going on?"

"Max needs me."

"Want some company?" he asks, his voice that sexy, half-asleep rumble. "Or do you prefer to be alone when you sneak off in the middle of the night with your ex-fiancé?"

I ignore his insinuation and add, "For Claire. I'll— Why are you getting dressed?"

"I'm coming with you." He pulls jeans on over his boxer briefs and then tugs a T-shirt over his head. "I'll drive."

Ten minutes later, we're at Meredith's door. Poor Max is so distraught that he doesn't even notice or care that Nate is with me.

"She's sleeping," Max says. "She'll probably stay asleep until morning, but I need to go." His whole body is a knotted ball of tension.

I swallow back all my questions and whisper, "Go. Claire will be fine."

He pulls me into a hard hug then gives Nate a nod and is out the door.

"What happened?" Nate asks after the door closes behind Max.

"Meredith was rushed to the emergency room. I don't know anything else."

MAX

It's late evening, and she's settled into a room in the psych ward before they let me see her. Hanna has stayed with Claire all day and required no explanations—because that's the kind of friend she is. That's the kind of woman she is.

"Hey," I say softly as I walk into the room.

Meredith is in a hospital gown, an IV in her hand. Her face is washed free of makeup. I can't remember the last time I saw her without at least something on her face, and I'd forgotten that her lashes are nearly as blond as her hair. She looks so fragile, I'm reminded of the girl I loved as a teenager.

"You must think I'm a real idiot," she mutters, staring at her hands.

The truth is, I've felt nothing but guilt since they loaded her into the ambulance and I had to wait for Hanna to arrive. I read the note.

If I'd read it outside of the context of her suicide attempt, I would have seen its contents as self-involved melodrama. But in the context, I see what I've been choosing not to for months. Meredith isn't well. She's depressed and desperate and irrational. And I feel guilty as hell for not noticing the signs. Was I responsible for pushing her to this?

"The doctor said I have postpartum depression." She's still not looking at me. "Which pretty much proves that I totally suck at this mothering thing." She squeezes her eyes shut and tears roll down her cheeks, each one knocking down another piece of my bitterness toward her.

"Why would you say that?"

She swipes at her cheeks with the backs of her hands. "Don't pretend you like me just because you feel sorry for me."

"I think you've done some rotten things, but the way you mother Claire is not one of them."

She sniffs. "I just don't think I was cut out for this mothering stuff. I love her, but some days I feel like…" She stops and takes a breath, and I can't tell if she's shocked by what she was about to say or if she's simply trying to find the courage to say it out loud. "Like I sacrificed my own life the day she was born. And one hundred times worse than missing my life is how shitty I feel about myself for missing it."

"I can help more, you know. Give me custody, and I'll—"

"I was never going to fight you on that. I wouldn't keep her from you." She leans against the back of the inclined bed and deflates. "It's not about the time she takes. It's about not knowing who I am and feeling like no one wants me."

"Can I ask you a question without you getting upset?" I flinch at my own terrible timing. I shouldn't ask an upsetting question to a woman in the psych ward, but she seems like she's in a sharing mood, and I could never bring myself to ask before.

"You want to know if I got pregnant on purpose?"

I draw in a breath. "Yeah." More specifically, did she get pregnant on purpose in the hopes that Will would think it was his? But there's no need to complicate the question yet.

"I really didn't. I wasn't ready for that."

"I wish you would have admitted she was mine sooner."

She shrugs. "I didn't want to admit it to myself."

"Ouch."

"Obviously I was an idiot, and I've realized that now. It never occurred to me that, someday, you wouldn't be there waiting when I needed you again. Then, yesterday, when you told me that you and Hanna had been broken up all summer, I realized that you weren't refusing me just for her." She cuts her gaze to me and then drops it back to her hands. "You really don't want me. Just like him." She doesn't have to clarify for me to know that the *him* she's talking about is Will. This has never stopped being about Will. Not since we were teenagers.

"Meredith…" But I don't know what to say. I can't be with her, and I can't pretend things are different just because she's in here.

"Thank you for being here today, but I'd like it if you left now. I'm tired."

I cross the room, smooth her hair back from her face, and press a kiss to her forehead. "Let me know if you need anything."

HANNA

The only thing that surprises me more than Meredith's agreeing to see me is that I came in the first place.

"Hey," she says when I walk into her room. Her face is scrubbed clean, and she looks almost sweet. "Max said you came over to watch Claire. Thanks for that."

"No problem." I settle into a chair opposite her bed and try to pretend this isn't as awkward as it is. "How are you feeling?"

"Like an idiot. A big, fat idiot." Something like embarrassment passes over her face and she says, "Not that there's anything wrong with being fat or…"

I sigh. Because, really, I'm not fat. Not anymore. I'm pregnant and my belly is heavy with growing twins, but I'm not fat. Maybe I will be again some day, or maybe I'll be able to maintain a smaller size because I'll be spending all my time running after the twins. But Meredith will probably always think of me as the fat girl because that makes her feel better about herself. But the difference between the old Hanna and the woman who stands here today is the understanding that her impression of me has more to do with her than it will *ever* have to do with me.

"I don't like you," Meredith says. "That's never going to change."

The feeling is so damn mutual, but I don't say anything because she's the one in the hospital bed, and unlike her, I don't think saying it out loud is actually going to make me feel any better.

She scowls at me, and when I don't reply, she says, "You honestly have no idea, do you?"

"Why you hate me?" I throw up my hands. "I just know that you were the girl who tripped me in the bleachers at high school football games. You were the one who made *sure* I knew all my body's imperfections. I never did anything to you, and it seemed to me that my existence alone made you hate me."

"Never *did* anything to me?" She rolls her eyes. "My father *adored* you."

I blink at her.

"The American history teacher in high school?"

"I know who he is," I say, shaking my head. "I just don't know what he has to do with anything."

"He was an asshole, you know. Said the cruelest things to my mother, cheated on her"— she raises her gaze to meet mine—"with your mother."

"What? My mother would never—"

"Oh, but she did. She was grieving for her husband and raising five girls on her own, and my father was the shoulder to cry on." She releases a long, slow breath. "She didn't care whose family she was destroying when she slept with him. She didn't care how my mother would feel when he decided he couldn't be with her anymore because he loved Gretchen too much. It was all so inconsequential to her, and after tearing apart my family, she cast him aside like he was nothing. Like mother, like daughter, I guess."

"I didn't tear apart your family." I can't speak to her accusations about my mother, but this I know for sure. "You weren't even *with* Max when he started dating me."

"You know what I got to hear that year he was fucking around with your mom? You were in his history class, and I was out of cosmetology school and trying to build my client list. *'Why can't you be more like Hanna? Why can't you be smart like her? Why can't you be sweet like her? Why do you have to be such a dumb slut?'* You were everything he wanted in a daughter, and I was everything he was ashamed of."

"Meredith, I had no idea." Suddenly, all of her cruelty makes a little sense. It's not okay, and she's still a bad person, but sometimes badness is easier to take when you understand the *why* behind it.

"Because you're so self-involved you can't see beyond your own nose." She releases her breath in a huff. "Max and Claire and I could be happy, you know. If it weren't for you."

"You didn't want him, Meredith. You had your chance." But her words still burn because they're probably true.

Just like Vivian was right when she said I would be standing in the way of her, Nate, and Collin being a family. I'm not sure if I get a family of my own or if I'm doomed to ruin everyone else's.

"You're no better than me. Look at you, playing house with that rocker while Max just waits for you. You think Nate Crane is going to move to New Hope?"

My stomach turns sour at the question. I already know the answer, and just because I understand why he can't doesn't make it hurt any less. I want the guy who will turn his world inside out for me.

No. I don't. Max was that guy. What I want is *Nate* to be the guy who will turn his world inside out for me. And it's not fair for me to want it.

"You really think he ever stopped fucking his actress?" she adds.

"Don't," I growl.

"Whatever. *I* didn't push you down the stairs," Meredith says quietly. "I don't care for you, and I don't think you deserve Max, but I would never intentionally injure someone that badly."

I take a breath and nod, but I don't apologize. Considering all she's done and said to me, I don't think my suspicion was unreasonable.

"But I wasn't the last person there that night either."

That gets my attention and I look up at her.

She's frowning. "I only remember because I didn't know about Nate then, but I was convinced you were sleeping around on Max, and this guy came up the stairs."

"What guy?"

She shrugs. "He kind of looked like Fabio, I guess."

My breath catches. "Was anyone with him?"

She shrugs. "We were in your apartment talking—fighting—and then you looked out your window and the Fabio guy was out there. You said you needed me to go because you had company." She frowns for a minute. "I assumed you knew who it was. Actually"—she shakes her head—"I assumed it was your lover—whoever you were cheating on Max with."

"I have to go," I whisper, grabbing my purse. "Thank you for telling me."

"Hanna," she calls as I reach for the door. "You're lucky. Anyone who receives Max's love is lucky."

I face the door and close my eyes for a moment. "I know."

TWENTY

HANNA

"I need to talk to you," I say.

Nate's in his room, packing his suitcase. He's heading back to California for Christmas. It only makes sense that he'd spend Christmas with Collin since this is the last Christmas that he won't have to choose between his children.

He looks up from his luggage and grins at me. He's seemed so damn happy lately, and I'm about to ruin everything by telling him what I suspect.

He throws some socks into the luggage and opens his arms for me. "Come here."

I step forward and let him wrap me in his arms. For a moment, I close my eyes and revel in the comfort of his nearness, his warmth, and his scent.

"Nix has never thought I fell down the stairs."

Nate straightens and pulls back to look at my face. "What does she think happened, then?"

"She's always believed I was pushed."

I feel his whole body tense and his arms tighten around me. "Who the fuck would do that?"

"That's what I've been trying to figure out."

"Shit, Hanna. Someone almost killed you and you haven't said a word about it to me? What if they're still out there? What if—"

"I'm telling you now."

He relaxes a bit and pulls my head against his chest. "I'm sorry. I just can't handle the idea of anyone hurting you."

I swallow. "I knew you'd feel that way."

"Do you remember anything? Has any of that day come back to you?"

"Not really." I step back—out of his arms so I can look at his face while I talk. "But some memories from the days before have, and I think I know who pushed me."

He raises a brow, and I can tell he has no idea why it's taking me so long to spit it out.

"I think Vivian did it."

He actually smiles. Smiles. "That's funny. What else ya got?"

I shake my head. "I'm serious. She wanted me out of your life. She came here specifically to ask me to let her have a chance with you."

His face has gone deadly serious. "That's a far cry from pushing you down the stairs."

"Listen, I never thought about it until today, but when she was in town last time, I went over to Asher's, and you and Vivian were fighting in the basement. Drake was at the top of the stairs and he said that, the last time he saw me, I was wearing Max's ring. Which means they must have been here the day of the accident."

"Vivian didn't push you down the stairs. She wouldn't do that." He drags a hand through his hair and cracks a sardonic smile. "Christ, have you seen the woman? She's half your size."

I wince. "Thanks."

"Jesus, Hanna. Seriously? You're accusing a sweet, loving woman of a serious crime and you're going to take offense to a reference to your size differences?"

"You don't have any idea how hard it was for me to tell you this," I whisper.

"She didn't do it, so let it go."

"Meredith was here that day too," I say.

"Well, *there's* a more likely suspect."

"She said I asked her to leave when a guy who looked like Fabio showed up at my apartment." When he looks at me blankly, I say, "Drake. Drake looks like Fabio in his romance cover days, and everyone knows Vivian doesn't go anywhere without Drake."

"So you're saying Vivian wanted you away from me so badly that she came to your apartment and, when she saw you were wearing his ring, she pushed you down the stairs?" He shakes his head. "Come on, Hanna. That doesn't even make sense."

"I just know she wanted me away from you. She told me as much."

"Of course she did. Do I wish she wouldn't have come here and asked you to stay away? Sure, but that's not *that* unreasonable. She wanted me back. She wanted our family back together. That's no crime."

"No. But pushing me down the stairs is."

He rubs the back of his neck. "Let it go. Please. It wasn't her."

"How do you know that? How do you *know*?"

"Other than the fact that I've known her most of my life and I know better than anyone that she's not capable of hurting someone like that?"

"Yeah. Other than that."

"She was in London the day of your accident. She didn't push you down the fucking stairs."

"What if she just *told* you she was in London? What if that was her cover because she was really here trying to make me forget—"

"I know," he says, and his words are so quiet that I finally believe him. "I know because she was in my bed."

My heart plummets because surely he doesn't mean... *"You really think he ever stopped fucking his actress?"* Of course that's what I thought. Why would I have believed anything else when I was so convinced I was the one he wanted?

"What?"

"You'd cut me out of your life and wouldn't even talk to me about it."

"So you took her to London with you?"

"It wasn't like that."

"What was it like, then? You took my virginity, told me you wanted me to leave Max for you, and by the way, a future with you meant a life in LA with no kids. And then, while I went home to search my heart and figure out if I could sacrifice everything I ever wanted for you, while I fought every instinct that said I should be with you no matter the cost, you were in London with your ex, trying to make sure you really meant the very fucking little you promised me. Fuck you, Nate. *Fuck. You.*"

"You chose him, Hanna." His shoulders sag and he studies me for a beat. "He's the one you were so sure was right for you. I'm just the guy who knocked you up."

We stare at each other, and my heart hurts so badly that I expect it to stop working at any minute. The silence pulses around us like an angry, living thing.

"I have to leave. Collin's expecting me tonight."

"Nate…"

"I have to leave. You and I…" He shrugs, and I feel like pieces of my heart have fallen into my stomach and are decomposing inside me. "Vivian's always going to be part of my life because Collin's always going to be part of my life. And you will always be a part of my life too. We're going to figure this out."

"That's what you keep saying."

Nate leaves the room, suitcase in hand. I feel broken and empty.

I need to go to the bakery. With the holiday rush, I have plenty there to keep me busy, and if the simple chemistry of baking can't busy my mind, nothing can.

I head downstairs to change. I'm halfway down the hallway when I hear footsteps behind me.

"Hanna."

Then Nate is spinning me around and pressing his mouth against mine. I'm so scared this is goodbye. I cling to him as I kiss him back. Our mouths are open, greedy, and demanding, and when he pulls back, he wipes a tear from my cheek.

"I'm sorry," he whispers. "I'm sorry I couldn't let you go. I'm sorry I couldn't keep my promise not to fight for you. Maybe you'd be better with him. He's the better guy, but I'm the *right* guy and you're *mine*."

"What about her?" I ask. "Are you sorry for sleeping with her?"

He shakes his head. "I don't even remember it. I remember her showing up. I was lonely. I was pissed. I missed you more than I ever thought I could miss someone. She showed up in the bar, and I wasn't alone anymore."

"So you slept with her."

"I thought I'd lost you. I got drunk. And I woke up in bed with her."

"You slept with her," I repeat.

His eyes meet mine. "Yeah. I slept with her."

I nod, and hot tears roll out of the corners of my eyes. "Do you still love her?"

"Not the way I love you."

"Do you still love her?" I am a broken record.

"She's the mother of my son. I'll always love her."

Vivian was right. I'm stealing something from him by being in his life. Would he even be here right now if it weren't for these babies?

"Go to her."

"Hanna, it's not like that," he growls.

"I'm not walking away," I tell him. "I'm letting you go."

"The fuck you are. I won't let you." He squeezes my shoulders and presses his mouth to mine, but I don't open under him this time. I'm stronger now. If only I'd been stronger sooner.

"You are too good of a father to miss Christmas with Collin just so you can stay here and fight with me."

"Come with me." He shakes his head. "I'm not asking you to move. Just come for the holiday. Janelle will arrange for someone to cover the bakery."

"We both know I don't belong there."

"Don't do this, Hanna. I'm sorry I didn't tell you about London sooner, but I hardly had you. I couldn't risk losing you."

"Tell me something." I force a full breath into my lungs. "If you hadn't met me, would you be with her now?"

He pales. "Don't make me answer that."

The kitchen clock ticks, and on the street, a snow plow's blade scrapes the street.

"But we both already know the answer," I say. "Merry Christmas, Nate. Give Collin a hug for me."

I walk away from him before my strength dissolves, and I shut and lock my bedroom door behind me. Time runs away from me. Minutes, hours, seconds—everything is meaningless but the measure of his steps against the floorboards toward my room, the space of the silence as he waits by my door, and the creak of the front door opening and closing.

I don't change clothes and I don't go to the bakery. I crawl into bed, curl onto my side, and fall asleep.

My bed feels cold. Empty. I reach for Nate and grasp at air. Slowly, I reorient myself, remember the argument, curl into myself at the memory of his confession.

"I thought I'd lost you."

My stomach hurts—aches—with grief.

I gasp and put my hand to my belly, where the cramps that woke me are making my whole core ache. Not so different than the cramps I got with my periods, the pain is low in my pelvis and wraps around to my lower back.

"No," I whisper, but there's no one here to hear the word. I'm afraid to move, but I know I have to. I grab my phone from the end table and pull up my contacts list.

A sob lodges in my throat when I see Nate's name, but he should be in California by now. I scroll past his name and dial Nix.

NATE

Drake opens the door when I arrive at Vivian's and inclines his chin. "Collin's already sleeping."

I'm lunging for him before I know what I'm doing—pressing him against the wall with my hand at his neck. "What did you do to her?" Because Vivian was in London with me, but I have no idea where Drake was that day. I always assumed he was somewhere in London—he never strays far from Vivian's side—but he could very well have been in New Hope assaulting the woman I love in some misguided attempt to protect the woman *he* loves.

"To whom?" he grunts. He barely seems fazed by the fact that I have him against the wall.

"Nathaniel, what are you doing?" Vivian asks behind me. "Let him go."

"What did you do to Hanna?"

Drake lifts a brow and points to his neck, indicating that he won't talk until I release him.

"You were there the day of the accident," I say, and I back up because I need to know what happened. "You saw her with the ring on."

Drake rubs his neck and looks to Vivian.

She nods. "Tell him."

"When Viv went to London, I went to New Hope to talk to Hanna one more time."

"If you hurt her," I growl, "I'll fucking kill you."

"No, you won't," Vivian snaps.

"I didn't hurt her." Drake throws up his hands. "Why would I have wanted to do that? I was just there to find out what she'd decided, and she was wearing that local boy's ring."

I flinch. "Did she ever say why?" I don't want it to matter to me. It shouldn't matter if I have her now. But it does.

"She said that she loved him," Vivian says, talking for Drake. "That she wanted to marry Max, and it was her final decision."

I push past them and into the living room and collapse on the couch. My gut aches, and I feel like I'm seconds from losing the tequila I had on the plane.

"I thought you knew," Vivian says behind me.

I rest my head in my hands. Of course I did. She was wearing his ring. My own damn sister said Hanna was leaning in that direction.

"But I didn't believe. Jesus. I don't know why it matters so much, but I needed to believe she'd choose me."

"Maybe she would have," she says softly. "I did something terrible."

I stiffen. I've known since the beginning of this conversation that something was coming. "Hanna?"

She nods. "I didn't want you getting hurt. I'd never seen you like this. I was afraid she was just some money-grubbing, celebrity-chasing…"

When Viv's eyes meet mine, I can see I don't have to explain. She knows now that Hanna isn't any of those things. "What did you do?"

"I went to New Hope and informed her I was still in love with you."

"So I hear."

She chews on her bottom lip and shakes her head. "I told her she was standing in the way of a *family*. That if she would move aside, you would finally have the thing you want most. What you need most."

"When?" My voice is hard.

Her face crumbles and she shakes her head. "I'm so sorry, Nate. I didn't realize how good she is or how very much you love her."

"When was this, Viv?"

She shrugs. "Back in August. Before I met you in London."

Before the accident. Before she put on Max's ring. Before I fucked up.

"Fuck," I mutter, dragging a hand through my hair. No wonder.

"She's lucky," she says to her wine. "I would have killed to have you look at me just once the way you look at her."

"Why didn't you ever tell me how you felt? Years ago, before your marriage, before Hanna?" I wait for her to look at me, but she stays focused on her wine, looking for all the answers there.

"I thought you didn't love me. I thought the problem was *me,* so I pushed you away. You don't let people in. You know that? You and Janelle are so close, but you shut the rest of the world out. When I realized it wasn't just me, I thought it was too late."

"I never meant to shut you out."

"You changed last summer. You smiled more. You'd been living like a zombie for years and suddenly you were awake. You were happier, and I thought we could make it work." Finally, she brings her eyes to mine. "By the time I realized *she* was the reason, it was too late. Sure, I was still married, but mentally, I'd moved on with you."

"Dammit, Viv. I never meant for you to dissolve your marriage for me."

"I had to. If I was willing to leave him for you, I shouldn't have been with him at all." She takes a sip of her wine, and her sip turns to a long drink until the glass is nearly empty.

"Tell me what I can do."

"Give me physical custody of Collin," I reply without hesitation. "Let me take him to New Hope to live with me."

She draws in a shaky breath. "I won't have half the country between me and my son."

"Don't make me fight you, Viv. I've learned the hard way I need to fight for what I want—for who I love."

HANNA

"The good news," Nix says as she scans the monitors beside the bed, "is that the medicine made the contractions stop."

I stare at the monitors, unsure what they all mean but too scared that, if I look away, they'll stop their beeping and wiggling and something terrible will happen to my babies.

"What's the bad news?" I whisper.

Liz squeezes my hand.

When I called Nix, she told me to have Nate drive me to Labor and Delivery. I called Liz and had her bring me. I don't think she's taken a full breath since we arrived. She's not the only one.

"The bad news," Nix says, "is that you're a centimeter dilated and you're looking at bed rest for the remainder of your pregnancy."

I dare to take my eyes off the monitors to look at Nix. "Bed rest? That's it?"

Nix sighs. "Well, this will all be up to your perinatologist, so it's just speculation on my part, but I imagine they'll keep you here to monitor you for a couple of days. If the medicine appears to be working and keeping your contractions at bay, they'll continue with it, put you on strict bed rest, and keep a careful eye on you. We want those babies to stay in there as long as they can."

The room is tense with the words she's not saying: the prognosis for twins born at twenty weeks' gestation is not a good one.

Liz looks like she might lose it and start crying any minute. "Do you think this is because of her fall?"

"I don't know," Nix says. "But that's highly unlikely. If that fall was going to create a problem, I imagine we would have seen it early on. Or we would have never known about the pregnancy."

My eyes are back on the monitors, but I feel Nix's hand on my shoulder.

"Try not to worry too much about why. Just rest. And get a hold of Nate. He'll want to know."

She shuts off the lights on her way out and leaves Liz and me in the glow of the light trickling in from the bathroom.

"Do you want me to call him?" Liz asks.

I shake my head, but I don't mean no. I just mean that I don't know. He's in California to spend Christmas with Collin, and I don't want to ruin that.

"He's upset with me," I finally admit. "I told him I thought Vivian pushed me down the stairs. And he told me she couldn't have because she was in London." I swallow. "In bed with him."

Liz gasps and chokes a little, and when I turn my head to look at her, her face is red and splotchy and she's crying.

"It's okay," I say. "I don't blame him."

She shakes her head. "I didn't know you really believed someone pushed you."

I shrug. "I don't know what I believe anymore."

"No one pushed you," she whispers. "Not intentionally at least." Then she sinks to her knees and rests her head on the side of my bed. "I'm so sorry."

"Liz?" Panic lodges in my throat. "Liz, what's wrong?"

"I'm so sorry," she repeats. "You're the most important person in my world, and I would never hurt you on purpose."

Oh my God. "What happened, Liz?"

She lifts her head and draws in a ragged breath. "The day of the accident, Sam called me and said you'd met with him. He said he was worried about you and that maybe you were about to rush into a marriage you weren't ready for." She pushes herself off her haunches and paces the room. "Of course, I didn't know anything about Max proposing at the beginning of the summer, and the idea of you getting married was new to me. And terrifying. You'd pulled away from me completely. You'd become a shell of your former self—exercised-obsessed and quiet and secretive—and in my mind, that was all associated with Max. I thought he made you like that. I thought that, if you married him, I'd lose you forever."

I force myself to steady my breathing. I know what's coming.

"I came up to your apartment to see if what Sam said was true and to try to talk you out of rushing into it. You met me on the balcony and you had a puffy lip and a swollen eye. You wouldn't tell me what those were from, and you were wearing the ring." She stops pacing and lifts her eyes to mine. "I demanded that you take it off. I'm your twin sister, and I didn't even know he'd proposed, and you were wearing his ring, telling me that I needed to trust you. You were doing the right thing, you said. But to me, it was all wrong, and I wanted my sister back. I tried to take the ring off you myself. I was desperate. I felt like it had you under some spell or something and if I could get it off your finger…"

"And I didn't want you to take it," I say softly.

"I don't even know how it happened. I had your hand and you were yanking away from me, and you told me to let go, said I was hurting you, and I did. But your back was to the stairs and somehow you lost your balance and fell." Tears spill down her cheeks. "I called 911 and got you to the hospital, and it was so much more terrible than I ever would have imagined a fall like that could be. I was terrified I was going to lose you. And then, when I didn't, I couldn't bring myself to tell you the truth because I finally had my sister back. I am so sorry."

"It was an accident, Liz."

"It was my fault."

"It was an *accident*," I repeat. But my mind is spinning and I wonder what would have happened if I hadn't taken that fall. Was I planning on telling Max about Nate? And when would I have learned about the pregnancy?

"Can I get you anything?" she asks. "Anything at all? Should I call him?"

"Don't call Nate."

"He'll come," she says. "He loves you."

I nod, and a salty tear runs into my mouth. "He does."

What was it he said to me the day we made love? *"I love*

you, and I'm afraid you're going to ruin your life because of it."
Turns out, it wasn't my life he needed to worry about.

TWENTY-ONE

MAX

She looks terrified and she's staring at the babies' heart-rate monitors like their hearts might stop beating if she turns away.

"She's doing great," Liz says, patting Hanna's arm. "No more contractions since they started her on the meds. Babies are healthy and strong. Now we just have to keep them cooking for a while longer."

"Have you called Nate?" I ask Hanna.

Liz speaks before Hanna can reply—or maybe she just knows she won't. "He's spending Christmas with his son."

"He can't be in both places at once," Hanna murmurs, almost to herself.

Liz frowns, exhaustion marking her features, but she pats Hanna's arm again. "He'd be here if he knew. Someone's being stubborn."

"Have you been here all day?" I ask Liz.

She nods. "It's no big deal. She's my sister."

"Take a break. I'll stay with her for a while. She won't be alone."

Relief lightens her smile. "Thanks."

"I'm so scared," Hanna whispers when Liz is gone. "I don't know if I can do this."

I sink into the chair between her bed and the monitors so she'll see me while we talk without having to take her attention completely off the graphs of the babies' heartbeats. "Everything looks good. They can do amazing things to stop preterm labor."

"It's not that. It's that I don't know the first thing about being a mom."

Taking her hand, I squeeze her fingers. "You're going to be amazing."

"I'm scared to do this alone."

"You won't be alone. We're all here for you. You know that."

A tear escapes her eye and rolls onto the pillow. "I'm so sorry for what I put you through."

My heart squeezes so hard and tight and painful that I can hardly breathe. "Hanna…"

"I am. You sacrificed everything for me, and how did I repay you? By doubting you? By stringing you along? By falling in love with another man? Will you ever be able to forgive me?"

"I will." I sigh and shake my head. "I already have."

"You, Maximilian Hallowell, are an amazing man, and someday, you're going to make some lucky woman very happy."

"You just say the word and it can be you." I don't even care that I sound desperate. It's the truth, and I need to know she understands.

"I'm in love with Nate," she says simply.

"Are you going to be with him? You deserve commitment, marriage, happily ever after."

"I don't know." She lifts her eyes to meet mine, and there's more determination there than I've ever seen. "But what will or won't happen doesn't change that my heart is his, and I never should have asked you to settle for me when I knew that was true."

"For me, it wouldn't have been settling."

HANNA

"Wowee!" Granny says, cocking her head at Liz. "You are so conflicted. If you could see your aura now."

Liz rolls her eyes. "I'm going to go clean up dinner."

"I'll help," Maggie says.

Mom looks at me. "Let's get you back to bed."

They let me out of the hospital this morning, and Mom insisted we hold Christmas Eve dinner at my house. I didn't even object. The idea of spending Christmas alone and stuck in bed is miserable. If I can't have Nate, all I want is to be by my family.

Liz and Maggie take stacks of dishes into the kitchen and quietly begin cleaning up, and Mom helps me out of the recliner they dragged into the dining room for me.

"I want to go to the living room," I tell her.

She props me up on the couch, positioning pillows to make it more comfortable. Then she sits in the chair across from me.

"Mom, I need to confess something," I say after a long silence.

"The only one you need to confess to is Jesus, Hanna, but you go down and talk to Father Douglas, and I have no doubt you'll find the forgiveness you seek."

I stifle an eye roll and take a deep breath. "I never wanted to marry Max for the right reasons. A girl should put on a man's ring when she knows he's the one she wants to be with. But I wasn't thinking about who *I* wanted. I was just trying to find a way that everyone could be happy."

"That sounds like you," she says with a sigh. She picks up her bag from beside the chair and pulls her latest knitting project from it. "I just hate to see you alone."

I want to tell her that I'm not alone. That I have Nate. But I'm not sure I'm okay with sacrificing his happiness for my own.

"Did you sleep with Meredith's dad?"

Mom's hands freeze in the middle of a stitch, and I have to remind myself to breathe while I wait for her answer. She starts working again without looking at me. "I never cheated on your father. Malcolm and I were friends." She sighs and finally lifts her head to meet my eyes. "You girls think I'm crazy for wanting you to get married, but you don't know how difficult it is to live in this world without a man."

I cross my arms and wait for her to finish, but my stomach hurts.

"I miss your father so much," she whispers, and her eyes fill with tears. "Not only because he was my husband and the father to my children. He took care of things. Life was so much easier when he was around, and when he left, I didn't know how to do anything. I'd never paid the bills or balanced the checkbook. I'd never changed my own wiper blades. I never realized just how much your father took care of me until he was gone, and Malcolm was a friend, and he helped me with those little things. I had no idea he thought our relationship was more than friendship until he left his wife. And we tried for a while, but then I saw his true colors and…" She sighs. "Good men aren't so easy to find, you know."

"Mom, if you didn't know how to do any of those things, wouldn't you want your daughters to wait on marriage? To be single and independent for a while first?"

She gives me a hard look then stands to take my hand in hers. "*Single* and *independent* are words women use to make themselves feel better about being *lonely* and *overwhelmed*. I want all of my girls to marry a good man and have a good life. I don't think that makes me a bad person."

"We can't just marry anyone and have what you had with Dad," I say softly.

Her smile is sad, a little hopeful. "But Max would give you that. You'd never be alone and you'd always have someone at your side to help you through the tough days."

"I already have lots of people to help me through the tough

days." I shift our hands so mine is squeezing hers, and her shoulders rise on her inhale. "And I count you among them."

She drops her gaze to our joined hands. "I know I'm far from perfect. Some days, I feel like I've failed each of you girls in a different way."

"You didn't *fail* me, Mom. I just…"

"You just felt like I wouldn't love you if you weren't thin. That sounds like a failure to me."

"No," I say firmly. "I knew you'd always love me. You pressured me to lose weight, to be thin, that's true. But I knew you wanted the best for me, and I never doubted that you loved me."

She sniffs and forces a smile. "If you want to raise these babies on your own, I will support you. Whatever you need, whatever my grandchildren need. You just say the word."

I don't reply because my eyes are glued to my open front door, and the tall, dark-haired man with a little boy in his arms.

NATE

"Hanna!" Collin calls when he spots her. I put him down, and he scurries across the foyer and into the living room. "How are my sibwings?"

"Sib*lings*," I correct, but then I close my mouth because Collin's gently cupping his hands over Hanna's rounded belly, and the vision brings me more joy than I can fit in my heart. She's lying on the couch, propped up with pillows behind her head and under her hips, and I want to scoop her into my arms and hold her close.

"They're good, Collin," Hanna answers, her eyes on me. "Did Liz call you?"

"No." I shed my coat and walk into the living room to crouch down beside my son.

"Max?" she asks.

"No."

Her breath catches as I place my hands next to Collin's. As if in greeting, a baby kicks, then the other.

"I feel them!" Collin says with wide eyes.

I lift my eyes to Hanna's and a smile stretches across my face. "Me too."

"Who told you, then?" she asks. "Why are you here?"

"I'm here because I want to spend Christmas with the woman I love."

At the sound of a sharp inhale, I tear my eyes away from Hanna's face and look up at her mother.

"You two need a minute," she says. She offers her hand to my son. "Collin, is it? You want to see if we can find any Christmas cookies in Hanna's kitchen?"

"Yeah!" He takes her hand, and Hanna's mom winks at me as they leave the room.

"I started having contractions the night you left. But I went to the hospital, and they put me on medicine to make them stop."

Her admission robs me of my breath, and I rest my cheek on her stomach. "Why didn't you call me?"

"I should have. I'm trying to figure out how to ask for what I need." She shakes her head. "I'm not very good at it. I've spent my whole life trying to make everyone else happy, and I'm starting to think that's not healthy."

I raise a brow. "Ya think?"

She shrugs. "The only reason I was in St. Louis the night we met was because I knew Maggie wanted me there. So it's not a terrible trait."

I brush her hair behind her ear. I want to kiss her, to hold her until the racing in my chest subsides and I know she's okay. "Not terrible," I agree. "But you aren't always so good at knowing what makes people happy."

"What do you mean by that?"

I draw a finger down her jaw, count the freckles across the bridge of her nose, memorize the exact shade of the pink of her lips. "You asked me if I would be with Vivian if I'd never met you. And the answer is *yes*. I'm sure I would be."

"Oh," she whispers. "I guess I knew that already."

"But, you see, you didn't ask the right question. Ask me if I would be happier if I'd never met you, Hanna. Ask me if a life with Collin's mother would have made me feel alive the way loving you makes me feel. Ask me if I'd take back our time together, even if you'd chosen Max."

I lean my head against hers, and she swallows so hard I can hear it. "I only thought everyone would be happier if I married him."

"Would *you* have been happier?"

She shakes her head. "No. Anyone paying attention would know you're the one for me. I gave you what I would never give Max—and not just my body. I trusted you like I never trusted him, needed you like I never needed him. I chose him for everyone but myself, but I *wanted* you."

She doesn't say any more because I'm kissing her—my mouth open over hers, my hands in her hair, my heart hers to keep.

I want to hold her until there's nothing in the world but us. I want to chase away the ugliness and protect her from any more hurt. But I know I can't, so I pour all of my love and hope into this one kiss.

She lifts slightly off the couch, her hand grazing my chest. "I feel empty when you're gone."

I cup her face in my hand and kiss her again. She's so damn sweet and perfect, and I love the feel of her tongue against mine, the way she moans into my mouth when I deepen the kiss.

"Hey now!"

Liz's voice pulls me from the kiss, and I lift my head to glare at her.

"The doctor very clearly said no shopping, no sports, no *sex*. Orgasms are an even bigger no-no, so stop while you're ahead."

I look to Hanna, who nods. "It's true. No sex until it's safe for the babies to be born."

I cock a brow and say, "Looks like Aunt Liz is going to

need to do a lot of babysitting so we can make up for lost time after they're born."

Hanna smacks me in the chest, but she's grinning.

"I'd be happy to," Liz says.

"Me too," another woman calls. The petite brunette steps into the room and offers me her hand. "I'm Hanna's oldest sister, Krystal. Nice to meet you."

I shake her hand and nod. "Nice to meet you too."

"Krystal lived in Florida for a while," Hanna explains, "but she just moved back home, and she's going to run the bakery for me while I'm on bed rest. Then, when the babies are old enough for me to go back, she's going to run the front for me."

"I'm tough to replace," Liz says, "but seeing as how Krystal doesn't loathe mornings like I do, she might be a better fit."

One by one, everyone joins us in the living room, talking and laughing around the Christmas tree. After putting Collin to bed upstairs and promising him that Santa will know where to find him, I sit on the couch with Hanna's head in my lap and her family gathered around us. No wonder she didn't want to leave this place. It's warm and loving and comfortable. It's home.

HANNA

I hear the television click off, and when I open my eyes, my head is in Nate's lap. "Did everyone leave?"

"A couple of hours ago." He's watching me, tenderness in his eyes. He tucks a lock of hair behind my ear and strokes my cheek.

"What are you looking at?" I ask quietly.

"My angel. My heart."

My throat grows thick. "I love you." Tears spill onto my cheeks as his hand settles on my belly. "I love you so much."

"Let me live here with you."

"You don't have to do that. We'll make it work. Somehow."

I swallow. "Like you said, we'll figure it out."

"Yeah, but I'm a selfish bastard who gets what he wants. I want to live here with you. I want to marry you and raise these babies by your side." He traces my lips with his thumb. "I want to make love to you every night and cook for you. Say yes," he says softly, and his Adam's apple bobs as he swallows hard. "Say you'll marry me and be my family."

My chest aches with hope and happiness and...guilt. "What about Collin?"

He looks to the stairs then back at me. "He likes the room he's sleeping in tonight, though, to be fair, it won't look nearly so tidy when we move his toys in." He smiles. "Vivian doesn't want to raise him in LA, so I've asked her to raise him here."

"And she agreed?"

He shrugs. "Not at first—she really is very jealous of you— but Drake talked her into it. Collin loves it here. He loves seeing Asher and playing by the river. She knows it would be good for him. She's going to start looking to relocate to Indiana after the holidays."

"Wow. That's amazing."

"You still haven't answered me, woman."

I grin. "I made a promise to myself that I wouldn't rush into any engagements until after the babies are born. But you have my permission to ask again then."

"That's fine," he says. He presses a kiss to my ear then whispers, "As long as you're planning on saying yes."

TWENTY-TWO

MAX

Meredith closes Claire's bedroom door softly behind her as she joins me in the living room. She's dressed for work in a tight black skirt and bright-colored, cleavage-showing sweater. Her hair is styled sleek and smooth, and her makeup is applied with its usual attention. But she looks tired. Drained.

The emotional exhaustion I see in her eyes slingshots me back to our teenage years, when she hid her hurt from the world and I thought I could save her.

"Come here," I whisper, opening my arms.

Her face crumples and she runs into my arms and buries her face in my chest. She wraps her arms tightly around my back, and I can't tell if she's crying or just breathing me in.

I run my hand over her hair and sigh. "I'm sorry I accused you of pushing Hanna. When I think of someone trying to hurt her, I lose my mind a little."

She pulls out of my arms and looks at the floor. Her tears left smudges of eye makeup under her eyes. "I kind of earned it by being such a bitch. I just couldn't accept that you'd rather be with her than me."

I tilt her chin up so she's looking at me. "And you'd rather be with William Bailey than with me." When she flinches, I add, "What if I told you we could be together and the next day Will said *he* wanted to be with you. Be honest here, Mer. You'd drop me in a second." She doesn't deny it, and I sigh and pull her against my chest again. "You deserve to be head over heels for the guy you end up with. And he should be head over heels for you. Don't settle for someone because you don't want to be alone."

"I don't know how to be head over heels for anyone but Will," she whispers. "And guys don't love me like that. You're the only one who ever did, and now you hate me."

"You've pissed me off enough times, but I don't hate you. I couldn't."

She tilts her face to mine and her gaze locks on to my lips.

Once upon a time, these were my favorite moments with Meredith—the moments when she dropped her defenses and let me in. And if I hadn't changed, I would drop my mouth to hers and kiss her softly. She'd turn it wild before I'd gotten my fill of her taste, and we'd end up naked and sweaty on the couch.

But I'm not that guy anymore, so I kiss her cheek before stepping back.

"Still holding out for Hanna?" she asks, but there's no sign of the bitterness that usually infects her voice on the topic of my once-fiancée.

"That ship's sailed, unfortunately."

"Maybe not. She's not in any rush to commit to the rocker, so there may be a chance for you two."

I collapse on the couch and lean against the headrest so I'm looking at the ceiling. "I don't think so. I think some relationships start out wildly unbalanced and they're doomed to try to survive on this rickety teeter-totter. That's the way it was for Hanna and me. I was always trying to make up for the beginning of our relationship—for not wanting her at the beginning, for dating her for the wrong reasons and taking so long to realize how great she was. We were off-balance from the start, and I spent every day of our relationship trying to catch my balance so I wouldn't lose her."

Meredith sinks onto the couch beside me and rests her head on my shoulder. "You mean by doing things like buying her a bakery you really couldn't afford?"

"Yeah. Like that." My stomach aches to admit this. "I think I knew I was losing her even before you shared those texts with her. She always held back part of herself, and she was so good and sweet I was greedy for her to let me in, even in those moments when things were good. Then you sent her those texts, and it's been wildly teetering ever since."

She stiffens beside me. "Will you ever be able to forgive me for that?"

"It was a really bitchy thing to do. It hurt Hanna and it hurt me." I wrap my arm around her shoulders. "And I think it hurt you too."

"I know my depression isn't an excuse, but I really wasn't seeing clearly. I'd like to think I wouldn't have done anything that terrible if I'd been in my right mind."

"You're going to spend the rest of your life alone if you keep acting like that," I say softly. Not to be an ass, but she needs to know. "Every bitter, angry thing you do and say alienates you a little more."

"And makes me a little more like my father." The words are so quiet I probably wouldn't have made them out if I weren't thinking the same thing.

"Go to Paris. Start fresh. Be the Meredith *I* knew. The one who'd sneak into bed with me and whisper about her dreams for the future."

"I don't know what happened to her."

"So find her. Who knows? Maybe you'll meet the love of your life in the process."

She sits up, tilts her head, and studies me. "And what about you?"

I shrug. "I've got Claire. Right now, she's the love of my life."

She throws her hand over her mouth and her eyes fill with

tears. "I'm so glad she has you," she manages, tears rolling onto her cheeks, "since her mom is so screwed up."

She pushes off the couch and grabs her purse off the kitchen table. I follow her to the door, but when I open it, she faces me again. "I am so sorry for being the reason things didn't work out with Hanna. So sorry. If I could go back…"

I take her hand and squeeze her fingers. "If we hadn't already been off-balance, anything you did or said wouldn't have mattered. It took seeing her with Nate to understand that. They're steady. Despite…everything. When the world throws them for a loop, they're fine as soon as they get their feet on the ground."

She nods and looks to the door of Claire's bedroom. "Tell her every day how much I love her. Tell her I'm coming back for her. I don't want her to feel…" She presses her fingers to her lips. "Stupid antidepressant clearly isn't working," she says, half smiling as more tears roll down her cheeks.

"I think they're working just fine. And you don't need to worry. I'll tell her. Every day."

HANNA

"This is the cutest nursery ever," Liz says. She's adorable with her blond curls pulled into a high ponytail, smudges of red paint on her cheek.

I can't disagree. I love everything about the nursery. The walls are a pale yellow with a bold, red accent wall. We used primary colors and found gender-neutral bed sets with colorful zoo animals.

"You think it'll be two girls or two boys or a boy and a girl?"

I shrug.

"I know, I know! We just want them to be healthy, but part of me is hoping it'll be two little girls." She slings her arm over my shoulder and eyes my belly. "Or not so little," she teases.

"I'm surprised I got to come over tonight, honestly. Nate hasn't taken his hands off you since the doctor told him it was safe to have sex."

I bite back a grin then sigh. Having Nate in my house the last four months has been amazing. Vivian and Drake bought a house in a ritzy little area outside of Indianapolis, not a bad drive from New Hope, and Collin stays with us during the week and stays with them on the weekends.

Everything was going so well that they took me off complete bed rest by thirty weeks, but only last week, when I hit the thirty-seven-week mark, were we released to have sex again. If I was worried about my enormous belly standing between me and Nate being intimate, I needn't have. He's plenty creative when it counts.

The thought sends a buzz of anticipation through me. I shift uncomfortably and move away from Liz to sit in the glider rocker Nate bought for the nursery. So many thoughtful touches for a man who never wanted more children. Or who told himself that he didn't want any more children. My heart pinches a bit at the thought. Nate's an amazing father, and I've never seen a man so excited about his unborn children.

"I need to—" I stop, eyes wide as I try to figure out what's happening. "Liz?"

"What, sweetie?"

"Either I'm peeing myself and I can't stop or my water just broke." A steady trickle of warmth runs down my leg.

She squeals and then claps. "Hospital. Come on. Let's go."

"We have plenty of time," I assure her. "Let's go across the street and get Nate."

"Are you sure? Should you be walking? Shouldn't I call your doctor?" She grabs her phone from her pocket. "I'll call Nate and then the doctor and then—"

"Liz." I put my hand on her arm. "It's going to be okay."

Biting her bottom lip, she wraps her arms around my enormous stomach and sighs. "I get to meet you two soon! You'll know me right away. I'm the cool one."

We grab my overnight bag and diaper bag and are halfway

to the door when Nate and Asher walk in. Nate takes one look at me and the bag slung over Lizzy's shoulder and says, "Yeah?"

I nod, and before I can say anything, he pulls me into his arms, slides his hands into my hair, and kisses me.

"Knock it off!" Liz says. "You can suck face later. Now it's time to have some babies!"

EPILOGUE

ṄATE

Three Weeks Later

"Hey, Crane!" Asher calls, waving me over. "Is it done?"

I find a seat in the chair next to his and hand him the finished version of the song we've been hammering away at since August. Hanna's song.

"What about that?" I ask, pointing to a new line in the chorus.

"Yeah." He nods as he studies it. Then he grins. "Yeah, that could work."

I've written a lot of songs in my life and co-written even more, but none of them fought me as much as this one. Or maybe I'm the one who fought it. I wanted it to be about how sometimes loving someone means letting them go, and it didn't work. Months later, it's turned into a piece about how love is worth all the pain and heartbreak that comes before and after.

I knew, if I touched you, it'd be more than a kiss.

I need you. I'll feed you. I'll be your dying bliss.

Staring at the chorus, I sense her. I lift my head, and Hanna's smiling at me, my daughter in her arms. Next to her, Liz cradles my other daughter, gazing into her little face like a woman lost in love.

My daughters, Sophia and Josephine, are three weeks old today, and the family is over to welcome them home and celebrate their healthy births. I'm exhausted and sleep deprived and generally the luckiest bastard in the world.

"Are you two going to sing for us or not?" Maggie asks.

Asher winks at her. "Sure. We've even got something new." He strums the first chords of the song, and Hanna's eyes go wide. She's heard me working on it and begged me to sing it for her, but I told her she had to wait until it was done. I guess it's showtime.

> *You met me in the darkness and invited me to see*
> *The path into the daylight wasn't what I thought it'd be.*
> *I wanted to slay dragons for you but didn't understand*
> *The dragons needing slaying were the ones inside my head.*
>
> *I knew, if I touched you, it'd be more than a kiss.*
> *I need you. I'll feed you. I'll be your dying bliss.*
> *I'll be your superhero. I'd do it all for this.*

The words aren't just perfect for the song. They're true. And when I look up from my guitar, I know she understands that every word is for her. She turns to Krystal and hands her the baby. Then she comes across the room and takes my hand.

"Are you ready to make good on your promise, angel?" I ask softly.

"What promise is that?"

I produce a ring from my pocket. It's an emerald-cut diamond framed by our daughters' birthstone. "Marry me. Be my wife and my family. Wear my ring."

She grins, and happy tears spill down her cheeks. "I was starting to wonder when you'd ask me."

THE END

ACKNOWLEDGEMENTS

First I have to thank my husband, Brian, and our kids, Jack and Mary. You make me remember what matters.

A huge thank-you to my friends and family for being amazing cheerleaders. From my siblings to my grad school buddies, to my ninety-six-year-old neighbor who has her visiting nurse hooked now, I couldn't ask for better book pimps.

To everyone who provided me feedback on this crazy twisty-turny plot—especially Heather Carver, Rhonda Helms, Adrienne Hogan, and Samantha Leighton. A special shout-out to Annie Swanberg, who threatened to write Here and Now fan fiction if I didn't have the guts to end this book the way it needed to end. You were right, of course.

Thank you to the team that helped me package this book and promote it. Sarah Hansen at Okay Creations designed my beautiful cover, and if I have my way she will do many, many more for me. To my editing team, Rhonda Helms, Mickey Reed, and Arran McNicol, you make my books better. To Chris, my assistant, who keeps me organized against all odds. Thank you to Christine at iHeartBigBooks for designing my gorgeous promo materials, and a massive shout-out to Julie with AToMR for organizing my promotional events. To all of the bloggers and reviewers who help spread the word about my books—you're amazing. Every one of you.

To my agent Dan Mandel and my foreign rights agent Stefanie Diaz for getting my books into the hands of readers all over the world—you're making my dreams come true.

To all my writer friends on Twitter, Facebook, and my various writer loops, thank you for your support and inspiration. Special thanks to the NWB—Sawyer Bennett, Lauren Blakely, Violet Duke, Jessie Evans, Melody Grace, Monica Murphy, and Kendall Ryan—you ladies make me smile on a daily basis!

And last but certainly not least, thank you to my fans all over the world. To those who read *Unbreak Me* and *Wish I May* and wrote begging for another New Hope story. To those who read *Lost in Me* and *Fall to You* and begged for early copies of *All for This*. You're the best fans an author could ask for. I couldn't do this without you and wouldn't want to. Thank you for buying my books and telling your friends about them. Thank you for being gracious and kind in your letters. And thank you for being the reason I have to pinch myself. You're the best, and you're the reason I get to live this dream.

~Lexi

PLAYLIST

Justin Timberlake—*Drink You Away*
Rihanna—*Stay*
Muse—*Madness*
Ingrid Michaelson feat. A Great Big World—*Over You*
A Great Big World—*Already Home*
Sam Smith—*Stay with Me*
Pink, Nate Reuss—*Just Give Me a Reason*
Ani DiFranco—*Falling Is Like This*
Norah Jones—*Come Away With Me*
Train—*Marry Me*
Oh Honey—*Be Okay*

Other Titles
by LEXI RYAN

New Hope Trilogy
Unbreak Me
Stolen Wishes
Wish I May

The Here and Now Series (A New Hope Series)
Lost in Me
Fall to You
All for This

Hot Contemporary Romance
Text Appeal
Accidental Sex Goddess

Stiletto Girls Novels
Stilettos, Inc.
Flirting with Fate

Decadence Creek
Just One Night
Just the Way You Are

Coming Soon...

Something Reckless Series (A New Hope Series)
Something Reckless (Coming December 2014)
Something Real (Coming 2015)

Contact
LEXI RYAN

I love hearing from readers, so find me on my Facebook page at facebook.com/lexiryanauthor, follow me on Twitter @ writerlexiryan, shoot me an email at writerlexiryan@gmail.com, or find me on my website: www.lexiryan.com

This paperback interior was designed and formatted by

www.emtippettsbookdesigns.com

Artisan interiors for discerning authors and publishers.

www.ingramcontent.com/pod-product-compliance
Lightning Source LLC
Chambersburg PA
CBHW031018030726
47497CB00004B/905